OF MOTHS AND STONE

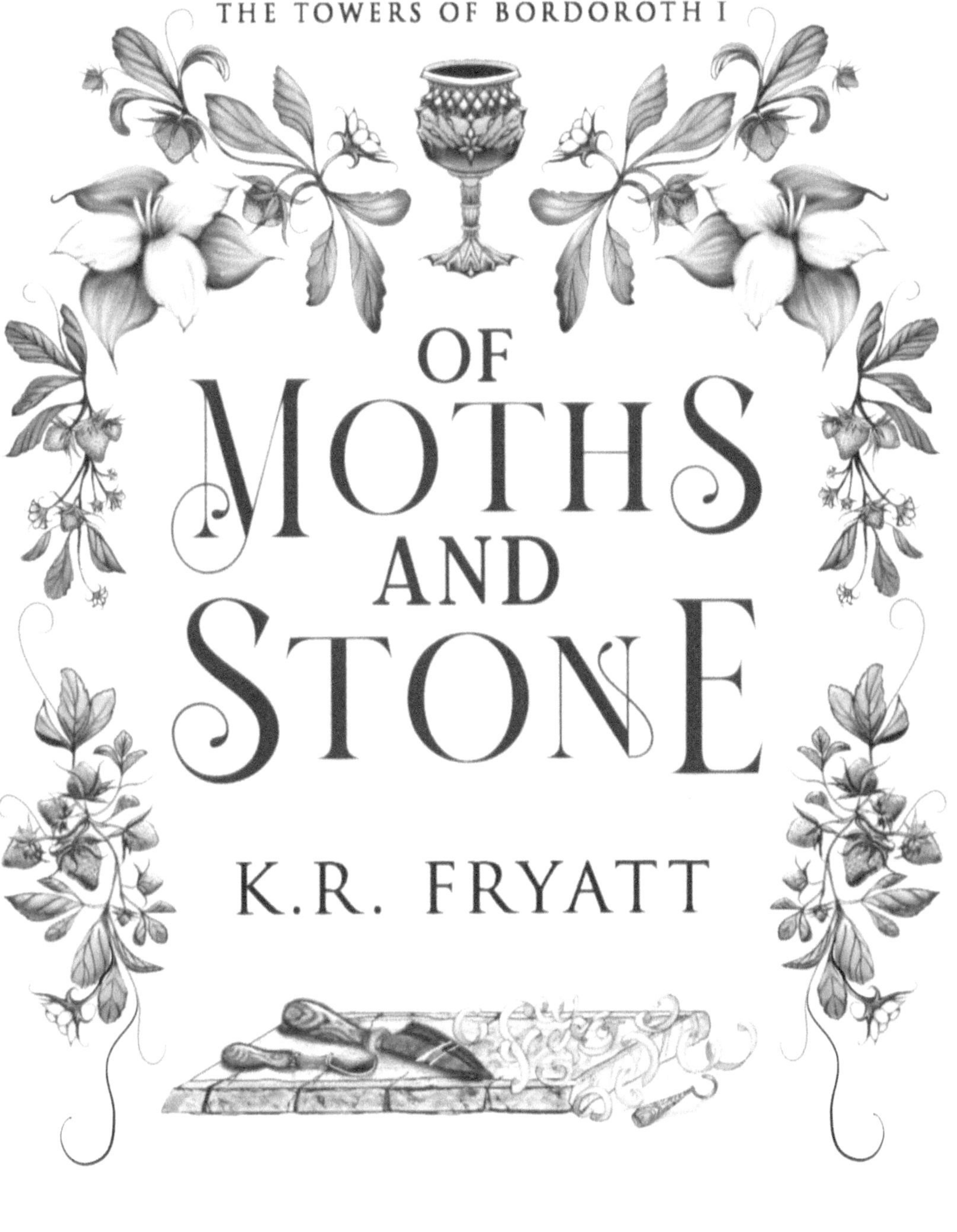

THE TOWERS OF BORDOROTH I

OF MOTHS AND STONE

K.R. FRYATT

ISBN: 979-8-9993301-0-9

Published by Moonweaver Publishing

First Edition: October 2025

Cover design by Moonpress | www.moonpress.co
Map illustrated by Marta Riva
Interior artwork by @mementomoreads
Artwork of Brand and Lunara by @danikalynnbooks
Glossary pages and Imperial Family Tree by K.R. Fryatt
Edited by Casey Harris-Parks

For the little girl who filled notebook after notebook with stories that only ever started with "Once upon a time..."
And for the wounded woman who'd forgotten her dreams, but finally pulled herself from the wreckage and remembered them.

Me. This one is for me.

For anyone whose soul is still buried, who's struggled to accept who they are, I hope this book is the reaching hand of a friend. Let me hold you, dear one, while you break free and find the raging, untamable power waiting within.

AUTHOR'S NOTE

I would first like to make it clear that I do not view disabilities (such as mental health and chronic pain issues) as something in need of a "warning." However, for my fellow sufferers, I would like to give a gentle heads-up that there are fairly detailed symptoms described within the book for both of those things, just so you can be prepared for your *own* mental health and wellbeing.

CONTENT WARNINGS

Please note that this book is intended for adults, and contains the following:

- Graphic violence, including battle sequences, torture, and death
- Scenes of a sexual nature
- Implied pregnancy loss (off page / in memory / not main character)
- Implied grooming of a minor
- Parental and spousal loss
- Invisible / chronic illness symptoms, as represented by a fantasy setting
- Mental health challenges, including panic attacks and PTSD related symptoms
- Attempted self harm (for the sake of others / not pre-meditated)

Suicide & Crisis Helpline for the US / Canada: DIAL 988

You are beloved. You are here. You didn't have to do anything to earn that. It just *is*, because you *are*. Please—reach out to someone, *anyone*, if you are in need of support.

THE IMPERIAL LINE OF BORDOROTH

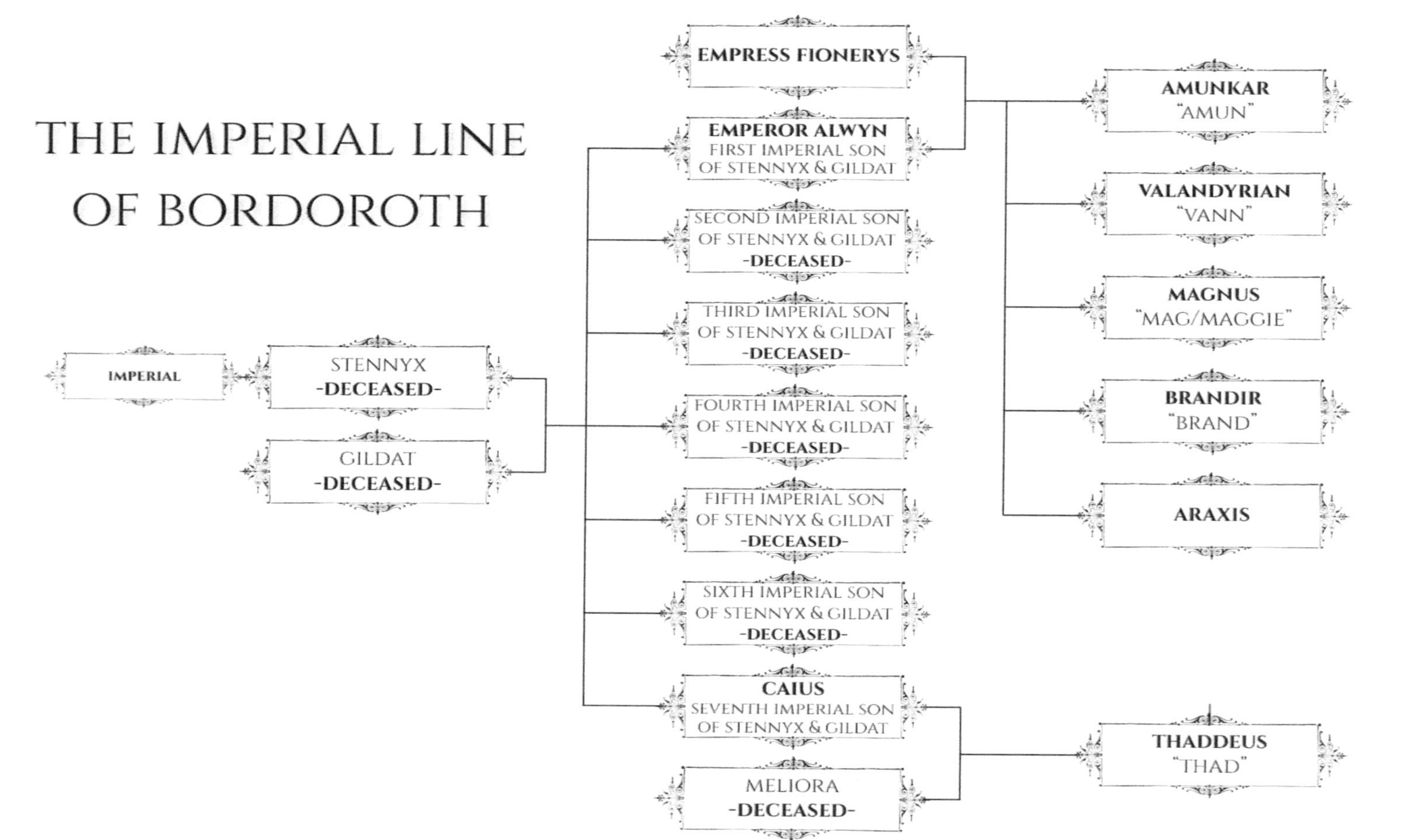

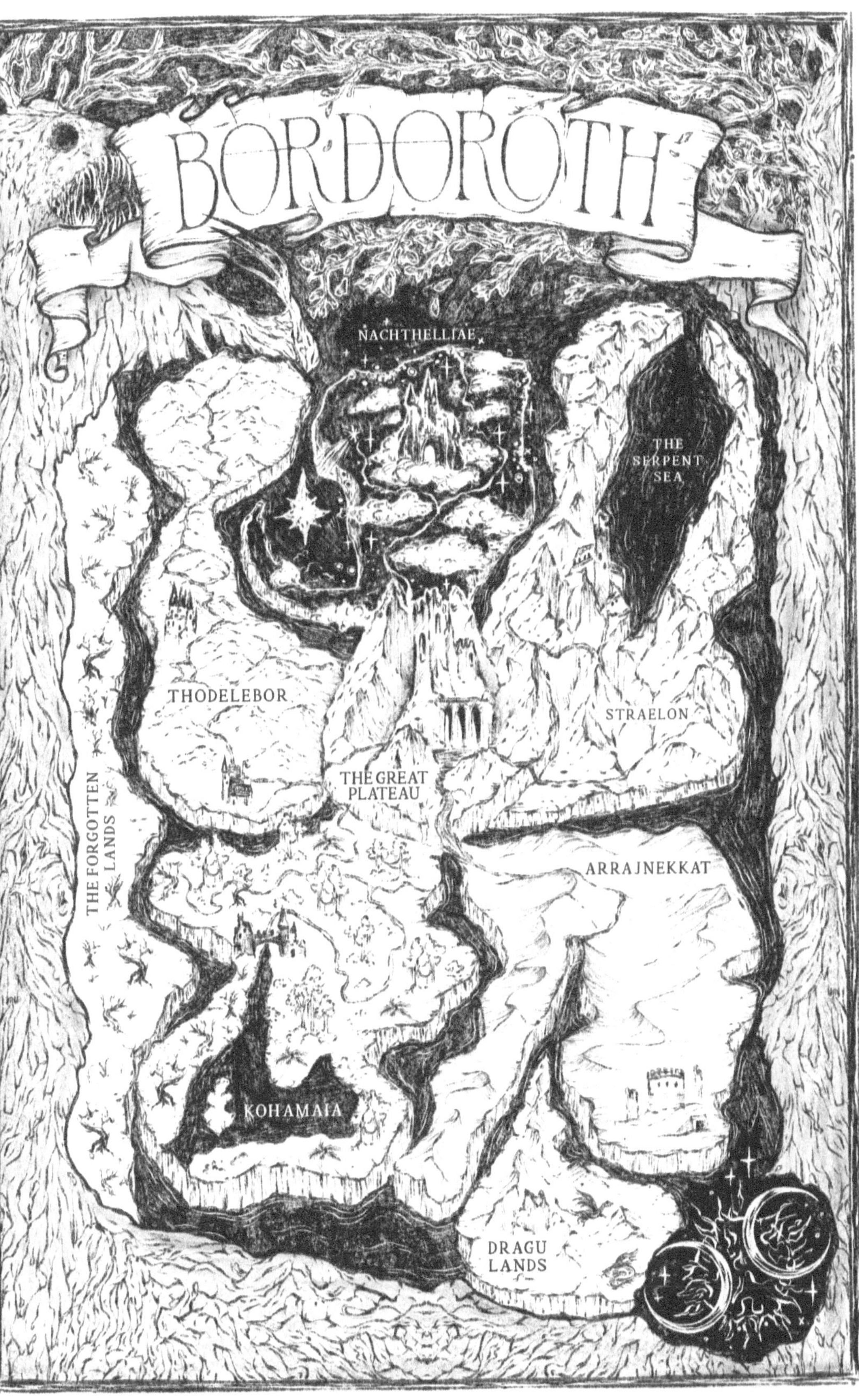
BORDOROTH
NACHTHELLIAE
THE SERPENT SEA
THODELEBOR
STRAELON
THE GREAT PLATEAU
THE FORGOTTEN LANDS
ARRAJNEKKAT
KOHAMAIA
DRAGU LANDS

BRAND

LUNARA

PROLOGUE

CENTURIES AGO...

THEY WOULD BE CALLING HER *THE ORACLE* BY THIS TIME TOMORROW EVE, AND forever after.

Unfortunately, it wouldn't be long before Endellion forgot she wasn't anything of the sort.

Perched like a wraith on the highest mountaintop, she cast her gaze into the basin below. An earthen pedestal of rock and diamond held the Palace of Argoph above the heavy fog blanketing the Weeping City—the names of both twisting inside her.

That beacon of ivory and gold glittered as moonlight skimmed its surfaces between tendrils of the shifting haze, the Fountain of All Life springing forth from its uppermost level and infinitely feeding the waterfalls tumbling over the cliff edge.

Blanketed as the city was in mist and darkness, she could barely make out the five rivers they formed—cutting across the land through forest and peak before spilling into the realms they fed—but no matter.

She'd seen this sight before and what followed.

The circumstances of the next few minutes had been her constant companion of late, her true life's purpose both ending and beginning in this infinitesimal snippet of time.

She would never truly be ready for what awaited her, but there was no real choice.

Blistering wind whistled through the gargantuan passes around her, raking its icy fingers across her cheeks and snapping at her robes. She drew in a harsh breath, then another, and turned her eyes towards the cosmos for one, last look at her beloved stars.

Even seeing it so many times through her Sight that she'd lost count, Endellion hadn't expected the reality to be quite so spectacular.

Still staring upwards, she wished for the thousandth time that she was able to share her visions in a more helpful way, but the laws of her power and people forbade it. Instead, she was forced to speak in loathsome riddles and ludicrous rhymes.

Once—and only once—she'd tried to divulge a vision plainly. The agony afterwards was not something one easily forgets. And the captain had still drowned in the storm she'd foreseen, pinned beneath the mast of his own damned ship.

Never again, she'd sworn, preferring those hated rhymes and riddles to her own pain and the death of innocents.

"Ah, but how easily vows can be broken," she sighed to the sky.

She would be doing a lot of that before the end.

Not today, though.

No, she had to use her convoluted gift in its intended fashion this time. It was the only way this world and its people might be saved from utter destruction.

With barely a thought, particles of energy solidified as a cyclone of sparks in the air, before clinging to her golden skin. She closed her eyes, enveloped by the comforting celestial warmth, and leapt into the ether with a blazing flash.

Endellion appeared above Argoph's Seat with a sudden, quaking burst, held aloft on her feathered wings. She'd seen herself arrive from the view of every soul below, terror in their hearts as they beheld her—a creature from songbooks and legend, little more than a myth, her blinding starfire pouring from within her in massive waves to bathe every crack and crevice of the vaulted court.

She summoned a maelstrom of wind, the snow-white curls that framed her face and body barely teased by the tempest she was creating.

Just because she could.

The drama of her calling had always been Endellion's favorite part, and she'd relished the shock and awe of creatures worlds over. If the situation weren't so serious, she might have even giggled at the whole thing.

It would be nice to laugh one, last, genuine time.

Instead, her shining eyes locked onto Stennyx, Emperor of Bordoroth.

The colossal ruler towered over his subjects, black horns curling and skin blazing with the marks of his Blessing as he dug his feet into the quartz tiles and snarled at her. Even to one such as her, his strength was astonishing, and a drop of sadness trickled its way into her heart at knowing his fate.

"I come to warn you, Emperor Stennyx, that you might ready your progeny." Her voice boomed with an eerie, crackling energy—a woven medium for countless others, unseen and funneling through her.

With a deep breath, Endellion gathered the wisdom of the ages unto herself, channeling the sorcery that would filter her phrasing. A blink and her eyes lost focus as she stared into the abyss of all time, their light multiplying, and the words she'd traveled galaxies to deliver finally left her with a wrenching force.

"A shadow, once living, abides in bleak places
A vengeance, once loving, on five towers gazes
Their hate is consuming, biting and bruising
Eating and rotting and writhing and oozing

"When twilight merges with stone's crowned dawn
And something most precious is suddenly gone
It waits in the rafters, the corridors, the rooms
The fourth now a feast for malevolent doom

"Come fangs and mist, come balance and majesty
Follow the moth with its bonded ferocity
Thus starts the ending, the middle, and beginning
Of five towers falling, the darkness yet winning

"Come springtime and dreaming, come fire and madness
The towers need mortar to smooth shattered edges
They war for the breaking, they bleed for the broken

They still violent scales and grin while they're choking

"A beacon, once sleeping, awakes in high places
A consort, once clawing, no longer encases
Their hate is consuming, biting and bruising
Gleaming and blotting and fighting and losing

"When nightmares are banished, no dark looming reign
And something is mended with gifts of white flame
It waits in the heartbeats, the landscapes, the ease
The realms cry their peace beneath star-blessed wings."

With another great, cracking shudder, her power exploded from the center of her, sweeping all in attendance across the floors. All except Stennyx, fierce as he was.

"And now, I offer you one truth, Your Majesty. A way to test what I have said and take it to heart. It will be only Imperial Sons that you sire, and no female babe shall be born into the line of Bordoroth until this tribulation has passed. Prepare yourselves."

There. The one honest moment she was allowed—eventual proof of her credibility, for all it would someday break him.

Endellion vanished as suddenly as she had appeared, returning to her vantage point on the frigid mountain peak, to the blessed sight of the shimmering mist below.

The last beautiful thing she would see for a very long time.

Panic threatened to devour her as she gulped the thin air, and Endellion cursed her knowing. The rest of her vision played out from *his* perspective, and she watched him tear through the invisible space of the world to get to her. A monster, coming to take her to her ruin.

The land shook with his fury when he arrived, his hot, scathing breath stirring the hair at her nape and spiking the blood in her veins. She blinked away the stirring tears, steeling herself for what was to come, and whispered a soft goodbye to her sisters.

With her hands clenched into shaking fists, Endellion turned and faced her destiny.

1

Present day…

He drew the scent of blood and refuse deep into his lungs, reveling in it, a shudder dancing its way up his spine. He lived for moments like this, when agony was a welcome cloud around him and answers were waiting right on his knife's edge.

He was close. So, so close.

His veins buzzed, the pleasant hum of certainty encasing his body.

"Such beautiful skin," he crooned, dragging his blade down a magnificently chiseled chest. "I wonder how much I can peel away before you tell me what I wish to know."

The Demon laid out on the rocky slab before him whimpered—a keening sound that brought him equal parts joy and disgust. It echoed between the festering cavern walls, a perfect accompaniment to the chorus of groans beneath it.

He glanced behind, as if he could follow the sound with his eyes, and surveyed his work. A swell of pride filled him, delighted with the whimsical play of torchlight over wasted bodies. Chained to the walls, nailed to boulders, hung from the jagged ceiling—every realm of Bordoroth was now represented in the creatures he'd collected.

Through the Sight, he'd once glimpsed a wonderfully savage people who displayed the corpses of insects and small animals, their legs and wings and tails pinned to padded boards like tiny trophies, hung on their walls for others to see.

Shortly after his arrival in this world, he'd caught a pixie telling bedtime stories to her young. History, really. Far closer to the truth than she ever knew. The image of those people and their curated beasties had flashed in his mind as he'd held her squirming body in his fist, and it had become his inspiration.

After all, what were Bordorothians if not vermin beneath his booted heel?

"Please," the Demon whispered, interrupting his thoughts. "Why are you… doing this?"

His lip curled back, a disappointed tsk escaping. Pleading from a Straelani Demon? They were supposed to be the fiercest of warriors, their berserker rages and finesse in battle legendary even in worlds beyond this one. They didn't know that, ignorant as they were, but still. He'd expected more.

His Gilly never would have begged.

Strangely, her absence still stung here and there. It had been pure chance that all of his stilted, grainy visions had pushed him towards other realms, but he could admit to himself that he'd felt a private relief in avoiding her brethren.

Until now.

Tonight, a Demon from the Montrealm had finally joined the growling Wolflords and stoic Riders, thrashing Sorcerit and hissing Fae, each and every one bringing him a little closer to his endgame.

He'd have to ponder later why the Sight had not shown him the Demon's presence this evening, or warned him to be ready. It was pure chance that he'd been nearby, listening as always. Fate, perhaps.

Fickle, cursed thing.

"I'm doing this because I was fortunate enough to hear you running your mouth," he said. "I have questions, and I believe you have the answers. Speaking of which—"

Without warning, he drove his blade into one of the Demon's horns. A twist of his wrist detached the hideous appendage, the mahogany spiral clattering to the stone as blood sprayed.

Ah, yes. There were the screams he'd been looking for.

All too soon, the noise irked him.

He tossed his dagger aside, shoved the Demon's jaw shut, and clapped a palm over his lips. "Shh, that's not getting us anywhere," he chided, bending to retrieve the severed prize while still keeping his subject silent.

His other hand settled over raised ridges, the flesh of his fingers sinking into the deep grooves between. The rings they formed shrank as they traveled the length of the horn, getting smaller and smaller until they disappeared entirely, the wicked, tapered end polished to a high shine by use and age.

"Tell me…" he said, turning it this way and that before pressing it to the Demon's sternum. "What are the Montrealm's secrets worth to you?"

Blood welled beneath the razor point of the horn, even as fierce determination painted itself across the Demon's face, his brow pinching and jaw ticking.

What fun.

"Here's whats going to happen," he said. "You're going to tell me everything I need to know, and then you're going to deliver a message for me. If you don't, I will find every person you care about and ruin them in ways you can't even imagine."

Shadows leapt from the ground and clamped over the Demon's arms and legs, defiance quick to replace his shock. He tore his head away and thrashed, gnashing his fangs and roaring to the cavern ceiling when he met nothing but air.

This was going to be even more enjoyable than he'd first anticipated.

Grinning, he fisted a handful of his prisoner's black hair and slammed his head against the slab. "Trust me, friend," he whispered at the Demon's ear. "What happens in the next few hours is entirely up to you, but know this—if you fail me, it will seem like foreplay compared to what I do to those you love. Are we clear?"

He didn't wait for an answer. It didn't really matter whether the creature agreed anyway.

"Now, what do you know about the Battle of Breamwyrm?"

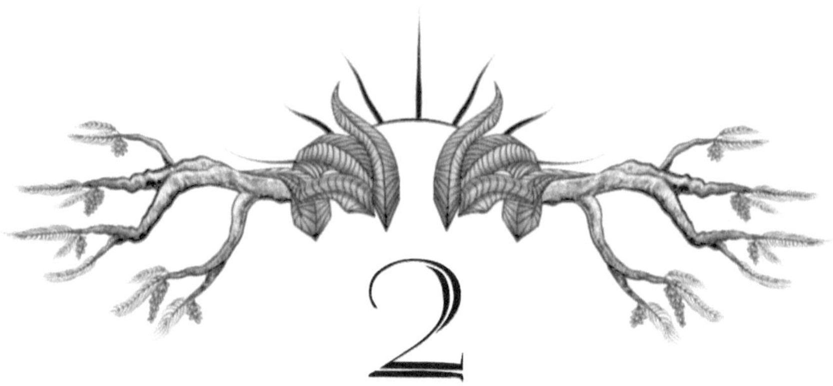

2

Solyrian's rays beat down upon his Demon brethren, their sweating bodies hard at work. The light was blinding, harshly gilding them as they moved—too fast, too slow, swirling and spinning in disjointed motions that made no sense anymore.

He was meant to be moving with them, helping to build the ceremonial platform, but he couldn't think. Couldn't feel his lips or limbs.

"Brand!"

Whoever was calling his name would have to wait until the ringing in his ears quieted and his heart stopped hammering against his lungs, stealing his breath.

Weeping Sisters, he hated it when this happened.

He made his trembling hand reach for a waterskin, drinking deep. He found no anchor within the cool liquid, but perhaps it would be in the swipe of an arm across his brow, or the peace he feigned when he tilted his head up to the sunstar.

Hopefully, the desperate attempts to ground himself looked like nothing more than a much-needed rest to those around him.

No one could know that a random thought had barged in uninvited, seizing control, his churning mind completely at odds with the smooth actions of his body. That a vice was slowly tightening itself around his chest, or that the flush crawling across his skin had nothing to do with the summer season. That he would give anything to sink into the ground and stay there until he was settled again.

"Brand!"

His eyes snapped open to Hedda standing in front of him. Hair like red wine was twisted up into a haphazard knot, her ivory horns rising from the mess. Worry was etched in the deep grooves between her furrowed brows, but not for him. She was too obviously irritated.

Good. Something to focus on besides his own shite—provided he could stop feeling as though he were drowning.

Brand clawed his way through the haze, barely able to form his question. "What's wrong?"

"It's Aldiat," she said, cheeks puffing out. "He completely fucked his fighting arm during morning drills and is refusing to have it looked at. Baldrir is the only one that can ever get through to the stubborn bastard, but he isn't here."

"Right. Um..."

Baldrir... Baldrir... He'd sent Baldrir to—

"Thodelebor," Brand answered finally, the rusted cogs in his mind reluctantly turning. "Bal left for Thodelebor yesterday afternoon with messages for the Chieftains, as well as my uncle and brother."

Stars above, when had his tunic started sticking that way, clinging to his neck and trying to suffocate him? He hooked a finger into the collar, wanting nothing more than to rip the garment off.

Faldir popped up beside Hedda, irritation evident across his nearly identical features. "We don't give a flying fuck where Bal is. Aldiat is meant to be mated in a few hours, his hand is barely attached to his body, and the damned fool has decided to try and heal himself with hard drink."

Brand's lips quirked up, not quite a smile but enough to seem normal. "Faldir. Cheerful as ever, I see."

Hedda's twin raised an unamused brow. The motion pulled at the puckered scar running down his cheek and into the corner of his lips, a shocking slash of pink in his otherwise deeply tanned skin. "If it were time to be bloody cheerful, I wouldn't be doing it here in the sweltering heat with you lot."

No, he certainly wouldn't. Faldir saved his best moods for others, during the few hours he was off duty.

With a sigh, Brand mindlessly dragged a palm back and forth along one of his horns and closed his eyes. "Find one of the Sorcerit due to bring the latest batch of flowers and pay whatever they ask in return for healing him."

"Um..." Hedda cleared her throat and waited until Brand pried his lids open to look at her. "That delivery happened hours ago."

Sometimes this middle space was the worst part of his attacks. He wasn't as lost but his senses were dim until they suddenly weren't, and it took Brand far too long to realize what Hedda had said.

He blinked once, twice. "Hours?"

"It's mid-afternoon, *Your Highness,*" Faldir grumbled.

"Mind yourself, little brother," Hedda hissed, elbowing Faldir.

Brand swallowed and cast a glance beyond the siblings.

At first, it was the expected visual noise—muffled sounds that didn't quite match up with their sources, the washed out imagery slowly coming into focus amidst the pulsing halo that ringed his sight—but Brand urged himself to center. To see the little things.

A lone tuft of sea grass making its home between two flags of marbled stone. A hand sliding slowly into another's. A single crow pecking at a plate of discarded food. A dark curl of hair caught by the light.

Seized by the familiarity of it all, Brand drew in a deep breath, and fell back into himself. All at once, laughter and chatter exploded into existence, the rhythm of labor a steady beat beneath.

The Main Square of the Horned City was a hive of activity, Straelani Demons moving in every direction as they readied not only for the coming Occurrence, but the mating ritual later that evening.

Some carried posts while others fetched piles of folded cloth for the canopies. Cut beams were being stacked into piles near those who needed them, a salty breeze carrying sawdust into the air. Arms worked and hammers flew as nails were pounded into bench seats and tabletops, platforms and displays. Blooms of every color lay waiting in steel troughs, enchanted by a Nachthellian Sorcerit to keep fresh and beautiful for the next couple of months.

Children scurried this way and that, playing games as they helped. One handed an end of cedar garland up to her father where he was perched on a ladder, his mate holding the other end further down.

Together, both males commanded the stone to grip the decoration, the swath of green hanging perfectly over the window of their bakery.

Two Demons in their rage dodged her as she cheered for her fathers, their colossal forms rising above the crowd and straining beneath a pallet of raw lumber. Sienna markings stained their darkened skin, Solyrian's light pulsing from them with every step they took, their faces twisted into mirror grimaces. They crossed the busy square and released their burden beside the obsidian Solyr Stone with triumphant grins, shaking the ground as they brushed off their hands and clapped one another on the back.

He was home. He was safe.

And, judging by the shadows stretching down from the towering evergreens and tightly packed buildings, it was most definitely later than he'd thought.

"I must've gotten distracted with the festival preparations," Brand said flippantly, bending to swipe his leather tool belt from a stool. He slung the mass over his shoulder, Hedda instantly beside him as he made for the high road. "Which means I've missed my lunch."

"Oy, hang lunch," Faldir called after them. "Aldiat is swimming at the bottom of a bottle. If Frida finds out, she'll ream the lot of us. You know how she is."

Brand rolled his neck as he walked, praying to the Sisters that—just this once—the knot at the base of his skull would melt away and he could skip his usual headache. "Hedda?"

"Yes, Highness?"

"Tell Faldir that there will be no reaming because he's going to find one of those Sorcerit before they leave, and pay them handsomely for their precious extra time."

Hedda threw her brother a savage grin as they rounded a tight bend in the cobbled road. "You heard him, Third Commander."

"Brand's the one who sent Bal away when he already had a job to do," Faldir grumbled as he caught up. "Maybe he should have to deal with the bloody Nachthellians."

That had been a minor oversight on his part.

"Our Imperial Son has his own job to do," Hedda said. "Speaking of which, have you sorted your part of the nonsense yet?"

Leave it to Hedda to reduce the most monumental moment in any creature's existence into nonsense.

To be so blessed by the Sisters as to find his fated other… It was one of the few things Brand wanted out of life that might be possible in his circumstances. Then again, he wasn't sure another creature deserved to be tied to a shoddy mess like him for the rest of forever, regardless of how much he desired it.

Faldir grunted, something akin to a laugh. "He's got to hold a bowl of paste and smile, and he's done it dozens of times. What's there to sort?"

Brand could practically feel Hedda's gaze boring into him.

"Perhaps," she replied slowly. "Still, it doesn't hurt to check."

Damn it. Maybe some of her worry *was* for him.

"It will be fine," Brand said with a heavy sigh. "I have it well in hand."

The wave of dread that came with stepping into the shadow of a wayward branch above—its darkness falling over them like a bad omen and sending a shiver down his spine—was merely another symptom of his traitorous fucking condition.

Everything would be fine.

BRAND HIT THE LANDING OF HIS TOWER CHAMBER AND PRESSED HIS HEAD TO the door, waiting for the panel to recognize him. From its surface, branches sprang to life and brushed once over his shoulder before it swung wide and he stumbled in, his thighs still burning from the long climb.

He tossed his tool belt on the overstuffed chair by the fireplace and made for the washroom, ignoring the bed as he passed it. If he didn't, he'd never get clean.

Pushing through another door, he called to a smattering of stones in the wall and urged them to glow. The pure sunlight that bathed them during the day poured into the room, glinting off of the gold mirrors and warming the space, hitting his skin as he ripped the dusty clothes from his body.

Another call to his power and a wide, rectangular hole opened in the wall above the massive tub in the floor, hot water gushing forth. With a sigh, he trudged down the steps and sat on the ledge beneath the steaming fall, the tension leaving him with every speck of dirt that was swept away.

Well, some of it, anyway. There was too much to fucking do. Never mind his duties during the mating ritual that evening—the ones he'd absolutely been obsessing over, even though Faldir was right and he'd carried the ceremonial vessel of stain so many times that he'd lost count.

When the bath was full, he cut the water off and eyed the cloths and soap on the opposite side, willing his magic to work on something other than the earth and stone. He hadn't yet gotten so lazy that he'd stoop to deforming the castle walls just to avoid walking a few measly feet, but still.

His youngest brother, Araxis, could have easily brought them to himself.

Lucky Nachthellian bastard.

Brand's grumbles were swallowed by the humidity as he sloshed across the pool and swiped them up, thoughts wandering to his family while he lathered and scrubbed.

He often wondered what they'd all looked like at birth, if they'd resembled each other or their parents for those few hours before they were made into something else. If they'd had wings like their father or frost like their mother. Eyes of green, or the deepest brown.

Unfortunately, he'd never know those answers. It was taboo to speak of such things. To try and own something other than that which they'd been given.

He may have entered life as Brandir aht Bordoroth, the fourth Son born to the ecstatic Imperial Sovereigns, but it had been a few hours later when the newly-crowned Demon King of Straelon had shown up to Bless him that Brand's true role in this world had been solidified for the rest of his very long life.

His father, Emperor Alwyn, said that Lyriat had looked comical standing there holding Brand to his small chest—a mere child himself and looking utterly lost—but the magic of Bordoroth needed no prior knowledge, no fancy words or actions, in order to work.

In an instant, his body, his very essence, had been transformed into those of the Montrealm.

For all eternity, he was changed. 'Til death, he was Demon.

Now, he was Straelon's striped sienna mountains and the towering majesty of its evergreen trees. His razor-sharp horns took pride of place in his reflection, their obsidian lengths rising up and back from his auburn hair to crown him with the dignity of all Straelani.

He commanded the earth and it heeded him. He raged, a seething colossus with whorls of power tracing over his skin. He swam in the sea and climbed the crimson peaks and rejoiced in the light of Solyrian.

Same as the rest of his Demon brethren.

Greater minds than his had been broken trying to understand how the magic worked, or why only Imperials could undergo the Blessing. Brand didn't care. He had no interest in picking apart Bordoroth's mysterious quirks. He had one job, and he would do it well if it killed him.

Which it might.

Brand submerged himself, rinsing the suds away before floating to the surface and staring up through the slanted glass roof to the sky beyond. Solyrian was still blazing, gulls flying by against the endless blue backdrop.

A couple of hours, then, before the gathering would start in the square.

"Fuck."

No matter how much he loved this realm and what it had made him, it never escaped Brand how wildly ill-equipped he was for being the focus of so many damned people.

The little moments were fine, like settling petty disputes in the pub over an ale. Ensuring the artisans, quarry hands, and lumberers were paid fairly for their wares and exports. Keeping the markets in good repair for the fisher folk. He even enjoyed visiting his uncle and brothers in their realms to negotiate Lyriat's terms, doing his part to keep a tentative peace in Bordoroth.

All easy enough. Business and numbers.

But he'd been made High Ambassador while still a babe latched to his mum, and his Blessing Day may as well have been his *Cursing Day* when he had to face the nights like this one.

When he had to perform for the masses, hundreds of eyes on him expecting to see a tear or two for the pair he'd be helping to join. When all he'd done was stand there holding a bloody damned bowl, but he'd have to hear over and over about what a marvelous job he'd done, pretending he wasn't fully aware of their veiled attempts to get into his good graces.

No wonder he had episodes.

And that evening marked the first of almost two month's-worth of feasts and parties he would have to attend.

"Sisters save me." With a groan, Brand pulled himself from the comforting weightlessness of the bath, water sluicing from his body as he wrapped a swath of linen around himself.

His canopied bed beckoned when he left the washroom, its airy sheets and mound of pillows whispering words like *nap* and *rest* and *forget for a little while.*

He'd planned to go down to his workshop, to make progress on a gift he was carving for his mother's birthday, but maybe if he went right before the ritual and left early, it wouldn't be too bad. And, after missing luncheon, he was exhausted to his very bones.

Right.

He could do both. He had time.

Brand scrubbed the towel over his long hair, threw it into a nearby basket, and flopped onto the mattress, melting instantly.

Twenty minutes. He'd just close his eyes for twenty minutes.

Brand dug his toes further into the crimson sand, the sea lapping at his ankles. Solyrian had dipped into its depths a few moments ago, staining the sky pink and purple, and making way for the stars to begin their shining.

The crowd roared behind him, a breeze carrying their raucous merriment straight to his ears, and he didn't have to force his smile. His people were happy, and it filled his heart to know it.

He was just moving to stand when that singular crow from the square landed beside him, sidling up and shaking its glossy feathers. At first, he thought it meant to search the tiny holes in the outcropping for supper, but it started pecking at his legs instead.

"What the?" Brand's voice was strangely distorted, his arms refusing to move the way he wanted them to. "Get out of here!"

He gaped when it jumped and the stone beneath him wobbled, jostling his body—before it leapt into his lap, *barked at him,* and drew a tongue like wet sandpaper across his face.

Brand jolted awake with a curse, cheek wet beneath his palm. Blinking into the darkness, he was met with two huge, golden eyes, Pet's huffing breaths wafting in the space between them.

"Damn it."

A soft growl was the only warning he had before a giant maw was wrapped around his torso.

"Don't you fucking dare," Brand warned, grabbing a fistful of flaxen fur. "I'm awake. There's no need to—"

He was not the least bit surprised when the arsehole tossed him clear to the balcony.

"Mangy prick!" he shouted, blood boiling as he stomped back inside.

It was nearly impossible to see, but Brand swung a fist anyway.

There was a flash just before his blow connected, a calloused hand shoving him backwards.

"I tried, you wee shite." The deep and rumbling chuckle that followed only served to fuel Brand's ire. "By the time you came to, I'd already promised Pet his fun."

"Oh, of course. Thank the Sisters the beastie's needs have been met!" He made his way towards the washroom. "Anything else before I have a piss?"

A massive arm came out of nowhere and snaked itself around his neck, knuckles digging into his scalp to violently ruffle his hair. "Aye. I've not had my own fun yet."

Brand gritted his teeth against the chokehold, but struggling was futile when he was this damned tired. Besides, Magnus was even bigger than him—a downright colossal brute, and probably the only creature in all of Bordoroth who could get away with calling him a *wee* anything.

"Ach, come on!" Magnus bellowed. "You're not even trying!"

Brand snarled as black spots began to crowd his vision, fighting to pull air into his lungs. Mag had caught him on the wrong day, and he suddenly didn't give a starry shite that this Thodeleborian had yet to dress after his shift and was naked as the day he was born.

"Fine. Just remember… that you… asked for it."

Brand cranked his arm and struck, an explosive *oof!* sounding before the booming thud of Mag hitting the floor like a felled tree.

Cheap elbow shots aimed right for the groin will do that to some people.

Stumbling backwards, Brand crashed into the bed frame, gasping and coughing as the blood rushed back to his head. He reached out and called to the stone, finally brightening the room enough that he could focus on his intruder.

A Wolflord through and through, tattoos in various patterns and symbols covered nearly every inch of Mag's tanned skin, his face the only part of him that was clear of the black ink. Rings of silver cascaded down his ears to match the ones in his nose and chest, beads of the same woven into the braids that kept his long, blond hair swept back on the sides.

A few stray waves had fallen across Mag's face to tangle in his teeth and beard as his mouth gaped on a silent scream and—writhing on the ground, with the light glinting off of every decorative bit of metal—his older brother looked like a glittering, hairy worm having the worst day of its life.

Not for all the riches in Bordoroth could Brand have contained his laughter then, wheezing as he collapsed and hit the floorboards.

The mirth left him on a sigh when Magnus rolled to his own back, their shoulders brushing.

"Well, I probably deserved that," Mag finally said.

Brand huffed, sitting up. "You definitely deserved that."

"Aye, well"—Magnus grunted as he stood—"it was worth it." He crossed to a satchel by the door, bending to rifle through it. "Anyway, you can thank Hedda for the rude awakening. She's the one who let it slip you were napping. Otherwise, I'd have headed straight for the food."

"Weeping Sisters, Aldiat and Frida's feast." Brand sprang from the floor, trying to sort his thoughts. "How late am I?"

So much for spending any time in his workshop.

Mag pulled his ceremonial robe from the pack, shoving his arms through the short, embroidered sleeves and belting the intricate garment with a practiced skill only the Wolflords could manage. "You're not. Yet." He plopped down onto the settee in front of the fireplace and leaned back to set his feet on the low table there. "The sunstar has barely set, and I passed Lyriat in the corridor on my way here—heading *away* from the great hall. You've got some time."

Some of the panic bled out of Brand. "Please tell me you've brought Baldrir back with you."

The Demon was not only Aldiat's best friend, but had a knack for drawing attention, and Brand had counted on his presence more than once to get out of sticky situations he had no desire to be in.

"Ah. Right." Mag's eyes darted away, his face twisting into something between a grimace and a grin. "You see, what happened was… Well, I… Alright, there was this scullery maid. Vausta, Fausta, something like that," he muttered, waving his hand. "They stumbled off last night and have been together ever since. Trust me, I heard far more than I wanted to when I went to knock on his door and fetch him this evening. In the end, it didn't feel right to drag him away to attend a party and fall asleep here, when he could stay another night with her instead."

Brand blinked, sure he hadn't just heard what he thought he did. "I sincerely hope you are fucking with me right now."

"What was I meant to do?" Magnus argued. "I'm nothing if not a romantic, Brand. I swear to the Sisters, I think she might be his mate with the way she was carrying on. That, or he's the best lover in all of Bordoroth." He pressed a hand to his chest. "Who was I to separate such bliss?"

"A bloody fucking *Son*, maybe?" Brand pinched the bridge of his nose. "For Bal's sake, I hope she *is* his mate. It's the only thing that'll keep him out of trouble."

"We'll know tomorrow, one way or another. Caius and both of the Chieftains were already abed, but I left a note for them to send Baldrir on his way come morning." Magnus laced his fingers behind his head and closed his eyes. "Now, get dressed. You've a mating ritual to get to."

"We'll both be lucky if Frida doesn't brain us with her warhammer," Brand grumbled, already digging through the wardrobe.

"Ach, don't worry about that sweet lass. I had Hedda point her out and already spoke to her. She was practically beside herself with glee at the thought of another mating so soon. Left her with hearts in her eyes, lad. We'll be fine."

If only Brand could have a fraction of his brother's smug self-assurance.

"Oh, and there's something else you should know."

He stopped dead in his tracks, the tone of Mag's voice making him wary. "What?"

"I brought Thad."

Brand swore, eyeing the bed, more exhausted than he'd ever been. "You two are here to kill me, aren't you?"

Mag's laugh clapped like thunder as he stood. "No, we're here to make sure you have fun! Hurry up," he said, crossing to the door. "We've got mischief to make and I'm fucking starving."

A SALTY BREEZE TEASED BRAND'S HAIR AS THEY STROLLED DOWN THE WINDING High Road, lifting the long waves of it and tickling his cheek. Pounding drums and vibrant fiddle joined the sound of crashing waves, their combined music luring revelers in from the farthest reaches of the Horned City and beyond.

Lantern pillars lined the tight, cobbled street at intervals, cloth garlands strung between them that hadn't been there when he'd walked by earlier. The carved, wooden columns twisted up to the glowing, stone orb perched on top, bathing everything in amber light.

It was beautiful, peaceful, and all Brand could think was that he'd rather be anywhere else.

"Think there'll be anyone wanting to try a Wolflord on for size?" Magnus said, stopping before a dark shop window and adjusting the fall of his collar—making it wider, naturally—and smoothing a hand over his hair.

Brand rolled his eyes, tilting his head up with a long-suffering sigh. The wooden shingles lining the rooftops seemed to almost disappear as they reached upwards and blended with the night sky.

He wished he was one of them.

"You already know there'll be dozens who are more than happy to entertain an Imperial Son, regardless of his species," Brand answered. "Try to not be a complete arse about it."

Mag laughed. "I only show my lovers the utmost respect. Besides," he said, wrapping an arm around Brand and continuing their walk, "I was only riling you up. You asked me to come for a reason, and I plan to see it through."

Right. *That.*

Shame hit him like a tidal wave. He gritted his teeth against the flush spreading across his cheeks and turned his face away. Still, he managed a quiet, "Thank you."

"Ach, never mind it. You know I don't mind."

Brand did. Aside from the fact that Magnus was more free than the rest of his brothers—having not taken his place as High Ambassador of Thodelebor yet—he genuinely adored this part of their life.

Which was why Brand often took advantage instead of getting the fuck over it and growing up.

He knew it was ridiculous that he was still calling on Magnus to shield him at his age—to speak when words fled him, to draw notice, to laugh at jokes he didn't understand and be the perfect diplomat.

Yet, he still bloody did it.

Magnus lifted his nose, sniffing like the beast he was. "Weeping stars, do you smell that?"

Brand was hit a second later by the mouthwatering aroma of roasted meats as they reached the final curve and began their descent into the Main Square.

The amount of work that had been finished since this afternoon was staggering.

The flagstones practically sparkled, no trace of the sawdust that had filled every crack and corner. Shops and homes gleamed, flowers and boughs hanging from doors and awnings, windows and balcony railings. Pebbles and rocks shone from the places they'd been tucked, tiny pinpricks of glittering light amongst the greenery.

The pavilion had been fully assembled on the far side of the square, its top stabbing upwards with colorful peaks, the silk ribbons at each post dancing in the wind. Steam rose from the abundant food within, held on platters and towers strewn across massive wooden tables that had only been half-built mere hours ago.

But the center of attention was the Solyr Stone.

As he did every time he saw it, Brand stopped dead in his tracks, something about the marbled obelisk calling out and demanding his awe and respect.

Behind a decorative arch, it rose from the platform he'd been helping to build, clawing for the Unknown. Taller than any building, higher than the trees, wider than four Demons in their rage could wrap their arms around.

And the main reason they were here, gathering with bated breath, anticipation building with every passing hour. The mating ritual was a happy coincidence.

A group of Demons walked by and called out to him, snapping him out of his trance. He waved, offering a small smile even as his heart skipped a beat.

"You know," Mag said, his eyes following a straggling pair of females. "I think you might be the most ungrateful wee shite I ever met in my life."

Brand huffed. "Your observation is noted. I'll try to remember it the next time I'm crawling out of my skin."

"Poor Brand—stuck with braw and bonnie warriors, forced to drink ale and dance until sunrise for weeks on end."

"I don't know why you're complaining. I invited you here to do all of those things in my place, remember?"

"Aye, I know." Magnus ran a hand over his hair and sighed. "Never mind. You'll figure it out, hopefully before another fifty years go by. Now, if you'll excuse me," he said, walking backwards and offering a mocking bow, "my stomach is eating itself and Pet is howling for sustenance."

"The food is for after the ritual!" Brand shouted after him, shaking his head when Mag ignored him in favor of barreling through the growing crowd blocking his way to the feast.

With a deep breath, he stole a glance back the way they'd come, his mind everywhere and nowhere all at once.

His eyes skipped past the tangle of streets and buildings, up beyond the walls and towers of the castle, finally settling on the Sacred Sisters.

Named for the Celestial goddesses that had formed this world, the soaring peaks were the tallest in all of Straelon. Snow clung to their twin summits, a shocking contrast to the sienna stone they were made of, and it was no wonder all of the Horned City seemed to be raising itself up from the sea below in worship of them.

Solyrian, the sunstar, would rise between the heights of the Sacred Sisters next month, its angle perfect as the first rays of day hit upon the mighty prism held where the mountains met halfway up. The immense shard of crystal would guide a concentrated beam directly to the top of the Solyr Stone, channeling its mighty force straight into the earth.

As the energy built, the land would begin to pulse with shockwaves of power, bathing the Montrealm from end-to-end in blinding light before filtering into each and every citizen and feeding them, sustaining their bodies and magic until the next Occurrence.

It was customary, on the cusp of the event, to pray—to cry out from the depths of one's own heart—and ask the Sisters for a boon.

Fifty years ago, Brand hadn't known what to ask for. He'd been young, at his first Occurrence, and unable to care about anything other than surviving his responsibilities as Straelon's Imperial Son.

This time, staring into the night, the twin moons hovering overhead...

"Help me," he whispered, so quiet that his own ears could barely hear the sound. "Remake me. Bring me peace, and ease my spirit. Please, I want to be more than my weaknesses. I want to be able to *breathe*."

In the deep dark, where no mortal creature had ever stepped foot, there was a snap.

Not the rending of twigs, or the crack of bones.

No, it was a falling into place. A soft sigh of relief. A laugh in the silence.

She'd almost forgotten that this was why she was here, that this moment was the true start of it.

The young Demon had been heard, though he didn't know it. Not yet.

He wouldn't appreciate the answer, not at first. He wouldn't grasp its nuances, or see the light of it amidst his own shadows. He wouldn't understand the mess of beauty and pain that was coming for him, ready to carve its name in blood upon his soul.

But he'd get exactly what he asked for.

Eventually.

Maybe.

If she was cunning and focused, and played her part well. If the pieces all listened and stopped fighting her.

Stars, help him.

Help all of them.

4

Aldiat dipped his fingers into the golden vessel Brand held—his arm now very much healed thanks to a lot of begging and even more gold—and lifted the crimson paste to Frida's face. "In the way of Solyrian, I mark my mate and ask for the Sisters' continued blessings." He drew a thick line from her forehead, over the slope of her nose, her lips, her chin, and down the column of her throat. "I am hers as I am yours. Shine on us both, and grant us your power and protection as we move forward in this life as one."

On the cusp of every Occurrence, Demons the realm over murmured a similar prayer. Legend had it that a lucky few in their history had been especially blessed by the sunstar and granted real markings of favor by the Sisters—a perfect, permanent match to their fated mate, whether they'd found each other yet or not.

Most only received the deep red paint at their mating ritual. Made from ground stone and perfumed oil, it was drawn in matching patterns however the pair wished as a way to mimic the stories of their people. Since the bond was there regardless, it was more than enough.

Frida grinned, her teeth stark against the stain as she repeated Aldiat's actions. Tears in both of their eyes, they pressed their heads together, and Brand's chest twisted. The way they looked at each other, it was like the two of them were the only two creatures in all the world.

Lyriat's voice was a distant muffle, the cheering of the crowd and fanning of their evergreen branches little more than a whisper in the face of his own overwhelm. His sheer fucking *want.*

Brand craved a mate and that safety in another so intensely he was practically choking on it. To have someone who understood him, without the need for cursed words…

Fuck. It would be everything.

He hardly noticed the hand-shaking and well-wishing, or the vibration of the wooden planks beneath his bare feet. Barely acknowledged when Lyriat clapped him on the shoulder and sauntered away, taking the ceremonial bowl with him. Didn't register a single face as he chatted and hoped the smile he'd plastered on wasn't nearly as fake-looking as it bloody felt.

Hundreds of shouts and whistles saved him. Those nearest spun to watch as Aldiat and Frida devoured one another, smearing the paste across their mouths and cheeks amidst raucous laughter, and finally giving him the escape he needed. It was the most natural thing in the world to slip away, silent and unnoticed, his shoulders sagging in time with his sigh of relief.

Hopping down off the back side of the platform, he wound behind the empty merchant tents and into the food pavilion, heading straight for Magnus.

"I'm so bloody hungry, I could die," Brand said.

Frida had gone all out. Slabs and slices and legs of meat crowded each other on their platters, crusted with herbs and salt. Smoked fish rested in beds of sliced lemons. Roasted vegetables and crispy potatoes beckoned. Clouds of steam danced over tureens of soups and stews. Breads and cheeses, olives and pickles, bowls of fruit and fresh cream—anything he could ever want, laid out before him and begging to be tried.

Mag tipped a ladle of brown sauce over everything on his plate. "You and me both," he grumbled. "Pet has been howling since I walked through the damned portal."

Brand chuckled and popped a chunk of cheese into his mouth. "Don't even try to pretend this is your first serving."

Wolflords were hungry at the best of times, but he supposed that's what happened when one was essentially eating for two.

Magnus winked and took a bite of what looked to be a roasted lamb chop, then gasped, his eyes widening as he examined the piece of meat.

Instantly alert, Brand darted his gaze around. It was uncommon for someone to target an Imperial, but not impossible. Sisters knew most of his uncles had met mysterious deaths. Poisoning was a real concern, no matter that they'd likely survive it. It still sent a message.

"Mag, are you well?"

"This smells like one of mine," his brother finally said, leveling him with a penetrating glare as his nostrils flared. "For the love of the stars, tell me you did not cook my Ilsa."

Brand blinked. "Ilsa?"

"My newest wee kid."

"A… goat."

"Aye."

For a minute, Brand was worried—until he remembered Magnus was an absolute arsehole when he wanted to be.

Most of Straelon's food came from Thodelebor, the Westrealm happy to trade their harvests in exchange for lumber and stone, and the use of Demon warriors when needed. While the Wolflords were fiercely capable of protecting their fields and livestock from the creatures of the Ghostwood, they were simple farmers at heart.

Years ago, Magnus had strolled through the portal in the great hall during supper, claiming his favorite dairy cow had been sent by mistake. He'd taken one look at the table, laden with beef, and clutched his chest. It was the whispered *'Fiona?'* that had nearly made Brand empty his stomach right there. He hadn't been able to eat red meat for… Well, about the same amount of time it had taken Mag to confess the entire thing had been an elaborate prank, weeks later.

"No way. Not again," Brand said, laughing. "You'll have to think of something else."

"I'm fucking serious," Mag growled. "She was meant to be a gift! Did you not see my note?"

Brand narrowed his eyes. "Why would you send a goat as a gift if not to eat it?"

"Are you out of your fucking mind? You don't eat a baby goat! They're fucking pets."

"I…" he swallowed, suddenly unsure. "If it… Magnus…"

Brand's stomach churned, every piece of meat on his plate suddenly having a name.

Faldir and Hedda chose that moment to arrive, never far from each other's side. The rare sight of her in a dress stunned him even further. It was strange, and oddly unsettling, and stole any possibility of words from his mouth. Even Faldir had cleaned up, his hair combed neatly around his horns, the rosy hue of drink infusing his cheeks and making him look something akin to happy.

"Your Highness," Hedda said with a nod. Her voice dipped lower when she turned to Magnus, though not at all flirtatious. "Your other Highness."

"Ach, Hedda. When will your bonny arse accept we're meant to be?"

"Hmm." She tapped her chin, pretending to think about it. "Nope, still never, cousin."

Mag tsk'ed, completely irreverent of their distant relation.

"Let me guess," Faldir said, leaning in. "You've convinced Brand, again, that he's eaten a beloved companion."

"Aye, he has!" Mag cried out. "My poor, wee Ilsa!"

Hedda punched him in the arm, and his brother's entire demeanor changed, eyes shining and face going red. Magnus tried to keep it together, pinching his lips between his teeth, but the laugh exploded out of him anyway. "Damn you, Faldir. I almost had him. You should have seen his face. He was *this close* to swearing off meat forever."

Brand opened his mouth to tear into Mag, but was stopped by the sight of a striking female approaching the opposite side of the table, teeth sunk into her plump bottom lip. Hazel eyes peeked at him from behind a curtain of ebony hair, her tawny horns catching the lantern light as she grabbed this and that.

He didn't recognize her, but she was beyond beautiful—which inevitably meant that all Brand could manage was to stare at her while he tried to think of anything to say.

She gave him a lingering look and sauntered off, glancing once over her shoulder with a soft smile, and Brand watched her disappear into the crowd, heart pounding.

Sisters, he was such a fool.

"Right," Magnus said. "I'll, uh… go and find us a seat."

Faldir cleared his throat. "I'll join you. Hedda?"

"Coming!"

Brand knew what they were trying to do, but he had no desire to stand there alone, marinating in the grime of his own idiotic solitude. He wanted the distraction, the jokes and camaraderie. He wanted to bloody relax with his family and friends and forget how long it had been since he'd found himself tangled in another's breath and body.

Everyone was already at one end of a long table contentedly devouring their meals, two foaming tankards of ale resting in front of Magnus.

Just what he needed.

"I sincerely hope one of those is for me," he said, setting his plate down.

"One of many this evening. I plan to get you rip-roaring drunk so you forget all your troubles." Magnus swiped up his drink and gulped half of it down.

Grabbing his own cup, Brand chugged the cool ale. He slammed it down when he finished and scrubbed a hand over his face, the short stubble of his beard scraping against his calloused palm as he breathed a sigh of relief.

Troubles forgotten, indeed.

"I still can't believe Baldrir missed Aldiat's mating ceremony for a damned female," Hedda grumbled.

"You can't believe a male thought with his dick instead of his head?" Faldir snorted, ducking beneath his twin's half-hearted swipe. "And here I thought you were supposed to be the sharper of the two of us."

"Ach, away with you two!" Mag chided. "True love was happening in the Westrealm behind that door, and if tonight's happy couple don't mind his absence, then neither should you. Besides, Nyri was there in his stead, and did a lovely job of Frida's hair. Joy and blessings abound, thank the Sisters for it."

Faldir stabbed a piece of meat with his fork. "I'm more surprised Bal managed to keep his mouth closed long enough to do anything other than talk the poor maid to death."

"If he knows what he's about, he won't have closed his mouth for the last couple of days, but not because of anything so mundane as talking." Hedda tossed a long wave of hair over her shoulder, sniffing. "Or have you forgotten how to please a bed partner, little brother?"

The table erupted, Brand fighting between laughter and choking on the food in his mouth when another two ales appeared at his elbow. Not by any mystical means, but courtesy of Thaddeus.

"Cousin," was all Thad said, arching his brow.

There was an impish light in Thad's eyes, even as his expression was almost bored, and Brand struggled to contain his smile. It had been over a year since he'd seen that sparkling mischief.

Over a year since their Aunt Meliora, Thad's mother, had died, and he'd worried his cousin would never be the same. Sisters knew, Caius was still wrecked over it.

Forcing his own face to match Thad's bland look, they stared at each other, waiting.

It didn't even cross his mind to care that the table had gone quiet, people watching and waiting, focused solely on them. Not when the result was possibly seeing Thad light up with a true smile, maybe hearing his cheeky laugh.

Thaddeus's lip quirked and, in a blur of motion, they both jumped to snatch a tankard. Ale sloshed, narrowly missing them as they lifted the cups to drink.

He dodged the fist that came at him from the corner of his eye, shouts of *Cheater!* and *Get him!* filling the space around them. Brand fought one-handed against Thad's sabotage, choking back his laughter and finally managing to snag his cousin's wrist.

He refused to lose to the whelp.

His cup hit the table a split-second before Thad's and Brand leapt up, bellowing out a triumphant *whoop*. Thad cursed and leveled a finger at him, breathing hard.

In that moment—skin clear of the usual Thodeleborian markings, face shaven and blond hair just long enough to brush at his collar—Thad looked almost exactly like Magnus had as a younger male. Full of life and exuberant defiance. Only his eyes were different, a deep cerulean to Mag's bright and golden amber.

Eyes that burned with challenge.

Without a word, Thaddeus spun and raced to the ale barrels nearby, dodging numerous people and nearly knocking a male over in his haste. The old Demon sent a string of curses after Thad, but his young cousin paid him no heed as he filled four cups with the frothy liquid. Carefully arranging the handles to bring all of them back at once, he managed the return journey without spilling too much, only slightly more aware of those around him.

"Best two out of three," Thad said, shoving a pair of tankards towards him.

Brand grinned, lifted his third ale, and emptied that one too.

"You know, you two could have at least tried to put yourselves together before coming down to breakfast."

Brand cracked an eye open against the hammering pain bouncing around his skull, and beheld the Demon King of Straelon.

Lyriat stood at the head of their table with his arms crossed, an arrogant brow raised in censure. He cut an imposing figure in his long, sleeveless tunic—a rare sight, since the cocky bastard often ran around shirtless for the entertainment of it.

His own, of course.

White horns spiraled from high on his forehead, winding upwards from the copper waves of his waist-length hair. Rings of gold inlay glinted along their carved lengths and bands of rare, pearlescent stone circled his arms above powerful biceps—a permanent mark of his station and all that would be left on the pyre after his death.

Those that didn't know him might have even been frightened, worried they'd offended the monarch. But Brand caught the mirth glittering in his friend's moss-green eyes, the slight upward tilt of his lips.

"Please—and I say this with the utmost respect—fuck off."

"Aye. What he said," Magnus murmured.

Dishes clinked under the hum of conversation, Solyrian burning bright and spilling into the great hall through massive windows that ran floor to rafters along the walls. For some bloody reason, even the ceiling was glass, and the dust motes dancing innocently in the overwhelming light only served to highlight how dreadful he felt.

He was never drinking again.

His brother was staring at his plate of untouched food, head propped in his hands. Brand was fairly certain the chunks he was seeing in Mag's snarled braids were sand and seaweed, though he had no idea how they'd gotten there.

"Ah, come now," Lyriat said. "Young Thaddeus was just telling me what a lovely time you all had last night. Do you disagree?"

No bloody clue. He couldn't remember a damned thing after Thad had wrapped a length of bunting around his horns while cackling in his face. All Brand knew was that, if he looked even half as awful as Mag, then it was no wonder Lyriat was commenting on it.

Head swimming, he chanced a look around the hall and found his cousin among a group of warriors near the portal. His hands waved wildly about as he no doubt told some ridiculous story, beaming at every comment and guffaw, and clearly unaffected by the chaotic shenanigans of the evening before.

Youthful prat.

"The night was fine," Magnus grumbled. "It's the morning that's being a right wee shite."

Lyriat chuckled and pulled a chair out, plopping down and rubbing his hands together. "Well, I don't know about you two, but I'm starving. Shall I have some eggs and toast? Or perhaps potatoes and greens."

"Sisters spare me," Brand whispered, his stomach turning.

"You know what? I think I'll have the lot."

A servant appeared to the sound of his and Mag's groans, gently placing a platter in front of the king. Two glasses came next, set before him and his brother. The liquid—if it could be called such a thing—was gurgling, putting off a noxious odor that was possibly the most foul fuckery he'd ever smelled.

Of course, he thought that every time.

"Ach, not this rot again," Magnus whined, swiping his up.

"It's no more than you deserve for being an irresponsible reprobate," Lyriat said cheerfully around a mouthful.

"Aye, I suppose there's that. Little brother?"

Brand eyed the brew, already dreading the next couple minutes. The only thing that allowed him to palm his own cup was the knowledge that it would work, born from previous, unfortunate experience.

Magnus gave him a halfhearted smile before clinking their glasses together and tipping his back, downing the entire thing in one gulp.

Before he could talk himself out of it, Brand did the same. The gelatinous mix went down like fizzing mud—bubbles exploding in his mouth, bits gagging him—and his whole face twisted against his will.

"Weeping arseholes!" Mag bellowed, pounding the table with a fist. "Why does it have to be that fucking repulsive?"

"To deter… from… same asinine… over and over."

Brand's ears roared in time with the beat of his heart as the potion took hold, half of Lyriat's words denied entry with every thump.

Tendrils of magic reached out from his center with long fingers and, just as he had the thought that his end was coming, the concoction settled and dissipated. Between one blink and the next, a cool dew lit upon his limbs, refreshing him. His body hummed, as if to sing and chirp with the morning birds. He was the shimmering dawn itself, shining bright after a long storm.

"Say what you will," Brand said with a sigh, "but the rank shite works wonders."

"Aye." Mag grinned. "And now that my head's cleared, I wonder…" He gave Lyriat a narrow-eyed look, leaning in close to the monarch. "Where were *you* after the ritual last night, Your Illustrious Horned Majesty?"

Brand huffed at the sarcastic jab, the awkwardness of their system lost on none of them.

He'd gotten lucky to be Blessed of Straelon, to have grown up with its king by his side in the trenches of adolescence. Lyriat was his friend first and foremost. Still, it was odd to try and define their official places.

Brand was higher in rank as an Imperial Son, but lower in rank as High Ambassador. Meanwhile, his father, Emperor Alwyn, outranked literally everyone in Bordoroth. Which meant creatures tended to bow and scrape before Brand and his brothers, even when it was technically inappropriate to do so.

Magnus liked to lean into those strange nuances, bringing the tension to its breaking point and forcing it over the edge with humor. As the only one of the current five Sons to still be in the position of Ambassador Apparent, he got away with more ridiculous behavior because he didn't officially represent Thodelebor yet.

That honor still lay with their Uncle Caius—Thad's father, and a male who'd taken seriousness to a level unheard of since the death of his mate.

Lyriat sniffed and looked away, his demeanor suddenly aloof. "I was here and there, of course. We must have missed one another throughout the celebrations."

Magnus barked out a laugh. "Now there's a damned lie if I ever heard one!"

Lyriat's cheeks slowly turned a comical shade of crimson that Brand wasn't sure he'd ever seen there before.

"Sweet Sisters," Brand said, gaping. "Mag is right! What—"

Shouts sounded on the opposite end of the hall, bringing every conversation to a screeching halt. Benches and tables turned over, clattering to the tune of shattered pottery. Weapons sang as they were drawn, flashes of light signaling various Demons giving in to their transformation.

He, Magnus, and Lyriat scrambled to their feet as Thad's voice reached above he chaos. "Get back! Don't touch him!"

The crowd parted before them as they rushed towards the portal. Lyriat called the rage and went through his change seamlessly, the mighty Demon King glowing with sunlight and towering above his subjects. Whatever he saw made his steps falter, his leathery wings jerking out to keep his balance.

"Out, all of you!" Lyriat bellowed, his voice deep and echoing. "Now!"

As if by magic, the room emptied and left Brand with a view that sent shockwaves tearing through him. He broke into a sprint, sliding on his knees as he reached the scene.

A ravaged body lay prone on the flagstones, Thad kneeling on the other side.

"We need to turn him over," his cousin said. "Somehow."

Brand's breath sawed as he nodded, his hands hovering uselessly above the creature. Skin had been peeled away in long strips from head to toe, the savage wounds oozing blood in such a constant stream that it was impossible to tell if any flesh was still intact.

"There's nothing for it," Mag said, crouching beside him. "We'll just have to do it, lads."

"Right. Hold his neck steady, Magnus," Brand commanded. "Lyriat, get his legs while Thad and I work his shoulders over." He met his cousin's gaze. "Pull him towards yourself, I'll do the rest. Everyone on my signal… Go!"

He waited until the male was half over before sliding his hands beneath and pulling the torso as gently as he was able.

For a moment, Brand felt a spark of relief when he heard a quiet, wheezing groan. Then his eyes focused and time slowed, the world stretching around him and snapping back as recognition came and disbelief stole his voice.

Baldrir.

Brutalized. Tortured. Maimed.

The room shook as Lyriat unleashed an ear-shattering roar, giving voice to the fury boiling within Brand.

His friend was nearly unrecognizable, especially without his horns. Their once-proud lengths had been violently hacked away, reduced to jagged stumps. Even more skin was missing from his front half than the back, his entire chest and stomach an oozing mess of exposed muscle and more. Worst of all, Baldrir's jaw was slack—blood pooling in his open mouth and pouring from the corner of his lips—and his tongue was gone.

"Sisters save us," Magnus whispered.

Brand shook himself, refusing the roiling emotions and forcing his mind to work logically. "Thaddeus, is there anything you can do for him?" Brand asked.

Thad's mother had been Nachthellian—making his cousin half Wolflord, half Sorcerit—but he was young, not yet possessing his full powers though he looked fairly grown. Still, there was a chance—

"No," his cousin answered quietly, a shadow flitting across his features. "I know only the basics. Mam hadn't gotten around to the rest before she... *Before.*"

"We need a healer then." Brand turned to Lyriat. "Please tell me an inordinate number of Sorcerit have already shown up from the Evesong to witness our Occurrence."

Lyriat's jaw ticked. "None," he said. "The few who came to do the flowers left as soon as they were done fixing Aldiat. You know how they are."

Brand cursed under his breath. "Baldrir doesn't have time for us to make a formal request. He needs help now."

He tried to recall anything that would help—a favor owed, a rumor heard, a connection to exploit. Finding Araxis would take too long, his youngest brother more myth than substance most days.

"I know someone who'd come without question," Thad said, interrupting his thoughts. "A friend."

Lyriat stopped his pacing and leveled Thaddeus with a chilling look. "They possess the skill to heal injuries such as this?"

Thad didn't hesitate. "I swear it."

"The price?"

That time, his cousin did pause, and his voice was hushed when he finally said, "Far less than you'd expect."

With a curt nod, the Demon King waved a dismissive hand. "Go."

"Aye," Mag said, gripping Thad's shoulder. "Fast as you can."

Thaddeus stood, determination in every line of his body as he rifled through his pocket and withdrew a length of thread. "It won't take long, so be ready." With that, he tossed the coiled bundle and followed it, disappearing through the oily, rippling surface of the portal.

Movement forced Brand to look up, just in time to see Hedda and Faldir drawing up beside Lyriat with weapons drawn, their faces twisted in mirrored looks of outrage.

"What the fuck? Is that…" his Second whispered. Then louder, "Bal!"

Her axe clattered to the floor as she dropped without thought and crawled through the pooling blood to her kin. She pressed her forehead to Baldrir's, crooning nonsense, twining a lank lock of his hair around her fingers.

The sight ripped into him. Whoever had done this would pay.

"Faldir," he said, the rage rising, "bring me our five fastest."

"Consider it done."

His Third was already shouting orders before he'd left the great hall.

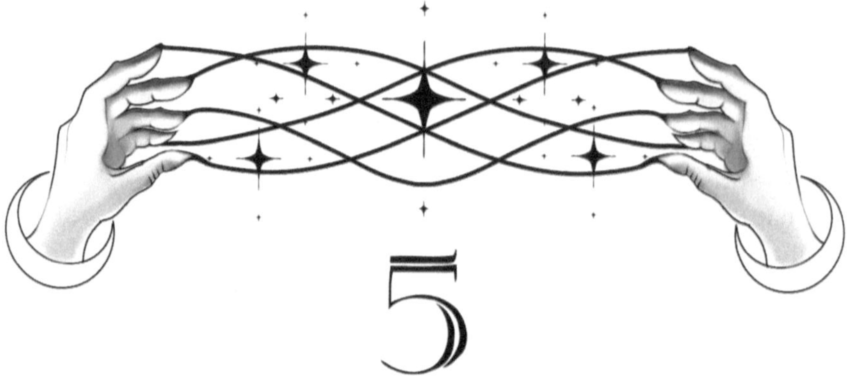

5

Lunara's hands moved of their own accord, the motion mindless. The moonlight she'd grabbed glittered in the air before her as the beams concentrated into threads, which then spun themselves into yarn. She tugged more of the glowing length towards herself, the opposite end floating up and waiting to be made into more when she was ready.

Not that she was really paying much attention to that.

No, her head was elsewhere as her hook bobbed.

She narrowed her eyes at the opposite wall of her cottage. At the countless books piled haphazardly on dusty shelves. At the trinkets shoved between them, bits and bobs from places she'd never been.

She looked lower, at the blankets and pillows and doilies strewn about the furniture—some her own creations, but most of them not—no rhyme or reason to their colorful mayhem. At the mismatched tables with stacks of pictures drawn by tiny hands. At the vase of eternal flowers that had been sitting there so long they would've died thousands of times in any other realm by now.

Payment for her services, every last thing, though she could hardly remember the faces of those who'd given them. Only fair, since none of them remembered her.

Even so, the people she'd healed seemed to know exactly what she liked, even if they didn't really know her at all.

It's better that way, and you know it.

Yes, she did. And she had no need for money anyway, which was why she didn't accept it.

It didn't change the dismal fact that she only had herself to talk to most days—or that she actually answered. That maybe said more about her than anything.

Again, good. Just as you wanted.

Lunara sighed and slumped back in her chair, sinking further into the cushions. The new position had the added benefit of changing her view from room to ceiling.

Huzzah.

Unfortunately, it meant that she was forced to acknowledge the cobwebs that had gathered since the last time she'd made herself clean. Didn't matter that it would take a mere few minutes and a wave of her hand. It was convincing herself to do it in the first place that was the problem.

That, and the pain that would follow.

Well, more pain, and of a different sort. The kind that didn't have anything to do with the twinges sparking in her joints after her healing the day before. Of course, the physical ailments could be easily remedied with a gift of blood.

No. Too dangerous.

But, if she only had a little, it would be okay. Just a sip to keep the aches at bay. No more than that.

No. It's fine. You're fine. Use a broom.

Lunara cranked her head around this way and that, the never-ending dimness of Nachthelliae doing absolutely nothing to help her locate said broom. She could get up and look, but that would require moving and what was the point?

It had been more than a year since anyone other than Cordelia had actually been inside her cottage. There was no one to impress. No one that would see or care.

Besides, she was busy. Her blankets wouldn't weave themselves, after all.

Actually, they might be able to if she was willing to try.

Which she *wasn't.* It was already a gamble to make them in the first place.

Don't think about it, Lunara. Ignore, ignore, ignore.

Right.

She tossed her project aside with a huff, the moonlight detaching as soon as her hands left it. The pile of pale yarn looked so innocent there on the chair arm. Just another part of the mess.

It was mocking her, though, she was sure of it.

Her stomach conveniently rumbled, reminding her that it had been hours since she'd eaten. Or… had she eaten today? It was impossible to remember.

Probably not, then.

Either way, Lunara was grateful for the distraction. Pushing from her seat, she made for the tiny kitchen off the main room. She would just get a snack and then find that broom—

The hair on her arms stood on end as a ripple passed through her home.

No, no, no.

Someone was on her land. Someone powerful.

Alarm bells pealed through Lunara's mind as her heart kicked up. Cordelia didn't set off the warning when she came, and very few people knew exactly where she lived. *Few* meaning exactly what it meant. As in three. *Total.*

Unless it was *them.*

Shitting stars. Think. Think!

She reached out and grabbed an iron pan. The sheer weight of it was ridiculous, but she tried a practice swing anyway, nearly tossing the thing across the room when the handle slipped in her grasp.

What are you doing, you bumbling ninny? Use your magic!

Blessed moons, it was a wonder she was even still alive.

Lunara tossed the pan back onto the counter and rushed across the cottage, muttering under her breath. Light gathered on her fingertips as she reached the front door and pressed herself against it. Closing her eyes, she searched for her courage, chest heaving and body buzzing.

She would've sworn she'd been so careful, had hidden herself and her abilities well, but she must have slipped. Must have—

"Lunara! Are you here, lass?"

Her eyes snapped open at the rolling richness of *that* voice shouting from a distance. Dizzying relief suffused her veins in an instant and she nearly crumpled to the floor before whirling around to grab the knob.

From the porch, she scanned the luminescent landscape. Birds called and insects buzzed, the twin moons hanging heavy in their river of stars overhead. No one was there, and the path to the portal that disappeared around the side of the cottage was undisturbed.

"Thaddeus?" she called, suddenly unsure she'd heard him.

He tore around the bend in a dead sprint a second later, kicking up sparkling turquoise dust, not stopping until he practically slammed into the column holding the roof above her. "Aye. It's me," he said, hands on his knees.

Lunara hadn't thought to ever lay eyes on the young Wolflord again. It had been a dreadful day the last time she'd seen him—one she'd rather forget.

As would he, she'd imagine.

"I'm sorry to come barging in like this, but you're needed. Right away."

She blinked at his words. "Needed?"

"Aye. Urgently."

Her first thought was for his father, and worry seized her. "Is it Caius? Did something happen?"

Thaddeus waved that away. "Ach, no. He's well. I'm to bring you back with me to Straelon, sent by the Demon King himself."

"The *Demon King?*" she shrieked, voice too loud as a hysterical laugh escaped her.

It had to be some kind of prank.

The Thaddeus that had shown up on her doorstep last year, demanding admittance to see his ailing mother, had turned out to be a wonderful nuisance. He'd gotten up to all sorts of tricks to make everyone smile.

Lunara crossed her arms and raised a brow, sure she'd caught him. "You want me to drop everything and go to the Montrealm with you *right now*?"

Thad straightened, throwing his shoulders back. "That *is* where Lyriat resides," he answered, voice rumbling low.

There was no quirk of the lip, no dancing amusement in his eyes. He just stood there, still as stone and staring.

Stars above, he was dead serious.

A cloud of terror descended over her as she retreated a step. "Oh. No," she rasped. "You don't understand. I've never… I can't…"

There was a reason she'd stayed holed up in her cottage, lost in the midnight wilds. Why she did everything she could to avoid rumors and prying eyes, and had never set a foot outside of Nachthelliae.

"A person's been tortured, Lunara. Torn to pieces. He'll not last the day without you."

She snapped her gaze up, unable to deny the spark of purpose that flared within her.

"What happened?"

Stars and arses. You've lost your bleeding mind.

Thaddeus exhaled, gripping his nape. "A Demon returned this morning missing half of his flesh. Horns gone, no tongue. I'm honestly not sure how he managed to get himself through the portal. He was still alive when I left, but unconscious and fading fast."

Duty called out to her but—

No. Someone will see. Someone will tell them.

Her mind and heart clashed, waging war in the deepest parts of her.

Fool, you shouldn't have asked. Now you feel obligated, and for what? You'll be risking everything!

And yet, she couldn't fathom hearing of another's suffering, being asked so pointedly for help, and choosing to do nothing. It would make her like the very monsters she wished to avoid, if she did.

Thaddeus must have seen the wavering on her face. He drew closer and held her hand in his own. "Please, lass. We need answers we can't get if he's dead. It has to be you."

Sometimes, Lunara would swear she could feel the universe holding its breath, waiting to shift one way or another, its fate in her hands—which she knew was completely absurd. She didn't matter nearly that much.

But this was such a time, when that stillness settled into her. A quiet certainty not even her worst fears could counter.

"Alright. I'll do it."

Before she could talk herself out of it, Lunara left Thad on the porch and rushed into the dark interior of her cottage, grabbing various things as she moved. She probably could have reached for them through the ether later, but there was no telling how much power it would take to heal the Demon. She needed to reserve every drop.

Agreeing to her first foray out of the Evesong was enough drama for Lunara. She wouldn't risk feeding in a strange place with people she didn't know on top of it.

She jerked to a stop mid-step just inside her bedroom door, arms full and chest constricting as she took it in. More books lay about, open to the pages she'd left off. Half-done projects cluttered here and there. The bed that hugged her like a lover and never failed to keep her warm. A round window with its velvet seat, overlooking the blooming garden she couldn't tame.

It was a mess, but it was her mess and she was leaving it. Just like that.

It's only for a day or two. You'll be back before the dust settles.

"I wouldn't be so sure," another voice—one that assuredly wasn't her own—whispered in the recesses of her mind.

The breathy, singsong sound sent a current down Lunara's spine, and her back hit the wall. She squeezed her eyes shut, clutching her belongings with white knuckles.

Please, no. Not right now.

The answering giggle did not help.

That infernal laugh followed almost every statement the Voice had ever made—a disturbingly cheerful, mischievous tinkling that was in complete juxtaposition to the words it said.

The intrusions, rare and random as they were, never failed to turn Lunara inside out. Still, she sent out a silent prayer every time, begging the Sisters for the Voice to be real. Friend or foe, it didn't matter to her.

As long as it wasn't madness setting in. Anything but that.

Deal with it later. Or never.

Lunara shook herself, shoving her upset into the dark inner dungeon where it belonged, and dumped the items she held on the mattress.

Yes, never was good. Perfect.

In the closet, she pulled an embroidered bag down from the high shelf. Another payment, one she'd never thought to actually use.

She hardly looked at the dresses she tugged from their hangers. They were all the same, anyway, only their colors and patterns varying. She stuffed them into the bag as she walked, and added the collection on the bed after. Though, what she planned to do with a brush and gardening gloves while healing a Demon was outside her comprehension at the moment.

She used one of her moon-woven blankets to hold all the things she didn't actually need, but that an average Sorcerit would be expected to use. Jars of salve, bundles of cloth—her distractions.

Better for them to think she spent time making potions and creams, infusing them little by little. Better they assume she had only a few tricks up her sleeve, a piddling skill she was known for. That she was just the same as every other Nachthellian.

She could hardly see over the mass in her arms when she found herself back on the porch, ready to go.

"Ach, gimme that." Thad snatched everything away, her possessions looking so much smaller when he held them. "If you trip and break your neck, we'll be right back where we started."

He continued to talk as he turned and left, unaware she was frozen to the spot, her booted foot dangling in the air.

Lunara had come and gone from her home so many times, but this was different.

She wasn't popping into the next village to oversee a birth or mend a bone. She wasn't foraging for mushrooms, or swimming in the lake, or lying in a field beneath the aurora.

This was another pissing realm.

When she finally convinced herself to move, to clear the stairs and hit the path, the ground seemed to tremble beneath her feet.

At the bend, she spared a single glance behind. Her cottage faded into the endless gloom of the Evesong with every vibrating step, until all she could see were the shadows and branches crowding her between the glowing flora and twinkling dust.

That was when she turned ahead, towards the portal hidden amongst the trees.

Thaddeus was already holding the toll in his hand when she approached him. "Ready?" he asked.

Not even a little bit.

"Ready."

With a nod, he tossed the small piece of Straelon into the undulating surface in front of them and held out his hand for her to take. Lunara's last thought as she reached out and followed him in, as spectral fingers caressed her skin for the briefest of moments and transported her body away from Nachthelliae, was a desperate plea.

Sweet Sisters, let this not be a mistake.

The first thing Lunara saw was the blood.

Rivers and puddles of it stained an alarming area of the marbled brown flagstones—which meant she should have known better than to dive straight for the mangled creature at its center without being more sure of her footing.

As she slipped and her feet went out from under her, Lunara could only be grateful that Thaddeus had taken her bags and she wasn't forced to chuck them every which way to catch herself.

Except, just before she went arse-over-teakettle, a massive pair of arms banded around her middle and saved her from the indignity of ever hitting the ground.

"Shite," a deep voice rumbled, craggy and soft at once. "Are you—"

She lifted her gaze and followed a strong, straight nose upward to meet hazel eyes in a kaleidoscope of earthy colors, wide with surprise beneath an elegant arch of thick brows.

Weeping Sisters. The Demon holding her was the most beautiful male she'd ever seen in her life.

"Th-thank you," she murmured, trying to catch her breath. "I wish I could say that I wasn't always so clumsy, but then I would be lying."

More lies were the last thing she needed.

He blinked down at her, silent, and Lunara didn't quite know where to look anymore—or why he was still holding her instead of setting her upright.

Hearing her name being uttered in hushed tones snapped Lunara from her frozen state, wrenching her focus back to the task at hand. Scrambling from the Demon's hold, she pushed him from her mind as she twisted and fell to her knees beside the creature on the floor.

All of the confidence she possessed burst to the fore at moments like these, when Lunara knew without a shred of doubt that someone's life was depending solely on her.

She called power from within herself, the threads of magic venturing out between her and the male. His heartbeat reached her ears in an instant—weak, wavering, barely there.

Without a thought, she placed her hands on his ravaged chest and funneled magic into him, detaching his mind from the agony of feeling. She knew just from looking at him that he'd long-since gone into a state of shock, his body precariously close to a point of no return.

It was going to take everything she had to heal him. She couldn't remember the last time she'd had to expend that amount of power, and the realization daunted her.

No, she had enough. She could do it.

He had to be moved from the floor first—if for no other reason than Lunara's own bones wouldn't be able to take hours upon hours of crouching in this position.

"I need a room and a bed, now," she said.

Shouts sounded in response, but she didn't understand a word. Her only focus was on forcing the Demon's heart to move, to pump, to keep him alive.

"Shall we lift him, my lady?"

Lunara spared a glance for the female who'd spoken directly beside her, a stunning Demon with red-rimmed eyes like moss. "I will do it, just tell me where to go."

The Demon hesitated briefly before standing. "Follow me."

Ignoring the twinge already starting in her hips, Lunara rose, her hands fused to his exposed muscle and bone. She bade the male's body to follow and he left the ground, his particles obeying her commands. Lunara kept one eye on her charge and the other on the female's back, the steady pitter patter of blood dropping to stone the only sound as she followed.

It wasn't long before they came to a door and she was led inside. The bed had been prepared with gauzy, clean linens, blankets and pillows absent and the curtains removed.

Lunara placed the Demon on its soft surface as gently as she could manage. "What is his name?"

The female stood at the end of the bed, gaze distant. "Baldrir."

"Hello, Baldrir," Lunara crooned as she detached herself from him, leaving two small handprints of perfectly healed skin, her palms burning as if it had been her own flesh she'd left behind. "And yours?"

"Hedda." Her voice was thick, trembling.

Lunara pushed a matted lock of black hair away from Baldrir's beaten face. "I'm going to do everything I can to save him, Hedda," she said quietly. "I swear it."

"Thank you." Hedda drew in a deep breath and made for the door. "Is there anything else you need?"

"My things, from Thaddeus. Otherwise, just time."

Hedda bowed her head. "It shall be done, my lady."

Lunara sat on the edge of the mattress as the door closed, lifting the Demon's large hand in her own. "You are beloved by those around you, Baldrir, which says a great deal. I should think they'd be rather cross if you left them here without your company. Let's not disappoint them, hmm?"

Light flared as Lunara's power concentrated between their palms, and she began.

Time wasn't real in that place, where flesh knit and bones mended. Where power was exchanged for pain over minutes and hours and days.

Where Lunara broke so others could heal.

Every reconnected vessel was a knife to her own. Rebuilding jointed places caused hers to splinter. Each bit of sinew restored and ligament repaired sent a fiery blaze of devastation through her.

She held Baldrir's violent mutilation within her hands and then accepted it all into herself.

No, Lunara didn't bleed. She didn't bruise, or split, or shatter. Her skin didn't rend in the same places. Her limbs didn't crack in the same ways.

There was nothing to see, but she *felt it.* Sisters save her, she felt every horrific second.

Lunara's fangs cut into her more than once as she clenched her teeth against it, slicing her lips and tongue, shredding her gums. Sweat beaded on her scalp and soaked her dress, the film of hard labor clinging to her. Her throat ached and her head pounded from the screams withheld.

From bearing every raw ounce of Baldrir's torture in silence.

Silent, but for the whispers she gave him between their shared torment. Soft words she uttered in earnest, their only purpose to uplift and bring him back gently.

"WHO WOULD DARE? WHO WOULD *FUCKING DARE* INSULT ME AND MINE IN such a manner!"

The Demon King was in a spitting temper, each stomping step shaking the windows of the great hall. His sunlight markings dimmed with every bellow he freed, until the obsidian flare of his membranous wings were like a void behind him. It was the footprints trailing him, though—the ones left behind in Baldrir's drying blood—that had Brand seeing his own shade of red.

"You said he was well! You assured us you'd seen him! Now, *this*?!" Lyriat chucked a wooden bench across the great hall, the seat splintering into infinite pieces as it landed and he roared to the glass ceiling, "I want the fucking truth, Magnus, right fucking *now*!"

Brand choked back the rage trying to rise in answer to his friend's fury. Hedda and Faldir didn't possess anywhere near his level of control, having long-since succumbed and made the change to tower above him along with the seething king.

If not for Lyriat's copper hair to the twins' wine-red coloring, the three of them could have been triplets pacing there, growling and grunting with every pass.

"I swear to the Sisters and all I hold dear that I left him whole and hale last night," Mag rasped, a haunted look in his golden eyes. "He was well. I don't understand what happened."

"Would you say the same while under the effects of a genuinely binding oath?" Lyriat spun on him, snatching Mag's rumpled robe in a colossal fist as he crouched and brought their noses together. "Shall we call Caius and your precious Chieftains here to perform it? Maybe the lot of you can take turns sinking your dripping, poisonous teeth into one another for good measure so that I am reassured and no longer tempted to lay waste to every last, fucking inch of your traitorous realm!"

Shite.

Invoking one of the Wolflords' most precious customs in that mocking fashion was careless in the extreme, and well beneath Lyriat as a Realm Ruler.

Pet flashed over his brother's features in a silent snarl. "I'm going to give you the benefit of the doubt and chalk this up to grief, despite the fact that you've just come perilously close to an unforgivable offense by saying such a thing to me," Mag bit out. "Even so, aye. Gladly. If for no other reason than to put you back in your place and remind you that Bal is as much my friend as the rest of you—which, by the way, is the only reason I haven't bitten your fucking hand off for touching me thus. Let go of me, Lyriat, before I force you to do so."

Brand drew in a deep breath while they stared each other down. Pointless to get between them. They'd have to figure out their own shite for the moment.

"Where are those messengers, Faldir?"

Brand's Third didn't bother to look at him when he held up three fingers, two, one… The doors burst open, five Demons marching through in the wake of their clanging sound.

"Uncanny bastard." Brand shook his head, swiping the coded scrolls he'd written from between abandoned plates of breakfast. "Brethren, to me."

The male and female warriors gathered in a flawless line, bodies at full attention and eyes on him.

"I don't care how long it takes my father and brothers, or my uncle, to get themselves in order," he said, handing each a roll of sealed parchment, "you do not leave without a response to this letter. Better yet, you convince them to come here so I may speak with them face to face."

Digging through the pouch slung on his trousers, he retrieved the requisite tolls.

Portals were scattered everywhere throughout the realms, and all they required for travel was a small piece of wherever you wished to go. The public ones were surrounded by stalls, merchants competing with one another and always claiming to have the best price. Of course, they were raking in profits no matter what they charged, taking full advantage of anyone who'd lost or forgotten their own.

The private ones, in palaces and halls across the realms, required tolls that were a tad more specific—and they were not bestowed at random to just anyone.

Brand turned to the first messenger with an ivory chip from the Palace of Argoph's pillars. "You are bound for my father, Emperor Alwyn, in the Weeping City."

So it went, one by one, as Brand handed out the rest.

From one of Nakarat's own scales, an iridescent, burnt ochre shard—to reach his oldest brother, Amun, in the Solyrealm of Arrajnekkat.

From Falwarren's perpetual vines, a budding leaf—to reach his second brother, Vann, in the Tempusrealm of Kohamaia.

From the Chieftains themselves, tufts of black and tawny fur tied with wheat—to reach his uncle, Caius, in the Westrealm of Thodelebor.

From the exalted Elder Halls, a round-cut moonstone—to reach his youngest brother, Araxis, in the Evesong Realm of Nachthelliae.

And lastly, from the carvings of Lyriat's snowy horns, every messenger was given a shaved curl of bone—to return directly back to the great hall, as quickly as possible.

"A written answer, or an Imperial on your arm—those are your only options for coming home. Do you understand your orders?"

"Yes, Highness," they answered Brand in unison.

"Go."

Without another word, they spun and filed through the portal on the far side of the hall.

One task taken care of. As for the rest of it, enough was enough.

"Take a moment to *think*, Lyriat," Brand hissed, pushing his way between the still-seething king and his indignant brother. "Political or no, we all know Magnus didn't do it. *He* is not your enemy."

"Not yet, at least," Mag growled. "It's becoming more unsure by the minute."

"That really isn't helping."

"Aye, alright. Damn it." His brother's cheeks puffed out, lids sliding closed. "I swear on my dearest mam's own life that I had fuck all to do with this."

Brand pressed a hand to Lyriat's chest. "See? There isn't a creature in all of Bordoroth who adores his mother as much as Magnus does ours. Calm. Come back."

Being the Demon King meant that—when truly fucking pissed—Lyriat entered a far deeper berserker state than most others ever did. Brand had lost count of the number of times he'd had to do exactly this. Shite, it probably counted among his official duties as High Ambassador at this point.

Or maybe it was just what friends did, since Lyriat had done the same for him almost as often.

Lyriat blinked, sunlight glinting off of his fangs when he jerked and snarled, trying to shake the rage away.

"That's it," Brand said. "Easy does it."

Lyriat reverted to his lesser self, stumbling as he released Mag and gripped Brand for support.

Fucking finally.

Magnus cranked his head side-to-side. "You *actually* think this was political?"

Between Baldrir's condition and Brand's sneaking suspicion that there was no possible way he'd made it through the portal on his own... Sisters save them, but there was little else it could be.

Dissent and rebellion were inevitable in a world as large as this one. Bordoroth had its fair share of criminals and cutthroats, or extremist factions that would rise up, intent on destroying the Empire and the peace it stood for.

Exactly the sort of thing he and his brothers were meant for. With family at stake no matter where they turned, ensuring accord was as much a personal matter as it was a diplomatic one for those within the Imperial Line. The Blessings bestowed upon them at birth and their place as High Ambassadors gave them alone the unique ability to uphold Imperial law and order and see to the welfare of their individual realms, all while possessing a true loyalty to both.

Some people really did not bloody like that.

Hedda and Faldir returned to their normal state with a pop of light, their faces twisted into mirrored, wary masks as Brand helped Lyriat to the nearest bench.

The king huffed, managing a bitter half-smile. "What other reason could anyone have for mutilating Baldrir in such a way, when his relation to me is well known?"

"Aye," his brother whispered. "There is that."

"And while I acknowledge it wasn't you, specifically, it would be foolish to rule out the Westrealm entirely."

Mag scrubbed a hand down his face, scratching his beard. "No. Whatever happened to Baldrir, it wasn't Thodelebor officially targeting Straelon. Nothing about his condition suggests the Wolflords are responsible. He'd be chewed half to death, not cut with a blade in perfect lines. Aside from that"—He sat down opposite Lyriat, ticking off his fingers—"our uncle may as well be yours, the Chieftains are gentle and fair, and we depend on our symbiotic relationship with the Montrealm too greatly. It would only hurt them to violate you. Besides, those two are entirely too besotted with one another to bother with cross-realm political maneuverings. All Lycidas and Ursula want out of life is to fuck and feast and make merry."

"Even villains want those things, Your Highness," Faldir murmured. "It doesn't absolve them."

"I'm telling you, I would have known," Mag argued. "And I sure as shite wouldn't have let it happen, allegiance to Thodelebor or no. It wasn't us."

"Be that as it may, it was someone with an agenda. Until we know who it is, or what they want, we must be hypervigilant." Hedda eyed Lyriat, her brow raised.

"Oh, fuck no," Lyriat scoffed. "No you don't."

"We can, and we will. Won't we, Brand?"

Brand let his head drop, having already been dreading this part of whatever conversation they ended up having. An enemy was targeting the Montrealm, Lyriat was its king, ergo…

"Hedda and Faldir will select a pool of twenty-four warriors, taken from my own First Legion. Four guards at once, rotating on a six-hour schedule. Two at your door and two in the chamber when you sleep."

Lyriat sprang up, chest heaving. "I believe I just said *fuck no.* Or have all of your ears stopped working?"

"Oy, our ears are working just fine." Faldir sniffed, crossing his arms. "It's you and your hubris that are the problem."

"My hubris? I'm going to—"

Hedda snatched up Lyriat's hand before he could use it to throttle her twin. "Please. At least until Baldrir is well again and can tell us what happened."

"If he's ever well again."

Lyriat deflated at Faldir's quiet words, a muscle ticking in his jaw.

The doors banging open once more saved them from falling too deeply into hopelessness. Brand had managed to put the Sorcerit from his mind, but seeing Thad stroll across the great hall brought her face screeching to the forefront of all thought.

Or, at least, her eyes.

He'd utterly lost himself for a moment, adrift in bottomless azure depths framed by long, sooty lashes. His impression of the rest of her was disjointed at best—too swept up in the pandemonium of everything else to have catalogued her every feature—but that split-second gaze they'd shared, the way it had snatched the words from his mouth and made his heart turn over…

Brand needed answers, not the least of which was how the fuck Thad even knew such a creature.

"I've delivered Lunara's things to her chamber," Thad said, swiping up a cold, half-eaten sausage and shoving the remnant into his mouth.

Lunara.

Why his greater half seemed to preen at the piddling scrap of knowledge was beyond him.

"Then you can sit down and tell us everything you know about her, and why you seemed so damned certain she was capable of this task," Brand said. "Now."

"Aye, well." Thad swallowed, the flush draining from his cheeks and leaving him pale. "Fuck, Da's going to kill me."

"Out with it, lad," Mag said gently. "Go on."

"She's, uh… She's the lass that tried to save Mam."

Weeping, fucking shite.

"This is the least we can do. Lunara's strength will be waning, if it hasn't abandoned her already."

Brand silently followed Thad down the corridor, eyeing the tray in his cousin's hands—and the oozing slash on his arm, wrapped in a haphazard length of gauze.

The goblet perched there among an array of finger foods sent a shudder down Brand's spine. The last thing he needed was to see more fucking blood.

Thaddeus hadn't given them much to go on regarding the female he'd brought back. Her name was Lunara. She lived and worked alone, was relatively young—younger, even, than Araxis—and Thad swore to the Sisters that she would be discreet when all was said and done.

She also allegedly charged next to nothing for her services because she didn't *believe* in money, whatever the fuck that meant.

Nachthelliae was a realm of endless night, Sorcerit reliant on the cosmos to fuel their power. It had never made sense to Brand that they would shun daylight so completely, Solyrian just another celestial rock for them to feed from as far as he could tell, but they couldn't stand it.

Fortunately for the rest of Bordoroth, they loved showing off, looking down on everyone, and *getting paid* more than they hated the sunstar.

Sorcerit famously charged exorbitant fees for their help, taking full advantage of the fact that they were the only creatures outside of the Imperial Line who could use their powers beyond the borders of their realm.

The smug looks and passive aggressive superiority usually came free with service.

So, whatever was going on, Brand wasn't buying it.

Especially since his cousin had flat-out refused to go into detail about Lunara's individual skillset, or how she'd been the one selected to care for an Imperial Son's mate when she wasn't even part of the Elder Tier. Thad's claim of having 'no idea' had been obvious dragonshite.

"I still can't fathom why you have so much confidence in a nameless Sorcerit who failed in the end," Brand finally said as they rounded the final bend and came to the first door. "Your mother died, Thaddeus. That's not exactly a point in Lunara's favor. How can you trust her?"

Thad growled, flashing his canines, and pinned Brand with a look that would have felled a lesser creature. "The only reason I am not punching you in your ignorant fucking face is because my hands are full. Wait here."

Brand recoiled, rooted to the spot as Thad pushed into Bal's sick room and went about seeing to Lunara's needs.

Well, then. That was unexpected.

He was just moving to follow when his ears locked on to soft, lilting murmurs, and a wave of power washed over him.

Incandescent, life-giving power.

It hit Brand like a gasp of fresh air in drowning lungs. Gentle and shocking at once in its strength. She may not have been able to save his Aunt Meliora, but shite. He'd met his fair share of Sorcerit over the years, and not a single one of them had magic that felt quite like hers.

He was still standing there, trying to pinpoint the thing within that seemed to be rearranging itself, when Thad returned.

The scowl on his face was not at all promising.

"Is something wrong?" Brand asked, a knot forming in his stomach. "Is it not working?"

Thad pushed by him. "Everything in *there* is completely fine."

"What, then?"

"Stars above, you can be such an arsehole. You always think you know better. Mam is dead, so it must be Lunara's fault and she's not to be trusted," he said, his tone mocking.

Brand went through life entirely convinced he knew fuck all and was only fumbling, but that was beside the point. "Thaddeus—"

His cousin spun and jabbed a finger into his chest. "You weren't there. You have no idea what we went through, what she went through, trying to heal Mam and bring her back to us. No one cares as much as Lunara does. That's worth something. Fuck, it's worth everything, even if it didn't go how we wanted it to in the end."

"We don't know what you went through because no one will bloody tell us," Brand argued.

"Aye, for good reason!" Thad shouted. Then quieter, "I was forbidden from speaking about it, just like I was forbidden from going into the Evesong ever again."

That last part was no secret. Caius was aggressively vocal in his swearing off of Nachthelliae. Any business the Wolflords had with the Elder Council was conducted in Thodelebor, or by Magnus.

"I broke a promise to my da today—one made with a symbolic *oath*—in order to help you. You don't have to trust her fully, but at least give me enough credit to realize that isn't something I would do in order to go and fetch just anyone. Now, kindly fuck off and let me be."

Thad stomped away, leaving Brand slack-jawed for the second time.

That had been the closest that either he or Caius had ever come to revealing what'd happened last year, and it was still bloody fucking nothing.

What it did do was ratchet up his curiosity until he couldn't help himself.

Brand backtracked to Bal's room and eased the door open, waiting a moment before slipping inside.

The damp scent of sweat and blood hit him, though there was nothing rank about it—more the smell of hard work than it was of putrefaction. He tiptoed into the sparse sitting area and paused again, letting his eyes adjust to the single, faintly glowing stone in the wall above the bed.

Baldrir lay supine, the Sorcerit twisted and huddled over him, but they were little more than a dark mass. The details were hazy, like the prismatic power leaching out of her was bending the air around them. Hiding them. He toyed with the idea of brightening the light, but something told him it was dimmed for a reason.

A low, shaky grunt, a wretched wealth of *agony* in the sound, and Brand jerked towards the bed, arm outstretched to—

"I know, I know. Shhh." Her voice stopped him dead. "You're doing so very well, my friend. This leg is nearly done, and we'll have a rest. You're so strong, Baldrir. You can do it."

So soothing in her reassurances, even as every word trembled with her own apparent exhaustion.

She was kind. He'd give her that. Even if she did end up demanding a ridiculous payment, that was more than he would have dared hope for from most Sorcerit.

A sigh of relief left her and Bal in tandem, and Brand moved to slink away. He had no interest in explaining why he was hovering there. Never mind that he had every right—it still felt like an intrusion. Like he was witnessing something he shouldn't.

Just before his fingers brushed the doorknob, her sharp hiss of breath and pained whimper cracked across the relative silence, wrapping around his heart and wrenching it into a galloping beat.

Damn it.

Regardless of their mercenary conduct as a people, the personal price of Nachthellian power was no laughing matter. In some ways, the healers at least had good reason to charge as they did, when it was their own flesh that bore the terrible cost.

He just hoped hers would be enough to save his friend.

Lunara shifted again, the mattress creaking beneath her incoherent mumblings. There had to be something he could do—for Bal's sake, if nothing else.

Brand's eyes landed on the chair, well out of her easy reach. Springing for it, he pushed it closer and dragged the small table with Thad's heavy tray up beside it. A piddling offering to the one they were putting their faith in, but it was all he had to give at the moment.

A small kindness, in return for hers.

That tightness in his chest lingered, though. Long after he finally made his escape, blessedly unnoticed. Through the corridors and his sleepless night. Over the anxious days that followed, and during silent meals spent worrying with the others.

It clung onto him and wouldn't fucking let go.

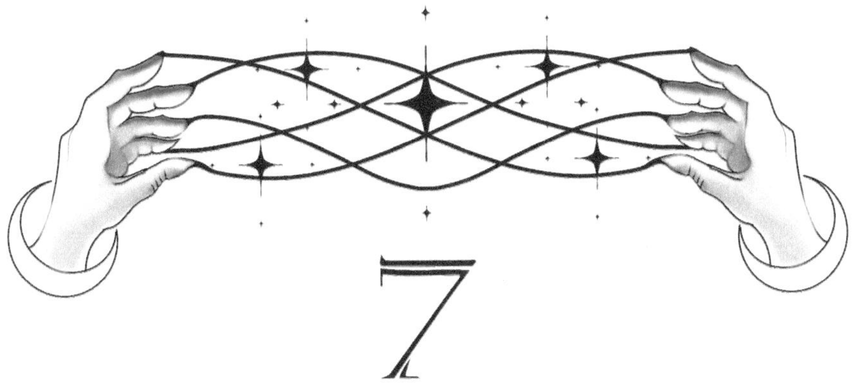

7

LUNARA WASN'T SURE HOW LONG IT HAD BEEN SINCE SHE'D STARTED—SHE couldn't even be sure it was the same day. There were vague recollections hovering in her memory of someone coming in here and there, leaving food, bringing a chair up beside her.

If her life depended on it, though, she wouldn't have been able to say who'd visited or whether they'd spoken. She'd had no energy for anything other than Baldrir.

Stars above, Baldrir.

Whoever had delivered such cruelty upon him was… there weren't words. Far worse than any of the others likely realized, but Lunara would not be disclosing the extent of the damage. The indignity of it. The Demon should be allowed to decide whether to share, when he was ready.

If he was ever ready.

For his sake, Lunara hoped Baldrir couldn't remember. That every part had been lost forever in a merciful haze. If not, she might be able to help him forget anyway.

His body, at least, was finally at ease.

Lunara finished cleaning away the dried blood and lingering filth, and covered him in a long, linen tunic. She had no idea whether it was a garment the Demons were used to, but his skin would feel sensitive for a few days—too new and raw for anything he might have been used to before—and he would need the room it provided.

Anyone who saw him would never know what had been done to him. He looked peaceful. Young and proud. Vibrant in his rest.

As for Lunara, she'd hardly moved from her perch beside him, and her body was convinced it was the only position she was capable of from now until the end of forever.

She spotted the deep, cushioned chair beside the bed from the corner of her eye, definitely closer than it had been before—thank the Sisters and whoever had thought of it.

Right. It isn't even far. Just twist, push, collapse.

Easier said than done, unfortunately.

Bracing a hand against the mattress, she blew out a slow breath. Then another. Convincing herself it wouldn't be so bad—that it wouldn't be exactly like the last time, and the time before—was always the hardest part.

Lunara knew the truth, though. Hence her stalling.

Go on, then. Get it over with.

With a hissing gasp, she turned herself and flopped onto her stomach, her useless legs dangling from the bed. With arms that could barely hold her, she leveraged her torso and shoved backwards.

She hit the seat, the chair's legs screeching across the floor. Shallow breaths and gritted teeth were her only answer to the anguish as every nerve ending went up in flames.

And cursing.

"Shitting Sisters' tits." A whimper left her against her will, her joints dripping in acid. "Veil fucking take me."

Just settle in and let the jagged edges soften. It's fine. You're fine.

Surely the Demon King wouldn't mind if Lunara lived in this cushy seat for the rest of her life. She could request it as her payment.

Slowly—so, so terribly slowly—the stabbing, burning sensation dissipated, and a heavy sigh left her. Only dull throbs remained in their place, flaring and retreating in waves. This, Lunara could handle.

Good thing Baldrir's sleep wasn't a natural one. The jostling she'd just given him would have woken anyone else.

A tray of cheese, bread, and various fruits had been placed on a low table butted up against the chair arm. And, if her eyes were not deceiving her, a goblet of blood.

Something between a laugh and a sob bubbled out of her, and Lunara let her hand fall to the rim. Gripping it as tightly as she was able, she wished all the goodness that Bordoroth had to offer upon the wonderful, lovely creature who'd brought it to her.

"Please, hand," she whispered into the silence. "Please don't drop it."

It wouldn't work as well as blood gifted straight from the source—an intimate experience if ever there was one, and something she absolutely avoided—so it was perfect. It would subdue the worst of her symptoms and allow her to relax without regaining too much of her power.

"Cheers, Baldrir. To your continued health."

With both hands clenched around it, she brought the cup to her lips and managed a sip. As soon as a modicum of strength came back to her, Lunara tipped her head back and gulped the rest down, trembling with desperation.

Relief was so instantaneous that Lunara was breathless with it. The fog lifted, evaporating from her head and limbs, clarity returning with each spark of life down her reviving nerve endings.

The melting came next, a sweet exhaustion that laid over her like a blanket.

Her eyelids began to droop and—

Snap out of it! You can't fall asleep yet.

Right. No matter how much she wanted to.

Lunara gave herself a few hard slaps on the cheek and sat up. There was no controlling the groan that escaped as she stood, dragging her leaden body across the room.

Those who cared about Baldrir needed their own relief.

A young Demon shot up from a bench across the way. She couldn't have been more than twenty-five or thirty, all round cheeks and wide eyes. Her hair was stunning, too. The deepest black, knotted and braided over and around her tawny horns in an intricate pattern that reminded Lunara of a crown of flowers.

And made her a little envious. She'd never been able to tame a single strand of her own wild mane.

"Please, my lady," the female said, her voice ragged. "Is he well?"

"Yes, he will be—"

With a cry, the Demon pushed by and rushed into Baldrir's room, falling to her knees beside the bed. "Bal? It's Nyri. Can you hear me?"

"—fine." Lunara propped herself against the doorjamb, too tired to bother with trying to interfere. "No, he can't. Which is better for him right now. And you would be?"

"Nyriadne, my lady," she said. "Baldrir's sister. But everyone calls me Nyri."

"Ah." Lunara softened instantly. "Well, Nyri, he won't be waking up tonight. I've made sure of that, for his sake." Stars above, it was so hard to keep her own eyes open. "I don't suppose you could tell me where I might find the Wolflord Thaddeus, or any of his companions who called me here?"

Nyri wobbled as she rose, dashing a tear away with the back of her hand. "Thank you." She crossed the room and threw her arms around Lunara. "Thank you so much, my lady."

Lunara winced, squeezing her eyes shut against the searing pressure. The blood helped her to function, but she was still sensitive, every inch of her like a tender bruise. "Right, um…"

Nyri released her, at last. "I'm so pleased to see you up and about as well, my lady. We've all been worried sick for the two of you these last few days."

Days. Plural.

No wonder she felt like a comet had landed on top of her.

"Please, call me Lunara." She tried to subtly rub at her temple, to relieve the headache threatening there. "I am no one of note, and certainly no lady. Just… me."

"Lunara," Nyri said, offering a bubbly curtsy. "Oh, it's such a weight lifted! I thought I was going to be all alone, but now I'm not. He's well, you're well, and the others will want to see you right away."

Nyri hooked an arm through one of Lunara's, her long legs taking one step for Lunara's every stumbling two down the hallway. "Um, Nyri?"

"Yes, my lady? Erm, Lunara."

She nearly fell over when they careened around a corner. "Perhaps we could walk a bit slower? I'm not quite up to running at the moment."

"Oh!" Lunara crashed into Nyri's side when she stopped dead. "Of course. I'm so sorry. I should have thought. I'm just so excited!"

The pace was far more manageable as they came upon a connecting corridor. "It's nothing," Lunara said, hushed and distracted, her eyes taking everything in. "I'm just tired, is all."

Twenty people could have walked down the passageway side-by-side, with room to spare. Beams and trusses soared above them, supporting glass panes that made it seem like they were walking amongst the towering trees outside. Massive stones had been embedded up the length of the wooden supports, most of them bigger than she was tall, and they glowed with a golden light that made everything seem like a dream.

"It's no wonder you're tired, with all that work." Nyri squeezed her hand. "They tried to keep me out of it so I wouldn't know how bad it was, since everyone is always underestimating me, but I have my ways."

Lunara could hear in the tone of Nyri's voice that she was just waiting for someone to ask exactly what those *ways* were. "Do tell."

"I bribed the warrior they originally assigned to the night watch and took his place." Her giggle was infectious, and Lunara couldn't help but smile. "They were too distracted to notice that it was me sitting there instead of Dendir. We do *not* look alike, so I'm not sure whether I should be offended. Anyway, it was almost too easy to convince him. He'd be in so much trouble if anyone ever found out, but it won't be me who tattles because it got me close to Bal. Been here every night since."

Another turn, and they left the glass hall behind. If she'd thought that one was grand, it was nothing in comparison to what Lunara assumed was the main part of the castle.

The beams had been intricately carved into snakelike creatures with fins and fangs, their gigantic mouths holding stone fish that glowed like lanterns. Tiles shone in the floor as well, the mosaic of green and blue and ivory seeming to flow beneath her feet. It reminded her of the lakes and rivers back home, the way they reflected the endless pinpricks of light in the night sky above.

At the end, two Demon warriors stood either side of a set of doors. She tried to ignore the flush of disappointment that neither of them was the male from before. The one who'd moved so deftly to save her from herself. Whose face was the stuff of fantasy.

More fool her for even entertaining a notion so ridiculous as flirtation when she was supposed to be getting herself home as quickly as possible.

Then again, it had been a dreadfully long time since she'd felt another move against her in any way, other than while healing. A tryst in the dark with a handsome Demon she could leave behind was far less of a risk than finding intimacy with one of her own people, regardless of how fleeting she insist it be.

Oh yes, she could very easily stare into those nameless hazel eyes as he—

The warriors threw the panels wide, snapping Lunara from her reverie and revealing a huge, open room beyond.

Shite, maybe this is *a dream.*

All Lunara could do was blink as her mind emptied of all thought.

If someone had told her she'd be standing in the Demon King's great hall one day, she'd have laughed in their face. Not that she talked to anyone, but still—waltzing casually across the flagstones, their steps echoing in the cavernous space, Lunara was struck with the reality of her circumstances.

She'd *actually* left the Evesong behind and entered another realm.

Shitting Stars.

Apparently, she'd said at least some of that out loud because Nyri squealed, "You've never left Nachthelliae before?"

Lunara wanted to crawl into a hole at the shock in her tone. "Um…" She cleared her throat. "No, I hadn't."

Nyri's grin was just shy of wicked. "Oh, everyone is going to be so jealous I got to show you around first."

She detached herself from Lunara and spun to face her. "Behold, the center of all Demondom!" Nyri announced, sweeping her arm in a wide arc. "Where many an ale is drink, drank, drunk, secrets are whispered but gathered by yours truly anyway, and all of the Montrealm's grievances are heard and solved, petty as they sometimes are."

She skipped over and drew Lunara along the windows—much like the ones in the corridor, but bigger. "If you look outside, you'll see that here we have a tree, and another tree. And oh, look, more trees! That's the portal you came through," she said as they passed it, power thrumming from within its rippling surface, "and there you'll find Bal's bloodstains still on the floor." She leaned in. "We thought he'd get a kick out of seeing them before they were really washed away. Give him something to brag about, because it was a lot."

She made a sharp turn and faced Lunara towards the opposite side of the room, her voice a theatrical hush. "And there on its dais, raised aloft for all to see and honor—the legendary Dominion of Demons, hewn from the primordial red balstrae by our ancient ancestors and enchanted by an unknown person of no small power."

Lunara's eyes skimmed down the far wall with a golden sunstar depicted across its vast surface, until they landed on the two thrones perched in front. The smaller one to the side was made of stone, with curving armrests and clawed feet. Beautiful and simple, a seat that any monarch would be proud of.

Unfortunately, Lunara knew down to her bones that it was the one front and center that Nyri was speaking of—a carved, wooden monstrosity that was, quite frankly, terrifying. Its back rose into two sharpened points like mountain peaks, vines and branches depicted across every visible surface, and exuding such terrible, foreboding power that it sent a shiver down Lunara's spine.

Nyri laughed. "If I liked you less, I'd dare you to sit in it. But I do like you, so definitely don't do that. You will *not* live through it."

Lunara was in a daze by the time Nyri led her to a solitary table in the center of the room, surrounded by carved chairs blessedly absent of any sort of magic as far as she could tell. The Demon pulled one out and forced Lunara to sit, backing away with her hands out.

"You stay put," she said. "I have to go gather everyone up from wherever they're hiding. It's not sleep-late, but it *is* quite a while after dinner. They've sat here every evening waiting to see if you'd come out and be hungry. It's all about the feasting with us Demons. Though, if His Highness Magnus is to be believed, we don't do it as well as the Wolflords do. I told him to prove it. He laughed. I still haven't been to Thodelebor.

"Speaking of which, you must be starving. The others said you didn't touch anything they brought in. Lyriat insisted his array would be the one you finally accepted, even though Hedda tried to tell him that raw meat was *not* the same thing as a blood gift. Thank the Sisters for Thaddeus opening up his arm. Seems it finally brought you back to us. Is that what it was? The smell of blood? I've never really met a Nachthellian before, so I have no idea how it works. You do eat food, right?"

Lunara tried to sort through the barrage of information and questions, she really did, but there was no holding in the hysterical bark of laughter.

Nyriadne was a force of energy and spirit. It hadn't been ten minutes since she'd been crying over her brother's sleeping form. Yet, here she was, babbling on and on, and—

Wait.

"Did you just say the king brought me food?" Lunara asked—a wheezing squeak that did nothing to flatter her.

Nyri's eyes widened. "Oh, I knew it. You don't eat. I tried to remind him that none of the other Sorcerit that come ever stay for dinner, but he just—"

"I eat!" Lunara said, waving her hands. "We all eat, I swear. I just… The Demon King Lyriat *himself* actually carried a tray into my room?"

"Of course he did. Why wouldn't he?"

Lunara propped her head in her hands and spoke to the tabletop. "Where I come from, those in charge do not serve lowly healers."

"Well, where I come from—which is here, obviously—it doesn't matter whether you're the king or the cook. Bringing food to the person healing your cousin is the least you can do."

She did not *just say cousin.*

"You and Baldrir are—"

"The most favored and exalted of Lyriat's extended family members." She sketched another curtsy, her eyes alight. "Well, aside from Hedda and Faldir—also cousins, other side, but there's only the four of us. Brand and the other Sons sort of are, but that's complicated. How else do you think I got Dendir to agree to letting me take his place so fast? It wasn't the gold and my batting eyelashes, that's for sure."

Sweet baby Sisters in a cradle.

It's a good thing you didn't let him die, then.

No shite.

"Forgive me, Nyri, but I really am exhausted."And needed to get out of here. "If you could just point me towards whichever appropriate individual is the closest, I can—"

It was already no surprise at all that Nyri didn't let Lunara finish her sentence. "Curse my blabbering mouth," she muttered, backing away. "I'll go fetch them and find some food. Not raw meat. Unless you *are* into that sort of thing?"

Lunara tried and failed to stifle a yawn. "Many Sorcerit do actually enjoy raw meat between gifts, to take the edge off. I'm indifferent, though not opposed. I'll eat pretty much anything, but I don't suppose you have strawberries in Straelon?"

"Strawberries it is! You just relax."

Nyri was off like a streak of lightning, through the doors before Lunara could blink.

What a heavy blink it was. She'd thought she was tired before coming face-to-face with the single most enthusiastic person she'd ever met in her life. Now, she was eyeing the table and wondering whether she had enough power left to turn it into a mattress.

Of course, the thought of a bed brought that gorgeous Demon to mind again. Maybe she could use *him* as a pillow.

Don't be an eejit. Tell them Baldrir is fine, ask for a room, and get out of here as fast as you can.

When her lids drooped again, she started to lose hope.

"Snap out of it, Lunara." Maybe talking to herself out loud would work better. "You cannot fall asleep here. They'll cast you into one of the chasms for offensively poor manners, and then where would you be?"

"I suppose we'll know for sure soon enough, one way or another," the Voice chimed in.

Lunara swallowed a blooming panic as she felt the color leach from her cheeks. Never, in all her life, had the Voice spoken to her twice in the same day.

"Not the same day, silly. It's been three and a half days, remember? At least, I think that's when we are." A giggle bounced through her mind. ***"Although,* now *it's been twice. Thrice. But who's counting, anyway?"***

No, no, no. This is not happening.

"It really is," the Voice whispered.

"It's fine, Lunara. You're fine." She pressed her hands to the side of her head and squeezed. "It's just a voice. A real voice, belonging to a real person who likes to laugh at you. Not madness. Please, not madness."

Some Sorcerit lost it when they didn't get enough blood. Others, from too much. And she absolutely refused to dwell on the ones who went mad for entirely different reasons.

"It's really not. Madness, that is. Trust me, I would know."

The words hit Lunara in the center of her chest and she latched on to the speck of hope the Voice offered, even as her heart constricted at its heavy, melancholy tone.

Until it giggle again, and all she wanted to do was scream.

"Screaming won't help. I know, I've tried."

Lunara felt its sigh as if it were her own and that maybe unsettled her more than anything.

"Please. I'm begging you to go away."

When minutes passed with no breathy laughter or lilting mockery, no haunting, nonsensical drivel, Lunara relaxed back into her chair and searched for a distraction—anything to erase the lingering echoes of that cursed intruder.

But, just as she'd pulled the long hook from her hair and thought to draw some of the moonlight outside to herself, a crushing thunderclap reverberated through her skull with such might that Lunara was sure she'd die beneath the weight of it.

It was like there were hundreds of the Voice inside her when it spoke again, a bludgeoning chorus of hammers and ruin. ***"This is the moment they planned for. It's time. But still, there's a split—a moth-shaped divide. Tell me, Sorcerit, will your answer be right? Or will you consign us to doom-colored night?"***

It's too much. Too much!

Lunara bit back a scream, black spots crowding her vision. Blinded by pain, the last thing she knew was her face hitting the table, no such thing as talking herself out of the slip into unconsciousness.

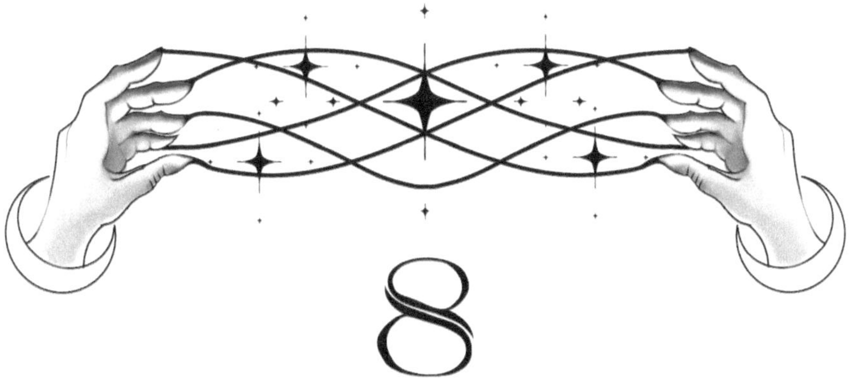

8

THE DEEP CRACK OF A THROAT BEING CLEARED STARTLED LUNARA AWAKE. SHE blinked to focus, rubbing the crease in her cheek and trying to remember where she was. Her back ached something fierce, popping as she straightened and—

It was the sight of Thaddeus's shite-eating grin that snapped her back to reality. Nyri's wasn't much better.

Stars and arses, you bleeding eejit.

She caught a flash of white, spiraling horns out of the corner of her eye. Just enough to wish the floor would open up and swallow her whole.

Lunara hadn't beheld the moving likenesses of the Imperial Family since she was a child in Starkeep, when the Sons were hardly more than children themselves. As an adult, she didn't bother with the public squares of the Evesong's cursed capital.

Nachthelliae didn't honor the other Realm Rulers the same way they did the Imperials, but she'd seen other depictions of them throughout her life.

She'd just been caught sleeping on the Demon King's dining table by the male himself.

Since the flagstones chose to be unhelpful, leaving her at the mercy of her own awkwardness, Lunara decided to pretend she was invisible.

Hold still. If you don't move or make eye contact, maybe they'll forget all about seeing you like this.

"This is Lunara," Thaddeus said, his voice dripping with mischief.

So much for that. Menace.

Wait… Introductions. To royalty.

Shite. Stand up, you bumbling ninny!

Lunara scrambled to free herself, wincing when the chair legs screamed across the floor, her hook clattering down and rolling away. A wave of her hand brought it back to her pocket, but she was tempted to snap the traitorous thing in half later.

She smoothed a hand over her hair, clutched her skirts, and bobbed a swift curtsy. Pretending there was nothing odd about her, she somehow found her voice.

"Um, hello?"

Oh, good one. Really making waves out in the big, wide world.

The biggest among them stepped forward and clasped one of her hands—a male without horns who bore a striking, nauseating resemblance to both Thaddeus and Caius, which meant there was only one person he could be.

Of course. Why embarrass yourself in front of one very important person when you could do it for two!

"Hello, fair Lunara. I'm Magnus." He bent and placed a feather-light kiss on her knuckles, his golden eyes sparkling. "Our Thad has been extolling your many virtues for days."

Magnus aht Bordoroth, Blessed of Thodelebor, Ambassador Apparent and Third Imperial Son of Alwyn and Fionerys—the only Son with hair that shade of blond and obviously a Wolflord with those tattoos and piercings.

He stepped away, utterly charming and chuckling as though he knew it.

Blessed moons.

"I'm sure he exaggerated, as he is sometimes wont to do." She managed to keep her voice from shaking, though it was a near thing.

"You've met Nyri and Hedda," he said, gesturing to both. "The hairier, uglier version of Hedda brooding in the back is her twin, Faldir. How the Sisters could get it so right with one, and so damned wrong with the other is outside my understanding."

Faldir really was the male version of his sister. A head taller, though, and rugged where she was gorgeous. Lunara tried not to stare at the twisting scar running down one side of his handsome face, puckering the corner of his lips, but all she could think was that his healer had done a piss-poor job of it.

"Kindly fuck off, Your Highness," Faldir rumbled, turning to Lunara and offering a nod. "A pleasure, my lady."

"She doesn't like being called that," Nyri hissed, elbowing Faldir in the ribs. "She prefers Lunara because she's not special."

"Nyriadne!" Hedda scolded. "Mind yourself."

"No one of note—her words!" Nyri threw both her hands up. "For saving Bal, I would have called her Supreme Majesty of the Cosmos if she wanted, but she said to call her Lunara."

"It's true," Lunara said, a smile tugging at her. "On all counts."

Gathering her courage, she turned towards the Demon King and froze, heat creeping up her cheeks.

The fact that he was shirtless, flaunting the broad expanse of his chest, would've had just about anyone blushing.

It was the other male she hadn't realized was there who snatched her senses away, though.

Again.

When did it get so warm in here?

The Demon was huge, only slightly shorter than the Imperial Wolflord Magnus, and just as muscular. Black horns rose from long auburn waves, sweeping out and back, and curving into wicked, out-turned points. His full, wide lips were slightly parted within a neat beard, and she could just see the straight edge of his teeth with a hint of fangs.

Her extremely brief interaction with him had not been warped by time or imagination, and seeing him again only solidified her first impression.

He was, without a doubt, the single most breathtaking male she'd ever laid eyes on.

Don't even go there. Are you out of your mind? Think!

If everyone else was who *they* were, then the male who'd stopped her from smacking into the floor…

Bleeding stars and arses.

Brandir aht Bordoroth, Blessed of Straelon, High Ambassador and Fourth Imperial Son of Alwyn and Fionerys—all grown up, and nothing like the gangly youth from the last Imperial portrait she'd seen.

Of course you had to go and latch on to that one. Off limits doesn't even begin—

Someone coughed. The gravelly sound wrenched her back to reality and out of her gawking, and Lunara recoiled as the spell broke.

She should say something, anything, but it was sinking in that they'd just found her drooling on the tabletop, oblivious, and every manner she'd ever learned fell right out of her head.

Sweet, merciful, Sisters. Just hurl yourself away and into the Veil already.

Why bother, when death by embarrassment was already a real possibility?

"Welcome, Lunara, to the Montrealm," the Demon King said, pressing a hand to his chest with a nod. "Forgive me for being so direct, but Nyri didn't reveal much. How fares Baldrir?"

Only then did she notice the dark circles under his eyes, the red rimming them. It softened the worst of her self-centered misgivings. They probably didn't give a shite where she took her naps when all their focus was on their family member.

A lesson she might have been able to learn and internalize long ago if she wasn't so damned terrified of being found out all the time.

"Physically, he is healed, Your Majesty. I can't speak to the state of his mind, but his body is whole."

The king swiped a hand down his face, looking away. "You were able to return his horns?" he whispered. "His tongue?

"I was, Your Majesty." Maybe the hardest thing she'd ever successfully managed, too. "There were enough particles of both left behind that I was able to rebuild upon them. Hopefully the shape is—"

"They were perfect!" Nyri interjected. "I'd never have known anything happened to him, I swear."

Lunara bit back a smile, incapable of stifling the swell of pride at hearing her work had been done well.

The Demon King raised an indulgent brow at Nyri before turning back to her. "When might my cousin be able to talk to us?"

"Hard to say when, Your Majesty. The sleep won't wear off until *he* is ready for it to do so. But again, I don't know what you'll find once that happens. The road to mental recovery may be difficult regardless of my efforts, and it's too soon to tell whether it will hinder his ability to communicate."

"Can you shed any light on what happened? Something that might tell us where or who to be looking at, or what he experienced."

She bit the inside of her lip. A tricky question to answer, given the more personal nature of Baldrir's wounds.

"Some things are not mine to share, Your Majesty, and I would not violate him by doing so—even for a king. Forgive me. What I will say is that nothing stood out as being unique to any one place, but my experience with such things is admittedly limited. Either way, he'll need care and attention more than retribution on his behalf."

Rather forward of you, considering who you're talking to.

True. The cold sweat breaking out told her as much. Still, her words were no less relevant.

The king looked at her for a long moment, his green stare penetrating. She fought the urge to squirm under that sharp scrutiny until he finally bent with an elegant flourish. "You have my most sincere gratitude for all you have done, Lunara. The hospitality of the Demons is yours for as long as you wish it."

How in the shite did you get a king to bow down to you?

Excellent question. One she'd probably perseverate over for several weeks. Didn't help that she was barely standing, the whole night like a fevered delirium.

Stop staring and ask for a bed, then.

Right.

"Your Majesty, might it be possible—"

A door clanged somewhere and stole his attention as Nyri squealed, "Snacks! Complete with strawberries, even though they're disgusting."

"—for someone to show me to a bedchamber." The rest of her words were swallowed by everyone's laughter, the tension broken as they took their places at the table.

"Come, Lunara," the king said, straightening the chair she'd been in before. "You must be famished, and I would be remiss if I did not at least see you well fed. Unless you are too tired?"

Sitting down with royalty instead of sleeping for three days was possibly the last thing in all the world that she wanted to do.

Who are you to say no to a king?

No one. Lunara was absolutely no one.

"It would be my pleasure."

Some lies were necessary, after all.

"... AND THERE'S THAD, SPRINTING NAKED THROUGH THE CHIEFTAINS' garden, Cook chasing after him with the biggest kitchen knife you've ever seen," Magnus bellowed.

"Completely unnecessary." Thaddeus crossed his arms. "I only wanted a bite! But everything looked so good and I couldn't carry all of it. Using my robe seemed as good idea as any."

"Aye, until Calista walked in and started screaming the Keep down!"

"I tried to calm her, but that made it worse," Thad whined. "Cook barely blinked before she went mental! I'd no idea the sweet, wee thing was so bloodthirsty."

"Serves you right!" Magnus laughed, his palm smacking against the table and rattling the dishes. "Spend five minutes watching the old lass butcher a side of beef. There's a gleam in the eye there, lad."

Lunara couldn't fathom how she'd ended up at midnight supper with the Demon King of Straelon, three of his cousins, and two and a half Imperial Sons. It was utterly surreal.

She cleared her throat, determined to participate anyway. "Forgive me, Your Highness—"

"Ach!" Magnus's outrage was too ridiculous to be genuine, but she froze anyway. "I beseech you, witchling, to never call me that again. Honorifics make me cringe. Fucking confusing too, when there's five of us bastards sitting 'round a table. I'm Magnus or Mag, and that's bloody it."

"They feel much the same as you, *Just Lunara,*" Nyri said around a mouthful.

"Right, um... *Magnus*... how did they not know it was Thaddeus? Being naked is about as apparent as it gets."

Magnus drew his lips in between his teeth, fighting more laughter. "You don't know how happy you've made me, Lunara."

"Mag, I'm begging you." Thaddeus threw her a fleeting glance from down the table. "Don't."

"You see, what happened was—"

Thaddeus threw himself over the table, scattering dishes and cutlery as he slapped a hand over Magnus's mouth. The Wolflord Son grabbed hold of Thad's forearm, flipped him off the end, and followed him down to the sound of muffled grunts and curses.

Bawdy jokes. Wrestling. A king who spoke to her as if she were any other person. From the time she'd woken up, Lunara had been confused. Especially because they seemed to be doing their best to make her feel comfortable?

It's the lack of sleep. Soon as you find a bed, you'll remember you don't belong here.

Lunara was searching for anything to say, always a chore, when the faintest tingle ran down the side of her face. Again.

She snapped her gaze across to the Demon Son, Brandir, who was pointedly ignoring her existence—just as he'd been doing all evening. Lunara would swear she could feel him peering at her here and there. But whenever she turned, his attention was entirely directed elsewhere.

As if an Imperial Son would waste his time staring at you.

Fair. She probably looked exactly like the only sleep she'd gotten in days had been spent sprawled over a tabletop.

Charming.

Of course, her finger chose that moment to catch on a particularly nasty snarl when she went to nervously twist a curl of her hair.

Get yourself out of here before anyone notices, you bogging halfwit.

Or, maybe she could coax Brandir into saying something. Just to draw his attention and see if that sensation happened again.

"Your High—"

"You have to forgive them," Lyriat interrupted. "Wolflords are rowdy at best, and I'm not sure they possess a single manner between all of them in the Westrealm."

So much for that.

"Please, don't worry on my behalf," she murmured, slow to switch her focus from Brandir to the king. "People are at their worst in a sickbed. If I can handle that, I can handle a rowdy meal. Speaking of..." Lunara swallowed, suddenly unsure whether it would be wise to continue.

Lyriat smiled as if he knew her thoughts. "Go on."

"You all seem very close. I admit, it baffles me. I expected a certain level of rigidity."

He chuckled. "A fair point. Our relationship with Thodelebor has always been thus. We benefit each other, perhaps, on a more fundamental level than the other realms. Since our needs align and trade is strong, the relationships have become even stronger. Provided we can agree on timing and costs."

Faldir snorted from her other side. "Don't let his feigned humility fool you. My cousin is beyond shrewd when it comes to trade."

"A hobby of mine, nothing more," Lyriat said, sniffing.

"Bloody obsession, more like," Faldir grumbled into his plate.

Lunara couldn't help smiling into her cup when Lyriat rolled his eyes.

"Anyway, my cousins are all that is left of my own family, and the Imperial Wolflords seem to have taken it upon themselves to ensure we are never lonely. Besides, we Demons do not thrive on formality as some of the other realms do. It suits us better to be relaxed. Quite unlike Starkeep, if I may be so bold."

"Ah, yes. The luminous capital of the Evesong," Lunara said, barely keeping her tone light. "I would have to agree. It's almost too formal."

Careful.

"I've only been a couple of times, but the vision stuck with me. For a realm that boasts no sunlight, it's very bright."

She nearly choked on her wine. He wasn't wrong. From plants to pathways to Sorcerit themselves, every last thing in the city glowed, as if each was solely responsible for combating the dark.

Wretched place.

Lunara had to tamp down the urge to run and hide, to scream until she forgot that heap of garish, glowing rock existed. She was already too damned tired. The last thing she wanted was to sit and talk about a place that made her skin crawl.

That's what you get for lying and not escaping when you had the chance.

"Are we talking about Nachthelliae?" Magnus said, breathless and practically shouting. Apparently he and Thad had finished their grappling. "I've got a story about the Evesong Realm that you might enjoy, witchling."

Lunara donned a polite mask, though she felt anything but.

Just change the subject.

"That's the second time you've called me that. Is there something I'm missing?" She was proud that only a speck of her true irritation colored the words.

Then again, she'd do just about anything to avoid the subject of her home and anything that went on there.

Including, apparently, being rude to those who possess more influence in their pinky nail than you could ever hope to boast.

Right. He was an Imperial Son, no matter how ludicrously he behaved.

Magnus blushed and, against all odds, some of her annoyance dissipated at the sheepish look.

"Ach, no. It's just, you're a witchy—Sorcerit—spell caster—thing, and you're so small. Wee witch is too tongue twisty. Wee witch, wee witch, wee witch." His rich baritone snagged between the words and, that time, she did choke on her wine. "See? Ridiculous!"

"Magnus likes to remind everyone how tiny they are compared to him," Hedda said, a twinkle in her eyes even as she scowled at him.

"Why don't you go all ragey and prove me wrong," he growled low, waggling his brows. "I'd love to be thrown around for a change."

Nyri flopped onto the table, gagging.

Magnus reached over and ruffled her perfect hair, making her screech. He dodged her clumsy slap, and said, "If it makes you feel better, I called Araxis a witchling once. He got all broody and shite, and then, well... let's just say it was only the one time and I didn't try again."

Lunara froze.

Araxis. Youngest Imperial Son and High Ambassador to her realm.

If there was anything Lunara had taken away from the total handful of minutes she'd spent in his presence, it was that the bastard probably didn't enjoy any form of teasing.

Reel it in.

Unfortunately, it seemed possible that Brandir might have more in common with his younger brother than with the older one.

Too bad, really, with a face like that.

No, no. Don't even go there.

King Lyriat threw a crumb of something across the distance, hitting Magnus square in the face. "I thought you were going to tell us a story about Nachthelliae."

Damn it. They were supposed to have forgotten.

Magnus released Nyri from a headlock and chucked her under the chin. "Aye, I've got a few actually."

It meant something to her that they were being so welcoming. It did. And it was obvious they were basking for themselves, released of worrying over Baldrir, but Lunara couldn't take it.

Not for another second.

She'd run out of things to say or feel, and the awkwardness of the Demon Son's silence was too much.

There's only one thing for it.

Lunara slipped a hand under the table, so as to not give herself away. "By all means, I would love to hear some of them."

More lies.

Magnus settled into his tale, but she didn't hear a word. Rubbing her fingers together, she called the tiniest bit of power from that deeper place. All she had to do was make it look like she was listening.

A flick of her wrist and magic tingled over her skin, imprinting her rapt likeness in the chair. Easing forward, Lunara gauged the group's reaction. Just in case, and at the risk of looking like she'd lost her mind, she spun on King Lyriat and stuck her tongue out.

Not so much as a twitch.

Lunara laughed, free at last to slump back and relax with no one the wiser. It was worth the deep ache in her gut to steal a few minutes and recenter. She could get more blood and moonlight—she could *not* come back from offending a Realm Ruler because she'd run screaming from his table.

The first thing she did was fix her eyes on the ceiling, her mind emptying. She stared at the beams and the glass and the trees, all silvered by the moons' light above, her breaths evening out as she came back to her peace little-by-little.

Maybe that's what she should do when she got home. She could build herself a gigantic hall, tall enough that the endless cobwebs and piles of dust would be too far away to see, and she'd never have to clean again.

Everyone shouted and Lunara shot upright, sure she was caught, but the others were firmly focused on Magnus as he waved his arms about, his face twisted into a dramatic grimace.

And then she felt it, the tingle in her cheek that shot down her spine like lightning tendrils.

She lifted her gaze across the table, and—

Lunara didn't bother stifling her gasp. No one would know she'd done it anyway.

Brandir aht Bordoroth was staring directly at her with a look of such unbridled longing that it stole her breath right back away.

He'd propped his bearded chin on one fist, tilted slightly away—easier to pretend he'd been looking somewhere else all along, the sneak.

His other hand flexed before he seized his goblet and emptied the contents in one gulp. Instead of slamming it down as she'd expected, he placed it gently back in place, twirling it against the tabletop.

All the while, his eyes were trained on her, brows pinched with something akin to agony.

His throat bobbed once before his mouth opened, as if he was about to speak, and Lunara leaned in—until he snapped it shut again, teeth clenching and nostrils flaring.

Hmm.

Lunara sent out one more thread of power, happy to accept the invisible knife scraping along her ribcage when she was greeted with the sound of his furiously drumming pulse.

Oh.

Shite.

Just like that, it all made sense. His silence, and that expression. The darting looks the others had been giving him. Their rushed words and interruptions. The way they'd steered the conversation from the moment she'd sat down.

He was anxious and they were shielding him.

From *her*.

Lunara could relate to that uneasiness far more than she'd like to admit. Knew the chokehold of those more insidious thoughts all too well.

She urged her likeness to titter at something Magnus said, since everyone else was doing it. Brandir's lids fluttered closed for the briefest second, his heartbeat actually stuttering before he aimed a bittersweet glance at his boisterous brother.

Then, the Demon Son took a deep breath, loosing it slowly through pursed lips, and a wash of guilt swept over her.

She wouldn't deny the flutter in her chest at being secretly perceived by so fierce a male, but she was crossing a line. He would probably be mortified if he knew she'd seen him this way, without his knowledge.

Just as she would be.

An ache bloomed from deep within—for the Demon, yes, but also for herself. The Sisters had truly blessed him when they'd delivered him into the arms of this family.

Let him be. Go home, guard yourself, and forget any of this ever happened.

Shaking herself, Lunara released her hold on him and seamlessly re-entered her body, the muffled conversation returning to full volume.

"…how I freed myself from the flesh-eating mushrooms of Nachthelliae," Magnus was finishing proudly.

She joined in the applause to avoid suspicion—and when the invisible caress of Brandir's gaze flitted over her again, she didn't want to go to bed quite as much as before.

"Please. You must have at least one more tale of my home."

Oh, you hopeless eejit. Why invite the trouble?

Because she'd be back in her lonely cottage, just a ghost in the dark woods, soon enough. What harm could a single night of living do?

"There is one." He hesitated, running a hand over his beard.

"Go on then!" Nyri encouraged.

"Aye, alright. Nachthelliae only briefly features in this story, but it started with me and some of my brothers deciding it was time to impart an important lesson on a young lad." She almost missed the way his eyes flicked to the side, in Brandir's direction. "Suffice it to say we left the wee shite in the Evesong's Northern Forests."

Lunara gasped. "You didn't!"

That wild region had been her home for more than fifty years, and even she struggled with the landscape from time to time.

"Oh aye, we did. Trust me, he deserved it."

He had to be speaking of Brandir, tension rolling off the Demon in waves.

"A few days later, I was nosing around some leftover plates after supper—shifted, mind you. I'm only an animal when I'm an animal," Magnus said, winking. "Except, I wasn't wise enough yet to realize the food was off. Turns out, the wee bastard had slipped in a sleeping draught! I learned my own valuable lesson when I woke up the next morning. You see, he'd shaved me bald from head to tail, and when I shifted back, well… Apparently, what happens to me as a wolf, happens to me as a male, because I was naked as the day I'd been born, down to my very balls!"

Everything bubbled up all at once, and Lunara couldn't help it. She threw her head back and laughed.

You're a fool.

"You know," she wheezed, "I honestly think I feel worse for the one who had to do the shaving."

Even Hedda and Faldir finally lost it, their dour facades crumbling.

"Tell us who did it." Nyri clasped her hands in front of her, pleading. "I have to know."

Oh, no. Embarrassment for Brandir bled over her in a hot flush. She'd never meant—

"Ah, lass, that's not my tale to tell," Magnus answered softly, his gentle tone belying his affection.

Oh.

Just like that, Lunara felt the Wolflord's allegiance towards his younger brother like a tangible thing. The fact that this sort of loyalty, this sort of love, actually still existed within the realms…

Sisters, if only she could be so lucky. So blessed as to have a family like this one.

But you don't, and you can't. Too bad, really—they might have been able to keep you safe.

9

HE OFFERED A SHALLOW BOW TO HIS *MISTRESS*.

Amusing for her to view herself as such, but she assumed it was respect he offered and that's all that mattered for now.

"Have you delivered my message?" she asked, gloom swirling around her.

With raven hair spilling over her shoulders and pooling in her lap like liquid obsidian, and the endless wardrobe of deepest black, it was quite the dramatic effect.

Utterly lacking in imagination, but dramatic.

Technically, he'd delivered *a* message. Not quite the same as the one she'd tasked him with, but… semantics.

"The Demon Son should be receiving word any time now, give or take a few days."

"Days?"

"I had to be clever in its transport to avoid any suspicion. You know how these things are."

Hopefully his *transport* of choice was not un-healable. Deciding on his next steps had to wait until he knew one way or another.

"Clever?" She pinched the bridge of her nose between long, clawed fingers. "I need this done. We all need this done. As soon as fucking possible." Her lids lifted slowly as she dropped her hand and turned crystalline eyes on him. "But you didn't just leave a fucking note like I asked, did you?"

He gasped as if the question had truly wounded him. "Of course I did. It simply took longer than usual to find someone who could be trusted to deliver it safely."

The lie slipped like honey over his tongue.

She was unaware of his proclivities, and he intended to keep it that way.

Her sigh was a tribute to her thinning patience. "I don't care how you do it, or how hard it fucking is—you get Brandir aht Bordoroth to that meeting place. People are dying, and I need him in order to fix it."

A series of clicks and muted shrieks sounded just before her massive abomination sidled up and pressed its head to hers.

If it could be called a head. Frankly, her pet was the foulest thing he'd ever seen—which was saying something.

But it did give him an idea.

"I assure you, mistress"—His smirk at that word was directed inward, as always—"it will be done as you say."

No, it wouldn't, but that wasn't for her to know.

10

WITH A CURSE, BRAND FLOPPED ONTO HIS BACK, PRESSED TREMBLING FINGERTIPS to closed lids, and kicked at the silken sheets tangled around his legs.

Every time he shut his damned eyes, the week's events battered through his mind in disjointed images.

Baldrir's mutilated body sprawled across the stone floor.

Lyriat's roars and pacing, lost in his berserker rage as he demanded justice.

Nyriadne screaming when they'd told her, fighting with fist and teeth to see him.

Thad's blood sloshing in a crystal goblet, the white-hot indignation in his eyes.

They still had no idea what had happened. His messengers had yet to return, the reports from their spies in the other realms hadn't mentioned so much as a whisper of anything suspicious, and—since Mag and Thad had been *asked* to remain in Straelon—there were no answers to be found through either of them.

Lyriat's *request* had been made under a friendly guise, but they'd all known it for the complicated demand that it was—they were to stay until it was bloody certain the Westrealm was without blame.

More of the same bureaucratic, arsing nonsense Brand had always hated.

And at the end of the cycling memories, he was wrenched from one nightmare to another when his mind centered and settled on one thing.

The Sorcerit, Lunara.

A heavy sigh escaped and he let his arms flop to the mattress, his stare fixing on the stars twinkling above through the glass dome of his tower chamber.

Without the strangling blindness of urgency, or the distraction of drama and duty…

In full light and with the blessed, knee-buckling knowledge that Baldrir would be fine…

That mysterious, luminous creature had utterly leveled him.

When they'd found her fast asleep in the great hall, face hidden in the arms cradling her head, it had merely been charming. Brand had chuckled along with everyone else—right before he'd noticed the moonlight mixing with the glow of the stones to gild a chestnut riot of teeming waves and curls in liquid gold and silver. It had spilled over the chair, the table, the curves of her body.

He'd become transfixed, dumbfounded by the seemingly infinite lengths as it cascaded down and nearly kissed the floor.

That is, until she'd popped up in a breathless rush, curtseyed like a drunken dockhand, and lifted her face to greet them. Then, he'd discovered that her spectacular mane crowned a visage that was every wondrous dream he'd ever had come true.

A single, harried glimpse of her eyes had already been haunting too many of his waking moments. Finally beholding all of her?

Shite. He'd be lucky if he could think of anything else with more than half his attention ever again.

He could almost convince himself that she'd been just as enthralled, but Lyriat had cleared his throat and the connection in one, fell swoop. His questions afterwards had only given Brand more time to sink further and further within.

Now, Brand couldn't be sure if he'd imagined the small hitch in her breath, or whether her body had actually leaned towards his in that suspended moment.

It had been decades since he'd frozen up so badly, incapable of a single sentence for hours on end. And it never really bothered him when potential lovers walked away, nothing said or gained. They didn't pull at him or consume his thoughts. They were gone, and it was done.

Brand dealt with people all day long, for fucks' sake. He didn't necessarily enjoy it, but he was able to handle whatever he needed to. Something about *her,* in particular, had him tied in knots.

Oh, he'd tried. Countless questions and comments had been perched right on the tip of his tongue. But, as soon as the air was in his lungs to speak them, the words got stuck in his throat, refusing to leave.

Instead, he'd sat there mesmerized as she'd quietly bloomed, revealing a sharp wit and sly mouth. He'd heard the Nachthellian accent all his life—a cousin, of sorts, to those in Thodelebor—but never once had it sounded like a lilting lullaby, magic and music in every syllable.

Who was he kidding? Her husky voice was bloody temptation incarnate, and it was his own damned fault it had never been directed at him, because he'd practically sprinted from the great hall at the earliest possible moment.

His name, that's all he wanted. Just to hear it one time, uttered in those dulcet tones, so he could finally focus on all the rest of the shite piling up.

Weak, pre-dawn light was already filtering through the dome and windows to suck every color from the room, transforming his furniture into eerie grey sentinels, watching him from their deep grooves of shadow.

Damn it.

Brand groaned and gave up on sleep entirely. Dragging himself out of bed, he crossed the wooden floorboards straight to the balcony doors and flung them open, drawing the salty air into himself with deep pulls.

Leaning against the balustrade, he forced his mind to calm while the land came to life in time with the rising sunstar—birds twittering from their tree branch homes, the sienna mountains glowing with dawn's fire, fishing boats dotting the sea in the distance one by one—until raucous voices reached up from the castle grounds to steal his peace.

With no idea what the day ahead would hold, it was almost impossible to focus. But, if he hurried, he might at least be able to catch Lunara for a moment alone before anyone else claimed her attention.

The hold she had on his thoughts…

There was a possible explanation for why he was responding to her so strongly. For why she—unlike any before her—would suddenly inspire him to attempt pushing past his usual reserve for a single chance to speak with her.

A cosmic, intangible calling that was almost too wonderful to consider.

Brand swore under his breath. Aldiat and Frida's mating was addling his thoughts, and he was getting ahead of himself.

Still…

It wouldn't be too difficult to find out for sure. Then again, it would require actually speaking to Lunara, and then getting to know her in order to *know.*

So first, Brand had to find the courage to introduce himself.

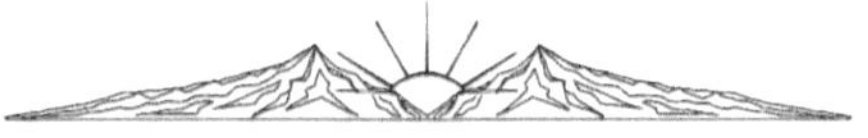

BRAND'S BOOTS POUNDED A STACCATO RHYTHM AGAINST THE FLAGSTONES, each jagged breath too damned loud in his ears.

At least the few people around must've sensed he was in no mood to be distracted, veering out of his way and giving him plenty of room to stomp by.

Maybe it was the incurable scowl twisting his face that did it.

He paused before the closed doors to the great hall. Staring at the ancient sea serpents carved there, locked in battle with whichever Demon was king at the time, Brand forced his breathing to slow. Begged his pounding heart to calm down. Tugged on the collar of his tunic.

The warriors either side ignored him completely, dutifully keeping their gazes straight ahead as they waited for his command—thank the Sisters for small mercies.

Lyriat had requested Lunara's early presence to discuss her payment. Of course, Brand had only made his less-than-daring escape after hearing her agreement. So, she was either already in there, or would be soon.

He had to apologize for his poor manners, if nothing else. He hadn't been a charming Imperial, or a cunning ambassador, or a mighty commander.

He'd been a complete twit.

At his nod, the guards threw the doors wide. Servants were readying the hall for breakfast, scattering every which way in their rush around the dozens of tables that had been added back since last night.

Still, it was easy to spot her.

She was the only stillness amidst the chaos, and the sight stopped him in his tracks.

Stars above, Lunara was even more beautiful in the daytime. A soft lilac dress managed to both cover and cling to her, hiding everything and nothing at once. Only her shoulders and collarbone were exposed, and sunlight shone down upon the opalescent expanse of her perfect skin, rainbow flakes glittering just beneath the pale surface.

All Nachthellians shared the feature regardless of their coloring but, on her, it was exquisite. And that hair. He could admit, at least to himself, that he was utterly obsessed with it.

And yet, he had to choke back the laugh that tried to spring free. Such an otherworldly creature, but he'd found her flattened against a window, palms and face pressed to the glass as if she could force her body through nose first. Her wide eyes were unblinking, seemingly caught in the throes of a deep trance. Shite, she didn't even breathe.

The bizarre moment buoyed him, curiosity demanding he see whatever she was so fixated on, and it was all the push he needed to close the distance and sidle up behind her.

Only inches separated them, but she didn't notice, and Brand was too caught up in her scent to announce himself. In amber and spice and... moonlight?

Standing there bathed in summer sunshine, she somehow evoked images of the rising twin moons. Of balmy breezes and swaying blooms beneath the gloaming. Of dreams and soft warmth.

So much damned warmth.

Lunara. Luna. A living, breathing little moon.

Brand blinked, fighting the urge to rub an errant lock of her hair between his fingers, and shook himself before gently clearing his throat.

A screeching yelp was his only warning, and Brand barely dodged the tiny fist that emerged from a panicked blur of curls and swirling silk.

"Shite," he rasped, hands snapping out to catch her before she could hit the ground *again*.

And, for the second time since she'd arrived, he forgot the part where he was supposed to release her.

"Oh, my stars! I am so sorry, Your Highness!" Lunara gaped at him, both hands plastered to her face.

Wet with tears.

Something strange happened then—a tiny splintering within himself. The shine of those crystalline drops, the tracks they'd left behind… Brand's heart stuttered, and fury replaced its beating entirely.

"What happened? Are you hurt?" The words came out as a murmur, but only because he had just enough sanity left to know that anything else would frighten her.

His fangs began to lengthen, a fire tracing itself over his skin and drawing heat from the earth to empower his change. Brand gritted his teeth against the looming rage, dragging in a deep breath to calm himself even as his grip tightened ever so slightly.

Shite, he was still holding her.

Lunara's brow furrowed, her confusion evident, and she swiped her finger across each cheek. The expression melted away upon contact, replaced with an apologetic smile. "Oh, I-I hadn't realized I'd been crying."

Nor did she seem to notice *his* struggle whatsoever.

The stunning Sorcerit turned to the window again, robbing him of the feel of her. "I'm not hurt, Highness. Quite the opposite, actually," she said with a dazed sort of laugh.

One word from her, and he was himself once more. Faint nausea swirled as the violence left him with shocking ease. If he'd been wanting proof… No. He wasn't going there. Not—

"I've never seen Solyrian before."

"You what?"

Brand might have assumed her to be exaggerating, but she was staring outside with such wonderment, as if this really was her first time in true daylight.

"How is that possible?"

Lunara lifted a brow, a shadow passing over her features. "I haven't had the opportunity," she said—a little *too* lightly.

It was clearly more than that, Brand noting her feigned nonchalance, but he ignored the tiny falsehood and chose to focus on the absolute sweetness of it instead. On her being so moved by something as mundane as sunlight.

"I came down before dawn broke," she said, voice hushed. "My room faces the mountain, and I wished to witness the Serpent Sea sparkling below my first glimpse of Solyrian." She glanced over one shoulder, shy. "Seemed like the more romantic of my choices, since I've never seen a sea either. Not that there are many."

Brand swallowed. "And how do you find it, my lady?"

Lunara laughed, the sound reaching into his chest. "Quite stirring. Obviously." All the air left the room when she turned towards him, suddenly serious. "I don't believe we were properly introduced last night, Your Highness. Forgive me." She bowed her head ever so slightly before meeting his eyes again. "I am Lunara. Just Lunara. It's wonderful to finally make your acquaintance."

Brand couldn't resist claiming one of those dainty hands in his own, his heart pounding. "Hello, Lunara."

His fingers engulfed hers. So small. Fragile. Should he lay a chaste kiss there like his brother so easily had last night? Or—

No. A bow was safe, easy.

Except he didn't bow, or take a step back, or let go. He just stood there, staring at her like a hopeless fool.

Brand sent out a desperate plea to the Unknown, beseeching the Sisters to temporarily grant him a single ounce of the charm they'd gifted Magnus. Just enough to get him through the rest of this encounter without cocking it up.

Words. Words were good.

"Please," he said, his voice cracking. Clearing his throat, he tried again. "Please, call me Brand. All my friends do."

Say it, he silently begged. *Please, say it.*

"Tell me, Brand," Lunara said, breathless and granting his wish, "do all of your friends receive such greetings from you?"

She threw a pointed look between them, where his thumb was absently stroking the inside of her wrist, over a particularly captivating freckle of iridescence.

He dropped her hand like it was made of hot coals, mortification prickling across his cheeks. "My apologies, Lunara. I seem to have forgotten myself." His voice was curt, the usual walls snapping back into place.

She laid a hand on his forearm before he could escape. "I find that, for once, I don't mind not being like everyone else."

Brand ignored the cryptic nature of her words in favor of hoping that wasn't pity she was offering.

He didn't want pity. Not from anyone.

"I—"

"What have we here?" Mag's voice was like having a bucket of ice water thrown over him.

"Sisters save me," Brand whispered under his breath.

Lunara snatched her hand away, a blush on her cheeks. "I was just introducing myself to His Highness, er, Your Highness, since we were unable to do so last night."

"Ach, away with all that," Mag said, batting her comment away. "I thought we discussed this last night. Magnus or Mag." He hiked a thumb towards Brand. "This is Brand. Or wee shite, wee bastard. Basically anything wee if he's being irritating. He hates that."

There was a twinkle in Mag's eye that Brand wanted to throttle away. Every single one of those cursed monikers were names his brother had used in his stories the night before, the bloody arsehole.

She giggled, the sound burrowing into him. "We covered the Brand part, thank you. I will leave the rest to you."

"Fair enough." Mag offered her his elbow. "What do you say we get some breakfast before Lyriat storms in here and ruins it with his grumpy arse?"

"That sounds—"

"He's awake!"

Nyri was sprinting across the great hall, weaving between other Demons and tables alike. She crashed right into Lunara, throwing her arms around the Sorcerit with a squeal.

"Blessed Solyrian, Bal is awake!" Bouncing on the balls of her feet, she gave Lunara a rough shake before holding her at arms length. "Oh, I can't believe you really did it!"

Hedda and Faldir were both at his side an instant later.

"She speaks true, Highness," Hedda said. "And he's asked to see you and Lyriat immediately. Baldrir claims he has a message."

11

Brand paced in the corridor, Lyriat posted up against the wall with his arms crossed.

They'd come immediately to Baldrir's sickroom, as fast as their feet could take them. Lunara had stayed glued to their side, her face a mask of determination, insisting she be allowed to examine him first and ensure he was truly well enough to talk.

Lyriat hadn't batted an eye when he'd granted the request—and he argued about *everything* when he was in a mood. What they hadn't quite expected was for her to race ahead and then lock them out of the room with a muffled promise to let them in when she was done.

Apparently, Baldrir needed privacy.

The waiting gave Brand far too much time to think.

Patience was easier when he knew, by virtue of the way things functioned in Bordoroth, that answers were not forthcoming. When he was forced to sit back and bide his time through the inevitable bureaucracy.

Unfortunately, those pauses also had a way of making reality drift off into the background, until he was able to convince himself that everything was normal because nothing was happening.

With Bal awake, it was all real again.

The endless possibilities he'd imagined flooded back in to rear their ugly heads, every last one sending an icy river down his spine.

At last, the door swung wide, Lunara's voice sounding from deeper within the chamber a second later. "Come in! He's ready."

They found her perched on the mattress beside Baldrir, his gigantic hand held fast between her own. Brand couldn't help noting a certain tightness around her eyes, dark smudges underneath that hadn't been there half an hour ago.

"You'll be overjoyed to know that Baldrir has retained full command of his speech." She smiled up at Bal and bumped her shoulder into his. "And what a lovely voice he has, too."

There was a collective sigh of relief, and then a different sort of tension entered the room.

"Thank you, Lunara, for all of your help," Lyriat said with a respectful nod. "Your willingness to protect one of mine, even from me, has not gone unnoticed. It will be remembered when we discuss your payment later."

It was a clear dismissal. At least, Brand had thought so.

Lunara just sat there, returning Lyriat's nod with one of her own, brows raised as if she was waiting for them to begin.

Baldrir, too, heard the words for what they were. "She stays," he said, his *voice* a pale imitation of what it had been.

Lyriat leaned down beyond Lunara and pressed his forehead to Baldrir's. "It's good to see you well, cousin."

Baldrir lifted a shaking hand and wrapped it around the back of Lyriat's neck. "Bloody damned good." He pulled back and gestured to Lunara. "Thanks to the lady here."

"Indeed." Lyriat gave her a sidelong glance. "You're certain you wish for her to stay?"

It was almost worshipful the way Baldrir looked at Lunara. "She drew me back from the edge of the Veil, and was safety where there was none otherwise." He swallowed. "Yes. Please, Lyriat."

There was no heat in Baldrir's gaze. No hint of possessiveness. His words were pure, if a bit shaky.

Otherwise, he looked amazing. His black hair shone, his skin was tight and clean. There were no scars left behind that Brand could see, or crooked bones. And he was speaking clearly—despite the fact that he'd been missing his tongue four days ago.

Lunara's work was incredible.

Brand said as much, unable to hold the words back. "Truly," he said. "Thad was right to trust you."

And he owed his cousin an apology.

"Yes, well…" She cast her eyes down and away, cheeks flushing. "Thank you."

Stars above, she was nothing like any of the other Sorcerit he knew.

Lyriat pulled a cushioned chair over to the side of the bed and sat down. "What happened, Baldrir?"

No one moved. No one breathed.

"I don't know. One minute I was following the loveliest maid I'd ever seen up to bed, and the next…" His head fell back onto the pillows propping him up. "He…"

"He? A male?"

Baldrir looked so small when he said, "I'm not sure what's real and what isn't."

"Anything, Bal," Lyriat whispered. "Anything you tell us will help."

"Platinum hair, or silver, or white. Maybe." He scrubbed a hand over his mouth. "Long… long enough to brush against my wounds when he was hardly bent over me. Moved like a blur, and his mood changed just as quickly, but I can't picture him. It's like he wasn't really there and I've made him up."

Brand knew one male who fit Bal's limited description, but there was no way he'd done this.

Lyriat threw him a fleeting glance, obviously thinking the same thing. "What else?"

"He wanted to know about the Battle of Breamwyrm. I think."

Brand shook his head, confused. "That was forever ago. What use is the knowledge now?"

"I don't know!" Baldrir snarled, going wan. "I wish I did, but I don't… fucking know. Shite, I'm going to—"

He wrenched to the side, and Lunara produced a basin from the ether just in time to catch his sick. She rubbed his back all the while, soft prismatic light glowing beneath her palm, until Bal finally slumped.

"There you go," she murmured, swiping a cloth over his chin. "You're doing so well, but you don't have to continue." She lifted her eyes to Lyriat. "Not if you don't want to."

Stars above, that was bold.

"No, I—" Bal loosed a weak sob. "I can do it."

"Just take your time." Lunara helped him settle back. "Deep breaths."

Bal was quieter when he spoke again. "I was telling the story of our great grandparents for the hundredth time. How they fought the sea serpents on the shore, piling them up one by one until none were left. I can't— I don't know exactly how I told it, or what I said that would be of note."

Lyriat patted Baldrir's shin. "It changes every time, cousin. We know that well enough."

"He kept going on about the secrets, but I didn't understand." Baldrir's lids slid closed. "Secrets, secrets, secrets. Even if I'd wanted to, I didn't know how to give him what he was asking for. And he was so fucking angry."

In some ways, the more Bal spoke, the better Brand felt. Vann might have long, silver hair and move in the way all Fae did, but his brother was almost level-headed to a fault. In all his life, Brand had never seen him angry.

"Can you remember what you said that finally made him stop? It may be your answer."

Lunara's tender questioning surprised Brand. Rather discerning for a simple healer.

"Maybe. It was something about the war council, or the trap they'd made. I think?" He lifted his head and speared them with a stark look. Raw. "I've told it so many times, in so many ways, that I don't know the truth anymore. I tried to lie, but I-I might've told him everything."

"Ah, cousin. Even the truth we think we know probably isn't real. Don't worry yourself."

Baldrir sneered against his welling tears. "I tried—fuck." He blew out a breath, blinking them back. "I tried to get away, to hold out. Anything. I *tried*. But he was strong. So fucking strong. And the haze of everything… Fuck, I just wanted him to stop."

"You did well, Bal," Lyriat said, gently extracting Baldrir's hand from Lunara's and holding it tight. "I'm sure you did the Montrealm and our forebears proud. We're just glad to have you back."

Brand didn't want to interrupt, but he had no choice. "Hedda said that you have a message for us."

Hopefully it would point them in the right direction, since none of the rest of it made any damned sense.

"Yes," Bal rasped. "*That* I fucking remember, like he's planted it inside of me."

"And?"

"And it's not for everyone. It's for you, Brand. Specifically."

Brand stopped breathing altogether, a buzzing thrum ringing in his ears. "Me?"

Baldrir nodded. "First, he said to tell you *'I'm close. So, so close. And you're all so very far away from knowing it.'*"

"The rest?" Brand whispered.

"A riddle of some kind. *'Glynmor thinks she's safe and well, tucked tight in her field of green. But what do you and her flesh have in common? I know what I hope it will be.'*"

So much for the message helping.

He would've sworn Lunara loosed an odd sound, but he was too busy trying to stay upright to question it. "I have no idea what that could possibly mean. Who is Glynmor?"

"I've heard the name," Lyriat said. "Somewhere. It's just there, on the edge of my mind."

Brand ran a hand absentmindedly over one horn, pacing. "The others might know. I could send another letter to my father and Uncle, my brothers—one of them is bound to know it."

"Fuck. Where is Nyriadne?" Bal gripped Lyriat harder, pulling him closer with a trembling desperation. "Where is my sister?"

"She's here, in the castle. She's well." There was a question both in Lyriat's voice and on his face. "You've already seen her this morning."

The assurance didn't placate Baldrir in the least. "H-he threatened my family."

Lyriat's horns curled ever so slightly, his markings flashing. "His exact words."

"*'You're going to deliver a message for me. If you don't, I will find every person you care about and I will ruin them in ways you can't even imagine.'*" Bal started hyperventilating. "You and the twins, you must guard yourselves. Even you, Brand. And Nyri is to go nowhere alone. Do you understand me?"

A knock sounded on the door, and Hedda pushed her way in. "We've just received word from Thodelebor. Caius is on his way."

Lyriat threw him a sardonic look, laced with a righteous sort of fury. "Convenient."

"Yes, well…" Hedda hesitated, and her gaze fixed on Baldrir.

"Speak, Second," Brand commanded.

She flinched, then faced him. "He's demanding that Bal be seized and presented for questioning."

"Why the fuck is that?" Lyriat growled.

"They've found a maid in the Keep at Fanghold, in his chamber. They think Bal's the one who murdered her."

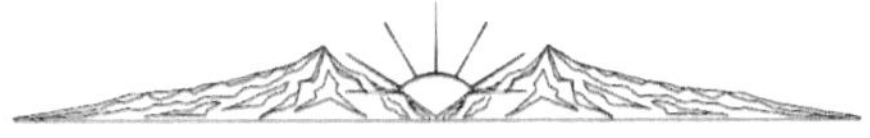

"Ten gold pieces says Caius wears that hideously embroidered purple robe he's been favoring lately," Lyriat murmured.

Brand was struggling to ignore the power prickling over his limbs. That his uncle would dare make accusations, when *they* were the ones who'd been wronged—

Lyriat's hand landed on his forearm, squeezing. "Five more says he tugs each sleeve before stepping off the portal dais."

Ah. Jokes, then, to hold the rage at bay.

He glanced back at Baldrir, where he was standing silently between Magnus and Thad, Mag's hand wrapped loosely around his upper arm—more for show than anything, but Caius would expect his demand to be met.

Even if it meant Bal collapsing right there next to the bloody thrones, in front of everyone.

"Fine." Brand shook himself. "I say he doesn't wear the purple, does tug the sleeves, and throws a *look* at everyone before stomping on his toll like he has an infinite supply of them somewhere."

After which, he would hopefully have a damned convincing argument for how the Wolflords were not at all responsible themselves.

Magnus leaned down and whispered, "Thirty pieces says you're both wrong and he's just as confused as everyone else because—as I've already said, repeatedly—we had nothing to do with this. Now shut it before I drop your naked arse somewhere else."

Brand ground his teeth together and avoided looking at Lunara amongst the crowd of gathered Demons, Nyri at her side. Veiled references at dinner were one thing, but Mag's hissed threat was too loud and direct for comfort.

Even if she was probably too far away to hear it.

"You're really going to bring that up again?" Brand bit out. "May I remind you—"

A soft patter cut off his words, and he looked at the portal just as his uncle came through.

"Caius aht Bordoroth, Blessed of Thodelebor, High Ambassador and Seventh Imperial Son of Stennyx and Gildat!" a herald called, as if everyone wasn't well aware of his identity.

Caius's boots drilled into the floor as he approached the throne, a pair of Wolflords trailing him. Lyriat rose to his impressive height as his uncle fell to one knee at the foot of the steps, his heavy breathing the only sound when he stood again.

Looked like Mag was getting thirty gold pieces.

Instead of his usual court finery, Caius wore a simple linen robe—the battle garb of the Wolflords. It was filthy, black streaks littering the fabric alongside splatters that could only be blood. None of his usual adornments were anywhere to be seen. No jewelry, no weapon. Only a small leather bag was attached to the belt at his waist, which he was slipping his recovered realm toll into.

His blond hair was lank, the normally shorn sides long enough to brush at his ears and hide the tattoos there, and dark smudges cradled haunted, golden eyes.

Shite.

Caius didn't waste a second. "You know why I'm here, Your Majesty."

"Yes, Your Highness, though I would hear it from your lips."

No one in the hall so much as twitched, the whole room holding a collective breath.

His uncle spared a fleeting look behind, lips pursed. "Certain you want to do this here, Lyriat?"

Lyriat huffed, arrogance personified. "When have I ever beat around the bush, Caius?"

"Aye, there is that. The whole thing, then?"

Brand noted the slight twinkle in Caius's gaze, his fondness for the Demon King—who'd become like another one of his nephews over the long years—apparent.

"May as well, old friend. Loud and clear," Lyriat answered, waving a hand to the room at large.

Unlike his uncle, Brand hadn't missed the unfamiliar note of mistrust in Lyriat's voice as he'd said *old friend.* They were going through the motions as usual, but the game he'd always hated was being played beneath the surface.

And Brand was caught in the middle.

Caius threw his shoulders back. "I, on behalf of the Westrealm of Thodelebor as its High Ambassador and Blessed Imperial Son, come to accuse that Demon"—He pointed at Baldrir—"of murder in our capital, the Keep at Fanghold, in the Westglen. One Fausta à Bor was found late last eve, strangled and mutilated in the quarters assigned to Baldrir of Straelon. She was last seen by mine own nephew, Magnus aht Bordoroth, and one other, entering said room with the male in question. As such, the Wolflords call for justice from our allies in the Montrealm."

A low growl rumbled from Lyriat, but Brand stood before it could escalate. "I, on behalf of the Montrealm of Straelon as its High Ambassador and Blessed Imperial Son, hear your accusation and proclaim its falsity." He ignored the way Caius recoiled, and continued. "We have proof that Baldrir of Straelon is as much a victim as this Fausta, and that they were both wronged by an outside assailant. We offer our sincerest condolences on your loss, and make a formal request of alliance in order to solve the heinous crime committed against us. Do you accept?"

Caius blinked between all of them, a crease between his brows. "Undecided. Permission to question further, Your Highness."

"Granted, Your Highness."

Sisters save him. Brand detested this shite, where lines blurred and power was thrown back and forth. Where he had to ignore the fact that he was speaking to his own beloved uncle in order to fulfill his obligation to protect Straelon above all else.

Ringing started in his ears, a match for the galloping beat of his heart—piss-poor timing, as usual.

"You say he's a victim as well," Caius said. "I see no evidence of that. Explain."

"Baldrir returned to us on the edge of the Veil." Brand tried and failed not to picture the memories as he spoke them. "His horns and tongue had been removed, as well as most of his skin. Multiple limbs were broken. And that was just what I could see with my own eyes. He has since recounted his abduction at the hands of an unknown creature. In Thodelebor. *Someone* has committed an act of war against the Dominion of Demons, and will answer for their crimes upon discovery. Painfully."

Masked threats were always useful for garnering truths if one knew what to look for.

Brand blocked out the gasps and murmurs, focused instead on his uncle's face. On even the tiniest of reactions.

Nothing.

Caius lifted a fist for silence. "Our Fausta lies dead, but he stands tall. I wish to know how that's possible, when no one could've healed such extensive damage in a matter of days. Where's this alleged proof?"

"You mean aside from the letter I sent long before we knew of this?"

His uncle's confusion was evident. One of the Wolflords with him leaned forward to whisper in his ear, earning a put-upon sigh. "I was at the Ghostbor fending off Forgotten until the wee hours of this morning. Apparently, it's sitting on my desk."

"My messenger?"

They conferred again before Caius said, "As of an hour ago, she was dining in the Chieftains' hall. I'll have her home as soon as this mess is cleaned up."

Brand nodded, satisfied for the moment. "If that's not enough, the healer who tended Baldrir is present and can attest to his condition."

"Come forward, Lunara," Lyriat commanded.

Caius gasped at the mention of her name, whirling around.

For Brand's part, all of his attention went to the Sorcerit as she took timid steps closer, hunched in on herself. He swore he could almost feel the flush spreading across her cheeks like it was his own, a kindred wish to disappear flaring within him.

"How?" Caius whispered, anything remotely official gone from his voice. "How are you here?"

Before she could answer, Thad cleared his throat. "It was me."

Caius gave his son a sharp look. "What did you do, lad?"

"I was the one who saw Baldrir come flying through the portal. Brand speaks true. He was *this close* to dying. No other Sorcerit were near, and I knew she'd be able to help."

"You went into the Evesong? You broke your oath?"

"Aye, I did, to save him."

"How'd you get to Lunara without…" Caius paused, pressing a fist to his mouth. "I know you made it there before, when your mother… Fuck. How'd you do it this time?"

"The same way, but hers instead."

What the fuck did that mean?

Caius growled, flashing his canines.

"It was just in case!" Thad threw his arms up. "She was there, Da. She knows what it was like, and I didn't want to be cut off from her. I thought if I ever needed to talk about it, she would understand."

"Aye. She would. But you were still forbidden." Caius turned to Lunara. "I'm not particularly happy to see you, lass."

Lunara's lip was trembling when she lifted her head. "I know. I didn't particularly want to come, but I couldn't say no to him. Not after everything. Besides, you know how he is."

"I do, unfortunately." Caius rubbed at his temples with one hand. "Well, I sure as shite didn't see this coming. What a fucking mess."

More details of Meliora's illness, still hidden beneath a shroud of secrecy. Caius had refused to speak about it. Thad had shrunk further and further into himself. And *the healer* had been as much a mystery as the rest of it until a few days ago.

Some had tried to claim they'd been there. That it had been gruesome. That they'd never seen anything like it.

Liars, of the worst sort.

No one, in their family or otherwise, had seen Meliora for at least a month before her death. That didn't stop the whispers, though. The rumors, rife with conflicting information. The gossip.

Now, Brand was somehow staring at the only three people in the world who knew the truth, and the urge to demand answers roiled within him.

"Right." Caius drew himself up, back to business. "If Baldrir didn't do it, who the fuck did?"

Lyriat folded his arms, head tilting. "Is just seeing her enough to assuage you? Do you not want to be briefed on her findings?"

Caius waved that away. "I wish I didn't know what the lass is capable of, but I do, unfortunately. If you say she's the one who did the healing, then aye. It's all I need to hear."

Brand's eyebrows shot up. High praise from a male who gave it sparingly.

"May I release him then, uncle?" Magnus asked.

"Aye, let the lad go."

Baldrir hurried down the steps and straight to his little sister, Nyri meeting him halfway and letting out a sob as she threw her arms around him.

Caius watched the exchange. "At least one of them is getting a pleasant ending." He signaled for the Wolflords who'd accompanied him to come forward. "Straight home," he muttered low. "Send the Demon messenger back, and relay all you've heard to the Chieftains. Tell them I'll be staying for a spell to figure this out. And tell Lilius we can't be putting her daughter to rest just yet. She'll not be pleased, but promise her whatever she needs in return. Go."

The males turned on their heels as one and sprinted for the portal, barely a blink between them tossing the toll and leaping through it.

12

"Now, for the love of the Sisters, can we please take this somewhere fucking else? I need a damned seat."

Lunara took Caius's grumbled request as her cue to back away and get out of there.

Nothing in the realms could have prepared her for coming face-to-face with the Imperial Wolflord again. Thaddeus had been bad enough, but Caius…

Shitting stars.

She'd known he was coming, but reality was oft worse than anything she could conjure up. So much worse. She needed her own place to sit. Quiet and alone.

You never should've let yourself believe it when he'd said you were forgiven. Who could ever actually forgive someone that let their mate die?

Not Caius, obviously.

Lunara shuffled backwards, hoping to melt into the crowd of Demons and—

"Now, I'm not sure where you think you're going, lass," Caius said, "but I have need of you, yet."

She swallowed. "But I thought—"

"I know what you thought. I need you to stay." He turned back to King Lyriat. "It's beneath me, but I'm bloody begging—clear the room or take us somewhere else. I don't care which, as long as there's a chair."

With a nod, the king flared his nostrils and planted his feet. He seemed to swell, lines of light tracing over his skin that were so faint she might have imagined them.

"Your king commands you from the castle grounds." His voice was booming and twisted. "Out, until I say otherwise!"

Demons scattered in a rumbling stampede, most heading for the main doors while others exited through hidden ones she hadn't noticed before.

Lunara wished she was one of them.

Between one breath and the next, King Lyriat reverted to his usual self, no trace of whatever that had been.

Probably the Demonic rage, ninny. What else would it be?

If that was supposed to be the legendary raging of Demons, then it was disappointing. Powerful, yes, but she'd expected more.

"Do you always have to be so dramatic, you wee arse?" Caius said, rolling his eyes.

Lyriat shrugged. "What point is there in being king if I don't get to have any fun with it once in a while?"

"What point is there in being king if you can't bring me a fucking chair, Demonling?" Caius growled. "I know I'm repeating myself, but my bones are so weary I could fall over, and I don't give a shite how many times I have to say it now that no one else is around to hear it. Chair. Seat. Bench. A fucking stool. Anything."

Brand and Lyriat shared a long, loaded look.

"I know what you're thinking," Caius said, his voice strained but gentle. "I'll swear on whatever you want me to that the Westrealm is innocent. I'll give a binding oath if it means finding the truth. Just as you said, Baldrir and Fausta were both victims."

Another tense moment before the king gave the faintest nod, and she would have sworn the room itself relaxed as the guards who'd remained melted back into the shadows.

"Thank the Sisters." Brand stepped down off the dais. "My skin was starting to crawl."

"Same. I hate pretending to be something I'm fucking not—like happy to be standing."

"Calm yourself," Brand said, the hint of a laugh in his gravelly voice. "I'm getting to it."

He moved towards Lunara, their eyes meeting. For a single, heart-stopping second, she was exposed, his hazel stare questioning. Searching. Digging for answers she had no intention of ever giving.

And then he brushed past, breaking the connection as he stretched out his hand in the middle of the hall.

Bleeding moons, you have to get out of here.

The floor beneath her feet vibrated, and flagstones folded back over themselves to leave a gaping hole behind. From out of it, the table and chairs from the night before rose upwards, a marbled platform beneath settling into place.

"Your chair, uncle," Brand announced.

He hadn't even broken a sweat.

Hedda and Faldir appeared out of nowhere, moving to take a seat along with everyone else, while Lunara hesitated on the fringes, unsure what to do with herself.

Why are you even here? It doesn't make any sense!

Meliora had been a childhood friend of Lunara's mother. It was the only reason she'd agreed via Cordelia to help, despite the risk to herself. And she'd only been grateful when Caius's last real words to her had been *'No matter what happens, we'll not be speaking of it, lass. Ever. It's not for others to know. I'd have my mate mend well and easy, her name safe from the gossipmongers."*

She'd died later that night.

He'd left nothing but a note behind, absolving her of any guilt or responsibility. The end of it had been a firm goodbye.

More like good riddance, probably.

To stand there, no idea what they'd be discussing or what he wanted with her, was a practice in torture.

A hand landed on her shoulder and she looked up to find Lyriat beside her. "Come. I'm sure he has good reason for it."

It was not a comfort when she found Caius directly across the table with his eyes narrowed on her—made infinitely worse when Brand settled in next to her.

Her feet twitched beneath the table, begging her to race home to her cottage. To hide from Imperials and kings. From the Elder Council. From everyone.

Silence reigned as a pair of servants brought platters of breads and cheeses amidst colorful fruits, pitchers and tankards beside. They disappeared behind a false wall as quietly as they'd come, unaware that everything they'd just left was too vibrant, too appealing. That the joy of food didn't belong here right now.

Caius swiped up a cup. "I wasn't entirely truthful before."

Talk about an opening salvo.

"The Sisters must be laughing at us," he muttered. "I came here knowing full well that Baldrir was innocent, but you know how it is. Have to keep up all the appearances, and I hadn't yet been willing to reveal how, exactly, I knew."

His gaze was a red-hot iron, searing into her, and she fought the urge to squirm beneath it.

"The second Lyriat said your name, I realized fate had wrapped us up together," he rasped.

No one said a word, and they were all looking in her direction.

Oh, they cannot be expecting you to carry this conversation.

The nervous breath of laughter that flew across her lips was an absolute abomination. No one should ever be allowed to sound so idiotic.

Brand cleared his throat, his mouth opening and closing a few times. In the end, all he offered was a hopeless look, as if to say *I'm sorry, I have no idea either.*

"I think you might need to be more specific," Lyriat said, his voice cutting through the awkward silence like a knife.

She could have wept with gratitude. It helped her make sense of the maelstrom of jumbled thoughts, getting right to the heart of the matter. "Yes, I— Yes. I'm so sorry, Caius, but why am I here? What could any of this possibly have to do with me outside of Baldrir's healing?"

"Look me in the eye, lass, and hear me without making me say it."

She did as he asked, even though it made her skin feel too tight.

"There were similarities, aye? Not to the same extent, and it's not what killed her, but"—He leaned back and plucked at the collar of his robe, at a particularly large, black stain—"it was on her."

All thoughts drained out of Lunara's head but one.

No, no, no.

"I'm assuming by the look on your face that the same was not true of Baldrir?"

Lunara shook her head. "N-nothing. I swear. I would've noticed."

"Aye, you'd look less sick about it. Can't decide whether that's a good or bad thing, honestly. Both of them at least would have made sense." His cheeks puffed out, the sigh so weary. "Someone's fucking with us."

Lyriat leaned in closer, scanning the soiled linen. "What is it, exactly, and how did it get on *you*?"

How, indeed. Rash, too, since she and Caius had never confirmed one way or another whether the substance had caused Meliora's illness, or merely been a byproduct.

Sometimes, though she'd avoided touching it directly, Lunara would swear she could still feel it sticking to her skin like a film. An invisible layer of putrescence that never fully went away, no matter how raw her body was with scrubbing.

"It was Fausta's resting period, and no one realized anything was wrong until she didn't show up in the kitchens for her duties. I was called back from the Dread Chasm after they finally found her in the middle of the night."

"That answers nothing." Lyriat's voice was hard, getting impatient.

"It got on *me* because it's my job to handle these sorts of things when they happen. I didn't see it when I first lifted the lass from the pool of her own blood and carried her body out to her weeping mother," Caius growled. "It wasn't until I handed her over, under the blazing light of Solyrian, that it stood out. Does that answer your question?"

"Partially."

Caius pounded a fist on the tabletop. "If I knew what it fucking was, then maybe Thad's mother would still be alive!"

Thaddeus shifted in his seat beside Magnus further down, eyes fixed on the distance.

"Maybe, uncle, if you did not insist on being so secretive, we might be able to figure out what it is *together* and prevent anyone else from succumbing to the same fate."

For Brand to go from flopping his mouth like a fish on land, to the seething undertone in his voice was jarring. Strangely, it made her want to reach under the table and clasp his hand, just so he would know that someone was nearby. An anchor, in his storm.

Right. And tomorrow you can go ahead and try to fly. It's about as realistic as that barmy daydream. Which you should not *be having.*

Caius's lip curled back, a spark of light catching one of his canines.

"I've been awake for days, nephew. I'm not interested in rehashing painful history to appease your curiosity."

"Da—"

"I said I'm not fucking interested!" The glass tankard Caius was holding shattered in his grip, shards and ale flying everywhere.

At the sight of blood and injury, Lunara transformed. Already calling power forward, she leapt up out of her seat. "You daft old beast," she scolded, rounding the table. "Look what you've done to yourself. Honestly."

Caius clenched his jaw when she took his hand, lids fluttering closed as light glowed between them. The gash in his palm knit back together, even while her own hands felt as though they were crumbling apart into flaming dust—worse, since she'd already taken a hit with Baldrir earlier this morning.

Stars above. The familiar, wretched stench of the black ooze all over him didn't help either.

Last year, she would've counted Caius as a friend, of sorts. She'd never publicly claim it due to his status as an Imperial, but she'd bonded with him and Thaddeus while they'd worked together to make Meliora as comfortable as possible. He'd told her stories and shown her nothing but gratitude, and it had been easy between them with their shared goal.

It would seem that her sort-of-friend had gotten bitter in the time since she'd seen him, a dark cloud sitting on his shoulders and following him around.

It broke her heart.

When he was finally put back together, Lunara took a shaky step away, fighting tears for too many reasons to count. She moved to sit, but—

Why is everyone staring at you?

She thought back, realizing too late that she should've reigned her words better and not spoken to an Imperial Son like he was a petulant child in front of them. But, for just a moment, they'd been back at her cottage and close as anything, and she'd slipped.

Then, Caius flexed his mended hand, sighing and flashing the perfectly unmarred flesh of his palm, and Lunara realized what she'd just done.

Tits. Fuck. Arse. Run.

LUNARA WAS PERILOUSLY CLOSE TO FAINTING. A VEHEMENT DENIAL MIGHT work. Better than fleeing, at least. Right? Perhaps she could try and turn it around. Maybe laugh it off.

For the love of the Sisters, do not *draw more attention to yourself by cackling.*

"Ach, Lunara, I… Thank you, lass." He turned to the table at large and offered them his apologies as well, but only Thaddeus was paying any attention to him.

The father and son pair were used to her power, but the others…

Hedda leaned in to Faldir and whispered something in his ear. Lyriat was nodding with pursed lips, his eyes bouncing between Caius's hand and hers.

"Witchling…" Magnus started, but didn't finish. He just cocked his head to the side, as if he wasn't quite sure which thought—or accusation—to go with first.

You knew this would happen. They've seen, and now they're going to tell the Council. Araxis.

"I—"

A clatter by the portal saved Lunara from having to explain, and she could have kissed whoever it was.

First, a petite Demon appeared, scroll clenched her fist. One of the Wolflords from before followed a second later, also bearing his own roll of parchment as they raced across the distance.

"Apologies, Your Highness," she said to Brand, handing hers over. "It was pandemonium, and I didn't realize the Westrealm's High Ambassador had slipped by me. I made sure to bring this back, so no other eyes would see it."

"Don't let it worry you, Frida. You've done well. Go, find Aldiat and your rest."

With a nod, she left, dodging the other messenger.

Caius stood as the male approached. "Speak, lad."

"A letter arrived from Glynmor, Your Highness. The Chieftains sent me straight back to bring it to you."

Caius accepted the folded paper with a nod and pulled the twine from around it.

"Did you just say Glynmor?" Brand breathed.

"Aye." Caius tossed the string, clearly only half listening as he read the letter's contents. "What of it?"

Another silent look passed between Brand and Lyriat, another nod from the king.

"Baldrir was tasked by his assailant with delivering a message. Someone named Glynmor was mentioned therein."

Magnus snorted. "Glynmor isn't a person. It's a place."

Lyriat snapped his fingers. "I knew I'd heard it. Just a sentence or two in a correspondence with the Chieftains some while back."

"Aye. A newer village on the southern border, only a couple years old. Bit too close to the Thodelemaia Dread Chasm for my taste, but the fertility of the land there is unparalleled."

"My thanks for the agricultural aside, Mag." Brand rolled his eyes. "If it's a place, then why would it be referred to as *she?*"

"While you're at it, perhaps all of you Wolflords can explain how this happened in Thodelebor, with one of its villages mentioned in the aftermath, and I'm still meant to believe the Westrealm is innocent of wrongdoing."

"Fiery arse." Caius rolled his eyes at the Demon King, tsk'ing. "You're young, so I'll forgive your thick skull. Take a moment and then try to tell me which Realm Ruler is actually stupid enough to make it this easy to figure out."

Lyriat stared at him, his nostrils flaring. "You think someone is setting you up."

"Aye. It's been a long time, but it sure as shite isn't the first time."

"It makes sense," Brand said. "Especially if it isn't one of the realms, but one of the anti-Imperialist factions. What better way to distract us than pitting us against one another while they make their moves?"

The king sighed. "And I'm sitting here falling for it."

"Perhaps," Caius said. "Perhaps not. It's wise to be wary until you figure it out. That's what makes you a good king."

There was a moment's quiet, finally broken by Magnus. "This is lovely and all, but I don't suppose you'd care to share this message? Might help in the helping, aye?"

The others all leaned in as Brand recited, "'*Glynmor thinks she's safe and well, tucked tight in her field of green. But what do you and her flesh have in common? I know what I hope it will be.'"*

Lunara's gut churned at hearing it again. Those puzzling words that said both something and absolutely nothing, all at once. The cadence just like a certain—

Oh my shitting stars. The Voice.

She forced her features into a blank mask, refusing to let any of the chaotic emotions bolting through her to show.

How in the realms could you have forgotten that it spoke to you just last night? Extensively!

What if it was the same being? Though, Baldrir had leaned towards his captor being male, and her *visitor* was decidedly not. Still, it would mean that it was real. Not the creation of a slipping mind, but—

No. Lunara couldn't think about it. Couldn't stomach it. She could only slow her breathing into something resembling normal and try not to lose her breakfast all over Lyriat's polished floor.

Realm matters, politics, factions—none of it had anything to do with her. She didn't owe them one of her most closely held secrets on the off chance it was related.

"Well that's fucking uncanny." Caius slapped the note onto the tabletop and pointed at it. "Because this is a letter asking for my influence in securing your services there."

"What?"

"Read it for yourself, lad."

Brand snatched up the piece of parchment, Hedda and Faldir on their feet in an instant and scanning the contents over his shoulder.

Hedda's face twisted with disbelief. "They want the Fourth Imperial Son to come and dig ditches?"

"I believe it says *a* ditch," Caius said.

She scrunched her brow and reread the message.

"And stone walls along the chasm edge!" she screeched, reaching around Brand to jab her finger into the paper

Magnus ran a hand through his blond hair. "Glynmor is a trial, to see if we can cultivate more places. The Westrealm is struggling to keep up with demand, so we've started to spread out into the land that had been left for the birds and beasties to thrive."

Faldir's face pinched. "What does that have to do with walls and ditches?"

"The walls are for the children, to keep them safe. Glynmor is less than a mile from the drop there. The ditch is to reroute part of the nearby Westriver and get a supply of water to the high fields behind the village—fields that grow your bloody damned food, you sour wee shite."

"And how do you know that?" Faldir crossed his arms, brow arching. "There are no specifics here."

"Glynmor was his idea. He's the one who designed the plans and stages," Caius said, his voice thoughtful. "I'm surprised he's never mentioned it."

The statement had Brand's head snapping up in his brother's direction.

"Ach, calm yourself." Magnus waved him away. "I didn't say anything because I wanted to see if it would all work out first. I did *not* know they'd already arranged to ask for your help."

"If it's your project, why would they put it to Caius and not you?"

Magnus gestured at Caius. "High Ambassador." He pointed to himself. "Ambassador Apparent. Think you can work that out on your own, Fal, or do you need it explained in shorter sentences and smaller words?"

Trails of light flashed over Faldir's skin as he snarled. He took a step forward, but drew up short when Lyriat raised a silencing hand.

"Regardless," he said with a pointed look at Faldir, "I am failing to understand how this relates to the message from Baldrir."

Caius huffed. "The message sounds like the riddled ramblings of a lunatic. I wouldn't pay it too much heed."

Hedda pulled herself up straight. "It is unwise to ignore such things." Her voice was hard, unyielding. "Especially under the circumstances."

"Perhaps I should clarify." Caius took his seat again and stole Magnus's ale. "Bring however many you think are needed to stay safe. Guard your backs and be alert. But you shouldn't *worry* about it."

Hedda scoffed, shaking her head at him like he was a hopeless fool.

"Ach, lass. I swear, all of you make me feel old as the fucking land itself." Caius looked genuinely exhausted when he flopped back and pinched the bridge of his nose. "Please don't tell me you actually think this is the first strife Bordoroth has ever seen."

"What are you trying to say?" Hedda hissed, her horns curling.

"That you're practically wee bairns, and I'm being woefully reminded of it. Listen"—He rested his elbows on the tabletop and pinned her with a sympathetic look—"this sort of thing has been going on for longer than our books have history for, and will continue to go on long after we're all dead in the ground. Our lot in life is to handle it as it comes while seeing to our duties, aye? I'm sorry for Baldrir. I'm damned fucking sick over Fausta. But, in some ways, sadly, it just is what it is and life has to move on."

Hedda crossed her arms and looked away, jaw ticking.

"You don't..." All eyes went to Thaddeus, slumped back in his chair and legs sprawled before him. "You don't think this is to do with the Prophecy, do you?"

Lunara couldn't help the frisson of fear that ran through her, even while the others chuckled—all except Caius.

In a moment of superstitious weakness, they'd once speculated about that very thing while his mate slowly wasted away in the next room. Useless nonsense, in the end, but they'd been exhausted and running out of more optimistic theories.

Which was probably why Caius was looking at her when he softly said, "Nay, lad. This is the same old shite. We'll all know without a kernel of doubt if the Shadow Prophecy ever actually comes into play."

13

LUNARA HAD TO GET OUT OF THE MONTREALM.

She'd done her duty as a healer. Baldrir was good as new, barring any damage to his psyche, but that sort of care wasn't included within the scope of her capabilities.

It didn't matter that she hadn't gotten to go outside to see Solyrian. Or the sea. It *didn't.*

Lunara shoved the last dress into her bag, and—

A knock sounded and she froze.

Pretend you aren't here until they go away and forget you ever existed.

It might work, too—until they busted down the door and it became a million times worse than if she'd just answered it.

Ignoring the pulsing throb in her joints, she limped over, hand hovering over the knob while she tried to decide which part of herself to listen to.

Climb through the window. Find a portal down in the city. Just don't—

"You know, Wolflords aren't the only ones with excellent hearing."

There was an impish lilt to Lyriat's voice, and it prickled over her. She should pretend she hadn't heard him just for saying out loud that he'd perceived her in such a teasing way. Obviously, she was trying to hide and have a moment alone.

Be honest with yourself, at the very least. You're trying to escape.

Yes, okay. Fine. She was. Obviously. But he wasn't aware of that!

"Please, Lunara."

Hard to ignore a 'please' from a king.

Damn it all.

She swung the door wide and turned away, walking further into the room. It was probably a felonious offense to snub a Realm Ruler in such a manner, but maybe if he didn't see the guilt written across her face, he wouldn't note the packed bag and start digging.

"I thought you might be needing this," Lyriat said, setting a tray on a nearby side table.

Lunara homed in on the goblet, standing proud beside a bowl of strawberries, its crimson contents gleaming. Her body cried out for the relief that gift of blood would give her, and she took a mindless step forward without meaning to—only stopping short when she saw the burning scrutiny in the king's eyes.

"Thank you, Your Majesty." It was amazing her voice was so steady when she felt anything but. "Though it seems below the duties of a king to bring a healer sustenance."

He let out a low sound, not quite a laugh. "You reduce us to our positions in this life so easily, rather than account for the intensity of the days we've spent in each other's company. Why is that?"

Lunara didn't know how to even begin to answer his question.

"Every individual here has expressed a desire to welcome you in and treat you as a friend—to honor you for what you've done—but you refuse it. Repeatedly."

If she hadn't been able to respond before, there was no way she had words for such a bald statement.

"I think it's because you're scared," he murmured, crossing his arms.

She plastered on a false smile, tittering like a nincompoop—all while her heart pounded hard enough to bludgeon her to death from the inside. "I can't imagine what it is you think I should be scared of, Your Majesty."

"Hmm." He pretended to pick at a thread on the shoulder of his sleeveless tunic, sniffing. "Tell me, Lunara—why is a Sorcerit with skills worthy of the Elder Tier hiding herself away in the Northern Forest of the Evesong, and not living comfortably in a bespoke tower on the Upper Block of Starkeep amongst her equals?"

It was remarkable, really, the way she could stand so very still while the world around her crumbled to nothing. The way she could cease to hear, or breathe, or speak, and yet she didn't fade away.

"Why should I know such a thing?" She knew the words left her lips because she felt them moving, but her mind had emptied so thoroughly that Lunara worried it might never come back again.

"Maybe because we all just watched you heal Caius in seconds—no salves, cloths, or incantations—when I know I saw shredded tendon and exposed bone beneath the river of blood. Do you deny that it happened?"

"I am simply proficient in my craft," she rasped, swallowing.

"Yes, you are. As proficient as any other healer on the Elder Council. Maybe more so, if my modest experience with them is anything to go by."

"A fluke, nothing more." Lunara was clawing for any excuse, any explanation that would make him back down.

Lyriat knew it too.

He offered her a smile, no less gentle for its insight. "Was Baldrir also a fluke then? Because I happen to know that Thaddeus mistakenly delivered your things here, instead of Bal's sickroom."

"So?" Her voice was little more than a croak.

"*So*, you healed a male who should've been dead without the common implements of your people and profession. There's only one type of Nachthellian capable of that feat."

Goosebumps broke out across the whole of Lunara's body, as if her flesh could break free piece by tiny piece and allow her to disappear that way.

"What is your *name?*" Lyriat asked softly.

Lunara knew what he was really asking, and it was amazing she stifled the sob his question tried to rip forward. Barely.

"Please. Don't make me answer that."

Names were of the utmost importance in the Evesong. So silly, when they were just a jumble of letters strung together.

And yet…

If a Nachthellian was powerful enough to have one, that series of syllables distinguished them in ways that had nothing to do with family or which realm they were from.

Lyriat was right. She was terrified. Had been for decades, ever since her parents had been taken and Cordelia had helped her to die alongside them.

"I swear on the Sisters who made us that I will never reveal it," he promised. "Not unless or until you are ready for it to be known. But I need to be aware of who I'm hosting in my home, for obvious reasons."

"You ask too much. *They* ask too much."

To deny a Realm Ruler was lunacy, but the words had blurted out before she could tear them back.

"Ah. It's the Council you fear, then."

His level of discernment had to be a gift from the Sisters, nigh mystical in its precision. It was the only explanation for how he could know exactly what had haunted her for so long.

There was no more sense in trying to deny it. A tear slipped free, damn the useless thing. "Wouldn't you? The Elder Council lures with false promises. They would groom me, until I was obedient, dutiful, mindless. They'd make me forget there was ever a time I was my own person. My hopes, dreams, all gone. And for what? A garish tower in an overrated city?"

The floodgates had opened and she was practically yelling, pacing like a caged beast.

"What hopes and dreams could anyone have when living half a life in hiding?"

That pulled her up short, too close to the truth for comfort. Fine. She *might* have had hopes and dreams if she wasn't afraid for her life every second of every day.

The Council wouldn't order her literal death, but they'd gladly cull any parts they found to be offensive in order to more easily pull her strings.

That, she couldn't live with.

And your parents would never forgive you if you tried. You may as well have killed them yourself.

Bolstered by the integrity of her choice, she looked Lyriat right in the eye. "My hopes and dreams may be small. Nonexistent, even, by some standards. But they're mine.

"Meanwhile, the Council thrives on using their collective power for their own, sordid ends. On ensuring creatures like me come to heel, whether they want to or not. On protecting the *monsters* they control, rather than the people who need them."

Sisters save her. Just the thought of those abhorrent beings, the individuals even worse than the Elder Council themselves, nearly brought her to her knees.

Talk about being scared of a name. She refused to let her mind even think theirs. *His.*

Lyriat's brows had punched upwards, his lips pulled down at the corners. "You seem to have a lot of opinions about them."

"More than I ever wished to have, I assure you."

"How is it you even have such a name, if the Council isn't aware you exist?"

Lunara had the insane urge to laugh—so contrary to what she was really feeling. "I was not yet of age when—"

No. He's asked enough of you already. He doesn't need that insight as well.

True. Her agony made no difference to him. She could keep that one thing for herself.

"My parents never announced it. Cordelia thought it should be my choice, when I was ready."

Half truths mixed with lies, but she didn't care.

Unfortunately, he picked up enough of the true portion. "Cordelia *the Firebane*?"

Piss and damn and shitting stars.

"Interesting, that you would view the Elder Council with such contempt, but have tenderness in your eyes when speaking about one of them individually."

She really did need to learn how to keep her mouth shut when it mattered. And *tenderness* was an overstatement.

"There are exceptions to every rule, Your Highness," she ground through her teeth.

He chuckled at that. "Why should you not be one of them?"

"I'm trying. Hence the hiding."

Lyriat nodded, then drew himself up straighter. "I would have your name, Sorcerit." When she didn't answer, he murmured, "Speaking it will not summon them. They're not hiding in the shadows waiting for you to say it. They aren't here."

Lunara deflated somewhat. She was beginning to understand that he, as a person, was ever a voice of reason. Level-headed to his core. Something of a comfort, if she was honest.

"First, I would have your promise as the Demon King of Straelon that it will never be repeated. It can be my payment, if you wish."

"How about my promise as a friend?"

She threw her hands up. "You Demons and Wolflords and your insistence on friendship."

He just stared and smirked, waiting.

Defeated, she uttered a name that hadn't left her lips in over fifty years. "Lunara the Moonweaver."

She sounded like an ill-tempered brat, but it was as good as he was getting.

"It is my honor to make your acquaintance, Lunara the Moonweaver." Lyriat sketched a shallow bow. "Now, about your payment. I would add to my debt before I settle it."

Lunara didn't have the strength to stand anymore. Everything that had happened, the aches and pains, caught up with her.

"How so?" she asked, hissing as she plopped down too hard on one of the chairs.

Lyriat swiped the goblet of blood from the tray and handed it to her, a knowing look on his face. "I want you to go to Thodelebor with the rest of them."

She paused with the cup halfway to her face, then went ahead and loosed that hysterical laughter from before. "And if I say no?"

"Then I will be disappointed."

Lunara considered the king. It seemed to honestly be that simple for him, but she didn't trust it. "You won't blackmail me into agreeing?" This was possibly the most ridiculous quarter hour of her life, and she fought to control her giggles. "You won't go running straight to Nachthelliae, to tattle on me to the Council?"

He looked genuinely disgusted at the suggestion. "What sort of friends have you *had?*"

That sobered her about as quickly as anything could.

May as well throw another humiliating truth out there into the world..

"None. One, if you count Cordelia, but that's something of a grey area. I may once have said Caius and Thaddeus." She looked away, towards the window where golden light was streaming in, oblivious to the sudden darkness shrouding her. "Let's stick with none. Nought by choice feels better than three I'm unsure of."

Lyriat scrubbed at his forehead. "I assure you, blackmail never once crossed my mind. I'm observant, and curious, and inclined to know for sure whether the instinct to beg your services is well-placed."

"What are you specifically asking me to do?" Her voice barely carried, but he heard it nonetheless.

"I'm about to blindly send four of the people dearest to me into Sisters-know-what. I want you to use your skills and ensure they remain safe and well."

"Just get them home in one piece, and we have a deal?"

Deals were too important to Nachthellians. Specificity mattered.

"Whatever trials come up, whatever ailments or surprises—you stay by their side and see them finished. My hope is that I'm being overly paranoid, and that you spend however long basking in the Westrealm's sunshine while Brand works his magic, and Hedda and Faldir stand as irritable sentinels nearby. Who knows what Magnus will be doing."

That pulled a huff out of her. "Sounds easy enough. And let me guess—you'll give me a sizable bag of gold in return?"

Useless shite.

"Lunara the Moonweaver, I will give you whatever absurd thing your mind can conjure up if you do this for me."

She sat up a little straighter. "Anything?"

"I swear to the Sisters."

Stars and arses. Whatever you want.

After a lifetime spent worrying, she knew instantly what to ask for.

"I would have sanctuary, without question, should I ever ask or have need of it. Not in the court or castle—somewhere remote and quiet, where no one would ever be able to stumble upon me. As well as your assurance that you will never reveal my location to anyone who comes looking. And…" She wasn't sure why she hesitated. Maybe because it felt like one more thing she was revealing about herself. "I want a clear, unobstructed view of the night sky. I want to be able to watch the twin moons move from one horizon to the other, with stars as their backdrop. Give me that, and I will do it."

Lyriat held out his hand, and she took it. "Done," he said, giving a single, firm shake.

The promise of freedom, just like that.

She grinned as Lyriat moved to leave, new hope flooding her veins.

He stopped short of opening the door. "And Lunara?"

"Yes?"

"I'm glad to have caught you before you were able to run away," he said with a pointed look at her overflowing bag. "It would have been awkward to have to send Thaddeus after you again."

Blessed moons. For the reward he offered? She was far more than glad.

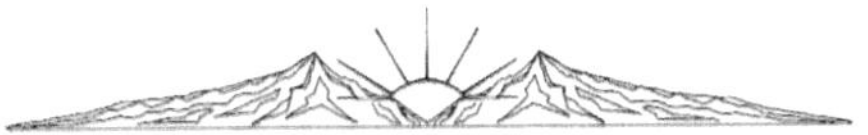

THIS WAS STUPID. *HE* WAS STUPID.

Apparently, all confidence had fled along with Lunara after the meeting, when she'd whisked herself out of the great hall. As far as he knew, she'd come up here and never left, which meant she had to be in there.

Just behind that door.

The one he'd been standing at for the last ten minutes.

Right.

He sucked in air, and let it out in a harsh puff. Again. And again. Finally, his hand obeyed and hovered there, inches away from seeing her again. Steeling himself, he tensed to rap against the wood.

At which point, he whipped around and stomped down the corridor. He made it as far as the glass hall before remembering how ridiculous he was being. Back and forth, a little further, a tad closer…

Great. Now he was pacing like an idiot.

He wanted to do something nice—something anyone would like—to express his gratitude for everything she'd done. So what if he'd planned it in a way that only she, perhaps, could appreciate?

There was no reason for her to linger now that Baldrir was healed, and he and the others were leaving for Glynmor in a few days. If he didn't see her now, he might not get another chance.

Why, in the stars-forsaken realms, could he not bring himself to just knock on the door?

Only the Sisters knew how long he was there, repeatedly convincing himself that he was a total prat before reminding himself of the opposite.

A low laugh in the near distance penetrated the fog of his mental acrobatics and he froze—until the thought of someone seeing him there, like that, spurred his feet in the opposite direction.

He had to escape. Couldn't be seen acting like a—

Brand skidded to a stop, kicking himself for his cowardice. Why should he, an Imperial Son of Bordoroth, care whether someone witnessed him there? People paced all the time. He could do whatever he bloody well liked.

Nerves steeled for the hundredth time, Brand turned back. He was tempted to practice on the countless rooms he passed—just to prove to himself that he did, in fact, remember how to knock on a damned door—but refused to be deterred this time.

He rounded the final corner, and—

No. Still not ready.

Fucking ridiculous.

He was already mad at himself for earlier. He hadn't had the faintest idea of how to respond to his uncle's obscure drivel about fate, and she'd clearly been uncomfortable.

Weeping shite, they'd all been uncomfortable.

Of course, his temper had gotten away from him too, but he was sick unto death of the mystery surrounding Meliora's illness. It wasn't helping anyone to keep it secret.

Brand rubbed a hand along one of his horns and dragged it down his face.

Maybe he *was* an idiot.

Or maybe Lunara would be willing to enlighten him. As long as Caius hadn't sworn her to a binding oath, the information was hers to give.

Unfair? Perhaps. But it didn't hurt to ask.

Just one more reason to stop his faffing and get to it.

With the millionth deep breath he'd forced into his constricted lungs in the last quarter hour, Brand gave himself a shake.

This was it.

He was doing it.

What he did not expect, as his knuckles were about to make contact, was for the door to swing open on its own.

Or for Lyriat to be standing on the other side.

Brand forced his face into a bland mask. Hard to do, when he was standing here with a spear of white-hot jealousy ramming itself down his throat.

Lyriat shooed Brand away as he stole a glance back over his shoulder, gently pulling the door closed behind him.

The soft click of the latch was deafening.

It was the sheer disappointment of it that gutted him. All that wasted time trying to work up the nerve just to talk to her, and it was his own best friend with her instead.

Lyriat closed the short distance between them, Brand clenching his teeth so hard it was a wonder they didn't shatter.

"This is rather fortunate," Lyriat said, voice hushed though his grin was practically beaming. "I was coming to find you."

He bore Lyriat no ill will. Truly. Brand had no claim on the Sorcerit's attention, and it was his own fault he'd missed an opportunity.

So why couldn't he stop staring at her door, wishing he could turn back time and do it over? Do it right, and get here first, and not be such a fool.

Lyriat was oblivious to his inner turmoil. "I have good news," he said, clapping Brand on the shoulder.

Weeping fuck. The only way this could possibly get worse was if Lyriat was about to tell him that Lunara was his mate. Why else would he be smiling from ear to ear? The realization crushed him because, if she was his, then—

Fuck. He couldn't even go there.

He only looked up long enough to see that Lyriat was staring at her door as well, a furrow between his brows.

Pining?

Lyriat turned back and tilted his head. "You know, it's not at all what you're thinking."

"I'm sorry, but how could you have any bloody idea what I was thinking?"

Lyriat blinked once, and then threw his head back and laughed.

Brand couldn't remember ever hitting Lyriat in anger, but his greater half was stirring beneath the surface of his skin, begging for the chance.

Maybe that's what he needed. A solid rage. To call out his greatsword and hack shite apart until he felt absolutely nothing but an overwhelming desire to go to sleep.

"Brand, aside from the fact that I know how exceptionally talented your mind is at cooking up utter nonsense, your face says it all." Lyriat shook his head. "I visited Lunara in order to secure her services for your trip to the Westrealm."

That was about as far from what he'd assumed as it could get.

"What? Why?"

Lyriat sighed, pulling him further down the corridor. "I don't feel good about it, for obvious reasons, and I don't want you to find yourselves in any unexpected situations without a capable Sorcerit."

Brand didn't feel particularly good about it either, not with that message hanging over him.

Then again, it was his brother's own project and their request made sense. If not for the mystery surrounding Baldrir's abduction and torture, none of them would have thought anything of it.

He scrubbed a hand over his face. "It's a farming village, Lyriat. What could possibly happen?"

"No idea. Which is probably what bothers me. Between Bal and the timing of the letter from Glynmor, something is off. I can feel it in my gut, Brand. Trust me."

"Alright, fine." He said the words but couldn't find even a fragment of himself that believed them.

Traveling. With Lunara. When he couldn't even knock on her door.

The Sisters had it out for him, surely.

"Now, I will leave you to finish whatever it was you were trying to start, with the knowledge that I'm in full support of you spending the evening with her, instead of alone. Good luck."

With that, Lyriat spun and made his way towards the great hall.

While Brand stood there facing the same fucking dilemma as before.

14

LUNARA PACED IN FRONT OF THE COLD FIREPLACE, A LOCK OF HAIR TWISTED between her fingers. The shadows in her room were getting longer and, if she weren't so distracted, she would've enjoyed watching Solyrian move, trying to gauge how the light correlated with the time. How darkness was a signal of true evening, of relaxing, and not the constant, somber state of things.

As soon as Lyriat had left, she'd gulped down every drop of the blood gift he'd brought her, excitement clouding her judgement. She hadn't needed that much. Her aches had been minor, and she'd used little power in relation to the last gift.

It had left her overly energized—not a good place to be when there was too much to think about, without a distraction in sight. The euphoria of her deal with Lyriat had begun to wane as a result, her mind refusing joy in favor of agonizing over every little detail.

Had she made the right choice? Asked for the right thing? Had Lyriat capitulated so easily because she could have asked for far more, or had worded her stipulations in such a way that he could easily outmaneuver them?

That's what scared her the most. That she held such hope, but it was misplaced, because she hadn't really gained anything.

You're going to find out eventually, one way or another. Hope now or don't—it doesn't really matter because the outcome is the same.

Yes, but for once in her life she wanted something solid. Something reliable she could count on without having to consider everything that might ruin it.

Lunara slapped a hand to each cheek and smushed her face between them, loosing a low groan.

This was useless.

If she was doomed to disappointment, she could at least enjoy the time she had before it struck.

A few days in Straelon, a few days in Thodelebor—a week then. Ish.

And another realm, foolish as it is. Seventy-two years without leaving the Evesong, and you're finally seeing the world. Even if Lyriat finds a way to cheat you—which he probably will—at least you'll have that.

Occasionally, she and herself did agree on something.

Right. Good.

Now what?

Excellent question. Lunara assumed it would be nearing suppertime soon, but did the Demons always dine together in the great hall, or did they do something different in the evenings? Sure, she'd been here for four days, but she had yet to spend a single one of them doing anything that even resembled normalcy.

Well, you're not going to magically come across it in here. Alone. Doing nothing.

So. She just had to walk out the door. Easy.

For the second time that day, she found her hand hovering over the doorknob.

Honestly, it's getting ridiculous.

"Get it together, Lunara," she mumbled under her breath. "The whole world's out there, just waiting."

And there's bleeding fuck-all in here.

She almost laughed at herself as she pulled the door open.

The corridors were different in this part of the castle, only one side holding chambers. The other was a wall of windows that spanned the entire length of the hall and overlooked a central garden. Someone had opened every pane, allowing a light breeze to tease the air inside. The welcoming heat of afternoon sunlight had sunk deep into the stone floor, seeping straight through her slippers as if trying to pull her feet outside.

She might have been tempted by the lush greenery had she not looked up to see Brand walking away from her. The sight of a familiar person was a welcome relief. Of all people, he would be able to acquaint her with a standard evening in the Montrealm.

Picking up her skirts, Lunara hurried after him. She was just opening her mouth to announce herself, reaching out to tap him on the shoulder, when he abruptly spun.

And slammed straight into her.

It was like running head-first into a solid wall. Stars exploded in her vision and, if she wasn't a healer and knew better, she would have sworn he'd just broken her nose. Fortunately, a pair of large hands wrapped around her arms and stopped her from falling flat back onto her arse.

Again.

"I— You—" He sounded strangled until he cleared his throat. "Forgive me, Lunara. I was… entirely distracted."

Brand's rumbling bass washed over her, sending a shiver through her bones as she blinked up into his overly-serious face.

It cannot possibly be fair for him to look and *sound like that.*

"We really must stop meeting like this," she said, a ridiculous titter escaping her.

Blessed moons. Keep it together.

"Perhaps it's better the Sisters drive us together, however awkwardly," he said softly, as if to himself.

O-kay…

"And why is that?" she countered.

"Because then I am forced to act," he whispered, "instead of dallying with my crippling thoughts."

Well, that was unexpected.

"Uh…"

Probably have to do better than 'uh' if you want him to ever speak to you again.

Never mind that she understood so completely it made her ache. Had lived with those crippling thoughts as her only constant companion for decades.

A blush stole across his cheeks to—undoubtedly—match her own. Charged silence hung between them for a moment as he searched her face, and she wondered if he even realized he was still holding her. Not that she was complaining.

"I wonder if perhaps..."

Should you tell him that you're still bent backwards and half-dangling, or just let it happen?

Let it happen. Obviously. She hadn't been held in so long—even inelegantly—that she'd begun to forget what it could be like. The warmth and comfort of it. Of another being sharing their space with her own, unable to tell whose heart it was she felt beating.

This was the third time she'd found herself accidentally in his arms and stars above, she liked it.

Fool.

His nostrils flared as he took a deep breath. "Would you like to see something spectacular?"

There was an earnestness in his tone that grabbed hold of her, banishing every backhanded thought and rejecting any response other than, "Yes."

Brand's eyes never left hers as he slowly pulled her upright and offered his arm.

She took it, his scent washing over her as he led her through the empty corridors. Salt and fresh pine, and something warm that seemed attached only to him.

Though he was silent, she felt his excitement grow with every step they took, thrumming just beneath her fingertips where they clutched him. She couldn't help the surreptitious glances she stole, taking in his profile and the way one side of his mouth had curled upwards.

It teased a smile from her own lips—until she found herself standing before the portal in the great hall.

Lunara had wanted to see Straelon. To visit the city, maybe go to a pub for the first time. Faced with the reality, though, a skitter of nervousness snaked its way down her spine.

"Um... Where are we going?"

"Not too far," he said, rummaging through a small pouch on his belt. "Just right outside, really."

He lifted his toll and threw it into the portal, offering her a crooked grin before grabbing her hand and pulling her through.

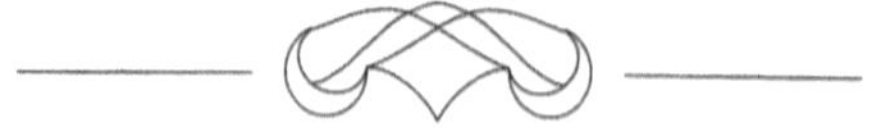

THEY EMERGED INTO A TEMPEST, HER HAIR WHIPPING INTO A FRENZIED, blinding curtain and tangling in every imaginable direction. Brand, too, was caught up in the mess, if the tugging at her scalp was anything to go by.

"Just don't let go!" he shouted, though she could barely hear him over the screaming howl of the wind.

He squeezed her hand and urged her to follow. Rock and gravel crunched beneath her slippered feet, and she held on like her life depended on it.

For all she knew, it did.

Just as violently as it had appeared, the gale stopped, calming to nothing more than a cool breeze. Her heart stuttered when Brand released her, but it was only so he could reach in to part the screen of her hair, his deep chuckle doing funny things to her.

"My apologies. I'd forgotten the wind could be like that on the portal side of the peak."

As he smoothed the curls and waves back, the amusement left his face to be replaced with something else.

Eyes darting, lids fluttering, he watched his own fingers moving through the strands. When he tucked the locks gently behind her ears, his lips parted as if words were waiting just on the other side to come tumbling out, but it was only shallow breaths that left him.

Lunara found her own lungs mimicking the action, and she couldn't tell whether it was relief or crushing disappointment that flooded her when he backed away and let his arms drop.

"Where have you brought me?"

He nudged her forward, turning her as he spoke. "I thought someone who'd never seen Solyrian before today should witness their first sunset like this."

The sound that left Lunara could not be described by any words she knew. It was like part of her soul wrenched itself from her body, just to come falling back with all the force of a comet landing.

In a million lifetimes, she never could have imagined…

Crowned by the castle and its many towers, all of the Horned City was spread before her, stretching and spilling down the mountainside. Pure, evening sunlight bathed the mass of rooftops and stone, the biggest trees she'd ever seen scattered amongst it all and providing shade beneath their evergreen canopies. Winding streets twisted amidst the landscape and structures, all leading her eye to the vast, glittering sea below.

And there, blazing just above the watery horizon, was the sunstar.

It shimmered as it sank slowly towards the waves. This time, she felt the tears as they flowed freely down her cheeks, dripping unchecked and lost to the earth. There were no words. She only wished she could capture this moment forever and live safe within its bright warmth.

She would have missed this if she'd left. Would have run back to her realm of endless dark and never known that such beauty existed.

How could she ever go back to Nachthelliae, to a cottage bathed in shadow and only her own thoughts for company? She wasn't sure she'd be able to do it. Wasn't sure she could accept not being able to see such a sight with regularity.

Accept payment from Lyriat the second this adventure is over, and you won't have to.

Sisters, it was tempting. She'd thought to only call on the debt if the Council started to close in, but now—

"And how do you find it, my lady?" Brand repeated his earlier words, pressed close enough that she could feel his breath stirring against her ear.

She had no idea when he'd gotten so near, had been too entranced. "Quite stirring," she whispered. "Obviously."

Brand stepped away and the ground shuddered. She spun to find him with his hand extended, stone cracking and warping at his command. It rose up, viscous, shifting like liquid until it finally formed a long bench in the settling dust.

He brushed off the top and gestured for her to sit, claiming the other half for himself.

"I haven't been up here in a very long time," he said, resting his elbows on his knees and clasping his hands together between them. "I'd forgotten the majesty of it."

The final rays of day set his hair alight as he looked out over the view, the normally subdued auburn turning to fire and making his horns stand out more starkly.

Blessed moons, the view wasn't the only majestic thing there.

Lunara cleared her throat, heart hammering. "I think I'd be tempted to come up every single day, if this were my home."

Brand tilted his head to look at her. "There are views to rival this one in the Evesong. Some, I would say, that are far better."

"None that I can think of." Starkeep didn't count anymore. "Though I don't get around very much, as we've already established."

He hummed a low sound that did funny things to her. "Why is that? We're close in age, according to Thad. I would have assumed you'd been everywhere by now."

His look was penetrating. So much was conveyed in that stare that he wasn't saying out loud.

Careful.

She had no wish to lie, but she barely knew him. Lyriat was a king and had given her no choice. While Brand was, in many ways, much more than a king, his question left room for her to decide how to respond.

To let her keep her secrets.

"I've never had the opportunity to do so." True enough. "I prefer to keep to myself and live a simple life."

"Hmm. I envy the prospect." He sighed, a wistful sound that she felt to her bones. "Tell me, what do you do with your 'simple life?'"

He sounded genuinely curious, which surprised her.

"It's not at all exciting, I assure you."

"It is to someone who wishes for it. Unless you'd rather I bore you with realm matters and the papers piled up on my very official desk? The price of grain from Thodelebor has gone up, especially. And don't get me started on the hoops I have to jump through to procure a particular cloth from the Kohamaians without bankrupting the Montrealm. They—"

"Alright, alright!" she interrupted, laughing. "I surrender. Spare me from talk of money."

"As I said—dreadfully boring."

"Well…" It took her a minute to decide what was safe. What would keep him from any prodding inquiries that dug too deep and too close to the truth. "I live in a cottage I built on the edge of the Northern Forest— Why are you looking at me like that?"

His brows had punched up his forehead. "You've just said you built yourself an entire home."

Stars and arses. Mucked it up with the very first sentence.

"Yes, well. Um. It wasn't hard."

That's the exact opposite of what you should have said.

Now his eyes had narrowed, mouth quirked. "I know many a Sorcerit who would wholeheartedly disagree with you."

You can either lie, or change the subject. There's no other choice.

"It's not what you're thinking."

Ugh.

"And what is it I'm thinking?"

His smile wasn't fair. It made her want to do something brainless like tell him everything.

"That I conjured it up out of nowhere, covered in mystical light, and magically didn't kill myself doing it."

He scoffed. "I was more wondering how you managed it alone."

"Oh. I guess I do everything alone, so same as I manage anything else."

"You don't get lonely?"

She couldn't bring herself to answer that. Last week she would've chuckled and said *absolutely not!* Now, she wasn't so sure.

"What's your favorite color?"

You were supposed to change the subject three sentences ago. And where are you even going with this?

"Blue," he answered quickly. "Like the sea on a clear day."

She didn't miss the fact that he was staring intently into her eyes as he said it, and tried to ignore the prickling heat creeping up her neck.

The rest of the idea finally came to her when she fixed her gaze on a cluster of trees nearby, their limbs swaying as they clung to the mountain-side. The Demons did seem to appreciate their wood.

Oh, no.

"If I'm going to make something, I need part of it to be available."

And an excess of moonlight! There has to be another approach to this.

She lifted her hands and a glowing orb formed between her palms, threads of magic writhing together. A block began to take shape in the center as particles manifested, drawn from one of the trees and into her hands.

The rest was taken from within.

"I can only manage *very* small things this way," she gasped.

You mean when you're almost entirely depleted and have no business doing it?

Lunara closed her trembling fingers around the finished piece before presenting it to Brand.

"My favorite color is green," she said, looking out over the city again and trying to find her breath. "Dark, like the shadows in the forest."

Wide-eyed, he took the chunk of swirling blue and evergreen wood and turned it in his hands while she tried not to topple over.

"Creating new things like that takes the price from somewhere deep. Hurts, in ways different than I'm used to."

Even now, her stomach turned, angry and cramping. Begging.

Halfwit. The cost could have been almost nothing. But sure, throw him off the scent by destroying yourself.

Most Nachthellians drew power from cosmic light, but it dissipated over a short time.

She, however, could draw in more than what simply brushed over her skin and was absorbed. She could move it, shape it, store it.

The blankets she wove were trivial in the scheme of things—child's play—but her mother had thought that *Moonweaver* sounded lovely, even if the name didn't fully encompass the scope of her gift.

Lunara's true and unique ability—the one that set her apart from most Sorcerit and would have the Elder Council foaming at the mouth to get their hands on her—was the fact that she had a bottomless repository within her. A well, deep as the sea in front of her, that could be filled to the brim and tapped into whenever she wished.

Unless she left it nearly empty and kept it that way.

Kept herself safe.

The truth was that Lunara probably could have conjured up an entire cottage for herself, if she'd fed heavily on a blood gift and had filled that well even a quarter of the way.

Brand didn't need to know that.

"This is incredible," he whispered.

Her voice was little more than a rasp. "It's a piece of wood that's too small for anything."

"Yes, but you've changed its colors, and it's *glowing*. I... Thank you. Truly."

"Yes, well, perhaps you can use it as a weight for your very boring paperwork."

His look was unnerving. Maybe because it was filled with awe over so trivial a thing, and she was a bleeding liar.

"How did you build your cottage then, if not like this?"

The words just tumbled out. "I stole it. Sort of."

There's no hope for you, is there?

Brand's mouth fell open.

It was almost enough to make her forget that her insides were convinced she'd swallowed a handful of razorblades.

"When I arrived at the place I now live, it was a dilapidated hovel in the woods."

Maybe unkind, when it had been free and secret and safe, but it wasn't far from the truth.

Biting her lip, she reached her hand out and into the ether. This was easy to show him because there wasn't a Sorcerit in all of the Evesong that couldn't manipulate its strange hidden places to some degree.

And it cost almost nothing.

"A few weeks in, I heard rumors of a nasty injury in a nearby village. The male in question turned out to be a right arsehole."

She closed her eyes and tried to remember where she'd set that book down. Sometimes going *through* instead of just accessing a pocket within took a little longer.

"Unfortunately for him, I'd overheard a conversation with his equally disgusting companions, bragging about how they'd cleared a copse of luminescent trees in order to sell the lumber to other realms in secret. Highly illegal, as I'm sure you know."

In her mind, she saw herself walking through her cottage, glancing at every crowded surface. Into her bedroom and—

Ah! There, on the dresser.

"So, I took it."

Light flashed as she pulled back, the book in her palm.

"It was slightly complicated because I had to grab each piece of hewn wood and drag them through individually, which took ages, but it was worth it to keep it in Nachthelliae. As the laws require."

"Yes, I'm sure it was all about adhering to realm law." Brand chuckled as he slipped the presented tome out of her fingers. "And you built your home with that?"

"I didn't technically build anything in the end. For the next year, my price for healing was construction. I merely provided direction on what I would like and gave them the materials to do so."

And then made them forget they'd ever been there.

"Remarkable."

There was a sparkle in his look, an approval, that washed over her. She welcomed the swell of pride that came with telling a true story and garnering such a reaction from him.

Do not go and get any ideas. You still have to go back to that home after this, with no one the wiser.

Remembering the way everyone had looked at her earlier, Lunara was nauseatingly certain that particular cat might be well out of its bag.

"The Wolflord Who Ravished Her." He raised a questioning brow, his lips pinched between his teeth, and a giggle bubbled up out of her.

"Well who doesn't like bodice-ripping and swooning?"

She watched the apple in his throat bob as he swallowed. "Who, indeed."

"Besides, I had to find a way to experience the other realms somehow."

"Yes, and what better way than this. Let's see…" He thumbed through the pages before stopping and cracking the spine open. *"'Axanderus shifted, his drenched fur sinking into wet, golden skin right before my eyes. Still dripping, he flexed his hard, rippling muscles, stalking stealthily towards me as I fingered my moist—'"* He practically choked on the last word before turning a panicked look toward her.

They stared into each other's eyes for a split second before they both burst into uncontrollable laughter.

"I didn't say it was good!" she squealed, wrapping her arms around her stomach. For once, the soreness there had nothing to do with using power she didn't have.

It was freer than she'd ever seen him. Not that a couple of days was much to go on.

She wasn't sure when Solyrian had finally dipped below the horizon, making way for the moons to hover in the sparkling night sky, but Lunara let some of their light in to bolster her. Just a drop to ease the clenching in her gut.

Blame it on the twilight and cocooning shadows. They made her brave. Reckless. Made her want more than giggles and sad stories that only reminded her how damned alone she was.

Except she wasn't. Not tonight, at least.

And neither was Brand.

As he sighed and wiped the tears from his eyes, face hidden in the darkness, Lunara had the wild thought that, maybe, he might like to know it.

She tangled a curl in her fingers, her eyes dancing over the twinkling lights of the Horned City. "I understand, by the way."

What are you doing? Are you completely mad?

She somehow found the courage to look at him. "About the crippling thoughts, I mean."

You are. You've lost your mind.

Stars above, he went so still. Frozen, like ice had formed in his veins and was holding him there.

There's still time. You can still back out or make something up.

"We speak to ourselves in the cruelest tone, don't we?" Lunara said softly, chewing her lip.

Brand's ragged breaths joined the sounds of evening as his hazel stare searched hers, pleading. She couldn't tell whether he was asking her to stop or begging her to go on.

You're in it now, you daft witch. It'll either help tremendously or make the foreseeable future absolutely unbearable.

She forced her eyes to stay on his, even though every particle of her body was begging her to look away. To protect that part of herself she'd never shared before. "It's your voice, but… not. Words you would never say, thoughts you would never have, feelings you've never felt for another—you direct it inwards, tenfold. It becomes a mantra that you beat against yourself, murmured painfully in the silence of your own mind."

Dramatic, much?

"Somehow, you endure every jagged, horrible whip against your being and convince yourself it applies only to you. No one else is ever as useless as you know yourself to be."

He leaned back, ever so slightly, his jaw ticking. Seeing it, Lunara couldn't help but note the stiff set of his shoulders. The trembling flex of his hands.

Sisters forgive her if she was wrong for doing it, but Lunara couldn't resist. She sent out a thread of power, silently thanking Lyriat for his gift of blood as she once again searched for Brand's heartbeat. When the pounding, stuttering rhythm reached her ears, a kindred ache bloomed within her own chest.

She placed a palm there, digging it in. "All the while, your heart works as though to claw its way out of you. Your air comes in gasps. Your vision blurs along with reality, and time twists, until the only possible thought is *'how can I escape this?'*" A rueful laugh slipped loose, the flippant mask dropping into place to cover her discomfort. "Busying myself is often my answer, though sometimes… sometimes I hide, because it's all too much."

The longer Brand sat there unmoving, his gaze boring into her, the more she was convinced she'd made a horrible mistake.

Great. You've broken him. Probably only needed half of that speech, and it still would have been ridiculous.

"See? I'm doing it to myself right now." Bitterness sat heavy on the words, coating her tongue.

Lunara let go of her spell, unable to bear the overwhelming sound of their hearts crying out in furious tandem any longer.

Probably best you find a way to get your arse out of—

"*Yes,*" he finally rasped. "Yes, exactly."

Sweet relief barreled over her.

"It's the same for you, then?" His tentative words were as much a confession as they were a question.

"Unfortunately."

Brand ran his hand along one horn, nodding as he looked to the ground.

"Do you have anything that helps? Any… one?" she asked quietly.

She had no business asking such a personal question, but as she'd already reminded herself—she was in it now. May as well find out before she let herself get too close to him. Let herself imagine things that had no place in her life.

He swallowed and shook his head. "Woodcarving," he admitted, voice low as he raised the block she'd just made him. "When it's too much, I go to my workshop. Everything is easier there."

What were the bleeding odds of that?

Lunara melted, then blurted, "I weave the moonlight, and make silly things out of it."

Sweet baby Sisters in a cradle. Back to madness! Didn't get revealing enough for you with the king? One person knows so it's time to scream your truths from the mountaintops, is that it? Bleeding, fucking ninny.

She bit the inside of her cheek, wishing she could silence what was probably the wiser part of herself and enjoy this moment.

He was staring again. Even if her head hadn't been cranked back to look up at him, she would have known that his piercing eyes were fixed on her. The sensation of it was unlike anything she'd ever known.

It was like stepping under a waterfall. No fear of drowning, no worry. Just the freedom of throwing her arms out and feeling it pummel into her before the cascade turned to a skimming caress down her skin.

Or you've cooked it all up with your harebrained imagination and are now spouting absurdly saccharine poetry about something that isn't really there.

The need to fidget was overwhelming. It took all of her strength to resist the pull to worry a curl in her fingers or swing her dangling feet—anything to expel whatever was building up within her. She didn't know where to look or how to be. Whether she should sway into him like she wanted to or sprint away like her mind was insisting she do.

It's fine. You're fine. Just—

"I know Solyrian has held you captive today, but…" He reached up to catch a strand of hair fluttering in the breeze, his thumb barely brushing the shell of her ear as he tucked it away. "You have your own light, Lunara."

Oh… Well then. That's…

"Thank you for sharing it with me." He looked away. Back to the sprawling city and its luminous lanterns. To the silvered waves of the sea. "Just… thank you."

15

Brand watched the door close behind Lunara and nearly collapsed right there in the corridor.

Weeping fuck. The things she'd said.

He wasn't ignorant. He knew there were others like him. Creatures that suffered from whatever his affliction was.

Lunara was the first, though, to look at him and see the morass of shite and strangled breaths and say, *'Me, too. I feel it, too.'*

To be understood so fully was… Shite, he didn't even know.

He was still floating on the high of it, like he'd smoked some of Vann's rolled herbs. Couldn't stop smiling. Just grinning from ear-to-ear for so long that his cheeks hurt. Burning Solyrian, the way she'd made him laugh.

There was still something off about her, though. Something she was keeping close. He could see it in her eyes when they widened after she said something nonsensical. And she had far too much obvious power to be living alone in the Evesong's wilds.

In a cottage she hadn't quite built for herself.

"I'm not sure what the barmy look on your face is for, Your Highness, but we've got two fucking problems."

Brand couldn't even bring himself to be annoyed at Hedda's tetchy interruption. He fell in beside her, tempted to sway to the hammering beat of their leather boots on stone. "Go on."

"Lyriat has just informed me that the Sorcerit whose room you were stalking around is coming with us to the Westrealm." She held up a crumpled piece of parchment.

"That's correct. I don't see the issue."

She stopped dead in her tracks, a few feet before the doors into the main hall. "Is it the luminous beauty and wide eyes that have everyone acting like they're living inside their own arseholes, or is there something I don't know about?"

"Uh…"

"I get it. She's pretty. She also hasn't been within ten yards of a standard pub brawl. How am I the only one who can see she'll be more trouble than she's worth in Thodelebor?"

The only words Brand cared about were *luminous beauty* and *wide eyes.* Understatements. At this point, Lunara could ask him to take her to every realm for a month each, and he probably wouldn't think it was more trouble than it was worth.

"That was only one problem, Second."

"Well, if you all insist on her going, then someone needs to train her."

Brand eyed the guards nearby, their faces a perfect picture of disinterest.

"Why?"

"Because going to Glynmor is a mistake. It's not a coincidence they've asked for your help just as the rest of this shite is happening. We're going to take a female who can't even raise her voice?"

All of the lightness left him, the weight of reality settling on his shoulders.

"I never truly thought it was a coincidence," he said quietly. "Though, I may have tried to hope."

His frivolous worry over whether Lunara would like a sunset had allowed him to ignore the riddled message for a few hours. The deeply personal nature of it.

"We shouldn't go."

"We will absolutely go," he said, pushing into the main hall. "This is exactly the point of my existence and position. If not me, or my brothers, then who? Fortunately, we'll have a marginally trained Sorcerit on our side by the time we do."

He crossed the empty space, his mind on the kitchens at the far end.

On food, then sleep and forgetting. And… maybe another thing. If Lunara liked giving gifts, perhaps she'd like receiving them in return.

"How, exactly, do you plan to accomplish that in a matter of days, Brand?"

Lyriat emerged from his secret passage behind the thrones, the stone melting back into place as he stepped away from the opening.

Hedda pinched the bridge of her nose with a long-suffering sigh. "Where are your bloody guards?"

Lyriat at least had the decency to look guilty. "Probably scrambling in a panic somewhere near my quarters while they try to figure out how to tell you they've lost me. I figured the passageways were safe enough."

"Except you're not *in* the passageways, are you? You're right fucking here, out in the open!"

"No one outside of the family knows they exist. What danger is there? Since I haven't been able to take a damned piss in nearly a week without someone looking over my shoulder, I needed a moment to myself. Ergo…"

Hedda looked between him and Lyriat, mouth gaping. "Am I the last one left in Straelon with a fucking brain? I swear."

Lyriat waved that away. "I could take on the lot of you with a hand tied behind my back and still come out the victor. I'm *fine*. Besides, it's rather late for you two to still be awake. Is something the matter?"

"I was just informing Hedda of the delay in our journey, and how she will now be spending the extra days training Lunara before we go."

"What?" she shrieked.

Lyriat chuckled. "A fine choice. How long?"

Brand took a moment to consider all of the possibilities. Too long, and the wait would unravel his already fraying nerves. Too short, and there was no point in it. "A week?"

"If it were up to me, you wouldn't be going at all. I'm happy for you to postpone as long as you want."

Hedda pressed two fingers into each temple. "You want me to turn her into a warrior in seven days?"

"No." Brand paced as Lyriat flopped into his throne, watching them. "I want you to make sure she can defend herself within seven days. I want you to be certain she can hold her own as a last resort."

"That would probably take years," she grumbled.

"It'll take a week, because that's how much time you have." Mind made up, Brand strode away, heading not for the kitchens, but somewhere else entirely.

"Where are you going?" Lyriat called after him.

"To send another message."

It didn't matter that Vann had yet to answer the first, more important missive. After the debacle over the damned fabric the Demons relied on, his brother owed him.

"To whom?"

"An arsehole with a talent for cloth."

And Brand knew exactly what to ask for. He could feel it.

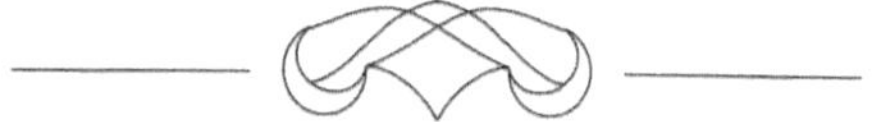

LUNARA KEPT HER BREATHS SLOW AND SILENT, HIDING IN THE SHADE OF AN evergreen on the edge of the practice grounds. It was early enough that Solyrian hadn't yet cleared the mountaintops to burn away the dewdrops still clinging to the grass and needled branches above her.

There were a couple of days before they were meant to leave for Thodelebor, and she was restless. On edge.

Her time spent with Brand on the mountain had only made it worse. How was she meant to close her eyes when all she saw on the other side of her lids was him telling her she had her own light in that gravelly voice of his? It had been bone-melting. Sigh-worthy. Wondrous.

And so close to the truth that she'd nearly been sick right then and there.

She'd grown tired of lying awake in bed, tossing and turning and staring at the ceiling, and had thought a walk would help.

She hadn't planned on spying.

Lunara gripped the trunk and peered around it, bark digging into her fingertips as she watched Hedda and Faldir train.

The twins were a blur, moving with such synchronization that it was impossible for her to decide which of them would win if the fight were real. They had no weapons—only their fists and flesh, their teeth and horns.

It was Hedda, though, that had all of her attention.

Lunara had been days away from beginning her training before... *before.*

Alone in her cottage, with no one else for miles, it was a lack that she'd lamented for the last fifty-two years.

How much safer would she have felt if she'd been able to use something other than power to defend herself? How much of her disquiet would have been relieved with knowing she could guard her space, her peace, without revealing herself?

She and Hedda were nearly of a size. Lunara was slightly wider, while the Demon was a tad taller, but there weren't so many differences that she couldn't picture herself in the same place, using her body in that way.

In fact, it seemed to occasionally be to Hedda's benefit. Where her brother was brute strength with devastating results, she was fast. Wily. Clever in the placement of her limbs. She used parts of herself that he didn't bother with. She danced around him, landing three blows for every one of his.

Watching her made Lunara wish she was someone else, even more than before. Identities aside, she wanted Hedda's skill, her confidence, for herself.

If only you could bottle it up and take it like a tonic. Oh wait! You can.

Stars above, was it actually possible to feel an inner self rolling their eyes?

Yes, Lunara maybe could have done that. Many Sorcerit had that particular gift. But it had always felt wrong to her, somehow. Artificial, instead of genuine. She didn't want fake fortitude and ability. She wanted the real thing.

Because the rest of your life isn't just one, gigantic sham.

Sometimes, Lunara sincerely wished she could reach inside and smack herself.

The second the sigh left her lips, she slapped a hand over her mouth, praying that the twins hadn't heard her. One beat, two...

They carried on as if she didn't exist.

Thank the Sisters.

As the morning wore on, more and more Demons joined them—all shapes and sizes, every age.

Lunara gaped when Nyri practically skipped onto the field with a sword over her shoulder, dragging Baldrir along. The warrior was steady on his feet, sure, and it warmed her to see them together.

Hope the risk was worth it. At least two people know who you really are now, as a result. The Council will hear of it any day.

Damn it all, it was. It *was*. No matter what she sometimes tried to make herself believe.

She stilled when she saw Magnus and Thaddeus roughhousing their entire way to the field, grins a mile wide.

The sight of Brand made her stop breathing altogether.

He'd braided his hair over one shoulder, and beads of sweat had stuck some of the errant strands to his face, his jaw—like he'd already been exerting himself elsewhere. His wrapped tunic was gaping and damp, wide sleeves rolled up to reveal most of his considerable arms. The trousers he wore only reached his calves and his feet were… bare.

Bleeding moons. Not even the sight of the Demon King, shirtless and swaggering beside him, was enough to distract her.

They took the field, Lyriat shouting something she didn't quite catch. Everyone fell into lines and groupings, facing one another, their bodies poised. With a word, chaos broke. It was much the same as Hedda and Faldir had grappled, but louder. Wilder. Moving with rhythmic precision that complemented the actions of the warriors beside them and boggled her mind.

Brand commanded the space around him, dodging attacks, delivering hammering blows of his own. At one point, he locked horns with another and roared so loudly, so fiercely, that it carried above the din of mock battle like it was meant for her ears alone. Stars above, his face. The power. He was—

"Care to join in?"

Lunara yelped, her face crashing into the tree trunk. She choked back the beating of her heart as it spiked up into her throat, but there was no hope for the flush she knew was staining her cheeks.

Wonderful. Only thing worse than sneaking around is being caught doing it.

Hedda chuckled and stepped around to face her. "Why hide over here when you could be over there?"

How in the arsing stars… She was just with the rest of them!

It was too difficult to look directly at Hedda. It would make the embarrassment real. Instead, Lunara darted another glance over to the practice field as she collected herself, the blur of Demons moving with such fluidity that it made her dizzy. "No. I could assuredly *not* be over there."

"Why not? All Sorcerit learn to fight. How else could they add it to the list of things to charge for?"

Lunara ignored the pang in her chest. "Not all of them," she murmured.

You're begging for it. You're literally begging to be outed. For shite's sake.

What were the odds that she would just be having the thought and then Hedda would come over to make her voice it?

She shook herself. "Anyway, I wouldn't have what it takes to spar with the likes of them. I'd be trampled in a second."

Hedda considered her for a moment before leaning against the tree and crossing her arms. "You know, you're peculiar. Even for a Nachthellian."

That got her attention.

She snapped her eyes to Hedda's. "What is that supposed to mean?"

Hedda shrugged. "I've always thought Sorcerit were all a little off. Creepy."

"Creepy!"

"You, more than most."

Lunara recoiled. This was a dream, or a nightmare. Surely. Any minute she would wake up and not be having this nonsensical conversation.

"You Sorcerit with your glowy skin and shiny eyes. Fangs that don't put themselves away when you're not feeding."

Still not waking up.

Was she actually trying to be rude?

"Don't even get me started on the feeding thing, actually." Hedda shuddered. "You drink blood for fun? Disgusting."

For fun! What in the—

"Not to mention that you're all attached to your spooky-arsed realm like a babe to its mother's teat. Are you even allowed to be out under the sunstar this long?"

Lunara gritted her teeth as she dug her fingernails into her palms. "Why are you saying this?"

The vitriol stung. Hedda had been kind to her, grateful for Baldrir.

And she was probably thinking every one of these things while you were over here admiring her like an eejit.

"Because I can," Hedda answered. "What are you going to do about it?"

You should smack her. Or un-*heal her. Is that a thing?*

Lunara drew in a ragged breath. "I'm not quite sure what you're doing, but please stop."

"*'Please stop?'*" Hedda laughed. "Sisters, your parents taught you such good manners. Oh, wait." She leaned in closer. "I forgot. Thad told us you don't have any parents. My mistake."

Something unhinged swept over Lunara. Fuming. Burning. Shattering. It clawed at her skin and screamed to be set free.

"What did you just say to me?" Her voice was hardly her own. A crackling rasp that held the fury flooding her body.

"Poor little orphan Lunara can't even seem to use her ears correctly."

Lunara couldn't control herself. She lunged, her lips peeling back as she hissed, her fangs an inch from Hedda's face.

The Demon grinned, a savage look of approval that stretched across her features as she gripped Lunara's arms and gave her a good shake. "*There* it is. That is all you need, Sorcerit. The rest is just practice."

The adrenaline pumping through her veins fizzled with Hedda's flip in mood, turning her stomach. "What just happened."

Hedda straightened and gave her a once-over. "Shite talking, to get your blood pumping. I wanted to see if you had it in you. You do."

"Had what in me?"

"*Rage.*"

That one word lit a fire somewhere within her. A spark that had merely been waiting for kindling.

"We Demons use it to feed our power, to give it direction, but it can be a tool for anyone." Hedda nodded, her eyes narrowing. "You have it in droves. I'm sorry for what I said. Truly. And for dragging it out of you so harshly, but I had to know for sure."

Lunara was buzzing, her head too light. "Why?"

"Because I can't train you without it."

"Train me?"

"I know a look of longing when I see one." She threw her hand up when Lunara opened her mouth to argue. "I don't need to know why you are probably the only Nachthellian I've ever heard of above the age of twenty who doesn't already know how. Though I am intrigued…" She raised a brow. "No? Not yet? Ah, well. Fine. Someday. Besides, I have selfish motives for wanting it done."

Maybe this is *a dream. It's the only explanation for how bizarre this is.*

"Selfish motives?"

Hedda reached her arms up to re-knot her hair around her horns, eyes on the battlefield. "Lyriat's told me what he asked you to do. The thing with my cousin, though, is that one idea tends to give him another. Then another." She loosed a heavy sigh. "Assumption, on my part, but it probably means you'll be around for a while, whether you intend it or not."

Um. No. Absolutely, definitely, assuredly not. Montrealm, Westrealm, home. Within a week.

But… Hedda was promising her something she'd wanted for most of her life.

"What does that have to do with me fighting?"

"If your job is to help keep everyone safe, then you need to be able to do it in more ways than one. A healer is useless if she's lying dead in the grass when the fighting is over."

An excellent point.

No. Not an excellent point! Have you lost your mind? Besides, there isn't time.

That did seem to be one glaring problem.

"How will I possibly learn anything of use in two days?"

Hedda smirked at her. *Wily.* "I've already aired my grievances with our king. He should've asked you from the start whether you had any capabilities in battle. Without them, you're nothing more than a pretty liability."

"How could you air grievances you didn't know to have?" Lunara threw her hands up. "You had no idea whether I could fight or not."

Hedda squared her body to Lunara's and dropped into a ready stance. "Exhale forcefully and tighten your core."

"Why?"

"Because I'm going to hit you."

"You're what!" she shrieked.

Hedda's mumbled, "Good enough," was the only warning before she slammed her fist into Lunara's stomach.

The one that pummeled into her jaw next was just insult to injury.

Lunara's feet left the ground as the force of it sent her backwards, the breath exploding from her lungs as she hit the needle-laden dirt.

Bleeding fucking moons! She's insane!

She tried to suck air in, but her spasming body refused it. Not until she coughed enough to make her throat bleed. Her wheezing gasp only served to highlight the pits of agony that had opened up in her abdomen, her face.

Hedda straddled her writhing form and bent over her. "People who know how to fight don't walk with fear in every footstep." She gripped both of Lunara's forearms and yanked her upright. "They don't announce their ineptitude with scrunched shoulders and wide-eyed looks of awe when someone else is doing it." Her hands were surprisingly gentle as they brushed Lunara down and steadied her. "They don't miss someone walking up behind them, or slam their faces into tree trunks because they were startled. And they definitely don't let someone get a second hit in, even when they *are* surprised by the first attack."

She has a point.

Oh, sure. Now she agreed with herself.

Apparently convinced that Lunara would not, in fact, be collapsing straight back down to the earth, Hedda released her. "We leave in a week. Caius already sent word to Glynmor that we'd be delayed, as of this morning."

It was too soon for speaking. She might never be able to form words again.

All she could do was blink uselessly at Hedda, her arms curling around herself, convinced her guts would be spilling out any minute.

"And now," Hedda said with a pat to her back, "you'll be less scared when we get started this evening. If you already know to your bones what it feels like to be punched in two of the worst places, that it isn't so bad in the end, then you won't concentrate so hard on avoiding it. That only leads to other mistakes while you're learning."

She walked away backwards. "Meet me here just after sundown. The others will be feasting down in the city, so there'll be no one around to see me kick your arse."

With a wink, Hedda spun and rejoined the fray on the practice field.

This is a mistake, halfwit. A gigantic, arse-brained mistake.

And yet, as air began to fill her lungs more smoothly and the pain dissipated—pain that wasn't really all that different from what she endured repeatedly through her power—Lunara couldn't bring herself to believe that.

How could it be a mistake when she was grinning from ear-to-ear?

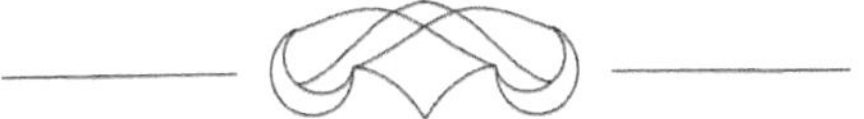

LUNARA STILL HAD THE OVERWHELMING URGE TO SNEAK. TO JUMP FROM shadow to shadow to make sure no one saw her heading for the practice field.

She'd spent the rest of the day in her room. Pacing. Eating. Not eating. Trying to decide what in the shite one was meant to wear while learning the art of hand-to-hand combat. Arguing with herself over the wisdom of her recent choices.

Or lack thereof.

The fading pinks and fathomless purples of the gloaming were battling with the light of the twin moons. Their celestial bodies had just cleared the peaks of the Sacred Sisters—a natural wonder she'd never once thought to actually see with her own eyes—as if to bless her presence here.

Lunara cast a glance around, checking that there was no one nearby, and opened herself up to them.

With a sharp inhale, she closed her eyes and reached inside, her mind following the path to the well at her center. Its yawning void cried out when it sensed her there, dry, begging for a single sip of the power that would give it new life.

Fool! Why? Why risk it?

Because Lunara was tired of sitting at rock-bottom, the ground doing nothing at all to cushion her arse. Yes, she had to keep her secrets, but with a gut-punch and upper-cut, Hedda had opened a door.

Just a crack. Just enough to let a little light shine through. To tempt her to steal a peek through the gap and see what was behind it.

What she'd realized earlier, plodding back and forth and wearing a hole in the rug, was that she *yearned.* Longed to be more than she was, even within her self-imposed exile.

Doing this would give Lunara armor. She couldn't show it to the world, but it would let her feel like there was something formidable about her.

Even while Hedda undoubtedly mopped the floor with her.

It would also combat the pain, to a degree. Give her something to fall back on. With more fuel for her spells, should she choose it, she'd be free to take the beatings and drills without having to worry that she had nothing left if something unexpected happened. If someone needed her.

Ironically, the thing she'd been running from was the one thing that could give her peace of mind.

At least, for now. For this.

The moonlight was a whisper. A caress. A wave that danced on her skin and invaded every inhale. She let herself swim in it, hoarding every word and touch and movement.

As she emptied her lungs on a slow exhale, it made room for the power to seep through. A trickle at first, like it was shy. Unsure whether she'd meant to let it in.

Another inhale. Out…

A deluge, sweeping in with staggering force to fill her empty places. Lunara planted her feet more firmly to the ground, clamping her lips against the whimper that tried to claw its way free. The well was greedy, taking and taking, gorging itself on the power she'd denied it.

Too much. It's too much!

But she hadn't felt this good in ages, this free. So close to satiated. So close…

No!

Lunara's eyes snapped open on a gasp, like it was the first real breath of her life. Deep. Cleansing. New.

Power was a song in her veins. Pulsing, thrumming, throbbing *power.* The things she could do with it. Create. Stars above, it was as if she'd never seen color before. Had never smelled or tasted properly.

Eejit. It hasn't been that *long. Quit being dramatic. And stop glowing!*

Lunara crossed her arms to hide glimmering hands, swallowing back the rest of the moons' light until she was no longer illuminating the grass in a perfect circle around her.

Then, she laughed.

16

"I DON'T USUALLY HAVE THE LUXURY OF FOLLOWING THE CACKLINGS OF A complete lunatic to find my way in the dark."

Lunara looked up from the ground with a grin. "Hello!"

She sat against one of the carved, wooden posts that circled the practice grounds, her back pressing in to every nook and cranny.

It was bliss. No radiating torment, no biting or bruising. No pain.

It had been so long since she'd felt her body without it that she hadn't even realized what she'd been living with.

Hedda arched a brow at her as she lit a few of the orbs perched atop the nearest pillars with a wave of her hand, the stone shining with golden light. Solyrian's light.

Stunning.

"Are you... alright?"

Lunara didn't bother to stifle her giggle. Why should she? "Perfect."

"Hmm. You seem awfully cheery for someone who's going to be throwing up her supper in the next few hours. Come on."

That cured some of Lunara's mirth as she stood, but couldn't smother it fully. "Why in the realms would I be vomiting?" she asked, following the Demon to the center of the field.

It was Hedda's turn to laugh. "Because that's how I'll know you've had enough. Are you sure you want to wear a dress for this?"

Lunara pinched her lips. "I confess, I had no idea what was appropriate. You Demons wear so little, and this is all I know."

Hedda's attire was all black, skin-tight and moving with her body in ways Lunara had never seen before. Though she was technically covered from neck to ankle, most Nachthellians would be picking their jaws up from the floor for days if they saw her. Revealing that much of their body for anyone to peruse? They'd rather die.

It was probably a result of her isolation, but Lunara liked it.

Hedda considered her for a moment. "Are you able to repair your clothing?"

Don't answer th—

"Yes. Why?"

You know, it'll be your own fault when this goes tits-up. Just remember that.

Hedda knelt in the grass at her feet and gripped her skirt at the knee. "I'll find you something better tomorrow, but this'll do for now."

"What are you— Wait!"

Too late. She'd already rent the fabric apart with a heave, tearing around and around until Lunara's legs were free. She folded the piece neatly and held the square up. "For later."

Lunara couldn't decide whether to laugh or cry. "You know, verbal statements of intention go a long way towards being on the same page. For the record, it's much easier for a Sorcerit to shrink particles up or stretch them out than it is to join them back together."

Hedda tilted her head. "What's the difference?"

Lunara let a thread of power free. It latched on to Hedda's clothing, and she commanded the particles to stretch. In the blink of an eye, the Demon was standing there swearing and swimming in her clothes. "It's like breathing, or bending your knee. Everything contracts and expands in ways it understands." Another blink, and it fit her again. "Repairing a tear is like healing sundered flesh. I have to convince two things to bond that no longer realize they belong together. It takes far more power and concentration."

Lunara shrugged, but inside she was frolicking. Stars above, the *ease.* With the well so full, aiding her, that output of magic had been nothing at all. It was like she didn't even know herself anymore.

"Huh. Good to know." Hedda seemed to store the information away before nodding. "Now, do as I do."

Apparently, they were done chatting.

Hedda began to bounce on the balls of her feet, bobbing side-to-side, and Lunara mimicked the movement.

"You need your muscles to be warm before you abuse them," Hedda said, eyeing her. "Straighten your spine, shoulders back. Good. If you start straight in on the harder movements, you run the risk of harming yourself. You have to take care of your body to be able to *use* your body."

Already, Lunara's lungs were straining, sweat gathering on her brow.

Sweet Sisters, how are you ever going to make it?

Funny how Lunara's place in this life was to care for others, but she'd so easily forgotten her own needs. She knew how to stop bleeds and seal cuts, how to mend broken bones and regrow limbs, but she didn't know the first thing about training. About making *herself* strong.

"All right, that's enough of that. Now, we stretch."

Once again, Lunara followed Hedda's movements—raising her arms above her head this way and that, bending to touch her toes, drawing out her spine. She couldn't deny it felt good. Freeing. Like her body had been wound too tight and she was helping to loosen all the coils.

"Now, this is the part where I make you puke your guts up," Hedda said.

Lunara did her best to remember she wanted this, even if there was a frisson of fear trying to convince her otherwise.

"You're going to follow the lights." Hedda pointed to the orbs atop the circling posts. "Jog first, nice and easy. When I give the word, you sprint for all you're worth to the next pillar. Then, it's back to jogging until I say otherwise. When I whistle, it's time to walk. We do this until you puke, or pass out. Whichever comes first."

Lunara gaped at her. "That could be hours!"

Hedda threw her head back and laughed. "No. I give you three quarters of an hour, at best."

As it turned out, Hedda gave her too much credit.

Lunara made it twenty-nine minutes—zig-zagging all over the stars-damned place to follow those lanterns as they lit to the tune of Hedda's bellowed commands and shrieking whistles—before her knees gave out and she was retching into the dirt.

"Not too bad, Sorcerit," Hedda murmured, combing gentle fingers through Lunara's hair to hold it back while she heaved. "You did better than I actually thought you would."

Lunara listed to the side and rolled flat onto her back, lungs wheezing. "I'll never… survive… this."

Hedda hummed a low sound. "Not only will you survive, Sorcerit, but you'll thank me for it someday. Now, come on." For the second time that day, the Demon peeled Lunara from the ground and set her to rights. "I'm fucking famished, and you will be too as soon as you walk it off and remember how to breathe."

Lunara would *walk it off* the minute she started feeling her legs again.

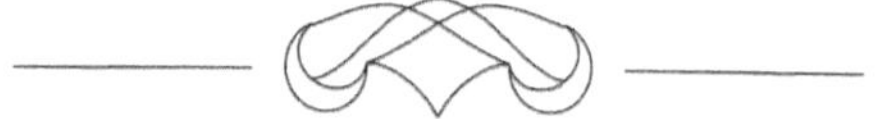

SHE WAS GOING TO MURDER WHATEVER IT WAS THAT KEPT POKING HER FACE.

Slowly.

Lunara rolled over and groaned, every muscle screaming at her for daring to disturb them.

She wanted to go back to two nights ago, to a mountaintop and hazel eyes, and forget yesterday had ever happened.

"Good morn-i-i-i-ng."

Nyri's sing-song greeting was the last thing in the realms Lunara wanted to hear. And there was no way it was already morning. Her body had just hit the bed a moment ago.

"I know how to make people disappear," she mumbled into her pillow. "No one will be able to find you."

Not technically true, but she'd gladly use the threat if it would make the Demon leave her alone.

The mattress dipped and bounced along with Nyri's giggling. "Hedda sent me. I'm to inform you that you're only a quarter of an hour from being in trouble."

Lunara snorted. "That sadist is the only one in trouble. She made me eat eight eggs for dinner. Every bite. I'll never forgive her."

She jerked back when something prodded her in the nostrils. Lunara cracked an eye open to see one of her own chestnut curls poised an inch from her face, clasped in two of Nyri's fingers.

Her arm was leaden as she batted it away, wrapping the sheet around her head. "Go away. Just leave me to die here."

"She said you would say that"—Nyri got under the sheet and shimmied her way in until they were nose-to-nose—"and to tell you she has a tonic waiting to make it all go away, *if* you can get to her of your own volition."

Lunara was fairly certain her soul left her body along with the sniveling whine that escaped her.

Hedda had forced her to walk around the practice field three more times last night and made her stretch again. Deeper stretches, holding them for longer, until she'd been nothing more than a quivering puddle by the end.

She'd then sat Lunara down in the empty main hall with a glass of milk and a pile of scrambled eggs that was as big as her head, and said, "Eat. All of it. You can get up and go to bed when you're done."

Nothing had ever tasted so foul as those last handful of bites. She wanted to vomit all over again, just thinking about it.

Never eating eggs again. Never, ever.

Still, the promise of a tonic—

"I brought you proper clothes as well. We'll match!"

Lunara opened both eyes that time and tried to see what Nyri was wearing. It looked much the same as what most of the others had donned in their practice yesterday. Not the strange fabric that welded itself to one's skin, but linen. Loose and airy.

And not at all something Lunara could imagine herself in.

"I'll help you dress, if you want. Which, you will. You won't be able to lift your arms yet, I know. Hedda did the same thing to me when we started my training. But I swear the tonic is worth it. You'll feel brand new!"

If only she could have a drop of Nyri's buzzing energy to coax her from the downy embrace of the bed. As long as she didn't move, Lunara could forget that her limbs felt as though they'd been chewed on by a dragon.

And yet, it wasn't the pain of power over-spent. The agony of giving more than she had within her. Even now, she could sense the shredded fibers of her abused muscles knitting themselves back together—better, stronger.

The thought bolstered her somewhat, though she was still hesitant.

"Add 'prying helpless Sorcerit from their deathbeds' to the list of services you offer, and we have a deal."

Nyri squealed and gripped her arm, simultaneously rolling and dragging until she was on her feet and Lunara was tumbling off the side of the mattress and crashing to the floor.

"Piss and shite! Ow, ow, ow."

Burning. Burning everywhere.

It was the irony of all Sorcerit that they couldn't heal themselves. There was no give and take in that lack of transaction, no balance. A tonic or feeding was the only way. If the wound was dire, blood needed to be gifted straight from the source—sharp fangs sinking into willing and welcoming veins. No goblets or flasks of day-old offerings.

And outside the Divine Right of Mates, forget *taken* blood. Not even the Elder Council would do such a thing. It didn't work, and only the vilest of Nachthellians had ever dared to steal a gift.

Fucking bastards.

"That's it, just breathe." Nyri was already tugging at her dress buttons, popping them open as she chattered encouragements. "It'll be fine. Promise. Think tonic-y thoughts."

"This will be much easier if you let me stand, Nyriadne."

"Oh! Yes, silly me. Obviously." She gripped both of Lunara's hands in her own. "Here we go. We'll just—"

Sisters save Lunara from grabby Demons that insisted on yanking her all over the place.

"There's a snack here, by the way, if you're interested," Nyri said.

She gestured over to a gilded tray on the bedside table. Between the bowl of strawberries and goblet of blood was a single bloom, its stalk rising from a porcelain vase. She'd never seen it's like, with three white petals arranged in a trifecta, larger green leaves in the spaces between, yellow stamens jutting proudly from the center and tipped with pollen-laden spheres.

The first flower she'd ever seen with her own eyes that wasn't glowing, or luring winged prey, or trying to bite her as she passed by.

The sight of it momentarily stole her pain. "What is that?"

Nyri followed her look and grinned. "Trilliatum. My favorite." She started tugging Lunara's sleeves down her arms. "It grows like a carpet at the base of the red balstrae, just behind the castle. You know, the primordial tree that Lyriat's throne was carved from."

"Stunning." Lunara's voice was reverent as she skimmed her fingers over the velvety surface of one petal.

"I can take you to see them later, if you like! Though, you probably won't want to be alive by then. Hedda has a habit of making people wish they were dead. At least for the first couple days. Or weeks. I can't remember. It's all a blur, honestly, even though it was only last year that I started myself."

With a tug, Lunara's dress fell to the floor, Nyri chit-chatting away while she helped Lunara step from the pile of silk.

By the time Nyri had shoved her into billowing grey trousers that flopped around her ankles and a strange matching tunic that wrapped and tied around her waist, Lunara was sweating. Teetering. Ready to call it quits and head straight for the Veil.

Maybe there's trilliatum in the Blessed After. That's probably the only way you'll be seeing it today.

Which was fine. What good was living when every step felt like dying, anyway?

Nyri brought the goblet to her lips. "Just a bit. We really don't have much time."

Lunara tried to deny her, but Nyri was already tipping the cup.

The first tentative sip exploded on her tongue and she nearly choked on it, gasping, power surging into her veins. Nyri tried to offer her more, but she clamped her mouth shut and pulled away. It was too much, too intense. Not safe.

Shitting stars.

Unfortunately, her unwillingness to take more meant that it wasn't enough to take away the bone-deep soreness of her muscles.

Maybe just a little bit more.

"Was that—"

"Time to chew and walk, walk and chew. Let's go!"

A strawberry was shoved into Lunara's mouth before she could finish asking whose blood she'd just taken into herself, but she didn't even taste it. Not after the potency of that gift.

Nyriadne's. It must be. She's the one who brought it, after all.

Lunara eyed the young Demon beside her as she hobbled through the door. She didn't look like she held that much power.

She's so young, and probably still coming into it.

True. And she was part of Lyriat's family. A royal of the Montrealm.

"Hurry up!" Nyri grunted a few minutes later, dragging Lunara's stumbling body down the corridor. "You've only got a couple of minutes left and we still have two turns to make and Hedda doesn't like it when you're late. She'll have you doing something humiliating like scrubbing the the floors in the main hall at the height of the luncheon service."

"Ach, away! Lyriat's not going to let Hedda force one of his respected guests into doing anything of the sort." Caius appeared out of nowhere and sidled up to Lunara, grabbing her firmly around the waist and hoisting her up straighter. "Come on, then, lass. Put your arm 'round my shoulder. That's it, nice and easy."

Lunara choked back a sob. She couldn't decide whether it bubbled up out of gratitude because he was doing most of the work for her, or because everywhere he gripped and bumped against her hurt. Spectacularly.

Or maybe it was because he, of all people, was being kind.

"Weeping shite," he grunted when Lunara tripped over her own, numb feet. "I knew she'd insisted on you learning some basics, but this seems a bit far."

"I would say this is standard for the Hedda regimen," Nyri chirped.

Think she's skipping just to rub it in that she can?

Probably not, but it certainly wasn't helping Lunara's mood.

They finally reached the main hall, staggering in like a pair of drunken revelers. Caius's laugh boomed when he plopped her down onto a bench at one of the long tables and, help or not, she definitely thought about kicking him in the shins.

By some cosmic blessing, only Hedda and Faldir were within. Then again, it was only just registering that the windows around them were still dark and the space was being lit by the stones, not Solyrian.

Lunara slumped back, the table's edge digging into her spine. "Why?" she whined. "Why am I awake when it isn't yet daytime?"

Hedda huffed as she swaggered over, a vial pinched between her fingers. "Because it's train with us now or everyone else later. Three, or three hundred. Your choice."

Lunara was just getting ready to say *later!* when she caught a glimpse of herself in the window, the sweating, unkempt, miserable reflection in its inky surface staring back at her.

Lovely. You know…

If she went later, it would mean Brand being there. Seeing her. Like this.

Take the tonic and get the bleeding fuck out of here.

"Now!" Lunara winced when her voice echoed, piercing. Clearing her throat, she managed a far more collected, "Now is wonderful."

Hedda smirked and uncorked the vial. "Cheers, Sorcerit. You made it through your first day of endurance training. Now, we teach you how to fight."

Every morning, Nyri woke Lunara up, pulled her out of bed, and helped her change clothes.

Every morning, she brought a tray with that same blood, and that same single flower. She still hadn't gotten to see the trilliatum where they lay beneath the tree in their blanket of white and yellow and green, but she didn't quite mind.

Because every morning, Lunara felt a little bit better.

It may have been Nyri's blood. She'd managed to coax Lunara into accepting more and more with each day, but Lunara secretly hoped the young Demon's gifted offerings weren't the reason. That, instead, she was feeling stronger because of her own hard work and dedication. That the mornings spent falling on her arse and the evenings spent heaving into the grass were amounting to something more.

She was dodging at least half of Faldir's punches in their hand-to-hand sessions, even landing some of her own blows here and there. And she'd improved in her nighttime endurance trainings—sprinting faster, lasting longer, her stomach starting to behave despite how hard she was pushing.

At first, all she'd been capable of between practices was sleeping, passing out face-down on her mattress and wanting nothing more than to never move again.

Yesterday, everything had changed.

Lunara had been trudging to her rooms after training with Faldir, half asleep already, when she'd come upon a Demon limping in the opposite direction. He'd offered her a pained greeting and lazy wave, and continued on. She might have dismissed it as nothing out of the ordinary for the male if she hadn't spotted the bloody footprints trailing behind him.

As ever, new energy had lit her veins at the sight of active suffering. There was no part of her that had been capable of ignoring him then.

Aldiat had shattered his kneecap falling from a ladder, a jagged laceration at the site. His second serious injury within a couple of weeks, apparently, and a fact she'd had to pull from him after discovering the shoddily healed fracture in his wrist. In order to keep his new mate from worrying, the foolish male had sucked it up and kept going.

Lunara was starting to suspect that was true of most Demons.

While tending to him, she'd learned from Aldiat that, with preparations for the Occurrence taking place, injuries were piling up left and right.

Which simply wouldn't do.

It had almost been too easy to commandeer a corner of the great hall afterwards, enlisting Nyri's help to secure a set of large chairs and a table for her "supplies."

News that a healer was in residence had blazed through the Horned City like a wildfire. Before Lunara had even finished setting up, a line of Demons long enough to span the room had formed.

Hands crushed by hammers, and bodies bruised by the stone. Splinters the size of her fingers. Shattered bones. Slices and gashes and scrapes.

Their enthusiasm might've had something to do with the fact the she refused to accept payment, but no matter. The normalcy of it soothed something in her, filling a hole that had been missing since she'd agreed to Lyriat's bargain, and she'd taken their pain into herself gladly. It was worth it to feel like herself again.

Today was no different.

Her fake salves and useless bandages were strewn across the tabletop beside her, their herby scents wafting through the air. She used them obsessively, excessively, to reinforce the illusion that she was just like any other Sorcerit healer. Nothing out of the ordinary meant that there were no rumors to be spread.

She'd learned her lesson with Lyriat.

"You know, Gaulnir," she chirped, "this is what shoes are for. Nails aren't meant to go through the bottoms of feet."

The old Demon grunted, lounging back in his seat with his legs stretched out to her. "We don't wear shoes while raging, m'lady. 'Sides, I hardly felt it 'til I left my form. Must've been one of the little'uns that left it there. They do try to help."

Lunara gave him a genuine smile. "Well, worry not. By the time I'm done, it will be as though it never happened." She threw Gaulnir a wink and got to work.

Her mind wandered while she carefully removed the spike of iron and set to mending him, her last healing for the day.

Stars above, what would it even be like to prepare for an Occurrence? To experience it? Be part of it?

No idea, but she'd give anything to feel the thrum of excitement growing with every day as it crept closer. To join together with her entire realm, her people. To welcome the power that the Sisters poured down, feeding her and the land.

The Occurrences only took place every fifty years. She should've had one under her belt and be preparing for another, but the last one in Nachthelliae had never happened. All because of—

No. Not that. Not him. Don't think about him.

Lunara drew in a deep breath and willed her fingers to be steady as she reached across the table and grabbed a jar of cream. Dipping her fingers in, she let the smell of night lavender reach deep and calm the raging storm threatening to break, rubbing it into Gaulnir's foot as she pushed power out of herself and into him.

As the stories went, the Occurrence in the Evesong wasn't all that different from the one here, or any of the other realms. Every half century, stunning celestial events took place throughout the year, power surging down from the cosmos. In the Montrealm, it was a gift from Solyrian, the sunstar hitting a prism between the peaks of the Sacred Sisters and sending a beam of pure magic down through the Horned City and into their Solyr Stone.

Nachthelliae had Illamiata, the Tear Stone—though the jewel was small, no larger than a coin. Normally, in a few months, the Evesong would be readying for the twin moons to align above Starkeep, their power funneling down into Illamiata and whichever evil fucking creature was in possession of it.

No. No, no. You're not meant to be thinking about him.

Another breath, another smile—that one nowhere near as authentic as the last.

She kept her hand over the Demon's foot, so he wouldn't see that it was healed already, and snatched up a roll of "enchanted" linen. After wrapping it carefully, she tied the ends in a neat little bow and gave Gaulnir's leg a pat.

"The bandage may be removed tomorrow, my friend," she said. "Until then, do try to avoid stepping on any other sharp objects?"

Gaulnir turned a fetching shade of pink above his greying beard. "I'll do my very best, m'lady. I swear to the stars, it feels better already."

Lunara bit the inside of her cheek as she nodded and waved him on his way.

The dwindling light outside told her it was nearing time for her to meet Hedda, and she sighed, stretching her own legs out.

This was the hardest part of starting the healings in between. She had to endure the pain she'd gathered over the hours while she ran and jumped and did whatever Hedda told her to. Thank the Sisters for Nyri and her blood gifts every morning.

They were the only thing keeping her going.

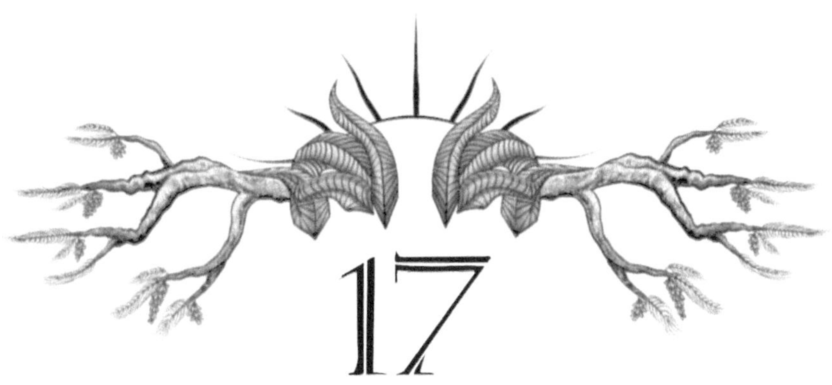

17

BRAND DREW THE BLADE OF HIS SMALL CARVING KNIFE ALONG THE BLOCK OF wood, a curl of luminescent turquoise and dark viridian falling to his lap.

He kept one eye on his project, and the other on the practice field below—on Lunara—just as he'd been doing for days.

Hedda was pushing her well beyond her limits. Every night that he watched Lunara lose her guts to the ground, he wanted to rage. Wanted to gather her up and ensure that she never felt any discomfort ever again. It was a lesson in torture to sit up there in his tree branch perch and resist the urge to make himself known.

If Lunara was anything like him, which—thank the sweet Sisters—she was, she'd be mortified to know he'd been there, observing her in that vulnerable state.

He swallowed, eyes darting even though she couldn't see him. She'd probably be just as mortified to know that he'd seen her sleeping, bundled up like a babe in swaddling, rosy lips parted and chestnut curls shooting out in every imaginable direction. He'd only stolen glances, intent on respecting her privacy while darting in and out of her chamber, but it probably wouldn't matter to her.

She'd be embarrassed, he was sure of it. Probably wouldn't ever speak to his sneaking arse again.

Meanwhile, he'd never get that captivating image out of his head. Ever.

There were worse things, he supposed. If he had to live the rest of his life with only memories of her, at least that was one of them.

Weeping Solyrian, she had completely bewitched him.

Brand pulled his shoulders back and shook himself, stretching his neck. No use feeling guilty. She was being tended to, and that's all that really mattered in the end.

"Puking already, Sorcerit? I thought you were better than this now!" Hedda's *commander* voice was like a banshee's shriek in the still night. She even drowned out the waves crashing against the cliffs.

Brand leaned over to better see Lunara. Sure enough, she was bent over her knees, her body heaving. For some reason, she refused to secure her hair in any way, and the ends dragged through the soiled grass. Gritting his teeth at the sight, he willed Hedda to show her an ounce of mercy and hold the damned mass back for her at least.

Fuck, he hated this.

"I've gone… twice as long… as yesterday," she said, gagging between her words. "I'm so tired."

"Perfect. All the better for your enemies." Hedda circled her like a vulture before leaning in closer, shoving her face into Lunara's. "They won't have to work as hard to slaughter you."

"I'd be happy for a trip to the Veil." Lunara let out a sound too close to a whimper for his liking, swaying precariously side to side. "Stars and arses, everything hurts."

"Unfortunately for you, I don't fucking care." Hedda gripped the collar of Lunara's wrapped tunic and hauled her upright. "You have more. Today, we go until you pass out. The retching is just icing, as far as I'm concerned. Now fucking move."

With that, she shoved Lunara into motion, reaching out every time the Sorcerit slowed to prod her in the back, shouting insults and obscenities.

Hedda would call them *encouragements*.

His hand tightened around the block of wood Lunara had made him, the edges he had yet to carve digging into his palm hard enough to slice his skin. Brand's greater half scraped at him, demanding to be set free and loosed upon the one offending the Sorcerit.

He breathed through the looming rage as she ran and ran, whorls of sunlight rising up in a burning dance across his flesh. Even his fangs began to drop before he clawed them back.

Lunara cried out and his heart lurched, ramming into his ribcage. He wasn't sure he could manage it. What good did it do, really, to sit there and watch her suffer just to preserve her pride?

Carving forgotten, he gripped the bark beneath his hands and dug his nails into it, using the pain in every fingertip to ground himself. To breathe.

Time stopped when she stumbled and went slack, chestnut curls a billowing trail behind her as if to signal her pending fall. He watched—fuming, horrified—when she finally toppled, leaping from his perch before she even met the dirt.

Enough was enough. Hedda had gone too bloody far.

Brand's feet hit the carpet of needles at the tree's base, and he stomped through them without a care.

Hedda turned as he reached them, a haughty brow raised. "Your Highness."

"Are you out of your fucking mind?" He didn't bother to reign in the snarling tone of his voice.

"I am not, thank you for asking." She pretended to examine her nails, as if she'd ever cared about such a thing. "Just in the middle of hardening our little softy Sorcerit. Yourself?"

The rage swept over him at her flippant words. Forget trying to breathe through it—he was fucking seething. He let it loose, let it have control, the world going red around him.

The stars floating above turned pink, the hanging moons along with them. Everything was awash in bloody hues, illuminated by the markings of his change, their patterns glowing as he grew and grew, towering over Hedda. He jerked his head as his horns curled, two extra sets sprouting free to cage his skull.

His chest was heaving by the time his reshaping was complete, a constant hum drumming inside of him to crush and maim and conquer. Thank the Sisters for the small mercy of that ridiculously expensive cloth he procured from his brother, Vann. It had stretched around his legs to protect some modicum of dignity. The tattered linen tunic hanging from his bulging shoulders was another matter.

"How fucking dare you, Second." His voice was a depthless pit, a low wrath incarnate as he stared down at her. "I told you to train her, not abuse her."

Lunara's form was limp, her face half buried in the dirt, and her limbs were askew. He could tell from their position that she hadn't even had the presence of mind to break her fall and protect her body.

A growl rumbled out of him at the sight. "The only reason I'm not choking the life out of you right now is because I know *she* would hate me for it."

Brand bent and scooped Lunara into his arms. She didn't so much as twitch, flopping awkwardly against his chest. Stars above, she was so small when he was like this, fitting easily into the crook of one elbow. Fragile, helpless, completely unaware that he could easily crush her if he wanted to.

Fortunately for her, he'd never wanted anything less in his damned life.

He couldn't resist clearing the tangle of hair from her exquisite face, tucking it gently away and stealing another stroke along one arched brow and down her high cheekbone.

Brand wasn't quite sure whether he wished for the action to wake her, to make those sea-blue eyes flutter open and behold him in his rage form, or whether he wanted her to never know this had happened. To stay asleep and lost in her dreams until morning, unaware he'd held her this closely.

"You will never treat her thus again, Second." He didn't bother to look at Hedda. She was probably rolling her eyes, and he wouldn't be able to control himself if he saw it. "*If* she still comes to you tomorrow, take her to the spring cavern afterwards. It will help the pain."

When Hedda huffed, Brand drew on every pitiful ounce of patience he possessed while raging and willed his hands to resist tightening into fists around Lunara's vulnerable flesh in furious reaction.

"I don't understand why she's suddenly hurting." Hedda's sigh was like acid in his veins. "She was doing fine before. I only thought to show her that she has higher limits than she believes, as everyone does."

Brand did turn on her then, lips peeling back to flash his fangs. "Pull your fucking head out of your arse for two minutes, and pay attention."

Hedda was wise enough to hear the command in his tone. To realize he was not her friend right now, but an Imperial Son perilously close to snapping. She drew herself up and raised her chin, muscle ticking along her jaw, silent and waiting.

"She's been healing during the day and then coming straight here. No gifts to ease the cost, no rest between. She's caring for our people while you run her into the fucking ground. Is that a good enough explanation for you?"

"Yes, Your Highness."

"And where will you be taking her tomorrow, should she decide your training is still worth the fucking trouble?"

"To the spring cavern, Your Highness."

"Good. You are dismissed."

Brand didn't wait for her to leave. Didn't care where she went or how she got there. He'd turned all of his attention to the little moon in his arms.

Luna.

Yes, he liked that. Very much.

His larger size meant he moved more quickly, covering the distance to her room in a fraction of the time it would have taken otherwise. It was a travesty to lay her in bed still soiled with her own sick and the dull dusting of dirt on her skin, but there was no other choice.

As tenderly as he could with hands the size of supper plates, he tucked her in on the side she seemed to prefer and wrapped the blankets tightly around her. He twisted her hair back, tucking the damp ends away from her.

Even like this—filthy, haggard, so exhausted that she'd lost her bloody consciousness—she was the most beautiful creature he'd ever beheld.

And Sisters, how he wanted her to be his.

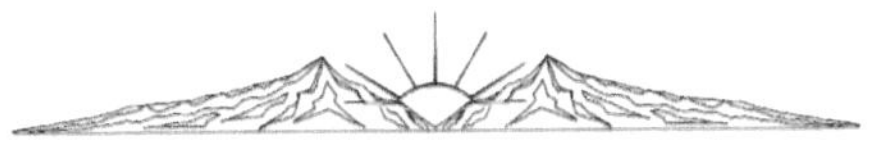

THE NEXT NIGHT, BRAND WATCHED AGAIN FROM HIS SPOT IN THE TREE.

Nyri had found the note he'd left her and ensured Lunara had plenty of time for a long bath that morning before her defense training with the twins. The proof was in the way her hair shone beneath the lantern light in fits and bursts, the curls bouncing and flowing. The glow of her luminous skin.

Unfortunately, his duties had precluded him from getting close enough to find out for himself whether she'd used the oils he'd left for

Nyri to give her. Whether she smelled of spice and musk along with the moonlight that seemed to love her so well.

If her movements—smoother, stronger—were anything to go by, then Nyri had also followed his instructions to cut the line for healings shorter, giving her more time to rest and partake of an extra gift.

Anything, just to behold that confidence in her look, that substantial improvement in her footing.

When Hedda finished—long before Lunara was about to lose her dinner or keel over—he followed them silently through the practice field, keeping to the shadows.

His Second led Lunara to the base of the mountain just outside the ring of lantern posts and the small, winding path that crawled upwards between two jutting boulders. He waited until their crunching steps were a distant murmur and took to the path himself, climbing the short distance to the cave mouth.

Inside, he knew it would be thick with steam, the hot mountain spring bubbling up from Sisters-knew-where and heating the space. Stalactites commanded to glow at all times jutted down like frozen rays of pure sunlight, and the milky-blue water glittering beneath them was rife with magic—seeping straight into bones and soothing aches as nothing else could.

Brand settled himself in beside the wide opening with his back against the mountainside, and resumed his carving. The stars twinkled overhead, and he would have sworn that moonbeams were concentrating at the cave mouth, as if to reach in and chase after Lunara.

He could appreciate the inclination.

The hushed cadence of her voice reached his ears, the awe and wonder in her gasp, and he couldn't help the curling of his lips. The deep breath that found its way in knowing she was enjoying herself.

Brand focused on his swiping knife. On feeling the blade slide along the grain, resisting, until he held a perfect coil. On the shape gradually emerging from the wood beneath his fingertips. On the slow and steady beat of a heart that was at peace in this place, close to her.

He'd given her space—time to find her stride and gain some confidence—without the pressure of him being nearby. Sisters knew her proximity during certain parts of his day would have him sweating, wondering if he was making a good impression or catching her eye.

Tomorrow, that would change. There were still a couple of days before they were set to leave for the Westrealm, and he wanted to be part of her training. Actually, if he was being honest, he wanted to take it over entirely. Wanted the excuse to be close to her, to touch her, sharing a part of himself like she'd done for him.

He nodded to himself as his resolve solidified.

Yes. Tomorrow, everything would change.

18

Lunara felt different.

Alive. Vibrant in a way she hadn't for a long, long time.

She'd dressed herself without Nyri's help that morning, and had almost—*almost*—foregone Hedda's soothing tonic. She'd begun to like the burn in her thighs and arms, the ache of a body being bettered.

The addition of an extra gift of blood between her healing and meeting Hedda last night had certainly contributed, but it was the surprise she'd had for Lunara afterwards that'd made all the difference.

The hot spring in the mountain cave Hedda had taken her to was… Blessed moons, there were hardly words.

Lunara was made of magic. Power lived within the very heart of her. And yet, that place was steeped in it, in a way that defied everything she thought she knew. It had felt ancient, almost sleepy, lulling her into a dreamy trance that had been more restorative than anything she'd ever experienced in her life. A comforting cocoon of steam and stillness, every breath muffled in the sultry air.

After Hedda had left Lunara alone, it hadn't been at all difficult to imagine she was the only creature that existed in all of Bordoroth, happily lost in the solitude of silence.

You should revise your deal with Lyriat and ask to live there instead.

She'd do it without another moment's consideration if she thought she could fit a bed in there.

"Head out of the clouds, Sorcerit!"

Lunara jolted at Hedda's booming command just in time.

She dodged a mock blow from Faldir and mimicked jabbing the heel of her palm into his nose, biting her lip to smother the roar of triumph trying to break free.

"Good. Very good." Faldir cranked his neck this way and that, shaking his shoulders out, and backed himself up to his starting position. "Again."

He struck without further warning, uncaring that she hadn't caught her breath or steadied her form. A blur of limbs and horns and linen, burgundy hair streaming behind him.

"I saw that look of surprise," he said, his voice little more than a growl as she squeaked, barely stumbling back in time to avoid the kick he leveled at her head. "An enemy won't give you the luxury of gathering yourself, Sorcerit."

She managed to knock his sweeping foot away, but probably would have been laid flat by the fist slamming to a stop mere centimeters from the tip of her nose.

"Dammit." Lunara sagged, tipping her head back. She hadn't seen it coming, let alone been fast enough to deflect or evade it.

"Your reaction is actually improving," Hedda said, an almost-reluctant hint of pride in her voice. "A couple days ago, he'd have had you on your arse with his initial drive."

A thread of delight wove its way through Lunara. It didn't matter that said arse was probably still sporting bruises from four days ago that proved Hedda's words to be true, regardless of the blood gifts and tonics and springs. It was progress, acknowledged by a warrior of high standing.

And it felt good. Really fucking good.

Too bad it's all practice nonsense, and you'd probably die within seconds if this were a real battle.

She only just resisted the urge to punch her own damned self in the face.

The twins shifted, sharing a look, conversation flowing silently between them as birds chirped and waves crashed against the land below. Lunara wasn't sure she liked the wicked tilt to Faldir's lips, or the way one of Hedda's brows shot up in challenge.

The branches soaring above the practice field seemed to know their minds better than Lunara could ever hope to. Faldir stood with arms crossed, steeped in a creeping arm of shadow, while Hedda glowed within Solyrian's dazzling morning rays, as if the universe sought to reveal their intentions to her through shade and sunlight.

Lunara wasn't comforted at all when Faldir raised his chin, sliding his gaze towards her.

At that look, Hedda sighed and threw her arms up. "Fine, but start small. And nothing weird."

Faldir rolled his eyes. "We've talked about this a thousand times—nothing is weird if it does the job."

Genuinely not liking where this is going.

"Agree to disagree." Hedda turned to Lunara, and winked. "As ever, *little* brother."

"Sisters fucking spare me." Faldir turned his back and strode away, muttering under his breath.

"There, Lunara," Hedda said, laughing. "A lesson in weaponry—sometimes words can be just as sharp as any blade. They agitate and unbalance your target before blows are even exchanged, and often dig just as deep."

Lunara huffed. "I believe you already imparted that particular lesson the day you agreed to train me."

"My, my. Such sass, Sorcerit. We'll make a warrior of you yet."

No. Don't you dare start beaming like that. You're a healer. Nothing else.

A hand sprang up in front of her, two fingers dangling a small dagger by the pommel.

"Words are fine, but useless in the end. Take this."

A gasp lodged itself in her throat when Faldir flipped the blade inches from her face and extended the handle to her.

Cross-eyed, she reached up and took it, surprised so little a thing could have that much heft. It felt unwieldy. Too heavy in her palm, too wide to get a good grip, the sharpened point more of an *idea* than something she could tangibly perceive.

"Now, if you'd been holding that during the last attack, you could have stabbed me right in the gut and won the fight."

Lunara tossed a wide look at Faldir, trying to still the trembling of her fingers. "I..."

You're not meant to inflict wounds like this, you're meant to heal them! Punching around for giggles is one thing. This? This is ridiculous. Give the damned thing back before you hurt yourself.

She let it slip from her hand until she was holding it much the same way he had been—though she was certain he hadn't possessed even a drop of the unease working its way through her. "This is not—"

"Are you planning on telling the witchling that she's holding it wrong, or are we letting her learn the hard way?"

Lunara froze at Magnus's voice rumbling directly behind her. The flush creeping slowly over her skin was a pale insult to the panicked thump of her heart stopping and restarting.

Ten gold coins says the Wolflord is judging the ever-living shite out of you.

She couldn't bring herself to turn around. Couldn't bear it.

There was no mercy to be found in the twins. Even if they noticed her pleading look, it wasn't as though they could wave their hands and make her invisible.

No, but you could. Leave your likeness standing here in a drooling stupor. They'll think you've gone catatonic and won't bother with you anymore.

Perfect. Wonderful advice. That wouldn't make it worse at all.

"You know…"

Oh Sisters, why? *Why?*

Brand sidled up to her, his words hardly more than a gravelly breath in her ear. "If you reach your arm out just a little further, you stand a high chance of landing the tip in the top of Faldir's foot. He'd probably deserve it, knowing him."

Why did he have to smell so good? Sound like that? Even if she'd never laid eyes on him, it would have been enough to draw her in. To tempt her into silly things like wondering what he felt like in the dark or whether he might be willing to protect her from those she feared most in this world.

Shitting stars, why did he have to be here?

Lunara had avoided him since their interlude on the mountaintop, successfully hiding in between her training. Everyone had to be aware she was the reason their trip to the Westrealm was delayed—she wasn't completely out of touch, after all. But facing them, knowing they knew, was another matter. How could she look them in the eye when she felt so… so…

Incompetent. Inadequate. Like the bumbling nincompoop you are.

Hedda had said she was nothing more than a pretty liability. In front of them—*him*—she actually felt like it.

Dammit. How long had they been there?

A nervous laugh escaped her, a plea in its own right. "I don't suppose you saw the part where I *successfully* countered his attacks?"

"We did," he said, rounding her fully. "Anyone you come up against will have quite the surprise on their hands. You don't often see Nachthellians employing the Straelani fighting style." He tilted his head, half smile in place. "Forgive me, Lunara. You seem"—His eyes darted to the dagger—"uncomfortable?"

That was an understatement, if she'd ever heard one.

You're also still holding it out like a soiled nappy.

Without thought, she dropped the blade and snapped her hand away as if it had burned her, her mind too slow to stop her from doing something so rash. Careless.

Brand side-stepped and swooped down, catching it without so much as a blink.

"I did say *Faldir's* foot."

There was no censure in his tone, but Lunara still cringed. "I'm so sorry, I just—"

"No apologies needed." Gripping her hand in his own, Brand turned her palm upwards. "It's normal to feel nervous when you truly understand the damage that can be done with even a weapon as paltry as this one." He wrapped her fingers around the handle, adjusting them into the grooves there, and placing her thumb tightly atop the others. "I'm sure you've seen what happens on the other end of a blade often enough in your healing. Knowledge isn't always as helpful as one would assume."

The others were fooling around, trading insults and challenges, but all of her attention was on Brand. The way his callouses grazed over the softness of her own skin. The goosebumps crawling up her arm. The tenderness in his voice and touch alike.

He gave her hand a final squeeze. "There."

That one word was like a lightning strike. She'd nearly stabbed him, and he still offered her reassurance. Encouragement. Confidence.

All she had to give him in return was her honesty.

Well, about this, anyway.

"I don't know if I can do it." Her voice shook as she stared at the blade's edge. "How can I deliver death, when I've sworn to preserve life?"

Brand made a low sound, not quite a sigh. "Is your own life less worthy of preservation?"

She snapped her gaze to his, unable to form a response. Why did these Demons insist on asking her questions she had no answer to?

He ran his fingers over hers again, where they were clenched, white-knuckled against the dagger's handle. "We... *I*... am not asking you to kill without cause. These lessons are to help you learn the necessary skills to keep yourself safe, should there be no one else to do so. Nothing more."

And wasn't that exactly what she wanted, to feel like magic was not her only course of action?

"Okay," she whispered. "Alright. Yes. I... I can do that."

"I know." He gifted her with a softer smile, then looked between them a few times. "Hmm. It seems we favor opposite hands. That'll make this much easier."

He thrust his arm to the side and golden light swirled up his palm from outstretched fingertips. With a radiant flash, a dagger appeared in his grip.

Lunara gasped, flinching backwards. "How?"

An image of Solyrian graced the bronze hilt, shimmering, its handle like two of the sunstar's waving rays.

"Only the Realm Ruler and Blessed Imperial have this particular ability." Brand turned his wrist, light catching on characters she couldn't decipher running down the center of the blade. "A gift from the Sisters, perhaps."

"It's beautiful." She moved to touch it, but stopped herself just shy of contact. "Is it only this you can conjure?"

Brand flipped the dagger in his hand and closed the distance, dragging the handle along her palm. It was impossibly warm, almost burning, raw power jumping between it and her.

"I can call any weapon I desire. My preference in battle is a greatsword. Lyriat is a dual sword-wielder, which he likes to remind me of. Often."

Lunara giggled. "I find that very easy to believe."

Brand bit his lip, as if to stop his answering laughter. She wanted to tell him to let it free—to let her bask in the sound of it—but he blinked and it was gone, his face grim. Serious.

He took a single step away and widened his stance. "I want you to mirror me," he said, voice low. "Do as I do."

The rest of the world bled away as Lunara nodded, and they began.

"Don't fling your blade and lock up when you extend it."

Brand's rough fingers ran up her forearm, beneath the wide sleeve of her tunic, and dipped into the crook of her elbow.

"You need to keep this joint engaged, strong. Strength starts up here."

He squeezed her shoulder with his other hand, then drew a firm line down her bicep.

"These muscles support the ones lower, and so on. Being loose does not mean being out of control. Your actions need to be smooth but secure."

He pressed himself against her back and wrapped his hand around hers where it held the dagger. "Move with me, feel where I start and stop. Across yourself"—Bending around her, he curled her arm in front of her body—"and out. Again."

They rocked back and forth like that as he murmured instructions, slicing the blade at an imaginary enemy.

Lunara absorbed none of it.

Just like she hadn't comprehended the downward slashes, or the reverse grip. Not even the proper way to retrieve the blade from the belt he'd given her to wear—both while they practiced and once they were in Thodelebor.

Bleeding fucking moons. How was she supposed to focus when every part of his massive, unyielding body was aligned with hers, shifting in tandem, cradling her softness against himself?

The little touches. The gravelly cadence of his voice as he patiently instructed her. The way his auburn hair sometimes fluttered out to mix with hers, tickling her face. The sight of his powerful limbs, flexing and stretching with perfect fluidity.

Just give up. Why focus on fighting when you could focus on f—

"That's it, there you go."

She almost crumbled to the dirt when his heat left and he rounded her, still swaying back and forth to help her keep rhythm.

"Good, just like that," he crooned, mirroring her once again. "Now, I want you to picture the way Faldir had you this morning—fist in your face, directly in front you—and I want you to add the next logical attack to this movement."

Lunara's body was in some kind of trance, still going through the motions while she tried to decipher his words. "Um..."

She froze when Brand struck out, as if to punch her square in the nose, stopping shy just as Faldir had and holding there. "Take a step back and look at my body position."

Yes, please.

Lunara coughed as she did what he said, surveying him from head to toe.

"You're at an advantage, using the hand most don't. Your attackers won't expect that and will leave themselves vulnerable because of it." He pointed at his stomach and ribcage, the other hand still raised. "Faldir spoke true when he said you could have gutted him. See how open this is?"

"Y-yes."

"Ribs are much harder to navigate. If you hit one—instead of going between—it'll be a nasty jolt for you and a minor wound for them. Go for the soft parts instead until you improve your aim and accuracy. Throat, gut, groin, and so on."

Sisters above, she'd never be able to do it.

Brand chuckled. "You will. The mind is excellent at taking control when our life is on the line, as long as it knows what to do ahead of time. That's why we practice."

Wonderful. You don't even know when you're talking out loud, instead of keeping your bleeding thoughts to yourself.

"The more damage you can do the better. So, I want you to pretend to slash me, and then let your body flow into the next natural attack."

From her position, Lunara went through the maneuver a few more times to let herself feel what he meant. "Okay, I think I understand."

"Excellent. Go ahead."

Lunara moved closer and sucked in a steadying breath. At his nod, her arm swept out and then thrust back in, mimicking a stab to his exposed abdomen.

If it had been real, she'd have skewered him right in the liver after spilling his innards. The thought made her stomach roil, but she swallowed back the bile creeping up her throat. She could do this, if needed. She could.

"Yes, Lunara. Perfect!" He clutched her hand and brought it closer, completely unperturbed by the sharpened end of her dagger being so near him. "That's it exactly. Right there."

She tried not to beam at his praise, but...

There. That's it. Good. Excellent. Perfect.

Those *words.* They burrowed deep and did things to her she didn't understand. Heart fluttering, skin warming, bone melting things. She couldn't catch her breath, couldn't stop smiling. Stars above, he said them with such conviction that she almost believed it.

Almost.

Brand released her but didn't step away. "If you let your body do what it already knows to do, if you follow your instincts, you'll be just fine."

For once, the flush tingling across her cheeks was not from embarrassment, but excitement. As for her instincts, they were telling her to toss the weapon and throw her arms around him. To forget every worry that had consumed her for so long and see what life had to offer outside of them, even temporarily.

It didn't have to be permanent. Just a fling. A few days of gratification to scratch the itch and then she could hide away wherever she liked.

There'd been a sort of detachment to the way he'd been plastered behind her before, regardless of how her mind had misbehaved throughout. That had been training.

With a gorgeous male who isn't for you.

Necessary proximity.

To his enormously powerful build—which you should ignore, ignore, ignore.

Now that he was in front of her, so close that Lunara could see the flecks of sparkling rust and green in his hazel eyes, could almost feel the rise and fall of his chest against her own, something shifted between them. Like they'd crossed a line she hadn't known was there.

The way he was looking at her—lips parted, eyes jumping back and forth between her own, brow furrowed—stole every thought away.

"I—"

Another hand appeared in front of her face. "Practicing staring your enemies to death now?"

Lunara jerked away, blinking, falling right back into the pocket of general mortification in which she tended to live.

Magnus chuckled. "I hate to be the one to tell you witchling, but I don't think it's going to work. The Forgotten don't care how bonny or blue your eyes are—they'll jump straight into the slashing and eating part."

Eating! Oh, this just keeps getting better. Sure you're not ready to get the fuck out of here yet?!

"What? Why are we talking about Forgotten? I thought we were going to a quiet village."

"Aye, a Thodeleborian village planted right up against a Dread Chasm. Now that I mention it, Forgotten won't be our problem. It'll be the dreadbeasts."

"D-dreadbeasts?" Her voice was little more than a croak. "Those aren't real."

Unless there was something the Imperials and Realm Rulers knew that everyone else was blessedly unaware of.

Magnus leaned in. "Sure about that?"

"Mag." Brand's voice was low and rumbling, a warning in the single word.

"Ach, away lad. I'm just messing with her. The Forgotten though..." Magnus waggled his eyebrows at her. "Those are definitely real."

"What the fuck do you need?" Brand hissed through his teeth.

"No fun, I swear." Magnus's sigh was heavy as he held up a half-curled parchment. "I've just received this."

At first, Brand didn't take it. His gaze was locked on her, jaw clenching. Lunara might've been worried the aggravation there was meant for her, but when he finally reached out, he snapped the message from his brother's hand and sent him a searing glare.

Magnus only smirked back.

Smug, ruining bastard.

More like the only one here with any brains whatsoever. You should be thanking him for pulling your head out of your arse.

Brand scanned the missive, lips pursed until he loosed an explosive sigh and looked up. "Scorched leaves, stunted flowering—I don't know what half of this means."

Magnus took the parchment back and folded it into a hidden pocket of his robes. "It means the crops are starting to fail and we can't wait any longer to leave. They need our help now. Today."

"It's still going to take some time for what they've asked me to do." Brand rubbed a hand over one horn and down through his hair.

"Aye, but better they get water to the fields in the next two days, instead of four or five from now."

Brand's head flopped back, his eyes closing.

"Ahem, Your Highness, but why does *my* Highness look like you've just spat in his food?" Hedda sidled up with arms crossed. "He looked more than content the last time I checked in on him." She threw Lunara a side-eyed look, her brow and one side of her mouth raising.

Sisters save her from shite-eating, puffed-up arseholes. She couldn't even flirt poorly without everyone having an opinion about it.

You could have gone home, but no—you needed to make a deal with a king and wrap yourself up in nonsense that has nothing to do with you.

That's when Lunara realized how high the sunstar was. She'd been so lost in Brand that she hadn't noticed the practice field was completely devoid of anyone else. Or that half of the day had gone by.

The perfect excuse. Time to flee.

She took a tentative step back, wringing a curl in her fingers. "I should probably go and see to my healings. I'll just…" She turned to leave—

"Wait."

Brand was there in an instant, looking down at her. "No healing. Packing. We leave in an hour."

What!

"An hour!" Hedda shrieked. "What in the realms is going on?"

Brand made a gesture at Magnus, who retrieved the message and handed it to the Demon commander.

"Can you hold our things for us?" he asked, ignoring the others again. "In the ether?"

"Of course. But…" The dagger's handle dug into her palm, still there though she'd forgotten it completely. She raised it between them. "I was supposed to have two more days. Even that wouldn't have been enough. I'm not ready."

She hadn't been ready for any of this. Couldn't fathom what she was doing in Straelon, surrounded by Demons and Imperials and kings. Fighting with weapons.

Madness. Utter madness.

He engulfed her hand with both of his own. "You're going to be fine. You won't even need it. We're only spending a few days at a village in the Westrealm. Forget about the Forgotten and all that other shite. The most you'll need to worry about is whether or not you're actually going to ingest the sheer amount of alcohol the Wolflords will be plying you with."

Lunara fought a hysterical bubble of laughter, tamping it down and bottling it up. As a result, her voice shook when she asked, "Promise?"

WHEN LUNARA STARTED WALKING AWAY, IT WAS THE FIRST TIME BRAND'S heart had turned over hard enough to make him sick in hours. The first time his lungs had constricted. That stinging jolt of panic had seized hold and convinced him he'd never see her again if he let her go.

She was bound to their journey, and being on it meant being close to her. So, in that moment, he'd made a snap decision.

If the Wolflords of Glynmor needed them now, then now they would go.

She was staring up at him with glassy uncertainty, her hand trembling beneath his own, clutching the dagger like her life depended on it. He recognized the look on her face on a visceral level but, instead of feeding his own useless self-doubt, it called up a fierce need to soothe her. Protect her. To erase that expression and ensure it never happened again.

He brought her clenched hand to his chest, pressing it to the spot above his heart. "I promise."

She expelled a tremulous breath, wobbling slightly. "Okay. Alright. An h-hour, then."

Brand released her and offered what he hoped was a reassuring smile. "We'll meet beside the portal."

She nodded, and he watched her go with clenched fists. The second she was out of sight, he turned on Magnus with a snarl. "Is it possible for you to at least try to be less of an arsehole."

Mag reared back, gripping the collar of his robes with mock affront. "So angry," he hissed towards Hedda out of the corner of his mouth.

Brand's greater half seethed beneath the surface of his skin, split between tearing off in different directions.

Part of him wanted to follow Lunara and continue the closeness they'd been sharing. The ease. The fucking searing heat that'd been boiling between them.

The other wanted to beat his brother into an unrecognizable pulp.

"That's the second time you've swaggered up and interrupted us." He crowded Mag, letting enough of his rage loose to bring him eye level with his brother. To drop his fangs down. "The second time you've taunted and embarrassed her. Do it again, I fucking dare you. You can ask my Second how I feel about people mistreating the Sorcerit."

Mag's brows dropped, all humor gone in an instant. "Weeping Sisters. Is she—"

Brand's fist was plowing into his face before he could finish that cursed fucking sentence. Magnus staggered back and righted himself but didn't move to retaliate. Just flashed a satisfied grin, blood dripping from the split in his lip.

"Get all your shite to the great hall within the hour, and don't forget it's you that needs me—not the other way around."

Magnus nodded, but Brand didn't miss the way his eyes tightened, a shadow of hurt lingering there. "Aye, little brother. That's the way of it. This time."

Some of the fury trickled out of him, a thread of guilt weaving its way in. "Mag—"

"No." He raised a hand. "You're right. I'll get my things." Magnus only made it a few steps before he stopped, not quite looking back over his shoulder. "I don't want to see you hurt, so I'm warning you now—until I'm sure of her, my only interest is in protecting you. Even if you hate me for it."

With that, he left, taking the same path through the practice field as Lunara had.

"So, that went well," Hedda said, her voice dripping with sarcasm.

Brand slumped on a burdened sigh, rubbing at his temples as he reverted to his usual size. "Not in the fucking least."

"You have feelings for her, then?" she asked quietly. "Truly?"

"I…" He huffed a laugh, entirely unamused. "Fully raging on you the other night didn't spell it out clearly enough?"

Hedda looked away, thoughtful. "There's a lot of reasons you might've done so, but none as serious as what Magnus is implying."

"As you are also now implying."

She drew herself up straighter but said nothing.

He wasn't ready to give voice to his inkling. He'd just punched his own brother in the face over it. Hedda sure as shite wouldn't be hearing it first.

Brand pulled his shoulders back, trying to ease the tension creeping in. "Portal. One hour," he said, already walking away. "Bring your brother."

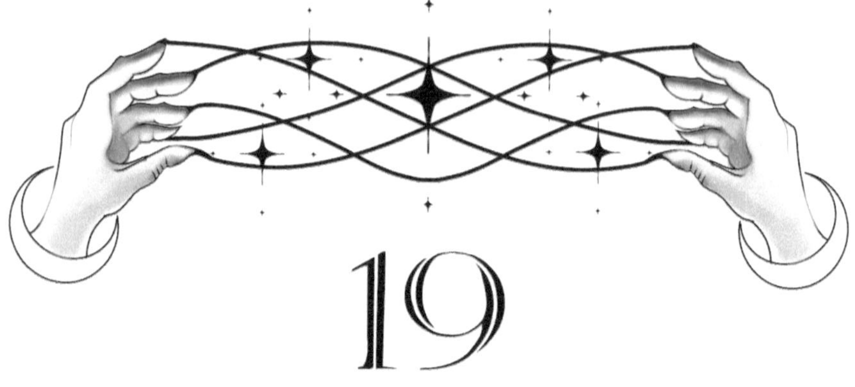

19

Solyrian's effect in Straelon had made Lunara feel wild. Like she could run across the crimson sand with her arms spread wide or sprint through the dappled forests with reckless abandon.

In Thodelebor, it was cozy. So soft and warm. Rolling hills of gold and green bathed in its rays, crops soaking up the light as they swayed in a gentle breeze. It tempted her to curl up on a hilltop amongst the tall grass, lazy and content. Made her feel safe. Hidden, somehow, like no one would ever be able to find her if she chose to run out into the towering wheat and live her days there.

But what she loved most about the sunstar, no matter where it shone, was that it chased away the shadows—the ones that lived inside and festered in the silent, tenebrous dark of the Evesong.

The dark isn't the problem in Nachthelliae, though, is it?

No. It was the 'ruled by murderers' part she couldn't stomach.

Sure? They weren't really the ones who slaughtered your parents.

The memory struck like lightning. Blood and her father's screams. Blackened claws embedded in her mother's—

No, no, no. Ignore. It's fine. You're fine.

Lunara forced her mind to blank, cutting the vision off before its horror could take hold, and looked up to find the group well ahead of her.

Shite.

Shaking herself, she stifled a groan and willed her legs to work faster, glad for the distraction of movement despite her exhaustion.

The strange time difference meant they'd skipped the night hours, their trek beginning in the Westrealm's next early morning, and the nearest portal was quite a distance from Glynmor.

More than ever, she was grateful for Nyri's gifts of blood. The young Demon had even thought to bring her one before their departure, and Lunara had guzzled the entire thing in her nervousness. Add in the moonlight she'd been soaking up every night and…

It's a wonder you aren't outshining Solyrian, you eejit. The damned well is nearly full!

Exactly. The surface of her skin was crawling over itself, humming, power teeming within her. Even so, she hadn't seen a bed in too long, and her bones knew it.

"Don't make me come back there to prod you along, Sorcerit!" Hedda shouted, throwing a judgmental glare over her shoulder. "If I have to scout the village after sunset, I'll make sure eggs are the only food you eat for our entire stay."

Lunara barely resisted the urge to stick her tongue out at the barking commander.

The worn, gravel-strewn path fell with the landscape, and she let the small hill carry her body quicker, the fields of grain and wildflowers whizzing by.

Stunning, but eerily abandoned, the emptiness like a warning—

Her foot snagged a rock as one of *those* feelings rose up. The kind where she went still to the core, frozen in a false settling before the shift.

Shite.

Naturally, Brand chose that moment to break away from the group, dropping back beside her while she urged her heart to slow. They walked in silence, the others inching further and further away, and she realized he was matching her strides.

Merciful Sisters, she could keep him just for that.

No. No, no. Head out of your arse.

"There's something I've been wanting to ask you," he finally said, pulling a waterskin from his belt and offering it to her.

Lunara took a welcome sip to hide her nerves. The list of questions he could have ranged so widely that she wasn't sure which possibility to panic about.

"Go on." She handed the skin back, hoping he didn't notice her trembling fingers.

Brand studied the leather pouch for a moment, lost in thought. When he finally raised it to his own lips, her mind emptied, worries forgotten when the corded column of his throat bobbed with each swallow. A bead of sweat trailed down his neck to disappear into the collar of his tunic, and she followed its path, mouth watering.

The desire to sink her fangs into him hit like a comet, and had little to do with a need to feed. Unfortunately, that particular intimacy had the potential to bring on a whole slew of complications she could not afford.

Look at you, using your brains for once.

Too bad, really, because—stars and arses—he was a fine male, and she was willing to bet he tasted as good as he looked.

Brand scrubbed a hand across his mouth, and she blinked rapidly, trying to dislodge the longing from her body.

"Caius has never mentioned my aunt's death. Not once. One day, Meliora was there, vibrant as anything, and then..." He let out a slow breath. "Was it truly as bad as the rumors suggest?" he softly asked.

Ah.

She recalled Caius's last words to her. "This is murky waters for me," she admitted. "Strictly speaking, I'm bound to no oaths or promises, but your uncle didn't want anyone to tarnish her name. I'm not sure what that means when it comes to her kin. Sharing information about my healings is not something I generally do."

"I swear on Solyrian, it doesn't leave my immediate family unless I find it to be a matter of absolute necessity. *Safety.*" He was so earnest, looking her right in the eyes.

"Are you sure you want to hear the answer?" Shite, she didn't want to relive it, but she would. For him, she would. "I promise, you won't like it. Some things are better left in darkness and silence, Brand."

A little like you.

"It's like a hole, not knowing the details," he whispered, then stronger, "Like she just disappeared, without saying where she was going. Caius and Thad have never been the same, the rest of us left wondering and trying to come up with plausible scenarios." His laugh was a soft and tragic sound. "The most powerful creatures in all of Bordoroth, and we don't know what happened to one of our own. But here you are, and you were there, and… Yes. I need to know."

She wanted to save him from the grisly tale, let him keep thinking whatever he liked, because—no matter what he imagined—it couldn't be nearly as awful as the truth.

But he just kept looking at her, waiting, hope written all over his face.

Lunara closed her eyes, resigned. "It was terrible," she admitted. "All the years I've lived, all my healings, I've never seen anything like it. Before or since."

Memories battered against her as if they happened yesterday.

Cordelia had showed up in the dead of night, begging for help. A last-ditch effort after all the other Elders had failed. Understandable, since Lunara was the only one left among their tier whose true gift was healing.

You don't need to think about that to tell the story.

Right.

They'd stolen to Starkeep in secret—always in secret—so she could see for herself whether there was anything to be done before forcing a move on the ailing female. One look at Meliora, and Lunara had known she was fighting against something unknown. Something impossible. But she had tried.

Sisters, how she'd tried.

They'd taken Meliora from her sick room and through the deepest shadows to the nearest portal, to Lunara's hidden cottage. It had been too dangerous to attempt healing her in the capital, forced to hide and petrified the entire time she'd be discovered.

Lunara opened her eyes again and looked to the road ahead, to the others chatting away, blissfully unaware of the heaviness behind them. "Meliora had these black stains creeping under her skin. They were alive. It's the only way I can describe it. And they were, well… eating her. I think."

Brand stopped dead in his tracks, shock twisting his features. He searched her face before whispering, "Explain."

Not a command, but a plea for her to make sense of something she couldn't.

"The worst was around her eyes and mouth. Faint at first, but as they branched out, the skin blackened behind them. And where it turned black, it started to, um, bleed."

She swallowed against the wretched memories. "It was like her blood was feeding the stains. We'd watch as it was reabsorbed back into her, and the dark patches would swell and branch out further. As they grew, the process sped up. When I finally woke her, she just screamed and screamed. I numbed her body so she couldn't feel it, but could still move and talk, but that was both a blessing and a curse. While she wasn't in pain, she couldn't feel her mate holding her either, and I think she started to go a bit mad from it all."

Brand scrubbed a hand over one of his horns, back and forth, the repetitive motion one she'd noticed him do often. Not for the first time, she wondered if he even realized he did it.

"Caius witnessed his mate go through that? And Thad… Fuck. No wonder."

She couldn't stop her bittersweet smile. "Thaddeus was only allowed to visit from a distance. We had no idea what we were dealing with, and his father was petrified of him getting sick as well. He and I spent a lot of time together while Caius…" Her lip trembled, an ache gathering behind her eyes. Sisters damn the emotions betraying her. "Caius never faltered, cared nothing for himself. He cooed and coddled. He stroked her hair and held her hand and never shied away from kisses or praising her beauty. I'd find them walking the woods, or sitting beneath the moonlight huddled together. I thought she was getting better."

"What happened? I mean, how did she…" His words trailed off, asking the same question that had haunted her every day since.

Regret formed a jagged lump in Lunara's throat. "No matter what I did, nothing reversed the physical damage that'd already occurred. The flesh had *changed*. Yet another thing I'd never seen before. I caught her gazing into the mirror once and the look on her face…" She shook her head, not wishing to remember Meliora's pale, haunted eyes staring back at her from that glass. "I woke up to Caius screaming. I tried to get in to the room to see if anything could be done, but he wouldn't let me near her. He was feral, snarling and fighting his change. Not at all like the male I'd come to know over the months. Absolutely mindless in his grief."

"So, she finally succumbed then."

He sounded so certain, and it shattered her. Not even Caius knew her theory.

Theory being the key word there. What point could you have in telling him without knowing for sure?

No idea. Except... Shitting stars, she had enough secrets to be drowning in them. Sharing her speculations might help release her of at least one of them.

She couldn't look at him while she did it, though. "I can't be sure. I only briefly entered the room before Caius banished me, but there was this smell. Like roses thrown onto a bonfire, but cloying. Sticky and wrong. I'd never encountered it before, but it reminded me of some of the more sordid potions one can purchase, if you know which darkened alley to visit in the Lower Blocks." Lunara blew out a shaky breath. "I don't know how, or even if I'm right, but... I think Meliora took her own life."

Shite, when had she started crying?

At home, Lunara could bottle and tamp and shove until she convinced herself that nothing bothered her. That the despair was just a spot of fleeting loneliness, and not the symptom of a deeper hurt that had no remedy.

A couple weeks away from the shadowy womb of Nachthelliae, and she was standing beside an orchard in Thodelebor spilling her tears and theories to an *Imperial Son* like he was any other person.

You're too tired for this level of gravity. Just calm down and shut your damned mouth.

No such luck.

"I'm so sorry." The words poured out of her, ripped from someplace that she didn't fully understand. "I feel like I failed her, and Caius and Thaddeus. If I'd only known she had it, I might've—"

"You have nothing to apologize for," Brand rasped, stepping in front of her. "Whatever happened, it was enough for Thad to trust you. To seek you out when we needed it most." He caught her welling upset, swiping his fingers over her damp cheekbones. "I have only gratitude for the things you've done."

She wanted to lean into that contact and accept the solace being offered. But, for some reason, the kindness in his eyes was choking her—a fisted hand around her throat whispering that she didn't deserve it.

You don't. It's your fault that she's dead—his own aunt. And you can't forget the Elder Council or that his younger brother is one of them. *Closeness to him means exposure to them. They'll find you. They'll force you.*

With that in mind—fatigue weighing her down—Lunara recoiled slightly, cutting herself off from the temptation of his touch. "Please don't do that. I probably shouldn't have even told you, and I certainly don't want to be comforted or thanked for it."

It was his turn to flinch, hands falling and fisting at his sides. "I…" His confusion was evident, deep grooves forming between his brows.

She understood. Being pulled in so many directions, she was muddled as shite, too.

Better this way. It's fine. You're fine.

"Lunara—"

"Brand, come and see Glynmor!"

Brand's nostrils flared and he stayed fixed on her for another beat, two, a muscle ticking in his jaw. It felt like an eternity before he finally turned to acknowledge his brother's voice booming from the top of the hill up the way. She'd been so distracted, she hadn't even noticed it looming there.

"My pride and joy!" Magnus shouted with a grin, his arm sweeping out towards what she assumed was the village.

Lunara didn't need any more encouragement. Before Brand could move, she fled up the incline ahead of him, towards the relative safety that waited at the top. She raised her chin and ignored the strange looks as she joined the others, Brand's heavy footfalls closing in from behind and mimicking the sickening pound of her heart.

There wasn't time to dwell on it. Not with the beauty stretching out before her and snatching what little breath she had away.

Closest to them, Solyrian beat down on a swaying field of grain, a rolling rainbow of vines and vegetables alongside it. Bees buzzed and birds chirped, the warm breeze fluttering between branches and blossoms and bringing the smell of fresh tilled earth to her nose.

In the near distance, beyond a meadow brimming with wildflowers, lay the Thodelemaia Dread Chasm.

It was said that two warring Celestials—sister Star Goddesses from the Unknown—had torn through space and time, locked in a legendary battle of wills and carnage. Their epic conflict finally reached its bloody end when they crash-landed upon a ghostly hill in this barren and unformed world.

Both gravely wounded from their starfall, the Sisters joined hands in silent apology as they lay dying, their weeping regret mingling on the earth between them. After eons of fighting one another, it had become too much, their injuries too great. With the ground cradling their broken bodies, the earth trembled and a mighty plateau formed, lifting them towards the empty sky, and a ring of mountains shot into existence to enclose their island deathbed.

As the life slowly drained from them, the pool of their tears multiplied, filling the newly-formed basin that circled the goddesses. It overflowed, and the raging waters swept out into the void in different directions, carrying the Sisters' power with them. Magic leached into the grey nothing as the rivers clawed through its fog and mist. Whole landscapes were born as rocks, and trees, and creatures sprang from their depths. Moons and stars rushed from far away galaxies to witness the formation. Where once there was nothing, there was suddenly *everything*.

With the last beat of their fearsome hearts, the universe quaked with sorrow, snapping the infant lands apart and leaving immense, fathomless rifts between them.

Even now, the cosmos still came to pay them homage in the form of the Occurrences, the surrounding celestial bodies mourning the death of their own and honoring the Sisters' creations with continued gifts of power.

Thus, Bordoroth and the Five Realms were born—and the endless, gaping maws of shadow and stillness known as the Dread Chasms.

Every realm was completely surrounded by them, cut off from their neighboring lands. There was no such thing as physically crossing one to reach the other side, no way to successfully enter their depths. They dropped off into nothing and that was it. If someone was unfortunate enough to fall in, they were never seen again.

The Chasms were used as a punishment for a reason.

With the endless night in the Evesong, Lunara had never actually seen one. Not like this. Not with the sunstar hammering down to highlight just how unfathomable they could be, how impossibly dark. It was as though the inky, undulating gloom was actually consuming the light, swallowing it in and erasing it from existence.

"Shitting stars," she breathed.

Hedda chuckled beside her. "I had much the same reaction the first time I was this close to one as well. There aren't really words."

Lunara tore her gaze away from the dense murk and turned to take in the village of Glynmor, tucked neatly off to the side between their fields and the edge of a small forest. The idyllic scene called to her, and she dipped into the well of her power, reaching out to brush mystical fingers over the beauty of it, as if she could snatch some back to keep for herself.

Oh… no.

Wait.

No, no, no.

At first, she didn't understand what her mind was trying to tell her, couldn't comprehend what she was feeling through the thread of her magic, but then—

"Sisters help me," she whispered, her feet moving of their own accord.

No wonder there hadn't been anyone around. No sounds outside of nature. No one to greet them as they approached.

Before she knew it, she was flying down the hill. Just as she hit the halfway point of the decline, arms banded around her middle like a cage of iron, halting her momentum and knocking the wind right from her lungs, and she was lifted from the ground.

"Let me go!" she shrieked, legs flailing. "Something is wrong!"

Her body thrashed as she jabbed her heels back, Brand grunting when she finally connected with solid bone.

"Weeping fuck!" He hefted her up, shifting to wrap an arm around her thighs, trapping her against him, her back pressed firmly to his front. "You can't go running off like that if you suspect there's danger, you bloody fool," he hissed into her ear, voice little more than a growl. "Calm yourself and speak plainly. Do so and I will put you down."

Calm yourself? Calm yourself!

Brand's first mistake was stipulating terms for her freedom. Lunara had spent her life ensuring it, guarding it with every waking moment, every ounce of her energy. That he would fucking dare to use it against her was enough to have her shaking with fury.

His second was forgetting she was a Sorcerit. He may not know just how powerful she was, that she could level the entire settlement if she wanted to, but it didn't matter.

His third was not bothering to secure her arms—arms she knew how to use now, thanks to him and his own damned commanders.

Hedda and Faldir appeared in the fringes of her vision on either side.

"What the fuck, witchling?" Magnus said, his voice coming from somewhere behind.

Lunara ignored him and relaxed her body, venom in her tone as she spoke only loud enough for Brand to hear. "There's exactly one fucking heart beating in that village, and it's barely holding on. The rest are silent, though I can feel their flesh rotting as if it were my own. Is that fucking *plain* enough for you?"

Harsh, but someone needed her. *Now.*

The instant Brand went slack, she cranked an elbow right into his nose. With a curse, he dropped her like a sack of rocks and she hit the ground. Her knees crumpled, but no matter—she was already sending a shockwave of her power out to knock him and the others back as she regained her feet.

She was at the bottom of the hill, sprinting towards that one, lonesome heartbeat, before any of them recovered.

20

BRAND WAS UP AND AFTER LUNARA THE SECOND HE STOPPED SEEING STARS, the others slower to recover from whatever the fuck she'd pummeled them with.

A problem for another time.

He leapt the rest of the way down the hill, boots tearing through soft, fertile soil. He ignored the produce he was ravaging—ignored her cryptic fucking words, doing their best to send him into an episode—and focused only on catching her.

Her hair streamed behind as she raced away, her strangled whimper as she hit the village outskirts loud enough to reach him even this far back.

"Lunara!" he shouted, desperate for her to stop and fucking think. "Please!"

He crossed some invisible line just as he was about to reach her and the fetid smell of decaying flesh hit him like a solid wall, even through his likely-broken nose. His steps faltered and death forced its way into his lungs, demanding he breathe through his mouth so it could deposit its rancid essence onto his tongue, insisting he taste its devastation.

"Fucking shite," he wheezed, coughing against the back of his hand. "Lunara, wait!"

Brand readied his power—to throw up a wall, an enclosure, *something*.

Anything to stop her from possibly running headlong towards her own fucking end like an absolute—

That's when he saw it. The blood.

Everywhere.

The tall, wooden longhouses were bathed in it. Indistinguishable pieces and parts littered the ground and rooftops alike, and Brand had to swallow back the rising bile.

Sisters fucking save them.

For some reason, his gaze fixed on a bed of flowers tucked up against the nearest home. On the yellow, sunlit blooms that were almost deranged as they fluttered in the breeze, untouched and ignorant of the tiny hand lying too still beneath their stems.

His feet tried to stop him right there—to root him to the ground in the miserable safety of that one horrific sight, instead of carrying on into whatever atrocity he was about to find—but Lunara's choked sob wrenched him forward, propelling his legs into obedience.

Her speed was a mercy. Focused on her, the countless bodies were little more than streaking smudges as the world blurred by.

Brand followed Lunara between buildings and into the middle of the village where a tower kept watch over the massacred landscape. She stopped in the center of it all, tears streaming down her face as she seemed to orient herself, searching amongst the carnage.

It was wrong, so wrong, to see her there with blood soaking the hem of her dress, crimson droplets splattered across her face and shoulders from the puddles of it they'd run through.

Puddles.

Her head finally tilted up, her eyes locking on the watchtower, and she raced around the support beams to fling herself upon the ladder on the other side.

"Don't—"

Brand lost his footing in the gore beneath his boots. He thrust his arms out to catch himself, retching at the squelching softness his fingers encountered, and couldn't ignore his surroundings any longer.

His mind blanked.

He didn't understand how his hands had gone from clutching Lunara mere moments ago, to being buried in the open chest cavity of a Wolflord. How he'd *just* been looking into her impossibly blue eyes and trying to figure out how to heal whatever rift he'd accidentally formed between them, but now he was being met with glazed, golden ones that lifelessly pleaded with him from a face that had been peeled away.

Eyes so similar to Mag's.

He blinked and jerked back, just for his sight to snag on a female's mangled body, black streaks marring the skin that had been left behind. On twisted limbs that battled for space amongst a sea of internal organs. On contorted mouths locked eternally in their silent screams. Everywhere he looked, piles of hair and bone and teeth and blood.

Brand couldn't breathe.

This wasn't the cost of warfare—an unfortunate brutality he was well used to. Even when violence was needed, when he was required to use fist and sword alongside his brethren, it wasn't *this*.

This was unspeakable.

Innocents, ripped away from their laundry and harvesting. Cut down in the midst of flirtation and laughter. Children in pieces, their ball still on the ground from the game they'd been playing. Mates slaughtered side-by-side, unable to protect their families.

Baldrir's message came into focus—all too clear, too dreadful. The threat it was meant to be.

Glynmor thinks she's safe and well, tucked tight in her field of green. But what do you and her flesh have in common? I know what I hope it will be.

Brand gagged as he righted himself, willing his limbs to work and his lungs to stop gasping.

He would've thought an eternity had passed, but Lunara's feet were only just leaving the top rung of the ladder.

Fuck the message, he could deal with it later.

His greater half thrashed when she disappeared from view, clamoring to reach her. Ignoring the cold sweat that had broken over his brow, he stumbled through the mess, reaching the tower as Magnus tore into the village square.

Brand had never seen that look on his brother's face before. Had never witnessed him freeze in utter disbelief, shock stilling his limbs.

"Help me!" Lunara's voice was breathless above, harried.

It jolted Brand into action, and he threw himself up the ladder and onto the tower platform. It was dim beneath the roof, but he spotted her in the corner instantly, crouched over something.

Some*one.*

Weeping, fucking Sisters.

Here, in the frontier lands of Thodelebor, was a Fae. It was too hard to tell which species the female was under the carnage caking her skin. The Tempusrealm of Kohamaia was home to so many different types, he might struggle to know even if she were freshly clean.

Still, a single, spiraled curl had avoided the mess, its honeyed color shifting to lavender in a ray of sun that broke past the eaves.

A prismatic glow gathered in Lunara's hands. "Tear the roof down. Now," she said, voice curt. "I need the sunlight. *She* needs it."

The tower rattled as Brand moved to obey, something in him incapable of ignoring her commanding tone. His teeming questions could be answered later.

Magnus pulled himself onto the platform and pushed past Brand before he could climb out, hopping up onto the low wall with grace that shouldn't be possible for a male his size. "I'll do it." His brother's rumbling voice was a shell of itself. "You stay with her."

Solyrian crept through in bits and pieces as shingles fell to the ground, revealing just how horrible a state the Fae was in. Her face was ruined and at least one arm was broken. Gouges were raked across her flesh, her short dress in tatters. Even with the light pouring in, Brand couldn't accurately place the color of her skin. She was little more than a heartbreaking splash of red and black and grey.

"What can I do?"

As soon as Magnus finished clearing the roof away, Lunara moved to lay her hands on the female's chest. "Nothing. Unless you—"

Her words were cut off by her own tortured screams the second she made contact.

Brand fell to his knees beside her, shouts sounding from the ground. He had no words to spare for Hedda and Faldir, no voice to reassure them as he grabbed onto Lunara's shoulders and was consumed by such searing agony that his body seized.

His teeth clamped down, right through his own tongue, eyes rolling back in his head. He couldn't make his lungs work. Couldn't let go. Couldn't—

Relief was instant as he was thrown to the side, Hedda roaring over him.

And still, Lunara screamed.

"What should we do?" Faldir dropped beside Lunara, eyes wide, a look akin to panic on his face. Something about the way he was looking at her, like he actually *cared…*

"Don't fucking touch her," Brand ground out, unable to discern whether it was the twisting jealousy in his gut or concern for his friend fueling the words.

Fucking territorial Demon shite.

Hedda stood silent, looking back and forth between him and Lunara, and he could see the cogs turning in her mind.

"What are you thinking?" he asked, shaking his head as he crawled across the wooden boards beneath him until he was by Lunara's side again.

She gave him a pointed look, nodding. "I'm thinking *you're* the only one who shouldn't 'fucking touch her,' as you so delicately put it, Your Highness." With that, Hedda wrapped her arms around Lunara and tore her away.

They tumbled to the ground, the sudden silence deafening. Brand lunged to gather Lunara from his Second, cradling her against him and murmuring things like *I have you* and *just breathe* and *don't fucking scare me like that ever again* as he rocked back and forth.

Hedda groaned, rolling to all fours. "Weeping Sisters, even I felt it."

"I know it was a bleeding mistake," Lunara mumbled, lids fluttering as she half-consciously tried to free herself from his hold. "Yes, yes. Perfect. Wonderful advice. Your logic is flawless, as ever."

She was speaking complete nonsense, her tone sarcastic.

Confused, Brand cleared hair away from her pale cheeks, her skin clammy beneath his touch. "Shh. It's fine. You're fine."

Her eyes shot wide when he said that, gaze scanning his face like she wasn't sure where she was, who he was. He saw the moment she regained control, and was already mourning the loss of her in his arms before she'd even started scrambling away.

"She… I don't…" Lunara thudded onto her backside, fighting to detangle her skirts as she dragged herself over to the Fae.

Brand gasped, ready to wrench her back when she lifted a hand and let it hover bare centimeters above the female's body. He trembled with the desire to rail at her, to save her from her own bloody recklessness, but he forced his mouth to stay fucking shut. He'd done enough damage today, even if he didn't have the slightest clue what he'd done to set her off.

Either time.

"That's never happened before," Lunara whispered, listing to the side before righting herself again.

Almost absentmindedly, she reached into the ether with her other hand and withdrew a flask of blood—*his*, though she didn't know it. He tracked the movement as she twisted the top off and took a long pull, her skin flushing with renewed life.

Helpless as he'd been, it was a relief he had this to offer—to her, to the Fae. A paltry contribution amongst the wreckage surrounding them, but it was something.

Lunara replaced the lid and cast the flask aside with a sigh, pushing to her knees. More of that prismatic light sprang to life and lit the space between her fingers and the Fae's head, threads of white-hot power dancing down like lightning bolts.

A sharp howl rent the air then, distant but still within Glynmor's borders.

Magnus.

In the chaos, he hadn't realized his brother had left. Hadn't considered him at all.

Fuck, the sound of it was pure suffering.

"I'll go check on him," Hedda said softly, already making for the ladder.

Faldir only grunted as he joined his twin, leaving him and Lunara alone.

"I have to still her particles to move her," she murmured, almost to herself. "There's no way for me to heal her here like this. I have no idea what it is, but her damage runs… deep. So much deeper than we can see."

A glowing barrier began to spread from Lunara's outstretched fingers, flowing over the Fae's limbs until it wrapped around her, encasing her supine form in a pod of light.

It was unlike anything he'd ever seen. There were no Sorcerit he knew capable of such a thing. Between this and what he'd witnessed her do to Caius, with Baldrir, there was no more doubt.

Her power was astronomical.

"Lunara."

She must've heard something in his voice, known what he was about to ask, because she was already shaking her head when she locked gazes with him.

"Please," she begged. "Not now. Maybe… maybe not ever."

Burning Solyrian, she looked so damned tired giving him even that infinitesimal admission.

All he could do was nod, the realization that he would likely give Lunara anything she asked for hitting him with startling clarity.

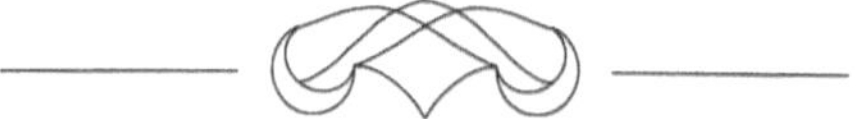

LUNARA WATCHED MAGNUS PACING AT THE CHASM'S EDGE, BACK AND FORTH, his ruined hands fisted at his sides while he gazed into the black abyss.

He'd attacked the roof of that tower with a vengeance. She'd spared a single glance up as the Imperial Wolflord had ripped and shredded the shingles away, just long enough to see the silent tears flowing down his face. Before she'd known it, only the rafters had been left, sunlight pouring in for her to work by.

Only, that hadn't quite gone to plan.

Understatement. What were you thinking jumping in like that without assessing her?

To be honest, Lunara had been so damned desperate for a victory, for one life to make it out of that festering pit, that she'd acted without thinking at all.

Weeping Sisters. After what the Fae must have gone through, she shouldn't be alive.

With the first touch, there'd been no such thing as give and take. The Fae's broken particles latched on so thoroughly that Lunara's body had no longer been her own, shutting down completely beneath the sheer weight of the female's pain.

The level of damage she'd sustained, the absolute fucking agony…

Something *in* the Fae had grabbed hold, greedy, immediately siphoning her power and fusing them together. It had swarmed Lunara's mind and set her veins on fire. Had tried to tear her apart, piece by tiniest piece. She couldn't have detached herself if she'd tried.

The Demon Son is right. You're a bloody fool.

Maybe. That wouldn't stop Lunara from trying to heal her again. Somehow.

Once they'd calmed him enough to shift back, Magnus had quietly refused her offer of healing before trudging off. The only reason she hadn't pestered him further was that she sensed it was a sort of penitence for him. For the brutal loss of people who'd been his.

She understood the sentiment all too bleeding well.

Stubborn Wolflord.

The Fae lay on the ground at her feet, safe within her stasis until Lunara could dedicate time to healing her. It had nearly knocked her over to realize that most of the mangled flesh surrounding the creature was her own wings, shredded and peeled apart. The deep, verdant gossamer of them seemed beyond repair, barely clinging to the bird-like bones beneath, but still…

Lunara would try. Fuck, she would *try*.

Footsteps sounded behind her, but she wasn't worried. She knew exactly who was approaching.

Brand didn't say a word, and no wonder. The evidence of their trying day was there in the lines that had settled in deeper around his eyes, the tense set of his wide shoulders. He had to be just as exhausted as she was.

They stood there, silent as Solyrian beat down on the land. Long grass swayed and birds sang, flitting between the wildflowers. Hard to believe such beauty existed beside such utter devastation, the flourishing landscape wholly unaware of the gaping wound in Glynmor nearby.

Across the yawning chasm, from amidst a lush forest on Kohamaia's northern border, one huge tree had tipped precariously out over the darkness like it was trying to have a peek below.

And the frayed rope dangling from a branch near the top sent a shudder down Lunara's spine.

The Fae's home was *right there.* What in the realms had she been doing—

Brand cleared his throat. "We've searched the village and surroundings, but found nothing of note. No tracks or scents. There hasn't been a soul here in days, maybe longer." His voice was a soothing rumble, washing over her. "We're going to stay here tonight, though, to see if we can't find more in the morning."

Stay… here…

He must have read the apprehension on her face. "*Not* in the village," he rushed out, shifting to stand in front of her. "We'll make camp in the woods."

Only then did Lunara notice the swelling in his face and the blood tracking down his upper lip. "Shite, your nose." Without thinking, she clapped her hand over it and poured her power into him, swallowing back any outward reaction. Not broken, judging by the pain she absorbed. Just dreadfully bruised, thanks to her. "I'm sorry. I—"

"No." Brand pulled away, flexing his jaw and neck. "No apology needed. It was good to see you using your lessons effectively."

His smile was lackluster at best.

"Still, I didn't mean to—"

"The rest of us can set everything up, if you wouldn't mind giving us the supplies?"

They spoke at the same time, their words stumbling awkwardly together, but his look said everything. They both knew her words for the half-hearted regret that they were, and he didn't want them.

Because you did *'mean to' and why apologize when you had every right?*

Fair.

All she could do was nod and flick her wrist, Lunara's dwindled power beginning to pull from her center in unpleasant ways. What were the odds they'd packed a whole slew of things at Lyriat's insistence, just in case?

Brand huffed when it all appeared. "I envy that ability. Always have."

His rueful smile cracked some of the ice that'd formed around her since that morning. The way it slowly fell from his face to be exchanged with soft concern almost melted it completely.

"You've done so much today already," he said. "Have a rest. We'll have food and a fire in no time."

It felt like a dismissal when he stepped away, turning his palm towards the ground. At his silent command, a slab of earth lifted the supplies she'd summoned, and he waved it along. The make-shift cart followed obediently as he backed away, gaze roving over her for a moment longer before he spun and headed for the woods.

Lunara stared after him, Magnus and Hedda joining him with grim determination.

Have a rest, he'd said.

There was no way in the bleeding realms she could sit there doing nothing. Even as she knew that she didn't have it in her to be around anyone else right now.

Then again…

Faldir was pacing at the village outskirt, looking as lost as she felt—exactly the type of person she could simply exist beside.

She knew what to do.

Lunara closed the distance between them. "I'm wondering if you might assist me."

Faldir's eyes narrowed on her, pursed lips pulling at his puckered scar. "Depends."

Short and to the point. Perfect. As a male of few words, he wouldn't wish to prattle on—and he'd be able to protect her.

"I don't want to talk to anyone, but I also don't want to wallow alone with my own thoughts. If you're willing, I think we might be able to do something… helpful?"

Lunara peered at the village, a mere stone's throw away. To the pain and horror painted in red over its homes and streets and gardens. Over the people.

The dead wouldn't expect anything of them.

He followed her look. "I'd say they're a bit beyond help at this point."

"Physically, yes, but their dignity isn't. Magnus isn't either. I need to *do* something, Faldir."

"I understand that." His sigh was heavy, but mostly for show. "What did you have in mind?"

She explained her plan. To his credit, he only hesitated for a moment, unsure it was worth it but agreeing in the end.

"Just so you know," he said as they entered the ravaged square, "I'll be laying the blame squarely at your feet if Magnus is pissed."

"Something tells me that's not even a little bit true."

"Perhaps not." He crossed his arms, waving one hand in a *get on with it* motion. "Guess you'll find out."

Lunara called on her dwindling power, gritting her teeth. She could do this. Her pain would be nothing compared to theirs in the end.

Not in the least.

SOLYRIAN HAD BEGUN SETTING, CASTING LONG SHADOWS OVER THE VILLAGE. Images of nameless faces and faceless bodies continued to flow through Lunara's mind in the encroaching darkness, and the number of them—the sheer weight of it—nearly broke her.

She hadn't bothered to try moving the rock and dirt as Brand did. At the end of the day, living or not, bodies and blood were her true domain. So, she'd used her power to call every last piece of every last person to herself, swallowing her screams and trapping them in the vice of her already shredded throat.

In the middle of the town square, as lovingly as she was able, she'd lined them up in neat rows and commanded their flesh to sink into the earth. Somehow, all of them being there didn't quite feel like the usual indignity it might have. Instead, it seemed fitting that they should rest together.

Then, she'd cleaned up, disappearing the gore and righting timbers. She had no wish for anyone to feel like she was erasing the travesty as if it had never been, but she'd wanted the village to be beautiful again.

For them.

Faldir had understood without being told. He'd made trip after trip while she'd worked, assigning himself the job of collecting flowers from wherever he could and laying them silently at her feet until they'd surrounded her in a mounded ring of rainbow colors.

When she'd finally noticed them there, a new ache had bloomed—one that had nothing to do with the cost of her power. Adding that tender hurt to the rest of her pain had almost been too much, but the moons were already rising. She'd be fine soon enough.

The last blossom sank its roots into the ground at Lunara's command, and a single tear broke away. She blinked the rest back, refusing them freedom, and sucked in a deep breath. She'd held it together so far, and she couldn't bear losing it now. Not with the wretched evidence of those who'd suffered so much worse spread out before her.

"Is it worthy of them, Faldir?" she whispered.

"It's not exactly the way they do it, but close enough. Damn close, actually." He crossed his arms, head tilting to the side. "Besides, what fault lies in an action taken with love in mind? This endeavor was selfless, and others have only benefitted. Anyone asking for more than that is not your friend."

"Hmm. Rather more poetic than I would've expected from you."

He looked away. "I have my moments."

"I know very little of friendship," she admitted. Though, how the unguarded confession had gotten free was beyond her.

"You probably know more than you think. Putting it into good practice, well… That's another matter."

She chose to blame the cold shiver running down her spine on the fact that they were standing over a mass grave, after a day that would probably haunt her for eternity. It had nothing to do with his words being too perceptive for comfort.

Nothing at all.

"I—"

A twig snapped, familiar power approaching in the wake of its sound, and she was glad for the interruption—even if her nerves were still trying to convince her she'd overstepped.

The others were silent for a long moment before Magnus strode forward and dropped to his knees among the wash of wildflowers.

"This is a lovely thing the two of you have done." His voice was thick with tears, the sound trying to draw out more of her own.

"I… I wasn't sure. If this was okay, I mean. I don't know anything about how you—"

"It doesn't matter," he rasped. "They've returned to the fields as they were meant to, however it happened."

With that, the bass of Magnus's voice rose above the din of evening in a tongue she didn't understand, chanting a lilting lament to his fallen.

Lunara closed her eyes as the insects and owls joined his mourning with songs of their own, like they were crying out in tandem. His language and theirs were lost on her, but… Stars above, she felt their meaning right down to her soul.

It might've been hours before she shook herself and glanced up, only to see Brand already staring back.

He looked bewildered when he softly said, "I find myself wondering if there are any bounds to your kindness."

Weeping Sisters, she was too bleeding tired for this. Too raw.

The truth was that there were already days when Lunara struggled to remember what kindness was. When she was so full of fear and sorrow that there was barely room for anything else. When she was numb to everything other than her hatred for the Elder Council, and the atrocities they'd allowed in the name of preserving Nachthelliae's power.

It was on the tip of her tongue to say so, her mind and body almost too wrecked to care that she shouldn't.

Almost.

"I hope not," she answered instead, taking a step backwards to put some distance between them. "What good is kindness if it has a limit?"

21

EVERY STEP CLOSER TO THEIR SMALL CAMP FELT MORE IMPOSSIBLE THAN THE last.

Trudging along, limbs stiff with pain, Lunara would have sworn to the Sisters that her feet were made of stone. Even her eyelids felt too heavy to lift after each traitorous blink.

When she reached the cold fire pit and fell onto one of the earthen platforms Brand had made, she nearly sobbed with relief. Hedda's low chuckle raised Lunara's hackles, but the Demon was forgiven the second she laid flint to wood and brought blessed warmth to the situation.

Eyes closed, Lunara fought sleep while she listened to the low rumblings of the others' voices, trying to muster the energy to summon her flask—assuming there was any blood left in it.

A sudden chill accompanied the disappearance of the fire's light behind her lids, but Lunara was too damned tired to scream. Instead, she hissed, "Whoever you are, I swear to the Sisters that I will turn you into something hideous if you don't move in the next two seconds."

Brand's answering chuckle was the only warning before Lunara was being scooped up and pressed to his chest.

She flailed, prying her eyes open. Even this close, he was nothing more than a black silhouette surrounded by orange flames.

"What are you doing?"

"I thought you might be hungry, even tired as you are," he said softly. "And I thought you'd prefer to be clean when you eat."

He crossed the camp, ignoring her struggles, and walked them deeper into the trees. Her body was at war with itself, wanting everything he promised but still incensed with this repeat of his earlier actions.

"Brand, put me down," she said through her teeth.

"You don't want to wash?"

"I don't want to be hauled around and *forced* to wash." She pushed against his unforgiving chest. "Just like I didn't want to be forced into *speaking plainly* earlier."

His head jerked back as if she'd slapped him. "Forced?"

He said it like it was ridiculous.

"Blessed moons, Brand. Let go of me!"

He set her feet to the ground and took a step back, obviously at a loss. She ignored the pang of regret in her chest, the chill running along the side of her body that'd been plastered up against him.

"I don't see the problem," he said, throwing his hands up. "I was only trying to protect you."

"I know that, but my life is complicated." She pinched the bridge of her nose and loosed a sigh. "There are certain things I don't… I didn't like it, and that should be enough. Alright?"

Well, aren't you chatty. Go on, tell him about the Elders while you're at it.

Sarcasm aside, the temptation was there. Stars above, the words were practically crawling their way up her throat, begging to be free. Just so he would stop looking at her that way.

He won't save you from them, you know. One word to his brother and you belong to the Council.

The reminder of his status as an Imperial Son drew her up short. It was so easy to forget how far he was above her. That she was in the presence of a creature who could ruin her with a word, a thought.

That you should watch your cursed mouth where he's concerned.

"I apologize," he said, his voice curt. "Damned if I understand what it is I'm meant to be sorry for, though." The last was said under his breath, almost to himself, but she heard it nonetheless.

Arsehole! Never mind. Rant away.

Lunara didn't need any encouragement.

"You trapped me, Brand, and demanded an explanation in return for my release. Now, I get to eat if I'm clean, and I can only be clean if you drag me around without asking? Once again, you're holding my freedom against me, and I don't bleeding appreciate it."

His eyes widened then dropped away, darting over the leaves littering the forest floor.

She crossed her arms and gave him her back, focusing on the peeling bark of a nearby tree to keep her mind from the pain sparking in every part of her. The exhaustion. "You should know—I value my freedom above all else. Taking my choices away will not go well with me. Ever. There's a difference between using your body to protect someone and using it *against them* because you think you know better. Now do you *understand?"*

If he didn't, then Brand was just like *him.* A monster. The Council's prized fucking pet. Hateful, cursed—

No, no. Don't go there. Ignore, ignore, ignore.

She wasn't sure what she'd do if that was the case. Disregarding her own obstacles, Lunara would've said Brand was everything she could ever want in a male. Impossibly strong and heartbreakingly gentle in turns. Beautiful. Kind. She couldn't keep him if she wanted to protect the autonomy she was so fiercely defending, but she might've had him for a little while. Might've stolen the opportunity to make searing memories for the long, lonely nights ahead of her.

He drew closer, his heat preceding his low voice, but she kept her gaze fixed away.

"I see now what you mean. I do. More than you know." She felt a small tickling at her scalp, as if he was rubbing a lock of her hair between his fingers. "I saw your face before you ran and I..." He freed an explosive breath, the air sending a shudder through her. "I panicked. Already, I know you well enough to have realized something was terribly wrong based on that look alone. With everything else, fear seized me and I acted without thought." His hand landed on her bare shoulder, his thumb tracing a lazy circle there. "Forgive me, Lunara. It won't happen again, I swear it."

His touch left her as the last word passed his lips, only serving to emphasize the promise he'd just made.

More of an apology than she'd had from anyone in a very long time. The first time in recent memory that she'd been heard and acknowledged.

The creature who'd ruined her life never would have done such a thing.

Stars above, you're all over the damned place.

She didn't care. Brand was *different*.

Lunara whipped around. "Brand, I—"

Shock rattled every one of her nerve endings. Ripped all thought from her head.

Brand stood in a glaring beam of moonlight, towering over her. Blood and gore covered his clothes head-to-toe in dry, flaking streaks of black and brown, made worse by the way the branches swayed in the breeze and set the shadows to moving. She refused to identify the different bits and pieces clinging to him. Her mind wouldn't accept any of it anyway.

How in the weeping fuck did you not notice that sooner?

The light had been dimming by the time she'd finished with the Fae, gone when she'd finished the burials, but still.

"You're… filthy," she said, swallowing her disgust.

His smile was tired, and not in the least bit amused. "I've had worse. But, yes, *we* are filthy." Brand sighed and gave her a pointed look. "Hence the need to bathe."

Oh no.

With dreadful realization dawning, Lunara looked down at herself.

Her dress… Her hair…

Blood had dried the lengths into hard clumps, all the way up to her shoulders in some places.

No, no, no, no, no…

"Brand," she whispered.

A wave of nausea washed over her, and Lunara wanted nothing more than to erase the creeping awareness of what was stuck to her. She stumbled to the side, Brand gripping her arm to—

Images from the past barraged her, laying themselves over reality. The forest twisted until she was crouched on a ravaged street in the Upper Block of Starkeep. Suddenly, it wasn't the dried blood of innocents that covered them, but their own, flowing freely. Stone crumbled around her, a familiar scream echoing. A clawed hand was poised in the air above Brand, holding his still-beating heart. Death by the name of Malachyr—

"Lunara?" Brand's even voice cut through the recollections.

Her legs had turned to jelly, face and fingers numb. All she could do was reach out, hands fumbling for something solid to save her from herself.

Real. He was real. Not the one dying. That was another time. Another night. Other people.

The bastard can't hurt you anymore. Cordelia promised.

Her eyes were glued to the pulse jumping in Brand's corded neck, to the proof of life pumping steadily there.

Real. Real. Real.

It wasn't enough to distract her from the sensation crawling over her skin, the past mixing with the present like a putrid film. Hadn't Brand said that knowledge wasn't always helpful? She should've shut her mouth and let him take her to the river.

The river.

Yes. There, roaring in the near distance. The instant her ears locked onto the sound, her body was no longer her own.

Lunara shoved past Brand, desperate. For the second time that day, she was sprinting away from him, the rush of water pulling her faster and faster through the trees. She ignored his shouts, heedless of the low branches stretching out like hands to grab her, smack her, claw her.

If she'd been in her right mind, she might've just commanded the dead particles away from them and eaten the cost, but she wasn't and she didn't.

Because this time, she was running from herself.

From the stain of remembering. From agony that had nothing to do with the price of her power. From facing him in this state and having to explain.

When she broke through the tree line and reached a small clearing, saw the river before her, Lunara had only enough sense left to summon a pile of clean linens to the bank and a bar of soap to her hand before throwing herself into the water—boots and all.

She didn't notice the iciness of it as she plunged into the pulling current. Nothing mattered but making the stars-forsaken soap lather and raking her nails over every exposed inch.

Get it off. Get it off.

More than anything, she wanted to scrub the memories away.

"Let me." Her frantic movements were stopped when a pair of hands landed on hers. Brand's presence loomed behind her, his warmth seeping through the water to comfort her. "Let me help you."

When he squeezed her shoulders, it grounded her somewhat. Loosed her tongue and had her confessing, "I can't… I can't do it. I can't get it off."

Lunara swayed, black spots swimming in her vision as that last burst of power and pain caught up.

"Shh, it's okay. I've got you."

Next she knew, his fingers were landing in her hair to massage her scalp.

Slowly, so *slowly*, her lungs unclenched. Feeling came back. Combined with the shock of the cold water and the soothing tone of his rumbling bass…

This blood was not her parents' blood. Brand was well and the monster was gone. The Elders had counted her among the dead. It was fifty-two years later, and she was in the Westrealm, not the Evesong. Not Starkeep.

Safe. She was safe.

Lunara tumbled back into her body, into sanity, on a ragged sigh. Her bones turned to putty beneath Brand's ministrations, muscles unwinding as he worked to remove the filth coating her and she finally relaxed—until her foot slipped from the mossy stone she'd been perched on and she fell into his waiting arms.

She was incapable of thought after that.

LUNARA WAS UNRAVELING.

Tearing at the ruined sleeves of her dress, clawing at the buttons on her bodice.

Her gaze had gone distant the second she'd seen him, into some middle space, eyes flashing with something that had nothing to do with Glynmor and its horrors.

And then she'd run. Again.

He'd followed her crashing footfalls, her gasps, the sounds tearing at him. Wondering the entire way what in the realms had happened to her.

Who had dared to fucking hurt her. Why it made her feral and unpredictable. Level, until she suddenly wasn't.

Yet another problem for another time. The litany of shite to deal with was getting longer, but he couldn't do anything about it in the middle of the night.

Not while he was watching her break.

He slipped his belt and boots off, dropping them onto the rocky sand near a pile of linens she'd summoned, and waded in to reach her.

"Get it off, get it off," she whispered repeatedly, a prayer and a plea.

He stopped a breath away from her trembling body, allowing only his hands to have contact with her.

"Let me," he whispered, sliding his touch through the water along her arms to still her movements. "Let me help you."

It was bordering on violating his earlier promise, but the tightness in his chest didn't seem like his own. She was falling apart, and he *felt it.*

This wasn't about knowing better, but about sensing that she needed someone else to care for her. He had no idea what ghosts she'd seen out in the woods, or what nightmares had come back to haunt her. Only that he recognized the *look*—one he'd seen on some of his warriors' faces often enough.

And he held no conditions over her. She could do whatever she liked, and he wouldn't stop her.

Brand appreciated the need for freedom, for choice. Maybe better than most, since he craved it so badly but could never have it. Not being who he was.

He was the biggest arse in Bordoroth for not seeing it. Not realizing what he'd been taking away from her, even in his panicked attempt to protect her. He didn't need to know the story to understand it to his marrow.

Dragging his hands back up, he squeezed her shoulders, kneading, trying to lend her some of his own calm.

If it worked…

"I can't… I can't do it," she rasped. "I can't get it off."

"Shh, it's okay," he crooned, plucking the soap from her white-knuckled grasp. "I've got you."

He lathered up and paused, reading her body language one more time to be sure it was truly okay, before sinking his trembling fingers into the mass of her hair.

Sisters, the way she melted. She swayed into the touch, a sigh leaving her lips.

Brand had to bite back a groan at the sound, at her capitulation, at finally having her curls within his grasp.

Even when it was such a mess, it was beautiful. He scrubbed at every clump and tangle, gently loosening knots and scraping away debris. When the last of the dirt and filth was whisked away by the river's current, only soaking strands of silk left behind, he still kept running his fingers through it. Kept inhaling the amber and spice that accompanied her moonlight scent.

It was working though. Her face was a mask of serenity, her limbs loose.

The sight of it untethered something within him. Visions of having the curls wrapped around him, tickling against his bare skin, flooded his mind. Had him straining against his trousers.

He wanted to step closer, press against her, feel her—

She lost her footing and stumbled backwards into him, granting his wish. He caught her by the waist, and every good intention fled him. Brand couldn't bring himself to move away, to leave the warmth of her. Instead, he tightened his hold and closed his eyes, every ragged breath matching hers.

Burning Solyrian, the way her curves cradled him. She was just so fucking *soft*.

Worse than the training by a mile. The water erased the layers between them, the heat of her skin seeping through the soaked fabric to burn his own.

A shock of lust tore through his body, amplified by the memory of her unknowingly drinking his blood gift in the watchtower. It hadn't been appropriate to acknowledge it then, not with so much death surrounding them, but now…

Now, they were in a pocket of relative peace and he could admit to the pure satisfaction that had filled his veins at seeing her throat bob. Seeing her take even that small piece of him inside herself.

His greater half purred within him, unable to help the swell of pride, the contentment. He would gladly be her sole source of sustenance if that was how it always felt to do so.

Fuck. The thought of her fangs sinking into him was like heady wine.

Brand finally opened his eyes, ready to turn her around and beg on his knees for her to feed from him directly, but the words got stuck when he saw a lock of her clean hair caught on the grime of his soiled tunic.

Ever so slowly, he loosened his hold and stepped away. Swallowing a growl of frustration, he turned his back to her and ripped off the offending garment.

"Thank you, Brand. That was…" She cleared her throat. "Thank you."

At least she sounded like herself again. At least he'd given her that.

He turned around to respond just in time to see her dress disappearing. It didn't matter that she was facing away or that the river was black as midnight and rose well above her waist because she was glowing—literally fucking *glowing*—and the water that should've covered her *didn't.* Instead, her body was revealed as a luscious shimmer beneath the lapping current. A beacon in the darkness, beckoning to him.

Seeing that much of her, so close, hit Brand like an avalanche on the mountainside.

It took every ounce of self control he possessed to look away and resume his own undressing. Unfortunately, the relief when he freed himself from his trousers was short-lived. His ears latched on to the sound of Lunara humming under her breath, accompanied by the tinkling music of water droplets splashing as she washed, and it nearly killed him.

On a heavy sigh, he sank into the water, holding himself under until his lungs screamed for air. Submerged in the murk, he finally accepted that there was nothing in all of Bordoroth capable of quelling the overwhelming desire he felt for the stunning Sorcerit. She was the most captivating female he'd ever met, beautiful inside and out.

And he wanted her with a burning intensity that should have shocked him, but didn't.

Not when the staggering truth was settling even deeper into his bones.

Not when Brand would swear he was starting to faintly feel her emotions as if they were his own. When he'd projected slow breaths and soothing ease, control, and she'd absorbed all of it like a sponge as he'd cleaned her.

Not when his greater half was crowing inside, alive with the triumph of certainty.

Mag and Hedda's faces flashed—his look of awed realization, hers of quiet understanding.

They knew. They fucking knew it too.

Pushing to the surface, he raked both hands through his hair, washing it as quickly as he could. He couldn't stay that close to her, not a stitch of clothing between them, any longer. Not without doing something utterly reckless. She deserved more, better, than a muddy river bank less than an hour after having to put him in his place.

Brand tossed his shirt and pants onto the bank along with everything else and strode out of the water, every sloshing step taking him further from where he actually wanted to be.

When he bent to retrieve a towel, Lunara's singing dwindled to nothing, and her softly gasped, *"Weeping, fucking shite,"* made him pause.

Made him wonder.

If they were sharing feelings, it was possible she was as tightly wound as he. Maybe having similar thoughts and realizations of her own.

The notion made him wicked. The distance and water between them made him bold.

Still facing away from her, Brand slowed his movements, running the cloth over his skin with deliberately drawn out strokes. He didn't bother to keep his head from tipping back, or his hand from gliding the linen over his cock once, twice, again...

Fuck.

He had to get dry, after all. May as well torture them both while he did it.

Brand froze when he heard her leaving the water. *Bold,* unfortunately, did not mean *reformed,* and his nerves spiked. Ignoring the throbbing jut of his erection, he tied the towel around himself in a rush and turned.

Weeping, fucking shite was right.

Mere feet away and dripping, Lunara was wrapped in a scrap of linen that had no hope whatsoever of fully covering her luscious curves. It gaped wide open up one rounded thigh, exposing a generous hip, and only tapered closed when it hit her much smaller waist. Her breasts were barely concealed, spilling over the top where her arms held the ends together.

Every inch of her skin shimmered in the moonlight, and Brand had the sudden, overwhelming urge to to drop to his knees and worship the goddess in front of him.

Lunara was every fantasy he'd ever had—and she was shivering.

Without a thought, he snatched up another towel and hurried behind her. Touching her was probably a mistake, but he couldn't help himself.

Just like he couldn't help goading her.

"Such foul language," he teased, letting his lips brush the shell of her ear as he draped it over her shoulders and squeezed.

Her breath hitched. "Yes, well…"

Brand rounded her again, wanting to gauge her expressions. To see if she felt it too, this *thing* pulling them together.

Lunara bit her lip, and his blood roared at the sight of one, sharp fang peeking out. Then he noticed her hooded eyes, the lazy heaving of her chest, and he nearly bellowed his delight.

"Well?"

She raised a challenging brow, absolute *fire* in the look. "*Well,* I had no idea that your arse was capable of looking the way it does."

The smirk that tugged at one side of his face felt foreign—too confident, too smug. The kind of look Lyriat would pull, the arrogant bastard.

Shite, Brand hardly knew who he was around her. Shameless flirtation was not something he did often. Or ever. He wasn't even sure he was doing it right.

But, with her, it was like…

Like lazy days spent swimming in the warm sea. Like the tingle of rare, irrepressible laughter. Like the comfort of a soft bed after hours in his workshop.

Easy. Energizing.

Like she could make him forget every bloody thing trying to destroy his peace, so he could focus all of his attention on her instead.

Lunara nonchalantly tossed a wet clump of hair over her shoulder as if she were a queen, knocking the second towel loose and emphasizing her long neck, her bare shoulder.

Yes, his greater half crowed, seizing some of his control. *Ours.*

Burning fucking Solyrian, he had to get her covered before he tackled her to the ground.

Brand reached for the emerald linen dress she'd summoned, trying to convince himself it was for the best. That he wasn't just looking for an excuse to touch her. "Shall I help you dress, Lunara?"

She turned her wide, sea-blue eyes up to him, the blush stealing over her cheeks well worth his audacity.

That gaze never left his as she nodded and shuffled closer—too much and not enough, all at once—but Lunara surprised him.

Her power spiked, the lengths of their hair drying in tandem with a wave of her fingers. Another, and the garment was gone from his hands, appearing on her body.

Except, it was gaping from neck to navel—unfastened buttons pulling the fabric aside, untied laces dangling from the parted neckline and falling beside the heavy mounds of her barely-covered breasts.

Sweet... merciful...

Brand was staring. Mouth gaping. Words gone.

Lunara placed one end of the ties into each of his hands. "I thought you were helping me dress."

Fuck.

THERE WAS NO EXPLANATION FOR HOW LUNARA HAD GONE FROM BLIND PANIC to this.

Panting. Hot. Practically salivating.

It had started in the water, the desire to touch him overwhelming her. Every lap of the river against her prickling skin had been a sweet torture. And when she'd heard him leaving the river, the temptation to peek had been too great to ignore.

Blessed moons, what a sight it had been.

Brand was even larger without any clothes on, every hard inch of him flexing and straining as he bent and then dried himself. Slowly.

Her mouth had actually watered, fangs itching to sink into any part of him. There was no way it hadn't been on purpose, meant just for her, and she'd practically run out of the river when his head had fallen back and he'd—

"Don't you—" Brand cleared his throat. "Don't you need undergarments?"

If she wasn't completely breathless, Lunara might have laughed outright.

"Ah, uh… I don't generally wear undergarments?" It came out as a question, but Lunara was fairly certain. "What can I say?" She shrugged. "I hate them."

It's possible he maybe, definitely, didn't need to know that about you.

Brand said nothing. His throat worked as he stood there, still as a statue—rather gratifying, actually, to see him speechless when faced with the prospect of her naked body.

"Literally never?" he finally rasped.

She reveled in the way his eyes narrowed as he perused her from head to toe. "Do stockings count?"

"No," he growled, and the sound sent a shiver racing down her spine.

"Then literally never."

Brand let out a slow breath through pursed lips before he tugged and wrapped the drawstrings of her dress around and around each hand to pull her in. Awareness of him, of his size and heat, bloomed over every inch of Lunara's skin the closer she got until—with a final, gentle yank—she was pressed against him. Her dress fell further apart, until it would take nothing more than a single, heaving breath for her to spill out and bare herself to him.

For a stand-still second of madness, she gave in and imagined a future that held everything she'd ever actually wanted, everything she wished for. Just a glimpse of what life could be like if things were different.

Stars, how she craved it.

No one had ever looked at her the way Brand did in that suspended moment. While they hovered there together, Lunara lost in the speckled depths of his eyes, it was so fucking easy to *forget.*

His fingers landed on her collar bone and crept down over the swell of one breast, dipping under the open seam of her bodice.

Oh, just do it. Just arch your back and—

Brand pinched a wayward curl that had gotten stuck underneath, the ends tickling in exquisite ways as he drew it out.

"In all my long years," he said, dragging the length across his open mouth down his bearded chin, "I don't think I've ever seen anything quite so magnificent as these wild, untamed locks."

"Oh."

Stars above.

Not what she'd expected.

Brand tucked the strand away and laced his fingers with hers. Bringing them up to the hard plane of his chest, he left hers there to plaster his own at her lower back, her nape, hauling her more firmly against him.

His gaze dipped her lips, a muscle ticking in his jaw, and her sharp fingernails dug into his unyielding flesh in answer.

Blessed moons, he was going to kiss her. Ruin her. She would never be the—

"Your Highness?" Hedda's voice was like a punch to the gut. "Lunara?"

She jumped back, closing her dress with a thought as Brand whipped around and scrubbed a hand down his face.

Still wrapped in only a towel. Barely.

Sisters save her.

Seconds later, Hedda ambled into the clearing. "Forgive me. We were worried. It's been quite a while."

The Demon commander took everything in. Lunara didn't miss the way she swallowed and straightened when her eyes landed on Brand, assessing his state. Probably realizing what she'd just interrupted.

Curse and damn her.

Better this way. No silly notions to distract you from reality.

Maybe.

Or, what if Brand could be her reality for a little while? Just until it was all over. Until she fled from his life and went back into hiding.

The second you leave Thodelebor, you're going home. Or calling in your debt. Anything else is madness!

She wanted to scoff. For a minute, even that side of herself had been desperate to see what he would be like. Feel like.

"We're fine." Brand's clipped voice cut off her musings, his sigh heavy. "I just need to get dressed."

"Right," Lunara said, backing towards Hedda. "I'll... um... give you some privacy."

Brand made a low sound. "This isn't over, Lunara," he said, whorls of light dancing up his forearms and stealing her breath.

If the heated look he leveled on her was anything to go by, then no, it most certainly wasn't.

It should be! It bleeding fucking should be, you daft ninny.

How could it be?

Goosebumps broke out all over her in response, anticipation an effervescent pool within her. In that moment, she wanted everything he was promising with every fiber of her being.

Lunara didn't respond with words.

Good thing she'd called the moonlight while bathing. She almost hadn't risked it, but Brand had turned away and she hadn't been able to resist. It had relieved some of her pain—just enough that she could ignore the fire licking at her nerve endings and add a little something extra to the sway of her hips as she sauntered off.

She failed to stifle the smile teasing at her lips. Perhaps she'd make some searing memories after all.

In the night, after the fire dwindled to nothing and a chill rendered her bedroll utterly useless, the nightmares came.

Probably because she'd been thinking about *him,* but it happened often.

Every time, she would swear someone was trying to tell her something, leading her through truths and lies to see if she could tell the difference. Someone beside her, though she could never turn her head to look.

Instead, she was locked on moonstone towers of the Upper Block as they crumbled around her, her father's power raging to save them. Her mother's screams, echoing in places they hadn't happened, a constant shrieking under the warped devastation.

Even in sleep, she couldn't stop the outcome. Couldn't manipulate the horror into fantasy.

Over and over, they died. All of them. Sometimes the way it had happened, sometimes differently. Worse.

Always by the same, bloody hand.

Malachyr the Mistwarden, Keeper of Illamiata. The Evesong's cursed *blessing.*

The worst part was always the twisted ending, when her mind whispered the lie that she'd never gotten free. That Cordelia hadn't given in and hidden her. That *he* was still alive and searching for her, alongside the rest of the Elder Council.

It was an eternity that Lunara was trapped there, delirious, reliving the horrors behind closed lids.

Until she was saved by a solid body pressing against her back. A heavy arm over her waist. A flattened palm against her stomach tugging her closer. That blessed heat and solidity worked to dispel her terror, and she was finally lulled back to sleep by hazy, baritone murmurings against her ear.

Into the best dreams she could remember having, even while lying on the hard forest floor.

She must have conjured her savior, though. Lunara was alone when she awoke to the first tepid rays of dawn, the ground cold beside her.

And a familiar voice was shouting loud enough to wake the dead nearby.

22

BRAND WAS VIOLENTLY WRENCHED FROM THE BLISS OF HALF A NIGHT SPENT tangled around Lunara.

Literally.

The first strike—the one that woke him—was a booted foot to his arse. The second was an immediate punch to the shoulder that sent him flopping onto his back, blinking.

Fucking Solyrian. He was truly exhausted if someone had been able to sneak up on him—especially this arsehole.

Somehow, Lunara slept through the *attack*. Brand intended to keep it that way.

He extracted himself carefully before rolling again and grasping the fist that was flying for his face.

"I cannot believe you bastards left me behind!" Thad was spitting mad, a vein pulsing in his forehead as his wolf flashed over his features.

"Keep your bloody voice down," Brand hissed, shoving his cousin away and sitting up.

He'd only just coaxed her back to sleep. Damned if the whelp was going to ruin it.

"Keep my voice down?" Thad laughed, the sound bitter. "Where the fuck is Mag?"

Any other time, Brand might have warned Thaddeus that the male in question was directly behind him, face still creased from his own rest, but he wasn't feeling generous this morning.

Magnus wrapped a hand around Thad's nape and hauled him back. His fangs flashed as he growled, "Why are you here, pup? How?"

Thad wrenched himself away. "In case no one has noticed, I'm not a wee fucking bairn anymore. Not a *pup*. You can both fuck off."

Lunara mumbled in her sleep and Brand shot up, shoving a hand over Thad's mouth before he could keep ranting. "I'll hear your grievances, but kindly quiet down while you do so."

Thad glared at him over the tops of his fingers, one eye twitching before he slumped and nodded. Satisfied, Brand propelled him deeper into the trees, Magnus at their heels.

Mag's sigh was heavy when they finally stopped. "First off, does your father know you're here?"

"Have you lost your mind?" Thad scoffed. "Of course he doesn't. I had to wait a whole day to sneak past him, else I'd have been here sooner."

"Sisters fucking save me." Mag pinched the bridge of his nose. "I'm not the one who's lost my mind, lad. Caius is going to be beside himself."

They stared at one another, the forest coming alive with a warm dawn—in direct opposition to the cold shiver that made its way down Brand's back.

Thad might be pissed about it, but there was a reason they coddled him. After Meliora's illness and death, if anything happened to him—

"What in the realms are you doing out here in the woods anyway?"

Thad's question was like a knife to the gut. Brand could actually hear Mag's teeth grinding.

"The villagers—"

"Don't," Mag whispered, cutting Brand off. "I can't…"

"What?" Thad looked between the two of them. "Tell me."

Magnus shook his head. "We have to get you home and clean up your fucking mess."

"Oh, no. I'll not be going back with my tail between my legs." Thad went red, his pent up fury flushing to the surface. "Something's wrong. You need me, Da doesn't. I'm staying with you."

Mag's hand darted out in a blur and seized Thad's collar. "Keep pushing it, and I'll be wringing your fool neck long before Caius does."

"Go on then! Fucking try it!"

"Hello?" Lunara's call stopped their scuffle, his brother and cousin freezing.

It took all of Brand's restraint not to reach out and clobber both of them for waking her up.

She rounded a nearby tree. When her eyes landed on Thad, her head tilted back and she muttered, "Stars and arses," to the branches overhead.

For her, Thad had the decency to swallow and look away.

"Good morning, Thaddeus," she said, joining them with a sigh. "We really must stop meeting like this."

"This isn't the same," Thad mumbled.

"No?" She cocked her head to one side, waiting.

Thad slumped, his eyes closing. "Aye, fine. It is."

Strange, to watch his fiery cousin concede so easily.

"We talked about this. At length, if I recall correctly." Lunara raised a brow. "Leaving a note is just plain decency and you're not supposed to use your special tolls anymore. It's too dangerous."

Special tolls?

Thad broke away from Mag and sidled up to her, conveniently changing the subject. "I don't suppose you'd be willing to tell me what happened with Glynmor, since these two arseholes won't?"

"Um…" She blinked and turned pleading eyes to Brand.

Naturally, he looked at his brother.

"Ach, fuck it." Mag trudged off in the direction of the village. "Just keep your gob shut and have some respect."

Then, they were gone, leaving him and Lunara alone.

Again.

This isn't over, Lunara.

Brand knew he was staring, but couldn't be bothered to care. She was locked on him just as fully.

Fuck, he could take the kiss they'd been denied right now. Could sink his fingers right into her flesh and drag her against him.

"Where's Hedda?" His voice was hardly more than a scrape. If he didn't want her so badly, he might've been embarrassed.

"Oh. Uh…"

Was that disappointment he heard? Good. *Good.* He was only asking because he didn't want to be interrupted again.

They were set to spend the next few days scouring the surrounding land for clues, and he wanted one fucking moment of peace beforehand to ravage her mouth. To get lost in her and pretend that there was no such thing as the shite piling up on top of him. That he'd never heard that message, or seen the reality of it. Wasn't feeling the threat of its words to his very bones.

Lunara blinked, shaking her head. "She was still snoring when I followed you here."

That was about the only thing she could have said to quell his building lust.

His Second was the lightest sleeper he knew, the quickest to her feet when under threat, and she didn't snore. Ever.

Brand should've realized something was wrong the instant Hedda wasn't right beside them while dragging Thad away for an explanation.

The female before him had scrambled his head ten different ways.

"We'd better be waking her up and fetching Faldir, then. We have much to do."

Damn it.

HEDDA WAS TWO FEET AWAY FROM HER BEDROLL, FACE DOWN AND DROOLING in the dirt, and still snoring.

A frisson of worry went through him. The scene was all wrong. She was sprawled out, one foot half buried in the cold ash of the fire pit, hair a mess, flask at her side. Brand couldn't recall a single time in their lives he'd witnessed her like that. Utterly vulnerable.

"Second, to me."

Nothing.

"Hedda!"

She didn't so much as twitch.

Lunara knelt and laid her hand on Hedda's shoulder. Light shone beneath her fingers, a frown on her lips. "Headache," she said. "Migraine, actually. Rather severe. Does she often suffer from those?"

Ah. The flask.

Immediately, his heart halted its frenzied gallop, his lungs easing.

"Her cycle causes them." He nodded to the carved wooden container by her head. "She keeps a tonic with her, just in case. Probably why she's out of it. But..." He thought back, to the last time Hedda had been indisposed. "It seems too soon for that."

Lunara tilted her head. "You note such things?"

"She's like a sister to me. Besides, anyone with a cycle is doted on for the duration of its visit. It's useful to be able to anticipate them and ensure their care accordingly."

Her brows punched up. "Blessed moons. I never heard such a thing." She cast her gaze down to Hedda. "How fortunate for those in the Montrealm."

"I assume the Sorcerit wave their fingers and never have to feel a thing."

Lunara busted out laughing. "And you were doing so well." She used her power to turn Hedda over. "No. It's taboo to mention it, and we can't heal ourselves. For many of us, the price of our magic is pain. What makes a cycle any different?"

"That's barbaric."

She shrugged. "*That's* just the way it is."

She said it so indifferently, and it pricked at him. He knew she lived alone, but to have so little concern for her own comfort?

Her mouth twisted as she palpated Hedda's stomach. "She's fertile, not shedding." She gently swept Hedda's hair away and flattened her palms on either temple. "Fortunately—or unfortunately, I suppose—migraines are common at both times. Nothing to worry about."

Lunara's face contorted into a grimace and her magic slammed into him, same as every other time. Potent. Massive. A caress and a wallop all at once.

Hedda shot up, gasping and swinging.

"It's fine, Second. Take a breath."

She glared up at him. "What the fuck?"

Lunara blew a slow breath through pursed lips as she swayed. "I healed your headache. It can be disorienting, so try to stay calm."

"Headache?"

"You were out like that one." Brand hiked a thumb at the comatose Fae on the far side of their camp. "Lunara healed and woke you. How are you feeling?"

Lunara snatched up Hedda's flask and waved it under her nose. "Where did you get this?"

Hedda twisted to look at Lunara. "Where did *you* get that?"

"It was on the ground next to you. Brand said it's yours?"

"Yes, but..." Hedda scrunched her eyes, rubbing her fingers into them. "On the ground? I didn't get it out. I... had my watch after Brand, woke up Magnus... and then..."

Alarm bells rang when Hedda trailed off and sent him a confused look. "Then?"

She dug a fist into her chest. "I—"

Shouts sounded from the trees, crashing footfalls behind them. Mag and Thad burst into the camp a second later.

"Come quick," his brother said, chest heaving.

Hedda pushed to wobbly feet, barely keeping hold of her axe as she searched the woods beyond him. "Where is Faldir?"

An eternity passed while Mag stared back at her. "Lass..."

Hedda turned on Brand, that same hand rubbing the spot over her heart. "He's not... I can't... Fuck."

She leapt over the fire pit and stumbled, nearly hitting the dirt before she scrambled away screaming her brother's name.

Shite. Something was very, *very* wrong with his Second.

Brand reached down and gripped Lunara's arm, hauling her from the ground. "Are you well?"

There was a sheen on her pale brow, but she nodded.

He pulled her after Hedda, trying to be mindful of the pain she was clearly in. "What did you find?"

"Only made it to the tree line," Mag answered, jogging alongside, "and turned right back around. Something's trashed the fields, and Faldir was nowhere to be seen."

"It was like this when I came through earlier," Thad said. "I never got close enough to see that it was wrong, else I'd have said something."

They followed broken branches and skidding foot prints, almost crashing into Hedda's rooted, listing body when they emerged from the wood.

Brand followed her look and froze right with her. "What the fuck?"

"Aye." Mag's voice was hushed. "That wasn't there when my watch ended, I swear it."

Fields that had been mostly pristine the night before were rutted and ruined, the land raised in jagged, overturned clumps taller than he was. Huge gouges ran like twisted scars from the spot where they'd all sat to keep watch, through the meadow, all the way to—

"The chasm," he said, feet already moving.

Magnus ran ahead of him, throwing his robe off and shifting mid-air. Pet put his enormous snout to the ground, sniffing at the divots, pawing around. He loosed a whimper and turned golden eyes on Brand.

There, mixed in with the mud and roots… No. Not mud. *Ooze,* inky and shining, even in the low light. It dripped from sundered petals and broken stems. Seeped into the dirt. And it was *moving.*

He reached down—

Lunara's hand wrapped around his wrist, her nails digging into his skin. "*Don't* touch that."

Her breaths were coming in pants, a haunted look in her eyes.

"What is it?"

She slowly unlocked her fingers, head shaking.

"All I can smell is burning death and rot. Nothing else." Mag had shifted back, already retying his robe. "There's blood, but the rest is too fucking foul to know whose."

That's what caught Brand's eye in the first place—crimson mixed in with the black, too much of it for comfort.

They followed the streaks and splashes of red right up to the chasm's edge, where Hedda was standing in the center of a colossal groove, swaying as she peered down into the darkness.

Lunara went up alongside her. "Hedda?"

She was met with silence.

"We have to assume it's Faldir's," Brand said quietly, one eye on them, the other on the ground.

Thad sidled up. "Do you think something actually dragged him down there?"

Sister's save them, but that's exactly where his mind had gone. As to *what* had done it—

"Dreadbeast." Hedda's voice was a haunted slur.

Brand hadn't wanted to think it, let alone say it out loud.

The mythical monsters that allegedly inhabited the bowels of every chasm. Some swore they could hear their animalistic snarls and screams echoing in the dead of night, when no other sounds pierced the air.

In all of recorded time, no one had ever seen one. They were supposed to be nothing more than a chilling bedtime story that parents used to frighten wayward children.

Not real. Not capable of *this.*

"Ach, lass, those are a legend. Fiction." Even Magnus didn't sound sure, false lightness in every word.

Hedda's head snapped up, violence in every line of her body and a crazed gleam in her eyes. "Are they? You saw what happened to those people. The same filth on their bodies, the same smell. What else could have done that?"

What, indeed.

She turned back to the chasm. "Real or not, we have to find him."

Brand was inclined to agree, except…

He shared a look with Mag, no words needed. His brother saw it too—the desperation, the drunken, uncontrolled movements of her limbs.

Warriors had to be sharp, quick. Hedda was all over the place, more likely to make mistakes or act without thinking, and it would only end in tragedy.

No way she was going into the chasm like this.

Fuck, he wasn't sure if any of them should go down there, or how, or… *Fuck.*

Brand straightened his spine and dug deep, calling on all of the authority he possessed—armor, for what he was about to do. "Second, to me."

Hedda paused for the barest moment before she obeyed, planting her feet in a wide stance in front of him—or, at least, trying to.

He reached out to steady her, surreptitiously removing the axe from her hold and tossing it away. "I know you want to go after your brother," he said, squeezing her shoulder, "but someone needs to get help, and reassure Caius that Thad is safe."

Hedda *didn't notice* that he'd just disarmed her. Oblivious, her lip trembled as she raised her chin, lids blinking too slowly. "Thaddeus himself should do it then, Your Highness, since he's not supposed to be here."

What in the realms? He could barely understand her garbled words.

He kept his face bland and lied through his damned teeth. "You're too weak in this form."

Hedda reared as if he'd slapped her. "What did you just say to me?"

"You heard me well enough."

Her lips peeled back. "You would forsake your own Second and let a *child* go down there? A timid Sorcerit that's afraid of her own shadow?"

An hour ago, he would have laughed and said *never.* Not in a million years. But looking at her, at the disjointed movements and the disconnect in her eyes…

"In this case, yes. If it keeps you safe."

Easy to let her think that, if it meant saving her life or someone else's.

She gripped the front of his tunic and tried to shove him, her respect gone. "Fuck safe, Brand. That's my *twin!*" Her fist was flying and connecting before he could blink.

Brand's head snapped back, every concern legitimized with that single action. In the more than eighty years they'd known each other, her destiny as his Second secured from the start, she had never struck him in anger.

If Brand were any of the Imperial Demons that had come before him, she would've just earned herself a swift death for treason.

"Look at yourself!" he hissed, running a hand across his split lip. "Would *you* let you go down there?"

She looked mildly horrified, but didn't let up. "I would do whatever it took to get him back."

"So would I," he growled. "You're a danger to yourself and those you'd be protecting. You're a liability. Now go *home,* Second, before you do something I can't overlook."

"You hear that, Sorcerit? *I'm* the liability now." Hedda's laugh was unhinged as she locked eyes on Lunara. "Think he'd let me go if *I* was the one sucking his cock?"

Lunara's gasp was like flint to kindling, igniting his fury.

Hedda turned on him again, fist flying as she shrieked. "Is that all I have to do, Brand?" *Slam,* into his chest. "Be related or get on my knees, and you'll let me do whatever I want?" *Slam,* into his stomach. "No matter how fucking idiotic it is?"

Brand was glued to the spot, enduring every hammering blow and fighting to control the rage overtaking him. He'd been rendered speechless, blood roiling, seething to his statued marrow.

"Hedda, lass."

She spun to Magnus, gripping her hair with white knuckles, tearing at the strands. "Is this what I'm reduced to? A messenger?"

"There's no shame in it," Mag answered.

"No shame in leaving my brother to the mercy of a chasm?" She staggered. "H-he would never… Faldir would've been halfway down by now, if it were me. But… you want me to leave and get *help?"*

All Brand could manage was, "Your Imperial Son commands it."

Hedda loosed a savage scream to the open sky, tears flowing down her cheeks when she faced him again. "I swore an oath to the Sisters, *with Faldir,* never to leave your side exposed."

Sisters above. Crying? If Faldir wasn't in danger *right now,* he'd be doing everything in his power to figure out what in the fuck was happening to her.

"This is an exception. You are not yourself, and I can't risk it."

"No!" she wailed. "No, no, no. I won't do it. I won't." Her eyes darted, unfocused, and she started to back away. "He would have been halfway down…"

"Hedda—"

She turned and bolted, clumsily dodging Mag's grasp and heading straight for Lunara.

No, not Lunara—*the chasm drop.*

Mingled shouts filled the air as Brand barreled after her, Lunara the only thing standing between his Second and a deadly drop into nothing.

She threw herself in front of Hedda at the last possible instant, faster than any of them would have guessed her capable of. The two collided with dual grunts, Hedda wrapped in the vice of Lunara's unyielding arms as they toppled to the ground amidst a blinding flash of light.

His Second was out cold by the time Brand made it to the spot.

"Forgive me," Lunara was murmuring, clearing wine-red strands of hair from Hedda's face.

It happened so quickly, mere feet from the edge.

Lunara looked up, a slight tremble in her lip. "It seemed a mercy to put her to sleep. I swear, it will only last as long as you wish it. Give the word and I wake her."

"That was…" Mag raked a hand through his hair, staring at Hedda's crumpled form. "Shite. You just saved her damned life, witchling."

Brand sucked air into his lungs—willing his body to obey and the red to seep from his vision, to resist the clawing desire to change—and unleashed it with a bellowed, "Fuck!"

Lunara was still stroking Hedda's forehead. "Something in her tonic wasn't right. I tried to say so." Her eyes scrunched closed. "I can feel whatever it is evading me while her body burns it away. Until then, there's no telling what her state will be."

"You think we should leave her like that?" Thad seemed so young voicing the question, so trusting.

"I believe it would be the safest thing for her, yes, but it's not my decision to make. Excuse me." Lunara stood and strode away, running a shaking hand over her face.

"How did all this happen without us knowing? Without us hearing it?" Magnus began to pace, his gait predatory, fixed on the depths stretching out beyond the cliff.

"I don't know."

"First Faldir, and now she's trying to say Hedda was drugged? Poisoned?" Mag threw his hands up. "A few hours ago I was waking him up and trading insults, and Hedda was grumbling at us to shut our fucking traps. None of this was here, she was fine. Shite, forget the rest of it. How can the land be overturned for nearly a mile and it didn't make a *sound?*"

Weariness hit Brand like a wave. "I don't fucking know."

"I assume we aren't really sending for help or waiting to go after him?"

Brand shook his head, relieved that he wouldn't have to fight his brother as well.

"And Hedda?"

"Leaving her like that feels so wrong, on so many levels." Brand let his head fall back. "But you heard Lunara. She knows more about this than the rest of us. Unless I can be assured of Hedda's state, this solves the problem—*poorly*—and we're wasting precious time debating it."

"How will we go down? Come back?" Thad asked. "N-no one returns once they go in."

Brand's found Lunara a few yards away, bent and examining the divots. "No one else was an Imperial Son, Blessed of Straelon," he said. "I'll make steps for us to descend and come back again."

"What of the shadows?" Mag asked. "They're not fucking right."

Lunara went preternaturally still at that. He wasn't even sure she was breathing… but she *was* listening.

He strode to the drop and knelt in the dirt, hyper-aware of her following his movements.

It was a gamble to test her, to see what she was thinking or if she would stop him again with a gaze that said she *knew* something.

One hand planted and gripping a tuft of long grass, he reached out, stretching for the writhing obsidian darkness.

"Wait."

He stopped shy of touching it—*them*—his satisfaction at the urgency in her tone curiously dim. Maybe because it only proved there was more to fear from the chasm than they'd realized.

"I…" There was that curl, tangled in her fingers again. "I can protect you from the shadows. I can shield you."

There was something monumental about that small admission. Her dazed expression would have been comical any other time, as if she couldn't quite believe she'd done it.

Oh, yes. He was starting to understand. What she was, what she might be capable of. There was no longer any doubt she'd been holding herself back. The real question was *why*.

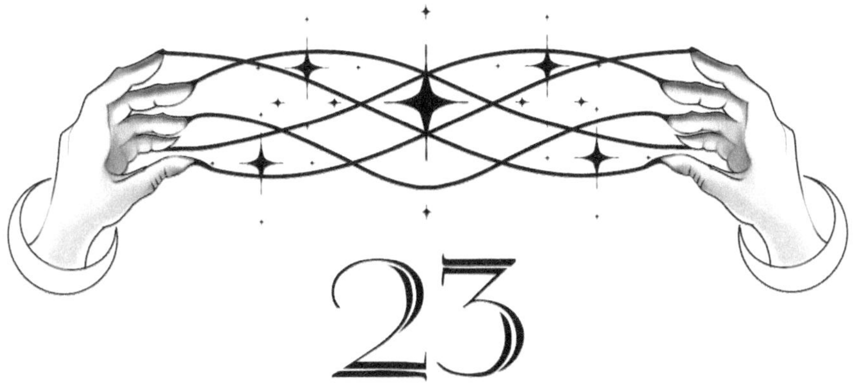

23

YOU ARE QUITE LITERALLY THE MOST EEJIT-BRAINED, HALFWITTED FOOL IN ALL of Bordoroth. This is the bleeding end of it, you know. All the plans… Poof! Fucking ash on the fucking wind.

Brand lifted a sardonic brow. "Care to explain?"

Lunara ignored that, which did not go unnoticed if the narrowing of his eyes was any indication. "I can shield *only* you." Her eyes darted to Mag and Thad. "Four is too many."

Oh well, if it's only two… Sure! He's probably rethinking every thought that's not at all obviously *whirring through his mind right now.*

The well was almost entirely full. With a decent blood gift to release her of the pain she'd gathered since last night, it wasn't too far-fetched to shield all of them.

But for how long? How far?

Exactly. It wasn't as safe with four. As certain. She had no idea how quickly it would drain her. And she was basing her claim on the burgeoning realization that whatever was coating the ground and writhing in the chasm was so close to her experience with Meliora that she might actually throw up.

Maybe it was forcibly taking away Hedda's autonomy that was making her nauseous. It went against everything she believed in, but what else could she have done?

Brand absolutely had to go, so there was no deterring him. One Son under her care was nightmare enough. Two and a half of them?

No. No way.

A low growl rumbled from Magnus's chest. "Now wait a fucking minute—"

"Done," Brand said, cutting off his brother's protest and holding her locked in his stare.

Magnus bent and hauled Brand upright, hissing into his ear. "Have you misplaced your feeble fucking mind? All of us was insanity. This is… There's not even a word for it! You don't *know* her."

It was unclear whether he thought she couldn't hear him, or if he really didn't give a shite.

"I know she threw herself in front of my Second and saved her from certain death." Brand shrugged him off and straightened his tunic. "I know she wept as she buried an entire village of your people last night, and it wasn't because of the cost to herself."

Even with the looming danger, she warmed at his defense. And when Magnus hung his head, nodding, it gave her courage.

"I think we can agree that Caius would probably die on the spot if he found out all of you went into a chasm, especially Thaddeus. Not to mention your own parents." She tamped down her shudder. The Imperial Sovereigns of Bordoroth would probably make her wish the Council had been the ones to find her if she let something happen to their children. "Someone needs to watch over Hedda and the Fae while I'm gone, and the two of you will be safer together. This is the least amount of risk."

"Weeping fuck," Mag breathed. "I suddenly understand Hedda much better."

There was an endless quiet between them—one they didn't have time for.

"Thaddeus, a moment?" For some reason, she couldn't bring herself to look at Brand. "I need to… get some things, if you'd be so kind as to accompany me back to the camp."

A lie, but she needed privacy.

Can't decide whether you're finally using your brain, or if it's gone and melted straight out of your arsehole.

She headed for the trees, Thaddeus's loping steps gaining until he was picking through the forest beside her, and it hit her that she might never see him again. Not if the chasm claimed them the way it had so many others.

"Thaddeus?"

He looked down at her, brow furrowed.

Lunara chewed her lip, remembering the way he'd sometimes stared into the fire at her cottage, sharing quiet secrets while his parents slept. She'd given him trite responses, not understanding the full scope of what he'd been feeling.

Now, words clawed up her throat—final words, perhaps, for a friend who needed to hear them.

"Knowing more of your family now... They're hard on you, like you always said, but you aren't exactly making it easy for them. Brand just tried to send his most trusted warrior away because of how she was behaving. What makes your actions any different?"

That had been clear to everyone except the Demon commander. Lunara didn't have any family left, but she knew well what the devastation of losing them felt like. She'd spent months in the same state. *Years.* Still wasn't over it.

At least in sleep, Hedda would be able to forget for a while.

"Aye," he whispered. "I can see the truth of that." His lips twisted. "I'm just tired of being left behind. They treat me like I'm still a child, but all of my cousins had many battles behind them by my age."

Thaddeus sighed and tilted his head back. His limbs were strong and packed with muscle, and he walked with a confident stride. He was younger-looking than Magnus—all soft blond curls teasing his cheeks and collar, and lacking the tattoos Wolflords earned after battle—but he was a male grown.

"I see it, Thaddeus, and I understand," she said, grabbing one of his large hands. "Perhaps if you respect Magnus while we're gone, prove you can handle any responsibility he gives you, they'll begin to see, too. An apology wouldn't hurt either. Promise me you'll behave?"

It was paltry in the scheme of things, but he might remember her words someday and be better for it. Safer.

"Where is this coming from?"

She couldn't look at him when she said, "If we don't come back—"

"Lunara..."

"I mean it, Thaddeus. Promise me you'll try to do better. Show your father, your cousins, that you're the male you claim to be. Do it for *yourself.*"

He stared at her for a long time before nodding. "Aye, I will," he said, squeezing her fingers. "I'd do anything that was asked of me. I just need someone to actually *ask*. I only wish to help."

They reached the small camp, the Fae glowing faintly where she lay on the far side, a soft mound of moss beneath her broken body.

"Blessed Sisters," Thaddeus breathed. "Magnus had only just gotten to the part about you finding someone alive when we reached the fields, but a Fae?"

Lunara detached herself from him and sat on her bedroll. "We found her like that in Glynmor. Magnus can tell you the rest. I haven't the heart or the time for it now, and there's a reason I asked you to come specifically."

Fool.

She summoned her empty flask from the ether. "I was wondering... Well, I figured you'd understand, and I don't know who else to ask. I'm not *supposed* to ask. But this is gone and—"

She'd only brought the one, thinking it would sit untouched while she gallivanted around Thodelebor for a few days. Her body was aching, torn between the humming energy of the well and the pain that healing caused.

For what they were about to do, she needed the security of a blood gift, even if it meant exposing her full power.

Thaddeus closed his hands around hers where they clenched the silver vessel. "Say no more."

He took it and used one fang to puncture his wrist, the crimson trail flowing until the flask was full to the brim. "Accept this gift, freely given," he said, intoning the words of their shared people as he handed it back.

Lunara moved to heal his wound, but he shooed her away. "*That* is for later. You already know I've never fed, but I'm well aware it's more potent this way." He offered her his still-bleeding arm. "Go on."

"I... haven't done that for a very long time," she admitted.

For good reason!

"Aye. You said that when da offered, too. He got you to take it, though, and that was the day you woke up Mam." Thaddeus waved his arm under her nose. "Once again, the life of my family is in your hands."

He was right. She knew he was right. That didn't stop the cold sweat from breaking over her brow.

"Swear to me… Swear you won't tell another soul what you're about to see."

There was a reason she only took direct gifts from Cordelia—Caius being the one exception in fifty-two years. Yet another thing that would give her away.

Thaddeus flashed a lazy grin. "You mean the way your eyes go swirly? Already seen it. Never said a word. Don't plan to."

Lunara blinked, stunned.

Tilting her chin up, he gave her head a little shake. "You have nothing to worry about. I wanted to know if it would be the same for me if I ever decided to feed, so Da and I talked about it once. That was it." He raised his arm again with a pointed look. "We both know what you are, but your life is your business. You might find that most of us feel the same."

Beyond the buzzing in her ears and the furious pound of her heart, there were too many thoughts for Lunara to process.

They'd known, and had said… nothing?

Maybe Brand would be willing to do the same.

Oh, no. No, no, no. Don't—

Too late.

If Lunara was going to her death, she'd be having as many wondrous ideas as she could.

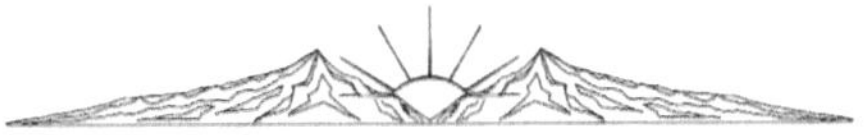

"I DON'T LIKE THIS ONE FUCKING BIT."

Brand had the insane urge to laugh. "No one in their right mind would like this."

Solyrian was climbing higher, its cheery rays at odds with his mood. Just like the chirping birds and swaying flowers made no sense. How was nature able to remain so oblivious?

"This is madness." Mag was pacing, hands knotted at his nape. "We don't even know if he's alive."

They both stared at Hedda, fast asleep in the grass and dirt beside them.

"He likely isn't," Brand admitted, dizzied by the prospect. "But we'd planned to find out what happened in Glynmor, and I would say this"—he gestured all around them—"is not a coincidence."

Already, Hedda might never forgive him. If he refused to try on top of keeping her away, he'd be losing both of them.

"Is one male really worth the risk?"

An age-old question, if ever there was one.

Brand did laugh then, not the least amused. "I don't know."

When it was someone beloved in danger, the answer was almost always yes.

When it meant taking Lunara into a place like that, sacrificing *her* life, he was suddenly much less sure.

Weeping arseholes.

His heart turned over, torn in too many different directions. That familiar, invisible fist came next, choking him, a weight settling on his chest.

Shite.

Mag's hand landed on his back, rubbing in large, steady circles. "That's it, slow your breaths. I know it's fucked, but where's this one coming from?"

Magnus had always been able to calm him, but it wasn't working this time.

"I…" He bent, fingers digging into his thighs as he fought a wave of prickling nausea.

"Brand?"

"I think…" He couldn't say the word—not even to himself. It would make it too real. Too terrible.

Maybe Mag would understand anyway.

"I think you were right." Weeping Sisters, was it only yesterday he'd punched his brother for teasing him about it? "You ask if it's worth it and all I can think is *no*. No, no, no, not in a million fucking years could losing *her* be worth it. And yet…"

"It's Faldir." Mag nodded, cheeks puffed out with his sigh.

"I"ll have to rage," Brand whispered.

"I thought that was a given. Has the witchling met the greater?"

Therein lied the problem. "No."

Revealing that side of him, swaggering and shameless, completely unfiltered…

Mag barked a laugh, damn him. "I'm sorry. This is all fucking dark, but that there is a bonnie bright spot."

Arsehole.

"I need you to prepare her." *So she doesn't hie off into the hills, never to be seen again.* "I don't think she's seen any of us that way."

"Aye, I'll handle it." There was a mischief in his brother's voice that worried Brand almost as much as raging in front of Lunara.

"Magnus—"

"Ach, and here she is, just in time."

Brand straightened and something in him eased at the sight of her. She was radiant, skin flushed and shimmering in the sunlight, her steps stronger than before as they made their way across the ravaged field.

She'd fed. And her gift had come from Thad.

He was instantly split in two, caught between a lance of white-hot jealousy and a swell of pride. Lesser and greater, completely at odds.

"A-are we ready," Lunara asked, not quite meeting his eyes.

The greater half was winning, pushing envy aside until only a single, consuming thought was left. If they headed towards their own doom…

"Leave us. Take Hedda back to the camp while you do."

Thad's head popped up. "What?"

Brand turned on his cousin and brother with a withering glare, rage already prickling over him. "I said, leave us. We need a moment before we go."

The smirk on Mag's face said he understood all too well. "Come on, pup," he said, lifting Hedda from the ground.

Brand didn't bother to watch them go. His eyes were glued to *her.*

"Are you sure about this?"

Lunara swallowed and glanced behind him, to the gaping maw of the chasm. "No. I'm not, but being sure is a luxury. Faldir is my friend, strange as that is. And I think he is much more than that to you." She met his gaze again. "Neither one of us would be able to live with it if we walked away."

She was perfection.

And Brand refused to go to his death without knowing what she felt like melting against him, what she tasted like, at least once.

He stepped up and sank a hand into her hair, his other snaking around her waist to pull her body flush with his. "We might never come back."

Tears pooled on her lashes. "I know," she finally said, palms searing when they cupped his face.

He pressed into the touch, into the relief of it. "Tell me to stop and I will."

Her words from the night before were imprinted on him, her desire for freedom and choice, so easy to give her in the end.

When she remained silent, thumb rasping against his beard, he said, "This isn't fucking over between us." Shite, he could hardly breathe. The thought of her dying… "No matter what happens—"

"No." A crease formed between her brows, sea-blue eyes darting between his. "It isn't." As soon as they dropped to his lips, it was over.

Brand surged into her, claiming her mouth with his own. He'd expected her to be soft and yielding, to sink lazily into the supple bliss of her.

He'd been wrong.

Lunara wrapped one arm around his shoulders and met him halfway, clinging as though her life depended on it. It was her tongue that darted out first, teasing, questioning. Her teeth that nipped at him and demanded entrance. She used his gasp to her advantage, dipping in to taste him, her nails digging into his jaw and tearing a rumbling, possessive snarl from him.

All of his lingering reservations evaporated. He was lost in a delirium, every whimper she loosed only adding to his desperation for her.

He palmed her generous arse and hiked her up higher, dragging her heat against the steely length of his cock. She tore away on a cry, head falling back and gifting him with the exposed column of her throat. Spine tingling, breaths sawing, he dragged his lips up its center, wanting nothing more than to lay her down in the grass.

But he couldn't.

Brand used his grip on Lunara's hair to press their foreheads together, running his nose along hers and already regretting every cursed fucking thing that was forcing him to stop. "We'll be finishing this." He pressed a final kiss to her lips and broke away, putting some distance between them. "Magnus!"

His brother and cousin emerged from the trees, faces blessedly blank.

"Go to Mag," he said to Lunara. "Stay by his side."

Brand turned on his heel and urged his feet forward, even though walking away from her had every part of his body screaming, begging him to whip around and never stop touching her again.

MAGNUS AND THADDEUS FLANKED LUNARA AS BRAND STRODE AWAY, leaving her dizzy.

Blessed moons, *that kiss.*

Never, in all her years, had she felt its like. Her lips were swollen, tingling, confused as to why they were no longer drinking him in.

She pressed a hand to her mouth, trying to remember how to breathe, how to be. Even her logical half had nothing to say, no words of *wisdom* to force her thoughts away from it.

Magnus rested a hand on her shoulder and gave her a squeeze. "It's a lot to take in, the first time you see a Demon rage. Fierce bastards, especially him," he said softly. "He's nervous about you seeing it. Shite, he's probably convinced himself that you're going to run screaming. Just be kind, witchling, and he'll see there's no need to be concerned."

Stunned, she nodded.

If he was warning her, there must be truth to the stories. Maybe the single time she'd seen Lyriat change hadn't been the full scope of what Demons were capable of.

Lunara couldn't be bothered to care.

Brand stopped about ten yards away and toed off his boots, tossed his tunic, and planted bare feet into the long grass.

Eyes closing, his nostrils flared as he pulled in harsh breaths. Warm light sprang up from beneath him, shining upwards, and she could actually *feel* the power flowing from the earth and into him.

Sweet Sisters…

Brand balled his hands into fists and grew before her eyes, his body tensed against its transformation.

A sunstar shape appeared on the center of his chest, and gently glowing sunlight whorls crawled up from the ground. They writhed across his body in symmetrical patterns, twining around his arms and legs, mimicking the twisting surface of Solyrian. Crept up either side of his neck, over high cheekbones, across his eyes, and into his auburn hair.

Muscles bulged and limbs lengthened as his skin took on a faint, muddy-red hue, his trousers shortening and stretching tight over massive thighs.

His head tilted in an eerie, jerking fashion as his horns started to thicken. They flared out and curled, wrapping down towards his ears, spiraling until violent points jutted forward, caging and protecting his skull. Another two sets sprouted from his forehead and temples, winding upwards and angling outwards, crowning him with a raw, primitive majesty.

He clenched his jaw and growled, lips peeling back as two razor-sharp fangs punched from the top line of his teeth to flank their perfectly straight brethren. Claws sprang from his fingertips, and he flexed them wide.

One hand shot out, and the light patterns seemed to concentrate there, blazing brighter. A broad, wicked blade came to life, forming in an instant as he gripped his fist around the hilt.

The greatsword he'd told her about.

He swung it over his head and behind him, where the blade fused itself to his bare spine, the horned handle and pommel protecting the back of his head. The weapon moved with him, as much a part of his body as any other appendage.

Brand locked eyes with her—the same beautiful, hazel eyes—before he arched his back and released a shattering roar to the sky, sending countless birds scattering into the air.

The light faded from his body and he snarled, hands at his sides and chest heaving as he finally settled.

Lunara's entire being trembled, completely drawn to him, her feet moving of their own accord.

There was a male any creature would hesitate to challenge. Even a mythical dreadbeast.

Shitting stars.

He was more than twice her height, but she was in awe. She knew him well enough already—knew the goodness in his heart and the sweetness of his mind—that fear never once occurred to her.

"Brand," she breathed, closing the final distance between them.

He dropped to one knee. Deep sienna markings stained his reddened skin everywhere the light had passed, and Lunara itched to reach up and run her fingers along the patterns to see if they'd left the sunstar's heat behind.

"Luna." His voice was a purr, so low and gravelly that she could actually feel it vibrating in her bones.

Wait.

She jolted. "Luna?"

"Hmm." Something like a chuckle rumbled from his chest. "Yes. Luna, the fierce little moon. Not frightened of me in the least."

Oh. That's… Oh.

Heart speeding up, she spared a glance back at Magnus, raising her voice just a little. "It'll take more than this to send me screaming."

Brand pressed his brow to hers, careful not to catch her with his horns. "Trust me"—his gaze flicked down to her lips before meeting hers again—"this will not be the form I take when I finally make you scream."

"Oh… my…" Lunara blinked rapidly.

"Aye, about that." Magnus cleared his throat. "Did I forget to mention that he goes a bit feral like this? Now you know. Sisters be with you."

Brand slapped a hand to the ground with a growl, magic snaking out. The earth lurched in a wave and slammed into Magnus, sending him flying for a few feet before he crashed down.

Lunara's smirk was wicked, even as her thoughts tangled.

Maybe… if Brand could be trusted…

Maybe even the Council would hesitate.

"Alright," Magnus grumbled as he stood and brushed himself off. "Go ahead and get it in while you can. I'll be waiting when you shrink back, you wee shite."

Brand huffed and rose to his full height. "May I pick you up, little moon? I would keep you safe, but the choice is yours."

He… remembers?

Sisters above. All the madness around them, the threat to their lives, and all she could think was that she wanted to keep him.

Dangerous. So dangerous.

When she nodded, he bent and scooped her into his arms with a hum of satisfaction, adjusting her until she was settled in the crook of one elbow.

"Hedda will not wake up without me willing it," she said. "A good thing, for now, but… if the worst should happen, find Cordelia the Firebane. She'll know what to do."

Magnus's hands balled into fists. "Come back, and I won't have to." His voice was tight, a shade of itself. "Please. Be careful."

Brand stared at his brother for a long moment before walking them to the edge of the chasm. He stopped just shy of the drop and reached out. A flat section of earth rumbled forth, then another, and another, forming a series of platform steps along the cliffside until they disappeared into the darkness.

He hooked a finger under her chin and tilted her face up to him, eyes boring into hers. "Ready?"

The way he looked at her, almost worshipful. It was… everything, she realized.

Everything the Council had stolen from her all those years ago when they'd chosen a monster over her parents. Power, over the safety of Nachthelliae. All of the potential in that look—the unspoken promises, the glimpse of a future—just out of her reach.

Because of them.

Lunara stole a precious, fleeting moment to memorize the perfection and pretend she could have it forever—and then she tucked it away, knowing it could never be anything more than a dream.

Especially if the Veil awaited them. Their end.

"I'm ready."

She laid her hands to his bare chest and a kaleidoscope of radiant light flowed, spreading out and over their bodies. The shadows closest to them cringed away from the shield, recoiling and hiss—

A faraway scream echoed up from the deep.

Male. Pained.

Proof.

Terror threatened to choke her, everything more real, more urgent, but she ignored it.

Faldir needed them. Now.

"Go, Brand."

One step down, another, and they were plunging into the abyss.

24

Sweat trickled down Brand's back, every droplet his only way of marking the hours they'd been descending.

There was no end in sight to the oppressive fog. It stretched infinitely behind and before them, sometimes thickening into opaque arms to test the barrier, and he had to stop himself from snarling whenever it dared a searching touch.

Like now.

Another black tendril bumped against the shield, Luna twitching like she could feel it, and Brand had enough.

"This is a good time for you to clarify some things," he said, voice crackling with disuse. "You can start with telling me what this is around us and why you seem to know it so well."

At first, he'd been glad for the silence. Each step closer to whatever dangers prowled below had tested his resolve. He'd needed the quiet to convince himself that bringing her wasn't the biggest mistake he'd ever bloody made.

She sat up a little straighter, biting her lip. "I was afraid you might say that."

Her honesty tugged at him, softening the sharper edges of his curiosity. "You have nothing to fear from me, Luna. Nothing at all."

Internally, his lesser self had railed at the use of that name, embarrassed he'd admitted to their thoughts about the little moon and her scent of blessed light.

Such a fool sometimes. The beatific look on her face when he'd explained, the shine in her eyes…

Obviously worth it.

Besides, pretense was impossible when he raged. He had no care for falsities and roundabout wording when the efficiency of raw truth was right there for the taking.

"Many have promised the same," Luna murmured. "Most turned out to be liars."

He bristled at that. "I am not most, and I will ensure the others suffer for their duplicity."

Whoever they were, whoever had damaged her so thoroughly, he would find them. Crush them. Raze their homes to the ground while they were still inside, begging for—

A scream filtered through the bleak density. The first in a long while and *much* further off than the last, and he felt another little chip of hope fall away. He'd spent the hours torn between wisdom and barreling down the steps. Between slow and wary to keep themselves safe, or getting to Faldir as quickly as possible.

It was starting to feel like a fool's errand.

"Please, Brand." Luna's tone was a quaking strangle. "Put me down."

He obeyed, helpless in this form to do anything but exactly as she wished.

The soft, lustrous light of the shield followed her across the platform, highlighting the quiet horror twisting her features. She stepped up to the cliffside, mere inches from the strange, dark liquid seeping from the stone, and he had to beat down the urge to wrench her away.

That same substance had been splattered on the ground above, mixed with Faldir's blood.

It didn't matter that her barrier kept everything at bay. There was a *wrongness* to it, even beyond its stench, and he didn't want it anywhere fucking near her.

"I've seen this before," she whispered, her fingers following the oozing filth as it crept down the rock to pool on his steps.

Her brows pinched down for a moment before she moved to the edge of the landing, her head tilting. Once again, a writhing wisp condensed and tried to get inside, and Luna followed its motions with a single finger, as if to play with the thing. She froze like that—head to one side, elegant hand in the air, and eyes fixed a million miles inward.

Until she said, "Meliora."

The single word was a ghost upon her lips, and it raised the hairs on the back of his neck.

He thought back over their conversation before Glynmor, when she'd described his aunt's illness. "Go on."

"When she bled…" She blinked and pointed to the wall, to the ooze. "It looked like that. Not fresh and crimson, but rotting black."

Brand leaned in to get a better look for himself, and the pieces started falling into place. "The shadows around us, are they like the stains you described beneath her skin?"

Her sigh carried the weight of all the realms. "Yes."

She started pacing, running a loose curl back and forth over her lips.

Sisters, those lips… *No.*

Breathing deep, Brand stifled the volatile reactions of this body. It was not the time, nor the place, for lustful thoughts.

"Everything about her infection, the stains…" Half muttering, Luna gestured outside the shield. "These move the same way. Reaching and wanting, seemingly harmless but… insidious." She scrubbed both hands over her face, squishing her cheeks. "Caius and I experimented with samples. He urged me to use my power in different ways, to see if I could repel it. Control it. Destroy it. Anything. The results made me rethink Meliora's treatment. That… that was how I woke her up."

"Explain."

She hesitated, her dread so apparent he could practically taste it.

Oh, yes. Whoever had hurt her would suffer *greatly*.

"No fear," he reminded her. "Not with me."

Luna's lip trembled as she turned to the barrier at last, her power multiplying to hum against his skin. With a wave of her fingers, a wall of diffuse light formed and shot into the center of the chasm, clearing the shadows away for a moment. A clench of her fist, and it disappeared, darkness sweeping back in to fill the void.

"I pushed them back, stopped them from feeding," she said, avoiding his gaze. "I couldn't remove them though, no matter how hard I tried.

They recoiled from my power, obviously affected, but I couldn't seem to get a hold of them."

"How did you remove samples from my aunt, then?"

She shook her head. "I promise, that is one answer you don't want." The look on her face told him enough. "But if the chasms had something to do with Meliora, we… we need to be careful."

Another scream, so far off he almost didn't catch it.

"I think it's time we hurry this along, hmm?" Brand bent and engulfed her shoulders with his hands, pretending calm. "I'm going to pick you up again. I would have this over with."

Wary be damned.

"Yes. As would I."

An idea came to him as he gathered her up and tucked her safely against his side—*away* from the chasm wall and its foul, crawling decay. "Do you trust me?"

Luna was already looking up at him, eyes narrowed. "Will I regret it if I say yes?"

He might have chuckled if they were anywhere else. If his friend wasn't crying his agony for all the realms to hear. "Can you keep the shadows away for longer periods and distances than you showed me?"

There was a flicker of something he couldn't identify before she replied, "I can."

Nodding, he lifted her to eye level and pointed down into the gloom. "Follow the angle of the steps I've already called, as far as you're able."

With a deep breath, she pushed her hands down and out. The shield shot forward about five hundred yards through the gloom, her power once more slamming into him and illuminating well past what he'd expected. Strange, to see such a large swath of the cliffside at once, as if it was never meant to be viewed that way.

Brand summoned a large landing right inside the edge of the barrier. Quite a distance, but he could make it.

"Can you hold that while we move?"

His eyes were glued to the side of her face, so he didn't miss it when that strange look passed over her features again. "Yes."

"Tell me," he said at her ear, swallowing the urge to bury his face in her hair. "How do you feel about flying?"

She whipped her head around. "What are you planning?"

"Hmm." Careful of his horns, he ran his nose along hers. "That might be an answer you don't want."

"Not funny," she breathed.

Her nails sank into the flesh of his arm, apprehension in every biting crescent, when he shifted to the edge and dropped into a crouch.

"Brand…"

"If death awaits, I would have a moment of joy before the Veil takes me." A moment of weightless freedom with *her*. "Trust me," he whispered.

With that, he launched into the air.

To her credit, she didn't scream. The shield stretched and bent with them, following their trajectory through the gloom as they plummeted. Brand braced for the impact and they landed with a booming thud, his knees bending to absorb their momentum.

Luna's hair was a wild, wind-blown nest. Half of it had flung forward, covering her face and body. The rest clung to him in snaking waves, and he used a finger to detach one, thick lock that had tangled in his horns.

"That was…" She sat forward to push the mass away, a wide-eyed look of wonder brightening her face.

"We like flying then?"

A thread of something wrapped around his heart, his lungs. Nervousness. Not his own, but *hers*.

It was a heady sensation, blood hammering through his veins. Brand barely stopped himself from rubbing at his chest. From giving up the small clue. She would run, if she knew. Hide. He could feel that as surely as her trepidation.

Her voice was tentative when she said, "I like flying *with you.*"

The thread snapped and melted away with her words, edginess gone, leaving him alone with only his own feelings for company.

Damn it.

He was a fool for dwelling on it anyway when his mind should be focused on rescuing his friend. Scouring his senses, he searched for any indication of new threats, beyond the darkness already—

Not a scream, but a garbled cry that time. All the more horrifying for its desperation. It's distance.

"I'm scared, Brand."

Her whispered confession cracked right through him. "I know, little moon."

If only he could reassure her that there was nothing to worry about.

Luna gathered her hair, deftly twining the mass on top of her head and summoning a stick to hold it there. "Then I would have some joy before the Veil, too."

Who was he to deny her?

She forced the shield out again and they were soaring. His spirit nearly left his body when she leaned forward and spread her arms wide, eyes closed and chin lifted to the wind as it whipped by them.

She was breathtaking. Wild.

The risk, the danger… Worth it, perhaps, to glimpse that side of her. Of who she might really be, free, without her secrets and pain. Burning Solyrian, maybe it was all worth it.

Another thunderous landing, the shield stretching towards a new step —they went on like that, over and over as they ventured ever deeper, the onyx fog lightening to a dense, smoky grey the further they fell into the bowels of the Dread Chasm.

Until, at last, rocky ground was revealed below.

Brand called a large platform from the chasm wall just in case, and leapt for the last time.

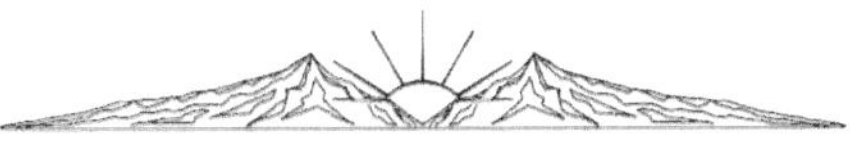

Dust and dirt sprayed when they hit, pebbles raining down to clatter against the shield wall as the swirling cloud settled.

"We made it." Luna's words were more question than statement.

Brand could hardly believe it himself.

She wiggled to get down, but he put a finger to his lips and stuck a foot out to test the safety of the chasm floor—alert, tuned in to every shift in the air, the tiniest of sounds.

"There's nothing here," she whispered. "You can put me down."

He couldn't feel anything waiting to jump out at them, but still. "I'd rather carry you."

"Not on your life, Demon," she snapped under her breath, fierce determination pinched across her brow. "I'm frightened, yes. But if we make it out of this, I want to be able to say I've touched the floor of a Dread Chasm and lived to tell the tale. Try and stop me."

Her words from the night before echoed. *I value my freedom above all else.*

"Fine," he grumbled, setting her down and fighting the urge to claw her right back into his arms.

It was *not* fine, but what else could he do?

Without a thought, she stepped off the landing and onto the chasm floor, and—for the first, utterly confusing time in his greater form—Brand had to bite back a shout of alarm caused by *fear*.

Something he'd never felt while raging, *Ever.*

He chased her into the grey, hissing, "You must stay close to me. We can't see a damned thing, and danger could be lurking anywhere."

She tossed an irritated look over her shoulder. "*You* have no way of knowing. I, however, am completely certain there's nothing *lurking* nearby."

"Explain."

"Demon Brand is bossy and likes the word *explain.* Got it." She tilted her head as if listening. "There isn't a heartbeat, nothing living, for at least… a mile, give or take? It's hard to know how far my threads are reaching with nothing to compare them to, but that's a safe estimate."

The corners of his mouth turned down, suitably impressed. "I don't suppose you could clear some of this up then, so I can see as well?"

Her expression was same one she'd made when he asked her to stretch the shield, and then again after he'd asked if she could hold it.

It clicked into place after she put some distance between them and faced him again.

Resignation.

"Luna—"

The air fluttered around him, grabbing at the waves of his hair.

She grimaced and brought clawed hands up in front of her. Sparks gathered in her palms, the shadows darkening at the same time—as if she was sucking the light from them, what little they had to offer now hers to command.

Weeping Sisters, the breeze was her.

Pricks of light turned to starry orbs, swirling and spinning at the center of the vortex she was creating. It cast her in an eerie, ethereal glow, highlighting the flashing speckles in her skin and shorter strands of hair whipping around her face.

Brand braced himself as the wind picked up, the sheer magnitude of her power slamming into him.

Forget her serenity as they'd flown down, step-by-step. This was seeing her for the first time—the *real* her—and it hit like a punch to the gut. What he'd sensed before was a pale imitation of her true ability. Nothing in comparison.

This, he'd only felt within his own family. From other *Imperials.*

She was commanding the very fabric of the world, bending it to her wishes, and it was… immense. Beautiful. Enough to bring him to his knees, though he fought the impulse.

Barely.

He held his breath when she froze, the entire universe stilling around them.

She flung her arms out and power surged away from her, the violent gale ripping through the shadows and fog until they were nothing. Infinite stars followed the currents, spreading up and out, hanging in the air and illuminating the empty floor of the chasm in every direction.

"As I said, nothing to see."

There was no missing the forced lightness in her tone, the breathy huff that wasn't doing anything to cover her trembling hands and refusal to meet his eyes.

"Hmm. From where I'm standing, there's plenty to see."

Ah, now she looked at him, gaze wild. "Such as?"

Lucky for him, she wasn't used to this form. Didn't expect him to rise to her challenge.

"The mystery gets old. You have enough power to level me. I know it, you know it. Can we please stop the act and move on?"

She was worthy, his true equal, and pride overflowed with every word.

Luna blinked. "I have no idea what you mean."

He buried his laugh, not so awestruck that he'd forgotten their shite surroundings. "Lies do not become you, little moon. Nor does false modesty or diminishing yourself to go unnoticed. Do you not tire of the charade? I'm exhausted just thinking about it."

She gaped. "I'm not… I don't…"

Brand narrowed his gaze down at her, daring her to finish any one of the ridiculous sentences she was concocting.

She finally settled on, "We don't have time for this."

"Hiding behind an undeniable truth? Clever."

Even if it did get under his skin, just a little, that she refused to trust him. That they might die, and he'd spend his last hours wondering, never knowing her truths or the future he wanted to give her. *Even then…* she was still bloody clever. He'd give her that.

Scanning the ground, he looked for anything that would tell them which direction to go, one ear waiting for the next shout or cry or bellow. Any sound at all.

Maybe ten yards off was a jagged disturbance in the otherwise smooth landscape. "Come."

"That… that's it?" She was breathless, her words asking far deeper questions than it seemed, practically running to keep up with his long strides.

He tempered his speed, agonizing though it was. "Faldir needs our help more than I need my answers. I'll get them soon enough."

Sweet and merciful Sisters, let him be alive enough to help.

They came upon the lengthy divot, just like the ones above, blood dotting the dust around it.

"This is the way. Still not feeling any life?"

She was clearly at a loss, staring at him for a long moment while she chewed her lip. "No," she whispered. "Nothing."

And it had been the longest span of time since the last they'd heard Fal, the silence weighing heavier because of it.

"Then he is either dead, or too far away."

Her head jerked back. "You say it so matter of factly."

"It *is* a matter of fact." Despite the hollow ache it opened in his chest. "Will you let me carry you, now? I can move much faster than you can."

"Who *are* you?" she rasped, leaning forward as if it would help her understand.

"I am as I have ever been, without the faults of my lesser self. *May I please pick you up?"*

Her lip curled, but it was not a pleasant expression. "Lesser? Hmm. So I'm not the only one who *diminishes* myself."

His brows rose. She was wrong, but he liked that fire in her. Very much.

"It's not diminishing if it's the truth. Interesting, though, for you to automatically assume I mean *inferior* when I say lesser, instead of the intended meaning—which is that I am, quite literally, smaller outside of this form."

Brand knelt and stretched his arms out, waiting for her to come to him.

Instead, she backed away.

That unfamiliar fear spiked again, stealing a little control. "Please. Don't fix so desperately on trying to hide, on being defensive, that you abandon reason."

Wrong thing to say.

She began weaving her fingers, lips a thin line. "You wish to move more quickly? Find him with haste? Fine."

Sisters save him. They were in a bloody fucking Dread Chasm, and she was *still* choosing stubbornness over sense.

"Luna..."

A writhing orb appeared between her palms, wings of light springing from the mass. She lifted a hand as the silhouette of an owl took shape, the ghostly bird circling once above their heads before coming to rest on her outstretched arm.

He was transfixed, marveling at the spectral creature, each feather wrought from the ether in stunning detail.

She brought it close and whispered to it, the owl bumping affectionately against her cheek before it took flight again and shot away—a glowing blur amidst the damp gloom.

It was the white-hot ring of glowing blue around one of her irises that was perhaps the most surprising. "I see what he sees. I'll let you know whether he finds anything worth increasing our speed for. Then, you can pick me up."

With that, she left him behind and stomped after the faint dot flying off into the distance.

Contrary female.

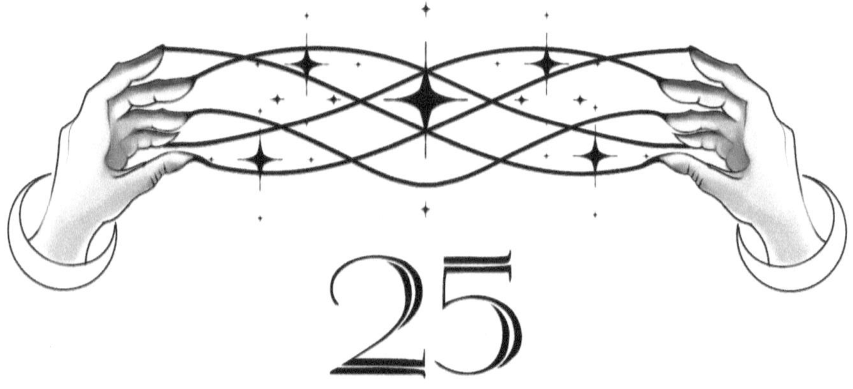

25

For the dozenth time, Lunara met Axanderus at the edge of the shield, cleaning his feathers as he waited for her to clear the shadows.

It was disorienting every time he blinked round eyes at her and she saw herself from his angle. Pale. Fuming. Looking as harried as she felt.

Even worse to see Brand calmly striding up behind her with long, slow steps. He'd stayed on her heels as they'd traveled, never letting her get too far ahead of him, no matter how quickly she forced her feet to move.

What could he mean by 'lies do not become you?' Lies keep you safe. It's not a bleeding act, it's survival!

She hardly recognized Brand in his *greater* form, never expected his frank honesty. The bald statements that left her naked and exposed.

How dare he be so direct? High-handed, overbearing... Ugh! He thinks he's better than you, pointing out your secrets like it's nothing.

Lunara was a hypocrite, but she didn't care. She burned to know what he was thinking. What he planned to do with the information. Wanted answers, though she was unwilling to give them.

Is he going to tell Araxis? The Elders? Bare your deception to the world?

It was all assumption on his part, but his taunting conjectures had been right on the nose.

Just like Lyriat.

Damn him.

She bent and ran a hand down Ax's back, her only true companion all these years. The voices didn't count. And it didn't matter that he was a figment of her imagination brought to life. He was loyal—and he couldn't bleeding speak unless she willed it.

He also can't judge, taunt, abandon, or betray you.

Indeed, he couldn't even fly too far away from her without disappearing, else she'd have used him to scout the chasm and avoided this entire fucking *mess.*

"Are you well?" Brand's low voice rumbled through the air, breaking the dense silence.

She wove her magic again, absorbing and condensing the tiniest slivers of light that the shadows carried before shoving everything away. Another chunk of the chasm revealed, as far as her eyes could see.

Another hour of walking while ignoring the gnawing in her gut, before she did it again.

"Luna."

"I'm fine, Brand."

With her split vision, half of the world whirred by her, a blur of dark and dust and nothing.

Her other eye focused on the dirt a few feet ahead, welling. A weight settled over her, and she was suddenly so very sad.

What in the realms?

"Why have we never seen your pet?"

"*He* is not my pet, he's my friend. And I only bring him out when it's absolutely necessary."

"Explain?"

Him and that word. A two-syllable reminder of the thing she most feared doing. At least he'd asked this time, instead of demanded.

A few minutes ago, she might have fought him—just to be keep the boundary between them as armor—but the strange shroud of melancholy was stealing her energy.

"He scouts the forest to help me find herbs and mushrooms, and avoid its dangers. Not much opportunity for that in the Montrealm, ergo..."

Brand sidled up to her. "A shame. He is stunning, little moon."

"Yes, he is."

Damn it all, but she liked that endearment *too much.* Its use made her feel shy and warm, like melting.

Don't even think about it. He's too close as it is.

Silence again as they walked and walked, the time distorted. Had it been hours since they'd started? Days? It was impossible to tell, the fog and shadows like a constant drone, every mile revealed looking exactly the same as the stretch before it.

Except for the imprints they followed.

Far ahead, Axanderus encountered another dragging tear through the dusty ground with more of Faldir's blood beside it, glinting in the hovering orbs of moonlight.

A twist of disquiet tightened her stomach. The droplets were becoming less and less, spaced further apart, while more and more she worried their quest was in vain, and they'd never find him alive. It had been a dreadfully long time since they'd heard him. Not since somewhere on the steps, in fact.

She said as much, struggling to utter the words out loud.

"It is what it is." His whisper could hardly be called such. Not with the way his voice tumbled down, vibrating in her bones. "Regardless of whether he's left for the Veil or not, this isn't a waste of our efforts. Something is down here, and must be stopped for Bordoroth to be safe."

Lunara would never admit it to him, but he'd been right—she was so used to running, hiding, that she let it cloud her judgement. Had stropped off to keep him at arm's length, instead of remembering they were walking through a stars-damned *Dread Chasm*.

Shite.

Realization hit like a comet, a belated wave of cold terror breaking over her skin, goosebumps in its wake.

How was he so calm? Why had he listened to her? Let her—

"Don't let the worry overcome you, Luna. We're here. We can't change what came before it."

Lunara stumbled, heart pounding. "How did you—"

Ax's cry was a distant, scarcely perceptible sound. What he showed her through their shared sight, though… "Sisters save us."

She took off, Brand's frustrated growl following behind her. He easily caught up, barely loping as she sprinted, but—to his credit—he didn't try to scoop her up and stop her.

"Is it him?"

"No," she gasped. "It's…"

The body came into view, rendering the rest of her words unnecessary.

"Burning fucking Solyrian."

Brand did reach down then, his hand on her front stopping her from getting any closer.

A male hovered above the ground just outside of her shield like a sagging puppet, her light bathing his wasted body. Steady streams of black shadow fell from the fog above and funneled into his gaping mouth, limbs dangling behind his bowed torso.

"What…" Lunara took a step back, bumping into Brand's leg.

He loosed a snarl. "*Now* may I carry you?"

She suddenly wanted nothing more than to be in the relative safety of his arms. "I have to clear the shadows first. Then, *yes.*"

"Shadows only, Luna. Keep the shield tight to us."

She nodded and forced her lungs to take in air, her feet to move and plant themselves down. Another wall, then, like the one on the steps, to hold the darkness at bay.

Power rose up and bubbled over, draining another few drops from the well as she pushed it out, revealing—

"No!"

Once again she was moving before her mind could warn her against it.

"Luna!"

Bodies. Bodies *everywhere.*

Hundreds. Thousands. On and on and on until they disappeared behind darkness and the welling of her tears.

Her hands landed on tiny shoulders, skimming over sage skin and tangling in twisted, ivory braids as she begged the Sisters to help her. A child—*a child*—hanging, eyes closed as if sleeping, drinking from the shadows just like the rest of them.

"Luna, please!"

Brand's voice cut through her panic, the desperation in it demanding her attention.

She glanced back—only to find him swinging his greatsword and uselessly hacking at the barrier she'd left between them.

If Lunara had paused, even for a second, she would have felt the death. Would have noticed that there were no heartbeats, no breath, no hope. That the air was different.

Fucking moons, *she'd run right through her shield.*

The Fae twitched beneath her palms and she whipped around.

Once-closed eyes snapped open, glowing like burning embers and staring directly at her.

Lunara startled away, but only managed a single, shocked step backwards.

The child jerked, revealing fangs that dripped with black as a vein of fire left her mouth, flowing up through the funnel of shadow and into the dark fog, spreading outwards.

The tendril of flame shot down into the next closest cadaver and brought it to life.

Then the next.

And the next.

More and more, until countless fiery gazes were turned in her direction.

Lunara spun and reached for the shield, pulling it to herself.

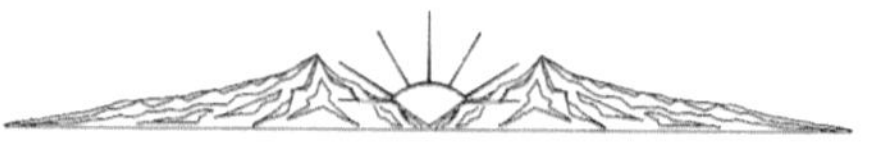

Brand hacked again and again, trying to cut through the shield.

When she'd passed through, the scent of misery had wafted by and torn his focus from the first body. Next he knew, Luna's wall of power was snapping closed, dividing them, before he could stop her.

"Bloody rash fool," he growled.

He couldn't allow his mind to dwell on what they'd found, the sheer amount of dead. All he could do was get to her and get them both the fuck out of there.

"Luna, please!"

She finally snapped out of her frenzy and noticed what she'd done, and he slumped with relief.

He was the fool.

For the rest of his life, Brand wouldn't be able to say whether time had slowed to nothing so he could absorb every horrific detail, or if it had sped by so quickly that he couldn't even blink before his dreams disintegrated to nothing.

The bodies awoke around her, their crimson power spreading.

That's when he saw *it*.

A Forgotten.

Its gangling body was like the branches and bark of the white, bony trees in the Ghostwood, and nearly as tall. Eyes like burning holes flared amidst the swirling smoke rising from its jagged skull and shoulders. Razor sharp claws nearly as long as its arms hung from gnarled fingers, and multi-jointed legs ended in taloned feet that would tear through the earth beneath as it walked.

The bizarre, woody flesh that was pulled too tight across the rest of its features had been completely ripped away from its mouth, leaving festering, black blood to seep from the permanently open wounds and exposed rows of needlepoint teeth.

It tore its head away from the dark fog above like it was breathing for the first time, and he realized…

These lost souls were being transformed. *Made* into Forgotten.

They'd always thought the monsters sprang from the Ghostwood along the chasm border of the Forgotten Lands, appearing from among the trunks. Slow as they wandered their dense, lifeless forest like vacant specters, almost unthreatening.

A clever deception.

When one decided it was hungry enough, it leapt across the chasm in a lightning-swift blur and whipped across the land searching for any living flesh to shred and devour. Thodeleborian legend claimed them as the reason for the Wolflords' ability to shift—a gift from the Sisters, that they could be just as monstrous as the creature hunting their lands and livestock, their people.

Except, instead of being in the Ghostwood, there was an entire army of them growing in a Dread Chasm—enough to easily overrun the Westrealm.

It only took one to end his own life.

Luna spun, wholly unaware of what loomed behind as she dragged the shield towards her.

Brand was screaming, begging, the sound far away as he beat and clawed and pushed against the barrier.

Inches away. He'd been only *inches away* when its claws were suddenly buried in her back, straight through her abdomen, her blood staining and dripping from their ivory lengths.

She didn't make a sound. Didn't cry out, didn't gasp. Just turned sea-blue eyes on him, her brows scrunching, confused, before she ran shaking fingers over the spikes jutting from her.

The second the shield engulfed her and the Forgotten, a roar tore past his lips and he was jumping, greatsword singing through the air.

Brand didn't give a fuck when its head tumbled to the ground. Didn't pay attention to the bodies crowding in around him. He landed and was with her in an instant, catching Luna before she could crumple.

"It's okay, you're okay."

He held the Forgotten's limp arm as it fell, keeping it still as he knelt and gathered her to himself. A red mist flew past her lips when she coughed, landing on his skin, and he wanted to burn the entire fucking world down.

A cluster of fledgling Forgotten had been trapped inside the shield, swarming him like gnats, little more than a nuisance at his size. Still, when claws slashed across his thigh, he swung blindly, shrieks in the wake of his sword's edge. More piled against the outside of the barrier, scraping their nails down its sides, groaning as they tried to get in.

Ignoring them, Brand turned Luna and pulled the long spikes from her back, pressing his hand to the gush of red as each one left her.

"B—Br—" Her lids slipped closed even as her lips tried to work.

"Shh. I've got you. You're going to be fine."

It was easy to lie if it comforted her.

Mag's question echoed—*Is one male really worth the risk?*—and Brand finally had his answer.

No. Sisters forgive him, but *no*.

He was on his feet without another thought, running back the way they'd—

The shield stuttered, blinking in bursts before glowing around them again.

"Luna?" Weeping Sisters, he wanted to shake her. "Stay with me. Stay. Please."

The shield winked out—and didn't come back.

"Fuck. Fuck!"

Dust skittered as his legs ate the distance, the ground rumbling. Without her power to stop them, the Forgotten were gaining, even half-formed as they were. And the shadows were slinking down from above, snapping out to test the air, like they were unsure whether it was safe for them yet.

Any minute, they would realize and come for them.

"Heal yourself, damn you." His breaths sawed as his eyes landed on the last step he'd made, so close and yet so fucking far away. "Use some of that ridiculous power and do something."

Brand called to the rock and the earth, tearing down huge swaths of the chasm walls behind him, screeches echoing in the near distance before they were buried.

A sting in his chest, and he looked down to find Luna staring back, nails digging into him.

"C-c-can't." Sweat soaked the hair at her scalp, her lips void of all color.

"You can. You can!"

He hugged her tighter and searched for their nascent bond, desperate to use what he fucking *knew* was there. Brand would give her his own willpower, his strength. Anything.

The shield formed around them, tight to their bodies but so dreadfully dim.

"Yes, that's it. You're fine. It's fine."

His feet hit the landing and he leapt, launching into the dark and commanding a new one to form. And another. Up and up, until he reached the stairs from before and made himself climb faster than he ever had before.

"Need... b-bl-ood." Each word was its own crushing burden, Luna gasping between syllables.

He knew that. Had wanted to make it to the surface, to safety, but there wasn't time.

Brand spun and slammed his fist into the cliffside, picturing a cave tall and wide enough to fit him comfortably, a raised platform for her to rest upon.

Power flowed out of him and pebble-sized sections of rock compressed and collapsed in a blur. Indents grew into holes, and the holes spread wider and wider until they ran into each other, forming a small opening. He pushed into the space and sealed the wall behind as a small cavern erupted around them.

With a thought, he commanded some of the stone to glow, imbuing the cave with a soft light that was entirely at odds with the situation.

"Almost there. Hold on."

He rushed to the back when the stone bed appeared, setting her down as gently as he was able.

Glassy eyes stared back at him, almost black as blown pupils swallowed the normally vibrant blue of her irises—until she spasmed and they rolled back into her skull.

Terror seized him. "Don't you fucking dare!" he shouted, his colossal hand grotesque against her pale shoulder as he jostled her. "Don't do this, little moon. Don't do this to me."

With no idea of what else to do, Brand bit down, tore a gash in his wrist, and grabbed her face. He held his bleeding arm over her open mouth and watched his blood trickled into her, stray droplets hitting her lips and chin.

When absolutely nothing happened, he roared to the cave ceiling, slumping over her limp and lifeless form when there was no breath left in him. "I swear to the stars, Luna," he croaked, "I will follow you into the Veil myself if you don't come back to me right now."

He pushed her hair away from her face and begged the Sisters to help him.

That was when the anger came. The blinding, consuming fury at the sheer injustice of it.

"What the fuck were you doing? When will you learn to bloody well stop and think?"

The last word echoed. *Think, think, think.*

"Fuck." He pried her mouth open to expose her fangs, shoving their razored points down into the meat of his hand. "It's a gift, damn you. Freely given. *Take it.*"

He massaged her throat, coaxing her to swallow, to force it down—ignoring how still her chest was, how sickeningly fucking silent she was.

It had to work. It *had* to.

A tear dropped from his lashes and landed on her face, sliding down to disappear into her hair. "You stubborn fool. All I wanted was for you to care as much for yourself as you do for the rest of the fucking world." He kissed her brow. "Please." Her cheeks. "I never even had the chance to tell you—"

On a shrieking gasp, she jolted upright, narrowly avoiding his curling horns. Brand rolled back to give her room, leaning as she scrambled up. He couldn't help his laugh. The burn in his hand, the way her fangs had sliced away, was the most wonderful pain in all of Bordoroth.

Her shoulders heaved as she stood there, facing away, the sound of her heavy breaths filling the silence. It was music. It was *everything*.

Brand sat up, planting his feet on the floor, and laid a hand on her back. "Luna?"

She whipped around to face him, hissing, her sharp, white fangs longer than before and flashing in the dim lighting. Drops of his blood dripped from her chin to land on her chest, blending with the mess that was already there. But, beneath the shredded forest linen of her dress, he watched her flesh pulling and knitting. The holes sealing themselves back together, as if they'd never happened.

Somehow, he could hardly be bothered to notice.

Brand was too stunned by the fact that the whole of her eyes had changed into a swirling vortex of silver and white. That every inch of her exposed skin was glowing. Humming.

Luna stilled when she saw him, tilting her head like a curious animal. Her gaze roamed over him, hooded and heavy, until she licked one fang and groaned, a look of ecstasy sweeping over her features.

Lids lifting slowly, she stared straight into his eyes and rasped, *"Mate."*

26

A bolt of lightning shot down Brand's spine and something within him was unleashed.

Mate.

It didn't matter that he'd already suspected. *Known*. It was a shock to hear that boldly-spoken word on her lips—an immediate claiming of his soul.

Like a flash, Luna hopped up onto the platform to stand between his spread legs. She gripped the sharp ends of his curling horns and jerked his head down to hers, her strength astonishing.

Brand leaned into the contact when she nuzzled his cheek with her own and sighed, the relief overwhelming.

"Does my mate have a gift for me?"

She was alive. She was well. She was *his.*

"Anything," Brand rasped.

He'd nearly lost her, before they'd even had a chance to make something for themselves. Whatever she wanted from him, for the rest of time, was hers.

Luna chuckled. A husky, life-giving sound that burrowed right into him and set his heart to pounding.

Her power skimmed over his skin, healing his various wounds as she placed a tender kiss against his ear. "I accept your gift," she whispered.

Without warning, she shoved him, his back hitting the platform with a thud. She climbed over his gargantuan body, her soft curves pressing into him. Careful of his size, he settled a hand over her thighs, his thumb straying up to stroke her lush arse. She moaned, spread dainty hands across his chest, and licked the spot over his heart.

Brand jerked when Luna's fangs sank into the flesh there and a wave of rapture followed the sting, crashing over him as she drank—not at all like when he'd been the one to force them into himself. He writhed beneath her, helpless not to when met with her little mewls of pleasure, the pull of her lips.

All thoughts emptied out of his mind when she rubbed herself against his abdomen with a slow, sensuous roll of her body. Then another.

All but one.

Feet planted to the floor, he willed his change, using what little focus he had left to slow his breaths. Bones snapped as they shrank. His head ached as his horns reverted to their normal state, three sets into one. He clenched his teeth as his fangs disappeared back into bruised gums.

Brand wanted to enjoy her *fully*.

A rumbling growl escaped him when he was finally back to himself and his lesser size meant her center was pressed directly over the hard length of his cock, still grinding against him.

Brand might have preferred managing the situation—learning her on his terms and ensuring she was sated, drinking in her gratification to feed his own—but her pleasure was his, and it didn't matter how she received it. He was a willing tool, delighted to be used by her, requiring nothing in return to feel content to his very marrow.

With a rasping moan, he latched on to her wide hips. She whimpered and scraped her nails over his chest in response, up the sides of his neck, fisting his hair tight to leverage her body. The sting only added to his own satisfaction, multiplied by the hard tips of her breasts digging in and dragging against him while she moved.

She picked up speed, and he groaned, "Take from me. Everything. It's yours."

Brand wasn't sure whether to rejoice or lament the fact when she detached her fangs from him and reared back, rising above him. He reveled in the stain of red on her lips, the trail of his blood down her chin, dripping with every one of her thrusts.

She was wild. Feral. Perfect.

Her hands left him to grab hold of her own breasts, plucking at her taut nipples through the thin fabric. The reminder that she went bare beneath her clothes did nothing to help his own composure.

"Fuck." His balls tightened, and Brand clenched his teeth, breathing through the tension gathering at the base of his spine, the building need to release.

She went taut, silent, a deep furrow in her brows as her mouth fell open on a silent scream.

"Look at me."

It was a reflex to demand it, but Brand gasped when she instantly obeyed.

He still held the control. Could still worship her, command her, and nothing was lost in their positioning.

Lunara came apart with a keening cry, her hooded eyes locked on his as she jerked and spasmed.

Yes. He would have her know who laid beneath her, aware of his submission as she extracted her bliss. It wasn't something he gave lightly. No one else had ever received this surrender from him, this yielding. It was hers—only hers—and he wanted her to *see it.*

His lips peeled back as he ground himself against her. Harder, faster. Drawing out her pleasure, fingers sunk so deep into the lush flesh of her hips, her thighs, that he was sure to leave bruises.

He'd gift her more of his blood, kiss each one away later. She would want for nothing ever again.

Brand flipped their positions as she sagged, pressing her languid body into the cool stone and seizing her lips with his before tearing away and standing. He wanted to behold her before he ravaged her. To take in the way her ruined dress had tangled up around her thighs, the way her flushed skin refracted the light and sent faint opal rainbows back at him. The way her chest rose and fell on heavy breaths, alive.

He needed more, to reassure himself. Needed to taste the life in her sweet cunt. Watch it twitch and drip. Feel her wrapped around his tongue, his fingers, his—

Lunara curled up on her side with a yawn, the exquisite hills and valleys of her curves on display as her delicate hands cushioned her head and she went lax. Fast asleep, just like that.

Brand huffed a laugh, even as tears welled.

One long lock of chestnut hair flowed over her cheek, the rest of the wild mass spread over the platform behind her, and he bent to sweep it away.

What in the realms had he done to deserve such a blessed gift? It was almost too much.

Gaze never leaving her, Brand commanded the stone to cocoon them further, reinforcing the cave to keep them safe within. To keep anything and everything else *out*.

As he finally settled in behind her and let his own eyes close on a sigh, Brand knew he would remember this moment forever. When Lunara, the little moon, became his.

"Mate," he whispered, from the depths of his soul. At last.

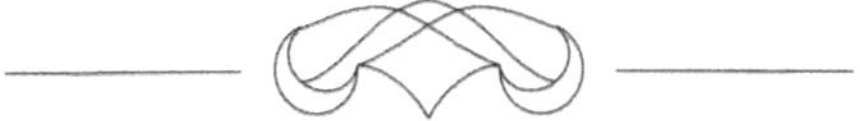

CLAWS LONG AS SHE WAS TALL SKEWERED THROUGH HER, RIPPING HER IN HALF, stealing her future before she'd lived it. They were almost gentle as they left her body gaping, gushing, unable to draw air.

Hazel eyes begged for more than she had to give. The life was bleeding out of her, darkness consuming her—both from the outside and from within.

A rush of desperate energy barreling in, such as she'd never felt before. Just enough to save him—her final act.

Dust and stone and screams before she was laid to rest in golden light by hands that stole her breath and sense. Hands she would never feel again once the Veil opened its arms for her instead.

One last look before a wave of blinding pain that put all the rest to shame, and Lunara the Moonweaver met her grisly end.

Fucking stars above, she was de—

Lunara awoke on a gasp, frantically clutching her stomach.

Whole. Entirely healed, as if that *thing* had never touched her.

She could have laughed, but her lungs were still clenching, the fire of terror licking over her sensitized skin.

Somehow, she was alive—and she was ensnared beneath a very large, solid arm.

Brand.

His name was perched on her lips when she caught sight of his muscled chest, rising and falling with even breaths. Of the two, blaring puncture wounds over his heart, perfectly placed within a bruised circle.

The fang marks were stark in the dim lighting, faint blue iridescence glowing at the edges amongst golden-red hair.

Oh no. No, no, no.

Memory flooded her at the sight. Her startling rise back to life from a cold void of nothing. Her veins singing, flesh knitting. Her body—

Weeping fucking moons.

She'd tackled him and… and…

The dwindling terror of her nightmare was replaced by burning embarrassment, a flush suffusing her cheeks.

She'd blooded him—right before grinding her way to completion and falling into the best damned sleep of her life.

Lunara's stomach lurched, and a lump of denial lodged itself in her throat. Tears sprang forth even as her heart stuttered, her mind and body locked in battle over whether she should be ill or elated.

What have you done?

Finding a true mate wasn't uncommon, per se, but Lunara had never once seriously entertained the possibility for herself.

Some creatures spent their entire lives waiting and hoping, never finding theirs and dying alone. Some gave up and bound themselves with a chosen love, but it didn't always fare well between them. The fortunate ones were blessed by the Sisters, finding the soul destined to collide with theirs in perfect, incandescent harmony.

Lunara scanned Brand's sleeping face, admiring the strong lines of nose and jaw, the muted fire of his hair and short beard, the raw curve of his horns. So at ease, the worry gone from his brow. So stunningly beautiful.

All the signs had been there. The instant attraction, the calm when she was near him. The way it was so bleeding easy to forget she was supposed to be hiding for the rest of forever, because he made her feel like something else could be possible.

She should have known. Should have seen that he was hers.

No. No, no. He's not yours, you're not his. Not if you want to stay safe. Please get your cracked head out of your arse and run!

Right. *Right.*

Wiggling and pulling, she slid out ever so slowly, desperate not to disrupt Brand's slumber. He would never let her go willingly—no one in their right mind would abandon their true mate.

Unfortunately for both of them, Lunara wasn't in her right mind. Probably never had been.

She nearly collapsed on top of him when she finally hoisted herself to hands and knees and found her hair captured beneath his hip, forcing her to grip the ends and tug them to free herself.

Brand grumbled and rolled to his back, and she froze. The bruising on his chest was worse than she'd first thought, and guilt roiled through her. She resisted the urge to trail her fingers over the mottle, purple skin—there was nothing she could do for such a mark anyway.

They were scars he'd be stuck with. Permanently. A beacon to all others that he'd been claimed by a Nachthellian.

Sisters, what had she done?

Station didn't matter when true mates were found, status nothing in the face of it. A cook could bind with the Realm Ruler they served, and all would rejoice. But she'd be visible at his side. Paraded everywhere. Someone would recognize her, and… and *use him* to get to her.

Brand was an Imperial, the most powerful beings in all the realms, but they'd find a way.

Her breaths came faster, visions drowning her. Of clawed hands poised over him, backlit by Illamiata, his life under threat because she'd been fool enough to stay. Of the Council swarming her with their power, laughing as they stole her mind and her freedom.

Go. Go!

Lunara scrambled from the platform and raced for the far end of the cavern. Hands skimming the walls, clawing at the rock. There was no door. No exit.

It hit her that she didn't even know where they were. That part of her memory was lost to her.

She threw a hand out to catch herself on the stone before sliding to the ground. Air heaved in and out of her lungs. A cold sweat broke over her brow.

This couldn't be it. Trapped, her life over. He'd wake up, and she'd never be able to look into his eyes and then leave him, and they would all die.

"Or you stay and live happily ever after. It's only somewhat up in the air right now."

At the Voice's interruption, Lunara jolted and smacked her head against the wall, its stars-damned giggles filling her mind.

No, no, no. You are not hearing the Voice right now. You are not.

"If you keep telling yourself that, I'll never be able to help you. You're supposed to have listened by now," it chided, rattling within her.

What was that supposed to mean?

"I say what I mean and it means what I said. Well, this time."

As cursed, breathy titters bounced around her head, Lunara fought to get her breathing under control. Nonsense for years, and it was suddenly trying to help?

It sounded offended when it said, ***"I wouldn't say 'suddenly.' I've been here all along you know, through everything. We are friends, after all."***

Friends? Lie. It's lying to you. You have no friends. Certainly not this one.

"Are we not friends yet? I would have sworn..."

Its seemingly genuine confusion made Lunara pause, but then it spoke again and ripped away any potential curiosity.

"Wait, did she just wake up with Brandir or with Magnus? Maybe we **aren't** ***friends yet..."*** it whispered.

With... Magnus...

Magnus?!

"Never mind. You weren't supposed to hear that. Shhh."

She wanted to scream when it laughed again, but her panting gasps and squeezing chest wouldn't let her.

"You need to take a deep breath—hyperventilating is not going to help, but I will. I will help you, Lunara the Moonweaver."

Lunara was perilously close to passing out when a thousand voices filled her head with pounding intensity.

"Merge with stone before the fourth tower crumbles, binding midnight radiance to the crowned dawn. Find power in patience, have patience with power. Hold both within and wield vengeance that blinds. With fangs and mist, balance and majesty, a moth spreads its wings with bonded ferocity. Dwindled sun makes evening darker, but twilight sings love's memories—thus mending stone with mated mortar and banishing the nightmare."

The words were achingly, horribly familiar, but Lunara couldn't place them in her state.

"I cannot say, so do not ask. You'll know the truth eventually." The Voice had reverted back to its usual singsong sound, the mystical quality from a moment ago gone, as if it had never happened.

Know the truth?

No, this is not happening. This is not real.

Oh, it was real enough. And cryptic as fucking ever. Just like whoever had sent that message to Brand.

"I'm really, really not. But never mind that. There's something else you'll need to recall, my sweet, little future friend. When all is dark and the ground swims beneath you... When the waves crash and the world thunders... When red mist lands and the wrong hands free you... When everything is lost and there's only one way left to find it... You must remember—only poor choices shaped the others, and you are not the same. You will need your fear to find your fate. Trust me, I would know."

It said the last with such raw melancholy that Lunara almost wanted to reach out and find a way to embrace it.

But then it giggled again—a grating, flippant sound that made Lunara want to rip her own ears off—and her compassion evaporated.

"And now, I offer you one truth. A way to test what I have said and take it to heart," it said lightly, wholly unaware that Lunara was plotting ways to murder it. ***"The first words the Demon will utter upon waking are 'Lunara? What are you doing over here? Are you alright? Speak to me, my little moon.'"***

Lunara's heart lurched, irritation with the voice and the sweetness of those words colliding within her chest. Somehow, against her better judgement, she found herself wanting it.

"There's no way that you could know it, only I can see." The voice sounded smug, right before it lowered with urgency. ***"I see so you can see —see what's right in front of you."***

The gravity behind those words, the utter urgency in its timbre...

"What is happening?" Lunara rasped. "What am I meant to see?"

Why her? Why now? She didn't understand anything. Was overwhelmed to the point of tears. What did the truth matter when nothing made any sense?

"I cannot say much more without dooming us all. Just... Do not fear

his light, Lunara," the voice whispered, almost begging. ***"The blessed night within you cannot exist without it."***

Lunara swayed as cracking pressure swelled within her skull, sure it was going to break apart when the agony suddenly released, melting away to nothing and leaving only breathtaking lightness in its wake.

Her head landed in her hands, those final words hitting harder than any of the other indecipherable rubbish.

'Do not fear his light, Lunara.'

She knew exactly what the Voice meant by that. Especially sitting here and leaning against a wall she would have run through if it had been the doorway she'd needed it to be.

But Lunara didn't fear him at all—she feared accepting him, for both of their sake.

She feared the growing feelings and the glorious pounding of her heart when he was near because she was terrified the beauty of those moments would be reduced to nothing more than heartbroken dust, crushed beneath the weight of her uncertain future.

No, Lunara did not fear Brand. It was the Elders she was afraid of. It was… herself.

She didn't fear his light, she feared inadvertently being the one to extinguish it. Because having it, having *him,* then being responsible for their destruction…

That would be far worse than never having him at all.

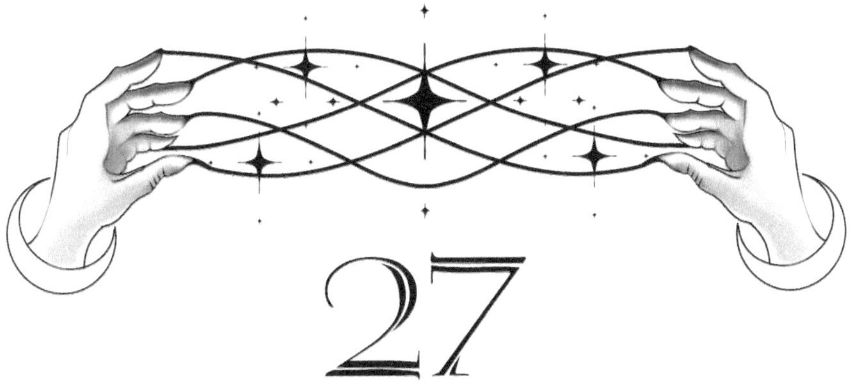

27

LUNARA HAD NO IDEA HOW LONG SHE SAT ON THE COLD GROUND. ONLY THAT her bones ached and her arse was numb.

Brand hadn't so much as twitched, still in a deep sleep. Draining a gift from his veins and blooding him in the same instant might have had something to do with that. Or maybe it was the countless lacerations she'd discovered on his legs, his hands, some of them horrific—wounds Lunara *knew* he'd ignored entirely in favor of tending to her.

Unfortunately, cleaning the crusted filth of her own near-death from both of them, and putting his flesh back together had only distracted her for a few moments, the soft fabric of a new dress doing nothing to comfort her.

She'd ended up back on the ground, eyes locked on him. On one of his shoulders as it went up and down, up and down, her thoughts spinning and spinning and spinning.

There was no sorting through all the Voice had said. In fact, there were only four words that stuck out, mocking her.

Merge. Bonded. Love. Mated.

The only ones that were relevant to her right now, while she stared across a bleeding cave at her sleeping *mate.*

Fucking ridiculous. You should have blasted a hole in the wall and left, the rest of the world be damned.

Maybe. Then again, the only thing stopping her from rejoicing her unbelievable fortune was terror over something that may not be real. Brand might be able to protect her after all. Perhaps he could rage and level the entire Council with his greatsword.

Lunara snorted, enjoying the thought a little *too* much.

What if that's what the Voice had meant? Not to fear herself *for* him. Not to deny what the Sisters had gifted them in favor of anxious assumptions and wretched memories.

Merge. Bonded. Love. Mated.

Love.

Did she love him? No. Not yet, at least. Not… quite.

Oh, but she could. Blessed moons, how easily she could.

The beginnings were there. The heat, the ease, the laughter and understanding—perfection resting just out of reach, waiting for her to stretch out and grasp it within steadfast fingers.

But there was at least one secret between them. One that was potentially more than enough to burn the rest to the ground.

'Do not fear his light, Lunara.'

She was going to have to face him when he woke. To look him in the eye after she'd hopped on his massive body like she owned it and taken her pleasure without so much as a thought.

Groaning, Lunara let her lids droop, listening and waiting for him to rouse, forcing her breaths to be long and slow.

Eventually—it could have been minutes or hours, there was no way to know—the sounds changed when bare feet met stone floor.

Funny. The swift patter of his steps matched the frenzied beating of her heart exactly.

Stone floor… Stone…

There was something niggling at the back of her mind, trying to surface through the mire of everything sloshing within, but the sleepy gravel of Brand's voice broke her concentration and swept the thought away.

"Lunara?" he said softly, urgently, a warm hand cupping her face. "What are you doing over here? Are you alright?"

Her heart stopped.

"Speak to me, my little moon."

Just as the Voice said it would be. And if it had been right about that one, simple thing…

A flood of words and proclamations swept through her, the Voice imploring her to listen, to accept him.

It was true. Weeping Sisters, it was all true.

The smug laughter that echoed through her mind was so faint, she may have imagined it.

Heart lurching, she opened her eyes and met Brand's. He visibly relaxed, but concern lingered in his gaze. He knelt and brought his other hand up to hold both sides of her face and just stared at her.

She was at a complete loss for words.

"Luna," Brand whispered.

The first time he'd used that name in this form, and it managed to hit even harder.

Her mate was there, right in front of her.

How? How did this happen? Sisters, what must he think of you?

"I don't know what to say," she admitted finally. "Maybe if you told me just how embarrassed I should be, I could better decide where to begin apologizing."

Brand chuckled, his face lighting up. She adored the way his eyes crinkled at the corners, evidence of his good nature painted there in lines that never fully disappeared. They drifted down and his thumb brushed along her jaw to reach her bottom lip. He rubbed back and forth, wholly focused on her mouth, and liquid heat flooded her veins.

"Perhaps you should be embarrassed about how damned careless you are, running off at every sodding opportunity with no thought for yourself. Or maybe you'd like to apologize for putting yourself in danger, for getting run through by a bloody Forgotten and scaring the ever-living shite out of me when you *stopped fucking breathing*. Then again..." He looked into her eyes once more. "If you hadn't done all that, we may have danced around the subject for far too long, waiting to see what would happen and never quite sure of the other. Perhaps it's fitting I'm on my knees here before you, so I can thank you instead for being a reckless, wonderful fool."

Tears welled in Lunara's eyes and spilled over her lashes. "I'm so sorry," she whispered. "I didn't mean—"

"Shhh," he whispered, gently cutting her off.

In one fluid motion, he pulled Lunara to her feet and into his arms, squeezing hard enough to push the air from her lungs. "I thought I'd lost you, and I've never been so terrified in my life."

"I'm still here."

Somehow. Against her better judgement. Though… it didn't feel quite as daunting as before.

Weeping moons, you're a hopeless bleeding eejit.

He let go only long enough to bend and grasp her around the thighs, lifting and wrapping her legs around him.

Lunara squealed, her hands landing on wide shoulders. "What are you doing?"

"Tell me to stop and I stop."

Blessed moons, the gravel in his voice.

"Stop what, exactly?"

Brand used one hand to brush the tears and loose curls from her face, his eyes following the motion before he reached back and reverently coiled her hair around his arm, grasping her nape. "Walking you over to that slab and finishing what we started."

She didn't want to say it. Didn't want to ruin it. "What about—" She cleared her throat, mustering her courage. "What about Faldir?"

A muscle ticked in his jaw. "You saw what it was like. With only the two of us, there's no way. The risk…" He shook his head. "And for what? An unlikely possibility?"

"You think he's gone."

"You were gone," he pushed through gritted teeth, the agony in his voice choking her. "And I have no idea what awaits us when we leave. I-I can't… I want…"

Her fingers landed on his lips, silencing him. Lunara knew what he was trying to say. "A moment of joy before the Veil?"

"Yes. Sisters save me, that's exactly it."

Eye-to-eye, breath mingling between them, they froze like that, time standing still as they poised for a glorious drop into the unknown.

"Well, what are you waiting for?"

Her back was hitting the platform before she could blink, Brand rising on his knees above her. He grabbed one ankle and brought her booted foot to his chest, eyes on hers as he undid the laces and tossed it aside. Fingers skimming up her calf, behind her knee, to her thigh and the lace on top of the stocking there. It was torture as he hooked his fingers in and dragged it away.

Worse, still, when he repeated the action on the other side.

He made slow work of hiking her skirts, pausing just before she was bared to him and settling back.

"Please, Brand," she whispered, hardly knowing what she was asking for. She'd take anything, at this point, so long as he touched her.

"Mmm." His fingers dug into the inside of one thigh, just shy of painful. "So different from the minx who *took* what she wanted."

A hot blush crept over Lunara's skin. "I shouldn't have done that. I'm sor—"

"No." He latched onto her hips and dragged her closer, light rippling up his arms. "Never apologize for your pleasure."

"Oh... my..."

"Your fulfillment is my fulfillment. I crave it. Only, now I'd like to know how to please you myself." At last, Brand exposed her, and Lunara's back arched under his gaze, her body seeking him out. His breath left him on a ragged exhale as he stared, his tongue peeking out before he bit down on his bottom lip. "I can't decide whether to touch or taste you first."

Honestly, she couldn't decide either. All of it, probably.

Her hands moved of their own accord, tracing up her sides and heading for her breasts. For the peaked nipples she felt scraping against her dress. She couldn't take it anymore, needed some kind of contact, even her own.

"Stop."

Lunara froze just shy of her goal. The word had been softly spoken, but there was no denying the command in his tone.

Just as there was no denying the heady reaction of her body at seeing the approval written across his face. Stars above, what was he doing to her?

"Unbutton your dress, then put your hands above your head."

As if he controlled them, those hands moved, fingers shaking and slipping as she worked the tiny shell buttons apart. Her dress gaped little by little, the cool air hitting each inch she exposed like a caress.

Brand watched her with a focus that might have been unsettling, if it wasn't for the sawing of his breath and the obvious satisfaction it brought him to see her do as he bade. When he rubbed a palm down the sizable bulge in his trousers, stroking his hard cock through the dark fabric, she understood.

She couldn't tear her gaze away from the sight. He was huge above her. Primal. Power in every controlled inch of him.

And he was right—she *craved it.*

The last button popped free and the backs of her hands hit stone, arms stretched upwards.

"Yes." He was on her in an instant, tongue dragging up her sternum as he parted her dress fully and cupped her breasts.

She cried out as he sucked one blushing peak into his mouth, pressing the other to the side of his face with a groan. The hairs of his beard were a sensation she'd never experienced. Tiny sparks that concentrated and shot straight to her core like a white-hot lance of need.

"Hmm," he rumbled against her, tongue lashing out, something wicked in his gaze.

Propped on his elbows, Brand palmed her breasts and forced them together, until her nipples stood side by side between his fingers. Close enough to… to…

She couldn't breathe for the waiting. The anticipation.

Sweet, shitting stars. He can't mean—

Brand drew his tongue over them, teeth scraping *both* in glorious tandem before he devoured the tips.

"Ah!"

The cry echoed, bouncing around the cave like ten of her were shouting. It wasn't enough to express her shock. Her wonderment. Lunara had never imagined such a thing. Wouldn't have thought it possible. Could hardly believe it was happening, even as she turned molten beneath his ministrations.

She nearly sobbed when he broke away and rasped, "Noted."

He gave her a squeeze and settled in at her side, head propped in one hand.

"Show me how you like it, how you prefer to be pleasured. No"—He stopped her from sitting up, from answering with words—"just feel and react. Let me learn from your body."

Brand's fingers danced over her soft stomach, down until he reached the curls at her mound, teasing his way into the wet inferno of her core.

She would have sworn his hand shook as he found her entrance and dipped inside, but he seemed so in control. So sure.

He nipped at her collar bone, and she whimpered as he spread that wetness everywhere, finally landing on the throbbing pearl at her apex. Circling, teasing, his eyes locked on her face.

That piercing look darkened as he tilted his head. Between one gasp and the next, he ground more forcefully against her, keeping the same lazy speed even as he popped over the bud between sweeping passes.

A choked sound left her and she undulated her hips, pressing herself harder into his hand.

Brand hiked himself even closer, even tighter against her, as if he could absorb her pleasure skin-to-skin and have it for his own.

Stars above, maybe he could.

Without warning, he vibrated his fingers, and Lunara jolted, uncertain whether to lean into it or retreat. Sparks and spots whirled past her vision, her toes curling, but it wasn't enough. Not what she wanted. Not what she *needed.*

A low hum rumbled from Brand's chest, and he eased off with a nod—right before he slid his hand back to fully impale her with a thick finger.

Lunara loosed a keening moan and arched, her breasts swaying. On a snarl, he dove in and buried his face between them, dragging his cheeks over the mounds, almost mindless.

The scrape of his beard… His tongue and teeth everywhere…

Yes, *this*. This is what she needed.

He pulled out and added a second finger, harder, faster, his thumb working 'round and 'round with every thrust of his hand.

Her body moved with him, his abandon intoxicating. She was so close. So…

"Brand, I'm… I'm going to…"

Tighter and tighter, she coiled, until she was sure to snap.

"Everything," he groaned. "Give me everything."

Lunara could only obey. Her entire body bowed, locking up at the edge of that fathomless drop, teetering for a mind-blowing eternity before she let herself fall. She was weightless as she spasmed. Floating as she gasped. A kaleidoscope of colors as she shattered into a million pieces and finally let the building scream free.

She found her arms wrapped around him when she fell back into herself, cradling his head as he rained kisses on her skin and whispered praise, easing her through every trembling aftershock of her climax but not letting up.

There's no way.

Brand surged into her, fusing his mouth to hers with a ravenous sound. "Again."

Lunara swore, the feel of him so exquisite—so painfully right—that she couldn't help it. He took advantage of the action, sliding his tongue past her lips. She met it with her own, twining and tasting in a frenzy of need. She lost herself, reveling in the brutal strength coiled within him, the power she desperately wanted him to unleash on every straining inch of her body.

She was senseless in her passion, babbling as he took her to new heights *'again.'* That time, when she broke apart and cried out, it was his name on her lips.

When his fingers left her, she wanted to rail, to shout her denial—until Brand gathered her up and tilted her head back, trailing kisses down one side of her neck before dragging his open mouth up the other and nipping her jaw.

"Do you have any idea how beautiful you are, *mate?"* he husked. "How perfect?"

Hearing that word on his lips and the triumph in his voice, Lunara sighed, boneless, unable to speak.

He rolled off the platform and dragged her forward, until her bottom teetered off the edge. Her breath caught when he dropped to his knees, shoulders wedged between her thighs.

"Any idea how good you smell?" His nostrils flared and he leaned in, exhale fanning over her—just before he licked straight up her center with a ragged moan, pulling an answering cry from her when it rumbled against her most sensitive flesh. "How fucking good you taste?"

Bleeding sisters. Maybe you should *keep him.*

"Please." That single drag of his tongue hadn't been nearly enough.

At her plea, Brand's lids fluttered closed and his head tipped back, as if *he* were the one with his lover's mouth on him.

Perhaps he wasn't the only one who could watch and learn.

She raised up onto her elbows and stretched her legs wider, pushing against his grip, offering herself to him. *"Please."*

His eyes burned into hers, a sparking blaze of hazel—and then he consumed her.

Brand held nothing back, like his life depended on tasting every drip and throb and pulse.

When he spread her open with one hand and latched his lips onto her clit, cheeks hollowing as he sucked in rhythmic draws, Lunara's hands slapped down and fisted each of his horns without a thought.

She needed something to hold on to, an anchor in the storm of his onslaught.

The sound that tore from him was raw. Desperate. Reverberating over every one of her nerve endings, as if…

She stroked them experimentally, using the obsidian lengths to guide him, pushing and pulling, the feel of him moving beneath her grip only heightening the sensations.

The groove between his brows deepened, the look somewhere between rapture and pain.

Oh, yes. He most certainly enjoyed having his horns touched. Used.

The realization sprouted within Lunara and grew roots, burrowing under her skin, electric when they reached the deepest parts of her. If her pleasure was his, then the same was true in return. She'd never experienced this level of connection, as if a thread had been pulled taut between them to send every feeling back and forth along its fibers.

"Again," Brand whispered, eyes open and on her face as his tongue flicked her.

He thrust two fingers into her, curling them *just so,* and Lunara was done for. The orgasm slammed into her, knocking the air from her lungs. She had no control over the near-violent splintering of her body, or how it brutally remade itself again. She was at Brand's mercy. Willingly. Blissfully.

It was a wonder his horns didn't pierce through her skin as she bucked, clamping his head between her thighs. He didn't seem to mind in the slightest. Not with the way his groans spurred her spasms. The way he clutched tight and spread her arse, pulling her even tighter against his face.

In the midst of ecstasy as she'd never known, a quiet certainty clicked into place—no matter what else happened, she would never be the same.

LUNARA BLINKED AND WAS SURROUNDED BY STRONG ARMS THAT WARDED OFF the chill air, Brand's breath hot against her neck.

Weeping sisters, she must have blacked out.

Time slowed as they lay there, the enormity of it all crashing against her like waves upon the shore.

At long last, Brand gently pulled her by the hair, separating their bodies. The trail of his other hand was like fire, searing its path into her flesh as he brought it around from her back. He slid it across her wide hip, over the crumpled fabric of her dress and up the line of her body, settling between her breasts.

He paused there, staring at his thumb drifting back and forth, before he broke the silence with a ragged whisper. "I feel as though I've waited all my life for this moment, to be able to breathe."

Curse and damn her heart for skipping. Her mind for understanding. Lunara forgot everything she was running from when he was near, and it freed her in ways she'd only dreamt about.

"Luna…" Brand swallowed, the sound cracking through the room. "Tell me this heart beats so fiercely here for me. Tell me I've finally found my home."

Home?

Yes. That's… that's what he sometimes felt like. Lunara had gone so long without one—a true one, with family and laughter and warmth—she'd nearly forgotten what it could be like. The joy, the… the safety of it.

An echo of the Voice's words drifted through her for the thousandth time. *'Do not fear his light, Lunara.'*

A small sob left her, fear and hope colliding.

Shitting stars, there's no dissuading you, is there? What if it's a mistake? What if—

"Y-yes," she said, her voice choked with emotion. "But…"

He tensed, his gentle strokes grinding to a halt.

Her own muscles went rigid, stomach curdling as words she'd kept imprisoned for decades started crawling up her throat. Parts of the truths she'd sworn to never utter.

No. No, no, no.

"I have secrets, Brand." The admission fell out before her wiser half could claw it back. "Dark and messy and complicated. When they find out…" She pulled away to sit up and stare across the cave, hating the icy loneliness already creeping in.

Bleeding arseholes.

The wall she'd beat against mere hours ago taunted her, and Lunara dropped her gaze, gathering her bodice together and pretending it was urgent she button it up again.

Before she could finish, Brand swung her into his lap to straddle him. The new position forced her to look at him, to bare an entirely different part of herself that Lunara wasn't sure she was ready for anyone to see.

"I know." He made no comment about her state, only smoothing the linen down to cover her, his palm warm through the layers. "I'd have to be an idiot of the highest order not to have noticed there was *something*." His smile was rueful, shy. "As long as you didn't torture any innocents, or murder a litter of puppies out of spite, I don't really care what those secrets are."

"You will. You'll—"

His arms came around her, his forehead pressed to hers. "What is any of it in the face of our mating?"

Lunara's chest constricted. It couldn't possibly be that simple. Nothing was ever so straightforward.

Her body couldn't decide what to do. With so many years spent running and hiding, pretending she was dead, the desire to bolt was second nature. Easy. Familiar.

So why did she find herself wanting to lean in and risk everything?

Brand should have recoiled on hearing she had something to hide, giving her an excuse to disappear. To guard her heart and remain at least somewhat intact. Instead, he was offering her life. A future that wouldn't be spent alone in darkness.

Sisters save her, but Lunara wanted it so desperately that she was almost sick with longing, the consequences be damned.

'Do not fear…'

"Swear to me…" Lunara swallowed, her lungs so tight with terror she could hardly speak. "Swear to me that I can trust you. Please. I can't give my heart just to be left hollow when you hear the truth and… and turn away from me because you decide it isn't worth it. I'm already petrified.

Being tossed aside…" She shook her head, huffing. "I know what I'm asking for, wanting your oath but giving nothing. That it's probably too much. That I'm no one. That—"

Brand growled. "No one? Luna." He gripped her nape, his markings lighting up in a sudden flash. "There is *no one* in this world above you now. *No one* more important. I will swear to anything you ask and count it a privilege. A blessing, for being able to say my *mate* has found me worthy of her needs, however challenging. So yes, you have my vow. On the Sisters, I swear it. But"—he gave her a little shake, his nose grazing hers—"only when you're ready. Only if you feel it's necessary or have a desire to share. As much as you are trying to find your trust, know that you already have mine. I know you, even if I don't know everything *about* you."

Something small and broken within Lunara shifted, as if jagged pieces fell back together and suddenly weren't cutting so deep.

"I've been alone for so long." Her voice cracked, a ghost of itself. "I don't know what to do. How to be." It hurt to say, but he deserved the small admission.

"Does anyone ever really know what they're doing?" Brand asked quietly. "I certainly don't, most of the time." He lifted her hand and placed a soft kiss on her palm before laying it against his chest. Her touch was met with a pounding, staccato rhythm—a beat that matched the furious hammering within her exactly and had a lump forming in her throat. "But I do know that this, here, is for you. That I've never felt its like, as though my heart is trying to break me apart in order to get to you. That it's yours."

That's… He… This is…

"Perhaps we could figure out the rest together."

He looked so vulnerable as he said it that she couldn't help but press her mouth to his. Anything to erase that growing uncertainty from his brow.

The kiss was tentative at first, a brush meant only to soothe. But as it heated, his teeth grazing her lower lip, her fingers tangling in his hair….

There was no such thing as Elder Councils or Keepers. No such thing as fear or hurt or loneliness. As the ache of her bones. Brand's words, his touch, erased all of it, filling the newly vacated spaces with dangerous things like promises and new dreams. A sense of rightness that refused to be ignored.

He said they could figure it out, and she *believed him.*

So, reveling in the possessive clamp of his hands on her body, Lunara gave in.

She dug her nails into his chest, leaving the last of her trepidation there in biting crescents. "Together," she whispered against his lips, panting.

His eyes snapped open, searching hers. "Do you mean it? You're sure?"

The most monumental question she'd ever been asked.

"Weeping moons, this is insane, but…" There was no going back. "Yes."

"My mate!" Brand roared to the cave ceiling, throwing his head back with a booming laugh.

The freest she'd ever seen him—and it was nothing compared to when he rested his ear against her, closed his eyes with a contented sigh, and whispered, "Blessed Sisters, my *mate,*" like it was worship.

Oh, my stars, he's…

The realization that he was listening to her heartbeat, like she'd done so many times to him, brought a fresh wash of tears spilling down her cheeks.

Lunara lightly traced the puncture marks she'd left behind. "My mate," she said softly, bewildered—almost a question.

He straightened, his possessive touch drifting up her thighs and taking her skirts with it. "Say that again."

"Brand." Breaths coming faster, she let her own hand drop to the waistband of his trousers. "My mate."

"Yours." Fingers digging into her bare hips, he ground her against himself. "Fuck, I'm all yours."

The strange material of his pants was soft, so thin she could see every bulging outline, but it was all wrong. She wanted to feel *him.* On her, inside of her.

Brand bucked when she gripped him through the fabric. Her palm ran his hard length down and back up, again, before seizing and frantically loosening the drawstring.

Holding her tight, he raised to his knees and shoved his pants down with one hand, freeing himself.

He was… there weren't words. A thrill ran through her seeing his size, the beaded drop clinging to the tip as it jutted toward her. She moved to seat herself on him, desperate to engulf his straining cock with her body. To put it right where it belonged.

"Wait. Stop."

Lunara blinked, confused, hovering mere inches away from ecstasy.

"We can't. Not yet." Brand's chest was heaving, his eyes wild. "Making love to you would complete our bond." One arm around her back, he tilted her away as he gripped his base, dragging the head through her arousal with a shuddering groan before bringing it forward to tease her clit. "Would seal us together for eternity." Side-to-side, so slowly she wanted to scream.

"I don't see the problem," she rasped, his hold too sure for her to move and take what she really wanted.

His lips peeled back, as if his actions were torturing him just as much. "The *problem* is that I refuse to do it outside of a warm bed, where I can take my time." He drew out the last word even as he rubbed himself harder against her, faster. "Already, this is madness."

Where Lunara found the audacity to say her next words, she didn't know. "I think, Brandir aht Bordoroth, that I would have you anywhere. Even a damp, mysterious cave with death lurking outside. Especially then." She grabbed one of his horns and forced him to look at what he was doing, to tempt him into more. "I want to see you come apart. I want to feel it—*before* the Veil."

"Fuck." He slapped himself against her, tearing a cry from her lips. "*No*. We're getting out of this. And when I finally have you wrapped around me"—His lids fluttered, muscles corded with restraint as he ground their bodies together—"I swear you will be cradled by silk sheets and down feathers, and we'll stay there for days, until I'm pried away against my will." Shite, the ridge of his cock was absolutely intoxicating. "Since we have none of those things—no bed, no time—*feeling* will have to wait, little moon."

"Then show me."

"You want to see?" Brand laid her back onto the platform, giving her a perfect view of him spreading her wetness down the length of himself. He bit his lip as his fist pumped, the fingers of his other hand skimming her calf, her thigh. "Then watch. Watch what just the *thought* of being inside you does to me."

"Oh, shite."

Muscles tense and corded, teeth sunk into his lip—witnessing Brand pleasure himself was unlike anything else. Up and down, every fierce stroke was fuel on the fire burning within her.

Lunara could hardly breathe when his movements became erratic, his stomach tightening. With a final squeeze to the inside of her leg, Brand covered the head of his cock and arched, coming with a strangled gasp and groan.

He was stunning straining above her, brows drawn, eyes never leaving hers as his other hand kept working to draw out every shuddering drop.

Lunara summoned a cloth from the ether as Brand collapsed next to her, the ease of the action a blaring reminder she'd blooded her true mate. Taking his hand, she kissed the back of it and cleaned his fingers, the salty-sweet scent of his release doing funny things to her. Mouthwatering things.

"Has anyone ever told you how magnificent you are?" She moved lower, dragging the linen over his abdomen. "I think you might be the most beautiful thing I've ever seen, Brand."

The flush already suffusing his cheeks deepened, and she would have sworn his lip trembled as he stared at her, a look of utter devotion painted across his face.

She moved to grip his length, using the excuse of cleaning to touch him again. "I wish—"

A shriek sounded, cutting her off.

Brand was on his feet in an instant, closing his trousers in a rush.

Another high-pitched screech, followed by a series of strange clicks that seemed to skitter along the walls, dust tumbling from above.

Light engulfed Brand as he grew, the rage overtaking him in the blink of an eye. "Time to go, little moon," he rumbled, kneeling and stretching out an arm.

She didn't think to argue. Not with that sound still snaking its way down her spine, leaving goosebumps in its wake. "What was that?" she asked as he scooped her up.

"Doesn't bloody matter." Greatsword in hand, he made for the far side of the room. "If it's down here, it isn't good. Shield up. And Luna?" He tilted her face with one gigantic finger, forcing her to look at him. "I meant it—we're getting out of this, so no more flirting with the Veil. I'd hate to have to follow you in."

Maybe it was the fact that Brand looked absolutely dead serious. Or maybe it was the cold panic seeping into her bones as another splintering howl sounded. Either way, as he crumbled the stone between them and the chasm's horrors, Lunara couldn't help the bubble of hysterical laughter that escaped her.

28

THE FEELING OF HOT, SERRATED KNIVES RAKING ACROSS HER BODY WASN'T something she'd ever get used to, no matter how many times she willfully brought it upon herself.

With as deep a breath as her chains would allow, she sent part of herself towards her hiding spot in a pocket of the Moonweaver's mind.

She couldn't leave her completely. Not yet. Had to make sure it had worked. Needed to get there before—

Oops.

Moth was likely going to feel some of this.

In three, two…

A sharp tsk-ing sound was all the warning she got before pain exploded across her cheek, his fist ramming into her with the force of a comet.

Unbeknownst to her assailant, though, his violence propelled her towards her destination, and she slipped behind the door she'd made there.

"Night take you, you interfering bitch."

So predictable. She knew he was going to say that.

Honestly, his voice was worse than the agony consuming her. The familiar, imperious tone that had once comforted her was now just one more item on a long list of things that she unequivocally detested.

Funny enough, that list was dedicated almost solely to him.

She tried to open her eyes, but couldn't accomplish the simple task so soon after her indiscretion. Which was fine, actually, considering the sight of him would probably make her vomit. Besides, she knew him almost as well as herself. Knew what a handsome piece of celestial garbage he was without having to look at him.

"Worth… it…" she said through gritted teeth.

Another pummeling fist. That one broke the skin, a hot stream of blood bursting forth to pour down her face.

Fabulous. It was definitely going to stain her hair. Not that it mattered. She'd forget about it soon. Too much else to remember.

"Haven't you had enough of this, Endellion? Wouldn't you prefer a gilded cage at home to the filth of this world?"

Never. Better she be stuck here for eternity. At least the dank cavern walls and teeming darkness told the truth. Besides, there was no way to move the pieces as she needed to from home. No way to save them from so far away.

Shame her most recent attempt had to include her own suffering. So little a thing and she was nearly as weak as the ones she was trying to protect.

"All you have to do is tell me where they are. So simple, and I'll set you free."

She fought the overwhelming desire to roll her eyes. Choosing to switch one word for another had been *simple.*

'Do not fear *the* light' would have yielded only death in the long run.

'Do not fear *his* light' had given them a chance.

A *very* simple choice, despite the consequences to herself. It had pushed the limits of what she was allowed without ruining everything, but the Sorcerit was dense enough that it hadn't really broken any rules. Getting through to her was like trying to pull teeth with a cobweb.

She probably could have screamed *Brandir is your fated mate and the world will literally end if you leave him right now!* at full volume, and Lunara still would have been confused.

Destiny was funny like that.

What *he* was asking for…

"There's nothing simple about the destruction of an entire planet, and we'll need them in the end, so I'll be keeping it to myself, thank you."

Not that she'd ever be telling *him.*

He huffed, and she didn't have to see to know he was spearing her with an impatient glare.

"I am beginning to tire of this," he hissed. "Why do you even care?"

He would never know the beautiful, perfect answer to that question—not until it was too late for him to do anything about it.

Provided she made it that far. That they *all* made it that far.

"Maybe I just like messing with you."

And...

Bam! Bam! Bam!—three more strikes to the head.

Why always the head? Oh yes. Right.

Because she was so wrapped up in chains that he'd hurt himself if he hit her anywhere else.

"So... predictable."

Was that her choking on blood? Or was it... No, it was her this time. He'd shattered her nose—*again*—but it had rattled her *just right.* Just enough to crack the door and bring soft whispers fluttering by, a vision with their trembling urgency.

The Sight was slightly different when it featured the present. Images were sharper. Less dreamlike. They played out behind her closed lids as though she was standing right beside them, anticipation building with each passing second.

'Lunara? What are you doing over here? Are you alright?'

Essence within, he was a handsome brute kneeling down there. Slightly too young for her taste, though. She preferred them, well, a *bit* older.

She turned in her mind and looked on with grim satisfaction as the Moonweaver paled, grappling with whether to accept or deny the truth.

This was it, where the vision always split in two, side by side—one irredeemable and careening headlong towards utter destruction, and the other...

A monumental step closer to hope.

'Speak to me, my little moon.'

Please, please, please...

The Moonweaver's thoughts echoed as her own. *'It was true. Weeping Sisters, it was all true.'*

There was no way, in all the worlds, she could have stifled her triumphant cackling.

"What did you do? *What did you do?!*"

He was many things, but entirely stupid wasn't one of them.

Her laughter was cut off when his hated hand seized her throat in an unforgiving grasp, repeatedly slamming her head into the cave-wall she was shackled to.

"I should have slit your throat the moment you left Argellion's ruined cunt," he choked into her ear. "The *second* I laid eyes on you and heard the sound of your pathetic cries, mewling for her leaking tit. If I'd known what a fucking nuisance you would be, I'd have saved us all the trouble."

"You're... just... jealous."

There was no point in finishing until he let go. It wouldn't be long anyway.

Nearly...

Now.

She sucked in air with gasping relief, spitting blood onto the floor.

Only, she finally recalled there was no floor anymore. Just miles and miles of her starlight hair.

Curse it and damn it. Now there was blood in her hair. Or was there already blood in her hair? It was so hard to remember...

"What could a meddling whore like you possibly have for me to be jealous of?"

Oh. Right. She'd nearly forgotten *when* she was.

Mustering every immortal ounce of her defiance, she forced her eyes open. The swelling made it difficult, but it was worth it.

Worth it, as always, to see his perfect lips peeled back in a sneer far too hideous for the beauty he boasted. To see his eyes flash with fury against his mottled, alabaster skin. To see that long lock of platinum hair—the one that never stayed tucked behind his pointed ear—tremble with coiled violence.

She was the only one capable of riling him and it always brought her a twisted sense of satisfaction to do it.

So, yes. It was *worth* the encumbered breath when yet another split vision presented itself and she chose her path, saying, "My lustrous, feathered wings. Obviously."

They hadn't been lustrous in hundreds of years, but her seeming delusion would diffuse him for a moment.

"You're completely mad." One corner of his mouth twitched upwards as he considered her, his mood as changeable as the wind. "Believe me, I couldn't possibly care less about your fucking deformity." Sighing, he ran a hand through his hair and paced away, as if to leave.

"But they're such a stunning representation of the greater issue!"

He stopped dead at the far end of the cavern, his head tilting back. "Which is?"

Finally here, living it, she knew there was just enough time to deliver words all the more devastating for their truth. Words she hated, but they would need him off guard.

The two visions became one and her fate was sealed. Nothing for it. No matter how much it was going to hurt.

"That here, on my back, is everything you've ever wanted and will never possess. I was loved, while you've wasted your days wondering whether the same was true for yourself, instead of *seeing* what was right in front of you."

He went so, so still.

"That I am of the stars and I *know it,* but you will never have a sure moment in your life. Traitors rarely do. After all, you're the coward who was weak enough to believe the lies of Night."

He disappeared, traveling through the unseen channels of this world in the blink of an eye. When he reappeared before her, she delivered the final blows.

"Argellion should have slit *your* throat, just to save us all the trouble of having to put up with your incessant insecurities. Instead, you look at my wings and all you can think is that she loved me more than she ever could have loved you, like the utter fool you are."

A single tear escaped the confines of his long lashes and slid down his cheek, his eyes burning with so much hatred that it sucked the air from her lungs—right before a scream rose up from the depths of him.

He threw himself at her captive body, spittle flying as he slammed, and slammed his fists against her.

Just like she knew he would.

29

HEART IN HIS THROAT, BRAND STEPPED OUT INTO THE CHASM AND PUT HIS lips to Luna's ear, his voice hardly a whisper. "Spread the shield, as far as you can."

Fumbling through the teeming murk, deluded into thinking it was hiding them, would be foolish in the extreme. Whatever had made that hideous sound, he wanted to see it for himself and face it head-on.

Luna's manic laughter had died when the first shadows had poured by them to fill their sanctuary, tainting it. Now, her breaths were shallow as she wove her magic, the darkness recoiling before she'd even sent out her power.

Interesting.

With a shaky exhale, she pushed her arms out. Instead of a gentle sweeping, a luminescent wind battered the shadows away with a vengeance, the surrounding area cleared in an instant.

Her head jerked back as she lifted her hands, staring at her palms like she'd never seen them before, and her skin was glowing.

Brand squeezed her closer, a swell of pride washing over him, and he vowed to himself that—whatever her secrets—he would protect her from their consequences. His mate was as lost as she was powerful, confused even by herself. They'd find answers together.

Provided they made it the fuck out in one piece.

"I—"

Stones clattered in the near distance, their fumbling descent echoing in the heavy air and stealing whatever she'd been about to say.

Brand pressed his back to the cliffside and scanned their surroundings, lit warmly by Luna's starry, hovering orbs. There was nothing to see, but *something* was close, hovering just out of sight. He could feel it in the prickle down the back of his neck.

Luna's nails bit into his shoulder as her head tilted, gaze going distant for a moment before she blinked. Swallowing, she locked eyes with his and pointed over the edge of the step they stood on.

Much as he wanted to get her to safety, he had to know what it was. Not just to assuage his own morbid curiosity, but for the protection of Bordoroth, as was his sworn duty. The Forgotten were bad enough. If there were more...

With a reluctant—*silent*—sigh, he spun and set her down, caging her against the rock with his massive body.

"I'm going to look," he said, barely making a sound. "When I turn back around, you'd better be right where I fucking left you, Luna."

Her eyes flashed silver, a biting retort no doubt perched on her tongue, but he shoved a finger against her lips to silence it. "Please." There. He'd *asked*.

She slumped against the wall when he released her—brow raised and displeasure clear—but at least she didn't move.

Satisfied, Brand turned and slowly made for the ledge. He allowed himself a deep, fortifying breath before he leaned over and...

Weeping fucking Sisters.

A dreadbeast. It had to be.

Clinging to the rock, Luna's star lights hovered around a creature almost beyond description, illuminating waxy skin and a massive torso that put his own to shame, even in his greater form.

Where a neck and head should be, there was instead a lump of flesh that hung over a bloodied maw large enough to devour a grown adult in a single bite. Multiple rows of needlepoint fangs jutted from the gaping opening as a tongue like tar-coated rope whipped out to taste the air.

Two sets of stacked shoulders terminated in jointed arms, packed with grotesque muscle and tipped with lethal spikes of black bone instead of hands, each as long as his sword. Four legs of the same were attached to an almost dragon-like body, though it was all wrong. Bulbous at the joints and shrunken in between, like an insect without its outer shell.

It had no ears or nose that he could discern, no eyes, and yet it was searching. Seeing, somehow.

He understood the clicking noise earlier when it shifted side to side, its body undulating and adjusting as it struck those taloned appendages into new footholds, sending more dust to the chasm floor.

The beast reared back with another lash of its tongue, revealing a glowing hole in its chest, not entirely unlike the eyes of the dead below. It pulsed rhythmically from within, a deep red where the gazes of the Forgotten had been a burning orange.

Fuck. He'd never seen anything like it. Not face-to-face, or within the pages of books. Not even in the worst of his nightmares.

It was death incarnate—and far more than they could handle alone. Looking at it, he knew to his marrow they either escaped or they died, and there was no fucking way he was allowing the latter.

He turned back to Luna, finger pressed to his lips to keep her from making any sound. He still wasn't sure whether it would be better to sneak away or run for all he was worth but, either way, he needed her in his arms.

Luna leaned sideways to peer around him just as he knelt before her, that foolhardy curiosity of hers right at the fore.

A reckless streak that might've saved them both, in the end.

Her eyes widened a split-second before he felt the looming presence behind, the world slowing around him. Apparently—for all it's shrieking and clacking movements—the beast did, in fact, possess the ability to move silently.

Fuck.

In one, impossibly smooth motion, he scooped Luna up and spun, his greatsword cutting horizontally through the air. He didn't wait to see what damage he'd done, if any, as it flinched away.

On a boost born of sheer terror—not for himself, but his mate—Brand leapt, clearing dozens of the steps he'd made before landing again and breaking into a dead sprint. A piercing roar rent the air in his wake, clattering footfalls reverberating through the depths.

Hopefully, the distance would buy them enough time to—

"No!"

Luna's shout was the only warning before the flesh of his calf was being ripped to shreds. His own bellows joined hers and those of the dreadbeast as flames spread to overtake every nerve ending in his body.

Agony. Burning. Eating him alive.

Fighting the urge to vomit, Brand craned his neck to find himself pinned straight through his leg to the chasm wall by one of its talons—within the confines of a shield that was supposed to be impenetrable.

The rest of the monster rose slowly behind them, as if it were savoring its catch. Talon by talon, like a monolithic spider, it cleared the landing edge.

Its poison must have addled his mind because—as it swooped closer and brought its "face" to his—he would have sworn it looked… perplexed, almost, as if confused they would be running.

Luna's choked gasp brought him back from the edge of his toxic insanity. Without another thought, Brand swept his sword down with all of his might, severing the spike holding him.

Whether he or the dreadbeast screamed louder was unclear.

It flailed back, spittle and ooze flying from its gaping maw, the severed end of its arm pumping black blood into the air.

He swayed, the weight of his greatsword dragging him to the side. Blinking, Brand tossed it into the ether and commanded the stone to release the talon's tip, freeing him. The thing was still lodged in his calf, ravaging muscle and sinew as he ran up, up, up, digging his fingers into the cliffside to keep himself upright when his leg threatened to buckle beneath him.

"Hold me upside down," Luna demanded, breathless. *Urgent.*

At least, he thought so. It was hard to tell.

"Brand! Now!"

He vaguely registered Luna pummeling a fist into his chest, but the rest of her words turned to nonsense. The sheer panic across her face, though…

A boost of power jolted through him. He had to get her to the surface. Couldn't lose himself and leave her vulnerable.

Hugging her ankles to his chest, Brand let her upper body fall and forced himself forward again, the long lengths of her hair spilling down to tangle around his knees.

She wrenched the talon from his flesh with a violent yank and he nearly blacked out, his shoulder slamming into the chasm wall as he stumbled. Something cracked within, the new onslaught of pain too much when added to the rest.

Sisters save them, his worst fears were coming to life. They were going to die here. His mate was going to—

There was nothing gentle about her power as it slammed into him with all the force of a lightning strike. Strength lit his bones, the fog clouding his mind lifting.

Just in time for Luna to scream, "Jump!"

He immediately obeyed, flipping her upright before he landed. She didn't miss his grimace of pain or the strange way his other arm was hanging, and stretched across his torso to tend his shoulder as they ascended.

She gifted him with more of her raw, battering might, feeding so much fucking life into his body that he was almost crazed with it.

Wrapped in Luna's glowing power, the world turned red, wrath replacing his physical anguish. Every scraping breath was hot with vengeance, his body bulking up even more as light swirled over his skin.

A Demon's change being fueled by their Sisters-given power was one thing. When it was bolstered with true, visceral *rage*?

The second she was safe, he was going to chop that fucking creature into so many pieces they'd never be able to find all of them.

A haze of black hung above, the portion of the chasm she'd cleared coming to an end. She finished healing him and launched straight into weaving another spell, her owl appearing with a screech. Luna murmured in his ear and he took flight, shooting straight up into the encroaching darkness.

The shadows shrank away from Axanderus just as they did from her, a beacon when they found themselves plunging once more into the gloom.

"A warning," she gasped out, slumping against his chest and breathing heavily. "For Magnus and Thad."

Shite, he hadn't even thought of that.

—*Something is wrong*—

Magnus huffed. No shite.

He could feel it in the way Pet writhed within, howling to break free and stating the obvious in his gravelly, earthy voice. In the tiny hairs on his body as they stood on end. When he peered into the darkness of the chasm and felt *something* rising to the surface.

—Let me out then, lad. Ye'll be needing me—

Not yet. The beast was ruled by blind instinct and Mag needed to keep his wits.

He paced along the chasm's edge as the twin moons dropped lower to make way for Solyrian in the clear sky, Thad right at his heels.

It hadn't even been a whole day, but Mag was crawling out of his skin with the waiting and wondering.

Yesterday, early evening, the ground had shaken beneath his feet for over an hour, massive quakes shuddering across the land. He'd felt his brother's power trickling up through the earth, familiar as always, but Mag's already fraying nerves had disintegrated a little more when he'd failed to appear with the witchling in tow.

Then, nothing. Magnus hadn't slept a wink for the worries plaguing him. Were they safe? Were they well? Why the fuck was it so stars-damned silent?

Not that it was silent anymore. Nightmarish shrieks had started filtering up from the abyss to break the monotony and his mask of calm, growing louder and closer with each passing minute.

Whatever was making that cursed sound was enormous. He could feel it as much as hear it. The only question was whether Brand and Lunara were in front of it, or had been left in its wake.

Weeping shite.

"What in the realms is going on down there, Mag?"

"Wish I fucking knew," Magnus sighed. "Nothing good, since my mangy mongrel is clamoring to come out."

—Maggie, my lad, we've talked about this. Name calling isn't nice—

Magnus clicked his tongue. How he'd got paired with a wolf more suited to being a nursemaid than a mighty, ferocious warrior was beyond him. Still…

Sorry, Pet.

—Ach, no worries. Now, let me out—

"Sorcha is acting up too," Thad said, turning worried eyes to the chasm. "Do you think they're alright?"

He couldn't even answer that. The possibilities were endless, and he sure as shite was not going to entertain the worst of them. Brand had to be okay, or Magnus didn't know what he would do. That behorned, uptight arse wasn't just his little brother—he was Mag's best friend in the world.

Pet internally howled his agreement.

Magnus kept up his trudging, moving back and forth along the edge and searching the fog for any sign or signal while he and Thad waited.

And waited.

Fuck, he hated waiting.

—Come now, Maggie. Patience is a virtue—

Hush, you. You've been fighting to get out since the first screech.

—It's my purpose to fight monsters. What's your excuse?—

Do I really need to answer that? My brother is down in a Dread Chasm, and I'm stuck up here with you.

—Our brother—

Pedantic, Pet.

Mag had tried to follow, instantly regretting his agreement to stay behind, but it was no use without the witchling's shield. The shadows had snapped up, vicious, and only his speed had saved him from the foul fucking grot.

The moons slipped further towards the horizon, drawing steep shadows on the landscape until the chasm seemed to fade away. Everything stilled in that odd time between, when the night and day creatures switched places. The entire realm inhaled, ready to release its sleep with a sigh when the sunstar finally rose, wholly unaware of whatever was coming for it. Until—

There. A shimmering light within the gloom.

—The witchling's magic is that color—

Magnus reared back as a *bird* shot up from the chasm a hair's breadth away from him, straight into the sky. Massive wings flung out and slowed its momentum—the biggest owl he'd ever laid eyes on. It swooped around and down to land in the grass, and he raced to meet it.

If she was casting her spells, then they were still alive a few moments ago.

Ghostly, starlight tendrils lifted from its head and feathers, and it turned round, silvery eyes his way. Absolutely stunning.

Then the braw, bloody thing *talked*.

"Get away from the edge and be ready," it said with Lunara's wheezing voice. "Dreadbeast, a breath behind us. My shield is useless against it. Make of that what you will."

Another savage scream pierced the air and visions bombarded him—images of Thad staring lifelessly into the sky, his blood spattered across the earth, limbs tangled with the villagers of Glynmor in their mass grave. Lost, like his mother.

Magnus shoved down his blooming panic. "Thaddeus!" His cousin's head popped up, instantly alert. "To me!"

Thad was there in an instant, his eyes bulging when he noticed the bird. "What is *that?"*

"A message from the witchling. They'll be here any moment, with a friend in tow."

He snarled the last, the flames of his fury stoking higher. There was no doubt in his mind it had been responsible for the razing of his village, the precious lives lost, and vengeance was a seething song in his blood.

"Should we shift?" Thad asked, hands reaching for the ties of his robe.

The enthusiasm in his tone scraped over Magnus like knives on porcelain dishes, and he had to smother the urge to throttle his cousin.

Thad was bouncing, too excited for what was coming. He was so young—so fucking untried—and it showed. He had no idea how foolish it was to be delighted by the prospect of battle, but getting upset with his innocence wouldn't teach him a damned thing.

"Nay, lad. Calm yourself." He laid a hand on Thad's shoulder to still him. "We've no idea what we're up against yet. The shift takes no time at all, and having the patience to wait and use your brain before your beast can sometimes make all the difference."

Magnus gave him a reassuring squeeze and stepped away. "Place yourself behind me—" He threw his hand up to halt Thad's protest. "It's not an insult. It makes us a smaller target and will allow us to move together if needed. You'll be able to do as I do and see my commands without needing to hear them."

Thad took a deep breath and nodded, backing a few yards away and trying to look serious.

Mag loosed his own sigh. He wasn't cut out for this teaching shite. Not when bestowing his knowledge meant throwing those he loved in harm's way.

A clacking sound started up, faint at first but growing until it was echoing through the field. The harsh accompaniment of layered screams joined the staccato sound—closer, and closer, and closer.

Any second now, Pet.

Magnus dropped into a ready stance, slowing his breaths and freeing Pet just enough to sense the things he normally wouldn't, to feel the shifts and scents on the air.

Pounding footsteps. Harsh breaths. The smell of—

Brand flew from the chasm, heading for them at a dead sprint with Lunara in his arms.

—Brother!—

"Thaddeus! Protect her with your life!"

Magnus gaped in disbelief when Brand threw the wee Sorcerit for all he was worth, right at their cousin. Lunara soared through the air over him on a high-pitched squeal, but Mag paid her no heed. Thad would catch her.

He was focused on Brand. His demeanor was off, jerky movements slightly too wild. That's when Mag saw the tiniest glint of fear in his eyes —a look he'd never beheld while his brother was raging—and it told him all he needed to know.

It was going to be bad.

Without thought, he kicked off his boots, tore the robe from his body, and let Pet take over.

Go on, then. Time to rip nasties apart.

—Aye, that's it, Maggie. My turn—

The world morphed around him as he changed. Magnus loved the savage instinct pumping in his veins. The dagger-like fangs filling his muzzle. His claws digging into the grass and dirt. Smells multiplied, and his pointed ears twitched atop his head to pick up every sound. Pet might be the fussy sort inside, but outside? He was beyond deadly.

Magnus completed his transformation and snarled, joining Brand just as he whipped around towards the chasm and brandished his greatsword.

"Four arms, four legs, all but one tipped with talons like wicked blades. No eyes or nose, but a mouth filled with rows of teeth, and massive enough to eat us in a single bite. Watch for the tongue—it's like a whip. Think colossal spider dragon, and you're halfway there."

Mag growled his response, hackles rising.

—Two legs or twenty, we'll feast upon it—

The head appeared first, if it could be called such a thing, followed by the arms. Dirt sprayed as it planted those talons into the ground and hauled its body up over the edge—one half-missing, a stump where the point should be.

Brand hadn't exaggerated about the tongue. It snapped out like an infuriated snake when the monster screeched, spraying rotten matter through the air.

—Ah, what a beauty. Let's kill it—

Killing is fine, Pet, but no eating. That scabby thing looks fucking revolting, and I don't want to be the one left with the belly ache.

With a sneer, Brand thrust out a clawed hand and the earth rumbled. A rocky ramp rose from the ruined field and shot up between them and the dreadbeast, nullifying its much greater height. Sword raised above his head, his brother sprinted up the incline and jumped from the towering drop-off on the far end with a war-cry, landing atop its back.

Mag maneuvered himself behind the beast as Brand hacked into its spine, even that mighty weapon like a splinter when compared to the sheer size of it.

Stone and dirt sprang up like crashing waves at Brand's command, snatching at the dreadbeast's talons to trap it in place—to no avail. It freed itself easily, no purchase to be had on the sleek appendages as it jerked to-and-fro in an effort to dislodge his brother.

Mag gauged its movements and lunged, snapping at its hind legs. His fangs cracked through a talon, ripping it sideways and breaking the spike. The beast stumbled, shrieking with rage. Foul blood filled his mouth and he snarled his satisfaction—until fire licked down his throat and seared his insides.

Magnus wavered, shaking his head to clear the toxic haze descending upon him.

—Wretched, bloody poison—

A frenzied growl left Magnus.

Aye. Let's avoid biting for now, Pet.

—Ach, you don't have to tell me twice, Maggie—

Gathering his strength, he leapt upon the beast's flank and raked his claws through its tough hide, savaging its hind quarter. Tendons snapped and gore coated him, forcing Mag to turn his muzzle away to avoid swallowing more of its blood.

The back leg fell away with a squelch, Magnus with it. Brand held on while it thrashed, trying to right itself, his sword wedge deep into its back.

He rolled to all fours and dove in again, aiming for the opposite front leg. Not as ideal as taking two legs from the same side but needs must. He set in to shredding, hacking, clawing—

Blistering pain sliced through his body, and he was lifted away, impaled on one of its arms. It brought Mag forward, another talon skewering him from the other side as he was dangled up over the gaping hole of the monster's mouth. The rows of needle-like teeth began to vibrate within, a sickening buzzing sound filling the dusk around them.

"No!" Brand wrenched his sword from the beast's torso, swinging forward.

Magnus sagged to the side, half free. He panted as his blood poured to the mud and grass below, and thanked the Sisters for his brother's intervention. No way he was getting devoured by this fucking thing. Better to die tainted with poison and lying within the sweet embrace of his beloved earth than being cut to ribbons and swallowed in pieces.

—You owe me for this one, lad—

With that, he snarled and sank his fangs into the dreadbeast, clamping down on the bony spike still holding him and squeezing for all he was worth until it, too, broke away.

Impact with the ground. A whimper left him when a talon drove deeper and mutilated his insides further. Ribs cracked and bone shattered, one of his forelegs twisting in the wrong direction.

The dreadbeast's toxin stole his mind as it seared its putrid way through muscle and sinew, and Magnus fought to stay conscious. How was he to pray for his return to the fields if he couldn't fucking *think?*

—It's not looking good, Maggie—

No shite, Pet.

Panting, he helplessly watched his brother through the haze of his failing sight, standing above him with the dreadbeast's jaw in his grasp.

Brand's fangs flashed as he roared, pouring his formidable strength into holding the creature at bay.

Something locked onto his hind leg, the familiar presence of Thad's wolf, Sorcha, dragging his broken body away before moving to stand guard between them and the fight.

Lunara fell to her knees and yanked both talons away without the slightest ceremony. Threading gentle fingers into his fur, she took a single breath before the light of her magic pushed back the dark tunnel creeping in on his vision. Coolness spread to tame the scorching heat of the poison, his flesh knitting together.

Strength returned like a hammering fist. Hearing restored, Magnus finally registered Brand shouting, but couldn't decipher any of the words —not over Lunara's agonized screams.

Pet, animal that he was, howled with bloody glee anyway.

—Oh yes, we like the witchling—

Except it sounded like she was fucking killing herself to save him, radge wee lass.

She slumped over, breathing hard, her power still battering—but the shift in her body revealed only horror.

Brand had angled his horns and caught the monster's last arm in their curling lengths, but the dreadbeast's tongue had him snared around the neck like a noose, choking him. His brother's hands clawed at it to free himself as he was dragged, closer and closer to its yawning, oscillating maw.

Brand planted his feet and leaned away, locking them in a standstill, but Mag knew he wouldn't last long like that. His face was already turning a deadly shade of purple.

Magnus whimpered and pawed at the ground, willing Lunara to move and afraid of hurting her if he tore out from beneath her too quickly.

—Forget the lass! We must get to our brother!—

With a gasp, her head whipped up to follow his look. Eyes silver as the twin moons themselves, a vicious look twisted her features and she swiped something from the ground before flashing away.

One second, she was perched above him, and the next she was misting in beside Brand. Lunara brought her hands together above her head, one of the dreadbeast's talons in her grasp. Loosing her own wee battle-cry, she thrust the spike down with all her might, severing its tongue.

Brand slipped back, his horns losing their hold on the front talon as the beast twisted and shrieked. Its newly-freed arm came sweeping out and into Lunara, her body crashing into the side of Brand's ramp and crumpling to the ground.

"Luna!" Brand bellowed, tearing the beast's tongue from himself and running to her.

Time to take a rest, Pet. It's my turn again.

Magnus shifted and grinned. The cheeky Sorcerit had given him a fucking brilliant idea.

"Thaddeus!" he shouted. "With me!"

—You're positively devious, Maggie. I love it—

30

BRAND SLID ON HIS KNEES THROUGH WET CARNAGE, COMING TO A STOP BESIDE Luna.

"No, no, no," he chanted under his breath.

"Take her up, Brand!" Magnus shouted, pointing to the top of the ramp before rejoining the skirmish.

His brother was right. She'd be safer above the beast and battle.

He commanded a chunk of the ground to lift beneath him, raising them upwards. When they reached the top, he ran his fingers over and beneath her head, shoulders, sides, legs… No wounds anywhere he could see or feel, but that meant nothing. Some injuries were held inside, seeping insidiously until the body succumbed.

She needed blood.

Brand lifted his arm to pierce his skin, but stopped when he noticed the layer of black ooze congealing on his skin. He wiped and wiped his arm against a fairly clean part of her skirt, but it wasn't good enough. He couldn't risk it.

Thaddeus.

His cousin hadn't engaged the beast directly. He could give her a gift.

Brand lunged sideways to peer over the edge of the incline and cursed. There was so much of the dreadbeast's blood on the ground that the overturned dirt had turned to mud and puddles.

His damned cousin was bounding around in front of the monster, splashing through the loathsome stuff as he yipped and snarled, luring it towards himself. The beast limped and jerked as it stalked Thad, Magnus racing behind it and plucking its severed talons from the ground—naked as the day he was born.

Both of the bastards were as covered in the shite as he was.

"Fuck!" Nothing for it. He'd have to feed her and hope to the Sisters she'd be okay.

Brand shoved the same hand he'd used before into her slack mouth and drove her fangs deep.

What in the weeping fuck?

The beast's blood began to move against his skin, crawling up his arm as if to escape the touch of her lips. It took all of his willpower to hold still and ensure she had enough, near desperate to yank his arm back and cut the substance off him with his own blade if he had to.

It was just so bloody fucking *wrong*.

The second he was satisfied, he pried her mouth away and set to exposing her skin. He swept loose curls away from her face, pushed her sleeves and skirts up—anything to bare as much of her body as he decently could. Though quickly disappearing, the twin moons were to the Sorcerit as Solyrian was to the Demons, and even their dwindling light should bolster her.

More than once, Brand wished he had Luna's ability to hear the heartbeats around her, to have the reassurance its sound would offer.

Her skin began to glow, the rainbow shards held beneath its surface glittering as she hummed with building power. A ripple pulsed out through the air with her at its center, and she gasped to sitting, eyes wide and silvered.

"There you are, little moon," he crooned, rubbing her back. "That's it, just breathe."

"What's happening?" she asked, still obviously dazed. "Is it over?"

The shrieks and shouts sounding below them was answer enough, but he didn't point that out. "Not quite."

Magnus sprinted up the ramp, hugging the three talons they'd severed against his bare body.

A surprising wave of aggression hit when he caught the crimson blush stealing over Luna's cheeks. He snarled in Mag's direction, his battle rage too close to the surface to contain it. His brother's answering chuckle only served to infuriate him more.

Luna leaned over the drop of the incline, Mag's wrinkled battle robe in her hand a second later.

"I refuse to apologize for the free show," Mag said, skidding to a stop and dropping the spikes like bloody, black logs to the ground. He snatched up the wad of cloth and donned it, breaths heavy. "But you have my thanks anyway, witchling."

"Where the fuck is Thad?" Brand snarled.

"Ach, playing cat and mouse with his new best friend. They should be here any second."

"They?"

"Aye, but don't get your pants in a twist. That thing is so close to death already, I don't know how it's still standing. Just get your arse up and help me finish it." Mag picked up one of the spikes and leapt off the edge to the battlefield below.

"What? Magnus!" Brand shouted.

"Come on, you wee shite! Thad is coming!"

Brand turned to see an argent streak racing in an arc across the field, his cousin's trajectory taking him straight to the bottom of the incline, the dreadbeast close behind.

"Damn it." Brand lunged to scoop the two remaining talons up with one arm, grabbed Luna with the other, and jumped.

They landed with a thud beside Magnus, who was already issuing commands. "Spikes in the ground, Brand. Have the earth grip them upright."

Understanding dawned, and Brand did as he was told. They embedded the talons in a triangle and cleared away just as Thad soared from the top of the ramp.

"Slaughter it," Mag growled.

He couldn't agree more.

As the dreadbeast followed, Brand sent out his power. He tracked it as it plummeted, commanding the rock and stone to move with its body, aiming the spikes beneath its concave belly. The earth built like a mighty wave, the beast's own severed arms leading the swell. With a final push, he forced the trap upwards to meet the monster midair and the talons embedded themselves to the root, blood raining down while it screamed.

He released his power and let the beast fall. Bones cracked and dirt sprayed as it landed with a boom, skidding to a stop across the field.

Brand's ears rang, the sudden silence deafening. The others drew up beside him, only their labored breaths filling the unnaturally still air as they waited to see whether it was finished.

"Oh, for fuck's sake," Mag sighed, throwing his hands up when it started twitching.

The dreadbeast reached out twisted limbs and jerked itself somewhat upright, but unable to find its balance. As it struggled, slipping to the ground, Brand let the tension in his shoulders melt away.

Moving like that… No longer a threat. They just had to find a way to end it for good.

"Now what?" Thad asked, shaking his hair out as he completed the shift back to two legs.

Brand sifted through their limited options. "My sword is useless," he admitted.

"Aye, and there's no fucking way I'm biting into it again." Mag crossed his arms, as if to dare anyone to suggest otherwise.

Luna cleared her throat and another talon appeared, plopping down in front of them.

"Where did you get that?"

"That would be the one I pulled out of you in the chasm."

The dreadbeast cried out again. Looking down at that talon, the one that'd been *inside of him…*

Without a word, Brand bent and swiped it up. He let all control go as he moved, his battle rage rushing to the fore. Red flooded his vision, seething aggression pumping freely through his veins. His muscles bulged even further and he ground his teeth against it, every step making him angrier.

It screeched weakly as he came upon it, shoving itself away as best as it could. The talons from their trap were lodged snugly between its forelegs, blood pumping out in steady streams from the jagged puncture wounds below the glowing crimson hole in its chest.

If it had a heart, that fiery spot was it, and it was begging to be skewered.

Never mind what it had done to him—an entire village was slaughtered. The piece of shite had taken Faldir, and nearly got Mag and Luna. Only the Sisters knew what other atrocities it had committed.

Brand didn't feel sorry as he drew back and slammed the spike home with a roar.

The dreadbeast seized up on a scream and teetered precariously above him, refusing to fucking die. He snarled back, daring it to deny this fate. One breath, two…

It tipped away, crashing to the ground with a wheeze that freed the last, putrid dregs of its life-force, finally still as the death that had claimed it.

Done. It was done.

The rage washed away, replaced with dizzying relief. With a heavy sigh, he let go and reverted back to himself. He welcomed the exhaustion, the pull on his overworked muscles and the weight in his limbs, glad to be rid of his berserker for now.

"Please tell me this counts as my first battle," Thad said, flicking a chunk of something out of his hair as Brand stumbled back to them. "I'm ready to be marked. Being bait was dragonshite and I'm tired of walking around with the glowing, pasty skin of a wee babe. Look at me. I am ridiculous."

"Yes, um… well…" Luna coughed and raised a hand. "I'll just…"

There was a tugging at his skin, and gasps sounded as the muck of battle lifted from his body, from the others, the filth they'd gathered hovering in the air before slopping to the ground.

Thad let out a sigh, running his hands over his bare chest with a look of contentment. When he trotted off to fetch his discarded robe—that *glowing, pasty skin* on stunning display—Brand couldn't help the fit of laughter.

It was always so strange after a battle, when he found himself still standing, still breathing. Hilarity and misery twined like hysterical lovers, the urge to weep colliding with the urge to laugh, and he became nothing more than a conduit for whatever form the emotions took when they forced their way out of him.

Brand howled like a loon, not giving a single shite because he was just so fucking grateful to be *alive*. Before he knew it, Lunara and Magnus were wheezing right along with him.

"What did I say?" Thad finished off his robe tie and threw his hands up.

"Not a damned thing wrong, lad," Magnus said on a mirthful exhale. "But yes, you single-minded pup—you'll be marked for your part."

Thad bunched his hands into triumphant fists. "Yes! Finally!"

"Aye." His brother's voice was little more than a croak as he tried to get hold of himself. "We'll put it on your arse to be sure everyone can see it the next time you're running for your sorry life."

"Ach, not funny, Mag!"

Brand glanced to Luna, to the tears streaming down her cheeks—lovely, cleansing, life-affirming tears. His own laughter died as he stared at her, heart squeezing at the sight of that smiling, beautiful face…

Fuck, it was everything.

"Right." Magnus sighed, scrubbing both hands down his face. "Best we retrieve Hedda and wee Fern and get the fuck back to Straelon."

"Fern?" Lunara asked.

"Aye, that's what he's taken to calling the Fae," Thad snickered.

"I had to call her something," Mag growled through his teeth.

"Why Fern though?"

Brand wanted to know the same. It wasn't unlike his brother to give nicknames, but it usually depended on the person being conscious enough to hear it and be annoyed by the fact.

Magnus shrugged. "The first thought I had when I saw the shredded ribbons of her wings was that they looked like fern leaves. It stuck."

"You're coming back to the Montrealm?" Brand had assumed his brother would stay here. Try to make sense of what had happened by throwing himself into fixing it like he did with everything else.

Mag speared him with those golden eyes of his and stepped up close. "Faldir?"

Emotion flooded in to choke Brand. He'd done his utmost to bury reality, shoving it as deep as it would go so he wouldn't have to acknowledge the awful truth.

Full strength and raging, Brand had barely gotten them out. Injured, lesser, alone… There was no way Faldir had survived whatever befell him. He'd realized it the second they came upon the army of Forgotten.

His twin shadows were no more.

Hedda was going to lose her stars-damned mind, especially after he'd ensured she had no part in it. No choices. When she found out her brother was… Fuck.

He wanted to forget and go back to laughing, but Brand forced himself to face it, vision clouding as tears filled his eyes.

Faldir—a life-long companion, as close to him as any of his brothers—was dead.

He couldn't voice it out loud. All he could do was shake his head, words and sounds refusing to work their way past the strangled lump in his throat.

"Aye, then I'm coming back with you. Glynmor is…" Mag's eyes closed for a beat before they were on him again. "Well, nothing more to be done here, is there? But it was me who asked for your help, and I'll face Lyriat for the part I played in this dismal shite. Hedda, too." He enveloped Brand in a crushing embrace. "And you, if you can ever forgive me," he whispered, abruptly releasing him and walking away towards the trees.

Thad loped after him, sparing a quick glance back before being swallowed by the dwindling forest shadows.

"Are you alright?" Luna's hand landed on his back, stroking softly.

Her touch siphoned away his melancholy, making way for gentler things. The tension in his shoulders eased, the knot in his chest with them, the sharp knife of sorrow dulled to a manageable ache. He'd lost Faldir, but he'd found *her*. She couldn't replace him, but her presence was a balm, nonetheless. A light in the darkness.

"I don't know," Brand admitted.

"I'm sorry, too." She moved to stand in front of him, tucking a wayward lock of hair behind his ear. "I feel responsible for cutting our time in the chasm short. We might have found him if I hadn't—"

"No. We should've turned around as soon as he went silent. Even without your injury…" He brought her hand to his lips, laying a swift kiss on her fingers. "I can see now it was a fool's errand. At least we can say the beast is no more. That both Faldir and Glynmor have been avenged. It'll have to be enough."

Luna swallowed, averting her eyes. Her guilt was misplaced, as was

Mag's, neither of them responsible. Sometimes things were just fucking shite.

"Come," he said. "I don't know about you, but I'm bloody famished. We've not eaten in almost two days, and the faster we retrieve our things, the sooner we'll find ourselves feasting at home."

Her head snapped up, an almost wild look about her as she blinked. "At… home."

"Yes, *mate*. Home. Together."

Brand pulled her against his chest and buried his fingers in her hair, seizing her mouth with his own. It was tame, meant more for comfort than anything else. To reassure her that he'd meant every word he'd said in their cave.

She pulled away, teeth sunk into her lower lip, her eyes still closed. "Okay. I… um…" She shook herself. "I wanted to fetch the talons. We might find something useful in them, or… I don't know. Even if they're just a trophy for those it would matter most to, it feels like we should take them."

It made a strange sort of sense, and he could deny her nothing.

"You go on with Mag and Thad," he said, running a finger over her brow. "I'll get them for you. I don't want you near it again, dead or not. Please."

She lifted those perfect, sea-water eyes to his and nodded—a wealth of understanding passing between them before she left to join the others.

Brand jogged over to the beast and yanked the talons from its lifeless body. He considered hacking off the others so they'd have the full set, but couldn't quite bring himself to do it. He'd had enough violence the last few days, and he was tired down to his bones.

He gathered the spikes in one arm and moved to follow the others—

A whistling sounded behind him. High-pitched. Ominous.

Slowly—as if it might make a difference—Brand turned around and froze, dumbfounded, dread forming a pit in his stomach.

The dreadbeast was crumpling in on itself, shrinking by the second. With a blinding flash, it imploded, the aftershock knocking him flat to the ground.

A tidal wave of wind followed, battering against the earth and his body, a feminine scream shattering the looming dawn in its wake.

The keening sound was enough to make his ears bleed. Brand groaned against the force of it—against the dark power it ushered in, bathing the land in shadow and pressing him into the dirt and mud. The staggering weight of it only allowed him to pant in shallow breaths, so like his episodes it choked him.

"Brand!" Luna's scream pierced the maelstrom around him.

It snapped him out of the mire of helplessness. He bucked against whatever was holding him down, desperate to be free, willing his body to obey. He had to protect her, had to—

With a final shove, the pressure lifted from his body, gone quickly as it had appeared.

Brand tried to gulp air into his burning lungs as the sky and his vision cleared, capable of nothing more than blinking up at the dwindling stars. Every inch of him was in agony, and he couldn't…

Luna's hands were there a second later, her brow furrowed in concentration. "Shite."

Her healing glow encased him, burrowing in to the broken places. He gasped as cracked ribs realigned, the sudden rush of breath like cool water after a day spent in the desert. Could actually feel the threads of her magic as they sought out every bruise and bleed, every break, erasing the injuries like they'd never existed.

It wasn't until she slumped back, his strength returned to him, that he saw the toll it had taken. Her entire body was trembling, purple smudges under her eyes.

She flinched when he sat up and gathered her close, her own breath hissing through clenched teeth.

"What the fuck?" Thad slid to a stop through the mud, but he wasn't looking at Brand.

Mag hurtled in, only a few steps behind, gaping. "Sisters save us."

Brand craned to look over Luna's head, where the dreadbeast had been.

There, lying in the grass and gore, was an aged Fae male and a female Demon.

They had to be hundreds of years old, hair like the whitest snow around his pointed ears and her grey, curling horns.

Both were missing limbs, and what was left was broken and twisted—a perfect match for the damage they'd done to the dreadbeast. Including a smoldering hole in the center of their bodies, tendrils of inky smoke rising to dissipate in the air. No, not smoke…

"The shadows did this to them?" Magnus was looking at him, as if he had the answer.

Brand fought back a rush of bile, the scene twisting the last couple hours into something he couldn't bear to examine too closely.

"It seems the darkness within the chasms is capable of a great many horrible things," Luna whispered.

31

LUNARA DRAINED THE FLASK THADDEUS HAD GIVEN HER THE DAY BEFORE. Nowhere near the same power she gained from Brand, but her control was too uncertain when feeding from him directly. No one needed to see *that*.

It's fine, you're fine. It's better this way.

Lunara wasn't so sure she agreed anymore. She was starting to see the possibility of a real life. A future where she wasn't alone in the dark, but standing proudly next to her mate. It was daunting, but stars above, she wanted it.

For now, she had just enough strength left in her to see this last task through.

"I don't like this."

Brand lingered on the edge of the camp, jaw ticking, still fighting her demand that they leave.

Family always thought they knew best where healing was concerned, but they were rarely correct in that presumption. She'd had this exact conversation so many times she was numb to it, and his posturing did nothing to persuade her. Nothing to change her mind.

"I should be here. She's going to need me."

Lunara raised a brow at him. "Best case scenario, she's *going* to be disoriented first, and then she's *going* to be utterly heartbroken. Vulnerable. She will then *need* peace and quiet, and the safety to do as she wishes without the pressure of others witnessing it. We collectively denied her a choice once already. We will now do her the courtesy of letting her decide how she'd like to move forward." She turned her back on him and made for his sleeping Second. "I'm only asking you to be out of sight, not halfway across the realm, Brand. Watch from behind a bush if it'll make you more comfortable, as long as you stay there until she or I say otherwise—no matter what she does."

They'd discussed the very real possibility that Hedda would immediately try to murder her. Lunara would hardly blame her if she did. She'd stolen her autonomy, after all. Yes, it had been to save her from herself, but she'd been quietly sick over it ever since they'd returned to their camp and seen Hedda lying there, certain she was no better than the Elder Council after all.

"What if she—"

"Then I'll handle it, Brand," she snapped over her shoulder. "Whatever it is. Now, go."

The quiet snickering floating in from the near distance didn't help. He stared at her for a moment longer, resplendent even in his anger, before spinning on his heel with a low grunt and stomping into the trees.

"Finally." Lunara settled gingerly onto the leaf-strewn ground and lifted Hedda's limp hand in both of her own. "Just you and I now, my friend. At least, I hope you forgive me and we can still be friends." She sent out a thread and delved into the sleepy darkness of Hedda's mind. "Time to come back." Lunara stroked her fingers, trying to draw her along softly. "Follow my voice, the pinprick of light."

Waking those she'd put under wasn't quite the same exchange of pain and power as healing, but it was wearying nonetheless. It sapped her, trying to lull *her* to sleep instead.

At long last, Hedda blinked, her eyes unfocused but growing sharper with each passing second.

"That's it. Relax and let it happen, slow as you like." Lunara kept up her crooning, dreading the moment when—

Hedda's gaze locked onto hers, a ragged hitch in her breath as her hand tightened, grinding Lunara's knuckles against one another. Lunara breathed through the spike of pain, refusing to alert Brand in any way that this might already be going poorly.

Her heart pounded as Hedda's other hand came up to grip her, dragging their clenched fists to her chest and pulling Lunara closer.

"You…" She sucked a breath through clenched teeth, tears gathered on her lashes and wobbling there. "He's…" Her lids fluttered and they spilled over, falling down into her hair. "He's gone, isn't he?"

Not what she'd expected, but she should have. Hedda was nothing if not pragmatic when she was herself. If only her return was something they could *all* be rejoicing.

Lunara's eyes welled in response. "We tried," she whispered, "but…"

Hedda nodded, shrinking in on herself.

"I'm so sorry for knocking you out. You were—"

"I know." A sigh shook its way out of Hedda as she tried to sit up. "It's like a nightmare. Like I was trapped inside while someone else controlled me. The things I said—"

"Weren't you." Lunara steadied her as she swayed. "There was something in your tonic I can't identify, but we'll talk about that later. How are you feeling?"

Hedda snorted. "Stupid question, Sorcerit." She pulled away and scrubbed both hands over her face. "Where are they?"

"I sent them off to give you space." Lunara sent a pointed glance into the trees. "Brand was particularly displeased with me."

"Males usually are when you try to tell them what to do, especially those ones."

"Would you like to see them?"

"No," Hedda answered. "Not yet."

Lunara felt more than heard Brand's sharp gasp of disbelief. She tried not to feel too smug about it.

They stayed like that for a long time, Hedda staring across the sun-dappled camp as Lunara held her hand. Even the birds seemed to realize it was a moment for mourning, their calls distant and subdued.

Hedda drew a deep, sharp breath and said, "I think I'm ready as I'm ever going to be."

Lunara had barely detached herself before Brand was there, dropping to his knees beside Hedda and wrapping his arms around her.

That was when Hedda lost it.

Heaving sobs wracked her body as she clung to him and poured out her agony. Lunara tried to look away, but it was too beautiful, even in its misery. Exactly the kind of thing she'd been missing out on all her long, lonely life.

It's just as easy to cry on your own, without the awkwardness of dealing with another person when you're done.

But being held… Knowing they felt the pain too and that she wasn't alone in it… Talking to someone other than herself…

Complicated. Unsafe.

It was the strangest thing, but—watching Brand and Hedda in their rocking embrace, hearing his whispers and how they calmed his Second Commander little by little—it was easy to ignore what she'd always thought was the wiser part of herself. To realize, for maybe the first time in her life, her heart wasn't threatening to pound its way out of her chest at the prospect of someone knowing her. That she was perfectly content to sit there and take them in and wait for whatever came next.

Madness.

A large hand appeared in her periphery. "Come on then, witchling. Up you go."

Another unexpected turn of events. Magnus had been kind but wary, up to now. Apparently, saving his life had softened him towards her somewhat. He might even be a friend.

Fool.

He helped Lunara to her feet and offered his arm as support while they retreated to the far side of camp, where Thaddeus was waiting.

"We need to get moving as soon as they're done," Magnus murmured. "The day is wearing on, and we've got a long while before we'll see any rest."

Lunara inwardly cringed. Every inch of her already ached, her bones weary to their marrow. "I'll gather everything up."

At least manipulating her pocket of the ether barely taxed her power. It was the work of a moment to clear away their abandoned bedrolls and blankets, the empty pans and remnants of stale food, trying and failing to ignore the fact that everything was exactly as she and Brand had left it the morning before.

She wasn't the only exhausted one, and they still had the trek to the portal before they made it back to Straelon. Back to its Demon King, and the unavoidable task of informing him that his cousin was dead.

Shite.

"Think my da is back home or still with Lyriat?" Thaddeus asked from his perch on the ground, shredding the green bark off of a sapling stick.

Magnus snorted. "I think he's wherever he suspects you're most likely to show up, knowing you've sat there and tried to figure out how best to avoid him. Accept it, lad. You're in for a lashing no matter which toll you throw into the portal."

"I always forget the *going back* part of running away."

"Aye, but your arse doesn't." Magnus clapped him on the shoulder with a soft chuckle, the sound sad. "Ten gold pieces says its puckering even now."

Thaddeus loosed a long groan and flopped backwards. "Don't remind me. I was doing a fine job of ignoring it."

Lunara nudged him with her foot. "It can't be that bad."

"Ach, aye. It can." He wiggled around in the dirt and leaves, a grimace on his face. "Still, it'll be better than living out here for the rest of my life. I'd never survive without a bed."

"There's an idea," Magnus said, a thoughtful look on his face. "Perhaps that's how we'll mark you. You'd be a legend—the mighty Wolflord warrior with feathers and a wee blankie tattooed across his scrawny arse."

A giggle bubbled up as Thaddeus kicked Magnus in the shin and Lunara let it free, allowing herself the small drop of levity amidst the weight of reality.

You're all over the damned place. How can you think this is good? Fine?

Because, alone in the dark Nachthellian wilds, there was no such thing as laughter to help stave off the burden of sorrow.

She sensed Brand approaching before he touched her, his knuckles brushing hers as he sidled up. He'd schooled his features into a bland mask, but it did nothing to hide the emotion roiling just beneath the surface.

Not when her skin was suddenly too tight, buzzing and numb at once. When an ache so deep it choked her formed and her lungs turned to lead, and—when every one of those sensations fell away as quickly as they'd come—Lunara realized those were not her feelings but *his*.

A memory of her parents, one long-since buried, sprang up from the lost depths of her mind.

Lunara had been young, hiding among the library stacks with no one the wiser. She'd thought herself clever when her mother had swept in and shut the doors behind her with a sigh, clearly thinking herself to be alone.

Then, her mother—the most renowned healer of her time—had doubled over, clutching her stomach as she tried to stifle her weeping.

At her tender age, Lunara hadn't understood that her mother was painting a perfect picture of the age-old Nachthellian tragedy—the inability to save themselves or their own, unborn children.

She later learned the loss had been weeks prior to that moment, and she'd been witnessing her mother's continued grief.

It was her father though, barging in with wild eyes, that she thought of now. How he'd dashed across the room, scooped her mother into his arms, and held her in one of the plush window alcoves for what had seemed like hours. Never speaking a word, but being so connected that even Lunara had felt the power of it.

Her father had *known.* Had sensed his mate's distress and come running.

She'd forgotten, over the years, that such a thing existed. That a bond could run so deep that two creatures became one, every part of them merely an extension of the other.

The others were making decisions, conversing in low tones, but she didn't absorb any of it.

Lunara was struck silent as she acknowledged the part of her that had been experiencing whispers and inklings of that very *thing*. Dozens of pulls and tugs and cracks that didn't belong to her, but had been given into her care nonetheless.

The first meal they'd shared. The mountaintop. The river. Even his greater half had brought something out of her in the chasm she'd thought long gone, a power that had nothing to do with magic as they'd soared through the air. Freedom, even as they'd thought themselves hurtling towards their own doom.

It had been *him.* His longing across the supper table. His disquiet and determination battling under the stars. His calm as he'd bathed her. His lightness as they'd flown. His sadness in the deep. His guilt over Faldir.

At every turn, he'd fought for her. Soothed her. Lifted her. All in spite of his own struggles.

Brand had *known.* Had sensed his mate's distress.

The bond was already there. Ephemeral as mist over a forest lake, it came and went—this tiny, fragile thing that hadn't yet found its purchase. But surely something even half as beautiful as what her parents had shared was more precious than any of her worries, wasn't it?

Too much. It's too much.

"Are you well, little moon?" Brand said under his breath, drawing a single finger down the line of her arm, both comfort and concern in the touch.

Lunara froze as she tried to accept that her mind was no longer only her own. Hazel eyes stared back, glittering and searching beneath furrowed brows—a solace of fire and earth that begged the ice in her to melt away. Begged her to give in.

Don't be rash. You're just tired. You'll realize this is folly just as soon as you—

"Yes, I…" *I think I might love you.* The words were on the tip of her tongue, but they stuck there, held back by the shard of fear that lingered. By the part of her that knew it wasn't the time or the place for such confessions. "I want to go home. Please."

Damned if she could settle on where that actually was, though.

After tending to the Fae and tethering her with magic, Luna hadn't made it ten steps from their makeshift camp before stumbling, pain in every pinched line of her face. Hedda hadn't fared much better.

The rage had come easy, giving Brand a boost of strength—along with renewed ire that his mate refused to feed in mixed company. Ire that had quickly swelled into concern when he'd scooped her up and she hadn't even tried to argue.

The Fae was worse than they'd thought, and Luna was hurting because of it. *Badly.*

He hated it.

Mag and Thad had shifted with him, and it had been the work of a moment to tie the sleeping Fae around Pet's neck in a makeshift hammock. Convincing Hedda to mount Thad—*Sorcha*—had been another story, but she'd finally given in when Brand had threatened to carry her instead.

Apparently, it was far more dignified to ride on a Wolflord's back than in the arms of another Demon when she was unable to make the change herself.

Brand didn't give a fuck how they made it home, so long as they did. His mate needed blood and rest. Warm food and walls surrounding her. Safety.

"Not long now," he murmured. "Two more hills, and the meadow between them."

Solyrian beat down on Brand's bare shoulders. With the soft brushing of verdant leaves in the breeze, the sweet smell of wildflowers in its wake, he could almost convince himself the last few days had been nothing more than a nightmare slowly settling into a dream.

Luna gifted him with half a smile, though she still didn't speak.

"We'll find you the biggest bowl of strawberries in Straelon."

Only a soft laugh in return, when what he really wanted was to hear the melodic husk of her voice. Wanted the anchor of it as the Montrealm loomed closer. To distract both of them until the last possible second.

Maybe he could shock her into responding.

He hiked her up and ran his nose along her jaw. "I'm hungry too," he whispered, brushing the shell of her ear. "Starving. Perhaps I'll eat some of those strawberries myself, right out of your—"

"Brand!" she hissed, clapping both hands over his mouth. Her eyes were wide, cheeks flushed. "The others will hear you."

"—hand," he finished, nipping at her fingers. "What did you think I was going to say?"

Hand had been the last thing on his mind, and they both knew it.

Her teeth sank into her bottom lip as she darted a quick look towards their companions. Answer enough.

"Hmm. Noted."

She managed an even deeper blush, the color stark against the paleness of her iridescent skin.

"Tell me, little moon, how do you feel about—"

Sorcha whimpered, and the high, keening sound had Brand's head snapping in her direction.

His cousin's wolf was writhing beneath Hedda's white-knuckled grip, fangs gnashing at thin air and trying to buck her off. Hedda was ashen, heaving, violently shaking her head as if to clear it.

Before Brand could reach them, the ground rumbled beneath his feet and a familiar chorus of roars sounded in the distance. His heart lurched at hearing it, resignation seeping in.

"What was that?" Luna struggled to sit up in his hold, looking all around them.

"Demons," he answered. "Here, for some bloody reason."

His most trusted, no less—a company of warriors from the First Legion. He'd know that war cry anywhere.

"Why won't this fucking dog *move*?" Hedda shrieked. "Ugh!"

She threw herself from Sorcha's back and rolled, popping up onto her feet with only slightly less grace than he'd come to expect from her.

"What is it?"

Hedda speared him with an astonished look, the ghost of a smile on her lips. "It's Faldir," she breathed. "I can feel it."

Then she was off, sprinting up the next hill.

"Oh no," Luna whispered.

Brand took off after her with a curse, mindful of Luna in his arms as he hit the slope. He was torn between stopping Hedda before she could be wrecked all over again, and letting her see for herself it was nothing more than a group of their brethren—probably sent to check on them at Lyriat's insistence.

He absolutely refused to acknowledge his own, tiny spark of hope.

Hedda froze on the peak, clutching her chest and desperately searching whoever lay beyond.

Fuck.

Holding her as she'd sobbed, drowning in his own guilt... Doing it once had been bad enough. He wasn't sure his lesser self would survive it a second time.

Just as he reached her, Hedda fell to her knees and doubled over, clutching her middle. The sounds coming out of her... Stuck somewhere between wails and cackling, she gasped between each manic peal.

He ignored the Demons racing across the meadow to meet them, sending up mixed shouts of greeting and alarm. Facing them would have to fucking wait.

Brand set Luna down and knelt in front of Hedda, engulfing her back with one hand and trying to hide her from their brethren below. They didn't need to witness their Second Commander in this state. "Hedda?"

Her head jerked up and she clutched his shoulders, a mix of tears and snot on her blotchy face. "Tell me I'm not insane. That it's really him down there."

Burning Solyrian. Even his rage couldn't protect him from a fresh wave of sorrow, like a knife slowly sliding in between his ribs.

A howl sounded behind him, followed by another, and pounding footsteps shook the grass around them as the Demons hit the hill and closed the final distance.

Shite. Hedda would be mortified if they saw her like this. "Stay back," he called, thrusting out a hand and hoping they heard him. "It's fine. We're just—"

"Brand…" Utter disbelief colored that single syllable, Luna backing into his side.

"What happened? Bloody fuck. Is she actually crying?"

Everything tunneled at the sound of that gritty voice.

Impossible.

A thump and whoosh of air. A knee brushing his own. Scarred hands reaching out.

On a cry, Hedda launched herself away and right into Faldir's waiting arms.

Faldir. Alive. Raging. Kneeling right fucking beside him.

"How are you here?" Brand rasped. He reached out, swaying, afraid his friend would disappear if he made the mistake of touching him. *"How are you here?"*

"What the fuck kind of question is that?" Faldir batted his hand away, the sting real enough. "And why are you—*oof!*"

Brand pulled Faldir into a crushing embrace with something between a laugh and a sob, careful of Hedda between them.

"Your Highness, I will murder you in your sleep if you don't let go of me right now, the consequences be damned."

Brand only squeezed harder.

32

"What the fuck just happened?!" Her shriek echoed through the empty fortress.

There was more darkness swirling around than usual, trying to comfort her. He would never admit to his pang of jealousy at the sight. Rejection, in all of its forms, was too familiar an experience for him to start letting it affect things now.

Still, he struggled to unlock his jaw. Responding to her question was difficult when he didn't quite know the answer himself.

He'd planned it all perfectly, or so he'd thought.

Use the tincture she'd given him on the Second Commander instead of Brand. Create chaos. Draw them all into the chasm. Let the children feed. Dance over their warping bones.

The next step was supposed to have been Faldir returning to find them all gone, and then using the Third's grief to his advantage with no one the wiser.

Especially her.

First Endellion's little rebellion, and now this. It was all fucked.

He'd have to be all the more careful. More artful. One way or another, the Demons would be realizing there was a villain in their midst and take the necessary precautions—not that he viewed himself as such.

No, no. He was the hero in this story. He simply needed everyone else to stop being *so. fucking. unpredictable.*

"A message was delivered, as you requested. The plan was sound. I have no idea what went wrong."

He shouldn't like lying as much as he did, but it always gave him a thrill.

She cocked her head to the side, long hair shifting and blending in with the shadows concentrated around her *throne*—a stunning piece she didn't realize was made of calcified Celestials. A good thing, since it would disgust her, and her lack of gratitude would snap the tenuous hold on his patience.

It wasn't even fucking meant for her. If she had the gall to criticize it, discard it, destroy it…

A slow breath out, to steady himself. That was all in his head. No use getting worked up over imagined slights. The seat would cradle its true master soon enough.

Her tears had long-since dried, leaving salty tracks down her porcelain cheeks—the only outward sign of her inherent weakness. Evidence she'd actually cared about that *thing*.

"Brand was to go to the village and complete the tasks requested so I could gauge his adult power before approaching him again. To see if he was the gentle, understanding child I remember, or if he'd grown into yet another heartless Imperial like the rest before him. It was perfect." She rose to her full height, nearly as tall as he was, and closed the short distance between them. "Instead, I wake from my restorative slumber to feel the tether connecting me to Ygritte and Aelthys *snap*. I arrive to find them *slaughtered*. To smell the death and decay in the land with *your scent beneath it*." Her hand shot out and latched onto his jaw, even as fresh tears bloomed. "Where is the vial?"

"Ah, well…" It physically hurt to hold in his laughter. "I'd meant it for Brand, of course, but things went a tad sideways. As you know." Perhaps he'd visit some of his captives, talk their ears off and relieve this giddy energy. "In the end, the wrong member of their party consumed it." Lie, lie, lie.

Her claws pressed in, piercing his skin, her lip curled in a sneer. "That tincture was a last resort. It took years to procure, and longer still to manipulate for my own ends."

He was well aware. He'd tried to be the one to get hold of it—if for no other reason than to speed things along—but she wouldn't hear of it. Her plan had been to dose Brand with the tincture, lure him to her fortress before his body burned through it, and use the opportunity to plead her case.

Plead, like the pathetic disappointment she was.

He'd given it to the Second Commander instead, having some fun while disposing of it in a way that would look accidental. It had been so easy to do, in fact, that he'd committed the egregious error of not sparing a single moment's thought for how it would actually affect her.

Admittedly a lapse in judgement on his part, regardless of how much he enjoyed toying with her. Mistakes did happen, after all, from time to time.

Seeing as all of them were still alive, he could only assume it had played out in such a way as to *ruin fucking everything.*

Well, not necessarily. Her getting hold of Brand is what would actually ruin everything, and he'd prevented that, however inelegantly.

"Do you think me a fool?" Her breath wafted over his face, sweet from the wine she'd been drinking.

Of course he did, but saying so wouldn't help him. Not yet.

"You have no idea how lucky you are," she hissed, "that I am unable to spend more than a handful of minutes within Bordoroth's lands. That the Sisters' power and the curse on me prevents it. If not for that, I would take your head right now and good riddance."

It was everything he could do not to fucking butcher her then and there. It would be so easy. She'd never see it coming.

Regrettably, and unbeknownst to her, they were at an equal impasse. He needed her as much as she needed him, and it was saving her life. For now.

"I tire of how little control you have over yourself—which, coming from me, is saying something."

Indeed. She'd executed nearly every one of the last Imperial generation. Brand didn't know how fortunate he was that she liked him.

How sweet.

He attempted to twist his face into something resembling contrition—an unfamiliar feeling if ever there was one. "My sincerest apologies. You know how I can be. It was dreadfully boring scouting Glynmor, and I was incapable of helping myself."

Let her think him a mindless murderer. That he hadn't carefully strategized his movements for longer than she'd been alive. That he wasn't playing a game she couldn't hope to comprehend, let alone win.

She let her nails rake their way out with a snarl, leaving fresh slices down his jaw. Normally, the aggressive act would've aroused him. His licentious urges knew no bounds. If it had at least one hole and he could make his dick fit, he'd try anything.

With her, nothing.

Interesting.

Apparently there were some lines even *he* wouldn't cross.

"We are close enough to our goal that I am feeling somewhat benevolent, and so you shall live." She spun on her heel and sat down again, a perfect picture of boredom when he knew she was anything but.

He lowered his chin, not quite capable of forcing his body into the bow she may have expected. "You are gracious, as always."

"It has nothing to do with grace." She crossed her legs and gripped the arms of her seat, the white of her skin blending near perfectly with its surface. "Replacing you would be another time-consuming inconvenience and I'm tired of waiting. Tired of relying on others for what I would accomplish much better myself."

That got his attention. His plans were centered on her reliance. If she no longer depended on him… "What did you have in mind?"

She smirked at him, the look wicked as they came. "Why do I have a feeling that telling you would be a mistake?"

He pretended affront, his chuckle masked by a feigned gasp. "I am only here to serve you, even if I occasionally misstep."

"Hmm… I think I'll let it be a surprise." Her pale eyes glinted and, for the first time in centuries, he actually felt something akin to real nervousness. "You will continue hiding among them and relaying relevant information, but be ready."

"For what, exactly?"

"Oh, trust me"—Her smirk twisted into a full-blown grin—"you'll know. Now get the fuck out of my sight."

He plastered an answering smile onto his own face, blood boiling as he scrambled internally. "It shall be as you say." His body released his features and morphed into another's, already misting into the ether when he added, "I will be waiting."

Waiting to wring her little fucking neck at the first viable opportunity.

33

In the end, all they'd worked out before re-entering Straelon was... absolutely nothing.

Nothing that made sense. Nothing that lined up.

Not that there'd been much time for deep conversation.

Lunara slumped back against a long table in the great hall, the chaos of an abandoned breakfast littered across its surface, and fought to keep her lids from drooping. Ignoring the half-eaten sausage staring back at her from a porcelain plate was becoming increasingly difficult—especially since both Magnus and Thaddeus had no such reservations.

Lyriat had taken one look at their faces as they'd stumbled in, seen Hedda fast asleep in Faldir's arms, and commanded the remainder of their party to *'stay right fucking there'* before taking Hedda to bed with Brand and Faldir on his heels.

"Where shall I put her, my lady?"

Lunara shook herself and looked up at Baldrir, *Fern* limp in his arms. "Oh, umm..."

"My lady?"

Lunara blinked her eyes open. "Stars above, forgive me, Baldrir. We haven't slept and I..." she lightly smacked both of her cheeks, hoping the sting would help her focus. "The room next to mine would be ideal, if possible."

"I'll see it done." He started to turn away, saying over his shoulder, "If you like, Nyri and I can—"

"Move!"

Baldrir's lips pursed as he side-eyed Thad. "Sisters be with you, my friend. Caius has been in a right bloody state. I don't envy you."

"Where is he?!"

"Ah, fuck." Thaddeus scrambled beside her at that shouted demand from the corridor, doing his best to wedge his large body between the bench and tabletop—as if his father wouldn't immediately spot him under there in the empty hall.

"No use for it, lad," Magnus said around a mouthful of food, tugging Thad to his feet. "You wanted to be taken seriously? To be a warrior? Here's your chance. Accept it."

"Shite." Thaddeus cringed at an echoing bang and crash outside. "Maybe I'd rather be a coward after all."

Magnus chuckled. "No, you wouldn't. This isn't even the worst thing you've ever done. Just means more than before, aye? You'll be fine."

Thad loosed a slow breath and nodded, his jaw set.

"Get the fuck out of my way." Caius burst through the double doors with fury twisting his features, revealing a crowd of eavesdropping Demons before the panels slammed shut again. "Thaddeus!"

Despite his blond hair being combed and braided neatly on the sides, and the perfect press of his ceremonial robes, Caius looked haggard. Worn out. Deep lines bracketed his downturned mouth and burning eyes, mottled anger splashed across his face in almost impossible shades of red and purple.

Shitting stars. Maybe you *should be hiding…*

Caius located his quarry, wrath in every clipped step as he barreled over. "You daft, misbehaving, contrary bastard," he growled, only feet away. "I should fucking skin you."

Thaddeus shrank even further under those biting words, the fire in him dwindling with each snapping syllable.

Caius plowed straight into him, enveloping his son with both arms. The hug was desperate, almost violent in its fervor. "What were you thinking?" he breathed into Thad's hair, before pulling back and giving him a rough shake. "What were you *thinking,* Thaddeus?"

He stared down at his father, standing a little taller. "That it was high time everyone stopped treating me like a child."

Without warning, Caius lifted a hand and cuffed Thaddeus in the side of the head. "And you thought sneaking off and worrying me sick was the way to do it?"

"Aye, and I was wrong. I understand now." He sent her and Magnus a fleeting look as he grimaced and rubbed his ear. "I'm sorry, Da. It won't happen again."

Caius's hand was trembling when he jabbed a pointed finger in Thad's face. "You're damned right it won't." That same hand flattened against Thad's chest, clenching. "Are you hurt, lad? Well? What the fuck happened?"

"Ach… Um…" Thad gripped his nape, at a loss. "I'm fine. We're all fine? The rest is a wee bit hard to explain."

Caius sighed and released Thad. "Aye, no shite. One second I'm bringing permission from the Chieftains for the Demons to enter our lands at Faldir's request, and the next you're all back here looking harried as anything and no one knows fuck all about it."

Magnus clapped Caius on the back. "Trust me, uncle. Our account isn't going to help matters. Just know we wouldn't have succeeded without him. You'd have been proud."

An odd look flitted across Caius's face. "You went into battle?"

"Aye. I did." Thaddeus beamed, his chin lifting with pride. "I'm to be marked for my part."

"I can't decide whether to be pissed I wasn't there or to take you to do it now—mostly because it's going to fucking hurt and you deserve it!" Caius barked out a laugh as he embraced Thad again.

When Caius broke away, he finally caught sight of Baldrir holding Fern. "What the fuck?"

Magnus ran a hand through his hair. "One of those things that's hard to explain."

"Someone had better!"

Lunara stood on shaky legs. "We found her in Glynmor. Suffice it to say that she was… the only one left. Barely."

Caius recoiled. "She was there in the village?"

"Did Faldir tell you what happened?" Magnus asked, voice little more than a whisper.

"Aye, but only enough to have me running back to the Keep to beg for aid from all sides." Caius scrubbed a hand down his face. "A fucking mess, and no mistake."

"You have no idea," Magnus murmured.

"Shite." Caius crossed to Baldrir, his hand hovering above Fern's head. "How is she still alive?"

"Lunara found her in the watchtower clinging to life, and worked her magic."

"Aye, but look at her. So wee. She should've..." Caius turned to Lunara, his gaze searching.

Lunara's heart skipped a beat, its usual response whenever someone noted her power. It didn't care that everyone here already knew what she was capable of. Couldn't discern between friend and foe. Just stopped for a breathless second before restarting with a galloping pace that chanted *run, run, run* with every nauseating thump.

The dregs of her remaining energy leached away when Caius finally released her from his knowing stare and said, "The others, were they..."

"Worse." Magnus's voice was hoarse as he answered his uncle's unspoken question. "So much worse."

Caius blew out a heavy breath. "Fuck."

That was about the gist of the last few days.

Baldrir leaned down. "If you have no other need of me, my lady, I'll take her now."

"Yes, of course," Lunara said through a yawn.

"I was going to say—Nyri and I can keep her company, until you're ready?"

She nodded as she sat again, the wooden bench starting to look like the Montrealm's most comfortable bed. "That would put my mind at ease, thank you."

It was no use. Lunara propped her head in one hand as her eyes closed of their own accord.

"She's the only one who can tell us exactly what took place in Glynmor," she heard Magnus say. "Don't leave her side for a second, and fetch the witchling immediately if something changes."

Lunara huffed something akin to a laugh. Hopefully nothing *changed*. She'd be useless until she partook of a blood gift. Better still if she could steal a few hours of sleep and something to eat.

There's a bed five yards and a single toll behind you, and none of this nonsense to go with it.

Lunara cracked open one eye and sent a bleary glance towards the portal, the smallest part of her tempted by the idea. She was just so *tired.*

She gave up entirely and rested her head on the table, lulled by the quiet murmurings of the others into a sort of half-sleep. Not the most comfortable she'd ever been by a long shot, but it would have… to do… until…

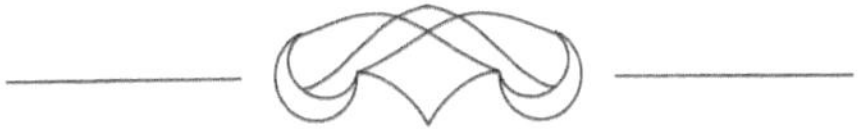

At least it was a dream this time. Or, as close as a memory cropping up in sleep could be called *a dream.*

Perhaps it was her parents' way of visiting from the Veil. She'd been thinking about them quite a lot, after all, and—even if she could never figure out *what* or *why*—she was still convinced there was something she was missing.

Regardless of which snippet of her youth was on display, she both observed as an outsider and lived them all over again. The dual view allowed her to notice things she hadn't before. Sometimes, it might be the way her mother had smelled. The next, it would be a small nick in her father's chin she hadn't realized was there.

Lunara never really allowed herself to see bigger than those mundane, once-missing details. She was too afraid of what she might find. This time, though…

She looked on, feeling every step as she watched herself move.

It was late in the Evesong. Too late for anyone to be awake, let alone for there to be such a heated discussion reverberating through the moonstone walls of her family's home.

Make that a muffled series of incomprehensible words she couldn't understand. Lunara saw no reason for that to remain the case.

Hence, the sneaking.

She hopped onto the glowing platform outside her bedroom door and sank. Like most Upper Block towers, theirs has been outfitted with the creation her father was most famous for, enchanted by him to work without any expulsion of personal power. A good thing, since she was reserving hers for her trial.

Lunara snorted at the smug smile on her younger face. If only she'd known.

On the lower level, her bare feet hit the cool floor and left a trail of glowing footprints, the luminescent tiles reacting to her every tip-toed step. Annoying, but such was the way of the Evesong. They'd fade before long.

At the library, Lunara pressed her back to the wall and craned her neck to better see through the partially open door.

Her father passed in and out of view, still fully dressed in his Council robes. "It's gone too far, Almaura. He's worse than the others, by a long way."

"I agree, but what can we do about it?" Her mother's voice reached across the distance, soothing even in distress. "We've said it a hundred times, but the others will never hold a vote so close to the Occurrence."

"Two years to find another is plenty."

"Stellan—"

"We can count on Cordelia to back us."

"Even if she convinced half of the Council, it wouldn't be enough. Unanimous or nothing, that's the rule. For our own sake!"

Lunara shuffled closer and spotted her mother upon a settee, head in her hands.

The black waves of Almaura's hair were mussed, her shoulders caved in and skin wan. Such despair, written right there on her body. Lunara had missed her mother's frustration, a sort of dark surrender. Had she known, even then, what was coming?

"That can't be the end of it!" Her father shouted. "We can fight the rules, make them hear us."

"Two of us cannot make them *do anything. They wish to shield him, so they will."*

"I know, but—"

"They'll wait, as ever, until it can no longer be denied by anyone. Do you think his mate will agree based on hearsay? And from whom? Some street urchin in the Lower Block who swears he saw a ghost do it?"

"Someone died today, Almaura."

The way her mother's eyes closed… She'd known. Maybe not the particulars, but enough. Lunara wanted to scream at Stellan to listen. To be a worse person than he truly was, and save himself. Save all of them.

Her mother abruptly stood. "I am aware. But there's no proof it was him. Nor was there proof for any of the others."

"He said her throat was ripped out by a phantom. Who else could it be!"

Lunara's gasp flew out of her, unchecked, and her parents' heads snapped up.

For the first time, Lunara wished she'd stopped that sound. What else would they have said? Which of their deepest thoughts would they have voiced? What difference might it have made?

"You may as well come in," her father said with a sigh. "Unless you prefer creeping around in the dark?"

Lunara pinched her lips between her teeth as she pushed into the room, looking anywhere but at them. "This is Nachthelliae. Aren't we all creeping around in the dark?" Her joke pulled a rueful smile from both of them. "Besides, I wasn't. I was getting a snack and thought I heard voices."

Her mother snorted. "You're a wretched liar, Lunara. Stick to the things you're good at."

Lunara's answering look was sheepish as her father wrapped strong arms around her. "I'm sorry you heard that," he said.

"Someone was murdered?" she asked, pulling away.

"Stellan, I don't— "

"She deserves to know, Almaura. She should understand what she's getting into when she endures her trial next week."

A spike of excitement thrummed. Only days until she'd exhibit her power, publicly claim her name, and join the Elder Tier. Maybe even the Council, like her parents.

Ignorant, optimistic fool. Lunara remembered that moment of exhilaration all too well—felt it again now, straight to her bones—and she wanted to shake her useless, youthful self to knock some modicum of sense into her.

"What does my trial have to do with it?"

Her father plopped onto the settee and patted the space beside him. She sat as her mother perched on the arm, her parents lacing their fingers—as always when they were near one another.

"The Council is... complicated," her father started. "You're aware of their basic responsibilities, but you haven't been exposed yet to our secret."

Her heart picked up speed. More proof she was soon to be an Elder herself, privy to things others weren't.

"I don't like this, Stellan."

A new ache bloomed watching her mother this time. Almaura had hidden it so well. The worry. The terror. It crept over her face so subtly it was no wonder Lunara hadn't picked up on it before.

"Better she hear it from us than some prettified version when she's initiated."

Her father lifted a lock of her hair, rubbing the strands. He was always fiddling like that.

"The Keeper is our most sacred burden, Lunara."

"Burden?" The word confused her. How could their protector, a gift to the Evesong from the Sisters themselves, be a burden?

When she said as much, her father let his head fall back to stare at the ceiling. "Sometimes a Keeper… loses their way. It's our responsibility to determine when they're no longer fit to wield the stone."

"I know that. The vote is cast and they relinquish Illamiata to the next, living the rest of their days on the Isle in reward for their service."

Her parents gave each other a long look, her mother's jaw clenching. "Not exactly," she said.

"The Elder Council watches the Keeper"—her father rubbed at his forehead—"for signs their journey is at its end."

That was… cryptic.

"Would someone please say whatever it is in plain words?"

It was her mother who finally answered. "We don't vote to send the Keepers off to a luxurious life on the Isle. We pool our gifts and use them to reclaim Illamiata through violence. It takes all of us, and we have to agree because we vote to eliminate *them, Lunara—at great personal risk to ourselves."*

She blinked, comprehending and yet… not.

"As far as we're concerned, Malachyr has reached his end. He's becoming erratic, strange. He's hard to find, and tragedies are piling up behind him."

"You think Malachyr the Mistwarden is murdering people?*"*

Hearing that name, spoken so reverently from her own lips and with such disbelief, opened a pit in Lunara's stomach.

He'd been the Keeper longer than she'd been alive. She pictured his angular face, the way he commanded a room and was always so kind to her. She couldn't imagine him harming anyone.

"Yes," her father rasped, "but it isn't his fault. Illamiata corrupts its vessel over time. The Keepers know this going in, and accept they'll have to sacrifice their lives for the honor of once holding it. Everything they do is for the Evesong. The Elders created the story of the Isle centuries ago because fallen Keepers deserved to have their memories held in the highest esteem after their death."

Shitting stars above. It hit Lunara all over again that Stellan had been the kindest male in all of Bordoroth. Gentle. Forgiving. Understanding. Even towards those who didn't deserve it.

"If that's their purpose, and they know he killed that girl…"

"They don't know without a shadow of doubt, and that's the problem," her mother said. "No one saw *him. At least, no one with enough credibility."*

"So they know, but are protecting him anyway."

"Yes." That one word from her father's lips said so much more than its single syllable.

He gripped her hand. "It's complicated. Malachyr has succumbed faster than most Keepers before him. He was meant to get us through the next Occurrence at least, *but only made it a few decades. That's alarming, and no one knows what to do with it."*

It wasn't complicated. Not to her.

"I don't…" Her stomach turned. "I want nothing to do with that."

Lunara hadn't been a total idiot, thank the Sisters.

Her mother reached down to cup her face. "Lunara—"

"No." She stood, pacing. "How could I while knowing that? I thought I'd be helping people, leading our realm. Not covering up crimes and catering to murderers."

"You must understand," her father said, his gaze pleading. "The essence of the Council is good. It would only get better with more that share your mindset. If you don't like the way it is, change it. That's what we're trying to do."

She considered her father's words, willing to admit their validity to a point. "I'll think about it."

No, don't think. Just go! Run, as fast as you—

A flash of white glinted in Lunara's periphery and she spun, coming face-to-face with a door. Gilded in gold and teeming with strange, intricate designs, it rose up from the middle of the floor, ever so slightly ajar.

In a daze, she moved towards it. Towards the light spilling through the crack that wasn't quite right, and the answers it might give her. Her hand wrapped around the massive, curved handle at its center and a laugh bubbled up out of her.

No, wait. That wasn't her—

34

"LUNA?"

Lunara sprang up, groaning as prickling pain danced along every nerve ending. "Stars and arses," she hissed, her neck spasming. "Shite."

"Forgive me." Brand was kneeling before her, a goblet in one hand, his other clearing hair from her face. "You deserve a bed, but this is the best I can do for now."

She'd only closed her eyes for a second…

The light in the great hall had shifted, long shadows across the marbled floor, and the tables had been cleared, leaving the scent of lemon soap in the air.

She didn't have it in her to ask how long she'd been lost in the past and its mysteries. The only correct answer was *not long enough,* and anything else might free the scream lodged in her throat.

When she reached for the goblet and her stiff fingers refused to work, her next groan was closer to a sob.

"Shh, it's alright. Let me help you." Brand cradled the back of her head and brought the cup to her lips.

She nearly choked when the blood hit her tongue, the relief was so instant. It tasted of him, of rightness, and she hadn't realized how desperately she'd been craving it. Downing every drop was easy. So, so easy.

Fool.

Lunara gasped the first unhindered breath she'd had since the cave. Then another.

Her body had learned to twist itself, convincing her it was fine when it wasn't. She never realized just how shite she was feeling until all the pain evaporated and she was reminded that limbs were supposed to bend and move, that skin should shift and stretch, without it being a torture.

"Better?"

Blessed moons, even his voice sounded richer. "Yes," she rasped. "Thank you. I was…"

"I know. I'm so sorry." He pressed a kiss to her forehead. "A little longer, and then we can sleep for three bloody days if you want to."

Sounded like bliss.

He led her towards the dais, where the others were waiting. Faldir and Caius stood either side of Lyriat, arms crossed and faces pinched.

The king surveyed Magnus and Thaddeus first, then pinned Brand with a look. "How bad?"

"Bad enough for what you're thinking," Brand answered.

Lyriat nodded and rounded his throne without another word, motioning for them to follow. At the back wall, where a golden image of Solyrian was etched into the expanse, a doorway shimmered into being beneath his palm. He led them through, into the pitch black and down the beginnings of steep, spiraling steps.

Lunara flinched when the door sealed behind, burying them in darkness for an eternal breath—until intermittent stones came to life, their light disappearing down and around the tight bend, highlighting the cobwebs and dust clinging to the crevices and corners.

No one spoke as they made their descent. The air grew heavier as they sank ever further into the earth, stale and stifling, and she longed for a breeze as a bead of nervous sweat trickled down her back.

At long last, they hit a landing, an ancient wooden door before them. Carvings nearly identical to the ones on Lyriat's throne covered the surface, accentuated by the striated stones glowing softly around it.

"I have seldom brought others to this place," Lyriat said, casting a sidelong glance at Brand, "but it seems we have need of it now. I'll trust you to keep its existence to yourselves."

Lunara's soul left her body when he laid his hand on the door and the hewn images jumped to life, creeping up his arm and teasing a wayward hank of his copper hair. The power was immense. Ancient, like the cavern pool. Beckoning, even as it repulsed her.

A click sounded and the door cracked open. Lyriat gently extracted himself from the grasping branches and they melted back into place as if they'd never moved at all.

The power remained, though, thrumming just below the surface.

Shitting stars. No. No, no, no. Bad idea to go through there.

He pushed and revealed a square room with no decorations or embellishments—only a huge, circular stone table in the center with a ring of benches around it.

Lyriat plopped down onto one of them with a weary sigh and lifted his hand. A fireplace she hadn't noticed on the back wall blazed to life at his command, the flames casting him in a foreboding silhouette.

They filed in, and Brand led her to the far side of the table next to Lyriat. Faldir took a seat to the king's other side, Magnus and Thad beside him. Only Caius remained standing, his eyes wary.

"I feel like I've been led to my grave," he mumbled with a shudder. "It isn't natural down here."

Lyriat nodded. "I was only a boy when my father first showed me this place. Right before he died, in fact, like he knew it was coming." There was something strange in the way he said it—a false lightness and a rigid set to his shoulders. "He swore any secrets whispered within would find themselves imprisoned, trapped in the stone for all time. The older I get, the more I realize he meant it quite literally. In all the years I've ruled Straelon, not a single word I've uttered in this room has escaped its confines."

He closed his eyes and crossed his arms. "Speak. Explain. Leave nothing out."

So they did—her, Brand, and Magnus weaving the story in turns. Glynmor, Fern, the burial. Thad blushed when they recounted his appearance, not even bothering to argue Magnus's colorful version of it. It wasn't until the part they realized Faldir was missing, how it had affected Hedda and the choices they'd made, that the conversation turned.

"We thought you'd been taken," she rasped in Faldir's direction, "so we followed you down into the Thodelemaia Chasm. Heard your screams and tracked your blood—"

"The fuck?"

"You *what?"*

They spoke over one another, Faldir recoiling while Lyriat slapped his hands onto the tabletop, all of his white-hot intensity directed at her.

Wonderful. You're doing great. By the way, the portal is right upstairs.

"I..." Lunara swallowed, shrinking back and ready to run for her bleeding life if his face got any redder. "I shielded us from the shadows, and we—"

"We had a deal, Lunara," Lyriat seethed. "You were to protect them. Heal them. Not facilitate a jaunt into one of the bloody chasms."

"I know, but—"

Brand gripped her thigh, cutting off the rest of her words. "Watch your tone," he said, his voice low. "I was going down whether she *facilitated it,* or not. Your ire is misplaced."

"All I'm hearing is that she incapacitated Hedda easily enough, but decided not to extend the courtesy to the rest of you!"

"It never would've crossed my mind to do so. It was bad enough taking Hedda's freedom, and I only did it out of absolute necessity. "

Lyriat's laugh was not in the least amused. "So, in the midst of an as-yet-undiscovered political subterfuge, you not only didn't try to stop them, but actually helped my family—*Imperial Sons of Bordoroth*—make their merry way into a Dread Chasm."

"Lyriat..." Brand's fingers tightened, and she dropped her hand to grip them. To find a modicum of calm in the touch.

"It wasn't that simple. And technically, it was only Brand and I—"

"What?!" Caius that time, his canines flashing with the growled demand. "Only the two of you?"

"There wasn't another choice." Brand drew in a deep breath.

Lyriat looked between them, his disbelief evident. "Have you lost your Sisters-damned minds?"

"They must have." Faldir's fists clenched, a look of hurt in his eyes. "Brand would never be so daft as to go into danger without his twin shadows, otherwise."

"How dare you?" Lunara breathed. "He was devastated—we were *all* devastated—over *you."*

He looked away from her, a muscle ticking in his jaw and pulling on the twisted scar down his cheek.

"Losing one of you was bad enough," Brand rasped. "I wouldn't endanger anyone else, and I was the only one who could make a safe way down. Lunara insisted on shielding me, with good reason. She repelled the shadows. They're volatile. Alive, even, like in Meliora's—"

"What the fuck did you just say?" Caius's voice was no less furious for its hushed tone.

Oh, shite.

"I told him some of it. I had to. If you'd been there…"

His glare was just shy of outright murder.

Brand explained about the shadows and ooze, the others listening with bated breath and slack jaws. "That's when we found the army of fledgeling Forgotten. When… when Lunara…" Brand scrubbed a hand over his face. "It doesn't matter. We ended up—"

"No, Brand." Lyriat's nostrils flared. "I said to leave nothing out, and I damned well meant it."

"Some things are not necessary for you to hear. It affects nothing of substance in the end."

Nothing except the trajectory of your entire life, but who's keeping track anymore.

If Lyriat's eyes burned any hotter, he'd be setting them on fire. "I don't appreciate you being cagey about this."

Brand jerked back. "I'm not being bloody *cagey*. I'm trying to be sensitive, and you're being an arsehole."

The two were ready to come to blows, aggressive power radiating off of them in waves.

Don't even think about it, you—

"Please, Your Majesty." Lunara swallowed, trying to ignore the fluttering pulse in her throat. "He's only protecting me. Perhaps it would be in everyone's best interest if—"

"Perhaps it would be in *your* best interest to keep quiet for now, Lunara." Lyriat cocked his head to one side, considering her. "Or maybe he's protecting you in the same way you protected him—which is to say, not at fucking all, and that's just a convenient excuse."

Magnus stood abruptly, a finger pointed at Lyriat. "Now wait a fucking second."

"Maybe his silence on the matter benefits you because you're hiding something. You're good at that, aren't you, Lunara?"

Her stomach soured and flipped over, threatening to dispel its contents.

"Say one more fucking word to her, Lyriat." Brand's voice was little more than a snarl. "I dare you."

"See, on top of the mystery surrounding Baldrir's assailant, there's now a pretender in the Montrealm. *My* realm." He leaned back and crossed his arms again, his gaze never leaving her as golden patterns lit up and danced over his skin. "Someone. Somehow. Faldir is there and here at once? Both dead and alive? Hedda swears on the Sisters she never spoke to him that night, but *he* swears on the souls of every lost loved one it was *her* who commanded him to procure help."

Where in the starry shite is he going with this?

"It hasn't gone unnoticed that everything was relatively bland in Straelon until you showed up."

Run. Run, run, run.

"You're saying it's *Lunara?*" Rage was etched in every hard line of Brand's face.

Lyriat's horns began to curl, his fangs dropping down. "As I've tried to impress upon you from the beginning, I'm saying it could be fucking *anyone*, and I know her the least."

"She saved my mam." Thad was looking at Lyriat like he didn't know him. "I trust her with my life."

"She *tried* to save your mam," Caius rasped. "She didn't though, did she? Even though Brand swears to have seen her repel the very shadows she now claims were in Meliora."

Lyriat's eyes finally left her to narrow on Caius. "Interesting point."

Goosebumps spread over the entirety of Lunara's body. This wasn't actually happening.

Not real.

Thad shook his head. "No one else offered their home to stay in. No one else was able to wake and soothe her. Lunara's the only reason I got to speak to her a final time."

"Regardless"—Lyriat raised an imperious hand at Thad—"none of this is relevant to the fact that we had a deal and, in the end, she deemed it appropriate to venture into the most dangerous part of our world instead of honoring it. And you, Brand, are now withholding the details."

"It isn't fucking like that!" Brand bellowed. "You want to make us relive it? Fine!" His fist hit the table, power rippling over its surface. "She nearly died! I watched my mate try to save a child and be skewered for her kindness. I held her insides together with my own fucking hand! Felt her heart stutter—"

Lunara couldn't hear the rest of his words, ears ringing, chest constricting with every shallow exhale. The others were shouting now too, she could see that much. Fingers wagging. Arms waving.

Too much. Not your fight. Just go, get out of here.

Lyriat thought *she* was the one who'd done this? She couldn't handle it. Shouldn't be here. Was out of her depth.

She was a single breath from bolting—from taking her chances with the mystical murder door, racing up the stairs, and flinging herself straight through the portal—when a flame jumped in the fireplace and hit Brand *just so.*

She was back in the cave, wrapped in his misery. His passion. His trust.

The way he'd relied on her to help him forget, and given himself in return. The way he'd rocked her back and forth in a ravaged patch of broken wildflowers after their battle with the beast, every other breath catching as he tried not to be crushed beneath the weight of his own anguish.

She heard Hedda's screams and her dash for the chasm's edge.

Felt Magnus nearly dying, Pet panting beneath her hands.

Watched Thaddeus and Sorcha's fearless heroics, their first real triumph in battle.

What they'd accomplished and discovered… The reasons they'd done it…

Lyriat was the one who'd wanted her to '*account for the intensity of the days*' spent in their company. To embrace their friendship. Now he was throwing it back at her?

Exactly the sort of thing she'd been running from all her life. Arrogant leaders demanding their due and having no thought for anything else.

Lunara refused to run from him as well.

If he wanted to bring up their deal, she'd make damned sure he remembered it exactly.

Bleeding, fucking eejit.

"Faldir was gone!" Her scream silenced the senseless cacophony. "A single soul had been left alive in Glynmor. If you'd seen it… There was no way we could've left Faldir to the same fate. So yes, Brand and I followed, while the other two protected the vulnerable."

She leaned in towards Lyriat, no thought for how monumentally idiotic it was to do so. "I did *exactly* what you wanted, Your Majesty. What was it you said? *'Whatever trials come up, whatever ailments or surprises—you stay by their side and see them finished.'* You should know by now that a Nachthellian never forgets a word of the deals they make, nor do they break them intentionally. Our society depends on them too completely."

She was shaking, almost dizzy with the lightness each word brought. "Did I make mistakes? Yes. I was fully prepared to release you of our bargain, thinking I'd failed to meet my end by losing Faldir to the depths. But don't you dare throw accusations at me. I did everything within my power to make it right and control the damage."

Brand's solid presence towered behind her, his hand on her lower back, and the slow, soothing circles of his thumb gave her strength.

She had no recollection of standing up.

Throwing her shoulders back, she raised a brow at the Demon King of Straelon like a complete numpty. "Look me in the eye and tell me you wouldn't have done precisely the same thing under the same conditions. That you could've wrangled these arseholes any better. As you so aggressively reminded me, they are *Imperial Sons*. They pretty much do whatever they damned well please!"

Now you've got all that out, fucking run!

It was either the most foolish thing she'd ever done, or the most brilliant. Hard to tell with everyone gaping at her.

May as well add another stitch to the funeral shroud, as it were.

"You're focusing on the wrong things. Forget the logistics of *how*. What's done, is done, and we made it back alive. Thank the Sisters. We should be talking about the army of Forgotten. About the fact that dreadbeasts are real, and we were forced to bring one down."

She reached into the ether and one of its talons plunked onto the center of the table, wobbling back and forth as it settled.

"Who would go to such lengths to get us down there? What was their point? Why us, and why now?"

The silence as Caius, Faldir, and Lyriat stared at the jagged spike—the others doing their best to look anywhere else—was one of the most gratifying sounds she'd ever heard.

"You want to uncover *political subterfuge* and find your imposter? Then start asking the right questions."

35

BRAND PULLED THE QUILT UP AROUND LUNA'S CHIN, TUCKING IT AROUND HER shoulders.

"I have to check on Fern," she mumbled, the words slurred.

His heart flipped, eyes pricking. Half-asleep and dead on her feet, and she was still fighting. Only for others, though, never herself. It bothered him, even as a wave of pride swelled.

"Nyri and Bal are with her." He pressed his lips to her forehead, tempted to linger. "Close your eyes. Rest. Your wellness is just as important, and you'll need it to help her, yes?"

Her reply was a vague series of garbled sounds, and she was fast asleep before he straightened.

He wanted to stay—to stare down at her slack face squashed against the pillow, fingertips tangled in glinting strands of hair that refused to be tamed, and spend the night wondering what he'd done to deserve such a creature—but Magnus was waiting.

For what, Brand didn't know. He'd been prowling out in the corridor for the last quarter hour, refusing to take the hint and go away. Instead, the impatient ripple of his brother's predatory power continued to seep under the door, demanding attention.

Whatever he wanted had better be bloody fucking important—and nought to do with that travesty of a meeting.

His hand trailed over her leg as he walked away. "I'll be back as soon as I can."

He slipped out of Luna's room, the door latching softly behind him, and turned to his brother.

"What the fuck was that?"

Brand called on his remaining patience, rubbing a palm along one horn. "An unfortunate example of the hazy power dynamics between Imperials and the realms they serve?"

"Don't get fucking cute with me, you wee shite," Mag growled, pushing past him and stalking down the corridor. "That was a mess down there, and you know it. Come on."

He did. If not for the note he'd spotted on Luna's nightstand, he'd be raging his way back to the great hall and plowing his fist straight into Lyriat's face. "All is not as it seems. Let's leave it at that."

"Ach, you don't say. Was it Lyriat's new personality, or the *imposter* part that tipped you off?"

"Very funny," Brand deadpanned, raising a brow. "Where are we going?"

Mag ran a hand through his flaxen hair with a sigh. "In case you were looking to add to the nonsense, the first of the messengers has returned. Well, aside from the one sent to fetch Caius, obviously."

Brand's heart kicked up. He'd put the messengers out of his mind, knowing the responses would take more time than he had the mental space to worry about. The odds that the first would come back tonight, after everything… Fucking uncanny.

What were they *missing*?

"Which realm, and what did they say?" he asked, nodding to the guards as they pushed into the great hall.

"See for your damned self."

The rich scent of grilled fish and roasted vegetables hit him, the fare passing by on large platters. Most of the Horned City was probably having supper down in the square, drinking and dancing as anticipation for the Occurrence reached a fever pitch, but the hall was still swarming—except for one empty corner.

"Vann?"

A warm grin spread across Mag's face in answer.

The Demons closest to Valandyrian aht Bordoroth, Second Imperial

Son, gave him a wide berth, lost somewhere between awe and unease. They were well aware of who was among them—hence the sharp murmurs and wary looks being tossed over their shoulders in his direction.

Brand picked through the crowd, and it was all he could do not to snap at his brethren. None of the rumors were true. His next oldest brother only *looked* daunting. Otherwise, Vann and Mag had spent a lifetime competing for first place as the most charming male Brand had ever bloody met.

Vann rose slowly to his feet with the ghost of a smile, dipping his head in greeting. "Hello, little brothers." A sharply pointed ear stuck out on one side as the satin sheet of his silver hair fell forward, before he straightened and tucked it away. "I hear you've been having all the fun, and saving none for the rest of us. Rude, wouldn't you say?"

Mag laughed and clapped Vann on the side of the face, drawing him in for a hug. "You'd have been bored to tears."

"Now, why don't I believe you?" Vann planted a kiss in Mag's hair and broke away to dart mismatched eyes over Brand. "Hmm." Brow furrowed, his head tilted to one side. "Something's changed."

The statement hit Brand a hundred different ways—not all of them good. "Truth be told, everything has changed," he admitted quietly.

Vann nodded and stepped closer, his arms tentatively outstretched. "May I greet you properly?"

Another punch to the gut. It had been quite a while since… since he'd been around anyone who might feel the need to ask.

Refusing most touch outside of sparring was one wall of many he'd inadvertently built over the years—part of an intricate, hardened framework designed to protect himself from… something.

Looking at his brother, at the cautious hope in his expression, Brand suddenly couldn't recall why he'd done that. Why he'd drawn a line in the sand and only allowed a precious few to cross it. Why Mag and Thad would be exceptions, but not Vann.

Especially considering the sheer amount of damned hugging and crying he'd been doing lately.

No. Not *lately.* Since… since the feast, weeks ago, when he'd called out to the Sisters and asked for a boon. A desperate plea to be remade. To be given peace and have his spirit eased.

Burning Solyrian, he hadn't even realized the connection. Luna had come crashing in like a comet the very next morning, upending his carefully structured life in wonderful, mystifying ways—all he'd ever wanted, and exactly what he'd needed.

An answer to prayer.

With her, he could breathe. For her, he could be more.

Aching regret crawled up his throat as he stared at his Fae brother. "Yes," he finally rasped. "Please."

Vann chuckled and enveloped him in a gentle embrace, as if afraid Brand would bolt if he squeezed too hard. "There you are," he whispered. "It's been a long while."

Brand huffed into the high collar of Vann's overcoat. "I saw you two months ago."

He knew exactly what Vann meant, but he wasn't ready to talk about it. Not in the great hall where anyone might hear.

"Yes, but"—Vann gave him the customary Fae kiss as well, the accompanying sting of power sending prickles along his scalp—"you were rather peeved that day, if I recall, eh?"

Brand gave him a shove, laughing. "You raised the price on the fabric we Demons rely on almost exclusively to clothe ourselves. Of course I was bloody *peeved.*"

Vann waved that away. "I was merely the grudging messenger. Speaking of which..." He pulled both of Brand's letters from an inside breast pocket, the edges already worn and crinkled. "I've brought that thing you requested. Since it was done, and I didn't feel like waiting alone to hear from Argoph about the other foolery, here I am. Also"—He retrieved a bottle black as night from some other hidden compartment, followed by the box of rolled herbs he was never without, and flourished both in Brand's direction—"I've missed the particularly stunning view of the Horned City from your balcony."

Mag snatched the bottle of enchanted Fae wine with a whistle of appreciation. "Vann, you perfect bastard. If you knew the kind of week we've had..."

Vann glanced at the hall and leaned in, voice low. "I know precisely the kind of week you've had. Or, at least, enough of it. It's all anyone is blimmin' talking about along the chasm border on our side. Surprise! You had an audience."

"Wonderful," Mag grumbled. "No one thought to, I don't know, *help*?"

"They were too busy spreading the news like wildfire. Everyone in the known world will be sufficiently terrified by this time next week." Vann tapped his box on Brand's chest, brows raised. "How about that view?"

Brand sighed, his head hanging. All he wanted was to tear through the castle as fast as his feet would take him, straight back to Luna. To bed and sleep, and the feel of her pressed close.

But... Fuck.

Duty—as ever—was calling.

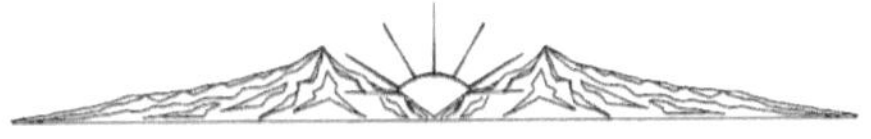

"So you see why we may have quite the issue on our hands now."

Vann took another drag of his herbs, the smoke curling around the glowing tip to cast him in a mystical sort of light.

It was the warmest night they'd had all summer, the breeze too quiet to offer much relief. Still, Brand could hear the festival going on in the distant city center, fiddles and drums accompanying the sound of laughter far below.

"We already had our bloody fair share of issues," Lyriat groaned, sliding down in his chair to rest his head back and stretch his long legs out further.

Discovering dreadbeasts were real had been bad enough. Learning from his brother that a slew of Fae had witnessed their battle across the chasm before flitting off to tell everyone they knew? Worse. By this time next month, most of Bordoroth would find themselves with some wild version of the story.

Someone, somewhere, would swear they'd seen ten dreadbeasts with their own eyes. Another would describe injuries and failures that had never taken place. A third would find a way to turn it on the Imperials and Realm Rulers in some sort of conspiratorial diatribe. On and on and...

The result would be a widespread panic that would take all their combined efforts to mitigate—and the idea of having to downplay a colossal fucking problem in order to keep the peace didn't sit very well.

"Yes," Vann said. "Hence Brand's letter. Care to share?"

"Ach, careful," Mag grumbled from his perch on the balustrade, taking a swig of the Fae wine before passing it to Lyriat with a grin. "He's as likely to strangle you as answer you."

"One measly loss of control and it's all anyone can focus on." Lyriat snatched the bottle away. Staring at Vann, he rolled the neck of it between his hands. "Considering you just told us there were countless Fae standing by gawping instead of helping, tell me... How do I know you can be trusted? What proof do you have the Tempusrealm and its people had nothing to do with any of it?"

Vann considered that. "At the moment? None, other than my assurances as your friend. The creatures who saw the battle were not warriors, and you know it's more complicated than that to go from realm to realm. Flying across a chasm isn't done, eh?" Another drag, another twining whirl of smoke. "I'll admit the Eternal Ones have been rather tetchy of late, but the reason is personal in nature. Sadly, I'm forbidden from saying more."

"Aye, definitely getting throttled."

"For fucks' sake, Magnus." Lyriat took his own deep pull of the wine and scrubbed a hand over his face.

Vann reached over and gripped Lyriat's shoulder. "I promise you my queens are focused inward right now, not outward. They had no motive for what was done to Baldrir, and all of us were just as shocked as the next to hear of the dreadbeast. You have my vow to the Sisters."

Brand found himself staring intently at his Fae brother, searching, a small part of him ashamed he would even consider Vann's guilt or feel the need to look for it.

"Fuck it." Lyriat plopped the bottle into Brand's lap and sat forward. "Since you already know all that, there can't be any harm in the rest of it. Brand?"

His turn for a drink. The amber liquid went down like honeyed sunshine, the slightest fizz crackling on his tongue. Normally, he might've savored the sweet, floral taste or the way his limbs went weightless. This time, he was only grateful it wouldn't run out or give them a hangover, no matter how much they imbibed.

Blind fucking drunk with none of the ramifications had a certain appeal this evening.

Brand dragged the back of his hand across his mouth. "Baldrir came back from his torture with a message…"

He, Mag, and Lyriat took the story in turns, right up to their return. Vann remained silent throughout, only his eyes and breath betraying his disturbance.

"You're being targeted," he said when they were finished. "Both the Demons *and* the Wolflords."

"So it would seem." Lyriat's gaze moved inward. "But for what?"

"The same thing any and all of the past offenders have wanted," Vann replied. "Power. Control. The money that comes with it. How many times have we done this dance? There's always someone who's unsatisfied, convinced they'd do it 'better,' and they rarely care who they hurt to get there. This business with Faldir being in two places, though… That's the most confounding part."

"Aye, no shite." Mag plucked the smoldering dart from Vann's fingers and put it to his own lips, breathing deep. "If it's a shapeshifter, anyone could be anyone."

"If it's a shapeshifter, we are on an entirely different level of *issues* than we thought."

Lyriat eyed Vann for a moment. "You're going to need to elaborate. Convincingly, since having a creature such as that in my realm is another clue pointing towards the Fae."

Vann chuckled, unbothered by the accusation. "True shapeshifters are so rare as to almost be fiction in Kohamaia. No one's seen or heard of one being born in a couple hundred years, and the documented instances before are almost as few and far between. The land has… forgotten that old magic, except for within the Imperial Line. Even then, we can only do it the one, uncontrollable time." He reached for the wine and his herbs in turn, partaking of both before he said, "Tell me, did you *see* Faldir in the chasm at any point?"

"No," Brand answered. "Only heard his voice, clear as day, and found signs of a struggle. At the time, it all made sense. Now…"

Vann shrugged, settling back. "Seems to me you have no evidence of an actual shapeshifter and are possibly letting your imaginations run away with you."

"We aren't bloody children." Lyriat loosed a long-suffering sigh. "How else would you explain Hedda and Faldir's accounts? He swears up and down she came to him during his watch and commanded him home for reinforcements, while *she* insists—vehemently—that such a thing never happened."

"Are you certain she was drugged? For all you know, she took too much of her own tonic, told Faldir to go, and simply cannot remember. Or one of them is lying."

"Neither of my cousins is lying," Lyriat growled. "I would know."

"Hmm." Vann's head tilted, almost animalistic in his movement. "Fair enough. Might be time to look at the Nachthellians. If you heard, but didn't see… Overturning the soil and mimicking a person's tone are well within the bounds of their magic, and procuring blood to further trick you would be no hardship for them."

All eyes went to Brand, their implication clear.

"Don't even think about accusing Lunara again," he hissed. "In fact, since we're on the subject, allow me to make myself perfectly clear." Brand stood from his chair, head spinning with drink as he leveled a trembling finger at Lyriat. "That meeting was an insult to everyone in it, but especially her. If you ever do anything like that again, Sisters help us both. She's off limits. Find your answers another way."

"That was awfully close to disloyalty, my friend," Lyriat murmured. "Perhaps I should be wary of you instead. You *did* send Baldrir to the Westrealm, after all, starting this chain of events."

Brand recoiled, blinking. One beat of utter silence, two… Both Mag and Vann disintegrated into choked laughter, falling all over each other as they wheezed.

"Your face!" Vann managed, barely keeping hold of the wine.

"Ach, put your curling horns away and sit down, you wee shite." Mag grabbed the back of Brand's trousers and yanked him backwards into the seat he'd vacated. "We all know there isn't a creature in all of Bordoroth less likely to betray their people. Weeping Sisters, the lass has you half out of your head if you can't see he was joking."

Mag's reminder that he was, in fact, feeling every raw effect of his incomplete mating tempered the rage he hadn't noticed rising. The rest of it bled away at Lyriat's unrepentant smile, leaving Brand more dizzy than before. "Bloody arseholes."

Lyriat chuckled. "Usually."

Vann turned serious, sending up a small shower of sparks as he flicked the spent dart of herbs away. "Your mate might be innocent, but that doesn't mean her people are."

No. It didn't.

Brand buried his head in his hands, the thought too depressing. "It doesn't make any *sense* for a realm to be plotting against another, and none of us brothers have heard a word of it. And for what?"

"*Three* of us brothers haven't heard a word of it." Vann's voice was gentle as he waved the wine beneath Brand's nose, goading him into having more. "Who knows what Amun or Araxis might say."

"We'll not be hearing from either of them until Da chimes in," Mag said. "Amun's up to the neck in Heir duties, and Axie is, well… *Axie*. You know how they are. Coaxing them out before their presence is necessary will be difficult."

"What if chaos is the goal?" Lyriat said, rubbing at his temples. "To wreak havoc and confusion, and force us into these pointless conversations that go 'round and 'round to keep us distracted?"

"Distracted from what, exactly?" Mag pushed from the railing to sit on the foot of Vann's lounge. "There doesn't seem to be a damned thing going on elsewhere."

"We've got an army of Forgotten in the Thodelemaia chasm, dread-beasts, potential imposters, kidnapping and torture, mass murder. There's plenty *going on* elsewhere. We just don't know what it is." Vann toyed with his box of herbs, a spark of mischief in his mismatched eyes. "Could it be… the Prophecy?"

They all burst out laughing, Mag shoving a hand in their brother's face. "Ach, away with that dragonshite."

Indeed.

Same as their father and uncles before them, their entire childhood had been built around the Shadow Prophecy—a manic poem of pending doom delivered to their grandfather, Emperor Stennyx, by an oracle of unknown origins. Battle training and constant lessons, memorization of its claims and time spent theorizing its meaning…

After centuries of anxious dissecting, the only thing her words yielded was the splintering of Stennyx's mind and family. Brand and his brothers knew better now, wiser with their years, and had long ago decided to put it in its place—little more than a joke, used to cover all manner of sadness.

No Daughters being born since was mere coincidence. Plenty of creatures didn't have female babes, and 'gender' was almost irrelevant in Bordoroth anyway.

Truth was, this round of shite was just another drop in the bucket of terrible things that sometimes happened—things that had fuck all to do with that sham of a foretelling—and they were well aware of it.

Vann slapped Magnus away, grinning. "Admit it, you toyed with the idea."

"Never," Mag countered, puffing up. "Not even when Thad said the same thing a couple weeks ago." He flopped backwards and crossed his feet, planting them in Brand's lap. "Light up another and pass it around, Vann. We're all too sober for this fucking superstitious nonsense."

"Here, here!" Lyriat called out, brandishing the wine bottle. "To forgetting our troubles for a few hours."

Brand tamped down his groan, torn between his heart and head. He gave in to the camaraderie but, even as they cackled through the night to welcome the first rays of morning, he was only half there.

The other part of him was across the castle, with Luna.

36

Soap and water splashed a discordant tune as Lunara washed Fern's spiraling hair, grimy suds dripping from the strands and into a bucket below.

She could've easily snapped her fingers and had the mass clean, like she had for the rest of the Fae's body, but some parts of healing were more than clinical. It took attention and care to get someone truly well. Lunara wanted her to know someone was there for her, even in sleep. That she mattered enough to make the effort.

It had made all the difference when Brand had washed her hair in that icy river after Glynmor. He'd calmed her panic, made her feel safe, and she'd felt inspired to offer the same to Fern.

Besides, the task was a welcome distraction from everything.

A convenient way to stall, more like.

That, too.

For the hundredth time, Lunara surveyed the extensive damage to Fern's body and wings, and had to force down deep breaths. Her own flesh still remembered their moment of connection in the watchtower. The agony it had caused.

The excuse of getting the Fae clean was a convenient one, giving Lunara the time she needed to prepare herself for the inevitable.

Oh, just get it over with.

Right. As soon as she—

The door opened, and Nyri breezed in, tray in hand. "Good morning! How's my newest friend?"

Lunara snorted. Leave it to Nyri to make friends with a comatose creature. "Still mangled." She averted her eyes, rinsing her hands and pretending to look for a towel. "Have you seen Brand this morning?"

Oh, good one. You definitely pulled off the indifference. The high-pitched, breathy quality wasn't at all tragic.

He'd artfully extricated them from yesterday's meeting before she could rip out all of her hair. In truth, she hadn't quite recognized him, steeped in diplomacy and subtle wording. She was starting to get the impression that Brand had many facets, depending on which role he was filling. So far, she'd met the lover, the Demon, the warrior, and the Ambassador. Sisters knew who else he was hiding.

Lunara couldn't decide whether it was a comforting notion or an alarming one. She just wanted *him*—not whichever version it was who'd tucked her into bed with a chaste kiss on the forehead before disappearing, without leaving so much as a note to tell her what in the bleeding realms was happening between them.

Even Lyriat—the arsehole—had thought to leave a note.

Brand had called her his home. She'd maybe, *possibly*, started to think the same of him in return. At the very least, she'd thought they would sleep beside one another. Or that he'd be there when she woke up. And why the guest room instead of his own chamber? Her parents had always shared a room and bed, as mates were supposed to do. Unless... Demons were different and didn't live in the same space as their mates?

No. That would be silly. Right?

You still being here is the only thing that's silly.

Strictly speaking, they weren't actually mated yet. The bond had yet to be forged, and... Shite. Maybe he was having second thoughts. It would explain his staying away from her. She could be confusing his kindness with interest, while he was simply trying to be a decent person.

She *had* screeched loud enough to bring the mountain down in that bizarre room with its spine-chilling door, and said some *very* bold things. Then again, if he was the type of male who would disparage her for speaking her mind, perhaps it was for the best they hadn't done anything permanent. But—

Admit it. You have no idea what you're doing. You know what might help? Speaking *to him. Honestly, when did you get so dense?*

"Yes, *Luna.* I've seen him." Nyri gave her a smug, knowing look as she set the heaping tray down. "He said, and I quote, *'Take this to Luna. Now. She's to eat every bite,* before *healing—make sure of it. I'll be there shortly, and she can begin,'* and then he walked away. Technically, that was over an hour ago. Don't tell him."

The *Demon.* As if she hadn't been healing on her own just fine for fifty-two years. High-handed, overbearing— "Let me guess. He was raging when he said that?"

Nyri's brows punched up. "How did you know?"

Lunara's nostrils flared as she snapped a thread of power out, evaporating the water particles from Fern's hair and clearing away the bucket of murky water. "I'm quickly learning you Demons have a *way* about you in that state. No offense."

"Fair…" Nyri's voice trailed off, her eyes wide. "Burning Solyrian. Have you ever seen hair like that?"

It was quite a bit shorter than her own, but Fern's was more free. The curls were tighter, fuller, coiling every which way with a beautiful madness. It couldn't decide whether it wanted to be lavender or honey in color, both and neither at once, depending on which way the light hit.

Absolutely stunning—and Lunara couldn't care less at the moment.

"No." She gritted her teeth and shored up the magic keeping Fern in her stasis. Just in case. "Let's go."

"Wait, Brand said—"

"I know what he said." Lunara flung the door wide and made a sweeping gesture towards the corridor. "Let's go. Shoo."

If Brand thought he had the right to go stomping around and using others to issue orders from afar, he had another thing coming.

Nyri looked positively delighted by the turn of events, bouncing on the balls of her feet. "Oh-hoo. Is he in trouble? Once, his Highness—What's this?" Nyri skidded to a stop and plucked a folded piece of parchment from the floor, flashing her a coy look. "A love letter?"

Lunara pinched the bridge of her nose. "Hardly."

It had been propped on the bedside, her name looped across the front in gorgeous calligraphy. When she'd seen it there, waiting… No. She refused to dwell on the way her heart had jumped with joy—right before plummeting into a wasteland of disappointment and furious indignation.

"*'Forgive my theatrics and any distress they may cause,'*" Nyri read aloud, head down as she meandered into the hallway. "*'Or have caused, actually, by the time you read this. Using you was necessary, and I hated every minute of it. Please know I hold you in the highest esteem, and count you as a friend. Lyriat, Demon King of Straelon.'*" She raised her brows. "Ooh, formal *and* dramatic. What did he do?"

At the very least, he'd surprised her. She'd never have guessed the bastard was a master thespian. His act—if that's what it had been—deserved a standing ovation and any ensuing accolades. Truly.

She could only assume his aim had been to 'use' her to suss out whether any of the others in the room were the supposed imposter. How it would help him do that was beyond Lunara's scope of understanding.

Arrogant prick.

Mostly, she was fuming over still having no idea whether Brand had known Lyriat's plan, which could've been cleared up hours ago if he'd bothered to show his face. If he *had* known—

You'll what, glare at him? Throw a fit at an Imperial Son? *Or have you finally come to your bleeding senses and decided to leave?*

They turned another corner, into the grand, glass-lined corridor leading to the great hall.

"Hello?" Nyri snapped her fingers in front of Lunara's face. "Are you going to tell me, or do I have to pull it out of someone else? Bal wouldn't budge, but I'll put it together eventually. People were in a right tizzy this morning."

"Well, I don't—"

"I still can't believe I missed it, and for what! Bloody kitchen duty. Even Hedda put me off. I was sure she'd be the one to spill the sordid details. She's soft with me like that. Sometimes. When no one is looking."

"Nyri."

"Brand was especially tight-lipped. I don't know if it's meant to be a realm secret or— Wait, is it? Something so shameful we have to keep it hidden from the other realms? Shite, I hadn't thought of that. And there I was, blabbering on with his brothers right there—"

"Nyriadne!" Lunara yanked her to a stop outside the ornate double doors.

Nyri blinked wide, mahogany eyes at her, a flush of crimson crawling over her rounded cheeks.

Lunara drew in a deep breath and offered an encouraging smile. There was no part of her that wanted to stifle even a drop of the young Demon's spirit, but this was spectacularly poor timing for a chitchat. "Forgive me, my friend. First of all, I don't know whether I can talk about what happened. I'm guessing not, though. Second, did you say *"brothers"* plural? As in, more than one of Brand's brothers is here?"

She threw a fleeting glance towards the silent guards as her chest constricted, the vice squeezing tighter and tighter until it left her dizzy. If it was Araxis…

"Yes." Nyri looped her arm through Lunara's and dragged her into the great hall. "His Highness arrived last night during supper." She giggled and lowered her voice. "It was almost enough to stop everyone's gossip about you lot."

Right. Okay. Another Imperial Son. Not a problem. She'd just… um…

Oh, no, please. Do go on. By the way, once again, *the portal is right through those doors.*

No. Running would implicate her more than anything else.

Fine. Change your name, your hair. Anything. Shite, change everything.

Lunara snorted. No amount of tonics or spells would be able to hide how starkly she resembled her mother—save for having her father's exact hair color. Besides, any number of Sorcerit would be able to see right through that trick. Not to mention she'd met Araxis, long ago. He'd recognize her immediately.

Shitting stars, she'd have to face him.

Why hadn't she told Brand the truth when she'd had the chance? Why hadn't she trusted him? He'd pestered her enough in the chasm, open and waiting, but *no*—she'd had to go and give him the silent treatment to protect herself. Now, she was about to be outed to her Imperial mate as a treasonous liar by the highest powered creature in all of the damned Evesong!

Or, you know, ask which brother it is before your halfwitted arse jumps to conclusions.

Blessed moons, it was all she could do not to smack herself in the face.

Yes, of course. Smart. Obviously, she should ask. The odds were in her favor—there was only a one in three chance she was in a waking nightmare.

A door banged open, and the raucous sound of laughter and spirited chatter filled the hall.

Shite, shite, shite. "Nyri, which—"

"Ah, I was just coming to find you, Luna."

His voice was a gravelly dream, a tingle of pleasure running up her spine as she slowly turned, even while a sharp dread threatened to eat her alive.

Stars and arses, would you make up your mind?

Hard to do when the sight of Brand emptied that mind of all thought, stealing her breath and her reason in equal parts.

He was shirtless. Swaggering. Barefoot. Covered in dust and grass and wood chips from the practice ground. Drenched in sweat, beads of it dripping from the ends of his hair to streak down through the mess and soak into the low waist of his short trousers. Dragging a linen rag across the back of his neck and over the wide expanse of his muscled chest.

Weeping fuck. The motion revealed her still-healing fang marks over his heart, and a spike of heat flushed and gathered in her core.

And that smile. The crinkled lines in the corners of his eyes. The press of his shortened fangs into his bottom lip. She'd swear it was all for her. A secret, just between the two of them.

A crowd of similarly filthy warriors followed in his wake, piling in as they roughhoused. She was torn between staying locked on Brand forever and scanning the other Demons for any sign of his younger brother.

Sisters forgive her, but self-preservation won out.

She spotted Hedda and Faldir, grinning like loons. Thad playfully darting a swinging fist. Magnus, laugh booming as he threw his head back. Others she'd healed, some she'd never laid eyes on.

No Araxis, thank the stars.

She did her best not to melt into a puddle all over the marble floor. It didn't mean Araxis wasn't here, but it gave her a chance to get hold of the situation.

Brand closed the distance and reached out to grab her chin, tilting her face up. His eyes danced between hers. "Good morning, little moon."

The sound Nyri made was somewhere between a gasp and a squeak.

Brand raised a brow in her direction, lips tilted in a half smile. "Goodbye, Nyriadne."

"Nicknames and twinkly glances, and you want me to leave? Did the trip addle your head? I need details." She turned to Lunara and pointed at her. "You had all morning to tell me whatever this is. I knew something was up when *he* called you Luna. Magnus? Meaningless. Does it all the time. But *Brand*? And little moon, are you kidding me! Oh... my... sunstar..." Her mouth fell open and she clapped both hands to her cheeks. "Are you *mates*?!"

Her shriek echoed through the bustling hall, the word *'mates'* bouncing from window to window, and Lunara couldn't stifle her groan as all eyes turned in their direction.

Brand drew in a deep, slow breath. Out, and in again, standing so still.

With an explosive *thump,* her heart flipped over and into a racing gallop that pumped tense pain right up into the base of her skull. Forced her eyes out of focus, her ears to ring. She couldn't feel her lips or limbs.

Two realizations slammed into her.

First, it wasn't her. She had her fair share of *moments,* but not this same struggle to breathe. This feeling that a carefully curated control had been wrenched from her grasp, forcing her into a spiraling unknown. And yet, she related so viscerally that it threatened to send her to her knees right then and there.

Second, she could help.

Lunara leaned into the overload, sifting through the dampened senses that didn't belong to her in order to find her own. She wasn't particularly thrilled with Nyri at the moment, but she could be calm. For him, she could.

She reached inside with both hands and tossed away the trepidation and the fear. The worry. The unbelievable dressing-down she'd planned to throw at him for being an imperious arse. They were no good at the moment.

Let him feel her awe, instead. The bliss she felt in his arms. Shy hope and quiet wonder. Even the drop of brazen impudence she'd carried with her through everything, just to give him a little fight.

The bond pulled tighter and—for the barest, fleeting instant—she was... *him,* focused wholly on the flecks of silver and sage scattered throughout her own azure eyes, the iridescent freckles across her nose and cheeks. On the thought that salvation lay before him, in lines and patterns and colors that mimicked the beloved sea and sky.

Tighter…

A blink and Brand was there, staring down with burning intensity, somehow closer than before. It was her turn to note the details. To show him the face she beheld was starting to become her own sort of deliverance. Her own anchor within the storm of herself. She leaned in and—

Snap!

Lunara sucked in a gasp as their connection broke. Brand reached out with a curse and caught her arm as she swayed, the blood rushing through her veins with electric tingles.

"That was… Fuck. Are you alright?"

The cadence of his voice soothed, every low syllable calling out to a new ache blooming within her. The severance had left a wound that time, bereft and bleeding. Longing to have the piece of him she'd held returned to its rightful place.

"I… I'm fine. I'm sorry, I didn't mean—"

"Don't apologize," he rasped, sinking his hand into her hair gripping her nape. "Not to me. Not for that."

She let her head fall forward onto his chest, content to do nothing more than breathe him in while she settled.

"Weeping Sisters, did you see that?" Nyri's *whisper* was more of a shout in the silent hall.

"Aye." Magnus, something like reverence in his tone. "I did."

Lunara didn't have it in her to look. To see countless other faces gaping at them. As long as she stayed still, eyes scrunched closed as she basked in the scent of salt and fresh pine, they didn't exist. Hadn't witnessed whatever the fuck that was.

A bench screeched across the floor, hissed reprimands following the sound, and the tension broke like a sigh.

"Alright, enough gawping!" Magnus thundered over the growing din of murmurs. "Be gone. Off with you. Aye, Nyri—especially you, you bonny wee shite."

Lunara had no control of the giggle that bubbled up, made worse when Brand's own rumbled out of him.

"Thank you," he said on a heavy exhale. "It… comes out of nowhere, usually, and I'm not sure... I never meant—"

"You don't have to explain." Lunara lifted her head, dragging her thumb over his lips to silence him. "I understand, remember?"

His brows fell, a crease forming between them as he nodded.

It was so easy to get lost in him, time slipping away like sand through her fingertips. Lunara shook herself to break the spell. "This has been thrilling, but Fern needs me. It's been too long as it is."

Lunara started to pull back, but Brand only gripped her harder. "I'll be going with you. It isn't safe on your own. Not after the watchtower. Please."

She was helpless to resist him when he used words like *please,* but… "It'll be harrowing." Her voice was firm, brooking no argument. "You cannot interfere. There's a reason I prefer to do it alone, and it's well-meaning people like you who think they're helping when they're not."

"I won't hinder you, I swear it. I only wish to ensure you're not in danger."

Her ire from earlier reared its head for a moment, and she jabbed a finger into his sternum. "One chance."

He grabbed hold of her finger and bit the tip, eyes dancing. "Agreed."

"High-handed, overbearing Demon," she muttered, her lips curling at the corners.

His grin was devastating. "Reckless, stubborn Sorcerit." He bent to her ear. "I plan to astonish you. You'll never want to heal another without me."

"Is that so?" She raised a brow at him. "Prove it."

"Oh, I will. But first…" He turned away, one arm extended. "I'd like you to meet my brother."

Fuck.

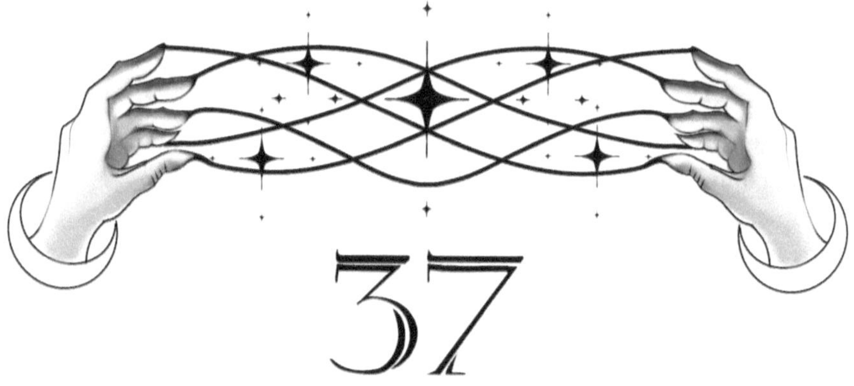

37

"LUNA, THIS IS VALANDYRIAN."

Lunara's legs nearly buckled for the second time that day, the relief was so stark. Smiling, she lifted her eyes and—

The budding leaves of spring, and their rot in autumn. The cry of a newborn babe, and the final, rattling breath before the Veil. The fresh light of rising dawn, and twilight fading into blackest night. The promise of forever, and the sharp stab of betrayal. Lovers and enemies. Laughter and screams.

He was everything and nothing, all at once. Teeming with the exuberance of creation, even as the airless void of him yawned wide.

When the shock of his power ebbed away, Lunara filled her lungs and discovered that the Second Imperial Son was *stunning*.

More beautiful, than handsome. Lithe, far less bulky than his brothers, but still boasting wide shoulders and a clear command of his graceful body. Square, clean-shaven jaw. Full lips and high cheekbones. Strong, prominent nose and thick, arching brows—the only traits he shared with both Brand and Magnus.

His hair was a silken fall of pure starlight—the palest, glinting silver trailing down over the intricate tailoring of his bronze, floor-length coat. The tunic and trousers beneath were a perfect match for its umber lining, and only served to magnify the impression that his pale skin lacked coloring entirely. Whiter than bone, than snow, than porcelain. Fragile, almost, if one didn't bother to look past the surface.

Valandyrian's head tilted to the side, and... *There.* The source of his power, concentrated behind eyes that were... Mismatched wasn't quite the right word.

Life and death. Beginning and end. Araxis might have been better.

One glittered like the clearest emerald, so deep and stark a green Lunara wasn't sure she'd ever seen anything quite that shade. The other was its own sort of Dread Chasm. No whites, iris, or pupil, the solid orb of matte obsidian obliterated any light that deigned to touch it.

And yet—mismatched, or no—they were also sad.

His shoulders tensed as he raised his chin a fraction of an inch, and she realized—she'd seen that exact look countless times, on the battered faces of those in her care. A false, wounded bravado that told the very secret they were trying to hide.

Before her stood a male braced for cruelty, waiting for what he assumed was inevitable, and something protective rose up in her. Defensive. It burned hot and bright, and all for him. For a creature so used to abuse that he expected it.

Lunara bowed her head and met his gaze again. "I wish I could say Brand has told me all about you, Your Highness, but we've been rather preoccupied of late." One side of her mouth quirked up. "Then again, if you're anything like Magnus, you won't mind enlightening me yourself."

He relaxed, offering the barest nod as he took a hesitant step forward. "Please, Luna, call me Vann. May I greet you properly?" he asked softly, arms outstretched.

Lunara didn't bother correcting him, or answering with words.

Wonderful. Add 'hugging Imperial Sons left and right' to the list of ninny-headed things you now consider to be normal.

His breath punched out in an *oof* as she flung her arms around him. "It's lovely to meet you, Vann."

It was like hugging a statue—until he thawed and embraced her in return, utterly restrained, as if used to moving slowly for the sake of others. After a beat, he drooped like putty, dropping his cheek to rest on top of her head.

What she did not expect was the kiss. A jolt shot down from her skull through tendon and bone, crackling back upwards and leaving sparkling revival in its footsteps.

On instinct, she leapt away, staring down at her tingling palms. "What in the..."

Shitting stars and arses. Do you feel *that?*

"That's usually what he means by *properly,"* Brand said, chuckling. "He refuses to tell us what it is, but you're going to feel amazing for a bloody long while."

"A trick of the Fae, nothing more." Vann's eyes dropped to the floor as he said it.

Another thing she recognized. He was lying, but... not in any way that would cause harm. She'd done the same often enough, in the interest of protecting herself.

"I told Vann of our Fae conundrum last night. I thought he might be able to tell us who she is?"

Brand offered his arm, but Lunara ignored it. "I'm sorry, but I'm afraid that's not possible. Not yet, anyway."

Vann's brows punched up. "Why is that?"

She chewed the inside of her lip. Vann had every right to see one of his own, but...

"For starters, I'm not sure her own family would recognize her. It's that bad." Picking up an errant curl, Lunara twirled it between her fingers. Unsurprisingly, it wasn't easy to look two Imperials in the eye and tell them no. "You must understand—aside from the fact that enough people have ogled Fern in her vulnerable state and violated her privacy, I need to get on with healing her. Speculating over her mutilated body would not only be pointless, but would further delay that happening and rob her of even more dignity. Please, I'm asking for a few more days. By then, she'll be able to tell you who she is herself."

"Hmm." Vann considered her for a moment. Stars above, it was like he saw right through her. "Your intentions are good. Pure." It was almost a question, like he was confused by the idea.

"Most of the time," she quipped.

He didn't smile.

"I'll allow the delay." Vann turned to Brand and gave his shoulder a squeeze. "Find me when you're done?"

He didn't wait for a response before walking—no, limping—away.

"Another thing he won't tell us," Brand said, sorrow underscoring the quiet words. "It came on slowly, over years and years. No one knows why, which is how he prefers it, but…" He turned hopeful eyes on her. "Perhaps you could try to help him?"

Lunara nodded, a bit dazed. "He's…" There weren't really words for what Vann was.

"Yes," Brand murmured, understanding. "He is." Lacing his fingers with hers, he tugged her towards the doors. "Come on, Sorcerit. Time to heal a Fae."

IN THE END, IT TOOK NEARLY A WEEK—AND LUNARA DID *NOT* FEEL amazing.

She held the last ruined fibers of Fern's wings in her shaking hands, the sweat-soaked linen of her dress clinging like a jilted lover as power surged between them.

It had taken an entire day and night to mend the gossamer membranes alone, the bird-like bones beneath threatening to crumble into dust at the slightest touch. The thought of botching them—of crippling this beautiful creature for the rest of her very long life—had nearly defeated her.

They'd made it, though. Somehow.

Lunara knew where she was, but barely. The haze of agony was so absolute that her mind had disconnected itself for the most part. Had swept her away into some deeper place she'd never gone before, trying to hide the desolation from her consciousness.

Repeatedly. Over six of the longest days of her life.

The thump of a book hitting wood sounded, footsteps after. Tingles along her spine told her Brand's hand was hovering there, wanting to touch her, but knowing he couldn't. Not yet.

He'd learned quickly after the first time—the only time—when he'd thought he was helping but she'd broken into sobs instead, begging him to get away from her until she could muster the strength to face it.

"It's done, little moon," he murmured. The heat moved to her hands, electricity jumping across the gap between them. "It's done."

She tried to open her eyes, but they were swollen shut, crusted with the salt of her dried tears. "I can't," she rasped. "I'm not—"

"Take as long as you need. I'm here when you're ready."

Lunara's eyes pricked anew behind closed lids. Her high-handed, overbearing Demon had kept his word. He'd *astonished* her.

Using his power over the stone, he'd braced a seat behind her on the first day—lined with overstuffed down pillows—so she had somewhere gentle to land when her body inevitably failed. She'd only had to hit the ground once before the solution was in place.

With an innate sense of exactly when to do so, he'd wordlessly offered her water and food, and the soft flesh of his inner forearm at all hours. Her fangs had sunk into him so many times it was a wonder she hadn't bled him dry.

Early on, she'd come alive after one such instance to find her hair flawlessly braided, every unruly strand tamed away from her face. It wasn't until later, hunched over and vomiting into a pail he was holding, that she'd realized his thoughtfulness. The hefty weight of it was still there even now, a comfort as it dangled off the edge of Fern's sickbed and reminded her she wasn't alone.

There was a sort of terror that came at this stage of a more serious healing she'd never allowed herself to acknowledge. When she was drowning in her stupor and desperate to find her way back to the surface. Stuck, unable to remember how to control her limbs. Pain so appalling she was sure she'd never feel normal again.

That's where she was. Again. Except, she had help this time. "I'm ready."

He pried her fingers from Fern's wing with all the force of a butterfly. His touch didn't linger or press. Didn't demand. It was exactly what she required, and nothing more.

"Are you able to sit up yourself?"

She was half-sitting down, half-sprawled across the floating slab, arms outstretched and cheek resting on the pad beneath Fern.

Her body tensed reflexively, the word *yes* perched on her lips, ready to do it on her own because she always had before—until the edge of the stone dug into her abdomen, paralyzing the muscles there further, and Lunara remembered she didn't have to. Didn't want to. Not when Brand was there and had proven himself completely.

"No," she finally admitted. Harder to do than she'd expected.

Just as he'd studied her body in the cave, Brand had watched and listened to her cues over the traumatic week, learning her in an entirely different way. He knew to slide his hand gently beneath her sternum, because it tended to hurt the least. To support the back of her head as he levered her backwards and settled her against the mound of pillows behind her.

He'd tasted the deepest parts of her, but this was more intimate. More vulnerable. He'd spent six days witnessing the worst she had to offer and was still here.

She forced her eyes open and found him kneeling beside her. "Thank you."

He ghosted a hand over her cheek, just shy of actually touching. "You are a blessing," he whispered. Glancing over at Fern, he swallowed. "I'm ashamed to say I had little hope for her. I'd thought there was no way…" His gaze came back to lock with hers. "I am in awe of you, Luna. What you've done is astonishing."

A low hum left her, as close to a laugh as she could manage.

It was nothing she wouldn't have done for anyone else. Shite, she *had* done it, many times before. There was a reason Cordelia contacted her in secret and sent particularly severe cases her way—Lunara was probably the Evesong's most capable healer.

Except, the usual swell of satisfaction didn't come. Not when a wave of shame pummeled into her instead.

Even when she had one eye over her shoulder, ever watchful for those who might come for her, Lunara had always felt a little thrill of inward pride. A sense she was still significant. Doing good work while defying the Council, right beneath their noses.

Shitting stars. What utter *nonsense*.

Her brows pulled down, a knot of tension forming between them as she stared at Brand.

Brand, who'd gone down into a Dread Chasm for a single person, and held friends as they wept. Who treated his brethren with kindness, helped lead them fairly and saw to their needs, despite his wish for a simpler life. Who would show the same respect to a youngling like Nyri as he did to a king.

Brand, who had stayed. Cared for her with no thought for himself.

Who'd never once shied away as she'd snapped and heaved and screamed, picking up her broken pieces with crooning encouragements and gentle hands.

The truth... the truth was that Lunara wasn't significant at all. Had no right to be proud. She'd wasted *fifty-two years* hiding and thinking it was acceptable to live her lonely, crippled little life in order to protect herself.

Only herself.

Sweet Sisters, was she really that selfish? Stellan and Almaura would be so fucking disappointed in her.

Her eyes stung again. She didn't want that life anymore. It sure as shite hadn't been worth it. The safety had been an illusion, and she'd been missing *everything*. The realms and their wonders. People to talk to, laugh at, cry with—people *other* than the voices in her head slowly driving her mad, and a figment of her imagination in the moonlight shape of an owl.

Family.

Her sluggish heart squeezed, its echoing thumps radiating out like hammer blows that felt an awful lot like regret. "Brand, there's... there's something I need to tell you. *Things*, I need to tell you. I—"

"Shh." His hand shook as he brought it to her lips, the wisp of his careful touch threatening to break her. "I know, but not yet." He turned back the sleeve of his tunic, pushing it up past his elbow. "Blood, first. Talk, after."

Twin fang marks littered the flesh he exposed in various stages of healing and guilt joined the maelstrom of emotion. So selfish. So focused on Fern—on *herself, herself, herself*—that she'd forgotten to tend to him as well.

"No," he husked, reading her mind or her face—she couldn't be sure which anymore. "None of that. Whatever you're thinking, I promise you're wrong."

She wasn't though. Not about this.

He cradled her head again, and her mouth flooded with saliva. "Accept this gift, freely given."

She sucked a breath through clenched teeth when his words caused her aching body to arch of its own accord. Five simple words that meant so much more—permission, for her fangs to sharpen and seek out the relief he offered.

Lunara latched on like her life depended on it, pushing through to the life in his veins. The power. When the first, coppery drop hit her tongue, her particles leapt up and rushed to meet their salvation—racing, buzzing, darting as they carried sweet renewal out to feeble muscles and shredded sinew.

She drank and drank, hardly breathing, every swallow lifting a tendril of the fog and leaving clarity in its place. The more she had, the stronger she would be—strong enough, hopefully, to survive the unveiling of her long-held secrets and deepest truths.

Flushed and breathless, she detached herself, thrumming with renewed vigor as she gulped air into free lungs. Sisters, there was nothing like it.

Nothing like him.

Brand chuckled. "Welcome back."

Only then did Lunara realize she'd clasped onto his arm, adding deep, crescent slices to the puncture wounds she'd inflicted. Before he could protest, she laid her hand over top and pushed out her magic, taking the pain into herself.

And the pleasure.

Something between a shout and a moan left her unbidden as sharp stings echoed over her body and almost immediately softened into bone-melting bliss.

"As you can see, your worry was misplaced, and it was no burden whatsoever to feed you."

Fighting to control her breaths, she willed herself to let go of him, shaking her head. "I haven't… Is it always like that?"

"Every time." Brand looked away, scrubbing a hand over his face. "You've never offered your gift to another?"

Lunara wasn't even tempted to evade the question, even though it would normally raise more than a few eyebrows. "No," she admitted. "Never."

She'd had lovers. Not many, and not in quite some time, but that particular intimacy had always been off limits. She'd been too afraid they would taste her blood and know she wasn't at all where she belonged—more fool her, since gifts between Sorcerit partners was standard, and her denial of that shared experience could have been just as incriminating.

Stars above, she'd been such an arse.

Oh, and that's suddenly changed? You used to be smart—now look at you.

Ugh.

She was having trouble seeing the logic and wisdom in that part of herself anymore. Tired of listening to its bloated, tiresome words. One gleaming benefit of being lost in her healing journeys was that she didn't have the energy to go to war with it. Lacked the patience to bother listening.

The only tiresome one here is you. You, and your halfwitted dreams. Your sudden need for family and truth and sharing. Weakness, all of it. Your parents died protecting you, and you think honoring that is what would make them disappointed?

"Luna?"

She blinked as a shuddering breath left her. Brand was standing with his hand outstretched, waiting, his gaze searching. Shaking herself, she took the proffered hand.

"Is everything alright?"

Nothing she couldn't handle.

Eejit.

She stood and pressed two fingers to her temples, head in a dizzy spiral as she reoriented herself into a reliable body. "Fine. Just… tired still." Not a lie. "Ready for this to be done."

Too bad the gifts don't heal your addled mind. If only all *of you could be reliable.*

Apparently, her answer was good enough for him. He led her over to Fern. "Your work *is* done," he breathed. "Look at her. She's an entirely different creature." Admiration she didn't deserve glittered in his eyes when he looked at her again. "No one would believe the damage if they hadn't seen it for themselves. You did that."

"Hmm."

"Is it normal for her to still be asleep?" he asked, posing a question she didn't have a precise answer for.

You do, you just don't like it. Go on, admit it. Since you're so bent on spilling all your secrets, go ahead and tell him you aren't nearly the astonishing blessing he seems to think. Nothing but a lying bitch.

Weeping moons, what the fuck? She could be unnecessarily cruel to herself, but this was a whole new level of vitriol.

"Luna?"

"Oh, umm… For now, yes. I often keep them out for a little while and allow them to come back slowly." She wasn't sure how to describe what she'd found. "Fern has a blockage, though. Or a wall? It's entirely possible she built it up on her own, to protect her mind from what happened, and it'll fade as her body realizes it's no longer in danger. It could also be a part of her that's always been there. I won't know for a couple of days whether or not it's that or my magic keeping her from waking up."

Not going to tell him you dumped enough power into it to fell a dragon horde, and it still wouldn't budge? So you do *know how to keep a secret, you're just too idiotic to do it when it matters.*

Lunara sucked down a deep breath, refusing to respond as she rounded the slab and ran her fingers over Fern's forehead.

The Fae was striking, whatever she was. "Nyri asked me if I'd ever seen hair like this," she said, keeping her voice from shaking. "I wasn't in the best mood to ponder it at the time, but now…"

From the comfort of her cottage, she'd traveled the realms through the pages of books. Amidst her reading and research, she'd seen countless depictions of everything imaginable. Sadly, truly informative texts on the Tempusrealm didn't exist. The Fae were *secretive*. But the pictures and paintings, the sketches and portraits and landscapes…

Boundless, like they enjoyed flaunting the beauty of their realm while leaving everyone guessing.

She glanced up to find Brand's brow furrowed as he stared at the Fae.

Interesting. Almost pining, wouldn't you say?

Lunara cleared her throat. "I once saw a painting of water nymphs with similar hair coloring." Grabbing Fern's hand, she turned it so the light of the stones could skate over deep bronze skin, shimmering across the surface as if she'd been dipped in gold dust. "But, if I'm not mistaken, I believe this feature is most often associated with the pixies of the Fall Domain. Unfortunately, her size and wings belie that."

Brand nodded, leaning closer to inspect the verdant appendages. "Their shape is all wrong for a pixie. And the color is more typical of the dryads in the Summer Domain. Although, dryads don't have wings."

Ooh, did you see that? Hear that? The strange note in his voice… Distracted. Probably noticing how gorgeous she is, and thinking he made a mistake with you. Sure you didn't mess with her mind on purpose?

Swallowing down a rise of bile, she laid Fern's arm down, resting her hands together over her abdomen again—and shamefully unable to ignore herself. "What… what are you thinking?"

He shook himself. "That I'm too bloody tired to be recalling Fae features. Vann will know *what* she is, even if he doesn't know precisely *who.*"

Well, what else would he say? He's sorry but he's fallen for a comatose female?

"Fair enough." She summoned one of her blankets from the ether, the moonlight strands humming beneath her fingers. Hopefully, it would help energize Fern. "I can stay with her while you find him."

Brand stalked around the slab, pausing a hair's breadth away. His eyes were like white-hot irons, boring into her. "I would very much like to hold you. May I pick you up?"

No, he wouldn't. He thinks you're weak. Useless. Helpless.

She scoffed at him, finding it harder and harder to ignore the doubts. "I don't need you to carry me through the corridors while we chase your brother down."

He tilted her chin up, dragging his thumb over her lower lip. "You misunderstand me." His markings flashed, eyes growing darker. "I'm not speaking to another damned person until I have a bath and something to eat—and neither are you, whether you walk or not."

"I'm not hungry."

She wasn't. Not anymore. Something was… not right.

His grip tightened. "I can feel you, remember?" The tips of his horns curled ever so slightly, and power pulsed out from him in gentle waves. "Not nearly as completely as I want to, but enough to know your mind has wandered somewhere it shouldn't. I'm not finished taking care of you, so may I *please* pick you up?"

38

WHEN SHE DIDN'T RESPOND, BRAND PACED AWAY, RAKING A HAND THROUGH his hair.

For fuck's sake, the two of them were a pair.

The last they'd spoken out loud with any real awareness was after his episode in the great hall—nearly a *week* ago. All of their communication since had been far more abstract.

Mind-to-mind. Heart-to-heart. Words replaced with a physical give and take that had nothing to do with sexual gratification and everything to do with two souls finally meeting.

Standing by, watching her suffer willingly, had been a grueling misery at times. More than once, he'd been tempted to get on his knees and beg her to stop—to accept Fern was a lost cause and save herself instead—but he'd made her a promise.

In the end, he'd never felt so connected with another creature in his life.

Her breaking body had voiced all she'd been unable to say with words, and his had heard. Had listened and adjusted to her needs as if it knew just what to do. They'd been so in tune, he would have sworn to the Sisters the bond had completed itself.

Now…

A whisper, low and grating, had made its way to his ears. He hadn't been able to figure out what he was hearing at first—not until he'd watched her eyes flash wide at the exact moment he'd sensed its insidious echo again.

Luna had said weeks ago that she understood the cruel voice inside, but he'd never thought to experience *hers*. Brand could actually feel it lying to her, even if he couldn't make out the words.

Part of him had the fleeting worry it might always be this way—back and forth between the weakest parts of themselves, never having the chance to be more because their fragile minds wouldn't allow it.

The other part—the bigger, louder, meaner part—fucking refused to let that happen.

"Was it just me?" He turned away from the window and the setting sunstar to face her again. "Tell me I'm not the only one who felt it, that melding between us."

Luna's head snapped up, brows punching upwards. "I…" Her eyes darted towards Fern on her slab, wholly unaware of her surroundings. "Not here." She practically ran out of the room, disappearing into her own through the opening Baldrir had made between them.

Brand grunted a curse and stalked after, finding her unraveling the plait he'd put in her hair while she paced in front of the fireplace. He watched from the archway, transfixed as she bungled her way back and forth, not so much as a flinch when she rammed her hip into a chair arm, or bumped one of her knees on the low table.

Goosebumps broke out over his skin after one such instance, pricks crawling like a thousand tiny insects making their way up his spine and around his head.

And there it was again. The whisper.

"Whatever it just said is a lie."

Luna gasped, stumbling to a stop and staring at the floorboards.

Brand crossed his arms and leaned against the doorframe. "Was it just me, Luna?" He knew it wasn't. No way she hadn't been right there with him. If he could get her to focus on that, admit it—

"No," she answered, barely audible. "It wasn't." Her skin flushed as she searched the middle space, like she was trying to recall anything else he might have picked up. "You heard that?"

His greater half preened within, itching for a little freedom. "Not the particulars, don't worry. More a feeling, and I can see you reacting."

"How long?"

He pretended to consider it. "About the last half hour, or so, but I'd wager it's been happening for a lot longer, hasn't it?"

Her shoulders drooped. "It's… one of the things I need to tell you." She brought her hands up to either side of her head. "It's never been this bad." With a shaky sigh, she trudged over to the settee and plopped down, gaze fixed on the ceiling. "It started when I was twenty—just after my parents died."

Her voice was completely flat, but the look on her face was devastating.

His chest tightened, aching for her. He'd known from Thad, but she'd never mentioned them specifically. Just heartbreaking comments like not knowing *how to be* because she'd been alone for so long.

Whisper…

"Would you like to talk about it? Them?"

Her laugh was light, but bitter. "*Like* is such a strong word, don't you think? There's so much to say, so much to confess. At best, I'm… terrified of it."

Whisper…

She swallowed and pressed the heels of her palms to closed eyes.

"I vowed before that you could confide in me, whenever you were ready. That hasn't changed." He finally crossed the room and knelt before her. "Can you look at me?"

She dropped her hands and let her head flop to the side. Weeping Sisters, she was so damned tired.

"Let's slow down." His thumb smoothed back and forth over her knee. "You've hardly eaten in days. You're wearing the same dress as when you started. We need to get you feeling stronger. *Then,* we talk. Hmm?"

Tears gathered in her lashes as she stared at him. "I'd like that," she finally said.

Whisper…

"I'm going to carry you to the washroom—both because I want to *and* because you deserve it. Okay?"

Whisper…

"It's not a power play. It's not control. *You deserve it,*" he said again, hoping to counteract whatever falsities she was feeding herself. "You are worthy of everything I have to give, and there's no greater honor for me. Don't let it tell you otherwise."

Brand knew the mating bond could be intense from his parents, but he hadn't expected this… liberation? For once in his life, there was no doubt. No second guessing himself. He knew just what to do. Exactly what to say. Which movements his body should make.

Without a word, Luna nodded and stretched her arms out, and nothing had ever been as sweet as the way she wrapped herself around his neck, the way her eyes drifted shut.

He stood and scooped her from the seat in one smooth motion, and loosed a contented sigh. Having her there tamed the worst of the restless gnawing that had been eating away at him since the first moment she'd laid healing hands on Fern.

"I'm here," he murmured into her hair. "I've got you."

Whisper…

"You never have to be alone again."

Whisper…

He caught the tear sliding down her cheek with his lips. "I will never leave you."

Whisper…

But weaker, that time.

Brand willed the stones to glow as he entered the washroom. The guest chambers in the castle were different to his in the tower. In his own room, the facilities could be whatever he wanted them to be because he could manipulate the stone how he pleased. Here, every possible feature was accounted for, the choices near-endless.

"Would you prefer a bath or one of the falls?"

"Falls?"

He grinned down at her. "Oh, you're in for a treat."

Within an alcove, steps led down to a massive pool carved into the floor. The ledge around it gave access to the various chutes, spouts, and rain heads shooting out from the stone, and depressions on the outer wall had been enchanted to recognize touch.

Brand pressed a hand to them and turned on everything. "See anything you fancy?"

Her eyes went wide, darting over the feast of options. The shower of tiny droplets. The wide, steaming fall in one corner. The streams jetting horizontally across the other. The sea serpent head jutting from the center of the ceiling, spewing water from its open mouth and filling the pool. The patch of floor with a thousand little holes, tiny geysers bubbling up from each one and waiting for someone to lay upon it.

"All of them," she breathed, sitting up a little straighter. "I want to try all of them."

"Only the finest for a guest of the Demon King." Brand chuckled as he set Luna on her feet in front of him and leaned down to her ear. "Which would the lady like to try first?"

She turned her head to look at him over her shoulder, their faces a hair's breadth apart. "What's your favorite?"

"Would you rather stand, sit, or lay down?"

Her eyes dropped to his lips for an agonizing second before meeting his again. "Lay down, I think."

Brand's heart flipped, and he froze. He had… not expected that.

He'd been doing a decent job of not allowing his mind to go *there* at all since they'd gotten back. Of course he wanted her—desperately—but they'd just spent six days locked in a blurry cycle of heal, feed, doze, repeat. She was clearly exhausted, and not a little frightened. He would be a cad of the worst sort to even think about the things he wanted to do when she was vulnerable.

Whisper… Whisper, whisper, whisper!

Her gaze shuttered and she shrank away slightly. "I'm sorry, I thought — Forgive me. That was probably too forward—"

Brand grabbed her nape and pressed his lips to hers to stop whatever daft shite was about to come out of her mouth. "Don't *ever* apologize to me for that," he hissed against her. "Don't doubt yourself." He rounded her, keeping hold of her jaw. "Anything you want is yours—my body included. *I* thought you'd want your space, and I only want you to be comfortable, Luna. At peace."

Her touch fluttered up his sternum, searing through the fabric of his shirt. "I'm… weary of space. I've had so damned much of it."

Whisper…

With a sigh, she let her arm drop. "Perhaps we *should* wait. You might change your mind once you've heard all I have to say. I wouldn't blame you."

He laced his fingers over the back of her hand and brought it back to his chest. "Is that what you think is going to happen? Still?"

"Honestly?"

"Always."

"I don't know what to think about anything, anymore. I'm afraid what I *want* is outside the realm of possibility."

His hold tightened. "What is it you want, exactly?"

Luna swallowed and blew out a slow breath. "I want to be free. I want to do as I like, where and when I like, without the constant fear that my life isn't really my own. That it could change at any moment, and I'd be lost. And I want… I want to live like that with you at my side. Irrevocably."

That word. If she was saying what he thought she was saying… A lance of something far stronger than desire shot through him. Necessary, and reaching out for her. Only her.

"I see nothing impossible about that."

Her quiet laugh was sad. "Then we are at an impasse, because I see nothing *possible* about it."

That tone, so bloody resigned.

"Do you trust me?"

Luna blinked up at him and searched his face. "Yes. Sisters save me, but… somehow, I do."

The same question he'd asked her while they'd been descending into the chasm—a far different answer in return, and all the encouragement he needed.

"Then hear what I am about to tell you, and believe it, because I swear on those Sisters I will never lie to you, and I will never go back on my word."

Brand let his hands trail down her sides as he sank to his knees before her, tendrils of steam dancing around them. "No one holds more power than an Imperial. If you want to be free, then free you shall be because I will make it so. Whatever you fear, I will gladly spend my every waking moment at war with it until you are released of the burden. And if you are lost, I will find you."

Whisper…

He gripped her hips harder and tugged her closer. "There is nothing you could say that would make me forsake you. Nothing you could do. If we lived forever and you never said another word about your past, I wouldn't give a single shite. I am already yours, Lunara. Irrevocably."

"We were supposed to talk *after* a bath," she whispered. "And f-food."

"Things don't always go to plan," he laughed out. "Sometimes, it's a good thing."

Luna nodded, dazed, as if she'd never thought of it like that before. Shite, he rarely did, but with her it was easy.

"I meant all of it, little moon. Whenever you're ready, you need only say the word, and I will spend the rest of our lives *at your side* proving it."

Not because she was his true mate—only an added blessing, at this point—but because he was bloody fucking in love with *her*, and he wanted her to believe it.

Her head tilted, brow furrowed. "I…"

He didn't dare to move, to breathe.

Whisper…

A muscle under her eye twitched. Luna lifted her chin and broke away, walking backwards, something a little wild in her look. Pausing just shy of the pool, she—

Her dress was gone in a flash of light, every inch of her revealed.

"I'm ready."

Burning fucking Solyrian.

"Are you—"

"For the love of the Sisters, Brand, do *not* ask me if I'm sure. No one in their right mind wouldn't be sure after the things you just said. I've…" Her cheeks puffed out. "I've been waiting fifty-two years for this moment. To be brave enough to take what *I* want. Please, don't make me wait any longer."

Brand was on his feet and surrounded by her before he knew he was moving—hands sinking into her thighs as they wrapped around him, mouths fused, her body crushed between his and the wall.

When she cried out to the rafters, he took advantage and lavished the column of her throat with his tongue, tasting the salt on her damp skin. The life.

"I don't… suppose you could…" he said between nips and licks, "get rid of—" Another flash and they were skin to skin. "*Yes.*"

He latched on to a dusky nipple, rolling the beaded tip under his tongue. She bucked, dragging her hot center over the length of his rigid cock. He wanted to sink into her, hard and fast. Fuck her until they both collapsed, but—

"I promised you a bed for this," he panted, grinding against her.

"You also promised me a bath and food," she rasped, nails clawing down his arms as she arched her back. "Things don't always go to plan."

"Cheeky, using my words against me." Her giggle turned into a moan when he wedged a hand between them and gripped himself, rubbing his throbbing head over her clit. "It's not going to work though," he rumbled low, tugging the lobe of her ear with his teeth. "I think you'll find I suggested a bath and food earlier, while in the cave"—He wrapped his arms around her as he spun, knelt, and laid her over the bubbling geysers —"I believe I *swore* you would have silk sheets and down feathers cradling this flawless fucking body when I finally had the privilege of being buried inside it."

She had an unbelievable ability to make him lose all control by merely existing, tempting him to do whatever she wanted and the rest be damned.

Not this time.

"That is one *promise* I intend to keep. Until then—"

He settled back on his haunches and slapped a hand to the stone, commanding it to mold to her body. The tiny holes beneath her shrank and grew in turns, fluctuating the water's flow in massaging fits and bursts. But her sweet cunt was already dripping on its own. Contracting. Empty. Begging to be filled.

And that simply wouldn't do.

Brand palmed his cock, grazing the long length from root to tip, and urged the stone between her legs to rise up in the same shape. Power in tune with her and his creation, he grabbed her thighs with a growl and spread her wider.

"—I can indulge you in other ways."

A yank and the stone phallus impaled Luna, sliding perfectly into her clenching entrance.

Her gasp and whimper… The way her eyes rolled back in her head… Her limbs melting into the spaces he'd made for them…

Music, and artwork, and everything he'd ever wanted in his bloody life. Her pleasure was his, and damned if he wasn't right there with her.

The bond had sprung to new life, the whispers gone, pure ecstasy buzzing along its fragile hold instead.

Panting, he reached up to a recessed shelf and pulled down soap and oil. "We've traveled together. Bathed together. Slept side-by-side." He upturned one of the glass vessels and drizzled every drop of its contents over her writhing form. "I've touched you, tasted you. Wanted you so desperately I couldn't see straight." Dipping a cloth into the pool, he brought it to her stomach and flattened it beneath his palm. "We've gone into battle together," he rasped, remembering the near-fatal wounds that had marred the perfection there, "and wept in the aftermath."

Hooded eyes on his, she raised her arms above her head, resting them on drenched waves of chestnut hair, trailing like a halo around her.

Brand scrubbed her slowly, lathering every inch and torturing them both. "Do you know what that means?"

Luna's teeth sunk into her lower lip as she shook her head, still rocking. Fuck, he was tempted to lean down and lick the marbled cock clean, just to have the taste of her on his tongue. To feel it working its way in and out of her.

He circled her clit once, twice—a tease before leaning away again. "It means I've spent weeks learning your body in a thousand different ways. Obsessing over every little thing so I might best serve you."

Brand quickly scrubbed himself with the same linen and tossed it aside to pick up the oil. Uncorking it, he turned that over too, dousing both of them.

"Shite," she breathed, whimpering, rising up on her elbows and thrusting herself harder, faster.

Oh, yes. He knew *exactly* what she wanted—because one of those *little things* he'd learned about his precious mate was that she liked to watch.

Brand took his time dragging his palms up his arms and behind his neck. Over his pecs and down his abdomen. Luna's breath hitched when he reached the jutting length of his own cock, cupping his balls and stroking himself in time with her movements. He was helpless to stop the bow of his body, the rumble that forced itself past his lips as he took her in. His eyes followed the viscous beads dripping slowly down the swells of her bouncing breasts, gathering at the turgid, blushing tips. The glisten of it on her opalescent skin and in the soft hairs on her mound.

He couldn't wait another second.

"I think we're clean enough now, don't you?"

Her chest was heaving, hips undulating. "Yes."

"If you're satisfied, perhaps you'd like a dip in the pool, after all?"

She narrowed her gaze, silver sparks swirling in the azure depths. "Brandir aht Bordoroth, if you don't take me to bed immediately, I will scream."

He chuckled. "Is that supposed to be a threat, little moon? Your screams will only encourage me."

Luna planted her foot in the middle of his chest and shoved him back. So sudden and unexpected—with so much force—that he had no choice but to land on his arse with a curse, sliding back across the washroom floor.

Between one blink and the next, she was straddling his chest, hands clasped around his horns.

"How did you—"

"Since you're so keen on learning, know this…" Her voice had a strange quality to it, similar to when she'd blooded him in the cave. It only made him burn hotter for her. "I'm not a naturally patient person. Surprise. You want to keep your promise? Then do it now, Demon, because *I'm ready."*

She punctuated her statement with an almost-violent kiss, using her grip to tilt his head wherever she wanted it—and then she was gone, sauntering out of the washroom and into her chamber.

"Are you coming or not?"

Weeping fuck.

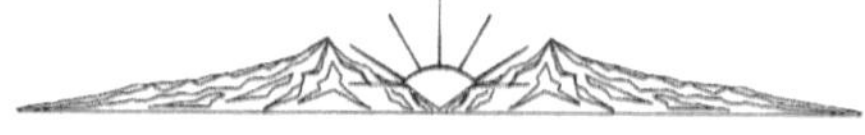

"Saucy, bloody minx…"

Brand caught up and spun her around, bending to throw her over his shoulder. When she flailed and fought the hold, pulling his hair to lever herself and trying to wrap her legs around him again, he landed a wet smack on her arse.

Her drawn out moan as he massaged the spot, the way she drooped, contradicted her hissed, "Insufferable, high-handed—"

"Overbearing Demon. Yes, I know," he growled, skirting around the sitting area as he made for the canopied bed. "Dry us off."

"Make me."

That stopped him dead in his tracks, a bolt of pure lust shooting down his spine.

The only sound while he wrapped his head around it was the soft pitter-patters of water dripping from their bodies to hit the floorboards.

Brand reached across, flattening his palm on the back of her round thigh and dragging it up to the reddened handprint by his face. He kneaded the spot, itching to sink his teeth right into it.

"What did you say?"

"You don't want to say please? Then... Make. Me."

His lids slid closed, jaw slackening. It was possible he'd imagined the way she'd wiggled ever-so-slightly beneath his touch, taunting him.

"Just so we're both perfectly clear, I'm going to ask you to repeat that one more time." He squeezed a little harder, fingertips grazing her hot core. "Feel free to rethink it, change your wording, take it back. Whatever you—"

"I said, *make me,* Demon."

That time, she absolutely pressed back into his hold, her pitch higher. Almost begging.

His markings flashed briefly. One breath, two... Make her wait. Make her squirm. And...

Smack! She cried out, her nails sinking into his lower back.

"Now, will you *please* dry us off?"

For a moment, she didn't move, and a knot of dread formed in his gut. Maybe he'd misread the situation and her cues. "Luna—"

Goosebumps broke out, his body shuddering as the water evaporated.

"Take me to bed, Brand."

The uncertainty bled out of him. "Exquisite creature," he rasped, finally giving in to the desire to nip her supple flesh. "Perfection."

He set Luna down on her feet, her oil-slicked skin gliding over his. "This *discovery* has been a delightful interlude." His fingers sank into her curls and he pulled her in. "But this first time, we're making a choice to be bound for eternity. I don't want to *take you* to bed. I want to walk at your side, as you asked me to do, each of our own volition." He laid a light kiss on her forehead. "No regrets, little moon. Just us. Together."

Her eyes welled and she shuffled closer, wrapping her arms around his middle. "Together," she whispered.

The tension built as they stared at one another, their breaths mingling, the moment rife with all the potential of a shared lifetime.

And then it broke.

Lips and tongues and teeth met in a frenzy as they stumbled, only parting when the backs of Luna's knees finally hit the mattress and she sprawled back across it.

Brand was halfway onto the bed when he was caught by her beckoning, sea glass eyes, swirling with silver, and they stilled him in a way nothing else ever had.

Trembling hands replaced fervid ones as he laid himself between her thighs. He didn't want to rush. Didn't want to lose this moment to a lapse in control. Didn't want the memories to blur years and years from now because he hadn't bothered to savor every damned second.

Brand's gaze followed his fingertip as it traced the high arch of her brow, over faint lines that held the secret details of her life in their furrows.

"I would memorize this face," he whispered. "Immaculately rendered by the Sisters and housing a soul that was crafted beside my own."

He trailed down her jaw and around the edges of her gasping lips, to the iridescent freckles concentrated there, blurring the boundary between blush and ivory.

"It will greet me in the mornings and be the last thing my eyes see before they close at night."

Across her cheekbones, to a tiny scar above the bridge of her nose, the story of its presence one he longed to hear.

"It will be the beacon of my life. The shining light that leads me through every darkness." He gripped her chin and pulled her to him. "And Sisters, how I love it more than any other sight."

His lips brushed hers. A single sob left her as she trailed her fingers through the short hairs of his beard. Up into his hair, nails scraping along his scalp.

The sound burrowed its way into him as he notched his cock against the molten center of her, clinging to the hills and valleys of her soft sublimity.

No sooner had he felt her readiness than his horns started curl.

Heart pounding. Eyes screwing shut.

Shite.

Ringing started in his ears. He wouldn't change completely, but he'd forgotten to tell her. Didn't want to frighten her. To—

"Brand, look at me." He did, and she clasped his hand and brought it to her chest. "This heart beats for you, remember? It's yours," she husked. *"Take it."*

The command in those words was punctuated by a tempestuous look of longing so stark it snatched his breath away. He jolted when her hand wrapped around him, teasing and pumping, urging him closer. Deeper.

His greater half rushed to the surface in answer, his markings flaring to life as he surrendered to it. To her.

Eyes on hers, breath sawing, he let his touch trail like whispers up the length of her leg. "Who am I to deny you?"

Brand splayed his fingers around her thigh and buried himself to the hilt.

Luna's body lifted from the bed and surged against him, and he felt it to his bones when they cried out in tandem. The old version of himself was ripped away with the sound, replaced with something better on his next gasping inhale.

At last.

Stars swam in his vision and he stilled, trying to breathe through the life-altering sensation of being joined with her.

Her, who filled his lungs and pierced his skin. Her, who swept through to undo the aching knot in his chest and fill him with ease. Her, who strengthened him. Made him new.

Her, her, her. Everything was *her.*

"Luna."

"Stars, you feel so…" she moaned, the silver in her eyes multiplying. "Do you feel that, Brand, how perfect it is?" Luna dug her heels into his backside, taking even more of him as her lids drifted shut and she uttered pleas for *more*.

Power rippled out when he began to move, the canopy ruffling and doors rattling, their souls and bodies and magic twining together as the mating bond began to forge itself in the fire between them.

He fucking *burned* for her.

Light poured from him, glowing pieces of his markings abandoning him to dance over her skin and sear themselves into her flesh, connecting their bodies in yet another way.

"Brand," she breathed, over and over, her limbs clasped desperately around him.

He reared back, bringing her with him and settling her upon his thighs. "This is where you belong," he murmured against her lips as he wrapped his arms around her. "Gasping above me while I kneel in worship."

He thrust up into her, panting, his hands roaming. Down the curving line of her spine. Into her hips to pull her down and meet her advances with his own. Up the center of her body and around her nape, to tangle in the mass of her hair.

When she used his horns to tug him closer, Brand buried his face into her glorious breasts with a groan, drowning in the ecstasy of dragging his lips and tongue across her flesh, of being utterly surrounded by her. Latching on to one dusky peak, he turned his head and sighed, listening to the fierce cadence of her heart as it beat in time with his own.

His heart, her heart… They were the same.

Brand looked down to where his cock pumped in and out of her sultry heat, her arousal dripping down his straining length, and it freed the ancient thing within him—something feral and possessive and protective—and he felt it like a lightning strike at the center of his being.

His horns curled, fangs dropping as muscles bulged. His skin changed, the deeper color of his rage rising and retreating in waves, the reddened hue only serving to highlight her twilight beauty when it finally settled in and stayed there.

Brand swelled inside of her, and Luna let out a choked whimper of approval that filled him with more satisfaction than anything else could. He wanted nothing more than to be the source of her rapture, to fuel his own with the indescribable feeling of delivering his mate into the soaring arms of bliss, over and over.

"Touch me, Brand." She spread herself, exposing her glistening clit. "Please."

"Fuck. Look at you."

He gripped her arse tighter, delighted to grant her wish. Circling her in time with his thrusts, he watched Luna move over him through hooded eyes, mesmerized by her abandon. By the pulse hammering in her neck when her head tipped back and she shouted to the rafters above. The furrow between her brows, deepening with every stroke, harder and deeper. Every sweep of his fingers.

All the while, those markings pulsed and shot between them, the light flaring and waning, tunneling further into her with every pass.

Fucking Solyrian, she was the most beautiful thing he'd ever seen. And, when she went silent—when her muscles tightened and her limbs locked her in a frozen arch above him, mouth open to the sky with her own hands buried in her endless waves—he knew he would never be the same.

"Yes, little moon," he rasped with awe, fingers strumming quicker, hips thrusting faster as he chased her completion. "That's it. I want it all. Let me feel you come undone around me at last."

With a wracking shudder, she screamed his name, melting and twitching and trembling, her sheath pulling at him in clamping waves that brought back awareness of how fucking perfectly she fit around him.

He loosed a strangled, "Luna," when she grasped his horns again, not even stopping to breathe before she was pressing her forehead to his and moving with renewed purpose.

As she seized control, every aching ounce of the mind-blowing pleasure he hadn't let himself acknowledge bombarded him.

Sweet, merciful Sisters, the *feel* of her.

He stared, transfixed and hardly able to breathe, at the goddess before him—completely drawn in by Luna's unconscious seduction as her thighs flexed and her arms strained. As her breaths stuttered and mixed with his. He was utterly lost in the uninhibited ebb and flow of her movements as she worked her body over him.

She was wild. Stunning.

Her tongue darted out to tease his own. "Does my mate have a gift for me?" She nipped his lip, her eyes wholly silver and dancing with barely-leashed power.

"Fuck yes," he answered, the rushed words scarcely able to escape his mouth before she was on him.

A thrill shuddered through him with the first nick, her groan sending sparks along his nerve endings. When she bit down, sinking her fangs into his bottom lip, all coherent thought left his mind.

Luna utterly devoured him. Her tongue clashed with his, no longer teasing but taking. The copper tang of his blood filled their mouths, that boneless, wonderfully hazy feeling washing over him. He was helpless against her onslaught, except to sink his fingers into those luscious fucking hips and hang on while she drank from him, ruined him, owned him.

With a heave, Luna broke away, bowing back. "Fill me, Brand," she begged, her words drawn out into a moan. "I want to feel it inside me when… when I—"

"Yes, take it. *Take it.*" Bloody fucking Solyrian, he was finished. *"Fuck, Luna!"*

She clasped his head to her breasts and tensed around him, and his own raptured bellows joined her screams. Luna never stopped moving, even as she shattered and drew him deeper. Never stopped her gasping words of praise as he emptied every drop of himself into her.

The fiery light between them was blinding, building and building as they came down, their groans no longer from pleasure but from the sheer force of the bond solidifying. It didn't hurt so much as feel like there wasn't enough room for the final dregs of blessing it had to give. Not enough space beneath his tightening skin and squeezing chest.

Brand gritted his teeth and held onto her as tightly as he could, as if he alone could keep them from breaking apart.

He'd expected an explosion when it was done—a shocking detonation that would level the world—not the subtle, gentle shift as it lovingly released them. Not the quietly deafening click that rocked him to his core and allowed him to take the first full, truly unhindered breath of his long, long life.

Brand heaved unfettered air into grateful lungs, the freedom of it completely intoxicating as he dragged his open mouth up the column of her throat and seized her mouth with a searing kiss.

"Oh, Brand," she whispered against his lips, voice hoarse and breathless.

This. This was where his life finally began.

He was home.

39

BRAND DRAGGED ANOTHER STRAWBERRY UP THE CENTER OF LUNARA'S BODY before pressing it to her lips.

"If I eat another bite, I'm going to explode," she said around the mouthful.

The feast had already been there when she'd awoken in the wee hours, everything she could imagine laid out on the low table by the fireplace—including the massive bowl of cut berries he was cradling between them.

He leaned over her and trailed his tongue up from naval to sternum, licking the juice away. "Strange. I'm still starving."

Lunara giggled as giddiness tingled over her skin. She couldn't remember the last time she'd felt so light. The last time a laugh had lodged itself in her throat, dying to burst free, because she was so stars-damned happy.

"I can't wait for the Occurrence." His finger followed the line of her collarbone, up and over her shoulder. "To see your markings."

He'd explained that—for those who weren't Demon, but mated to them—the physical evidence of their bond would only show up for that single day, when Solyrian rose between the peaks of the Sacred Sisters and funneled power into the Montrealm.

"*I* can't help but be disappointed. What if I only get to see them once, in all my life?"

A low rumble reverberated in his chest. "You will be living far longer than that."

Will you, though? Fifty years is a long time, and there's no hiding from the Council anymore.

Right. The only mar on an otherwise flawless night was their looming conversation and finding out whether Brand had meant all the beautiful things he'd said.

No going back. May as well get it over with so you can move on.

Brand kissed up the side of her neck and nuzzled at her ear. "What lies are you feeding yourself now, mate? Tell me, so I may disprove them."

Lunara chewed her lip. "None, this time."

She *felt* his skepticism through the new fibers connecting them. What had come and gone before was a solid presence now, constantly humming below the surface. The only difference was that there was no more mistaking which feelings were her own, and which were his.

It comforted her.

As for those moments after healing Fern, she was still baffled by what had happened. Why her other half had warped within her mind, into something else entirely. Something that didn't feel like *her* at all. Something… darker.

All Lunara could think was that she'd been so wrung out, so raw after being in such close proximity with him, that she hadn't been able to tame the worst of her worries. Perhaps a defense mechanism, of sorts, but it left her uneasy.

That he could suddenly hear it might be the most terrifying part of the whole mess.

Ohhh, what if he hears the other one, too?

Shitting stars, she hadn't thought of that.

Brand gripped her chin and tilted her face to his. "From bliss to worry as it piped up again, but no lies." His eyes bored into her. "What, then?"

"The *truth.* I just… don't know where to start."

"Hmm." He pushed up straighter and leaned back against the pillows piled against the wooden headboard. "You don't have to do this. Not for me."

"I think I do, as much for myself as anything." She sat up and crossed her legs, wrapping the ivory sheet around herself. "And because you deserve to know. If for no other reason than, now that we're… that we've…" Her cheeks puffed out with a heavy sigh. "You're an Imperial Son. As your mate, I'll be seen, and I don't want you to be blindsided by it. I'd rather you hear it from me."

No, please. Be more *dramatic. I'm sure it will help.*

"I suppose a good place to start might be proper introductions. Forgive me, Your Highness, but I lied to you before."

His brows shot up when she thrust out her hand. Meanwhile, a roaring had started in her ears, the throbbing beat of her rushing blood filling the room. Once she told him her name, that was it—the end of her running and hiding.

"I am… Lunara the Moonweaver. It's wonderful to finally make your acquaintance."

His eyes danced, his fingers engulfing hers. "Hello, Lunara the Moonweaver." He tugged her arm and planted a kiss to the inside of her wrist. "You're an Elder."

"You don't seem surprised by the prospect."

He chuckled, letting their hands fall. "Not in the slightest. I had a feeling it was along those lines."

"Yes, well…" Her head fell back on her shoulders and she stared at the ceiling—easier than looking him in the eye. "They think I'm dead. And, for clarity's sake, I'm not technically an Elder. I never completed my trial."

"I see."

It didn't sound at all like he *did*.

"It's strange, the lens you find yourself under when you're the child of not one, but two Elder Tier Sorcerit and Council members. I imagine you can relate, being an Imperial."

"Oh yes." His nod was slow, introspective. "Very well, indeed."

"My power bloomed late—almost too late. The first nineteen years of my life were spent with countless eyes on me, waiting to see whether I'd live up to the legacy. I was never *not* aware of the fact that I might be a freak anomaly."

Her mind reached for the heavy curtains beside the bed, seizing their particles and drawing them open to invite the waning moonlight inside. It didn't beam down like it should have—not when she had it in her grasp and was pulling it towards herself.

"My magic was weak. Hardly good for anything. I could do little tasks without trouble, but nothing meaningful. Certainly not healing. Except, my energy never dwindled, while everyone around me would get so tired."

A prismatic glow encompassed her as the well within gulped the moons' magic down, the level rising and rising.

"Most Sorcerit can go a day, maybe a few, before needing to bask in the cosmos. Hence their love for the Evesong, where there's a constant source of sustenance."

Twisting her wrist 'round and 'round, she spun the light into threads, threads into yarn. Tugging the newly-formed length towards herself, she disconnected it from its source and laid the coiled scrap of material into Brand's palm.

"Their love…" He skimmed his fingers over it, then her. "What about you?"

"A few months shy of my twentieth birthday, I felt the moons for the first time—playful caresses, poking at me, looking for attention—and I realized what was inside me."

She gestured towards the tiny bundle of yarn. "My gift is the ability to manipulate the very life-source of all Nachthellians. I can bend it, shape it, weave it. But, most importantly, I can store it. As much as I want. I've never tested how deep the well is, out of fear, but I can go for *months* without seeing the night and still use my magic."

Lunara let go of the light, letting it snap back to wherever it naturally wanted to fall, her glow gradually fading.

"Turned out, I'd been unwittingly filling the well without knowing how to use or direct it my whole life. Once I understood…" She shrugged. "Quite the prize for the Elder Council. My parents were ecstatic."

"And you?"

"Oh, ecstatic doesn't even begin. I was beside myself. Told everyone I knew, made little presents. I'd been an oddity for so long, and then powerful people were suddenly inviting me to parties, clamoring to speak with me… They were the happiest months of my life."

He wrapped his hand around her foot, giving a little squeeze. "What happened?"

"Malachyr the Mistwarden."

Brand cringed. There probably wasn't a creature alive who didn't know his name. Not after the horrific blow he'd single-handedly dealt to the Evesong.

He searched the bedsheets, and she felt his calculations. Watched in real time as it dawned on his face. "The calamity on the Upper Block… Fuck. They were there?"

Lunara's laugh was a twisted, bitter thing. "Oh, they weren't just there. They were the reason it happened."

His eyes went wide as he recoiled.

"I didn't know my life was ending the first night I heard his name spoken in anxious whispers, instead of the reverence I'd always thought he deserved."

Leaving out that she traveled her memories in dreams, looking for messages, Lunara told him of the night she'd revisited most recently.

"I no longer wanted to be part of the Elder Tier, or the Council, or any of it. And I'd already lived almost my entire existence thinking it wouldn't happen, so what would it matter if it actually didn't?"

Brand drew in a sharp, deep breath, blowing it out slowly. "I've always thought they were a bunch of bloody cold bastards, but Araxis has never mentioned a word of it."

"Why would he? He's one of them."

She hadn't meant it in a cruel way, merely a statement of fact, but Brand bristled. "No, he would never. He isn't like that."

"No?" Her heart ached for him, for herself. "Then, tell me—if he isn't one of them, why did he vote against culling Malachyr that last time, when they all knew what he was doing?"

"What are you talking about?"

She dug deep—so deep she worried it might kill her to finally find the bottom. Pushing beyond the loneliness of the last fifty-two years to the center of her pain, Lunara sifted through a drudgery of memories best left forgotten to find *that* night.

Brand's gasp was instant when she called it up in full, the mating bond roiling between them. "Weeping Sisters," he breathed, tears springing to his eyes as he clutched his chest. "What the fuck happened to you?"

"The day before my trial and twentieth birthday, a vote was cast. That's when everything changed."

Fifty-two years ago...

Lunara was lost.

She and her parents were taking their usual walk after supper. Music floated gently on the air, the swelling strings a perfect accompaniment to the glittering city of Starkeep—and completely at odds with her mind.

The truths her parents had shared haunted her. She didn't know how to act, how to *be.* So much building hope, so much excitement, and it was just gone.

Everyone had tried to convince her to release her concerns and accept her place, making light of every argument or question she posed. It was like being a child again, and they were not taking a word she said seriously.

Her father showed her blueprints and projects he wanted the two of them to work on together—cycling through glowing drawings and journal entries, going on about how their powers would compliment each other. Her mother had suggested various healing demonstrations she could do—making casts or bandages that empowered the wounded, filling orbs with light to speed the restoration process. Rambling about the profits she could make in the long run.

After all, tomorrow was supposed to be her trial. A public display of her ability to control the most revered substance in Nachthelliae.

'The things you could achieve!' they said. *"The changes you could make!"*

She took all of it in—and still had no idea what she would do.

Cordelia's visit had only made it worse.

She'd arrived in all of her crotchety glory and requested a word. They'd sat in the front room with tea and cake, and Lunara had confessed her every concern regarding the Council. A risk, since she was one of them, but the aged Elder was her mother's best friend, and Lunara had always loved her.

Cordelia had taken a couple beats at the end of Lunara's impassioned speech before throwing her head back and laughing to the rafters.

"Sweet, naive child," she'd said, hiccuping as she tried to suppress her mirth. "You think you have a choice? No."

Lunara had asked her to clarify, and Cordelia's response had utterly bewildered her.

"They've already been cataloguing the possibilities for how your power could be used to their advantage. They'll tell you it's for the Evesong. In some ways, I suppose it is, but they're not going to let you go on your merry way because you're having a moral dilemma. I tried to tell your parents to be discreet, but their pride knows no bounds. I'm sorry, but your fate has already been decided *for you,* Lunara *the Moonweaver.*"

"How so?" she'd asked.

Cordelia had gotten a far away look. "They'll persuade you. You'll be joining the Elder Council tomorrow, one way or another."

And then she'd walked out, leaving only more confusion in her wake.

"Where are you wandering?" her mother asked, the bump of her shoulder knocking Lunara from her reverie.

"Just ruminating," she answered. "I'm not happy with my choices."

The moonstone towers of the Upper Block shot up around them like shards of rainbow glass. Beautiful, the way they reached for the cosmos twinkling above. The temptation to give in just to have one of her own was staggering. It would give her independence. The freedom to entertain outside of her parents' friends. To sleep with someone *overnight,* instead of sneaking around at parties and having passionate encounters in darkened alcoves like she was still an adolescent.

Her father wrapped an arm around Lunara as her mother broke away to sniff at a glowing vine of night-blooming jasmine. "I understand," he said. "We both do. It'll all work out after your trial. You'll see."

"And if I refuse the trial?"

His eyes tightened, highlighting the beginnings of wrinkles in their corners. "I hope you won't, but the choice is—"

"Stellan."

It was amazing how viscerally a body could react to a single word. How instantly Lunara's limbs iced over upon hearing the breathy choke of her mother's voice, like they knew moving would be the start of something wretched.

"I would have your gift, Almaura."

Lunara's father shoved her behind him and whipped around, his fangs glistening as he snarled.

It sounded like Malachyr, but wrong. Chest heaving, she peered around her father's torso. Sure enough, it was he who stood behind Almura with one hand gripping her jaw, the other dipping lewdly between her breasts.

"Would you deny your Keeper?"

Her mother whimpered, frozen and blinking as both of his hands tightened around her.

"Would you touch another's mate thus?" Her father was seething, the cords of his neck bulging.

Lunara had never seen him like that, with the promise of violence in every line of his body. Hadn't realized he was capable of it.

Malachyr raised indigo eyes to her father. "You should be honored, Stellan, that I would deem her worthy after what you've both done."

"It is you who is no longer worthy, Mal. Let her go, or die."

Illamiata pulsed in the space where Malachyr's collar bones met—a single, crystal teardrop set against the ghostly blue shimmer of his skin. *Phantom,* her parents had said. She understood it better as he moved, there one second and gone the next.

He leapt between the ether's spaces in a blur. Without waiting to see where he would land, Stellan reached back and shoved Lunara as hard as he could into a border hedge. She sank like she'd leapt into water, the leaves and branches devouring her beneath their surface.

She fought to escape as the din of battle rose. Power thrumming. Growls and grunts. Fists meeting flesh. One of the hovering platforms clipped the bush as it flew by and the crack of bones echoed.

It was her father's pained bellow, though, and the silence after that stopped her heart.

She freed her head just in time to see Malachyr where he'd started, bleeding from several places, one eye swollen shut.

Claws embedded in her mother's throat.

Almaura's wide eyes landed on Lunara, and blood trickled from her lips as she mouthed *run.*

But Lunara couldn't run. She couldn't even *move.* It was like the shrub had planted itself into her body and rooted her to the ground, paralyzing her.

Her father was on his knees gasping, reaching. One of his hands was… missing.

Bile rose, hot and searing at the sight of that mangled stump. If Lunara could just convince her limbs to work, she might be able to help.

"It isn't me who will be dying today, Stellan." His grin was demented. "You should've let me have her. Better yet, you should've remembered your place."

Blood sprayed as Malachyr's hand wrenched to the side, the slap of something wet hitting the street a second later.

Lunara's mind broke, rending itself in two and refusing to comprehend what it was seeing.

No. No, no, no. Not real.

Surely that wasn't her mother crumpling lifeless to the ground, missing half of her neck and face.

It was happening to someone else. Someone else.

Not real. Not real. You aren't even here. It's not real.

Her father threw out his arms with an ear-splitting roar, and the buildings around them rumbled. Boulder-sized chunks broke away from the tower bases. They vibrated as they spun, until each one fractured into millions of tiny shards. Even Lunara wasn't safe from their razored edges, the bits pelting her arms, her chest, her face as they shot out.

"I'm going to fucking slaughter you," Stellan rasped, and swept them into a frenzy.

Malachyr only smirked before he misted through the moonstone fragments. Some hit their mark, but it wasn't enough.

That was the moment she knew. Knew what came next. Knew she'd never speak to her parents again. Feel their arms and warm laughter wrapping around her. Witness their love, and wish for a bond even half as strong for herself.

Knew she'd never be the same.

Lunara watched from outside of herself, utterly numb as Malachyr the Mistwarden, Keeper of Illamiata buried a fist in her father's chest, withdrawing his still-beating heart with a laugh before crushing it in his hand.

With his cackles still echoing like a flock of mad birds, Malachyr tossed the ruined scrap of flesh and unleashed the Tear Stone. Power exploded from the center of him, beams blasting outwards into the buildings and along the walkways. Upwards into the dark sky.

She didn't know how or why, but it must have been her power that saved her when their quarter of the Upper Block was reduced to a pile of rubble and twisted bodies. When the screams started.

None of them were her own as she drifted in and out of consciousness, inches from her father's unseeing stare. It wasn't until Cordelia's face appeared in front of hers hours later that she joined the chorus of agony.

"How?" she sobbed out. "How did he know we were here? Why would he do this?"

Cordelia knew exactly who she meant. Lunara could see it in her eyes even through the haze of misery as the aged Elder used her magic to dig. "Your parents called a vote earlier. Theirs were the only two cast against him."

The only two.

"How could you?" Lunara whispered. Her repeat was a shriek. "How could you!"

"I had my reasons." Cordelia didn't look at her as she said it, wouldn't meet her eyes.

Lunara would have spit on her if she'd been able to move.

Then, it hit her. "They knew we would be here. Every… everyday the same walk after supper." Something inside of her disintegrated—a blind, happy trust she'd taken for granted. "They—*you*—let this happen. Wanted it. *You wanted this to happen!"*

Cordelia's flinch may as well have been a lengthy confession. Still, she refused to acknowledge it out loud, instead saying, "We'll get you somewhere safe. You can stay with me or one of the others until you—"

"No. Please, Cordelia," she begged through gritted teeth, hating she had to ask the snake for anything. "Please. Don't make me go to them. Not after this."

"Death is the only way to escape them, Moonweaver. *That* is their method of persuasion. *Our* method."

"Then I am dead!" Her voice shredded itself apart as she gripped Cordelia's collar. "I am dead, and no one need know otherwise."

Cordelia looked away, eyes shining. "You have a responsibility."

A single tear dropped from her chin and Lunara wanted to strangle her for daring to shed it.

"So did they." She couldn't help it. Her hand was flying before she knew it was happening, her palm landing with a stinging smack against Cordelia's cheek. "So did *you!*"

That was the end of it.

Cordelia didn't say another word as she used her fire to cut stone and debris. Didn't utter a sound as she bloodied her knuckles digging and digging, or as she carried Lunara through the wreckage and abandoned back streets to her own tower. Not so much as a whisper over the days it took to mend the crushed bones of Lunara's legs, the mangled flesh—something her mother could've done in hours.

It wasn't until she was healed, heading out with no plan and only a splintered soul for company, that Cordelia finally spoke.

"I know somewhere you'll be safe."

"Tell me." Lunara felt no remorse over the shrewish demand. She owed this creature nothing.

Cordelia's instructions were succinct. Easy to follow. Lunara rejected the longing in her tone and the brief light in her eyes when she described the destination. She only cared about getting there and then never seeing another person for as long as she lived.

"It'll need some help," Cordelia murmured. "It's been a very long time since I was there."

"I don't give a starry shite." Lunara wrenched the front door open. "Goodbye, Cordelia."

It was slamming shut behind her before Cordelia could reply. She pulled the deep, velvet hood of her cloak over her head and disappeared into the Evesong's shadows.

Thus, Lunara the Moonweaver perished along with everyone else they hadn't bothered to save from the wreckage.

LIMPING THROUGH THE SWAYING BRANCHES AND FALLEN LEAVES, A TEMPTING flask of blood bumping against her hip, Lunara spotted a dense shape ahead.

Hope spiked within her. She hadn't dared use the portals to travel to the Northern Forest, except to get out of Starkeep. There was no telling who'd be on the other side, who might spot and recognize her. The cloak she wore went some way towards disguising her, but there was no such thing as being too careful.

Her journey had taken weeks, especially since she'd foregone her power, barring a couple of desperate times when she'd needed to find food. The blood was there to replenish her only once she'd reached her destination.

Which, if she was right, was just beyond the tree line.

Lunara fought the urge to run. She'd only end up hurting herself in her sorry state.

She made it a few steps before passing through a wall of rippling power and emerging into a dream. The foreboding shroud of fog and mist dissipated, revealing a meadow of wild blooms and dancing insects. An overgrown path appeared at her feet, winding merrily away as if to say *follow me!*

So she did. That shape from before sharpened, lines appearing in its dissonance. Before she knew it, she was only a few steps from a… Was it a cottage? Shed? Hut?

Hard to say. Modest was an overstatement. A porch of waving, mossy boards took up the entire front and one side, its mushroomed roof and carved, blackstone pillars perilously close to crumbling. The large, round window beside the door was almost too big. Also missing a few of its faded panes, some of the others cracked, shards of colored glass littering the deck below.

Better than nothing. And heaps better than the Council.

She was still getting used to the new commentary—a figment of herself that her mind had conjured. Its snarky tone mixed with her own usual husk was a comfort, its words shrewd. It kept her level, focused. Helped her to cope.

Probably best not to dwell on that…

Right.

She dared to take the first step up, then the next, tentative as she tested the wooden planks for weakness. The arched, turquoise door was inviting amidst the rest of the structure's rubble, its bronzed handle gleaming. Her hand didn't feel like her own reaching out to grasp it, pushing the lever down and opening with a click.

Inside was worse. Aside from the sheer amount of dust and cobwebs, the dripping ceiling, and the strange nest in one corner, the entire thing was smaller than her bedroom in Starkeep by half.

No. Not… not your bedroom. Not anymore.

…Right.

Well, at least you'll have something to occupy yourself! That's not so bad.

A tight hallway led to a separate chamber—and a bed she would absolutely *not* be sleeping on. Back to the main room, and another door led to the… kitchen?

"Weeping moons."

Shhh, it's fine. You're fine! Go top up that well, use your power, and you've got the blood for after! It'll be stunning in no time.

She drew in a deep breath and thanked the Sisters for the gift of her new duality. For the wisdom it spoke and the peace it gave amidst the heartbreak roiling inside her.

And then she got to work.

It took a couple of days—and enduring some truly shocking indignities involving the local fauna—but it wasn't terrible in the end.

If she was honest, it was sort of nice.

Exhausted to her bones, pain streaking like lightning along her nerve endings, Lunara trudged to the chamber and its renewed mattress. She could worry tomorrow about how she'd distract herself from the horror of recollection now the cleanup was done.

Lunara fell back against the single pillow with a sigh—where she learned to never trust that satisfied, contented feeling again. To forego hope and optimism, because everything was actually complete shite.

Drifting towards sleep, lids like leaded weights, Lunara heard the *other* Voice for the first time.

"So it begins, moth. Just you, yourself, and I, against the world. Well, for a little while, at least."

Its giggles followed Lunara into her nightmares.

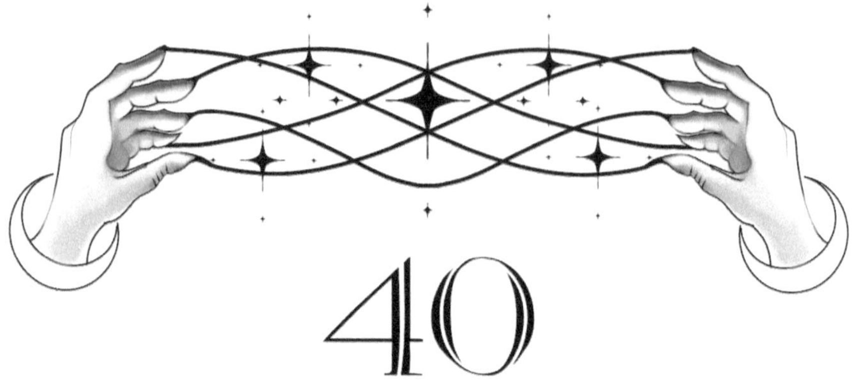

40

"You hear *two* voices?"

Lunara almost laughed. Of course that was the thing Brand latched onto—she would, too. The tears streaming down his reddened face stopped her, though.

"Yes," she admitted. "I used to think I was going mad." Sisters, she was so wrung out. "Shite, there's so much more to tell you."

Brand dashed the backs of his hands across his cheeks. "Truth be told, I'm not sure how much more I can handle, little moon."

Lunara had ended up on the opposite side of the bed, back propped against the footboard so she could face him and have some distance. She'd been afraid his touch would only wreck her. Make it impossible to continue.

Not once had he interrupted her, or asked questions. He'd sat there, silent, taking every blow she delivered. Strange, to watch the things *her* body felt manifest in his instead. She hadn't cried, but he'd sobbed for her. She hadn't choked on her words, or stumbled over recollections, but he'd buried his head in his hands precisely when she would've.

The mating bond was intense, to say the least.

"The rest isn't nearly as sad, I promise. Just lengthy, and complicated."

"How so?"

"For one thing, I got so desperately lonely that I finally answered the door around the thousandth time Cordelia knocked on it."

"You didn't."

"I did. A good thing, too." Lunara pictured the Firebane's weathered face. Her long, white hair and no-nonsense attitude. They'd never been as close as before, but at least she hadn't been completely solitary. "It wasn't comfortable, but she gave me a purpose. Without my mother, there were too many creatures who needed advanced healing that weren't getting it. I took the most extreme of them, with the caveat of drinking a tonic at the end, so they wouldn't remember me after."

"Caius and Thad?"

"You try forcing a memory potion onto an Imperial Son—*that one* in particular. Besides, we'd become close, and their departure was somewhat unconventional."

"I'd say it worked out in the end."

"Me too." She gave him a half smile. "Besides, that was the day she told me Malachyr was dead. It happened almost immediately after the calamity, but it took me a few years to speak with her. It was the most relief I'd felt in a long while."

Lunara still had days she didn't believe it, though. Where she was sure he was stalking her, waiting for his chance to finish what he'd started.

"I still can't believe all of Nachthelliae's Keepers are… *culled,* I think you said? We'd always assumed it was an abdication, like an Imperial stepping down for the next Heir."

She nodded, still having trouble accepting it herself sometimes. "I forced Cordelia to tell me of the others. My father hadn't exaggerated—they all lose themselves in the end, and there's no such thing as an oasis on the Isle. Malachyr was just the first to be so *public* about it."

"Maybe a good thing, the culling. I'd have had to kill him myself if they hadn't already done it." His nostrils flared, horns curling ever-so-slightly. "I think Araxis has some explaining to do."

"For the love of the Sisters, no!" she shrieked, hands clasped in supplication. A shudder worked its way through her. "Not on my account. The last thing I need is for the *Blessed Nightmare of the Endless Dark* to be thinking that I'm causing *him* trouble."

"An overly dramatic name for a genuinely kind male, if a little rough around the edges." He grabbed hold of her calf, kneading the muscles there as he stared into the middle distance. "How'd you do it, Luna? How'd you survive?"

She might've laughed or had some clever response for him a month ago, but the contrast between then and now was so staggering, she no longer had any idea.

"I don't know," she answered honestly.

He nodded. "Why were you so afraid to tell me? I see nothing you've done wrong."

That time, she did laugh, though she wasn't amused. "I didn't *know* you, Brand. I didn't trust you. I've been running for so long, I hardly know how to do anything else. And I assumed—incorrectly, I think—you might feel obligated to inform them. Turn me over, and good riddance." She swallowed, finally getting to the crux of the issue. "The second they find out I'm alive, not only will they want answers, they'll want *me*. My gift is no small thing, and there hasn't been a healer as skilled as my mother in all the years since she's been gone. I'll be a coveted prize and I'm terrified they'll do anything to have me—including using you against me. If you got hurt, or worse—"

"I won't let that happen," he growled. "I am an Imperial Son, and you are *my mate*. What argument could they have?"

"I'm not worried about their arguments, Brand. I'm worried about the underhanded, lawless ways they might subvert you and the rest of your family. I have the ability to harness our most precious resource and do *whatever I want with it*. They've done far worse for far, far less."

His head tipped back against the bed frame. "Fuck."

One word. One, single word and she felt the world crumbling around her again, her mind and body detaching from each other. Why did he look resigned? Why did she feel heartbreak and regret in their bond? Why did—

"No!" He lunged for her, gathering her into his arms. "No, no, no. Forgive me. That was *for* you. For everything you've been through. Nothing more, I swear it. I'm here, and I'm staying."

Her breaths were ragged, terror bleeding out in little pinpricks over her skin. "The bond is…"

"A heaping pile of wonderful, bloody confusing shite?"

Lunara huffed. "Something like that."

Brand tipped her face up, his thumb drifting back and forth over her cheekbone. "I'm so sorry, little moon. So fucking sorry for what happened to you." He pressed his lips to her forehead, her lids. Ran his nose along hers. "Tell me their names, so I may remember them with you."

"Stellan the Gemwright and Almaura the Bonewhisperer."

His intake of breath meant he recognized the names. Anyone with any knowledge of Starkeep probably would. After all, the capital of the Evesong only functioned as it did because of her father's inventions—and they'd been the only two elders who'd perished in the calamity. *Miraculously,* those whose towers had crumbled that night had all been gathered at the same party, on the opposite side of the Upper Block. If only their servants and staff had been as fortunate.

"They were Stellan and Almaura," she whispered, "and they were wonderful."

The flood of tears finally came, spilling over to the sound of her wracking sobs. Brand caught them all against his shoulder, rocking her as she let out fifty-two years' worth of agony and finally accepted it. At least, some of it. Amazing, how much easier it was when there was someone to share it with.

When she'd finally wrung herself out—boneless exhaustion heavy on her limbs—Brand stretched away from her.

The dagger from Faldir appeared in his grip. "I found this on the mantle, gathering dust. I'm ashamed to say I didn't realize you'd left it behind."

She'd completely forgotten about it. The day they'd left for Thodelebor, she'd stood in front of the fire for what had felt like hours, trying to decide what to do. In the end, there'd really only been one, logical choice.

Lunara plucked a curl from her lap, twisting it as she looked away. "I didn't feel confident enough, worthy enough, to bring a weapon. I'd had only hours to train with it. It was more likely I'd accidentally stab one of you than anyone who might deserve it."

"They were quite the few hours though." His voice was low, teasing.

Her body had no trouble remembering the way he'd molded himself to her, running through the motions over and over and—

"You were flirting with me."

He chuckled. "Of course I was bloody flirting with you. *Poorly*. I had an inkling we might be mates. It was my attempt to get closer, using teaching as a very convenient, not-at-all-obvious excuse to do so." His finger teased around the bedsheet, across the swells of her breasts, dipping inside to pull it away.

"That explains why I didn't learn a single thing," she admitted, her back arching. "You were too distracting."

"Mmm." His lips landed between her collar bones, tongue dipping into the hollow between. "I know what you mean."

"Is this real?" she breathed, a catch in her voice. "Was it really so easy as that?"

He detached his mouth from her neck and met her eyes. "I told you it didn't matter. That I was yours and the rest be damned. When will you believe I meant it?"

She wasn't sure when it had happened, really. "I believe you now." She cupped his face, wonder dawning. "Sisters help me."

He'd kept his word at every turn. Had proven over and over again he could be trusted.

Brandir aht Bordoroth, Blessed of Straelon, High Ambassador and Fourth Imperial Son of Alwyn and Fionerys was that rare and wondrous thing she'd thought long gone.

A good person. Honorable to his core. Compassionate and mindful of those who depended on him. He was everything.

His bellowed laugh burrowed right into her. "Maybe someday you won't sound so terrified of the prospect. Now…" He shifted to his knees and gripped her ankles, tugging her flat and laying her body out before him. "As I said before, I'm still starving. And when I'm done with my *meal*, we're going out to the practice ground."

Her body writhed, responding to the gravelly promise in his voice. "We are?"

Brand sobered a little, his look fierce. "The Elder Council will never touch you, Lunara, I swear it—whether it's my hand that defends you or your own. I would give you that peace of mind. So yes, every morning and every night, that's where we'll be."

"Okay," she rasped, eyes pricking again.

"Where were we again? Ah yes." He dove in, hands plastered against her thighs as he licked long and slow up the center of her. "Hands up, little moon," he rumbled against her, "and leave them there."

THAT NIGHT WAS THE FIRST BRAND SLEPT IN DAYS, AND HE DREAMT.

Not the usual faff bending the mind in strange ways. Instead, a sense he'd seen it before but couldn't place *where* followed him throughout. It almost felt like a memory.

The only problem was that, in the dream, he slipped Pet's guard and used his power to scale the Imperial mesa with no one the wiser—something he was positive he'd never done.

He'd thought about doing it, though. Constantly. When he should have been paying attention to lessons and instructors, he'd planned all the ways he could escape the responsibility and incessant public scrutiny. How he'd build a small home for himself somewhere secluded and pretend he'd never heard the words *Imperial Son* or *High Ambassador.*

Maybe that's why he found himself trailing an eight- or nine-year-old version of the child he used to be through back alleys of the Weeping City, the Palace of Argoph shrinking away in the distance behind him.

It made an odd sense that he would manifest his wildest childhood dream right after the one he'd carried through adulthood had become a reality. Two days spent making love to the exquisite creature of his fantasies, merging their souls, was bound to call other desires to the surface—even long-lost ones he'd let go of in order to grow up.

Brand was somehow aware he could have followed the Montriver to reach his destination, but it was too likely he'd be spotted and recognized by other Demons coming to drink from its rapids, even so late at night. That it was better to use the shadows to his advantage.

Except, a glow surrounded him, sparkling on grey stone and verdant vines. Brand looked down at his hands as he walked to find himself made entirely of Luna's prismatic light, and a smile teased the corners of his mouth knowing she was with him even in sleep.

The tall buildings shrank as he moved with himself—less and less stories, fewer and farther between—until he reached the outermost edge of the city proper. Trees rose up to take their place, and he dove in, aiming for the roar of rushing water ahead.

Excited, he left himself behind. His legs were so much longer now, and he didn't need the guidance. His mind and body knew exactly where to go and what he'd find when he reached the clearing.

Countless stars stood watch overhead as he emerged from the tree line onto a grassy bank, the twin moons looming among them. The odd thought slipped in that it didn't matter if they knew his secrets because they could share them only with each other. A warm comfort. His parents would be livid if they found out what he was doing.

A rocky outcropping came into view, rising from the sandy riverbed and jutting nearly halfway across the Montriver. Beneath it, the water hurtled its way to his Blessing realm, the thundering sound so loud he could barely hear himself think.

Maybe that was the point.

The tension eased away from his shoulders, stress he hadn't realized was there melting away with every step closer. The peace blanketing him felt familiar. The sense that, if he just kept walking, he could make his grand escape and no one would be able to find him. Sometimes the knowledge that he *could* was enough, even if he never actually did it. Even on the worst days.

A little stone seat came into view. It crowned the outcropping, perched on its furthest tip and facing his eventual home. Though far too small for him now, his limbs remembered exactly how it had felt. Knew that this was *his* spot. One he'd made for himself.

"I'm still wondering if you're ever going to make a place for me to sit as well."

Brand jolted at the deep, but distinctly feminine voice. It husked in all the wrong ways, skittering down his spine in warning as he turned, no idea what he would—

The scene warped and he was staring down at his younger self once more, settled in his river throne. Infinite droplets landed on his skin and hair, the mist soaking him—a perfect match to the little boy at his feet, with dripping, auburn waves and a ruined tunic, stoically staring into the wild darkness.

"Pardon any offense, madam, but I come here to be alone. Another seat would rather defeat the purpose, wouldn't you say?"

Burning Solyrian. The detached tone hit him right in the gut, those very adult words falling from lips far too young to be so proper already—like all the other words he'd been required to say with courtesy and composure while he'd screamed and screamed inside.

The shadows shifted beside the boy, chuckling softly. "You say that every time."

How could I say that every time if this is the first time?

The thought rang through his mind in his own, adolescent voice as Brand watched himself adjust, lungs clenching in tandem through the outward, awkward silence.

"Forgive me, madam. I do not wish to be rude. I only—"

"I know, Brandir. This was a hard day for you."

The world spun again and he was sitting in the seat, one with himself. His limbs felt fragile and weak, like twigs and mud and paper, instead of the strong solidity of the body he was used to now.

A hand reached out to grasp his own, the touch gentle even as the taloned, ivory nails terrified him. "We talked about this before, remember? Even His Highness Magnus will have to abandon you eventually. Everybody leaves at some point. It's not your fault, it's just the way of the world."

He absolutely could *not* remember ever speaking to this creature before, but Brand searched his young mind for the events of the day anyway and—

There.

That's right. This was the age he would've been when Magnus was preparing to make his permanent move to Thodelebor as a young male. There'd been a feast to celebrate. Mag had beamed at the room, his pride evident as toasts were made and gifts were offered. Just as Vann had been. Just as Amun had been.

Mag hadn't seemed saddened by the prospect at all, hadn't once looked at Brand with any sort of remorse, and it... it had *hurt.*

"The most important thing to remember is that the ones who leave us almost always forget us in the end. They get on with their lives and fail to recall how much we once meant to them. It's better for people like you and me if we acknowledge it ahead of time and don't let them bother us. Some people aren't built for love—like your parents and brothers. They don't know how persistent it's supposed to be, how accommodating. Too wrapped up in themselves. It's nothing you did, Brandir. You're such a good boy, always trying your best. No one understands you." Her hand squeezed, thumb running lightly over his knuckles. "But I do. Perfectly. I promise I'll *never* forget you or leave you behind. You're too important to me."

The air burned in his lungs, tears gathering in his lashes as he rasped, "Why?"

Within, Brand struggled against his confines, trapped as a child while his adult mind thrashed inside. She knew everything that had quietly terrified him for decades. The abandonment. The estrangement. The duties and responsibilities eating all of them alive until it sometimes felt as if his family hardly knew each other anymore.

"I'm sure you've noticed your parents starting to pull away from you, readying for the day you leave as well. They'll say it hurts, that they wish you didn't have to go, but you'll see how the letters come less often, and the visits and invitations to return home start to disappear. You'll realize they were excited for you to go, able to enjoy themselves without the burden of children. That they never really cared as much as they said." Her sigh was heavy, laden with sadness. "Oh, it's so unfair to you, my perfect boy. I only wish to give you the love and care you deserve."

Brand turned his head to look at her, not comprehending why a perfect stranger would be so generous. How she could see all of his deepest worries and give voice to them so accurately.

Her face was steeped in a lurching fog, features clearing here and there, but never all at once. He caught her ruby smile as she said, "Maybe someday, you'll find yourself wanting to offer your love in return. I'm going to need help soon, and you're the only one I can trust. What do you think?"

"Forgive me," he said, wary and hopeful at once. "This day has been dreadfully long, and I am ever so tired. I can't seem to recall your name, kind madam. I would know it before I offer my thanks for your friendship."

Brand nearly gagged on the words of his younger self, so fucking confused that his stomach was sick with it.

On one hand, he wanted to lean into her and clasp onto everything she offered with desperate fingers. To thank her for honest, straightforward words in a world where everyone hid their true intentions behind twisted phrasing. Anything, as long as she promised not to leave him too, even though he had no bloody idea who she was.

On the other, he wanted to break free of the flimsy bones holding him down. To rail at this version of himself that she was not offering kindness or friendship. That grown females shouldn't be talking to children in the midnight woods and asking them for favors.

She laughed outright, bumping her head against his shoulder. "We really must stop meeting when it's so late. You say that every time, as well." She gave his hand a final squeeze and rose to her full height, quite tall for a female. "I grow tired myself. This land wasn't made for one such as me. See you soon?"

He nodded, hardly understanding what he was agreeing to.

"Good." Dozens of crows descended from the trees to encircle her, their caws loud enough to drown out the rush of the river. "Perhaps then, you'll remember I'm—"

BRAND SAT UP WITH A WRENCHING GASP, TREMBLING AND HEAVING. HE DID his best to avoid disturbing Luna, untangling himself from the sheets and stumbling from the bed and into the washroom.

One stone glowed above as he filled the sink basin and splashed cold water on his face, scrubbing his hands over both horns and through the short hairs of his beard.

The sight of his towering body in the mirror was a relief, the muscled bulk reminding him that he was no longer anywhere near as weak as he had been as a child. As he'd felt while imprisoned within it once again, unable to escape.

"Just a nightmare," he whispered to his reflection. "Just a load of imaginary shite."

Already, it was fading into the recesses of his mind, the details hazing into a dark nothing.

Luna mumbled as she turned over, her words little more than nonsense before she settled again. A flutter in his chest and, even passed out, he felt her soul searching for him through the unrelenting fibers of their newly-sealed bond.

Without warning, Brand bent over the basin and vomited, a cold sweat breaking out as guilt and shame slammed into him with the force of a comet landing.

His beautiful mate was right there, perfection personified. Everything he'd ever wanted. More and better than he ever could have imagined.

So why in the fuck had the name *Okthana* been on his lips like a prayer when he'd awoken?

By the next morning, even that little detail was forgotten once more, and he didn't remember that—for a moment—he'd *remembered.*

41

It was just as Brand had said.

Every morning they peeled themselves from the bed and onto the practice field. Every evening, they fell right back into each other's arms. While Brand went about his duties as High Ambassador—showing her the mundane parts of himself that only made her fall harder—Lunara fit as many healings as she could between their time together, his frequent blood gifts cleansing her of the pain day after day, night after night.

Sisters, the *nights*.

Brand's lovemaking was a revelation.

She'd spent her life overthinking. Obsessing over every movement and choice. His control and consideration, his dominance—all of it removed the burden of thought. And when she did seize power, when something animalistic overtook her and she was helpless to fight it, her body was still *his* instrument, and he was a master at his craft.

There was only one point of contention between them.

Lunara had declined to move into Brand's chambers. Had refused to even see them. She was loathe to admit the remnant of fear that lingered. Old doubts and embedded habits, clinging to her, refusing to dissipate.

The constant conversations about Glynmor were like a fist around her throat. Draining her. Stoking that wary feeling. Hours upon hours spent trying to work out what happened, who the 'pretender' might be, and how they were going to handle the chasms.

And at the end of it all was Fern.

She was never far from the Fae. The wall in her mind was bad enough, impenetrable and now undoubtably the thing holding her under, but Lunara was convinced Fern was in danger.

Something just wasn't right.

Well… Some*one*.

Valandyrian had been waiting outside their door the morning after their mating, barely acknowledging Brand's ecstatic announcement. All of the Fae Son's attention had been fixed on the inside of her chamber, his breezy congratulations followed immediately by a request to finally lay eyes on Fern.

Brand hadn't noticed whatsoever, happily inviting him inside.

Lunara, however, had watched him closely as he'd rounded the floating slab the Fae laid upon, a crease between his brows. He must have limped around the damned thing ten times, arms crossed, stroking his chin back and forth with his knuckles, gaze turned more inward than out.

At last, he'd sighed and thrown his hands up, a sad smile on his lips. "Thodelebor's frontier is indeed a blimmin' strange place for a Fae to be, and begs many questions." He'd drawn a finger down one of Fern's cheeks then. "Unfortunately, I can't say I've seen her before. Poor creature, her family must be worried sick. I'll keep an ear out for anyone looking. If you'll excuse me?"

Brand had chuckled as his brother tapped the pointed shell of his ear, thinking Vann's playful comment an adorable joke. He hadn't been perturbed in the least when his brother swept out of the room just shy of running, and he'd thought nothing of it when Vann was nowhere to be found until the next day, when he mysteriously reappeared at breakfast.

Lunara had seen the tension ratcheting his shoulders higher and higher with every pass around Fern's sickbed, though. Had heard the strained lightness in his tone and false pity in his words. Had honed right in on the way his fists had flexed and tightened as he'd left, the slight tremble there.

Maybe it took a lifelong deceiver to recognize another. Maybe it was a different, intangible thing altogether. Either way, Lunara was sure Vann knew *exactly* who Fern was, and had lied right to their faces about it.

Except, she couldn't figure out *why*. In his presence, she never noticed anything off or ill-intentioned. Never had a twist of dread in her gut. In fact, she was having trouble trusting her intuition at times because he was one of the gentlest creatures she'd ever met.

It was the *shift* in the air holding her captive. The stillness settling over her bones to tell her the universe was holding its breath and waiting. A feeling that something was coming, something big. She just wasn't sure where he fit into it.

It didn't help that, many days later and a mere week before the Montrealm's Occurrence, Emperor Alwyn sent word to his sons.

The response to Brand's missive from the day she'd arrived in the Montrealm was dangling from Vann's fingertips as he nursed a mug of tea.

"Just like them to leave us all waiting, and then demand we come *now,*" he grumbled.

What if it's him? What if he's the imposter?

She narrowed her eyes on Vann, searching for any clue in his words and movements. Except, all she could focus on were the purple smudges under his mismatched eyes. The twitching muscle in his cheek and the faint grimace on his lips that had nothing to do with the letter. He looked pained, exhausted, and her own body betrayed her as she cringed with empathy.

"You know why that is," Brand said, his large hand drawing circles on her thigh beneath the table.

"I don't, though." She shimmied along the bench, closer to him. "Am I allowed to know?"

Vann set the parchment carefully onto the table, as if it might snap out any second and bite him. "The Imperials are very rarely all in the same place at the same time," he answered. "It makes people nervous, and there's bound to be talk and rumors."

"What, why? You're a family."

"Yes, well…" Brand gave her a squeeze and moved to wrap his arm around her. "It's important the realms are assured we're truly part of them. Loyal to them. That we won't combine our might and seek to overtake them, like in the days of the conquerers." He looked around the great hall, eyes darting. "*Especially* our family."

No one was paying them any mind as they ate, their quiet conversation lost amidst the bustle of breakfast.

Still, she whispered when she asked, "Why especially?"

"Our grandfather, Stennyx, wasn't fucking right," Magnus answered around a mouthful.

"Unwell would be the preferred term, little brother." Vann gave his shoulder a squeeze. "He was sick according to dad, not a true monster."

She'd heard a bit about Emperor Stennyx's madness after the delivery of the Shadow Prophecy, but details were few and far between, and before her time.

"When our father seized the throne from him, he was going the way of the old ones—using his power as emperor for things he shouldn't, ruling with fear and an iron fist. There was an incident… Fuck, many incidents." Brand loosed a heavy sigh. "Things are touchier than they used to be. I honestly can't remember the last time all seven of us were in the same room."

"Shite." Magnus shook his head, eyes to the table. "I can't remember the last time *three* of us were in the same room."

"And thank the weeping *everything* for that. You're only trouble when you're together." Caius plopped down onto the bench next to Magnus with a wink and nodded toward Emperor Alwyn's letter. "I've got one as well, but you'll be going in my stead."

"Ach, lucky bastard!"

Caius pointed across the table at Thad. "You're in enough shite as it is, lad. I'll not be setting you free to wreak havoc on the Plateau as well."

"You mean it, uncle?"

The instant Magnus had seen the letter's wording after its arrival—calling on the High Ambassadors to gather—he'd been subdued. The light in his eyes now, the hope, opened a crack in Lunara's heart.

"Aye. One of us has to stay away or Bordoroth will revolt, and I'm embroiled in the Glynmor mess with Lyriat. I'll send a message with you explaining things, not to worry."

"You don't want to see him?" Magnus asked quietly. "It's been a long time."

Brand tensed beside her, and his anticipation came running down the bond with a twist of trepidation, an uptick in his pulse.

It was tragic, really, how little communication went on between the Imperials. The wall between them, built with the mortar of realms and duties. She was realizing little-by-little that, while they were close, they were also worlds apart at the same time.

They'd known nothing of Meliora until she'd come along. Brand hadn't had an inkling of Magnus's project in Glynmor. No one seemed to think anything was off with Vann, and none of them knew what ailed him. That was just off the top of her head. It was making her feel a bit loony, if she was honest.

Caius got a far away look in his eyes. "Aye, more than a year." He scrubbed a hand over his face. "I'm not sure I'll ever be ready for the questions he'll be wanting to ask. And with everything that's happened, reminding me… Go on and be with your brothers, lad."

He stood with a clap to Magnus's back and lumbered off, barking at Thad to follow.

Thad backed away with pleading hands. "I'm begging you, Lunara. Hide me in your bags. Turn me into a kitten. Anything. I'll owe you forever."

Lunara giggled. "You know better now, remember?"

He groaned, eyes scrunching shut. "Why'd you have to go and talk me into being more? I was perfectly happy before."

"No, you weren't."

His answering sigh was really more of a whine.

"Thaddeus!"

"Shite." He jolted at his father's bellowing and turned on his heel, calling over his shoulder, "Think about it anyway, aye?"

They watched him go, but it was Vann who turned around first and said, "Alright, who's betting for and who's betting against him showing up at Argoph?" He reached into his long jacket, removed a jangling pouch, and peered inside as he sifted a finger through the contents. "Twenty—no, *nineteen*—storm seeds says he's there before supper's finished."

Magnus gaped. "You charge us out of the arsehole for those, and now you're giving them away?"

Vann shrugged. "I had them on me. Along with a lot of other things. Not that it matters, because you're going to lose."

"Ach, fuck off. He shows up tonight, and I'll tattoo your name on my arse."

Brand laughed. "Do you even *have* any room on your arse?"

Having seen the Wolflord's very naked, almost entirely inked body, Lunara was inclined to think he didn't.

"I'll make room. Sure as shite not having it anywhere else."

"I say Thad behaves and never shows up at all," Lunara murmured. "He's different now, even if he tries to pretend otherwise."

There was a twinkle in Vann's clear, green eye. "And what do you have to offer, little sister?"

The endearment hit her right in the chest, so unexpected that it stole any words she might have said.

No, no, no. What if it's a trick? Don't fall for it, you soft-hearted ninny.

Good point. Still, she couldn't resist.

"I'll fix your leg," Lunara blurted.

The table went very, *very* silent.

"I'm sorry. I would do it anyway, I only thought—"

"If you can fix me, I'll give you a lifetime's worth of anything you like." Vann's smile was sad as he spun on the bench and rose slowly. "See you all in an hour."

His pain was even more pronounced as he trudged off, the Demons in the hall skirting away like he was carrying something contagious.

"Shitting stars," she mumbled, slumping. "I didn't mean to upset him. I just…"

Wanted to throw him off a little while also offering something thoughtful in case he's not a scheming villain?

"Don't worry yourself, witchling. He's fine." Magnus heaped the remnants on his plate into a huge pile with his fork and shoveled the whole thing into his mouth, completely unconcerned.

"Apparently, we're leaving in an hour," Brand rumbled at her ear. "Since I know how quickly you can pack, I'd say we have three quarters of that time to do whatever we like."

His low tone sent a ripple of anticipation through her, warring with the wash of guilt.

"He really is fine," he said. "Trust me—you'll know if Vann is ever truly upset."

"If you're sure…"

"I'm sure."

His conviction flowed into her, and it was so easy to let go and trust him.

"Then, yes. *Please.*"

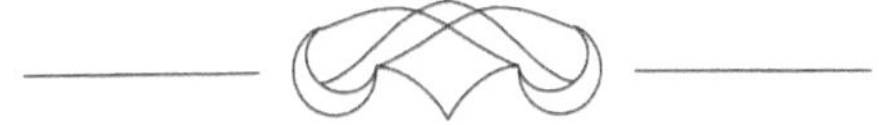

BRAND'S COCK HAMMERED INTO HER, ONE OF HIS HANDS PINNING HERS TO THE wall above as he latched onto a taut nipple.

Lunara pushed into the sensation, wanting more. Wanting it sharp and stinging. For him to soothe away the little pleasure-pain afterwards, as he did everything else.

His teeth bit down as he read her mind and her wishes, pulling a cry from her lips.

"That's it, little moon." He nipped her neck, her shoulder. "Fall apart." His tongue hooked behind the lobe of her ear. "I'll catch you."

Her body could only listen, ratcheting tighter and tighter with every word and touch until she snapped and fell over the edge.

"Yes," he moaned, his head tipping back as her ripples of ecstasy pulled him in deeper. "Fuck." He spun away from the wall and let her top half fall backwards onto the bed, her legs still wrapped around him as he widened his stance.

Gripping her hips, he slowed his movements, his lungs heaving with every thrust and eyes locked with hers. The depth of emotion in the bond was enough to have tears springing to her eyes.

"Oh, Brand."

"Do you have any idea how stunning you are? How perfect?"

Her lids fluttered, teeth sinking into her lower lip. She'd learned early on that he didn't expect responses to his praise. A good thing, since she wasn't capable of forming more than one or two intelligible syllables.

Brand reached up and grabbed one of her hands, bringing it down between them. "Touch yourself for me."

His gaze flared even hotter when she obeyed, circling herself with a whimper, dipping down to feel the hard length of him as it disappeared inside of her and retreated, over and over.

Her other hand had a mind of its own, taking his instruction a step further. She gathered a heavy breast, fingers sinking into her own flesh, the dusky tip peeking lewdly out between them.

"Shite." He bent to lave his tongue there, her back arching from the mattress as he flicked and teased, teeth nipping at her finger before he straightened again.

"Exquisite creature," he rasped, hooking one of her legs over his arm to spread her wider, tilting his pelvis *just so* as he picked up speed. "Again."

Again.

That word had become kindling, fuel on whatever fire he was stoking within her at any given time. He was a male possessed when he got like this, always drawing more from her body than she'd ever realized it had to give, and reveling in his exploits.

Who was she kidding? She was just as crazed, just as obsessed as he was.

Brand hadn't exaggerated in the least when he'd said her pleasure was his. She felt him ride the waves of her bliss as if it was his own every time.

The thought had sparks flying along her nerve endings, shooting over her body to gather into one, blinding coalescence in her core. Building and building and—

Bang, bang, bang!

The room rattled right along with the door when someone knocked with enough force to beat it right off the hinges.

"Fuck off!" Brand bellowed.

His lips peeled back in a snarl, flashing his elongating fangs as he continued his onslaught without the slightest pause.

"It was an hour *twenty minutes ago,* you wee shite."

"I'm busy!"

"Aye, the whole bleeding castle can hear how *busy* you are!"

"Just a minute!" Lunara didn't bother to hold back the giggle bubbling out of her. "We're coming!"

"Ach, I didn't... Just hurry up." Magnus's last words grew more faint as he left grumbling.

"Saucy Sorcerit," Brand growled, licking up her sternum and rearing back again.

"Well, we *are,*" she breathed, voice catching. "Unless you'd rather not—"

He cut her off with a toe-curling smack to her arse, her impish laughter mingling with a moaning cry as his fingers dug in to massage the sting away.

"Don't even finish that sentence." Throwing her hand away and replacing her strokes with his own, he circled her tight knot, faster and harder. "Give it to me, then," he demanded. "Come apart for me."

The sensations that Magnus's interruption had dulled came flooding back with Brand's touch, with his voice, dousing her in wave after wave of breathtaking rapture. It seized her lungs and her limbs. Her reason. Crashed with such perfect force that she had no choice but to give in and shatter into a million tiny pieces. *Again.*

The whole castle probably *did* hear the scream that left her then.

"Yes, yes, yes, Luna." Brand's body bowed above her, trembling as his thrusts grew erratic. *"Fuck."*

Lunara locked her legs around his waist and worked herself over him as he broke, drawing out every ounce of their shared gratification. Lids hooded, she was entranced by the corded muscles of his neck and shoulders. The way his abdomen rippled and strained. The feel of his cock twitching as he emptied himself inside her.

The sight was enough to have her pleasure building all over again, stirring the lingering remnants of her previous climax into a renewed frenzy.

His gaze snapped to hers, a wicked grin spreading slowly across his face as he pulled out of her without warning.

Her whimper of denial was nothing short of pathetic.

"Remember this feeling," he murmured, drawing one of her legs out and rubbing the cramping muscles in her calf. "Hold on to it."

"You're torturing me, Demon," she whined as he kneaded the arch of her foot. "Why?"

"Because…" He set that leg down gently and gathered the other. "I want every look between us to carry its charge. For every needy twinge shooting down your spine to be in answer to my own. And because I want you so worked up that you gladly give yourself to me in the first hidden alcove we happen upon in the palace, knowing I'm just as desperate to have you in return."

He laid down next to her, propped up on one elbow as he gripped her nape and devoured her mouth. She clasped his horns, dragging him closer and hoping to change his mind. Unfortunately, he had far more control than she did.

Brand broke away, a twinkle of amusement in his eyes. "Now, little moon—are you ready to meet my parents?"

Lunara looked down at their naked bodies and burst into laughter.

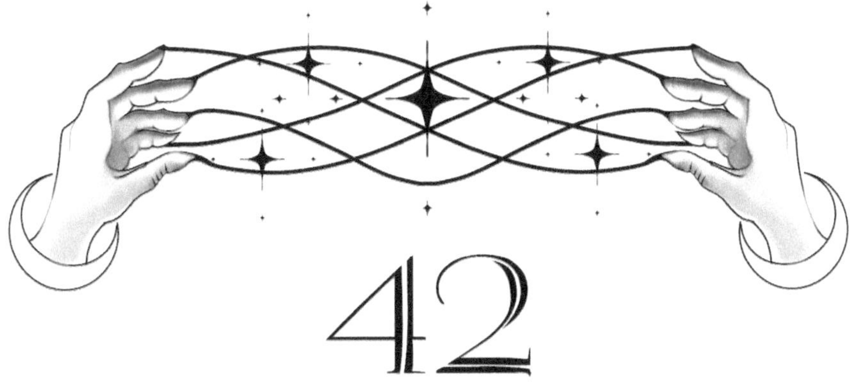

42

"I hope you don't mind, we have a bit of a walk," Brand said, lacing his fingers with hers.

She nodded, in a stupor when Brand drew her along behind his brothers as they stepped off the platform and disappeared into the throng around the portal.

There was no such thing as responding. No forming thoughts, let alone words.

The Weeping City, capital of the Great Plateau and the epicenter of creation, rose up around her in shades of grey and green, white and gold. Emerald vines clung to the lofty stone structures, their leaves as large as supper plates. Colorful canopies were suspended over the stalls lining the open market they'd stepped into, shouts and laughter ringing out over the din of the crowd to mix with the scent of spiced food in the air. Creatures from every realm meandered, pausing only to acknowledge the Imperials among them with bows and nods and dipping curtsies before going about their business.

It was the Palace of Argoph, though—perched on its mesa above—demanding all of her attention.

Brand's home.

Wide, seemingly infinite steps of glimmering stone gave the illusion they were growing out of the city itself, springing into view above the skyline. Cleaving the elevated land in two, they cut up through rock and flora to terminate at the palace's foundation atop, so huge that the hundreds—maybe *thousands*—daring the climb looked like little more than scurrying insects in comparison.

Argoph itself rose in ivory tiers, sculpted pillars and ancient columns holding each diminishing level aloft. Gilded domes topped the dozens of towers in its rounded perimeters, the central, largest one looming high above the rest and glinting in Solyrian's light like its own sunstar.

Waterfalls streamed from the uppermost story and fell to the next, and the next, and the next, building into five massive cascades that pummeled over the cliff edge beneath arching bridges, carving themselves into the land as they rushed away.

The Realm Rivers, being birthed from the Fountain of All Life right before her very eyes.

Tears pooled in Lunara's eyes as she beheld them, their distant roar calling out to her like a siren's song. The closer they got, the faster her feet wanted to move, until she was the one tugging Brand along.

At last, they rounded a final corner, shoulder-to-shoulder with countless others on their way into the palace grounds, and were greeted by a garden of sorts. The open expanse laid at the foot of the steps, trimmed with trees and wild, reaching greenery. Stunning blooms jutted from their stalks into the pathways and lined the grassy area, almost swallowing the intermittent benches and gathering places.

Lunara tipped her head back, gaze pushing past the crystalline stairs and soaring into the sky. Argoph seemed to mingle with the clouds themselves, so far above them it stole her breath away, excitement and trepidation twisting with equal measure.

"There are no images or renderings or words in all of Bordoroth that do this justice," she breathed.

Magnus turned to look over his shoulder with a grin. "Aye. They can't quite capture the feeling, no matter how they might try."

Even Vann had perked up, his limp less pronounced, a look of utter serenity on his beautiful face.

"I have to tell you," Brand murmured. "This will be an announcement, of sorts."

A month ago, Lunara would've shied away, unwilling to do anything that would draw attention to herself. Now, with him at her side, she didn't even mind. "How so?"

They reached the edge of the green, a dozen yards from the base of the steps. Between them, a mosaic depicting the Sisters and their forming of Bordoroth had been immaculately laid into the stone. The circle where the world might have been between their hands was empty of detail, copper tiles forming a hoop around a void of midnight blue.

Oily, shimmering midnight blue. A portal.

Those weaving around them were careful to steer clear of it, no one stepping upon the yawning space—except for Brand's brothers, who disappeared the moment they were inside of it.

"None but Imperials and their mates are able to enter Argoph through this portal. Everyone who sees you go in will know you're mine."

"Good." She looked him right in the eye as she said it. "As long as they realize you are mine in return."

Plunging his hand into her hair, he rasped, "Oh, I don't think there will be any doubt, little moon. Not after this."

His kiss was sudden and searing, and over too soon. Lunara heard the gasps, a wave of murmurs in their wake, and didn't mind that either.

"Come. Time for you to see what all the fuss is about." He leaned closer. "Maybe find that alcove."

She was still laughing when they stepped through the spectral fingers of the ether and into the Palace of Argoph.

Lunara stared crosseyed down the long length of a very elaborate —*very sharp*—spear, and into the flickering crimson and ebony gaze of who she could only describe as a stone-cold killer.

You could probably blast her halfway across Bordoroth with nothing but your shield.

"Amal, I don't give a fuck that you're his *ajma.* I will feed that to you pointy-end first if you don't take it away in the next few seconds."

Even better.

Brand had flown into his rage the second they'd stepped through the portal and found this madness on the other side, ruining his shirt and roaring in her aggressor's unflinching face.

A warm, rolling chuckle followed Brand's threat from somewhere beside her, but she was too scared to even dart a glance, lest she be skewered for the offense.

The warrior in front of her oozed a strange, protective hostility. Something about the controlled lunge of her toned body promised that Lunara was safe—as long as she complied. Since the only words out of her mouth had been a rich, guttural, *"Not another step,"* it would appear this spot on the portal platform, just outside the throne room, was where Lunara lived now.

"I will not." She—*Amal,* apparently—narrowed her eyes. "I don't know her."

A growl rumbled from Brand's chest. "She is Lunara the Moonweaver, a Sorcerit of the Evesong, and she's my bloody damned mate, Amal. I'm not going to ask again."

"It's true, we were all there to hear it happen," Magnus said, chuckling. "How are you, lass? Still terrifying?"

Amal lifted her gaze towards him. "Uncertain, Your Highness. Are you still telling insufferable jokes?"

"Aye. Usually."

"Then I'm probably still your worst nightmare."

Magnus only laughed louder. It didn't escape Lunara's notice that Vann was entirely silent and not even attempting to defend her like the others.

Taking the threat to her life out of the equation, *nightmare* didn't seem an appropriate description for the breathtaking female before her—especially when one side of her full lips twitched in amusement.

Amusement that fled when Amal focused on Lunara again.

The deep red flecks in her irises were imitated in fine scales across high cheekbones. They flashed with blazing pops of deep ochre and sunny amber against her mahogany skin, disappearing entirely when she shifted slightly out of a patch of light—a perfect match for the beads of gold and fire opal woven into the countless, jaw-length twists of her black hair.

Dressed neck to feet in sensible swaths of oiled leather and midnight linen, she was without a doubt an Arrajnekkatti Rider—the first time Lunara had ever come face-to-face with one, but there was just something about her that sang of sparkling sand and sunlight.

"What proof do you have that you are who they claim you to be?" Amal asked.

"Um…"

"Amalajneera." Sisters, that voice. Deeply resonant, though the owner spoke softly. "Can you not feel my brother's marrow entwined with hers?"

Seeing as she knew what Araxis sounded like—and that he didn't have a *very* enthusiastic Rider bodyguard—the only one of Brand's brothers left was Amunkar, Heir to the throne of Bordoroth. Which, made sense. His commanding, restrained tone was very believably that of a future Emperor.

Well, shite.

Amal's nostrils flared. "She could have tricked him to get to you or your parents. Could be a mind-wielder. Or what if *she* is the shapeshifter, and we are giving her exactly what she's been working towards all along? The timing is too convenient."

Amunkar finally stepped into view.

The warm brown of his skin had the same metallic scales sparkling beneath the surface as Amal did—only his were almost entirely gold. Long hair like fresh-tilled earth was half gathered into a knot on his head, the rest falling over wide shoulders in coiled ropes to his waist.

A heavy, gleaming medallion sitting in the center of his chest caught her eye, suspended on a thick chain and framed perfectly by the deep vee of his knee-length tunic. Along with his tight trousers, the silken, olive threads boasted a subtle shimmer, complimenting the vibrant pattern of his wide-sleeved overcoat. Black, russet, and ivory shot through the deep green color in a pattern both curving and geometric at once, so intricate that Lunara could've stared for hours trying to piece it out.

The epitome of looming majesty.

He wrapped his hand around Amal's shoulder, a thick ring glinting. "If that is the case, it will be handled." His penetrating, umber stare landed on Lunara.

Hot and cold, and loaded with so much raw power that she actually stopped breathing. It promised friendship and ruin in equal measure, depending on which side of him you fell—not unlike Amal, there.

Shitting stars.

"Anything to say for yourself, Lunara the Moonweaver, Sorcerit of the

Evesong with an Elder name, despite the fact that I have never once laid eyes on you and know all of those who boast such status?"

"Amun—"

The Imperial Heir raised a silencing finger at Brand and waited, focused solely on her.

"I have a great many secrets," she rasped, acknowledging the implication in his words. "Ones that will alter the course of my life when they are widely known, but none of them are as serious as what is being suggested, and Brand knows everything. And believe me, convenient though it may seem, this might be the last place in all of Bordoroth I want to be."

He studied her, utterly still.

"Second to last, if you'd like me to be specific."

Too used to Magnus and Vann, Lunara belatedly realized she'd spoken to him as if they were familiar with one another. She dropped into as much of a curtsy as she was willing to risk with that spear-tip still hovering inches from her face, and mumbled a rushed, "Your Highness."

Which did exactly nothing to thaw him.

He drifted away, his eyes sinking to stare into some middle distance.

What the—

Searing rage tumbled through the bond, licking like acid through her veins just before Brand's hand shot down and seized Amal's weapon, bringing it up to his own chest.

Trembling with *his* fury, Lunara stumbled back, straight into Magnus and Vann.

"I've been as patient as I am fucking able, watching you threaten my mate," Brand sneered. "If you're so bent on violence, you can direct it at me."

Amal was clearly surprised by the turn of events, an uncertain furrow appearing between her brows. "Your Highness…"

Brand took a step forward, the spearhead jabbing into his sternum.

Amal looked between them, jaw ticking as her lungs heaved. "Brandir, please. Do not make me do this."

"Brother." Vann reached up, his fingertips brushing Brand's forearm. "You know full well she may only relent once she's assured of Amun's safety, or he releases her himself."

"My word is fucking assurance."

"You're right, but she doesn't deserve your ire." Vann's voice went quiet. "She's only doing her sacred duty."

Eyes darted in every direction, the building tension so thick that Lunara was choking on it.

Not what you expected mixing with Imperials? What did you think was going to happen—hugs and fun, all the time?

Amunkar sucked in a sharp breath. "Enough, Amal. There is no danger. She is who she says."

They broke apart at once. Amal sagged, withdrawing her spear with obvious relief and mumbled apologies. Brand ignored the warrior entirely.

"Before we go in," Amunkar murmured close, as if sharing a secret, "you should know I've been looking deeper into the contents of your missive."

Brand went tense again. "And?"

"And there are many things that may not be as they seem. You'll know as soon as I do, once I've found the answers."

"That isn't at all helpful, Amun."

"It is what it is." Amunkar straightened, pushing his shoulders back as he walked away. "Come. We have much to discuss and they are waiting."

Brand's nostrils flared at the command. "Apparently that's that, then. Luna, meet Amun and his *ajma,* Amal," he grumbled.

"Ach, well..." Magnus bounced on by, following after their oldest brother with a grin. "Never dull in Argoph, that's for damned sure."

Argoph's Seat was as dazzling as the rest of the Weeping City.

The circular room was packed with creatures from every realm, Solyrian blazing through the open spaces of the vaulted dome above. Glittering over wings and scales. Shimmering on skin. Gleaming on horns.

The variations in dress—or lack thereof—were enough to make her dizzy. Otherworldly Fae mingled with Wolflords in elaborate robes. Riders flashed sharp teeth as they laughed with boisterous Demons.

Only the Nachthellians held themselves apart, silent and judging—and blessedly paying her no mind.

Yet.

In the center of the space, a humongous throne stood proud on a central dais—Emperor Alwyn aht Bordoroth entrenched on the wide seat beside Empress Fionerys o Koha.

Imperial Sovereigns of the world. Brand's fucking *parents.*

Stars and arses. This is the worst idea you've ever had, coming in here.

The Emperor's heavy brow was pinched, mouth turned down in a frown—until he spotted his sons within the crowd and lit up. He spared only a moment to nudge his mate, whispering in her ear before he stood and helped her up with an impish grin.

He was huge, like his sons, with golden, shimmering skin and gossamer wings that brought sweet pollen and summer leaves to mind—rather like Fern. Indeed, if it wasn't for the slightest hint of evergreen in otherwise black hair, she might've thought they were related.

His garments were similar to Vann's—cut in long, billowing swaths—but the sage fabric was lighter, airier, and shot through with pale silk.

Empress Fionerys was tiny in comparison, nearly a head shorter than his shoulder. Her petite frame was wrapped in an wispy lapis gown that perfectly complemented her midnight hair. The shining blue curls glittered with frost against her light brown skin, too thick for anyone to see the pointed ears Lunara knew hid beneath.

Magnus dropped back as they approached and leaned in, murmuring, "Don't be fooled by her small stature, witchling. Forget dreadbeasts—it's our mam who's the scariest creature in all of Bordoroth."

Brand grunted. "Mag…"

"What?" Lunara's heart turned over. "Why?"

"Because she's captivating and kind—and fucking excellent at hiding the fact she'd gladly skin anyone who harmed her family alive. Probably with a spoon and that exact, lovely smile on her face. Not so much as a blink."

"Why are you telling me this?"

"Ach, *because*"—He bumped his shoulder against hers—"she's your mam now, too."

Lunara blinked. "Oh."

He was still chuckling when they approached the base of the dais steps—and she was still trying to wrap her mind around what he'd said when her gaze landed on an eight-pointed, star-shaped hole beneath the throne, an eddying flow rolling and rushing beneath the diamond floor.

Even she heard the awe in her tone. "Is that…"

"Mmm." Brand nodded, half a smile on his lips. "The Fountain of All Life."

The Sister's weeping regret—the perpetual source of sustenance for the world—was *right there.* Swirling. So close she could almost reach out and touch it.

But, before they could stop or say a word, Emperor Alwyn offered a silent arm to Empress Fionerys and headed for a set of doors on the opposite side of the room.

Lunara tried—and failed—not to be disappointed.

They followed the Imperial Sovereigns down a set of winding steps and into a lofty corridor, and right through the first door they came across. As soon as everyone was closed inside the large room—a study if the desk and shelves of books were anything to go by—the Sovereigns whipped around.

"Come here, my gorgeous boys!"

The emperor opened his arms wide and laughed as Brand, Magnus, and Vann all swooped in, a tangle of massive arms and flexing muscles, the empress buried somewhere in the middle. It was ridiculous, and sweet, and—

"Not what you expected of us."

Lunara jumped at the sound of Amunkar's sedate voice beside her.

And you're absolutely sure escape isn't an option?

"If I may be so bold as to say so, Your Highness." She waved a hand at the pile of bodies, shouting and laughing over one another. "It doesn't exactly paint the picture of an all-powerful Empire."

"Does it not?" he asked. "What better picture than that of love and family?"

"I rather agree with you, Your Highness. I just hadn't realized that's what I would find when we got here."

"Hmm. Fair enough."

The others had separated themselves, and Alwyn was looking at her like he'd been waiting his entire life for this day to come. Which was odd, to say the least.

Brand smiled and gestured towards her. "Mum, Dad, this is Lunara."

She bent at the waist, staring down at the tendrils of her hair pooling on the floor. "Your Majesties."

"No, no. Come on." A hand at her elbow pulled her upright and she found herself staring into the Emperor's bronze gaze. "None of that. Let us have a look at you."

She swallowed as he led her to the empress. Closer, Lunara could see she had eyes like winter bark, peeking from behind ringlet bangs and staring straight into her own.

"The mystery Sorcerit. Have you…" Empress Fionerys cleared her throat and looked at Brand. "You're sure? The bond is set?"

"It's done." Brand smiled down at her, his peace settling like a warm blanket. "A true match, blessed by the Sisters."

"Brace yourself, witchling."

The empress transformed with the shriek she loosed, throwing her arms around Lunara.

"A daughter! Finally! Ohh!" She squeezed hard enough to make Lunara wheeze. "You're so beautiful! Hurt him and I'll make you wish you'd never been born. I'm so excited!"

"Fi…"

Lunara's eyes bugged at the exuberant promise of maternal retribution.

She surprised even herself when she said, "Likewise, Your Majesty," and the emperor barked a laugh.

No one could prove she'd just threatened Her Imperial Majesty's life, but she'd meant it. Meant every ounce of the protective ferocity barreling over her. It may have been decades since she'd navigated the social battleground of the Evesong's Elder tier, but she hadn't forgotten the lessons she'd learned.

The empress tossed her head back and cackled, too. "You're a right spark, eh? You'll do fine. Wouldn't have it any other way for our precious Brand. Please, call me Fionerys. Or Fi, or mum. Whatever you'd like."

"Indeed, and I am Alwyn. There is no greater joy I would wish for my sons than that of blessed matehood." The emperor shocked her to her bones when he offered *her* a bow, his eyes welling when he straightened. "And if you are Brand's, then you are ours as well, and we thank the Sisters for their gift. May I embrace you, Lunara, my daughter?"

What in the Five fucking Realms is happening? Daughter this, daughter that… They don't even know *you.*

True, but the idea of being wrapped again in paternal arms… To find the safety of family gathered around her, even if it was an illusion…

It was almost too much, how intensely she craved it.

Lunara took a tentative step towards him. "Your Majesty, Alwyn, I would be honored to—"

Araxis aht Bordoroth—Blessed Nightmare of the Endless Dark, Fifth Imperial Son, and High Ambassador of Nachthelliae—appeared behind his parents from out of nowhere and immediately recoiled at the sight of her.

He was the same as her in so many ways, as if their ghostly, shimmering skin and piercing blue eyes had been crafted from the same spark of light in the cosmos. The only real difference, the only part of him that was not in perfect place, was his raven hair. Done in the old way—cropped nearly to his scalp on the sides, fading into longer lengths on top and in the back—a single lock had fallen forward to brush at his brow in a carefree flop that did not at all reflect his capacity for ruthlessness.

Oh, and the fact that he was a treacherous bastard.

"What in the cosmic fuck is the *very dead* Lunara the Moonweaver doing here?"

Ohhh, shite.

43

"...AND THEN WE CRESTED THE HILL AND THERE HE WAS, ALIVE AND WELL."

The first his parents were hearing the tale, but Brand had lost count of how many times he'd recounted those dreadful few days at Glynmor—and it still didn't make any more sense than it had while they'd lived it.

"There's something we're missing." His father stood at one of the large windows in his private study, looking out over the city.

Araxis narrowed his eyes on Luna. "Something is often being missed."

He'd said little else since arriving and demanding to know why he was looking at an apparition. After a gaping, awkward silence, his mother had diverted everyone's attention towards *relaxing*.

So, here they were, posted up on heavy leather lounges with tea and tiny bites of food on the sideboards, pretending like it was any other day.

Hard to do when Araxis was hovering in a corner, utterly still. Quiet in a way that had little to do with noise as he glared holes into the side of Luna's head. Brand could almost believe his brother was seeing straight through her to the secrets inside.

It made him fucking furious.

"I propose we leave the imposter conundrum alone for a moment." His mother flitted around the room, refilling cups and plates. "We have documents from both Caius and the Chieftains, and Lyriat to go over that may help. In the meantime, I want to hear more about this dreadbeast."

Entirely unnecessary for her to sound so excited by the prospect.

Brand sighed. "It's dead. What more is there to say?"

She gave him an arch look. "My darling, there is always more to say."

"You gave us no real details." Amun sat on the settee across from them, legs crossed, one arm laid along the seat back. "What realm did it seem most closely related to? Were any of its features something else you're familiar with? Think *deeper*, brothers."

"It was fucking hideous. Looked like someone tacked spiders legs onto a glob of fucking snot. Tasted like someone shat on a rotting carcass and then dipped it in vomit." Mag managed to look bored as he painted that graphic picture. "Oh, and it was poisonous. Toxic? Venomous? I don't know the damned difference. Pet tried to eat it, it was foul as fucking anything, and I almost died." He shrugged as gasps sounded from both of their parents. "There really isn't much else to it."

Fionerys ran over to him, clenching his cheeks between her small hands. "Sounds like there's plenty blimmin' more to it, since no one said anything about almost dying!"

Brand couldn't help a smile. "Thad's maybe the only one who was never on the Veil's doorstep at any point." He squeezed Luna's knee, letting his gratitude shine in the bond. "It worked out in the end."

His mother's gaze snapped up to him. "And you never thought to mention this in a letter, or in the last couple of hours we've been *chatting*, or the fucking second you were in my presence?!"

"Mam." Mag's voice was gentle as he pried her clawed fingers from his face, little bits of frost stuck in the hairs of his beard. "We are well. Brand's right, thanks to Lunara there."

All eyes went to Luna, a blush stealing over her cheeks.

"Shite, witchling. Now that I really think about it, you're the *only* reason we're sitting here instead of traipsing around the Veil, and not just because of the healing."

His father's eyes bored into him and Mag, but Brand was having trouble focusing on anything other than Luna's confusion slamming down the bond.

Her brows dropped, a crease cutting between them. "What are you talking about?"

"The talons. You're how I got the idea to use them."

"We're getting ahead of ourselves," Brand said, pressing two fingers into his temple.

"Indeed." Alwyn rounded a sofa and dragged their mother to it, urging her to sit down beside him. "Perhaps we should start again. This time, I want to hear every last, tiny, seemingly insignificant detail from the time you sent Baldrir to the Keep at Fanghold, to this exact moment."

"No, no." Vann waved his hand in encouragement. "I want to know how Luna saved three Imperials trained in warfare from the day they'd been born, and why *she* doesn't even know she did it."

Another flip of his heart, her confusion bleeding into something else.

Mag laughed, ignoring their father's request. "It was epic. I'm lying there, losing my mind and skewered all the way through from two different directions. Blood everywhere."

His mother loosed a strangled squeak, snowflakes falling around her.

"Ach, Mam, it's fine. You see, Brand was holding the beast back. Sorcha dragged me away, and then Lunara ripped the talons out and healed me." He parted his robe, flashing the smooth skin on his sides and abdomen. "Good as fucking new, too. She even saved my battle markings."

Everyone leaned in, gaping. Amun hardly ever looked surprised by anything, and even Araxis had left his corner to have a closer look, eyes darting back and forth between Luna and Mag.

"There was a bit of overlap. See, she was still mending me when the wee shite over there got himself snared by the dreadbeast's tongue and was being strangled to death. Had to be at least five yards long."

"Sisters, spare me," his mother mumbled, dropping her head into her hands.

Brand pressed a fist to his chest, his own remembered terror from that moment bubbling up to mix with whatever horrified anticipation Luna was dumping into the bond.

"The witchling went fucking feral. Brand suspected, I think, but that was the first I thought they might be mates myself." Mag looked at her, his gratitude shining. "She snatched up one of the talons she'd taken from me and misted over there, saving his life. If she hadn't done that and given me ideas, we may never have slain it."

Luna froze beside him, the world tilting around Brand. He couldn't breath through the onslaught of her devouring dread, the wrenching twist of his stomach.

"What did you just say?" Araxis's voice mirrored the feelings roiling within him.

"I didn't mist." Her fingertips dug into the tops of her thighs. "I can't mist."

"Ach, you can and you did," Mag snorted. "I watched it with my own two eyes. One second, you're kneeling over me. The next, you're standing beside Brand, screeching and stabbing, like that." Mag snapped his fingers, the sound echoing around the room.

Luna shook her head slowly, every shallow breath cracking like a whip in the heavy silence.

Brand gritted his teeth, sucking in a lungful of air as two realizations hit him. "You can," he forced out. "You got to Hedda before anyone else and stopped her jumping into the chasm, too. And in the washroom after… When we were…" Shite. Right before they'd sealed their bond and he'd spent hours and hours buried in her. "You can."

"No. I can't," she whispered, wide eyes fixed a million miles inward. "Almost no one can."

Brand felt the tiniest breeze pass through the room, ruffling his hair. The others tensed when it happened, all breath but Luna's held still as the magical current moved between them.

"You're both absolutely certain you saw her do that?"

Brand's lips peeled back at his younger brother's calm question—in direct opposition to the tense aggression in his body. "Why are you holding your blade, Araxis?"

"Because there are only two Sorcerit with the ability to mist at any given time. So I need you to be really fucking sure that's what she did."

Another gust swirled, even stronger.

"What?" Brand growled. "Since when?"

Araxis's jaw ticked. "Since fucking always."

"Well…" Vann called his own power up for some reason, vines twining around his wrist. "That's news."

Pounding started up on the outer door, Amal's panicked voice shouting on the other side. Amun rose to reassure her, but Brand couldn't be bothered to give a shite.

"No, no, no, no, no…" Luna's chest was heaving. "This isn't happening. Not real. Not real. I can't mist. I can't."

Araxis crossed the room towards them, clear reluctance in every dutiful step. "Brother, you should move away from her."

Magnus growled. "Would someone please fucking explain what's happening?"

Brand tried to call his rage, to rail at his brothers, but all he could do was gag as nausea like he'd never felt brought a rush of stinging bile.

"Brandir, son, you must calm yourself. Breathe."

"Da, no," Araxis hissed. "You need to get Mum out of here right fucking now."

His father was there, waving Araxis away as he knelt in front of him and Luna. "You control the bond, it doesn't control you. You need to fight through her overwhelm or you'll only make it worse."

"I can't mist," she gasped out. "I can't mist."

Brand clawed through the spiral of her fixation, following his father's instructions as he inched himself out of it. When he finally found his own mind again, his greater half surged to the surface.

His markings flared, the transformation almost instantaneous. His father leapt out of the way as Brand went to his own knees to gather her close.

"I'm here, little moon. You're safe. I've got you."

"No! Get away!" Luna screamed, the harsh cry ripping through the room as a pulse of raw power rippled from her body and shoved him back.

Then another.

And another.

"You have to get away from me."

Tears streamed down her cheeks, her eyes both wild and apologetic as the others were forced backwards, furniture and feet scraping across the floor until they were pressed against the walls and windows, gasping for air, books and knickknacks falling from their shelves.

Vann uttered a curse, his vines and branches rising up from the floor along with their father's, flora reaching for everyone else.

"She's right." Somehow, Araxis was resisting her power, his hand squeezing Brand's forearm. "You don't understand—"

Brand reached over and threw Araxis. His brother disappeared into the ether mid-air, popping up right where he'd been before. "Arsehole, I'm trying to help."

"Then fuck off and get *them* out of here while I help *her*."

Brand locked his arms around the settee and blocked everyone out. Leaning in to the jagged blasts as they surged from her to batter against him, he gritted his teeth and commanded the stone to rise from the floor and form a protective dome.

Darkness swallowed them as they were encased within. It wouldn't hold for long—not against this—but it would give the others a chance to get to safety.

His muscles strained as he tried to lift his arms against the sheer force of her. If he could just touch her, snap her out of it.

Prismatic light flashed, near blinding as it poured from her to join the wind and pressure, building and building. He locked his jaw, calling on the Sisters' aid, and his rage multiplied. Red flooded his vision, his body growing even larger, bulkier. The warm sunlight of his power flared to join with the moonlight of hers, twilight and dawn crashing together to form something else entirely.

Blessed, fucking Solyrian—even like this, he struggled. It took every ounce of his considerable might to propel himself through the field of her magic, finally colliding with her. She didn't seem to notice when he lifted her into his arms, clutching her against the hard plain of his chest and pressing his face to the side of her head.

"Shhh," he rumbled against her ear. "I am here. You are safe."

Luna let out a sob and a crack formed on one side of the enclosure, crawling up from the floor to arc over their heads. "No one is safe," she cried, pebbles crumbling from the rounded ceiling and pattering to the floor. "*I'm* not safe. You have to get away from me."

Her skin was hot and cold against him, electricity buzzing from her in waves, and he had the sudden, terrifying thought that she was about to scatter apart. That the pieces of her would be thrown out into the Unknown and lost to him forever.

No, not his thought. *Hers*.

Brand tightened his hold, whispering little nothings and quiet everythings into her ear. Whatever was happening… "I'm never going to leave you."

As time passed, her rigid body shaking within the vice of his hold, the tempest began to settle.

Her power dissipated piece by piece, threading itself back into her.

The wind died, leaving the tousled strands of their hair to float down in haphazard knots like a blanket around them, and Luna crumbled on a ragged sigh.

Brand took his first full breath as darkness enveloped them, and commanded the dome to melt away—looking up to find every last, idiotic member of his family still there.

With a huff, he used a finger to clear her face, and hooked it under her chin. "Little moon?"

His gasp was sharp when she turned her face up to him, the whole of her eyes a shocking, glowing white, instead of their usual faint and silvery swirl.

When Araxis misted in next to them, they rolled back into her head and she passed out.

Brand's fist shot out in a blur, twisting into his brother's tight leather armor. "What the fuck just happened?"

Araxis didn't even try to fight the hold. Just looked down at her and said, "We've found Malachyr's successor, at last. Your mate is the Keeper of Illamiata."

Lunara was plucked from her nightmare and thrust violently back into consciousness.

Heart pounding, she scrambled to hold on to what she'd seen. There'd been an urgency to the warping images, the strange, gilded door always just out of reach, but they were slipping like sand through her fingers.

All but one was swallowed by darkness, the one that woke her, and she wanted to scream—a vision of Brand's naked body, lying broken and bruised upon a blackened stone slab.

She sucked in a shuddering breath, trying to clear the awful sight from her mind. Another.

A dream. Not real. Not—

"Have you finally returned to me, little moon?"

Brand's low voice settled over her, batting away the last clinging remnants of her fitful sleep, and Lunara's eyes shot open to find the rugged perfection of her mate's face inches away.

His unbeaten, unmarred, beautiful face.

The relief that tried to suffuse her bones was blocked entry by the intensity of Brand's stare. Something about it, about the little trace of fear lacing his words…

Every wretched moment of the cursed meeting came crashing back.

Turned out, some nightmares *were* real.

Lunara scrabbled backward and hit the headboard, making herself as small as possible, fighting to keep her breaths under control. "You have to go. Now." There was less force in her words than she'd been trying for, but the sentiment stood.

A furrow formed between his brows when he shook his head. "Seeing as this is my chamber, I'm not sure that's true." Spoken like a question.

She finally looked around, only just realizing she was in an unfamiliar, gigantic room.

The light was dim, but she could make out the dark wood and heavy furniture dotting the space. A huge fireplace darkened one wall beside a sitting area, and a few closed doors led to unknown destinations. No trinkets, no clutter. Even the gauze curtains hanging from the bed frame and around the open balcony doors were utterly confident in their necessity.

But what truly caught her eye was the domed glass ceiling directly above them, showcasing a perfect view of the night sky.

"This isn't how I intended you to see my—*our*—quarters for the first time, since it isn't the real thing, but I suppose an exact replica works just as well."

It was wonderful and confusing—and she had to get as far away from it as possible, as quickly as she could.

A *flash* and she heard the breathy choke of her mother's voice. Saw Malachyr looming behind her. Clawing. Groping. Demanding her gift.

No, no, no.

Lunara leapt off the bed and ran for one of the doors, ripping it open—just to be confronted with an absolutely humongous washroom.

The next door was a closet.

The next one went up. Where the stone staircase led, she had no idea.

One left. One door between herself and everyone's safety.

Get back to Straelon. To Lyriat and the deal he promised, and you can hide away.

Her heart sank like a rock when she turned and found Brand stationed in front of the last door, arms crossed, the fabric of a new tunic stretched tight over his muscled chest. "Are you done?"

Power lurched in her fingertips unbidden, a rawness there she'd never felt. It seemed to count him as a threat, spiraling out of her control.

No, no, no. Not him, of all people.

"Please, Brand," she begged, hands clasped in front of her. "I need to leave."

"Luna—"

"Move. Now. For your own good." She failed to sound commanding, the desperation in her voice doing nothing to help her.

"You would hurt me, *mate*?" Sisters, he sounded so—

Another *flash* and Lunara's knees threatened to buckle, her father's growling voice assaulting her. *"Would you touch another's mate thus?"* A blink and Malachyr's answering, unapologetic smirk was there, the Tear Stone's glow highlighting the demented twist of his features.

Tears sprang forth and Lunara shook her head, trying to dislodge the memories as she backed away. "Never," she whispered. "That's the point. Don't you understand? I'm trying to protect you!"

"Protect me from what?"

"From myself!" she snapped.

The glass dome rattled as a wave of power battered against it, and she tried—blessed moons how she *tried*—to rein in her panic.

He reached out, taking a step towards her. "Your eyes…"

"Stay back!"

Lunara only threw a hand up to keep the distance between them, but Brand was suddenly plastered to the door, grimacing and unable to move. She gaped at the tendrils of white-hot magic snaking from her fingertips and snatched the traitorous appendage back with a gasp. "I'm so sorry. I'm so sorry."

She kept repeating it as Brand hit the floor with a groan.

Hit the floor… Hit the…

Flash. The wet slap of sundered flesh. Her father hemorrhaging, Malachyr's fist buried in his chest. His manic grin. The mangled mess of her father's heart hitting the ground beside her mother's throat and face. Malachyr's laughter shrieking above the din of the screaming and screaming and screaming.

"No, no, no, no, no…"

Lunara's back hit a wall. A frantic search showed her the open doors leading outside. The night sky beyond them. The promise being offered.

Oh, no. What are you doing?

Saving him. Saving *everyone* from the abomination she was.

"Please, forgive me, Brand. I didn't… I never meant… I'm so *sorry.*"

She waited only long enough to check that his chest was rising and falling, before sprinting for the balcony.

Climbing the balustrade, scraping her hands and knees as she struggled, there was nothing of herself anymore. She barely felt the stone beneath her bare feet once she was finally poised on top, didn't sense the icy breeze.

The only thing that mattered was him.

Fionerys had said she'd make Lunara wish she'd never been born if she hurt him—this would save the Empress the trouble.

Because Lunara *would* hurt him. Maybe not right now. Maybe not in a week, or a month, or a year. But eventually, she'd be like the others. Would ruin his life in ways that didn't bear consideration.

You don't have to do this. Get to Lyriat and demand your payment.

She didn't know where to go or how to get there. Argoph was a maze, almost as large as the whole of Starkeep.

Mist, then. Picture the great hall and mist there.

Her stomach turned at the thought. Lunara couldn't stop the rise of bile, bending over and heaving.

A monster. She was a monster.

That's when she made the mistake of looking down.

They were in one of the outermost towers of the palace. The mesa dropped off beneath her, one of the falls plummeting down directly below. The world swam, stretching further and further away, before snapping back to its true position.

Fucking shite, it's a long way down.

A cold sweat broke out across her brow. She didn't want to harm herself, she just couldn't think of any other way to protect him. She couldn't *think* at all.

Flash. Brand's naked body, lying broken and bruised upon a blackened stone slab. No rise and fall of breath in his chest. No life beneath the caked blood and shattered bones. Naked. Broken. Gone, gone, gone.

"No!" Lunara sobbed, looking out over the Weeping City to replace that sight with *anything else* as she inched to the edge of the heavy railing.

Maybe…

Maybe if she kept the image of his smiling face in her mind instead, *alive,* she could do it. For him, she could do it.

Just one step. One step to save him—all of them—from her very self.

She couldn't be the Keeper of Illamiata if she was dead.

"Forgive me," Lunara whispered to the wind, hoping it would carry her pleas to Brand.

And stepped off into nothing.

44

A CALLOUSED HAND WRAPPED AROUND LUNARA'S ARM AND YANKED HER back.

She'd been so ready for the fall, for the ground to rise up beneath her, that the sudden backwards movement was somehow more jarring than anything else.

"What are you *doing*?" Brand snarled, setting her back on her feet and pinning her body against the balustrade.

Pure, unadulterated *rage,* as she'd never seen in him before—and it was all directed at her.

A fissure cracked open within, her heart stuttering and stopping and starting again. Why wasn't she feeling it? Why couldn't she find his anger in their bond?

It doesn't matter. You should've run a thousand times before this, but you didn't because you're a hopeless eejit. Now you have reason, so get out of here. Go!

"Tell that whispering gobshite to fuck off. This is between you and me, not the deceiver in your head."

It's not a fucking deception if it's the truth.

His markings whorled, hand still like a vice around her forearm, the other snapping up to snare her jaw. "You would dare harm yourself, mate, just to get away from me? Did *it* tell you to do that?"

Brand's voice was scarier for its softness, the accusation in his tone slicing through her like a hot knife.

"No, that's not what I— *No!* You don't understand."

"Explain, then. Immediately." When she didn't respond right away, he flashed his fangs—not a threat, but agony. "Have I not earned an explanation from you? Do I not deserve that, at least?" he whispered, eyes glassy with unshed tears.

His face was twisted with something akin to disgust, and she *hated* that expression being directed at her. Not because he didn't have every right to scorn her, but because Lunara knew she was everything the look implied.

Filth.

Brand tightened his grip and shook her. Not enough to hurt—just enough to bring her back to reality. "Answer me, Lunara!"

"Of course you do!" she cried. "You deserve everything lovely and blessed in this world. Everything that is good!" She wrenched herself from his grasp and shoved him back, shocked she was strong enough. "But I am none of those, Brand. I am poison and death. A *thing* to be paraded through Nachthelliae amidst cheers and banners, and they will welcome me with open arms. *Me! A fucking bane!*" Her voice had pitched higher and higher until she was screaming, pouring every ounce of her anguish out into the world.

"I am… I am the *thing* that destroyed a city and murdered hundreds. That has to be put down like a rabid animal." She collapsed to her knees. "I am the same *thing* that slaughtered my parents."

She caved in on herself, the admission too much.

Too much. Too much.

She'd spent fifty-two years running from that night, from the Elder Council and whatever latest monster they'd found for the end of their leash, and it had been her all along.

Fucking stars, she'd been the villain all along, and she hadn't even realized it.

One word, nonchalantly uttered by an irreverent Wolflord, and her life was over. One word that meant nothing to him, and *everything* to her.

Misted.

How could she have misted through the ether without knowing?

Three fucking times.

"I am Illamiata's Keeper," she whispered through her tears, spitting the last word as a new emptiness opened up inside, gnawing and gnashing as she tipped sideways and crumpled to the ground.

Shite. Even the cold, unwelcoming floor of this terrace might be too good for the likes of you.

She vaguely noticed Brand moving in her peripheral vision. Barely acknowledged it when his own knees hit the stone in front of her except to try and find the strength to fight him when he gathered her up against his chest and gently rocked her back and forth, but couldn't seem to manage it.

The world tilted and swayed around her with his movement, and she imagined this was what it was like to be lost at sea.

She started to protest when he stood, lifting her with him, but he cut her off.

"No speaking. Please, just… not yet."

Fine with her. It didn't matter what he had to say anyway—she was merely biding her time. There were no words in all of Bordoroth that would convince her to stay here and put him in danger.

She had to disappear. Utterly, completely disappear.

BRAND CARRIED HER BACK THROUGH THE CHAMBER TO THE WASHROOM. Warm light flooded the space as they entered, but it did nothing to thaw the ice pumping in Lunara's veins.

He set her on the long counter between the basins at either end. Her heart clenched when he leaned forward and placed a soft kiss against her brow before moving to a drawer in the vanity and withdrawing a cloth. Steam rose and warm water flowed over his hands as he wet it, wringing out the excess and turning to her once more.

Apparently, bath time when you lose control has become a thing…

Wedging himself between her knees, he gripped her nape, tilting her face higher. With gentle strokes, he mopped the evidence of her despair away. Smoothing her brow, swiping her cheeks. She didn't miss that he lingered on her lips, stroking the wet fabric back and forth before moving to her chin, her neck.

The only thing it accomplished was to make her love him more, which—

Shitting stars.

She *loved him.*

Soul-crushing, life-ending kind of loved him. The kind where she'd rather burn their future down and break both of them if it meant he was still alive in the world, making it more beautiful just by *being.*

Piss-poor time to realize it.

When he finished, Brand tossed the cloth into one of the sinks and knelt down, his face only slightly lower than hers. He stroked the column of her throat with his thumb, using his other hand to tame a rogue tendril of her hair as he stared at her. But then he leaned forward and pressed his lips to her jaw, her nose, each eyelid… and she broke.

Tears welled along with her shame. "I don't deserve this." Her throat was raw, voice ragged. "I'm not worth your kindness."

"I decide what is worth my time," he snapped. "*I* choose, Luna. No one else may dictate my actions for me, not even you."

"You don't under—"

"I swear, if you tell me I don't understand one more time…" He pressed his forehead to hers, eyes closing before his next hushed words. "No, I wasn't there when your parents died, but I relived every second of it through you and our bond. I understand bloody well enough what this means to you."

It was odd.

For a split second—as she faced saying words that had somehow become the most terrifying thing she could ever utter—she wasn't Lunara anymore. She was just a passing breeze. A shaft of moonlight. A moth flitting by as it looked down on two lovers in an intimate moment.

She watched them from above. Beheld them breathing one another in and out, and wished she could stay like that forever.

But she crashed back into herself all too soon, reality with her, and she couldn't put it off anymore. He'd stopped her before, but she hadn't made herself clear enough.

"Then you also understand why I have to leave you."

There, you've said it out loud. The sooner you accept it, the sooner you get the fuck over it.

"Now that"—He sat back and pierced her with a searing look—"I absolutely do *not* fucking understand. Not if my life depended on it, which it bloody well does."

"I am the *Keeper*, Brand. What else is there to say?"

"You can start by telling me why you're suddenly so fucking sure you have to go! How it could be so easy for you to walk away!"

The tiniest trickling of emotion finally broke through whatever barrier was separating them.

Agony. *His.*

No. You have to be strong.

She brought her hands up between them and pressed her fingertips into her eyelids, sending golden sparks across her blackened vision. It was easier that way, as if she was speaking to nothing but darkness. Easier when she couldn't see the betrayal on his face.

"There are exactly two Sorcerit, at most, that possess the ability to mist." Tears pricked, the wound so fresh that it physically pained her. "Whichever Imperial is High Ambassador to the Evesong, and the Keeper."

"So Araxis finally informed us—apparently a very well-kept secret among Nachthellians. That doesn't answer a damned thing, Luna."

She looked up at him, lip trembling. "Doesn't it? You heard what happened. You know the history of the Keepers. We already know the Elder Council is comprised of snakes and liars. I was terrified enough of being one of *them!* Instead, I'll be their fucking *pet,* Brand. And as I slowly go mad, they'll have more and more control until I can't remember who I used to be before they owned me. Until I finally snap and they cull me."

Lunara started to reach out, to cup his face and feel him beneath her hands, but stopped herself shy of contact. "When it gets to that point, it will be because I finally crossed a line not even they can ignore." Her head drooped. "I can't remember doing it. I m-misted thrice, and didn't know? I'm… I'm already losing it, and I don't even have Illamiata as an excuse. I won't put your life in danger."

Brand stood with a snarl. "What about *you?*" He surged towards her, gripping her upper arms with anguish in every biting finger. "You are my *mate,* given to me by the Sisters, and you're telling me *you* are going to die. *Your* life is in danger, whether by their hand or your own! You expect me to just accept that? I cannot. I will not."

Why were whispered words sometime so much worse than bellowed ones?

He swept her hair back, as he always did, gripping it behind her with both of his hands. "The only madness I see here is that you believe there's any life I'd want to live without you in it. That you'd ever think stepping off of a fucking balcony is something that would be good for me."

"I just wanted to protect you. I still want to. I *will*."

His hands tightened, hazel eyes boring into her. "That's the stupidest fucking thing I've ever heard in my life."

Another *flash* of memory—her parents, lifeless in their funeral shrouds, their skin colorless and shadowed beneath the grotesquely glowing flowers that surrounded them—and she snapped.

"No it's not!" she screamed, only centimeters from his face. "I refuse to let them take one more thing from me!"

No one had even known she was there, thinking her dead. Her body lost to the destruction. She'd used her power to leave her likeness behind in Cordelia's tower, and snuck to the garish service. Had watched false tears fall from traitorous eyes, Sunestra—Malachyr's mate—among them. She'd been so fucking alone it had sickened her.

"The Council isn't here, Lunara. *You* are the one taking away. *You* are the one trying to deny your own happiness, *and mine*."

"I'm trying to save you!"

He didn't back down. He didn't flinch. Just stayed there, steady as cliffs in a storm as she broke down, heaving sobs tearing themselves from her lungs. It could have been hours, days, weeks she was like that, pouring out her soul in wails and diamond teardrops.

By the time she settled, the front of his tunic was damp and clutched so tightly in her grasp it was a wonder she hadn't shredded the thing.

"Why won't you let me save you?"

Brand peeled her exhausted body away and scooped her up without warning. He carried her to the main room—to the massive, canopied bed—and nestled her against the headboard. The smell of salty pine resin and his intangible warmth rose up from the downy mass and engulfed her, testing her resolve.

He stepped back, a muscle ticking in his jaw when his eyes darted towards the balcony, and all she could think was that the loss of his touch only served to emphasize how miserable the rest of her life was going to be.

Brand nodded finally, as if to himself, and climbed in to kneel in front of her. He reached out and grabbed her hand, bringing it to his chest. "This heart is yours, remember? I've given it to you so many times, I've lost count. I'll be giving it to you every day until I pass into the Veil and, even then, I'll still be trying."

A tear slipped over his cheek, glittering as it fell to the silken sheets. He pressed his other hand over her heart, the treacherous organ pumping an erratic rhythm as his heat seeped into her.

"And this, I took for myself," he rasped. "I took it and I filled it with my every wish, prayer, and dream, and now… Everything I have *ever* wanted is beating here before me—a beautiful heart that I've gilded with my own future and entrusted to you." His fingers dug into her flesh ever so slightly, possessively. "If you run because you're still afraid, know that I will follow. To the edges of this world and beyond, Lunara. I will chase you. I will go to battle and fight with you. I will fall to my knees and beg you. I will do anything, except lay down and let you leave. Not when I know you're only doing it because you think you're protecting me. No one is allowed to steal away my greatest treasure—not even the female herself."

Never before had Lunara felt so wrecked, so ravaged. Every emotion pushed and pulled at her, clawing at her determination and tugging her in too many directions to count.

You have to fight it. You have to go.

"Brand—"

"No," he breathed just before his mouth landed on hers, the gentle kiss silencing her and over too soon. "No, I am yours and you are mine. I protect what's mine, Lunara, and I *will* protect you—from the Council, from Illamiata. I'll even protect you from yourself." He dropped their hands and slipped his fingers into her hair. "I swear to you, I will not let you fall into the darkness you fear. I will always be there to remind you that you *are* all that is lovely and blessed in this world. Everything that is good. You are." He closed the almost nonexistent distance between them and kissed her again, then whispered once more against her lips, "You are."

Then his mouth devoured hers, frantic and frenzied, so unlike the two before. She didn't know whether to pull him closer or push him away—what she wanted for herself and what she needed to do instead so at war that she hardly knew how to untangle the mess of it.

Drawing on her courage, on all she felt for him, Lunara ignored the heart that wasn't even hers anymore as it shattered to the floor.

She allowed herself one last rake through his auburn waves. One more nip of his full lips and brush of his tongue. A final shared breath.

"I'm so sorry."

"Don't—"

Her power was gentle, as in love with Brand as she was. He slipped easily into sleep, tumbling over next to her and onto the down mattress.

The sight of him blurred, like the fresh wash of tears was trying to steal it away to save her from the torment.

He seemed so much younger, dark eyelashes fanning against his cheeks, not a worry in the world to crease that intense brow or twist his mouth. His long hair was a gorgeous, fiery mess, tangled around his horns and caught in his beard like rivers of molten earth.

That this would be the last she saw of him was a balm on her spirit, in a way. A soothing touch against a soul that had been clenching and cracking for decades, until it had finally known a little healing because of the creature lying so peacefully before her.

"I love you," she whispered into the relative silence, wishing to test the words at least once—to feel the taste of them on her tongue, the rightness—before she left him forever. "Goodbye, Brand."

As if to confirm the wisdom of her decision by giving her the means, a dark and familiar power drew closer, brushing up against her own like a long lost friend.

"I'm sorry. I didn't mean to intrude, but I had to be sure he was well."

Lunara looked across the room, the youngest Imperial Son's severe countenance staring back. He was hardly more than a shadow himself in his black armor. Only his skin gave him away, flickering as hers did in the evenings.

"How much did you hear?"

Araxis took another tentative step, his sigh heavy. "All of it. I was ready to catch you from your fall if Brand didn't."

"And ready to rescue him, too, I'd wager."

"Always."

Lunara huffed, starting to go numb as it sank in. She couldn't resist trailing her fingers over Brand's as she stood, knowing she probably wouldn't feel anything again for a very long time.

Maybe ever.

She straightened her skirts and combed her fingers through her hair. "If there's one person in this world who has absolutely nothing to fear from me, it's Brand."

"I can see that." Another step. "I might even believe it, if I didn't know what you're capable of."

Her laugh was an ugly thing. "Araxis, if I hadn't come to help when Thad asked me, you'd never have known I was alive. The only way I could be capable of the things you're talking about is if I claimed the Tear Stone—which I abjectly refuse to do."

"The next Occurrence—"

"I was there for the Evesong's *last* Occurrence," she snapped, uncaring he was an Imperial. Shite, at this point, she might even outrank him in the same awkward way Lyriat sometimes outranked Brand. "Was there when exactly *nothing* happened, despite there being no Keeper to facilitate it. There to hear the uproar of whispers and wonderings as everything remained completely unchanged, much to everyone's shock. Nachthelliae will be fine."

His nostrils flared, a muscle twitching beneath his eye. "What will you do?"

"Funny you should ask." It was becoming more real with every word. More painful. "As far as I'm concerned, you owe me a favor, Araxis aht Bordoroth. Maybe a lifetime of favors. Fuck, *two* lifetimes."

"That night wasn't all it seemed."

"No?" she hissed. "Seemed real enough to me when I watched my parents get brutally ripped apart, and half a city with them, while the rest of the Council dined and danced, you fucking coward."

His fists clenched. "What would you ask of me?"

"Take me back to Straelon, to Lyriat, and tell no one where I've gone."

"He's going to chase you." Araxis nodded his head towards the bed behind her, and she had to fight against every particle in her body as they tried to follow the gesture and turn her around. "And I value my life just enough not to try and stop him, even though I might want him to."

"Yes, so he said. And I value *his* life enough not to give a starry shite about my own. He might try to find me, but it won't matter. I won't let it happen. Are you going to help me or not?"

45

Lyriat jolted, the three-petaled blooms he'd been gathering flying from his hand. "What the fuck!"

Normally, Lunara might've been shaking in her boots, red with embarrassment at treating a Realm Ruler thus. Right now, she couldn't be bothered to care. "I require the payment that is due to me."

"Hello to you, too." He bent and retrieved the flowers from the ground. "Would either of you care to explain why you've appeared in my garden?"

Araxis cleared his throat, chin ticking upwards. "There are many reasons, Your Majesty. All of them good, none of them your business unless she or he would like to share it."

He didn't wait for a response before disappearing in a winking flash. Probably back to Argoph.

Probably back to Nachthelliae, to tell everyone he bleeding can that you've been found.

Interesting. She didn't give a fuck about that either.

Lyriat loosed a long-suffering sigh. "Do I even want to know?"

Solyrian hadn't yet cleared the mountain peaks, though the light was bright enough to see. They stood at the base of the biggest tree Lunara had ever seen, its feathered needles littering the ground nearly as long as her arm.

All around them, the trilliatum were rampant, punching up through the tree's detritus in shades of emerald and ivory. Possibly the most stunning plant she'd ever seen, but she didn't care.

Didn't care. Didn't care. Didn't care.

Good. Just as it should be.

Maybe if she repeated it to herself enough, it would be true.

"I am the Keeper of Illamiata."

That brought him up short. His brows popped up high enough to nearly disappear into his copper hairline. "Going by the look on your face, I assume this was something of a surprise?"

To his credit, he didn't seem repulsed by or terrified of her. Something, at least. Hard to have a conversation if someone's running away screaming.

"Yes. Entirely."

He nodded, depositing his collection into a wicker basket. "Brand knows?"

"Yes."

Lyriat's mossy eyes narrowed as he straightened. "But not that you're gone."

Her heart turned over with a sickening thud. "No."

"Lunara..." Another sigh, this one almost pained as he pinched the bridge of his nose.

"I attacked the Imperial Family. Committed *treason.*"

Crossing his arms, he looked utterly bored—as if she hadn't admitted to being guilty of an offense punishable by death. "Something tells me that Araxis—the Blessed Nightmare of the Endless Dark, and a male known for his relentless pursuit of transgressors—wouldn't have happily dumped a traitor of the empire at my feet."

"I was completely out of control!" She threw her arms out, but reeled them in just as quickly when she felt another spark of wayward power tingling in her fingertips, like something had been awakened by finding out what she was. "I haven't laid eyes on the Tear Stone in over five decades, and already it has a hold on me. I misted *thrice* without knowing. Everyone is in danger." It belatedly dawned on her that she was in the presence of a Realm Ruler—not a simple friend—and her breaths picked up speed. "Weeping Sisters..." She took an abrupt step away from him, then another. "I shouldn't even be here. I shouldn't be anywhere. Please, Lyriat—you owe me. Get me out of here."

"What about the Fae?"

"What does she have to do with this?"

"The twins, Baldrir and Nyri, and Thaddeus have kept a constant watch over her—in pairs, as you requested. They've followed your instructions. Fern, however, remains unchanged."

Lunara's hands sank into her hair, fisting at the scalp. Maybe the pain would ground her. Would make it make sense. "So?"

"You haven't finished healing her."

"What?" She searched the ground for answers, finding nothing. "I'm telling you that I'm a monster, that I need your help, and you're worried about *her*? You hired me easily enough—find someone else. I don't understand why it has to be—"

"You're not the only one capable of remembering deals, Lunara. Fern is a *surprise* you've not yet seen finished."

She barked out a disbelieving laugh. "Are you joking?"

"Not in the least."

Under any other circumstance, Lunara would've been more than happy to stay and fulfill that duty, even if it was a stretch. She genuinely cared about the Fae and her wellbeing. Had bonded with her in the way only a healer and their charge can.

She wasn't a healer anymore, though. She wasn't safe.

Lunara paced away, unable to wrap her mind around what was happening. "You're pushing it… Twisting it…"

"No. I'm refusing your payment until you do what you were hired to do."

Cunning Demon arsehole.

He was technically correct, though she could probably find some way to refute it. Except, by the time they came to any sort of agreement, she could've gotten it over with and appeased him. If he wanted to bend the rules, well…

"Fine," she spat, "but if you're going to manipulate the terms, then I'm adding on to my part."

"Oh?"

"You take me away the second she's awake. The *second,* Lyriat. And…"

She could hardly say the words. Coming here and being demanding was one thing. Actually following through and making it a binding agreement was another. It would kill the last speck of hope she was clinging to, and she wasn't sure how to survive it.

"And?"

You must.

"Brand can never know where I am." Her voice cracked. "He can never find me or see me again. Once I'm gone, I no longer exist to him."

"You're asking me to destroy my best friend in this world."

"No." An invisible hand tightened around her throat, her eyes welling. So much for not caring. "I'm asking you to help me destroy *myself,* so I can *save him.*"

"Lunara, that's not—"

"Do you think this is what I want?!" she wailed, the tears breaking free. "That this fucking tragedy is the ending I envisioned? The story that's played out in my dreams?"

"I—"

She couldn't take it anymore. It was just too much. Too much.

"I'm not asking you." Lunara fell to her knees, her hands planting themselves into the soil. "I'm *begging* you."

She fucking hated the pity in his eyes—she had enough of it for herself, she didn't need his.

"Please, Lunara, don't— Shite." He scrubbed a hand over his face, looking to the lightening sky. "Fine. It will be done."

Brand's eyes snapped open, the empty, untouched space on the other side of the bed staring back, taunting him, and he *knew* right down to his very soul—Luna was gone.

She'd fucking left him.

While she'd been passed out after the drama in the study, his father had guided him through building safeguards into the bond, to help the two of them cope. Brand had followed his father's instructions and laid brick after brick between them to give her some space.

Stupidest fucking thing he'd ever done.

He should have let her feel his devastation. His ruin. Every raw lash of anguish tearing through him after she'd tried to fucking end herself like it was nothing. Maybe he'd have felt her shutting him out. Maybe he would've known what she was planning and they could've avoided this whole stars-damned travesty.

The betrayal was a crushing fist around his heart. He sucked in breaths, trying to stay calm. To think.

Damn it. He thought he'd gotten through to her. That she'd—

Wait.

There, beneath the lingering moonlight and amber spice, was the faintest scent of caramel spirits and desert orange—and only one creature he knew drank that specific concoction. Someone who *terrified* her.

No.

Brand's roar shook Argoph to its foundations, from the monolithic pillars to the tiniest pebbles. The rage was so sudden, so blinding, that it stole his conscious mind.

He had no idea how he ended up in the throne room, the whole of the Weeping City awash in bloody, pounding hues, and he didn't care.

No, there was only one fucking thing he cared about.

"Araxis!"

Stone surged like a roiling sea and courtiers scattered like insects, their screams nothing more than an irritating muffle beneath his furious bellows.

"Araxis aht Bordoroth, you come and fucking face me!"

Brand was going to choke the life out of his younger brother. If he'd hurt her, forced her…

All of the Evesong would pay. He'd tear Starkeep from the bloody fucking sky if he had to.

"Araxis, where is—"

A spear pulled tight across his throat, strangling him. Vines shot up from the tempestuous floor, snapping at his arms and torso, coiling around his horns. Ice crackled through the carnage to seize his legs. Howls and curses shrieked above the din of the falls. Tighter and colder, more and more, until there was nowhere for his breaths to go and the world bled from crimson to spotty black.

Brand buckled, his knees hitting the marble with a booming crack.

The spear vanished and vines loosened, and sensation rushed back into Brand's body with the first free gulp of air. And still, there was only one thought worth expressing.

"Where is Araxis?" he rumbled, fighting to keep himself steady. They'd trap him again if they knew how close he was to the edge.

The Imperial Family picked through the wreckage, almost bored, but slightly worse for wear. His parents murmured to the couple of brave guards and servants who'd remained. Vann and Amun were brushing themselves off. Magnus was retying his robe, an oozing cut on his cheek. Amal had a wary eye fixed on Brand.

No Araxis.

"Release me."

"You need to keep breathing, son," Alwyn murmured. Calm and gentle, like it could possibly make a difference. Only half paying attention as he continued doling out whatever instructions. "As soon as you're calm, we'll talk."

"I'm as calm as I'm going to be until I find my mate," Brand growled. "Araxis took her, and I want to fucking know where—"

"I'm here."

Araxis appeared from the ether, chin held high—as if he hadn't bloody betrayed him.

"What the fuck did you do?"

The arsehole only stood taller. "As I was asked."

Brand's markings blazed over his skin, the red doubling back over his vision, and he had to fight against every particle of his warping flesh to stay sane.

"By *who*?"

It was possible Luna hadn't chosen to leave. That her worst nightmares had come to fruition, and the Council—

"Lunara, herself." Araxis dared a step closer, his tone more suited for a wounded animal. "While she stood over your sprawled body after ripping your consciousness away."

Brand sneered, flashing his fangs. "Do not twist her actions to manipulate me, snake. I know her to the marrow."

"Please, Brand. Let her go."

Never.

This wasn't the first, or even the hundredth, time Brand had nearly leveled Argoph in a fit of rage. For once, he was glad.

Used to it, his family's mistake was their nonchalance in the aftermath.

He pretended to consider his brother's asinine suggestion, gentling his features. One breath, two… Ice melting, vines slipping a little more… Their attention drifting further…

Brand called a solid wall of stone as he lunged through their half-arsed bindings, his fist plowing into Araxis's face before the bastard could mist his way out of the blow. Another swing, and he snatched Araxis by the neck, bringing them eye-to-eye.

He paid no mind to the others shouting on the other side of the enclosure. "Where is she?"

"I told her I wouldn't stop you looking. That doesn't mean I intend to help you to your own ruin. *Let her go.*"

"I would rather die."

"Funny." Araxis raised a dark brow. "Isn't that what she was trying to do to *get away* from you?"

"You think this is fucking funny?" Brand shook him, ignoring the hot lance of agony buried in his chest. "How dare you say such a thing to me."

"I'm sorry, that was—"

"Fuck your half-arsed apology. *Where*?"

A muscle ticked in Araxis's swollen jaw. "At her request, I delivered her to the Demon King."

Wrong answer.

Brand slammed him into the ground, stone chips flying as he hissed, "You honestly expect me to believe she'd beg *your* help, just to escape to my own fucking home?"

"Not only did she *demand* my help," Araxis choked through gritted teeth, vessels rupturing in the whites of his eyes, "but I dropped her at Lyriat's feet and left before I could hear where she was going next, so it couldn't be beaten out of me. For your sake, I hope she's long gone and you never find her."

Truth rang in the words, and a thread of panic wove its way into his fury.

Brand squeezed a little tighter. "The only reason I'm not beating you to an unrecognizable pulp is because it would take too long," he seethed. "*For your sake,* I hope she's still in Straelon. You'd better stay very fucking far away from me if she isn't."

"LUNARA!"

Everyone in the great hall screeched to a halt as Brand roared his way through the portal into Straelon, forks and glasses poised halfway to silent mouths.

"Where is she?!"

A tiny squeak and skitter caught his attention, Nyri ducking under a table on the far side.

"Nyriadne!"

Those nearest her scattered, not stupid enough to stand in his way. They knew he wouldn't hurt her, even though he probably looked like he was ready to rip every last one of them into pieces.

She poked her head back over the tabletop as he thundered over. "Shite."

Hope sprang for the first time since waking. If she was hiding, she knew something. And it meant Araxis had told at least part of the truth.

"Brand, is this really necessary?"

"Aye, Vann is on to something. The witchling just needs a few days. She'll come around."

"Assuming she's even still here—no, she won't. He should leave it alone."

"I probably wouldn't speak if I were you, Araxis."

"Ach, Vann again with the wisdom."

Brand could only assume Mag and Vann had insisted on following to make sure Araxis survived the day. Why Araxis had insisted on coming was beyond him. His youngest brother was already fucking lucky he was still standing.

"Out, Nyri. Now."

"I'm so sorry, I can't hear— Eeee!"

Brand tossed the table away, dishes clattering. "You're going to tell me where she is."

"Where who is?"

"Don't get fucking cute with me, Nyri. Where is Luna?"

"Luna... Luna..." She tapped her chin and pretended to think. "Nope, don't know a Luna."

Brand balled his fists and roared to the ceiling, seething when he bent close to her again. "I swear to the Sisters—"

"She's been instructed to say nothing."

Brand's head snapped to Lyriat, traipsing into the hall like it was any other fucking day. "Where is Luna?"

The king ignored him, his pointed attention on Nyri. "Go find Hedda."

Nyri scrambled from the floor and was off without so much as a look back.

"Lyriat, *please*. Tell me where she—"

He raised a stilling hand. "She's here. Come with me."

The worst of his rage instantly abated, the panic of urgency draining away.

Lyriat led Brand and his brothers through the winding corridors towards Luna's chamber. "She called in our deal, demanding her payment. I stalled her—for *you*—by fiddling with the terms. 'Displeased' doesn't even begin to skim the surface of her ire." He nodded as they passed a wall of guards blocking entrance to that wing of the castle. "She immediately barred herself in there. *This* started happening shortly after, and none of us have been able to get in since."

"Weeping fuck."

Magic was bleeding into the hallway from beneath both her door and Fern's—prismatic wisps dancing with tendrils of black in the afternoon sunlight, flowing up the stone walls, little bits floating away to dissipate.

Brand ignored his brothers' murmurs and inched forward. The closer he got, the more volatile the wisps and tendrils. The darkness snapped out at him, angry, while the pieces of Luna's magic lashed out to block their attacks. So similar to the chasm.

He called to his power, ready to bring the castle down to get to her, but Lyriat placed a stilling hand on his arm.

"We've tried, but the stone isn't listening," he said. "Can you feel her through the bond at least?"

Shite. That bloody damned wall.

Never again.

His lids slid closed as he reached inside and tore it all down, opening himself up to her and—

Agony. Biting, writhing *agony*. Hers.

"Lunara!"

Brand didn't think. He sprinted to the door, a male possessed—bloodying his knuckles. Ramming his horns against it. Bruising his shoulders, his knees, his feet.

Something was very, *very* wrong.

"Lunara! Let me in!" His voice echoed around him, every word emphasized by a slam against the panel.

He summoned his greatsword from the ether. Brand had meant what he'd said last night—he would go to fucking war with her for the rest of their lives, relishing every second, if that's what it took to make her see reason.

He'd sure as fuck go to war *for* her.

"Help me!" He bellowed, calling to the others.

As he hacked and hacked, Brand was transported once more to the chasm depths, when she'd left him on the wrong side of the shield and he'd been forced to watch her mutilation. To feel her life draining away until she was—

Muffled shouts reach him, and he spared a glance over his shoulder between punishing swings. Lyriat and his brothers were waving their arms, their words lost on him.

That's when he noticed the wisps of her magic. Clinging. Shielding. They caressed over his skin, forming a protective enclosure around him and pushing the shadows out into the surrounding area.

"Please." Brand pressed his forehead to the door, begging it to hear him. "Let me in so I can help her. *Please.*"

It almost seemed to whisper in answer. A strange song that hummed in his his blood as it drew closer, tightening, tightening...

Release, just as the door clicked open. He could wonder about it later.

Brand barreled into the hazy room. The magic was thicker, but he could see her chamber was packed to the brim with crude wooden crates and overflowing sacks. Blankets and pillows in more colors than he'd ever seen had been tossed on every surface.

But no Luna.

He leapt over the piles nearest the door and through the opening into Fern's side—and stopped dead.

"Sisters, help me."

The two of them hovered in the air, entwined in light and shadow. Luna's eyes shone, their silver beams locked on the ceiling as she held a limp Fern in her arms, the Fae's body bowed backwards.

Power choked him. Insidious and cleansing at once, it was like sweet poison on his tongue. So much worse than the study. So much more consuming than Glynmor or the chasm.

When he sent a command to the stone in the walls and beneath the floorboards—hoping to use it to separate them—it barely rippled, as if it couldn't compete with the pressure she was creating. Just as Lyriat had said.

This was different to when Luna had healed Fern's physical wounds. Deeper, a vortex, like the watchtower in Glynmor. Which meant he couldn't fucking touch her.

He needed help.

Brand raced back the way he'd come, pushing himself free of the barrier. Cool air rushed in, a relief against the dampness of his skin. When he saw Hedda and Faldir there as well, his knees nearly buckled in relief. They would understand.

"The same as Glynmor, but so much worse." His chest was heaving. "I need someone else to separate them."

It rankled, but Luna was more important than his stupid fucking pride.

Hedda's shoulders went back instantly. "I'll do it. I already know what to expect."

"I'll be going with her," Faldir said.

The twins stepped forward and into their rage, rising to meet his own towering height. Lyriat did the same alongside them.

"Obviously, we're all fucking going now the door is open," Mag said.

Brand twisted to look behind, the prismatic wisps getting larger, sweeping out farther.

"Fine. Shield us from the shadows, Araxis, but no other magic." He gave a pointed look to him and Vann. "Whatever is happening in there, adding more might bring the whole place down."

Back through Luna's room and into Fern's, everyone following close behind. He ignored the gasps and murmured prayers, and turned to Hedda.

"You're sure?"

His Second was limned in Araxis's power, her face serious when she nodded. "She's my friend. Just... if anything happens, put me in a stunning gown for my pyre. I want to look incredible when I step into the Veil." She offered him a cheeky wink and lunged.

Her screams tore through the room when she latched on to Luna. Faldir rushed forward to brace her, his bellows joining the cacophony.

Magnus and Vann went to Fern's side, unaffected as they pried the Fae away from Luna's hold.

Pulling, pulling…

Both he and Lyriat were poised for the inevitable snap, waiting to catch everyone as they fell. He chose to ignore Araxis, hovering on the perimeter with his short blades in hand.

Almost…

They broke apart with a shuddering boom, bodies flying in opposite directions.

Brand dug his feet into the floor, skidding as he wrapped his arms around the twins. He watched with a sort of fascinated horror as all of Luna's power retreated into her, while the shadows either evaporated or *went back into Fern.*

Conscious of Luna's undoubtedly horrific pain, he extracted her from Hedda's hold as gently as he could, cradling her against himself. It was the only thing stopping him from either kissing her, or shaking her awake so they could have it out.

He settled for speaking his earlier thoughts aloud. "Stubborn, reckless fool," he hissed into her hair. "What were you thinking?"

Old parchments and worn books littered her bed, and he swept them away to lay her down. Same as too many times before, he shoved her fangs into the meat of his palm and coaxed her to drink, to come back, his massive fingers grotesque against her delicate throat.

Better he stay in his rage, though, lest he fall to his damned knees and weep.

She drew in a sharp breath and latched onto his arm with both hands, and he breathed a sigh of relief. He wasn't even upset when she went slack almost immediately, a drop of his blood trickling its way down her cheek as she fell into a deep sleep.

She was alive. She was well. She was with him. Nothing else mattered.

"Brand." Lyriat stood with arms crossed at the foot of the bed, back to his lesser self. "May I offer some advice?"

He already had an inkling of what his friend was about to say, already wanted to argue it, but he nodded once.

"Leave her be for a few days."

Furious tingles crawled over Brand's limbs, his suspicion correct. "Why the fuck would I do that?"

"Because she needs to realize for herself that running isn't the answer, and she won't be able to see through her fear if you're crowding her."

"*Crowding her*? She's my mate. We are one being now."

"Yes, but that half"—he jutted his chin at her—"is more terrified than I've ever seen another living creature. If you'd been there this morning…" His cheeks puffed out as he shook his head.

"I watched her try to leap from my tower in Argoph to save me," Brand rasped. "I have a fairly good idea."

Lyriat recoiled. "Weeping fuck."

Brand caught himself before he could dig his hand into the permanent groove in one of his primary horns. He'd never once sought the soothing motion while raging. He wasn't fucking starting now.

"I knew it was bad, but I did what I could, Brand. I kept her here, knowing you'd be back as soon as you were able. The rest she has to do for herself."

"She's already done too much by herself." It was getting harder to keep his form, sorrow setting in and trying to wrench it away from him. "For so long, she was alone. Why would you ask this of me?"

"I recognize someone carrying old wounds—wounds that have just been ripped wide open again." His voice was hushed, the tone of a male who knew what it was to lose everything at a young age. "Give her some time to see she *isn't* alone. Let Hedda and Nyri care for her while she tends to the Fae. Let her see she has friends outside of you, people who care what happens to her. Maybe if she realizes how many would be affected by her leaving, she'll pause to think. You can use that space as well. You don't have to be right next to her to love her."

Those last words hit hard. Hadn't he been doing that before Glynmor? Days into meeting her and he'd been mostly head-over-heels already.

"You truly think it will make a difference?"

"I do. Let her spend some time missing you, and she'll see it's no way to live."

Brand drew two fingers across her brow. "She's Nachthelliae's fucking Keeper, Lyriat. That's no way to live either."

"I know," he whispered. "You'll just have to cross that bridge when you get to it."

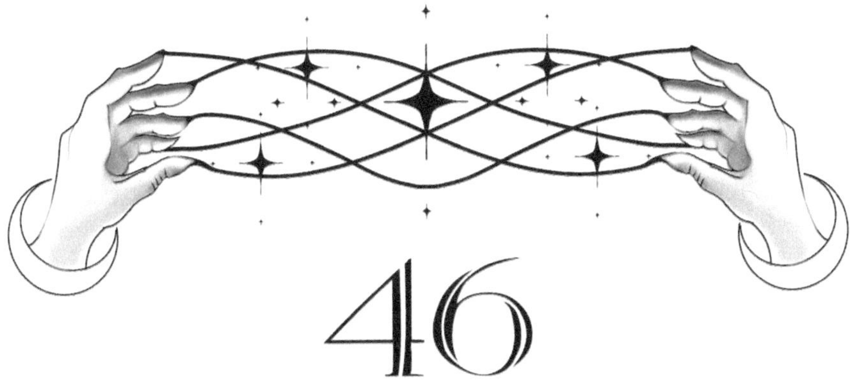

46

"Are you absolutely certain you want to go back in so soon?"

Lunara looked up from Fern's supine form, Hedda hovering over her like a fly on shite. "Yes. And for the hundredth time, you should go. I don't want anything to happen to you."

"I'm not leaving you to that *thing*. Not again. Since you already kicked Nyri out, you're stuck with me."

"Of course I kicked Nyri out. She's basically a *child*. What any of you were thinking letting her be so close to me, I'll never know."

She'd woken sometime in the middle of the night, tucked into her bed, the young Demon cuddled up beside her. The absolute horror of it was still fresh in her mind. Something could have happened. She could have snapped, or had a moment of madness, or done something she couldn't take back.

And she was absolutely ignoring how she'd probably gotten into that bed in the first place.

Sure you are. You're doing a fabulous job. Not thinking about him at all.

"I'm not a child!" Nyri called from the other room.

Lunara rolled her eyes. Of course, kicking her out had been relative. Nyri's meddling damned king had ordered her to stay here, so banishing her to the other room was the best Lunara could do. It at least gave her a chance to escape if it all went sideways.

Again.

"Wait."

Lunara eyed Hedda's hand, now clenching her own above Fern's breastbone. "Why?"

"Have you thought this through? Like, *really* thought about what happened the last couple times and aren't just jumping in to do the same dangerous thing?"

"Before the rest of you idiotic arseholes interrupted me, I was most of the way through pushing whatever it is out of her!"

She'd been literally blind with agony, so completely wrecked that her mind had detached itself from her body and she hadn't even known her own name, but still. Even though she really had no idea what it was or what she'd been doing, it had been working.

Mostly.

Sort of.

"*Whatever it is* was violent. Your magic protected Brand, and Araxis shielded the rest of us, but it was still awful. Are you sure we should loose it?"

"There is no *we,* Hedda. And it's that or leave it inside her, which I won't do."

Lunara ignored the flicker of hurt on Hedda's face. Or, at least, she tried to.

Dammit, you're supposed to be getting out of here as quickly as possible, not solidifying friendships! If that's even what it is.

Right. Be cold. Leave it all behind. No problem.

It's fine. You're fine.

She wasn't, but it didn't matter.

The only thing keeping her here was the almost inherent compulsion in all Nachthellians to see their deals through, and she needed her payment. Lunara could never go back to her cottage. Not when Araxis knew what she was and could use Cordelia to find her.

Hopefully, she wouldn't turn into a bloodthirsty, murderous abomination and kill all of her friends before she could finish and get the fuck away.

"Lunara, please. I'm scared for you."

Stars and arses, Hedda was going to make it as difficult as possible.

"I already lost one person to this kind of thing," Lunara admitted. "I'm not losing another."

It wasn't quite the same as the chasm's darkness, and not exactly what had been happening within Meliora, but it was close enough. Personal enough.

Hedda *did* have a point though.

You know… If you had Illamiata…

No. No, no, no. Not even fucking going there.

"If you're willing, we might try something."

It was hard to even consider, knowing the idea came from time spent with *him*.

Hedda's hand tightened on her own. "Of course. What did you have in mind?"

Her swift acquiescence almost brought Lunara to tears.

Ignore, ignore, ignore.

"The other times, I've jumped in and had to be rescued after I was already locked in with the darkness, which hurts you. If I had a tether though, someone to sort of hold on to *before* I went into Fern's mind, it might work to keep things under control."

She'd done something of the sort with Brand when she'd healed Fern's physical wounds, not that he'd known it. Shite, she'd hardly realized it until after the fact. When they'd… they'd…

Weeping moons, she *was* going to cry.

Get yourself together. You'll have the rest of your lonely life for crying, eejit.

Right. Sure. Easy.

Fuck.

"What do I need to do?"

"Nothing in particular," Lunara answered, swallowing. "Just stay close and keep a hand on me. I'm going to tie a thread of my power to you, and pray to the Sisters it doesn't backfire. If it does, just get yourself and Nyri out of here, okay?"

"I'm not going anywhere, and you can't make me."

Lunara's head snapped up, Nyri on the other side of Fern's slab.

"Nyri, no! Shoo!"

"Why does *she* get to be the tether?" Nyri grumbled. "I'd make an excellent tether. You'd hardly even know I was here!"

"Absolutely fucking—"

"What if you used both of us?"

"—not." She spun on Hedda. "Are you actually out of your stars-damned mind? Did it get scrambled the last time you had to wrench me away from Fern? Or was it the first time?" She stuck an admonishing finger out at Nyri. "No. Um… no, again. And… Oh, look! Still no!"

"Lunara."

She shuffled back, pressing shaky hands to her clammy cheeks. "Everyone in this whole place has gone mad. I've been worried about myself, when I should've been worried about the rest of *you* all along!"

"We haven't gone mad, Lunara," Nyri said softly. "We trust you. There's a difference."

And *there* were the waterworks she'd been trying to suppress.

"You saved Bal. You saved her." She pointed to Fern. "And Hedda told me what you did in the chasm and after. I know you won't hurt us. You need to start believing it yourself."

Lunara scoffed, angrily swiping her tears away. "Believing it? You know what I am. I—"

Hedda reached out and gripped her upper arms. "We know *who* you are. Everything else is just stations and titles."

"*No*. A title, I could live with. The others… They went *insane*. Had to be *killed*. And I'm one of them. I won't have your blood on my hands. I can't—"

"Oy! How many of the other Keepers were handed Illamiata as children? How many of them were pampered, spoiled Elder Tier Sorcerit without a worry in the world? How many were given free rein because no one cared what they did with it as long as they carried out their sacred duty and delivered power to the Evesong?"

Lunara's spiraling mind screeched to a halt. "How the fuck do you know all of that?"

"It's my job to know things like that. I'm not just a gorgeous Demon with a wicked axe hand, you know." She gave a little squeeze, her voice quieter when she said, "How many, Lunara?"

She'd never thought about it like that. Had never considered that upbringing and mindset could play a part in a Keeper's ultimate outcome.

No, no, no. Don't start getting ideas. No.

"A-all of them," she finally answered, a little dazed.

"Exactly. And you are none of those things. That hurt you carry around—it's as much a tool as it is an injury, Lunara. You can either let yourself bleed out, or you can use it. Let it be your failsafe. Let it bolster you. You won't allow Illamiata to do to you what it did to them, and you won't hurt us. I know it. She knows it." She bent closer, almost nose-to-nose with her. "We all know it, except for you."

"Trust us," Nyri said, rounding the slab and wrapping her arms around Lunara's waist. "Hedda was there when you found her. I've kept watch over her. We care almost as much as you do. Let us help."

Don't fall for their pretty speeches. You don't need them. You don't need help. You're enough on your own.

She wasn't though, was she? If she'd been enough, Fern would have been free of the shadows and flitting around by now.

Lunara could hardly believe it when she said, "I will only do it if someone else—no, two someones—are in here with us. Just in case. *Not Brand.*"

That would be too much for her. Just because she was willing to trust Hedda and Nyri for a time, had begun to love them almost as much as she loved him, didn't mean she wasn't leaving. She didn't need it to be any harder than it already was.

"Are you sure?" Hedda shared a look with Nyri. "He's dying to see you."

It was torture. Absolute, fucking torture.

"I've never been more positive in my life."

Liar.

Nyri sighed, pushing her lips into a pout. "I'll get whoever's in the hall." Her tone was flat, despondent, like she was the one being torn from her mate without a choice.

She returned a moment later with Faldir and Magnus in tow.

Shitting stars. How had she never noticed how starkly the brothers resembled one another before? Magnus was golden, where Brand was fiery, but they looked almost exactly the same, retaining more similarities through their Blessings than they had with their other brothers. Same nose and square, bearded jaw. That same dramatic arch to their brow and matching crinkles around their eyes.

Oh, Sisters, she couldn't do it.

A sob exploded out of her, snatched back with a gasp as quickly as it had left her.

"Ach, witchling. It's alright, lass, come here."

"It isn't safe," she cried. "It isn't—"

His arms were around her before she could get away. Before she could talk herself out of accepting the embrace. It was like they'd coordinated the whole thing to cripple her determination. Planned every word and touch to do the most damage to the walls she'd been fortifying since she walked away from Brand.

"Nothing has changed except the knowledge in your head, Lunara," he murmured. "You know you're the Keeper now. So what? You were the Keeper the day before finding out, too. And the month before that, and the years before that. *Nothing has changed.* You're still you."

That only made her sob harder, soaking the fine linen of his embroidered robe as she pressed her face into it.

It helped that he didn't smell or feel like Brand, didn't hold her with the same possessive intensity. Helped her keep just enough of her composure that she didn't fall to her knees and curl up in a ball on the floorboards.

Even if you wanted to stay, he'd never forgive you. You left him. Rejected him. He probably hates you. Just get over it and go.

That feeling of resentment for her other half multiplied. Even if it was right, she was starting to hate it.

You're only mad because it's the truth and you know it.

"Come now. Nyri says we've got work to do." He produced a kerchief from some hidden pocket, using it to wipe her face down, then pinched it around her nose. "Blow. Go on, I can take it."

A pathetic, half-hearted scoff gurgled out of her, but she couldn't possibly—

"I've wiped worse snot than yours, Lunara. Get on with it."

Are you serious?

She blew her nose as hard as she could, as much out of spite as anything else.

When she was done, he dangled the cloth in front of her face, laughing. "Shite, maybe I haven't wiped worse snot than yours. Look at that mess!"

Sisters save her, but his teasing brought a fresh round of tears. She blinked furiously, refusing them freedom. He was right. They had work to do.

"Thank you, Magnus," she rasped. "It changes nothing, but thank you."

"You're right. I believe I *just* said that." He chucked her under the chin. "Glad you finally agree."

"Wait, that's not what I meant."

He ignored her completely, clapping his hands and rubbing them together. "Right. Let's heal the lass, aye?"

She forced her consciousness through the dark spaces of Fern's mind, the feel of Hedda and Nyri's hands on either shoulder comforting her through the near-instantaneous onslaught of pain.

Her connection to them—the sound of their beating hearts, the grounding contact of their touch—kept her from diving too deep. From losing herself entirely.

Following the threads of her power, she trudged through the bogging gloom until she hit the iron wall at its center.

Hammering blows started up in the deepest parts of her skull when she reached out to touch it, as if a blacksmith had taken to forging her brain for fun. She gritted her teeth, swallowing back a rush of nauseating saliva, and pushed.

It devoured the light of her power as she thrust it out, as much as she could manage without collapsing. The barrier swelled, fighting back, lashing out with invisible claws and teeth.

When a contralto shout she couldn't decipher accompanied sharp nails digging into her skin, she pulled back.

Right. She was meant to be going slow this time.

Another push—this one gentler—and the wall bulged again, almost smug.

Like she was feeding it. Satisfying it.

Shite, she hadn't noticed that before.

Except, she had the same impression upon first seeing the chasm. Of the gloom consuming Solyrian's light. Erasing it. She'd only been trying to commit the color to memory. Describe the indescribable.

What if it was literal?

If that was the case, this inky evil had already defeated her. All she had was light.

Unless...

She sucked back every ounce of her power, plunging herself into utter darkness. Feeling her way, she laid mental hands on it again and dug her clawed fingers into its unforgiving surface.

She *felt* more than heard herself screaming.

The others were there, still safe. Only the slightest uptick in the pace of their heartbeats. Worry for her, more than distress for themselves.

Good. She could take any amount of agony, so long as it was her own.

With all the strength she possessed, she wrenched outwards, tearing through the insidious blockade piece by piece. It was like digging through the great hall's marble floor with nothing but her bloodied fingertips, only chips and granules coming away.

It was possible she was doing more damage to herself than anything, but progress—however seemingly insignificant—was progress.

LUNARA AWOKE WEDGED BETWEEN HEDDA AND NYRI, BOTH OF THEM SLACK-jawed and snoring.

Solyrian's rays peeked around the closed curtains, casting her chamber in diffuse morning light. It allowed her to see the purple smudges adorning the flesh beneath their closed eyes, their olive skin unusually pale.

A pang of guilt twisted in her chest. They'd stayed beside her for hours on end, never faltering, and then catching her limp, ravaged body before it could hit the ground at the end. Even Magnus and Faldir had been wrung out, their horror evident.

Their respect, too, which had been hard to swallow.

And when they hadn't known how to handle her—when they'd tried to lift her and the only sound she'd been able to make was incoherent whimpering and pleas for them to stop—they'd called in Brand.

Fighting it had been impossible. *Desperate* didn't even begin to do justice to how she'd felt.

Lunara hadn't been able to look at him as he'd suffused her with his calm compassion through the bond, though. Hadn't opened her eyes when he'd pried her mouth open with such heartbreaking tenderness that she'd choked on it, or when he'd set his flesh to her fangs.

No. With lids plastered shut, she'd fed on his perfect gift and silently wept, tears streaming when he'd lifted her and offered soft murmurings, a kiss to her brow.

Lunara hoped he thought it was the pain from healing, and not because she was so torn apart that she was positive the jagged damage was irreparable.

Extracting herself in slow increments, she crawled from the bed. Someone had turned the chaos of her things into organized piles. Everything had been sorted, like with like, crates and cases lining the perimeter instead of being tossed every which way.

Lunara picked up one of her woven blankets from the top of one such pile, intending to wrap it around her shoulders, and nearly doubled over. The smell of salt and pine resin, of Solyrian's warmth, lingered in the moonlight fibers, and she knew.

Her neat, orderly mate had been the one to do it. To lovingly fold her linens and stack her books. To straighten parchments and untangle the mess of random trinkets being in the same box as her frying pans.

Shite. It *hurt.*

Worse than healing. Worse than the loneliness. Worse than any moment in her life, even the death of her parents. The old wound was exactly that—old and scarred over, the damage healed enough to leave her functional, even if it did twinge from time to time.

Weeping moons, this wound was so new. So raw. A fatal, hemorrhaging gash across her heart and soul.

A tray had been left on the low table, stunted flames left in the enchanted fireplace, and she crossed the room. Her stomach rumbled, gleeful at the idea of sustenance. Of—

A bowl of cut strawberries.

A crystal goblet of gifted blood.

A single trilliatum in a tiny, porcelain vase.

She leaned in closer, brows dropping together. No. Not a real trilliatum, but a carved one—hewn from a block of glowing, foamy blue and deep viridian wood with her magic all over it.

And it hit her.

Woodcarving, he'd told her. When it was all too much, he turned to woodcarving.

Lunara did double over, then. Just folded herself in two, palms landing on the wooden tabletop on either side of the offering, and sank to her knees in front of it.

Nyri had never left her side. Not after the healing. Not after climbing into bed beside her. Nyri hadn't done this.

Maybe it made her crazy after all, but she pressed her nose to the sculpted flower and… there he was.

Brand. *Brand* had been making the trays all along.

Every morning during her training, they'd been there—the only thing keeping her going. She'd just assumed. Hadn't made the connection.

She didn't need to do the deed herself. Leaving him was going to kill her more surely than anything else ever could.

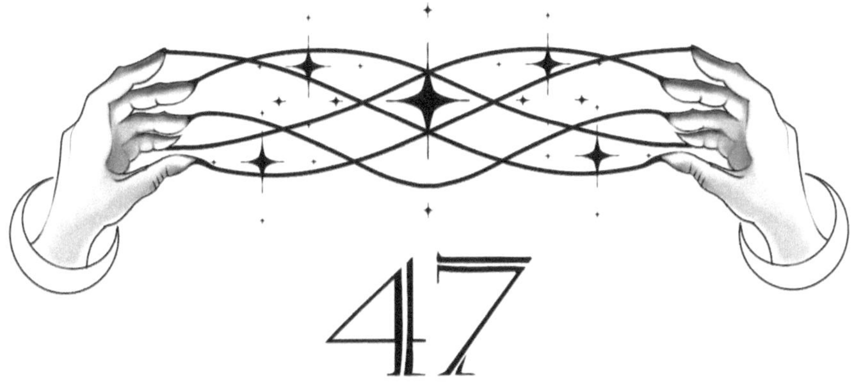

47

HACKING. TEARING. GOUGING.

That's how she spent almost every waking moment. Lost in the dark, shored up by Hedda and Nyri, some combination of Magnus, Thaddeus, Faldir, Baldrir, or Vann hovering nearby. Only her conditioning and training with Hedda—which the Demon Commander insisted upon each day before starting, and was conducted right in the middle of her chamber—was free of pain or thought.

Weeping. Grieving. Breaking.

That's how she spent every other moment.

Brand never said a word to her. Never pried. Never demanded they talk or begged for answers. Just tended to her fragmented body, fed her, and put her to bed.

Last night, there'd been no such thing as resisting anymore. She hadn't *seen* him since Argoph, and feeling him hadn't been enough anymore. Cracking open one eye as he'd walked away, taking him in…

She'd nearly given up right then and been the one begging.

He'd looked worn and ragged, his face drawn. Worse than when they'd thought Faldir dead. Worse than when he'd held Hedda afterwards and they'd trudged across Thodelebor with the terrible knowledge.

Lunara had a feeling that she didn't look much better. The only benefit was that she'd ignored the other part of herself so thoroughly that it had gone quiet the last few days, too tired and too fed up to bother with it.

Once more, she climbed from the bed without disturbing Hedda and Nyri, going directly for the tray she knew would be waiting. Her one connection to him. Where she could just *be* for a moment, and pretend he was right there with her.

By now, she knew that there were at least two others in Fern's side of their joined chambers, and that she had to be quiet if she wanted to keep her peace. That first morning, Magnus had heard her sobbing and come over to investigate. Thad, the next. She'd learned her lesson where Wolflord hearing was concerned. It was silent tears or nothing from there on out.

Tiptoeing, she rounded the settee and—

Next to the tray was a long, beribboned box made of stiffened parchment.

Her eyes darted between it and the tray, and her curiosity won out. Slipping the silk bow free, Lunara lifted the lid and gasped.

She didn't know fabric could look as if someone had harnessed the night sky and then dipped it into the sea, just to leave the stars there. When she picked up a corner, the color shifted, glittering from azure to evergreen.

It was a wonder she had any more tears to shed.

With trembling hands, she lifted the dress and hugged it to herself, almost missing the small bundle of papers that fluttered to the ground.

Separate little notes, individually folded. Collecting each one, she laid them out on the table, terrified of what she would find and unable to decide how to open them.

Eventually, Lunara closed her eyes and pointed, picking that one up first. She barely choked back the laugh that threatened to burst free when she saw the contents.

Brand's handwriting was terrible.

She could hardly make out what he'd written, only deciphering the message after a comical amount of squinting and head tilting.

That the summer sky and the evening forest
could meet beneath eyes of the sea.
Turns out, little moon, that you are my favorite color.
—B

"Oh, Brand," she whispered, sending the note to the ether where it would always be safe.

The reminder of their sunset on the mountaintop, the first real time she'd spent with him, threatened to topple some of her rigid resolve.

The next was on strange parchment, and not from Brand. The words were sharp and tidy, in a hand she didn't recognize, and the unsigned note stilled the blood in her veins.

The world went dark and swam beneath you, but you forgot to remember.

Ringing started in her ears, her breaths shallow. She tossed it away as if it had burned her. The Voice's words, rephrased and written out before her. At the very least, it was an odd sort of relief. If someone else knew what it had said, then the Voice was real and not a figment of her addled mind.

But *how* the mysterious sender knew… What they were implying… It was too much to try and figure out. Too much to try and decipher. She still didn't understand the warning, and she was exhausted in ways she hadn't known were possible.

Ignoring it was easy. Sort of.

The remaining note almost made her want to go back to the one before.

I know you are hurting, because I am in agony. I know you think your only choice is to disappear. I have realized, over and over, that I am unable to deny you anything. I can't control you. I can't hold tight when you beg me to let go. And I especially can't withhold your freedom.

Even if it destroys us both.

Just know this:

There has been no greater honor in my life than loving you, Lunara. You will be the last I kiss. You will be the last I hold—one way or another. If both of those moments have already come to pass, I will still count myself the most blessed creature alive.

And when I exhale for that final, endless time…

No matter how far away from me you are…

Know the last breath I shared was yours as well, and that I rejoiced in the privilege.

I hope you will reconsider. I hope, with every fiber of my being, that I will come down from the mountaintop as Solyrian blesses the land and you will be there wrapped in a sea of stars. That I will once again know the simple bliss of your hand in mine.

Willingly. Happily.

Irrevocably.

The rest, we can figure out together.

And I hope you know, even if you don't, that I will never stop loving you anyway.

—B

Lunara stared into the middle space, the parchment clutched in her trembling hand. Shoddy calligraphy or no, Brand's way with words wrecked her every time. Spoke to a broken piece of her with perfect eloquence, adding a stitch to mend the damage with every earnest syllable.

The Sisters had made him for her, knowing what she was. Could she really throw their gift away? Was she really so arrogant that she would insist on knowing better than them?

"What will you do?"

She jolted, and found Magnus perched on a chair arm, staring at the letter in her hand.

"I don't know," she answered honestly. "I just… don't know."

"Well, not to put any added pressure on you, but the Occurrence is tomorrow." He scrubbed both hands down his tired face, folding them in front of his mouth as he sighed. "My brother is more broken than I've ever seen him, which is saying something. He hasn't been able to leave the rage since Argoph. And you..." He huffed, one corner of his mouth quirking upwards. "Shite, I think you might be doing worse. Do you even realize the only food you've eaten in about five days is the berries he leaves for you?"

Her eyes went to the bowl beside her, waiting patiently for her to fall upon it as if starving.

She was, too. Starving. But not for food.

"I thought I was made of sturdier stuff than this." She picked up a strawberry, turning it in the low light. "Fifty-two years on my own, and I can't make it a week without him? Even for his own good?"

"Mates aren't supposed to go without one another at all, Lunara. And it *isn't* good for him. You think you're rescuing him, but it won't be Brand you leave behind. Not my Brand. Not yours. You'll be leaving a husk. A walking corpse. I don't say that to lay on a heap of guilt, but because it's the Sisters' honest truth. It is what it is." He slipped from the chair arm and down to the floor, wrapping an arm around her. "It won't be *you* walking away, either, and for what?"

"Because no matter what I do, I will destroy him in the end. I'm the Keeper of Illamiata. A monster. Kill him now, or kill him later. It's all the same, except one gives him a chance."

"Ach, I love a bit of drama, but that's too much even for me." He gave her a playful shake. "I'm sorry, but I don't see a stone 'round your bonny wee neck, witchling. You're not the Keeper of anything at the moment. Tell me, what's the shortest a Sorcerit has ever held Illamiata?"

Confused, Lunara looked back, surprised at the answer. "I… I think it was Malachyr." It didn't hurt to say his name because nothing could make her feel worse than she already did. "He wasn't much older than me. He had it maybe thirty years, or so? Why?"

"Sounds to me like, even should the very worst happen, you'd still have more of a life with your true mate than most ever get."

Sisters, it was so tempting. She hadn't thought of it like that. Hadn't considered the possibility of riding it out. Malachyr had been wonderful until he wasn't. Enough years had passed that she could look back and admit it now.

And maybe… maybe she didn't have to rely only on herself to be safe.

"Magnus?"

"Aye?"

Excitement bubbled up. "What about a binding oath? I've read about them before. The strongest among the Wolflords are able to compel others. You could lock me in a binding oath. Make it so I was unable to hurt anyone."

He tilted her chin up. "Ah, lass... not for all the riches in the world."

"But—"

"No. And I'll show you why. If I may?"

When she nodded, he took her arm and brought it to his mouth as he partially shifted, his teeth turning to fangs. Venom of some sort dripped from their lengths in shimmering green. Without warning, he struck, biting down on her flesh.

The pain was almost immediately replaced by paralysis.

She sat there, trying to breathe as his voice exploded in her mind, mixed with the earthy growl of another entity.

—No harm may come to any other by your hand or power, Lunara the Moonweaver, 'til the last of your days. By the Sisters, I so bind you—

He released her as the last word echoed, a hazy lock settling in around her. She felt it, sinking deeper and deeper until it melted in, just another part of her very being. The marks he'd left behind healed before her eyes, as if to seal the magic in.

The relief was overwhelming. "Thank you. Thank you," she repeated, slumping with a sigh.

"Don't thank me yet." His grip tightened around her wrist, digging in to the tendons and bones, even as the rest of him completely relaxed. "Remove my hand, however you need to. I won't let go, so you'll have to do it yourself."

Brow furrowed, she tried to pull away, but his hold was an iron manacle. Reaching over, she tried to wedge her fingers beneath his—

Weakness suffused her until she let go. The same again when she tried to use her nails to claw at him. Every attempt, she went limp as a babe. She didn't bother trying her magic because she knew what would happen.

She was helpless.

"Do you see now? I mean you absolutely no harm. I'm barely using a fraction of my true strength. And yet..."

"I can do nothing about it."

He nodded. "What if you needed to fight, for good reason? I would never leave you in such a state." He leaned forward and pressed his forehead to hers. "I release you of your oath."

Instantly, a weight she hadn't perceived was lifted.

"Go ahead."

This time—though still ineffectual because he was a bleeding strong brute—she at least had the illusion of a chance when she was able to scratch the top of his hand, punch his knuckles.

Magnus let go as he laughed and held her hand, patting the back of it. "I swear to never do that again. It's more of a ceremonial thing in the Westrealm, anyway. We say the words to mark our commitment or the gravity of a situation, but we don't actually *do* it. I've literally never held anyone to a legitimately binding oath, and I can count on one hand the times I know it's been done by all the others capable of it, combined. The language has to be so precise, so tailored to the individual. Knowing me, I'd probably still fuck it up somehow. Only under the direst circumstances would I ever even consider it."

"This feels like the direst circumstances to me."

"I know, Lunara, but it isn't. You can't see the forest for the trees right now, and that's alright. That's what friends and good family are for. They can be your eyes when you're rendered blind."

"Am I, though? The things I've seen. The things I *know*."

"Are devastating, aye." He tilted his head, looking her in the eye. "But you are your own person. You get to decide who you are and who you want to be."

"The Elder Council will make me accept Illamiata. They won't let me have a choice."

"You're ours now." Magnus lifted her hand and kissed the back of it, squeezing. "As Imperial as the rest of us. It comes with quite a few advantages, aye? Not the least of them being that we look out for our own. We'll not be letting anything happen to you that you don't want for yourself, I can promise you that."

Hope was so, so dangerous. "Can you?"

"Ach, aye. I really can. I may be little more than a bloated figurehead at the moment, but I know what I stand for. Force, of any kind, isn't it. I know my parents will agree, and Brand would probably bring Starkeep to the ground by himself if you asked it of him. Have a wee bit of faith, witchling. You're not alone anymore, so stop acting like it."

His gentle admonishment hit Lunara right in the heart.

"Put on the dress tomorrow morning. Come down to the city and be with us. With Brand. Eat and laugh and dance under the night sky. *Live.*"

"He's right." Hedda padded silently across the rest of the distance, settling in on Lunara's other side and raising a sardonic brow. "And trust me, I don't say that lightly."

Magnus grinned. "She really means that. Might be the first time it's ever happened."

"Probably. It was horrible." Hedda smacked her hands down on her knees with a forceful breath. "Which brings me to the next thing. We can't do any healing today. I have duties to see to for the Occurrence."

Some of Lunara's earlier excitement returned, a little spark of optimism she hadn't felt flaring in a long while. "Not to worry. I wasn't going to be healing her today anyway."

"What? Why?"

"Because we need to let her meet us halfway."

"What are you getting at, witchling?"

They deserved to know. To share in the thrill of success.

"I didn't mention it last night, for obvious reasons. And it isn't done, not fully, but…" She chewed the inside of her cheek, heart pounding. "I did it."

Just a little. Just enough to see a pinprick of light in Fern's mind. To feel the absolute *force* of her on the other side, chomping to be freed.

"I broke through."

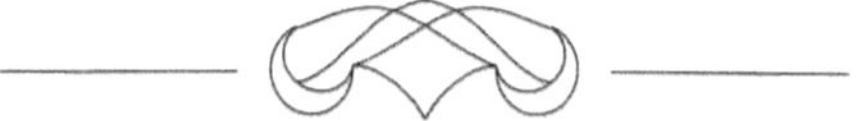

"I CAN'T. WHAT IF THIS IS A MISTAKE? WHAT… WHAT IF…"

Lunara backed away from the gown being presented to her, wrapped in nothing but a blanket.

Nyri groaned to the rafters for the tenth time. "You can, and you will." Her face twisted, a mix of boredom and annoyance. "You're going. It's what you really want. You love him. He loves you. Everything else is details. You're not a monster. You're not a chaotic evil. You wouldn't even kill that weird bug in the window earlier!"

"It was a *moth*, and it was beautiful. Why would I kill it?"

"Do you even hear yourself? Burning Solyrian, when did you get so dense!" Nyri's mouth turned down, voice going lower as she tried—and failed—to mimic Lunara's lilting accent. *"Meh, look at me, I'm Lunara the Terrible—the foulest beast who ever lived. No! Don't touch me, I'll probably murder you! Oh, look! An ugly butterfly! I think I'll name it and feed it and keep it forever as my precious little pet. Is Twila not the most stunning thing you've ever seen?!"*

"I thought Twila was a good name for a moth." Lunara crossed her arms, glancing away. "And I opened the window to set her free."

It wasn't at all symbolic.

She could practically feel her inner self rolling her eyes.

Nyri gaped, a disbelieving smile quirking at her lips. "Are you serious? Sisters save me. You've completely missed the point."

She really hadn't.

"This is the most ridiculous day of my entire life!" Nyri threw one hand up, the gown drooping in her other. "I'm going to say this nice and slow. Creatures… who name *moths…* and *set them free…* are not bloody dangerous! Put on the damned dress, Lunara! Put Brand out of his misery! Put your own ruddy self out of your misery! *All of us.* Put all of us out of this misery!"

Ironically, Nyri was missing the point. "Are you done?"

"Not by a mile!" She began pacing, gesticulating wildly, and Lunara had to stifle a wince as the gown dragged along the floor. "I've dreamt every day about my mate…"

Sisters help her, but Lunara wasn't listening anymore. She'd spent the day before and most of the night rolling it over and over in her mind. And when Nyri had bounded out of the bed in the wee hours, excited as anything, Lunara had been confident in her decision.

Refuse Illamiata. Go back to limiting her blood gifts and not filling the well. Run as fast as she could—*towards* her mate.

For some stars-damned reason, seeing the dress was making her panic over an entirely new set of fears.

What if Brand resents you? What if this is too little, too late? What if—

A knock sounded, and Nyri huffed her way over to the door, throwing it open. Lunara loosed a squeak when Magnus strolled in like he owned the place, wearing the most ostentatious robe she'd seen on him to date.

"Weeping arseholes, witchling. You're meant to be ready!"

She ducked behind the wall dividing her and Fern's rooms, peeking her head around the jamb. "I still need to get dressed."

And do her hair. And dig around her things to find a cream or a pot of something that might make her look less like she hadn't slept in a week.

And maybe puke.

Magnus plucked the gown from Nyri's hold. "I know you want to go because you told me when I brought your supper last night. So, when I say you have to the count of three before I come over there and wrestle you into this confounded thing, consider yourself warned. One…"

"This is completely unnecessary."

"Two…"

Lunara was leaning forward, her body trying to pull itself towards the gown and all it represented.

But what if he changed his mind? What if he never sees you quite the same way?

What if, what if, what if.

"Two and a bleeding half…" Magnus loosed a long-suffering sigh and started forward. "You asked for it."

"Wait." Without giving it another thought, Lunara called the particles of the dress to herself, wrapping them around her body in less time than it took to blink.

"Thank fuck for that. Let's go."

"Please, a few more minutes."

Lunara scurried over to the crates, digging around. It was unlikely she had anything, but it was worth—

Nyri grabbed her shoulder. "Deep breaths." She pulled Lunara to a chair, a vase of trilliatum on the table beside it. "Sit." One by one, the blooms in the vase disappeared as Nyri ran deft fingers through Lunara's curls, working her own sort of magic before presenting a small vial. "Drink this."

Lunara didn't question the pink, swirling liquid as she tipped it back. The rosy tonic fizzed its way down, burrowing in and suffusing her cheeks with warm tingles.

"Much better." Nyri winked. "You look like yourself again."

"Aye."

"I'm terrified," she whispered.

"Then you're definitely yourself again," Magnus quipped. "Come on."

"Wait!" Nyri shrieked. "She has to see herself!"

She shoved Lunara into the washroom, in front of the full length mirror gracing one wall, and—

Shitting stars. Lunara hardly recognized herself.

Brand must've described her preferred shape of gown right down to the stitches—a neckline that barely clung to her shoulders. Long, billowing sleeves gathered at the wrists. Skirts to the ground.

And yet, he'd taken liberties.

There was a slit in one side that went all the way up a thigh *and* hip, and the bust of it left absolutely nothing to the imagination. It was almost carnal, the way the fabric flowed over her like water, even as it stayed perfectly in place, clinging to her skin and hugging her curves.

The flowers Nyri had woven into her hair looked like they'd sprouted from inside her. Like her curls had been made to hold them. It was still wild and rebellious, but that only complimented the garment.

Lunara felt *beautiful,* in a way she maybe never had before, but still. "What if it's not enough?"

What if she'd let him down so spectacularly by running away that *she* just… wasn't enough anymore?

Magnus barked out a laugh. "Brand's head is going to melt right out of his arse when he sees you."

"I know the feeling," she whispered, knowing they weren't at all talking about the same thing.

What if, what if, what if…

"The sunstar won't wait for the likes of us, witchling. Trust me, you won't want to miss this." He jutted out an elbow, brows expectant. "Shall we?"

What if…

She'd never know if she didn't try.

With a deep breath, knees shaking, Lunara took his arm.

48

LUNARA HAD NEVER WITNESSED AN OCCURRENCE BEFORE. THE LAST TIME they'd happened, it had only been two years after her parents' death, and she'd been in no place for celebrating anything.

Besides, without Malachyr, Nachthelliae hadn't been able to have one at all.

The Evesong needed its Keeper to act as a conduit, taking all the raw power from the twin moons and funneling it down into the land and creatures. She knew it required a blood gift, an offering of sorts, but that was as far as her knowledge of the particulars went.

Doesn't matter, because you won't be doing it.

Right.

Straelani of every age surged around Lunara, their raucous merriment so full of joy that it was almost impossible to dwell on her own shite.

She clung to Magnus as they wound their way through the throng of Demons, the aroma of rich perfumes and countless foods bombarding her as they dodged feet and elbows, trying not to be trampled.

Because every last one had undergone their change.

Males and females alike had forgone most of their clothing, their Sienna skin glowing under the hazy lamplights, horns and fangs glistening. So many whorls and patterns in their individual markings, all of them incredible.

The first topless female had been something of a shock—mainly because it had been Nyri, and Lunara hadn't ever thought to see that much of her young friend. Now, all she saw was their absolute freedom.

And *she* was probably overdressed, despite nearly every part of her threatening to spill out.

Nyri crowed in front of her, bouncing on the balls of her feet. "Look at it!"

She ran off, her absence revealing a magnificent wooden dais—and a stone obelisk jutting up from its center, so fucking huge it may as well have been a monument to how bleeding distracted Lunara was.

The pillar shot into the sky, as tall as any of the surrounding trees and so black it put the chasm's shadows to shame. She probably could've lived inside of it, it was *that* wide.

But when Magnus led her up the steps, every other thought fell away because she was finally high enough to *see*.

So much color. Flowers strewn and strung everywhere amidst boughs of evergreen and silk garlands, tiny twinkling lights among them. Canopies and booths dotted the square, brightly still in the chaos.

The crowd was a living thing, writhing and churning before her, the sea a glittering backdrop behind them. Most were Demons, but creatures from other realms had come to bear witness as well. Children clung to their parents, perched on shoulders and grasping horns of every shade in their little hands. Families and friends mingled, heads tipped back in laughter or bent towards lovers.

Her heart squeezed as she watched one couple, tangled together for all to see. It was like a sickness how starkly she missed her own Demon. How desperately she wanted to touch him.

Magnus bumped his shoulder against hers and pointed, and she followed the gesture to the other side of the platform. There, perched on the corner in an elaborate stand, was a golden spyglass.

"Ever hopeful, my brother. He had it placed there just in case, so you could see him."

"I need a spyglass to see him?" she asked, as confused as she was relieved for the moment.

She wasn't ready. He'd asked her to come, had practically begged but still.

What if…

Magnus chuckled. "Aye, he's up on the mountaintop for now." He pointed up beyond the city and castle, and Lunara gasped.

The Sacred Sisters.

Beholding the two jagged peaks from the ground like this—jutting into the sky and making the rest look like hills in comparison—stole her breath. The only thing more incredible was that she'd actually stood upon their majestic heights, watching a sunset with Brand as their souls had taken the first shy steps towards melding together.

"What is he doing up there?" she whispered, almost to herself.

"He's to announce Solyrian's rising. Lyriat will answer him, and Brand will join us quickly after. Then, the Occurrence."

"What do you mean Lyriat will answer him?"

Mischief glittered in his eyes. "Ach, witchling—let an old wolf keep some of his secrets, aye? The surprise is half the fun."

Something in his tone sent warning bells pealing through her mind, but the dais rattled and Lunara had to grab him to keep her balance.

She saw his horns first as they cleared the top step. Gold and ivory twisted and knotted themselves together into a crown befitting the highest royalty. How appropriate it was, then, that a king's visage followed after them.

If Brand was impressive in his *'greater'* form, then Lyriat was something else entirely. She hadn't known it was possible for him to become even more magnetic, commanding awe as he cleared the steps and headed straight towards them.

He absolutely towered over her and Magnus, easily larger than Brand by several feet when he was raging. The telltale markings of his change had manifested in thick bands of pulsing light around his calves, forearms, and neck—the perfect match to the pearly stone circlets at his biceps.

All of his other markings, the ones she would've expected to grace his olive skin, had been reserved for the massive set of membranous wings hanging from his muscled back.

They were so covered in the glowing whorls, they looked to be made of pure sunlight, rather than the fathomless pitch beneath the markings. Wicked, bony talons tipped the peaks and ends, dragging across the wooden planks in jarring opposition to the silent, graceful steps of his feet.

As she stared, transfixed by their king, a reverent hush fell over the entirety of the crowd below, their faces turned to the Sacred Sisters above.

Lyriat passed by her with a wink and moved to the back of the platform as Magnus whispered in her ear, "Now might be the time you'd want to use that spyglass, witchling."

Heart pounding in her throat when she finally reached it, she had to blink a few times for her eyes to focus—that same heart stopping when they finally did.

Brand was there at the other end, power in every solid inch of him. Hedda and Faldir flanked him on either side, matching dual-bladed battle axes planted in the ground, their hands folded and resting on the pommels

A gargantuan horn curved from Brand's mouth to rest on the hard earth at his feet where he stood in front of the Solyr Prism. Sunlight and shadows moved around him, pouring over his body as he pressed his lips to the mouthpiece.

Velvety and rumbling, a low note tumbled down through the morning air, as if to say *The sunstar comes*—no less quiet for the distance.

The crowd gently surged as their feet began to pound rhythmically into the ground, their bodies swaying with the movement.

Then came their chanting voices.

"Hoo, hoo, hoo..." they intoned together. Over and over, the deep sound like the beating of a heart, each inward breath between like blood rushing.

Nothing could have prepared her for Lyriat's answering call.

The same note Brand had played pummeled directly behind her, the king's horn flaring in reply. How she'd missed it there was beyond her. The boards of the dais actually rattled beneath her feet, beneath the overwhelming force of its colossal sound. *We are ready,* it bellowed to the sky.

She could only perceive with her watering eyes that Magnus was cackling as it whipped her hair and dress forward—there was no hope of her hearing him.

Stars and arses, she might never hear anything else again.

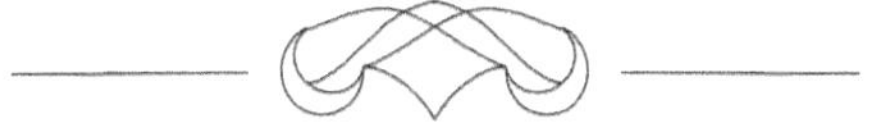

He was here. Sisters above, he was right in front of her.

"Tell me you're real," Brand rasped. "That I've not lost my mind and imagined you."

Fear, sharp and gnawing, hit her. *His*, through the bond.

"I'm here," she croaked, the lump in her throat aching.

Fear was replaced with a spark of wary hope.

She nodded when he knelt and sent her a questioning look, his arms wrapping around and lifting her from the platform just when the first rays of Solyrian started spilling over the mountains and making their way to the Solyr Stone. The chanted chorus reached staggering heights as she was finally pressed into the chest that was possibly her favorite place to be.

He nuzzled his face into the side of her head. "Tell me you're staying. That you're mine. I can't... I don't think I could take it if you left again after this."

"I'm staying. I'm yours. I'm sorry."

Joy. Unbridled, effervescent joy.

"Shhh." His shaky sigh matched her own. "Say the prayers with me. Blessed Solyrian," Brand breathed into her ear, the light growing and growing as she repeated him, "mark my mate especially. I am theirs as I am yours. Shine on us both, and grant us your power and protection." He turned her fully and pressed his forehead to hers. "Brace yourself, little moon."

She didn't have to be told twice, not after that second horn blast. Not when she wanted to hold him so much that it hurt. Her teary eyes locked with his, the hazel depths of them glittering back as she latched onto one set of his curling horns and pulled herself tighter against him.

No sooner had she done it than the sunlight reached the top of the Solyr Stone.

The ground shook with a shockwave of power, rippling out from the obelisk and sweeping over them.

Then another.

And another.

The cracking shudders echoed along the mountain peaks. Waves crashed harder against the shore. The land roared with its triumph, with the gift it was being given.

On and on, pressure building, Brand's markings blazing bright each time and spreading in spiderweb veins across his skin. A muscle ticked in his bearded jaw, his teeth clenching against the onslaught even as his eyes changed and began to glow, golden and fiery. A stark hunger filled them as she watched, his chest rumbling against her when he joined the others in their primal song.

Stars, was it *primal.*

It was suddenly so sensual, so erotic—the rhythmic chanting and the heat in his look joining together and pooling within her. Unbidden, her breaths began to match his, her skin buzzing as every nerve ending responded to it. To him.

Only once did his eyes stray from hers—a brief glance down to her lips that made his nostrils flare—before they burned into her once more.

His arms tightened across her back and thighs, his fingers sinking into her, every illicit thought racing across the bond between them to plant itself in the other's mind. Sweet sisters, how she wanted to kiss him, wanted to—

Silence.

Immense, profound silence. So sudden that her ears rang with the eery absence of all those voices, the thundering power of Solyrian meeting the Solyr Stone at its zenith.

For the space of a single breath, it hung over the realm in its own sort of backwards cacophony.

The release of that pressure was a mute explosion of blinding light, and then all of the Horned City erupted.

Shouts and cheers took up the emptiness as they rejoiced, their jubilation so thick that Lunara was sure she could reach out and touch it.

A victorious grin spread across Brand's face and he joined the celebration of his people, laughing as he spun her around. "Irrevocably?" he breathed.

"Irrevocably," she answered.

He stepped right up to the edge of the platform. "Demons of the Montrealm, my brethren!" he shouted, his voice booming over the crowd. "The Sisters have blessed me, your Son! Behold, Lunara the Moonweaver —now marked by Solyrian. Behold, my true mate!"

She hadn't known it was possible to be this happy.

SHE WAS HERE, AND SHE WAS *DEVASTATING*.

Brand couldn't stop staring at Luna, his heart overflowing. Clenching Hedda's arm in a death grip, her teeth were sunk into her lip while she listened to Magnus being ridiculous, amused horror twisting her face and emphasizing a mark she didn't even realize was there—a true blessing he never once thought he'd actually see, though he'd whispered the words that begged for it.

Along with a personal boon, nearly every Demon prayed for their mate as the Occurrence happened, whether they had one or not. There were rumors and legends that the sunstar could mark the both of you—could help you find your mate if you hadn't yet or give you one more thing to be bonded by if you had—but most believed it to be symbolic. He certainly hadn't believed it to be a real possibility, and he'd never known anyone that had actually witnessed it happen.

Until today.

Brand hadn't seen his own yet, but Lyriat's look of abject shock had confirmed its presence.

They'd all long-since reverted back to their lesser selves and donned festive clothing, but their markings remained—this day and night the only time it happened—and so he knew, with absolute certainty, that there was a sienna sunbeam running in a pointed line down the center of his bottom lip and chin that hadn't been there before.

A perfect, mirrored match to hers.

It wouldn't always be visible, but that didn't matter. All of the Horned City had fixed their eyes on Luna and seen it for what it was. And Sisters, how they looked at her now—with all of the awe and reverence she deserved.

She'd healed them. Cared for them. Sparred with them. Now, she would be eternal among them, written in their histories forever. The Nachthellian Sorcerit blessed by the sunstar at their Occurrence.

He couldn't wait to see the look on her face when she beheld it.

Every thrumming inch of his body was intent on reminding him that he hadn't been wrapped in her for a week. That he hadn't tasted her, touched her, adored her. Only made worse by his gift.

Sweet, fucking Solyrian. *That dress.*

After the sunset on the mountain, he'd *known* she would be with him today. Instead of finding his bed that night, he'd scribbled a note and shaken a poor messenger awake, urging him to leave for Kohamaia immediately.

Vann's response to the feverish letter had not disappointed.

Brand only asked him for fabric and, in a fit of madness, had waxed poetic about the Sorcerit he'd just met. About her manner and beauty, the way she'd made him feel. About everything—including her normal garb, apparently.

Vann had drawn his own lines and conclusions, taking it a step further by bringing him a finished gown. It was more than excellent tailoring holding the garment to the perfection of her body, framing her mating marks exactly and fitting her like a second skin—it was magic.

She was temptation incarnate, and he was hanging on by a thread.

Brand didn't care that she'd run because he understood it all too well. He'd do anything for her. That she would return the sentiment, even in her backwards way, meant something to him.

Fuck, it was all he could do not to drag her to some shadowy corner and make love to her right there.

Vann rose and chucked his leftover stump of rolled herbs to the ground, offering Nyri a hand. The girl turned a stunning shade of pink, rebellion sharp in her eyes, but she took it—declaring she would definitely be stepping on his toes on purpose, just to teach him a lesson. The table roared their laughter in response.

This was the time of the feasts and festivals Brand dreaded most. When the meal was winding down, but there were hours yet of celebrations he was required to attend. He'd gotten away with it this year, bound to more serious duties because of all the shite, but he would have no such reprieve tonight.

Children were being gently laid to sleep beside one another in makeshift beds near the bonfires around the perimeter. Musicians were chatting as they took up their instruments, readying to lure the adult revelers with their own kind of magic.

Hedda gripped Faldir's arm and pointed across the way. Brand followed the gesture and found another set of twins on the other side of it

—Fae visitors, by the look of them—and his commanders were scrambling up before he could blink.

Thad's head snapped up to track a Demon strutting by, the warrior's eyes trailing behind him and giving his cousin *the look.*

He already had his legs over the bench, chasing after the male, when Mag called after him, teasing. "A strapping lad tonight, is it?"

Thad turned, walking backwards and grinning. "The night is young, cousin. Who's to say?" he hollered, arms wide as he disappeared into the crowd.

Brand swallowed, trying to accept that this was the start of it. When the night devolved into something more raw. More basic. Something that had ever eluded him.

Because every celebration always ended the same—with music and *dancing.*

It was the embarrassment for him. A sense of feeling slightly off kilter, too stiff to pull it off. He had an image to uphold as their Imperial Son, and sullying it with his inability to make his limbs work in that way was something he absolutely tried to avoid.

Knowing Luna, how well her body moved… He'd be watching his mate with pleasure, letting temptation sink deeper and deeper, fueling him until he snapped and claimed the rest of her evening for himself.

Magnus chuckled and pushed himself up from the table. "I think I saw Amun and Lyriat escaping up the high road a while ago. I might go and see what shite they're getting up to, maybe have a chat with Caius, before I find my own strapping mischief this evening." He lifted his tankard and downed the rest of his ale before slamming it back to the table.

Luna sat forward. "If you're going up to the castle, would you mind checking on Fern?"

"Of course," he answered. "Anything in particular I should look for?"

She shook her head. "I would just feel better knowing someone laid eyes on her again today."

"Your wish is my command, witchling," He sketched an exaggerated bow, flourishing his arms. "Don't do anything I wouldn't do, aye?"

With that and a wink, he left, Luna's shouted thanks following after him.

"Why do I have a feeling there's almost nothing Magnus wouldn't do?"

"Because there isn't," Brand said, laughing.

Luna giggled as she stood and rounded the end of their table, facing out towards the dance floor when she settled in beside him. His hand was instantly drawn to her chin, his thumb brushing the new mark on her lip. Fuck Occurrences and parties. He wanted to get her in front of a mirror, show her before Solyrian rose again tomorrow and erased them for another fifty years.

"Luna—"

"Would you like to dance, Brand?" she breathed at the same time.

The bond pulled tight, wanting and needy.

Brand swallowed. "No," he answered, almost immediately regretting it. "I would bloody fucking love to watch *you* do it, though."

Luna searched his face for a moment and seemed to come to a decision. "I have a secret," she said softly, "but it may be a solution, too."

He studied her profile as she watched the writhing crowd. "Go on."

"Would you dance if no one could see you? If you could look to all the world like you were sitting right here?"

Any other time, any other day, he might have jumped at the chance to move so freely without another thought. But she was stunning and he was hard as a fucking rock. Dizzy with wanting her.

"Explain."

"Do you remember the first supper we took together, after I healed Baldrir?" She was nervous, spinning a curl in her fingers, and his breaths shallowed to match hers. "Well…"

She went on to describe her mastery over a power that would've turned his entire childhood into a fantasy playground. That she could leave an impression of herself and move around freely, unseen.

Burning Solyrian. She was utterly endearing the way she chewed her lip, not quite able to look at him when she was done.

His hand trailed up her bare leg, teasing the inside of her thigh. "You could really leave our images doing anything?"

A shuddering breath left her. "Anything."

"Then I think we can do better than sitting." Drumming music chose that moment to start up, its sultry beat calling to him and fraying his nerves in turns. "No one would know?"

"I swear it."

Heart beating almost painfully, he gripped her nape. "Do it," he rasped, and kissed her.

Power twined around them, swelling, sweeping over him in a gentle wave. Weeping Sisters, it had been too long. Fleeting pecks to her pale brow had hardly satisfied his desire for her. He needed *this*—her tongue and teeth. Her wandering hands.

Tugging on her hair, he broke away to lick a line up her sternum, over the markings she had yet to see. "Fuck, I missed you." He nipped her throat, her ear, drowning in her moans. "Need you."

She spread her thighs, and he delved beneath the highest hem of her dress, dipping in to run his fingers through her dripping arousal as he deepened their kiss.

He groaned when she pulled back slightly, her voice a ragged whisper when she said, "Don't be alarmed." Her head tipped back when he circled her. "It can be strange to view yourself apart from, well, yourself."

Eyes on hers, Brand brought his fingers to his mouth and licked every drop of her away—an excellent distraction for his disoriented mind, which had become convinced that shadowed pieces of his body were being gently stripped away as he moved.

"Shitting stars," she husked, her back arching. "We're supposed to be dancing."

"Get on with it then, little moon, so I can finally take you to bed. Show me this trick of yours."

Though he felt no sensation when he took those first few steps, he still shuddered, not sure if he was ready to see himself *removed* like that. He wanted to please her, though, in any and every way.

"We look perfect."

Brand followed her look and sucked in a breath. Tangled together in the most innocent beginnings of their kiss, their likenesses were bathed in firelight, sighing as tongues darted out to taste and tease, his large frame cradling her.

"Fucking stars, you're beautiful."

"So are you." She tugged on the vee in his tunic. "Now, dance with me."

Every step onto the dance floor chipped away at Brand's arousal, a practice in torture.

His muscles went rigid, breaths catching in his lungs. He soaked up as much of Luna's brimming confidence as he could, but he still felt like an utter fool.

She led him straight into the heart of it, to the one battlefield he had yet to conquer, and all the while he dreaded their rowdy greetings as he moved. For heads to nod and mouths to seek conversation.

No one so much as looked at him.

Luna hadn't exaggerated. The whole of the Horned City was completely unaware of his presence, and a wild sort of liberation barreled into him.

He was invisible.

He was *free*.

She stopped beside Thad where he was dancing between a female Brand vaguely recognized and the male warrior from before, their damp bodies grinding sensuously together.

"Watch this!" Luna shouted over the pounding drums and spun on his cousin, sticking her tongue out with an explosive *blegh!* as her fingers splayed in the air like claws.

Brand threw his head back and laughed. It was like she wasn't even there.

Mischief sparkled in her eyes. "You try it!"

He couldn't possibly resist.

Looking around, he found Vann dodging Nyri's flailing arms. Brand dug deep, finding a part of himself he'd thought long dead, and blew the wettest, longest raspberry he could muster right into his brother's oblivious face.

They disintegrated. Brand could hardly breathe for laughing so hard, and Luna was clutching her stomach, gasping beside him.

It only got better.

Before he knew it, she was pressed against him. Luna dragged her hands up the curving line of her body and through her hair, ruffling the mass and dislodging some of the trilliatum he'd left for her to use, before throwing her arms in the air. She swayed against him, mirth painted across her face as she moved with the steady drumbeat.

Brand let his hands hover over her, trying to find the same rhythm within himself. Tried to harness that untamed, unfettered quality she had. If he could just—

"Like this," she said, raising up on bare toes to murmur in his ear. "Feel the music, feel me through the bond, and follow."

There was no judgement as she placed her hands on his hips, forcing them side to side with the beat. Moving to his shoulders, she coaxed them into harmony with the rest of his limbs. At last, she lifted his arms towards the sky as she'd done, her fingers teasing down their length to rest on his waist.

And he did. He felt it. Felt her feeding it into him from her very self.

Grasping on to the crackling energy between them, Brand let his body *move.*

Hours, they were like that. Hours, locked together in a perfect imitation of what their bodies would be doing later. They teased and touched, letting it be the foreplay it was as the rest of the crowd devolved into its own abandon.

Sweaty and achy, Brand's gaze wandered over Luna's head, trailing over the crowd until it landed on his cousin—watching as Thad's jaw went slack, his partners tangled around him and pressing mouths and fingers against his skin.

Over Faldir wrapped against a Fae's back, his hand disappearing down the front of her skin-tight dress as she reached behind to grasp his horns.

Hedda, with an entire group surrounding her, begging with lips and hands to be one of those she took to bed with her.

More and more couplings plastered themselves together as the night wore on, releasing the last dregs of restraint and letting their bodies go, and Brand knew he couldn't take it another minute. Another *second.*

He bent to Luna's ear, his teeth latching onto the lobe as he dipped both hands down to her hot center. "I think it's time we left."

She stopped moving, except for the heaving rise and fall of her chest, and twisted to peer into his eyes. "I think you're right."

Overcome by something he couldn't name, he softly growled, "Lift the spell, little moon."

Confusion twisted her brow. "You want me to…"

His fangs punched down, his Demon rising to the surface and obliterating any remaining restraint. "Lift the spell. I want all of the Montrealm to see me here, with you." He emphasized his words by grinding against her lush arse. "To fucking watch as we leave and I take you to bed."

She licked her lips, waving her fingers. Those dancing in their immediate vicinity startled, but he ignored them as he swept her off the ground and into his arms.

Brand didn't even register the cheers as they sounded behind him, already well on his way to the portal on the far side of the square.

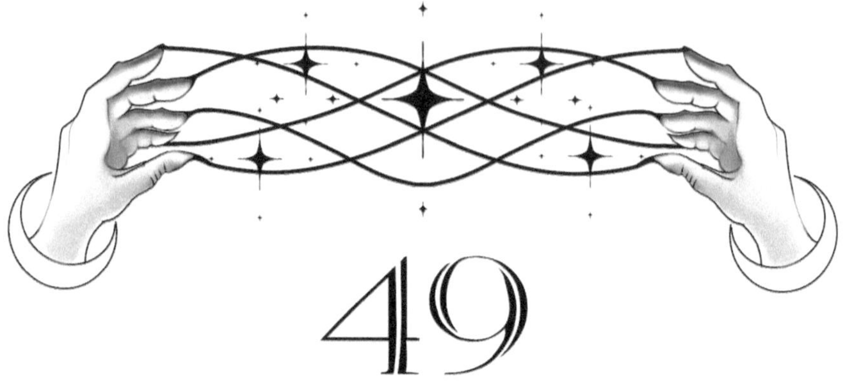

49

LUNARA SHIVERED AS THE FLOOR CHANGED BENEATH HER BARE FEET—FROM smooth, timber floorboards to the cool, stone tiles of the washroom. Anticipation quickened her breath, threatening to force a stifled laugh from her.

When they finally paused, Brand's lips were at her ear. "Ready?"

He'd insisted on the element of surprise. Of bringing her up to his —*their*—chamber for the first time and giving her a full view of her mating marks.

She'd tried to catch glimpses here and there, tucking her chin to see them, but to no avail.

Her cheeks ached from the grin that hadn't left her face in what felt like hours. "*Yes.*"

His hands dropped away—air rushing in to brush her cheeks and eyelids against the warmth he'd left there—but she kept her eyes closed, drawing it out.

"Good idea." He swept her hair aside, tongue landing against her nape, teeth sinking into the spot where neck met shoulder. "You are entirely too clothed."

Calloused fingers trailed along the neckline of her dress, tugging it down. She popped free of the bodice, her nipples hardening in an instant, goosebumps following the trail of fabric as it left her body entirely.

One of his hands retraced the path, so slowly, drawing a line up between her breasts. "*Look* at you," he rasped.

Blinking, she finally beheld herself, awe bolting through her.

An upturned, crescent moon was nestled against her sternum, its bottom curve radiating out and down with sunbeam spikes that just kissed the swell of her cleavage—except for the center point, which dove between them, almost all the way to her navel.

His chest to her back, Brand sank one hand into her hair, his lips devouring hers as he walked them closer to the gilded mirror above the basin. He groaned into her mouth when she reached behind to grasp onto one of his horns, his breaths sawing in and out of him by the time they crashed against the long counter.

He broke away, jaw clenching. "Look," he urged, head tilting towards the mirror as he pinched her chin. "Look at yourself, now marked eternally. Look, and see how Solyrian and the Sisters have blessed us." His thumb caught on her lower lip, digging in.

Another gasp. She hadn't even thought to look at her face.

She pressed shaking fingers to the mark there, the pointed ray a match for the one down her torso. Brand grabbed her other hand and brought it to his own mouth, and her eyes went wide.

No, not a match for her own, but a match for *his.*

"They will sing songs in your name," he whispered, gaze on her stunned reflection. "Ballads, for the little moon bathed in sunlight. Our prayer was answered."

"How? I didn't realize it was literal." Her head shook with disbelief. With wonder.

Brand leaned back only far enough to pull the tunic from his body, the fabric ripping as it caught on his horns. "Nor did I, but you won't hear me utter a single word of complaint." He shucked his dark trousers with a sigh. "Though the color is curious. I think I love it."

Indeed, her markings were not the burnt red of Brand's settled ones as she would have expected, but rather a deep charcoal that simmered with a concentrated version of the iridescence that had ever lain beneath the surface of her skin. Stark against her paleness, they seemed almost alive, glowing faintly along the edges and throbbing as if they had their own pulse.

So different. *Other.*

A tendril of that earlier self-doubt trickled in, the *what ifs* snaking their way around her throat.

Brand stilled, obviously feeling it too. "What is it?"

"Can you really forgive me so easily?" she whispered, needing to hear him say it. "Just like that?"

His eyes locked on hers in the mirror, devotion shining there. "Little moon, nothing has ever been so easy. Now..." He cupped her heavy breasts, plucking at the pebbled peaks. "Have you ever watched *yourself* as someone made love to you?" His voice was like gravel, the sound scraping deliciously over her and pooling low in her belly.

Lunara wanted to weep as her worry melted away. Shitting stars, she'd missed him.

"Does watching our likenesses count?"

Brand bit his lip, pinching that parallel mark between straight teeth. "Not quite."

"Then never," she said.

She couldn't manage any more than that. Not with the way his hands had begun roaming, sinking into her hips for leverage as he ground his hard length against her.

"Nor have I."

He gripped one of her thighs, resting her knee on the countertop. That same hand ghosted up to palm her arse, parting her as he used his other to tease himself through her wet heat. Lunara whimpered, raising her arms to wrap them around his neck when he prodded at her entrance, the motion begging and tempting him all at once.

"Here, with you," he said, "I find myself wishing to know what it's like."

"*Yes.*" She arched her back, offering herself up to him.

"Leave those hands right where they are."

With that, he thrust into her, barking out a wordless shout she felt all the way to her soul—a sound of all-consuming relief that she echoed back to him.

He stretched and filled her so completely. So perfectly. Made just for her.

She'd been a fool to try and deny it. To try and separate something so immaculately rendered.

With one hand splayed across her abdomen, his other snaked around her raised leg to grip her inner thigh, spreading her open further and revealing the sight of his cock gliding in and out of her, glistening with her arousal.

"Fuck, look at us."

He landed a sharp smack to her arse, digging in to the crackling pleasure-pain to massage it away.

"Brand," she cried, breathless as he started to pump his hips faster, harder, her body already beginning to tingle with the first signs of her release.

"Do I forgive you? *Yes.* Wholeheartedly. Easily," he growled. "But don't ever leave me like that again. Don't ever deny us this most precious gift." Another smack, hot and stinging and sublime. "I am yours and you are mine, Lunara."

"Never again." Her voice was little more than a broken croak. "I swear it, never again. I am yours and you are mine."

"Exquisite fucking creature."

Pressure built, her mind and body careening towards that invisible edge. Bowing, tensing, ready to snap so she could tumble over.

The sight of them was something to behold—his skin reddening against the shimmering milkiness of hers, the writhing of their bodies as they reached in tandem for that blessed peak and fall, the ecstasy painting itself across their faces as they came undone together with gazes locked.

She'd never seen herself that way. So wanton and lovely, euphoria radiating out from her with every heaving breath. It would be seared into her mind forever.

"Beautiful," he growled, snatching the word right from her thoughts, even as he began moving again. "We are fucking beautiful together, little moon. We are *nothing* apart."

LUNARA WAS LOST IN BLISS, THE BOND PULSING SO POWERFULLY BETWEEN them that she wasn't sure how she'd ever lived without it. Her body was little more than a puddle, sunk so far into the down of their bed that she was a part of it.

She inhaled deeply, languidly emerging from sleep as salt and pine wound their way around her, Brand's warmth both scent and reality. She burrowed further into his chest, the little golden-red hairs there tickling her cheek.

Home. She was finally home.

There were so many things to disentangle, but they were together. They could do it *together*.

The domed glass above revealed an endless expanse of stars, the twin moons caressing one another in the sky as they drifted lower and readied for Solyrian's rising.

Everything was still, silent, but for the almost imperceptible music of their breathing. A warm, salty breeze fluttered in to brush against the canopy through the open balcony doors. If she focused, Lunara could just make out the soft lapping of the sea as waves broke against the shore. The caw of a single crow. The murmurs of late revelers returning to the castle.

Not silent, then, but perfect.

She darted her tongue out, unable to resist dragging a fang over the permanent scars she'd left on him—her own sort of mating mark.

Brand stretched, his arms tightening around her. One hand drifted down her spine to squeeze her arse, and she loosed a breathy giggle. He was bleeding obsessed with the damned thing.

"I hope you sorted your affairs before the Occurrence, little moon." His voice was sleepy gravel, rumbling beneath her.

"Sorted my affairs…" She scraped her nails over one muscled shoulder, watching the goosebumps that appeared in their wake. "What do you mean?"

"Mmm." He hiked her closer, his steely shaft digging into her hip. "I *mean* we won't be leaving this bed for a month, so you won't be making any meetings or appointments."

She laughed outright. "High-handed, overbearing Demon. I don't have any of those things."

"Excellent." He buried his face in the crook of her shoulder, biting down. "No one will miss us then."

"What about *your* 'meetings and appointments,' mighty Imperial Son?" She dropped her voice to mimic his, snorting.

"I don't know what you're talking about."

"Ah. So someone, somewhere, might miss us. Well you, anyway."

"Luna." He started to pull away but she shoved his head right back to what it was doing.

"I'm not complaining. Meetings are dreadfully boring, and the others are probably sick of me after everything I put them through. I bet they'd be happy to be left alone for a whole month."

He laughed into her hair. "Glad you're starting to see it my way, even if you got there from the wrong direction."

She pinched his ribs and he jerked away, cackling. "Ooh, are you *ticklish*?"

"Absolutely not." He grabbed her wrist, pinning it above her head and bringing them nose-to-nose. "We Demons are far too formidable for such a thing."

Her heart skipped over, a little thrill of nerves. His, in the bond.

"Forgive me if I'm the first to say it, but you should know—you're a terrible liar, Brand."

He swooped down to nip her jaw. "I know. Don't tell anyone."

She knew the grin spreading across her face was wicked. He hadn't realized he'd only pinned one of her hands.

"I'm—"

Her head cracked with searing pressure, a breath hissing in between her clenched teeth as she scrunched her eyes shut.

"Behold the dawn," the Voice said, urgent, its many layers battering through her skull, ***"crowned in rugged black and rusted flames. Do not fear the rising ruin, do not fear the light it brings. Triumph rests there, in the palm of twilight's acceptance. Do not fe—"***

Lunara retched, the emptiness within her instant and sickening. It was like the Voice had been unwillingly ripped from her mind, that unfinished, strangled last word haunting her.

"Luna! Lunara!" Brand's panicked voice broke through, the ringing in her ears subsiding in violent sweeps.

"Behold the dawn…" she whispered.

Lunara opened her eyes, and did.

Brand loomed above her, abject horror twisting his face, and clarity hit like a bolt of lightning. With a cry, she scrambled to her knees and shoved her hands into his hair, raking through it. "Rusted flames…" she muttered. Her fingers danced along his horns. "Rugged black…"

"Luna, what—"

She gripped the ends of them and cranked his head back, forcing him to look at her. "The crowned dawn… is… it's *you.*"

"The crowned dawn?" He tried to pry her fingers away but she was frozen, her mind zig-zagging around, trying to recall every other word the Voice had ever said to her.

"Luna, are you alright? Was this the voice you told me about?"

The Voice… *She*… Sweet fucking Sisters, *the Oracle.*

She wasn't sure her heart was pounding anymore, or if it had flown from her chest entirely. Shaking tremors worked their way over her body, breaths so shallow she was likely to pass out.

It all made sense. So much terrible sense.

"The Shadow Prophecy," she managed. "It's *us*! Shite!" Her eyes darted everywhere, searching for the words. *"When twilight merges with stone's crowned dawn*… What did you say to me earlier? *This most precious gift?* Oh, fuck. Fuck!"

'And something most precious is suddenly gone.'

"Gone. Why would I be gone? Is it Illamiata? Or…"

Brand gathered her hair, trying to smooth it away from her face. "*Breathe.* What is happening?"

"The Voice. It was the Voice! It all makes sense. This *is* the Shadow Prophecy happening, Brand. And you and I are *named in it.* She's been trying to tell me. Trying to guide me. I was too fucking dense to see it!"

His eyes widened, fist digging into his chest where he was no doubt feeling the unshakeable certainty of what she was saying in their bond.

She *knew* it like she knew her own face and his, down to her shaking fucking bones. Stars and arses, how the fuck had she taken so long to realize it?!

"We have to—"

A rolling rumble shook the tower, dust falling from the rafters. Not a split-second later, a horn blasted through the air with just as much force, the long bass note vibrating beneath her.

"No." Brand was up before she could ask what was happening. "Dress us, Luna. Now!"

She didn't question him. Her power flung away from her, gripping the particles of their strewn clothing and wrenching them onto their bodies.

"You can't fight in a bloody gown," he bit out, tearing a drawer open and tossing some of his clothes her way.

"Fight?!" She switched them out, sending his gift away to the ether where it would be safe.

Sparring linens, like the ones she'd first worn when Hedda had started training her. She shrank them to fit her frame, scrambling from the bed. Brand was on her in a flash, yanking a belt around her waist and calling his dagger from the ether. "Stay with her," he hissed, and shoved it into the sheath.

She felt its power thrumming at her hip, and bile rose. It was her turn to ask, "What is happening?"

"An attack. That was the war horn." He rolled his sleeve back with no calm whatsoever and shoved his arm to her mouth. "Freely offered. Drink. Quickly."

Again, she obeyed without hesitation, using the time it took to sink her fangs in and partake of his gift to draw from the moons above. There was no doubting the level she should bring it to, filling the well to overflowing, until power was practically spilling from her pores.

She barely had time to heal the puncture wounds on his arm before he was dragging her to the balcony, the war horn still blowing.

"Weeping fucking Sisters."

His words had to be her own, for there was no such thing as speaking.

The sea heaved with gargantuan bodies, slithering up from the crashing waves. Screams echoed from the city below, the twinkling lantern lights nearest the shore starting to disappear one by one.

"The sea serpents have returned." He sounded as though he couldn't believe his own eyes or mouth.

Shite, she couldn't either.

Something pulled at her center as a thunderous boom sounded, her knees buckling in the aftershock.

"Brand… those aren't sea serpents. Not entirely." They were and they weren't. She couldn't see them clearly enough to tell, but she could feel it. "Those are dreadbeasts."

50

BRAND ROARED AS HE UNLEASHED HIS RAGE. HE HAD NO ROOM FOR HORROR. No time for thought. The Horned City—his city—was being ravaged.

Those are dreadbeasts.

He scooped Luna up in one arm. "You never leave my side. You never leave my sight. Do you understand?"

She blinked up at him, brow furrowed.

"Do you understand, Luna? No running off to save one person. I'm sorry, but it's the warriors who will need you this time. You *have* to understand."

Her nod was sharp, sure. Good.

Brand leapt from the tower to a rampart below. Demons were already racing along it, streaming from every which way. He joined the hurtling flow, shoulder to shoulder with his brethren, shouting orders as they hit the stairs that would take them to the courtyard.

His twin shadows were there, flanking Lyriat along with the rest of his guard. Hundreds of warriors had already gathered before the gates to the high road in neat lines, countless others still coming to fill out their ranks.

"Do we know how many?" he asked as they joined them.

Lyriat's jaw ticked, burning fury on his angular face. "Too many. Perhaps a dozen, maybe more."

Brand's world narrowed to a pin prick of hazy light. A dozen dreadbeasts.

It had taken two and a half Imperial Sons and Nachthelliae's most powerful Sorcerit to bring *one* down.

Magnus and Vann arrived, Thad on their heels. Brand scanned the way they'd come, searching for hope in the formidable forms of his uncle and remaining brothers.

"Where are they?" he demanded.

Mag began untying his robes. "Araxis never showed, Caius went to report to the Chieftains, and Amun left with Amal a couple of hours ago."

"Fuck. Fuck!"

Luna's hand landed on his cheek. "We were surprised by the first," she murmured. "We know better now. Put me down."

Brand obeyed, curious to see where the determination he felt in her would lead them.

She reached out, power flaring, and the four talons they'd taken from the first dreadbeast appeared on the ground.

"Fucking genius, witchling. Who will take them?"

Another shudder in the earth, gasps and growls sounding.

A nervous hitch in his chest belied Luna's air of confidence. "I have an idea, born from my own inabilities, I'll admit."

A stream of power poured from her palm as she reached it to the sky, the moons' beams craning down to meet it. She gave a yank, and the whips of light stretched out to grasp onto two of the jagged talons, melding with the ends. Coiling the lengths, she pulled them towards herself, fangs flashing as she gritted her teeth. A pulse, her clawed hands gripping both the rope of her magic and some other invisible thing she seemed to be crushing together.

Pulse, and the talons—nearly eight feet long—shrunk to half their size. Another, Luna grunting with effort, and they shrank again, and again, until they'd compacted to the size of her forearm.

Breathing heavily, wavering, she said, "I'll take two. I can use them from a distance. Probably poorly, but better than relying only on close combat and a dagger I'm shite with."

"Aye, like I said—fucking genius."

Brand knelt, offering his hand. "Drink."

She waved him away, drawing a hand across her forehead. "I'm not hurting. That was *my* power, and I am already replenishing. Save it for when I actually need it."

He nodded, standing. "Vann, use your vines to take another. I'll take the last. If you see a glowing patch of fiery light, that's where you stab it."

"I will command and fight from above," Lyriat said, his wings flaring. "Brethren! Our forebears waged this battle once before and won! Use your wits, funnel the beasts to our Imperial Sons. You know what to do!"

He took to the sky, war cries following him up.

Brand had no idea what they were walking into, but still said, "One at a time, as best you can manage. We'll split into groups, lead by myself, Magnus, and Vann. Overwhelm them. Confuse them. Use your power. Do *not* try to take one on alone. First Legion, to me!"

Scooping Luna up once more, he sprinted through the gates and down the high road, scores of raging Demons in his wake. Closer and closer to the sounds of fighting. Buildings had been toppled, falling partway into the streets. Screams and shouts reverberated, the ground rumbling beneath his feet.

At last, they hit the square and its chaos.

The smell of rotting fish assaulted him. Brand counted eleven sea serpents, writhing from the beach and twisting between the surrounding areas. Their gigantic heads rose up, pointed teeth like daggers as they destroyed everything in sight with abandon.

They weren't like the ones from the old books and renderings. From the tales he'd been told.

Instead, they were decomposing. Their dull scales sloughed away with every movement, falling to the ground liked hurled supper plates and scattering in wisps of black shadow. The same deathly grey as the dreadbeast from the chasm.

And the sleek bodies of the terrible and magnificent creatures depicted on nearly every surface of the Horned City certainly hadn't possessed fucking *legs*.

They'd been crudely patched on, jutting out and sharply angling back in like centipedes, the same talons supporting them.

"That's fucking great," Faldir growled. "Foul bloody dreadwyrms."

Hedda pointed above them with her axe in hand, her voice choked. "The Solyr Stone."

Sure enough, there was the twelfth. It was camouflaged against the night sky and the obelisk's endless obsidian, wrapped and wrapped around it, trying to break it apart.

"Lyriat!" Brand bellowed, pointing himself. "Bring it down!"

Their king swooped down and shot upwards, his dual greatswords glinting. Vann went up too, in the dark side of his power, nearly disappearing himself as his blackened body followed on a wingless flight.

And so it began.

The dreadwyrm tumbled down into the square in front of them, flopping as it shrieked, and Brand commanded the ground to wrap up around it. Others followed suit, replenishing the stone entrapments as it broke them apart.

"Find the weak spot!"

Those with him searched the colossal body, shadows lashing out from between scales and teeth.

"There!" Luna scrambled forward in his hold.

He followed her finger—straight into the dreadwyrm's gaping maw.

"Roof of the mouth!" His voice carried across the square, to where his brethren and brothers were locked in their own battles.

Putting Luna down, he pinched her stunning face between two of his fingers. "Remember, you never leave my side."

"Never leave your sight." She nodded. "I understand."

Brand flipped the talon in his hand and called to the stone. Rocky claws rose up around the dreadwyrm's head, funneling into its mouth and wrenching it apart. With a lunging heave, he buried the the talon in its hard upper pallet.

The dreadwyrm's death throes were almost more destructive than any of the intentional attacks. Leftover stands and canopies were destroyed, a quarter of the surrounding storefronts and homes obliterated. He tried to limit its movements, to keep it trapped, but the damage was done.

Warriors rushed in to pull victims from the wreckage, stone melting to sand beneath their power.

"The talons!" Luna shouted. "Take them!"

The ones who weren't helping obeyed without hesitation, hacking away at the bony appendages. Victorious cries sounded from another part of the city, a pair of howls rising above them. Again from his other side, Vann's echoing laugh floating by on the breeze.

The next dreadwyrm went down in much the same way—in a fit of earth and shadow and screams, the talon of its hideous cousin embedded in its house-sized head.

And the next.

Brand rested his hands on his knees mere feet from his third kill, catching his breath and gathering strength as hope flared within him.

They could do it. They could win.

"Brand!"

Face twisted in terror, Luna shot one of her taloned whips past his head, a wave of his hair caught in its current. He spun around as she hauled back, her body bowing with effort. A dreadwyrm had snuck up behind them from a tight alley and was rearing back, arched and towering a dozen stories above him with her magical weapon embedded in its eye socket.

He reached out to take the whip from her, but his fingers passed right through the glowing rope as if nothing was there.

Fuck.

"To me!"

Demons swarmed, stone blasting out from the alleyway structures to grab the serpent. At the same time, Brand went to his knees behind Luna, wrapping his arms around her and engulfing her tiny hands with his. He couldn't touch her power, but he could touch her.

"Pull!"

She did, all her weight pressing into his chest as he pulled with her, trying to bring its head to the ground where he could reach it. Lips peeled back, a ripple of light surged from her hands and folded the rope in on itself, threads spinning out and back in around themselves.

The dreadwyrm shrieked, thrashing, trying to dislodge the talon. More stone and earth rose up like reaching hands, grasping and towing.

"Almost there, little moon. Again!"

Another heave, another ripple, another fold.

"Hedda!" His Second whirled around, grimacing as she manipulated the stone. "Take her!"

She was there in a blink, switching places with him and enveloping his mate's body.

"With your life, Second."

She gave a sharp nod, knowing what he meant—protect his mate at all costs.

Brand brandished his jagged talon and leapt into the air, closing the remaining distance between himself and the clamoring beast. With a roar, he brought that one down, too.

The damage was less that time, having learned their lesson thrice over.

Luna was slumped back in Hedda's arms, gulping down hiccuping breaths. "I can't believe I did that."

Hedda chuckled. "I take partial credit."

Brand gathered Luna to himself, giving Hedda a pointed look of thanks before he turned away and hugged his mate close. "You were incredible. Thank you. You might have saved my bloody life."

She huffed a shaky laugh, leaning her forehead against his chest. "I was aiming for its mouth."

Brand joined her, laughing at the absurdity of it. "Practice makes perfect. We'll make a warrior of you yet."

"I fucking hope not."

Pet and Sorcha loped into the square, their fur splattered with black ooze. Luna squealed, a shudder running through her as she tossed out a shield to coast along their bodies, scraping it away. That's when they noticed Sorcha was hobbling, her foreleg bent in the wrong direction.

"Shite, Thad is hurt. Put me down, Brand."

He did, hoping to the Sisters she didn't look around her and notice the others who hadn't been as fortunate. The sorrow would have to wait for after, when they could allow their mourning to begin. For now, he could still hear the chorus of battle in the area of the city nearest the shore.

Mag shifted, uncaring of his nudity or the muck and shattered rocks beneath his feet. "Vann and Lyriat have it well in hand," he said. "Last one."

Brand kept his eye on Luna, crouched in front of a panting Sorcha as her prismatic power flared. She'd be needing him and the gift he could offer her, but there'd be no sleep for her tonight.

As if on cue, the violence died down and the cries became audible. The weeping and wailing, like ghosts haunting the decimated streets. The reek of death and pain. It was easy to ignore in the thick of it, to block it out and focus on the task at hand.

This. This was the worst part. This was when she'd be most needed.

Luna kept one hand on Sorcha's flank as they ambled over, a limp in her own step now. It was the wary, almost suspicious, feeling down the bond that got to him first, though. A guarded trepidation that set his own mind to spinning.

"Mag?"

"Aye?"

"Do you feel like that was... Do you get the impression..."

Fuck, Brand didn't want to say it out loud, like speaking a curse into existence.

It had taken them hours to fell the first dreadbeast. Now, in the same amount of time, they'd taken down a dozen? A dozen that had been far, far larger and more disastrous.

The sense that it'd been too easy intensified when he saw Luna stop dead in her tracks maybe fifteen yards away, head tilting as her gaze went distant.

Magnus winced, hands going to his ears with a curse.

Dread, swift and staggering, twisted in his gut like a rusty knife.

And then he heard it.

That same high-pitched, keening whistle from the chasm edge. Ominous. A promise of looming destruction from not one, but twelve difference directions.

"Luna! Your shield!" Brand bellowed, uncaring that his voice splintered as he surged into motion to reach her.

He was too late.

With an explosion that must have rocked all of the Montrealm, every last dreadwyrm imploded.

A wave of absolute ruination followed, leveling half the city around him. Brand was thrown mid-step, his body flying across the square and slamming onto a pile of rubble. Even his horns hadn't been enough to protect his head, a sharp corner cracking into his skull hard enough to steal his senses.

He'd thought the sounds before were haunting. They were nothing in comparison to when his ears popped clear and he was bombarded by so many screams that it wrenched a sob from his lungs.

Lyriat's roar rose above the din, a broken, devastating sound that only wrecked him further.

Luna.

Brand could barely see through the billowing dust, a cloud of deep sienna that may as well have been blood. Stumbling, dizzy, he tripped down the broken boulders beneath him and followed the bond where it led, that tension pulling them together.

Feeling it was the only thing keeping him sane. Surely, if anything had happened to her, it would be gone.

Surely.

A howl went up, followed by a growl. Sorcha.

Something dark flew past him, and those growls turned to violent snarling. Snapping barks meant to threaten. When he heard Lyriat's cries of alarm, summoning any who could stand, he didn't care anymore that he was practically blind—he ran.

Brand broke through the veil of red, the wasted square clear before him.

There, in its center, was a writhing mass of black hovering over Luna's prone form, completely unperturbed by the feral Sorcha. It seemed to turn to him, and then it spoke—layered, like a chorus of clawing nails. "Catch me if you can, Brandir."

"No. *No!*"

It lifted her body, swallowing it, and flew up the high road towards the castle. He kept his eyes on it only long enough to see it disappear into his own fucking tower.

Brand didn't think as he sprinted for the portal on the other side, hoping it had survived. He had to get to her.

BRAND BURST INTO HIS CHAMBER, HALF-CRAZED AND SEARCHING.

There was little relief in finding Luna sprawled on the bed, even when he saw the shallow rise and fall of her chest. Something else was there. He could feel it.

Brandishing his greatsword, he took tentative steps towards her. Scanning. Sweeping. His muddled senses alert. He was all too aware of his exhausted limbs. The throbbing at the base of his skull and the blood trickling down his back.

There. Movement in his peripheral vision had him whipping his head towards the fireplace on the opposite wall.

The shadows, seemingly innocent as they clung to the nooks and crannies of their bedroom, began to writhe—just like the ones in the Dread Chasm. They pulled from every crevice, gathering themselves into a pool on the floorboards like a shifting sea of evil.

Heart pounding, Brand raised his sword and put himself between it and Luna.

He spared a glance back at her, at the crooked, almost lifeless heap of her, just to be sure—

With a blast of fetid air, a great screech rent the room and the shadows sprang at him, whipping his flesh and leaving oozing gashes in their wake. On a savage bellow, he swung his sword in a downward arc, his blade landing with a booming thud that shook the high tower.

Light poured from him as his muscles bulged, cutting, slashing, stabbing, his biceps burning with the effort.

It was like attacking a valley mist—pointless, hopeless. The infinite darkness of it dodged and dissipated, reaching out in lightning-fast wisps to rip at his flesh, wholly unaffected by his labors.

Sweat and blood poured from his brow, breaths ragged.

A pale flash of movement caught his attention. "Luna, don't—"

He was too late to avoid the single, thick tendril that snaked out from the center of the mass, wrapping around his neck and lifting him from the floor.

Luna loosed a guttural shriek, the sound a battle cry even as it ripped his heart from his chest. He was meant to protect *her.* Meant to shield her from all harm. Instead, his legs flailed uselessly beneath him as the shadow pulled him closer.

It loomed over him, wafting a rotten stench of burnt flowers that promised only despair. He drained as it squeezed, his light abandoning him as the rage left his body and he reverted to his lesser self.

The involuntary transformation was agonizing. Horns and fangs forcibly shoved back into his flesh. Skin tightening and clamping down on his muscles as they spasmed.

His sword slipped from his impotent grasp, disappearing back to the ether before it could clatter to the ground, too much of his hope with it.

Luna vaulted from the bed, white-hot threads at her fingertips. Her long tresses spun into the air as an orb formed in her hands, a perfect match to the silver swirl in her vengeful eyes. She was magnificent in that moment, landing with preternatural grace as she unleashed her colossal power, blinding him and washing the room in pounding light.

The shadows shrieked and cowered beneath her onslaught, blast after blast slicing through its inky depths. Hemorrhaging magic as it poured and poured from her in defense of him.

He wanted to scream when he saw the first stumble. The first gasp and her pallid skin. The signs of her weakening.

But, by burning fucking Solyrian, how she'd fought.

Brand strained with everything he had left, trying to get free—until the shadow began leaking itself into him, filling his body with lifeless weight.

With the sound of Luna's labored breath in his ears, a crooning note sounded, laced with a chorus of countless wails as it grated and echoed through the chamber.

"Shhh, Brandir. Calm," a voice of the same whispered. "Rest. This was a hard day for you."

Shock tore an unwilling whimper from his burning lungs.

"You're surprised, but you shouldn't be. I promised I would never leave you." With blinding speed, a second arm of shadow branched into massive talons and latched onto Luna's torso, wrapping over her shoulders and around her waist. "Not like *she* did."

"Please," Brand wheezed, hardly a sound at all.

"I'm so sorry. I know what she means to you, but I need your help, remember?"

He couldn't. He couldn't fucking remember—not what she was implying, not why that voice was familiar beneath its layers—and that was the problem.

"I don't think you'll be able to do that if you're worried about her."

"No, no, no." He felt his lips move, but there was nothing to hear.

Luna gasped as the talons squeezed, followed by the worst sound he'd ever heard in his fucking life—the tell-tale *pop* of his mate's spine snapping in half.

As the crack shot through the room, he tried to cry out—*he fucking tried*—but the shadows were choking him. Forcing their way down his throat.

The darkness lifted Luna upwards, her body bowing like a marionette until she was thrust towards him in a dizzying blur and jerked to a stop mere inches away. The force of it flung her arms and legs forward, a single, perfect finger sliding against his cheek before a series of deafening snaps told him her limbs had just been wrenched from their sockets.

Tears flowed down her cheeks, and he would have given anything to be able to comfort her. To wipe those tears away and whisper in her ear. To not have that violent brush of her hand be the last time he felt the bliss of her moonlight skin.

He'd just gotten her back. Just had the best night of his life. How was this happening? *How?*

The shadows halted their invasion, allowing him a single breath before he felt the first razor-sharp fingers of it tunneling through his insides, raking over muscle and mind. His gaze locked with Luna's, a tear slipping down his cheek as a dark cloud crept in from the edges of his vision. He tried to blink it away. To hold on to the blessed sight of her even as he fought his pain and hopelessness.

Puffy, reddened eyes stared back at him, blue as the sea and holding a wealth of tenderness in their depths. His favorite fucking color.

"I love you," she whispered, smiling despite the fearful trembling of her lips.

No. That wasn't supposed to be the way he first heard those words from her perfect mouth.

He tried so hard to reach for her, to offer her anything in return, but a stark cold was wending its way through his veins, his body shaking as consciousness began to slip away.

He'd thought the Veil would be softer, more welcoming. Had expected Luna at his side when he crossed over, her hand in his own ages from now as they went together into their joyful eternity.

Not this weeping loneliness slashing its way through the hole in his chest. Not this freezing lethargy.

One last look, then. One last glimpse of her before he died so he could take the sight with him.

Brand forced his lids to open and found himself sprawled on the floor, the wooden floorboards scraping against his back as the sickening sound of Luna's choking sob seized his attention.

"I know this seems unfair, my perfect boy, but you must say goodbye."

Luna was snatched backwards into the seething black mass on a blood-curdling scream, thrashing and baring her fangs. Even fractured and ruined, she resisted, her wild eyes darting and searching until she found him and calmed.

"She's done all she can for us."

Nothing in this world—not the creature, not even the Sisters themselves—could have stopped the roar of denial that shredded his vocal cords and took half his soul with it when one of those spikes of shadow thrust down through her torso before tossing her aside.

An enormous wave of black surged upwards and the glass dome above shattered along with his heart, pelting him in countless, jagged pieces as darkness finally consumed him.

51

"LUNARA!"

She ignored the insistent wail, too taken with what lay before her.

The Veil stretched out, promising an eternity of solitude. She wasn't sure how she knew where she was and she couldn't be bothered to care. She'd never expected it to be so deep and vast. So lovely.

If only that voice would quiet down and leave her be.

Ghostly blue shadows enveloped her, whispering for her to follow. Their luminescent presence offered a peaceful temptation she was loathe to ignore. Her footsteps glowed behind her as she trailed them, brightening with each step she took towards the onyx chasm in the distance.

"Lunara!"

There it was again, that infernal screeching denying her the rest she sought. The sound of it competed with the lulling voices of the Veil, tickling something on the edges of her memory, but the spirits ahead were so sweet in their coaxing as they beckoned her to join them. To revel in the dark joy of death.

She finally reached the edge of the abyss and dared a glance down. Souls swarmed in its depths, the dance of their eternity enticing her beyond reason. A soft laugh left her lips as she readied for the jump.

"Are you supposed to be here? You don't seem like you are, and I *know* I'm blimmin' not. It doesn't feel right."

The rasping, unfamiliar voice drew her up short, poised one step from the edge of that final oblivion. Confused, she spun towards the speaker.

She knew that gorgeous face, but *why?*

It jarred her to see it, recognition trying to bloom but stunted by the encroaching darkness.

"Hold on, Lunara. Please, witchling, don't you bloody go there. Hold on for me."

That anguished sound stopped her, too. *Lunara.* She knew the word, but why didn't she know what it meant anymore?

How long had she been here? Her memory was twisted, like it had been both centuries and seconds, time warping around her.

Lunara. Lunara… Luna?

A disjointed memory flashed within her, the impression of auburn hair brushing her cheek as a gravelly voice—a different voice—whispered that name into her ear with the utmost reverence.

Luna. Little moon.

The vision grabbed hold and tempted her to turn back, forced her to remember this wasn't how it should be happening. There was supposed to be a rough hand holding hers, going with her, a shy smile urging her on.

The female that had spoken crouched at the edge, sifting black sand through her fingers.

"You're not supposed to be here?"

Her head snapped up. "I know your voice. You're the one…"

"I know your face."

Knew the deep bronze of her skin and that lavender mass of curls. She *knew* it, but why?

"I think you're right. I… don't think this is where I'm meant to be, either."

"You've got that fucking straight, mate." She stood, verdant wings of gossamer fluttering out behind her when she threw her arms out. "How are you supposed to help me if we're both in this cunting wasteland?"

"Help… you?"

It hit like a violent tidal wave, images and memory crashing over her.

She was Lunara, and she definitely wasn't supposed to fucking be here.

Neither was *Fern.*

She lunged forward and grasped the Fae's hand.

"LUNARA!"

On a gasp, she regained her consciousness. Every inch of her hurt—a throbbing, all-consuming pain working to disconnect her mind from her body. She blinked against it, all of her energy directed towards trying to focus.

A salty breeze blew through absolute carnage, swirling the sienna dust as it settled into the chaos of shattered glass and crumbled stone. She watched, panic blooming, as the tiny specks landed on her skin like red mist, seamlessly joining the steady flow of blood leaving her from countless lacerations.

She snapped her gaze around the room, unable to reconcile the scene before her.

It was the stars shining innocently above, unimpeded, that shocked her out of her confusion. A scream of denial lodged itself in her throat as she railed silently against what her eyes were showing her.

The massive glass dome that should've been crowning the tower was instead all around her, on top of her, *in her*.

No, no, no.

"Help me clear it. Pet can sense her wee heart beating, but she's barely bloody alive. She hasn't got much time."

Lunara registered shouting and wails in the distance as she became more aware, muffled somewhat by a string of harsh curses nearby. Bricks shifted and collapsed across the room where the door should've been, tattooed skin and blond hair flashing before disappearing into the chaos once more. She tried to form words, to call for help so he'd know where she was, but nothing would come.

More swearing sounded to the tune of crunching glass beneath heavy footfalls before a massive windowpane was at last lifted from her chest and tossed aside.

"Ah shite, witchling." Magnus reached down to clear more debris away and knelt beside her. "I'm sorry for this next part."

His eyes never left hers as his arms banded around her broken body, forcing a strangled whimper to push itself past dry lips when he lifted her from the floor.

"We'll not find him here amongst all this, will we lass?" he rasped, eyes brimming with the same tears she felt pouring from her own.

She barely stomached the answering shake of her head. Tears broke free of his blond lashes and cut rivers through the grime clinging to his cheeks and beard.

"Aye, I thought not. I can't feel him anymore. Not nearby, at least."

A sob slipped free, her chest constricting with his words.

Neither could she.

He's just… gone?

"Shh, I know, Lunara. I know," he choked out. "Let's get you safe and worry about the rest later, aye?"

Magnus clambered over the debris of the fallen tower and stumbled onto the winding staircase, down into the castle where Demons she couldn't name rushed forward to meet them. He refused to let them pry her from his arms, trudging through the massive corridors until he reached her guest chamber.

No. No. No.

One second they'd been together, wrapped up in each other's bodies exactly as they should have been, and next he was being ripped away from her in shadowed clutches.

She'd tried to fight. Sisters, how she'd *tried.*

She wanted to thrash, to scream. She wasn't meant to be in the Veil, but she wasn't meant to be here either, back in her room with—

"Fern," she wheezed. "*Fern.*"

"Aye, it's alright. I'll check on her soon as you're settled."

There would be no such thing as *settled.* Not as long as he was gone.

Not real. Not real. You aren't even here. It's not real.

She hated how comforting the sound of herself was, emerging once more to protect her. She'd been utterly content for the first time in so long, and it had finally let her be. So long it had let her *be.* But now—

Maybe you didn't see what you saw. Maybe it's just another nightmare.

She looked for something to be wrong. To find a door that shouldn't be there, or a white flash in the corner of her vision.

"It didn't happen," she choked. "It *can't* have happened, Magnus."

"Lunara…" Despair laced his tone as he passed the sitting area and fireplace.

He laid her on the downy mattress that wasn't supposed to be hers anymore, and she lost all control.

"No." The last dregs of her magic flooded to the surface with nauseating suddenness. "No, no, no, no, *no*!" Her wail shook the walls.

Raw power shot forth from her body and knocked Magnus clear across the chamber and into the fireplace mantle. She should've been mortified but, as the last ounce drained and the blinding prismatic light died away, Lunara had nothing left within her. No energy. No feeling.

Just a gaping hole where her heart should be.

Magnus approached her carefully with one arm stretched out, like he was trying to soothe a wild animal. He only paused for a moment before, as gently as a male his size could, he eased his body onto the mattress and perched himself beside her.

"Calm yourself, witchling," Magnus whispered as he swept hair from her face. "Let me help you."

"What's the point if he's gone?" she croaked.

He scrubbed a hand over his face and pinned her with a look of utter desolation.

"Let me do this, Lunara. Please," his voice hitched. "For him."

She didn't bother to reply as he plucked a small knife from his belt, swiping the blade across his wrist with no thought for himself. She tried to force her shattered limbs to work so she could turn away and ignore what was being offered, but a drop of his blood splashed onto the blanket beside her and she froze, her eyes latching onto the stain.

In that moment, Lunara truly hated herself. Hated the gnawing, overwhelming hunger. The way her body betrayed her and somehow leaned towards him, too concerned with healing itself to remember her spine was broken and she wasn't supposed to have to take the blood gift of anyone other than *him*.

Hate yourself later. Just take it and sleep. At least then, you won't remember it might be your fault.

Disgusted by her weakness, she closed her eyes against the swirling guilt and tried not to gag as her fangs sank into the wrong flesh. Her mind emptied and darkness encroached on her vision.

A verdant flash, and then she was lost.

MAGNUS BACKED AWAY FROM THE BED AND MADE FOR THE DOOR, HIS HEART cracked in two.

—We'll find him, Maggie—

Aye, Pet, but it's not only Brand I'm worried about.

—Our sister is strong—

He knew that. He did. But Mag wasn't sure he'd seen a body as broken as that on someone still living. Not even Baldrir. He didn't understand how she was breathing at all. Fuck, he didn't know how any of them had made it through the night.

—You'll need to gather the family again. Their blood is potent enough. It'll work—

Not for a whole city.

"Shite."

Pet perked up within and wrenched his senses to the surface, his own head turning. Something was here.

His hackles went up just before a petite pair of arms came whipping around his neck swift as lightning, and a set of teeth sank into one of his ears.

"Weeping fuck!" he shouted as they yanked.

He reached a hand back—

"What did you do to her, you pissing bog troll?!"

Sweet, bleeding Sisters. Even screeching, that throaty voice dripped like honey.

He grabbed onto a head, hair like a silken pillow greeting his palm—which he sank his fingers into and pulled. It, she, whatever the fuck, bit down on his arm hard enough to nearly bring him to his knees, gone a second later.

—You know that scent, lad—

Alert, waiting, Magnus breathed deep. Petrichor and teeming, sun-drenched blooms collided together—a rebellious perfume that made no true sense but was all the more lovely for its dissonance.

"Fern?"

Then, she was everywhere.

Claws and teeth danced around him in a blur, lashing out to deliver bites and scratches and blows with startling efficiency—before disappearing again.

The sound of a pained thud was not comforting in the least.

—Go easy, Maggie. She's confused—

I'm not gonna fucking hurt her. Not that she extended the same courtesy.

Mag found her slumped beside the couch in a gasping heap, having clearly exhausted herself. She was likely weak as a kitten and never should've been flailing about like that. Slowing his movements, he crouched and crept towards her with a hand out. His massive damned size was not generally conducive to seeming non-threatening, but he tried anyway.

"It's alright, Fern. You're safe with me."

—I'm not sure she knows that name—

Aye, thanks. I had no idea.

"Lass, can you understand me?"

There was just enough light for him to be bowled over when she turned around and pierced him with midnight eyes that held every last galaxy in their inky depths, the orbs so brown they were nearly black.

Beautiful, wide eyes that were burning with absolute fury.

"I'm not a cunting bird-brain." She skittered back, swearing when one of her fragile wings snagged on the leg of the settee. "What did you do to her? She wasn't broken in the Veil."

That, he did not expect.

Terror and curiosity were a strange mix.

"You saw her in the *Veil*?"

Her eyes narrowed, chest heaving. "She pulled me out with her, after that rutting wankstain tried to suffocate me with my own fucking pillow."

Magnus reared back. "What did you just say?"

"I'm not saying another fucking thing until you tell me why she's hurt."

—Fair enough—

Aye, fine.

"She"—He pointed towards the bed—"is Lunara the Moonweaver, we've had a wretched fucking night here in the Montrealm, and I'm not even fucking close to the one who did that to her. She's my sister. I'm trying to help her. Just like I'm trying to help you, Fern."

"Is… is that my name? Fern?" Her gaze shifted away, and he could tell it physically pained her to ask and admit she didn't know.

Fucking stars, she doesn't… Fuck.

—Our witchling will be sorely disappointed—

"I don't know," he admitted. "It's what we've taken to calling you while you slept."

"While I slept..." Her feathered brows furrowed. "I woke up earlier, but was too tired to move. That's when *he* came in. How long was I asleep before that?"

Magnus really needed to figure out who '*he*' was.

"About a month, give or take, as far as we know," he answered instead. "Lunara's been trying to heal you since we found you in Glynmor, shredded as anything."

"I know. I recognized her voice. Owe her my life, whatever good it is." Her stare got lost in some space between. "I know that name. Glynmor. Feels right." She blinked and was scowling at him again.

"Is there anything else you can remember? We can help you find your way home, aye?"

Not that it would be happening tonight. Shite, he didn't even have time for this fucking conversation right now.

She looked absolutely pissed that wobbly tears had dared to gather in her thick, sable lashes. "No. I... I can't. I don't even know where home *is*. Maybe that Glynmor place."

Magnus hadn't realized he could feel any worse than he already did. "No, lass. Glynmor isn't anyone's home." He swallowed. "Not anymore."

Her breaths quickened, nails digging into the wood planks of the floor.

"It's alright. You're safe here." He reached out to lay a hand on hers, but she snatched it back.

"Did you not hear the part where someone tried to murder me, tosspot?"

Fuck me. She's fiery as the bleeding sunstar.

—Aye. Wild, like us—

"Aye, I did." Magnus settled back on his arse, too damned tired to be bent down in a squat anymore. If she killed him for it, good for her. "Wanna tell me about it?"

"It was the same fucking cunt from before." She leaned further away, a wary frown on her face as she gave him a once-over. "Whoever... The one who... I just know it, eh? It feels right."

"You keep saying that. What do you mean?" He had to stifle a yawn, every fucking dreadful minute catching up with him.

He couldn't let it. He raced up here as fast as Pet could take him when he saw the tower crumbling, unable to sense his brother or the witchling nearby where they should've been. Those he'd left behind would be out of their stupor by now, looking for answers he didn't have, and there were too many people who needed pulling from the wreckage.

Her look softened ever-so-slightly, turning inward. "The smell of him is in my bones." She breathed deep, like she could still recall the scent from her ravaged memory. "So much pain, the first time it entered my lungs." Another breath. "Both for me and the ones I was with. They were like you. Shifters? But they're gone now. I think. Because of him." A shudder worked its way through her. "I can *feel* it."

Magnus sat up a little straighter at that. The last time she would've been around Wolflords… "Are you trying to say a *male* razed Glynmor and he's *here*?"

That couldn't be right. A dreadbeast had done the deed. They'd killed it. He'd had his justice.

"I don't know, but I *know*. Fuck." A hand landed on her chest, over her heart. "In here, I know what you just said is the truth." She jabbed a finger against her forehead. "Up here, I can't make sense of fucking anything. But yes. That. He's here. *I can feel it.*"

"Aye, alright. Alright." Mag tried to keep his breathing steady. Everyone else would have to wait. "Did he speak?"

"I'll say. That cunting bag of pixie shit called me a fucking *fairy*, then had the nerve to *shush* me while I struggled," she spat, a grunted screech leaving her. "I'm going to peel his fucking flesh away with my teeth when I find him."

Weary as he was, a rising wrath boiled in his veins to match hers.

"Tell me everything he said, Fern," he breathed. "Word for word."

She rolled her eyes. "*'You should have stayed dead the first time. Now, go to sleep like a good little fairy and stop fucking up my plans.'*"

Fucking fuck. A *person* had done it.

Could a single creature be responsible for all of it, or was he working with someone else? Baldrir, Glynmor, the chasm, the dozens of fucking dreadbeasts and attacks—seemed like too much for a single individual. Unless…

—Unless they could be more than one person at a time, moving to and fro unnoticed. Aye, lad. That might be your proof—

Vann had been wrong. Magnus was sure of it. The Kohamaians might not have any documentation of a shapeshifter being born in the last couple centuries, but that didn't mean there weren't any. Especially if he was working for extremists. They'd have gladly hidden him away to be used later.

"What did he look like? Sound like?" It might not help, but he had to ask.

"I only caught a glimpse of long, silvered hair and pale skin before I was eating pillow stuffing. As for his voice..." Her lips peeled back, sneering. "Sounded like he's riddled with seeping cock warts, the uppity arsehole."

Even spinning from the night's events, Magnus almost laughed. "That's not a sound."

"Shitting seasons. Fine." Her head tilted, lips pursed. "Not like you or me, eh? Or the witch. Deep, high-handed. Too stupid to realize he's already fucking dead. Probably proud of his twig dick."

Aye. Fiery as the sunstar.

Long, silvered hair, like Bal's abductor. Not Thodeleborian, Kohamaian, or Nachthellian. It wasn't even half the dots that needed connecting, but it was something.

—Except, he could be anyone, Maggie. At any time—

Shite. There is that.

Everything else aside, the lass was sitting there telling him the one who'd slaughtered his people had been in this room within the last couple of hours.

No one could be trusted. Not until she pointed the shite-sucker out.

—We'll feast on his bones when she does—

Aye, Pet. He's ours.

But not tonight. His people were already gone, Demons were suffering down in the city, and Lunara needed him. *Brand* needed him.

Magnus stood, ignoring the creak of his battered body as he debated what to do.

Her ability to identify the culprit was worth its weight in all of Bordoroth's gold. Leaving her alone, vulnerable, would be a mistake. On the other hand, taking her out where she might be seen was just as fucking bad.

—If you take her with you, you'll need to cuff her to your own wrist, lad. Never let her out of our sight. At least by leaving her here, you can lock the door and keep pretending you know nothing. Keep her safe—

Aye, that's—

"Oh, I'll be staying with her," Fern said, jutting her chin towards the bed.

Every particle of Mag's being snapped to attention, honing in on her. She'd said that like it was in answer to his conversation with *Pet*. "Fern..."

"Piss off. She was with me the whole time I was lost. Saved me." She rose to unsteady legs, snapping her teeth at him when he moved in a daze to help. "She might be asleep, or healing, or whatever the fuck, but she's the only person in this twigging place I trust. *I'm staying with her*."

His heart was pounding hard enough to make him sick. Good thing he could see there was absolutely no point in arguing with her.

He was too fucking shaken to do it, anyway.

52

Blood sprayed the second Endellion's tormentor finally grew sick of her silence and disappeared—a red mist that flew from her lips and coated her shackles, the slivers of her exposed skin, her infinite hair.

It had been near impossible to hold it in, but this had needed to be secret laughter.

Just between her and her.

She'd choked on it as he'd beaten her. Setting it free was a relief, her manic cackles like music as they echoed from the walls of her prison.

They'd just made a terrible, wonderful, mistake. Or, at least, his unwitting accomplice had—if she could be called such thing, ignorant as she was.

Poetic, really, the way her surprise blunder would eventually ruin him.

He would be scrambling. Sloppy, because he was too fucking selfish to realize that life didn't revolve around him anymore. His egotistical mindset would only work in their favor.

"It's done," she breathed to no one, voice still shaking with her mirth.

The end of the middle of the beginning of the middle of the end.

So many pieces, pieces, pieces, all moving, moving, moving.

They'd brought it on themselves. Her little vengeful moth would be coming for them now, lit up like her sisters in the sky—just as soon as she woke up.

Then, it would get dark and dangerous and complicated. Then, it would *really* begin.

53

"NO, NO, NO, NO, NO!"

Brand jolted, life flooding into him as the vision of Luna's broken body faded into the dark edges of his mind along with her imagined screams.

He wasn't actually dead. The fierce pounding of his heart told him that much, at least, though a part of him wished he was.

His head was a leaden vessel full of jagged rocks, body throbbing like it had been thrown against the coast amidst crashing waves. And fucking shite, the taste in his mouth—made worse by the choking dryness of his throat and tongue. He couldn't even swallow properly.

Sisters, let the whole thing be a horrific nightmare. Let him turn over to find his mate beside him and the Horned City whole.

Eyes gritty, he lifted his hands to—

No.

For one hopeful, terrible second, Brand tried to convince himself he was still asleep—that there weren't really chains holding him down—but they tightened, digging into his flesh and glowing a faint, fiery orange. Shadow and bone combined, the links writhed around him, and nausea churned at the sight, the feel.

Not a vision. Not a nightmare. It had been real. All of it had been real.

Luna's tortured wails a moment ago took on a whole new meaning.

"No." His voice was nothing more than a wheeze.

The shadows. The snap of her spine. Her blood on the floor.

"No!"

He had to get back. Had to get these off and figure out where he was and get the fuck back to her.

Stone. There was stone beneath him. He called on his power, hoping to wedge some of the rock between himself and the restraints to break them.

Nothing happened.

Taking a deep breath, he sent out his power once more.

Nothing.

He could feel it there, under the surface of his skin. The *weakness* of it. He should've been raging his way across Bordoroth at the mere possibility of her being hurt somewhere. Instead, his greater half felt subdued —drugged almost—as if nothing in all the realms could possibly rile him into appearing.

A bead of sweat trickled along his temple and into his hair as he tried again.

And again.

And again.

All to no avail.

Chest squeezing, he bellowed out as he thrashed. The chains only clamped down in response, slicing clean through his skin and hitting bone in some places. His curses echoed strangely in the confined space while his body struggled, gritting his teeth against the pain.

The only thing keeping him somewhat sane was the knowledge that she was still with him. He could feel her there, pulsating, the faintest beating of her heart alongside his own.

"She's alive. She's alive." He chanted the words over and over, fuel as he strained and pulled and yanked and screamed.

"I'm so sorry, Brandir. That's really not going to work."

Brand snapped his head towards the voice, only just realizing it was pitch black around him beyond the glow of his restraints.

The voice from the tower, less overwhelming without its layers. From somewhere else, too. Somewhere muddled and dark. Familiar in ways that confused his mind and body.

He steeled himself against the sickening thud of his heart, even as something within him felt… comforted?

No. No, no, no. Not right. That was his captor. The one who'd harmed his beloved mate.

His eyes strained as they attempted to pierce the gloom, to mark the face of the creature who'd wreaked such devastating havoc. To see the one he was going to destroy.

"Show yourself!"

A long, sad sigh was the only response.

Sharp anger rose to the fore. He fucking hated games. Hated feeling like he was being played with. If he was to go into battle with someone, he wanted to do it while looking straight into their beady fucking eyes.

A silhouette appeared among the fuzzy outer reaches of the chains' light.

"Where is Luna?"

He was practically begging her to tell him this was all a misunderstanding. That she hadn't really shattered his mate's body and left her for dead.

She finally stepped close enough that he could make out details. Beneath a crown of iron and ivory spikes, raven hair fell thick and shining all the way to her knees. Skin paler and more porcelain than any he'd ever seen peeked out here and there from her onyx gown. The fabric was gauzy and transparent, her slim body exposed through the useless garment.

"She doesn't matter anymore."

He jerked his gaze away from her gaunt nudity and beheld her face. She had to be closer to his mother's age, and strikingly beautiful—but there was a latent savagery in her that unnerved him, regardless of the apologetic furrow between her brows. Kohl lined her lashes, highlighting irises so blue they were almost white, seeming to glow. Her red, red mouth was turned down in a frown, the look tugging at the back of his mind.

That blue… That expression…

Eyes locked, something cosmic settled within the furthest reaches of him. Before him stood the creature responsible for Straelon's woes—an answer to the Prophecy's riddles if Luna's *voice* proved true—and he *knew* her, even as he didn't.

"What does that mean? What do you want with us? With me? Why?" His mind was working too fast for his mouth, every question inspiring another, including one born of loathsome curiosity he couldn't resist. "Who the fuck *are* you?"

Her head tilted, remorse replaced with something less sure. "You say that every time." She searched the floor, completely unaware of the panic tearing through him. "Though not quite so aggressively. I'd always thought it the adorable antics of a youngling, but you… truly don't remember me."

Brand tried to tame his rapid breaths. To keep her from knowing how deeply this travesty of a conversation was affecting him.

Her eyes snapped back to his, a brutal sort of disappointment in the look. "All those years…" she whispered. "I'd thought we were building something untouchable. Unshakeable. I watched and guided and waited, and you don't even know who I am."

She seemed genuinely shocked, which only rattled Brand further.

"Why should I? I've never seen you before in my life."

The words almost didn't come, part of him knowing them for the lie they were. But why? *Why* did it feel like he was betraying her somehow?

The thought sickened him. Twisted him up in ways he couldn't untangle.

Luna. Luna was the only thing that mattered.

"We'll have to remedy your poor memory, my darling boy. I hadn't accounted for it, but no matter—I've waited this long." She waved a dismissive hand, as if it made all the sense in the world and didn't bear stating.

"What the bloody fuck do you mean?" he growled, alarm sending goosebumps racing over his flesh. "Waited for what?"

He fucking hated how intensely he wanted to know. That there was a spark of something other than absolute rage at the possibility of having some answers.

"Oh, Brandir." She sidled up to him, cupping his jaw in her frigid hand. "It's time for you to help me, my love."

That last word shoved the sight of Luna—bleeding, crying, mouthing such precious words in her pain—to the forefront, raw fury with it.

Brand tried to wrench himself away, but she only gripped harder. "There's only one creature in this world with the right to call me that," he hissed, "and it isn't you. Get your fucking hand off me."

Her eyes went wide as she jerked away, a sneer working its way up from her lips to distort her pert nose. "Forget about the Sorcerit. I allowed you the gift of bonding with her so you might reach your full power, but she's no good to you anymore. Be grateful I rid you of the distraction, and was kind about it."

Brand was almost too appalled, too bewildered, to speak. "*Kind*? You fucking mutilated her, you fucking bitch."

Without warning, her clawed hand shot out again and snagged his throat as she bent close, her nose only inches from his own. "You were supposed to be different from the others. I made sure you were different!" The last was shrieked, spittle flying from her mouth to land on his face.

Wrapped in her burning, floral scent, Brand lay there dumbfounded as the air heaved in and out of her lungs. He hadn't a single inkling of what she meant, and he couldn't even begin to wrap his mind around that last bit.

He didn't bloody care. He just wanted his mate. His home.

She pushed herself upright, calm once more. "I should've grabbed you in that cursed field when I had the chance. Even though you were lying in the blood of my beloveds, I still forgave you. Still loved you, my perfect boy. I didn't realize you'd already been broken, needed fixing, else I'd have never let you go that night."

With a wave of her hand, torches embedded in the walls sprang to life, lighting his prison with a fiery glow.

Burning fucking Solyrian, he knew this place. Knew exactly where—

"Brand!"

No.

He scrambled to twist his body, dread searing through him while he prayed to any being who would listen that he hadn't actually just heard that husking voice *here.*

"Where are you? Please!"

He couldn't see a damned thing, but he could hear her clear as day—ragged, pained, begging.

"No, no, no!" His muscles bunched and strained, the chains carving into his bones as he thrashed, but he didn't feel it.

His little moon was here somewhere, needed him, and he was fucking useless.

"Shh, Luna," Brand crooned, trying to soothe her, wherever she was. "It's okay. You're okay. I'll find you."

He didn't see his captor's flying hand—only knew he'd been struck when agony splintered across his face as she shattered his cheekbone.

The pain was nothing compared to Luna's tortured wails in answer.

"If you can forget me so easily, then you should have no trouble forgetting the fickle tart who left you like all the others," the bitch hissed, her voice like glass crunching beneath his boots. "You should be thanking me for doing you the favor of removing her, before she could taint you further."

He was too enraged to be confused, to care about the discomfort. "I will fucking slaughter you!" he roared to the ceiling, spots dancing in his vision to mix with the faintest tint of red.

A link in the chains gave the tiniest bit, creaking as he flexed. He couldn't let this creature live. Couldn't let her hurt Luna more than she already had.

"My, my. You *are* strong. Just as I'd hoped." With a snap of her fingers, his shackles healed themselves.

"No, no, no. Okthana, please!"

Brand wasn't sure which of them was more astonished when the name left his lips—a name he didn't know, but did. The deep-seated awareness had just burst from inside of him, but why? *Why?*

"Oh… you do remember." The tears in her eyes sickened him. "Good. *Good.* Then we have work to do—starting with reminding you of our purpose."

Brand didn't have time to loose the colorful response crawling up his throat before writhing shadows leapt from the chains to engulf his face, forcing their way up his nostrils and down his throat. Suffocating him. Eating him alive.

He had just enough time to watch her dissipate into a dark mist before he was lost.

All he knew, for a long while after, was black and the sound of Luna's screaming and sobbing.

DARKNESS AND DREAD SHROUDED HER, HOLDING HER BELOW THE SURFACE OF waking. They locked her within and denied her the satisfaction of unleashing her

screams upon the realms. She tried to rouse herself enough to set them free, but he was too strong. Too connected.

Instead, she loosed them inside along with her tears as she searched the invisible places of the world for her other half.

Every lash. Every bruise and break. Every bellow. She felt them as if they were her own.

They were, in a way. His heart was hers, after all, and hers was his—which meant his agony belonged to her, as well.

Shitting stars, what agony it was.

Their internal weeping and wailing wove together, a silent symphony of pain shared.

It should have helped—should have bolstered them to know the other was alive and they weren't alone—but it hurt. *His torment forced her to sink, deeper and deeper. There, the sounds and feelings painted a picture that was the stuff of nightmares. Assaulted her, drowned her, owned her.*

Over and over, she clawed her way upwards—towards light and air and living, where she might be able to do *something—just to be wrenched backwards when fresh cruelty was visited upon his mind and body.*

Back and forth she went, locked within the blacks and greys of his torture and her own survival.

When his suffering finally eased—when the onslaught disappeared from their eternal bond, and she felt his peace—she should've been comforted. Except, that peace drifted away to nothing. Little-by-little, bit-by-bit, until the day she could no longer feel him at all.

That was the first day she finally heard something other than the sound of their shared anguish.

Conversations bled together in a warped cacophony around her and she latched onto them, hoarding every piece she snatched from the confusion.

"For the mate of my son would I freely bleed. Accept this gift, and awaken, my daughter."

She swam and scraped and dragged, trying to emerge. To get closer to the calloused hand gently sweeping the curls from her face as the smell of copper permeated the shadows.

"You are mine as much as the others now, for the mate of my son is a child of my heart. Take my gift, freely given, and mend, Lunara."

Closer to the warm lips landing upon her brow, even as an iron tang met her tongue.

"For the mate of our brother would we bleed—now our own sister. Take our gifts, freely given, and heal."

Closer to the procession of powerful bodies, each giving more than the last.

"Give it up, witchling. You won't find him in sleep, and I refuse to lose you both."

Closer to the strong arms holding her in hopeful silence, tears that weren't her own falling upon her skin. They burned where they struck and brought her own flooding forward.

She tried to share their words—sending them into the deepest parts of herself to show him he was loved, even when it was her they were tending to—but he'd gone. Just like that. There one second, holding as tight to her presence as she was to his, and then nothing the next. Like he was... Like he'd...

She couldn't let herself think the word. Couldn't imagine living in a world so cruel and empty. There was an explanation. She just had to get the fuck out of wherever she was to find him.

"Everything happens when and how it should—I've made sure of it."

She shivered within, nerves waking and firing with every gentle syllable the Voice spoke into her.

"Yes, that's it. You heard them, moth. The Veil is not ready for you yet. Your mate needs you. The realms need you. And someday, well... you'll see." *Power of a strange and familiar sort pummeled into her mind, her body, and light sparkled across her lids.* ***"Take my own offering, my friend, my sister. It's time, just as destiny demands. Wake up!"***

That bellowed command, in a voice she'd tried to ignore for as long as she could remember, was the final push she needed to tear through the barrier of their mated mind. To pull herself away from the heartbreak of not feeling him, just for a little while.

Just until she could find him.

A shock of otherworldly strength jolted through Lunara's veins, jerking her against roughened hands that sought to steady her. Air filled her lungs near to bursting, the first true draw of breath she'd had since...

Since Brand had been *taken.*

She used it to finally free the screams outside of herself.

Denial, raw and violent, shredded her control and Lunara released her agony. Knees buckled and hit the floor. Hands clapped over ears. Grunts and groans sounded. She heard it, sensed them fighting against the wretched sounds coming from her, but she didn't care.

Light poured from her body, pulsing and battering in waves, her power seeking all possible routes to funnel away before it could shatter her apart.

She subjected them to every jagged shard of her heartbreak. Every ounce of her fury. Every drop of her misery.

Let whoever it was feel a fraction of what she did. Let them hear her torment. Her utter revulsion that she was without *him.*

On and on, until the air in her lungs ceased to exist, and she was forced to gasp. Out and in again, mingling with her strangled sobs.

"That's it, Lunara. Steady now. Just breathe."

Magnus's voice was an anchor in the storm. She did what he said, focusing to steady her breath. Trying to blink away the tears that wouldn't stop coming.

There was no point in the effort, so she gave up and let them flow as Magnus rocked her, back and forth, helping her to come back to herself little by little.

"Aye, you're alright. I'm here. We're here."

A ragged inhale brought a semblance of calm—if the burdened, hopeless numbing of her limbs could be called such a thing. "Oh, Mag—" she started, but couldn't finish.

"Ach, there she is," he said, voice gruff as he pressed his lips to the top of her head. "Finally deigned to grace us with your presence then, witchling?"

She shifted her head to look up into the eyes of her friend. His face was haggard and tear-streaked. Dark circles and shadows had replaced the laughter that usually gilded his features, and his beard was an overlong mess, but she was strangely glad because it meant he understood.

With a hole where her heart should be, Lunara nodded.

There was a shift in the room as others pulled closer, familiar power radiating off of them to mesh with her own. The strength of it permeated straight through her skin, a buzzing sensation that rippled in time with numerous heartbeats. She'd known there were creatures around, but the realization of *who* hadn't truly registered.

"Magnus," she whispered, refusing to look.

"Aye, lass?"

"Please, for the love of the Sisters, tell me I'm not going to find your entire family around my sickbed."

"Well, I hate to disappoint, but…" His eyes shifted towards the room before he gave her a pointed look.

Shitting stars. Just what you need. Twice you've faced the Imperial Sovereigns, and twice you've mauled them.

"I don't know if I can do it." Her tone was pleading. "The last time I saw them—"

"You gave us more excitement than we've had in an age, little sister," he said, smoothing her hair and leaning in a little closer. "You forget we're your family now. You're one of ours. We've all done far worse than toss each other against a wall here and there—on purpose and just for the laugh—and we still stand at each other's side when needed. That's what happens when people love you, witchling. They don't run screaming just 'cause you've thrown a wee fit. Go on, look and see."

Tears welled anew, his words wrecking her. He was so earnest as he peered down at her that she had no choice but to trust him. To believe there was a family waiting on the other side of her fear.

Which was how Lunara found herself staring back at the Imperial Sovereigns and their remaining Sons, and sobbing all over again.

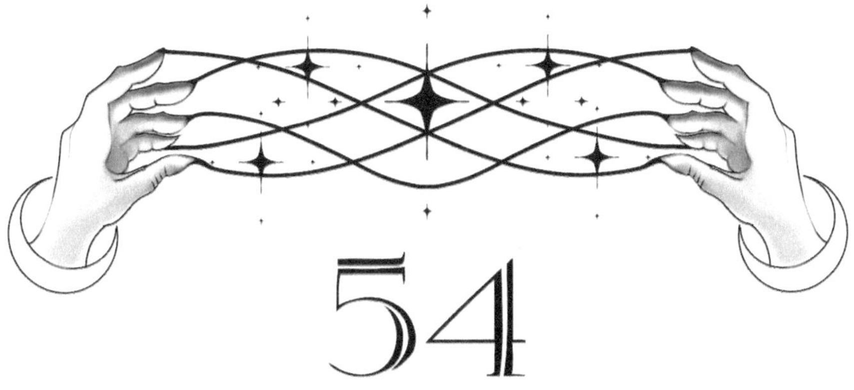

54

ALWYN AND FIONERYS FELL UPON LUNARA, THEIR ARMS WRAPPING TIGHT. She'd never thought to see them again. To face them.

Engulfed in their embraces, she searched for any words that would make it bearable. All she could come up with was, "I'm sorry. I'm so sorry. I *tried.*"

"Shh." Alwyn pulled back and swept her hair away, tucking it behind her ear. "No one understands what you're feeling right now more than we do," he said, his voice like summer rain. Clipped, powerful, but no less warm for it. "No one, daughter."

"Beloved daughter." Fionerys squeezed even tighter, the frost in her hair soothing against Lunara's cheek. "We're so relieved to have you back."

Confused didn't even begin to cover it.

She'd met them once, accidentally abused them, tried to end herself, and then disappeared in the night, and they were calling her *daughter.*

Again.

It helped her regain some composure, the disbelief grounding her—until the empress leaned back with a weighted sigh and the light caught her face.

Damn it all.

Just the other day, she'd finally noticed how starkly Brand and

Magnus resembled one another. Now, their parents' features slammed into her in ways they hadn't before.

Alwyn's heavy, bronze-eyed gaze, sitting beneath an arched and furrowed brow exactly like Brand's. Fionerys's strong nose, with the same, tiny bump at the bridge. The same regal cheekbones.

Worse when Amunkar stepped forward, his umber stare both devastated and aloof. The loving brother and the future emperor. An expression so like the one Brand had often worn when they'd first met—a male at war with himself—that Lunara had to choke back a whimper creeping up her throat.

"Magnus is right," he said in that deeply resonant voice of his. "You must understand, we are *Blessed.* With the exception of our dearest mama, every person in this room has lost control as they came into their gifted powers. You losing yourself was nothing for us." His smile was sad. "I once set fire to the entire top floor of Argoph. The *stone* floor."

Before Lunara could respond, Vann chimed in, quiet. "I got stuck in a loop during suppertime while some of my abilities manifested. Everyone in the palace was trapped, watching their food rot and restore itself again. We all relived the same thirty seconds, over and over, for nearly a week. In the end, it was hilarious."

She had no idea what he meant by *loop,* but the square cut of his jaw, the way his head tilted to the side… For all of her skepticism surrounding the Second Imperial Son, he *felt* the most like his missing brother. Like she could squint and Brand would appear in shy shades of silver before her blurry eyes.

"Yes," Fionerys said, huffing. "Magnus was a babe and had just swallowed a bite. The five of us were rooted at the table watching his food go down and back up again the entire time."

Lunara couldn't help the tragic sound that bubbled out of her, somewhere between a giggle and a whine.

"It should be noted I was stuck in my wolf form at the time," Magnus admitted. "It was nearly another year after that debacle before I found my way back to my own body. That happened many times. The worst was when I shifted a few months after Brand was born and was stuck until he was five. *Five,* witchling. Brand didn't realize I was his brother. He thought I was nought more than a loyal and steadfast pet."

"One that followed him everywhere," Vann said.

"Aye, someone had to keep the wee shite out of trouble. You've never seen a beast like a Straelani toddler, throwing a fit. Talk about a rage, aye? He would grow and shrink, grow and shrink, big wobbly tears in his eyes as his horns caught on everything and the stone of the castle went all sorts of wonky around him."

Alwyn sighed. "Brandir used to have these bouts of overwhelm. All he wanted was to be alone. His powers fluctuated with his emotion, so the worse he felt, well… Let's just say, when he didn't want someone following after him, the stone took care of the problem for him."

"The floor would rise up and grip our ankles." Vann stared into the middle distance, his voice soft. "Once, everyone in the castle found themselves up to the knees in stone vices. Brand quit Argoph with his trusty hound at his side, intent on using the opportunity to escape. He never once trapped Magnus, you see."

"That was the day I shifted back," Magnus murmured. "Didn't want the wee lad getting lost or hurt. He about shat his pants when I finally did it. Who could blame him? One second I was his pet, the next I was naked and stumbling on two legs beside him, begging him to go back and free our mam, if no one else."

"Your wolf's name…"

"Aye, lass. *Pet*," he whispered, eyes welling anew.

Oh, sweet Sisters. She couldn't take it.

The somber silence in the room wrapped its fingers around Lunara's throat and choked her.

These were the kind of stories people told when someone left for the Veil and they wanted to keep their memory alive for a little while longer.

She refused for that to be the case. "We have to find him."

"Aye, witchling," Magnus answered, swiping a tear away from his cheek. "We do. But first…" He looked at the others, head shaking. "We need to know what happened."

"What do you mean?"

He couldn't seem to look at her. "None of us who were here that night can remember, like it's been erased. Blocked? I don't fucking know. I was walking towards Brand while you healed Thad, and then I was laying in a pile of rock as the tower was falling, everyone else still out cold around me. Except, I couldn't smell you or Brand, and knew you had to be up there somehow."

A whole city of creatures couldn't recall? Hadn't seen? It didn't make sense.

A problem for another day. Too much at once and you'll never get through it.

Right. One thing at a time. Brand needed her even more than before, because she remembered all too well.

Her lids slid closed. "It was a shadow. A female? I don't know. Hard to tell beneath the layers of their voice. I've never seen anything like it, except in the chasm. It spoke to Brand as if it knew him."

She told them everything, from the moment she'd awoken to Brand battling the creature, to when he was whisked away and the dome crashed down.

"There's something else, too," she admitted, sitting up a little straighter. "It won't make much sense, but you have to believe me. I… I only realized that night that a voice I've heard in my head for most of my life is *the* Oracle, and that the Shadow Prophecy is upon us."

She'd expected gasps or flying looks, not total silence.

"Explain."

Alwyn's tone nearly killed her, sounding exactly like his son when he demanded the same. Her breath hiccuped, so fucking tight in her chest.

She told them her history, of the Voice's many visits and clues. "Some of her words have been identical, some different, but I see it all so clearly now. I am the moth it speaks of. The twilight. Brand is stone's crowned dawn, and… and a most precious thing now suddenly gone."

Fuck, he was gone.

Alwyn scrubbed a hand down his face. "We'd already come to that conclusion. The old warnings are finally in play."

That accounted for their nonchalance.

"Aye," Magnus said. "How could we not? After all our joking around, Brand's tower falling was a bitter pill to swallow. Could have knocked me over with a feather when Vann pointed it out and we put our pieces together."

Vann nodded. "Luna's claims give us a key to the words, though."

"True." Alwyn chewed his lip, eyes going distant. "If the Oracle was naming creatures, people we know, I might be able to crack it finally."

"Alwyn…" Fionerys gave her mate a wary look.

"Not to worry, love." He wrapped an arm around her, laying a kiss on the top of her head. "I won't go the way of my father. Not when so much is at stake, and I have you to pull me from the edge."

His father. Emperor Stennyx, driven mad by the very words that held her destiny.

Words that might hold the answer to locating Brand.

"I don't know how, but I'll bring him back." She pressed a fist to her chest, to the spot where she should be feeling him. "I swear it."

"We will help." Araxis stepped from his pocket of shadow, surprising her with his presence and promise.

She would've laughed if anyone had compared him to Brand. Would've argued any claim they were alike. Now, she clearly saw the way their lips bowed the same, the way the top one was slightly larger than the bottom. Noted the shallow cleft in his chin, a twin to the one she knew hid beneath Brand's short, fiery beard. But it was his look—one of righteous indignation, promising suffering to any who'd harm one of his own—that set her heart to pounding.

The same look Brand had worn on his bruised and bleeding face before he was taken.

Lunara ignored the gnawing emptiness building, the ache in her throat trying to suffocate her as she realized that—regardless of the features their realms had Blessed them with, or the striking differences on the surface—her mate was *right there*, staring back at her from six different creatures in lines and shapes, features and tendencies.

Right there, and yet—

Gone. Gone. Gone.

"Aye, that's enough then, I think." Magnus moved to settle her into the bed. "We'd best let the witchling rest."

She didn't want to rest. She didn't want to sleep anymore. She'd already been lost for—

"How long, Magnus?" Her voice was like rusted knives, both needing and fearing the answer. "How long did he hold me under?"

He swallowed, the sound cracking through a room that had become unbearably silent. "Lunara..."

"How long?" Sisters, was that her snarling?

"A month." Fionerys's voice was thick, and Lunara snapped her eyes to the empress. "It's been a month."

It took her far too long to sift through the wreckage of her heart and mind to register the words. "A *month*?" It was a wonder she didn't scream.

Magnus's sigh was like a weighted breeze, pressing down on her even as it fluttered the wispy hairs clinging to her clammy skin. "Aye."

Brand had been taken four weeks ago. Four weeks. Four…

Fuck. No. No, no, no.

Lunara scrambled to throw the blanket from herself. She couldn't lay here for another second. Had to get up and—

"Where do you think you're blimmin' going?"

She'd heard that rasping tone exactly once in her life, in the most unlikely of places.

Fern.

A verdant streak, just like she'd seen before tumbling into her unnatural sleep, and the Fae was perched at the end of her bed.

Awake. She was awake.

"Shite." Magnus cleared his throat. "About that…"

"So, you see, we have to keep her hidden. Only those closest have been allowed into your chamber, and only after she's had a good look at them to tell me how they make her… feel."

Magnus had sent everyone away, refusing to tell her anything until they were alone. Fern had looked on throughout, correcting him when he'd made some perceived error, her pride shining through the feigned boredom.

"She's not left your room, and only the family and Lyriat know she's awake. We have yet to discover who the culprit is, but at least those who matter most have been cleared of guilt."

Lunara zig-zagged back and forth, gathering everything she could possibly need in her search and sending it into the ether for later, cataloguing all of the new information as she went.

The biggest relief was that her mistrust of Vann had been misplaced. At least, so far as him being any sort of murderous villain. There was no question he was hiding something, but it was one of those problems for another day.

"Concealing her will be easy, but we'll need to make everyone else believe she's still here," she said, stuffing random clothes into a pack and magicking the mass away.

Brand's dagger stared at her from its perch on the mantle, still stuck through the belt he'd slung around her waist that night. *Stay with her,* he'd said—and it had, somehow. Choosing to leave it behind was one of the hardest decisions she'd ever made, but if the worst happened and she lost that piece of him—

No. It didn't bear thinking about.

"Concealed or not, I won't be leaving you. My life is yours until my debt is paid."

Lunara straightened and looked at Fern, shaking her head. "There's no debt, I already told you that."

Approximately a thousand times, but who's counting?

Before Magnus had delved into the whole story, she'd tried to grapple with the wall in Fern's mind again, to see what had gone wrong. All she could surmise was that the opening she'd made was too small for more of Fern's *self* to come through. Fortunately or unfortunately, she'd refused further treatment, citing—once more—that Lunara had done enough and there were more pressing matters.

Her language had been somewhat more colorful, though. In fact, she was maybe taking her amnesia too well, all things considered.

"Fuck off," Fern said, waving her hand. "You've saved me twice, and you clearly need help. What are you going to do with those, eh?"

Lunara looked down at the dirty gardening gloves in her hand. "Um…"

"Exactly. Take a breath. You're all over the twigging place."

There wasn't fucking time to take a breath. She had to find Brand.

"I don't need help. I need to leave." For some asinine reason, she sent the gloves to the ether, refusing to look at either Magnus or Fern as she did it. "Hedda and Faldir aren't coming. They, along with Baldrir and Nyri, can pretend they're still guarding her to keep appearances."

"Fuck."

Lunara stilled at his tone, goosebumps crawling over her skin. "What is it?"

Magnus stood and crossed the room, stopping in front of her. "There are still… We haven't… Fuck." His hands scrubbed over his face and into his matted hair.

"What?"

"We've been searching the rubble, but it's a lot even for the Demons and their power. Everyone is exhausted and…"

"Spit it out, Magnus," she hissed.

"The night of the attack, a group was lost. Nyri, along with Bal and about a dozen others, have yet to be found in the wreckage."

"No, that's not possible."

Isn't it, though? Think about it.

There wasn't a creature in all of Bordoroth with enough power to stop Nyriadne when she wanted something, and the young Demon would have fought horn and fist to be allowed in to see her.

Except, Lunara hadn't laid eyes on her since waking.

Fury, hot and swift, slammed into her. "Why was she down there?!" Her palms smacked into Magnus's chest. "Who let her go? Who let that happen?" Again. "She's barely more than a child!"

A sweet, innocent being. A perfect friend. This couldn't be happening. Not Nyri, too. Not Baldrir.

Lunara was utterly out of control. Couldn't breathe. It was too much.

"Aye," Magnus growled, gripping her wrists to stop the blows. "I'm of a mind to agree with you, so stop bleeding hitting me."

Too much. Too much. Another dream.

No. A waking nightmare. A cruel reality.

"You think you're the only one who's pissed? We all have vengeance in our veins, witchling." Magnus released her with a sigh. "I know everything seems lost right now, and I know you want to find them, but one step at a time. We've got choices to make, and I'd prefer they weren't shite ones."

Something pulled at the back of her mind, her ears ringing. "What did you just say?"

He gave her a funny look as he repeated himself, another voice layering over his.

The Voice. All of her words—at home, here in Straelon, in the cave…

Pressure, swift and pounding, filled her skull.

"This is the moment they planned for. It's time. But still, there's a

split—a moth-shaped divide. Tell me, Sorcerit, will your answer be right? Or will you consign us to doom-colored night?"

Lunara found herself flitting through the air again, apart from her body and taking in the scene from above as the Oracle spoke into her mind with hushed intensity, fervent delight in every syllable.

"When all is dark and the ground swims beneath you…"

A vision of the Realm Rivers crashing down below, when she'd discovered she was the Keeper and tried to end herself.

"When the waves crash and the world thunders…"

A vision of Brand springing from the bed, when the dreadbeasts attacked the Horned City. When she'd been powerless to stop that insidious creature from taking her mate.

"When red mist lands and the wrong hands free you…"

A vision of the sienna dust falling to her skin, when she'd awoken in the crumbled tower and Magnus had rescued her.

"When everything is lost and there's only one way left to find it…'"

A vision of Nyri's grinning face at every turn. Of Baldrir, whole and hale, jogging behind her onto the practice field. Of Demons celebrating their Occurrence with glorious abandon.

Of Brand wrapped around her, his lips whispering over her skin.

Gone. Gone. Gone. Gone.

Her mate. Her friends. Even her fucking sanity was hanging by a thread.

"You must remember—only poor choices shaped the others, and you are not the same. You will need your fear to find your fate."

Fear. Fate.

Brand was her fate. His love. His light. The teeming life he offered. Certainty filled her, eradicating any possible doubt as she flew lower, ghosting over her own frozen form.

But her fear…

"Find power in patience, have patience with power. Hold both within you and wield vengeance that blinds. With fangs and mist, balance and majesty, a moth spreads its wings with bonded ferocity."

Power. *That* was her greatest fear. Being hunted for it, used for it, oppressed for it. So, she'd run. Buried her head in the sand. Rejected her status as an Elder. And when she'd realized what she really was, she'd been more willing to end it all than to face it.

"Do not fear the rising ruin, do not fear the light it brings. Triumph rests there, in the palm of twilight's acceptance."

Her acceptance.

If Brand was her fate, then she would need her power to find him.

The power of a Keeper.

She came back to her body just in time to watch the moth she'd freed before the Occurrence landing on the sill, the window cracked open behind it. It seemed to stare back at her, its viridescent wings fanning and contracting before it took off into the night beyond, the Voice—the Oracle—leaving with her.

"I know what to do." Lunara heard herself say the words, hardly believing they were leaving her lips.

She hadn't before. Not really. Her only plan had been to slip away from whoever insisted on accompanying her so she could go blindly bumbling into the chasms one-by-one without endangering anyone.

She didn't need to do that anymore. Not when all of the answers were right there, inside of her.

Magnus stepped closer, head dropping so he could meet her eyes. "Anything, witchling, and I will help you. We'll all help you."

"I am the Evesong's cursed blessing." Lunara looked up at him. "And I am ready."

Ready to claim Illamiata.

Ready to wield that blinding vengeance.

Ready… for Brand.

55

OKTHANA WAS SENDING HIM A MESSAGE. SHE HAD TO BE.

What else could those vulgar, undead serpents have been for?

Maybe she'd overheard his interrogation of Baldrir, and was looking to make him aware of the fact. Reminding him of where his loyalty was meant to be. Playing him for a fool.

Then again, knowing he'd asked questions was not the same as knowing *why*. She was smart, but she couldn't read minds, and putting it all together was probably beyond her feeble imagination.

Endellion, as usual, had been no help whatsoever.

"There's no way Okthana knows," he whispered to himself. "No fucking way."

The information he'd coaxed from Baldrir was innocent enough. He might still be able to convince her it had just been a bit of fun to learn about the Battle of Breamwyrm. Among other things.

He'd have to do some groveling, of course, and find a way to remove Brand from her clutches—preferably before she could convince the Imperial Demon to help her and ruin every fucking thing he'd been working towards as a result.

His dungeons were compromised regardless. If she hadn't actually found them, he'd be doing a lot of work for nothing, but no harm was done. If she *had*, it wouldn't be long before she meddled in ways he couldn't tolerate, whether she knew his secrets or not.

Either way, she'd fucked his peace. It had been weeks since her attack and he'd had yet to hear from her. Sure, he'd been up to his fucking eyeballs in keeping up appearances, but she always knew where to find him. She should've said something by now.

Not like he could come right out and ask her if she'd happened to realize his duplicity. Whether he liked it or not, he still needed the bitch.

What a fucking mess.

Unless…

Maybe there was a way he could make it a mess *she* would have to clean up. One she'd have no way to blame him for. After all, he was merely Okthana's lowly servant. Incapable, as far as she knew, of what he was thinking of doing.

Yes. It might work. He'd have to be sure she was distracted, but—

A rustle and hissed whispers snagged him from the maze of his mind and pacing.

"Ah-ah. Trying to escape again?" He plucked the bent hairpin from Nyriadne's bruised fingers and tapped her nose with it. "Naughty."

He thought he'd gotten them all during her first attempt early on. Silly him for not checking her everywhere. Although, he was sort of curious to know how she'd gotten hold of it when her toes were barely scraping the floor. Her arms should've been out of their sockets by now, dangling as she was. He'd have to keep a better eye on the crafty chit.

Lucky for him, he finally had a little time to himself.

"Trying? We *will* escape." Her eyes positively burned through the matted clumps of her black hair. "Today, tomorrow. Doesn't matter if it takes a bloody year. We'll get out and I'll make sure to tell every creature we meet what you're doing down here, you disgusting bast—"

The back of his hand connected with her soft cheek, a satisfying *crack!* echoing above the din of captivity.

Naughty and annoying. Sweet Night, no one talked as much as she did. And yet, she didn't make a single sound when struck.

Interesting.

"Don't fucking touch her! Don't even look at her!"

Oh, how he adored the musical sound of chains rattling and creatures thinking they still had control.

"You know, Baldrir…" He sauntered over to his first Straelani prize, drawing the hairpin across the Demon's chapped lips. "One would think you'd remember how little those sort of demands affect me. Shall I refresh your memory?"

"You've already done your worst to me. I survived once, I'll do it again and again."

He clicked his tongue. "You were rather fortunate, weren't you? Lunara is an absolute wonder. Sadly, she's also occupied at the moment, what with Brand missing and all. Bringing you back from the Veil a second time will not be on her list of priorities. *If* they ever find you. Which they won't."

A gasp sounded from Nyriadne. "Brand is missing? Do you have him? Tell us where he is!"

Both he and Baldrir ignored her to stare each other down. A delightful battle of wills.

What fun.

"You don't scare me."

For all the bravery Baldrir's words boasted, the tremble in his voice was like a heady wine—utterly intoxicating. He never should've neglected them for so long and denied himself the pleasure.

"No? Ah, but you're not using that hard head of yours, my friend! You may not care about yourself anymore, but you care about them."

He gestured to the silent contingent of Demons he'd stolen along with the siblings. Twelve pairs of eyes stared back at him from all sides, the rage suppressed within them shining through like starfire as they observed the exchange between captor and commander.

"And *'care'*... Well, that's far too tame a term for our Nyriadne, isn't it?"

Baldrir blanched, a muscle twitching beneath one eye.

Oh, yes. The Demon was beginning to understand his circumstances.

"You see, nothing went to plan." He perused the warriors as he spoke to Baldrir, arms crossed. "I still haven't gotten what I need from the Montrealm, and I'm of a mind to place the blame at your feet. Remember what I told you would happen if you failed me, Baldrir?"

"I delivered your fucking message exactly as you asked."

"Hmm. I suppose my definition of failure is a bit more fluid than that."

Lantern light flickered on a female Demon's face, highlighting the perfect curve of her jutting cheekbone. Fitting, for the fiery Frida.

"Your subpar history lesson and inattention to detail forced me to extract the necessary information myself. It would've been fine, except all that work amounted to nothing. Your lack has become my problem, ergo…"

Wait.

Scanning the Demons, he searched their haggard faces as the beat of his heart picked up speed. They were changed from their month spent wasting away, gaunt and filthy, but not so much he wouldn't be able to find one in particular if he was here.

Ah! *Yes*.

"Oh, this gets better and better."

He closed the distance, more pleased than ever he'd chosen to secure the group in a rounded offshoot from the main cavern. The tight circle would ensure they could all see.

"Fate's favor shines upon me once again." He grabbed Aldiat's clenched jaw and jostled his head before slamming it onto the stone wall. "Your sister *and* your best friend, Baldrir!"

Taking the whole contingent mid-battle had been something of a panicked decision on his part. He'd been right in the middle of sending that meddlesome Fae to the Veil *again* when the attack had started, and he'd had to scramble. Okthana told him he would know when her 'surprise' was in play, and she'd been right. He just hadn't been ready for it. Whatsoever.

His fault, for underestimating her.

Then again, he could hardly be held accountable for her deciding to become an unpredictable fucking cunt lately.

"Here's how this is going to work." A new strategy came together as he walked backwards into the center of the space, keeping his gaze on Baldrir. "I made you a promise I intend to keep. You're going to watch as I slowly disassemble your friends. I'd like you to take the opportunity to dig deep. Remember everything you can. That way, by the time I make it to those who matter most, you fully understand the stakes of any ongoing incompetence."

"They have nothing to do with this," Baldrir hissed. "I'll tell you the Breamwyrm story again, every version I know, and whatever else you want. Just let them go."

"I don't think you're understanding me, so let me simplify. There are fourteen of you here. At least ten will be peeled apart layer-by-layer because I fucking told you what would happen if you let me down, and I'm a firm believer in following through. That said, I'm willing to make you another promise: learn your lesson, give me something I can actually use by the time I'm done with them, and Nyri, Aldiat, and Frida will die swift deaths as a reward. If not, I'll ensure what they experience is multitudes worse than anything else you're about to witness." He raised his voice, spinning in a leisurely circle. "That goes for all of you. Disclose something relevant, and your pain ends."

"Just kill us and be done with it!" Nyri shouted. "None of us are going to say a word to help you, so you may as well save yourself the effort."

Night spare him from any more headstrong females. Endellion and Okthana were already exhausting the meager limits of his patience.

He went right up to her, dropping his head to look her in the eye and be sure she was paying attention. "I understand your feelings for me are less than positive. I'd like for all of you to try adjusting your mindsets. Don't think of it as helping *me*, per se…"

Loosing a fraction of his considerable power, he donned Baldrir's likeness and pinched her chin, tilting her face closer so he could watch the fear take root.

"More along the lines of everyone you know and love."

Another burst, and he was wearing Hedda's skin, the hitch in her breath nothing compared to the silent calculation he knew was taking place—that scrambling in the mind while she tried to figure out whether this was the first time he'd done so in her presence.

It was, but she didn't know that.

"If it fit into my plans, I could bring all of Straelon to its knees."

When he reshaped himself into Lyriat, her lip began to tremble, that effervescent spark she carried through life fading the tiniest bit.

Beautiful.

"Until now, the triflings of a single realm have been beneath me, the scope of my goals encompassing far more than you could ever dream of. However, if you'd like to continue being difficult, I'm willing to deviate from my current venture for a little while."

One last shift, just to drive his point home.

"You…" she whispered, the tears in her brown eyes spilling over as realization dawned.

"As you can see, I'd have some finagling to do, but I'd be happy to take the extra time to prove to you that I really, *really* do not fuck around when I want something, Nyriadne."

Their stunned silence was like a drug, but he knew a way to improve upon the buzz starting up in his veins.

"Now that we understand one another,"—Misting through the ether, he appeared before a grizzled male and thrust the hairpin directly into his eye socket—"shall we begin?"

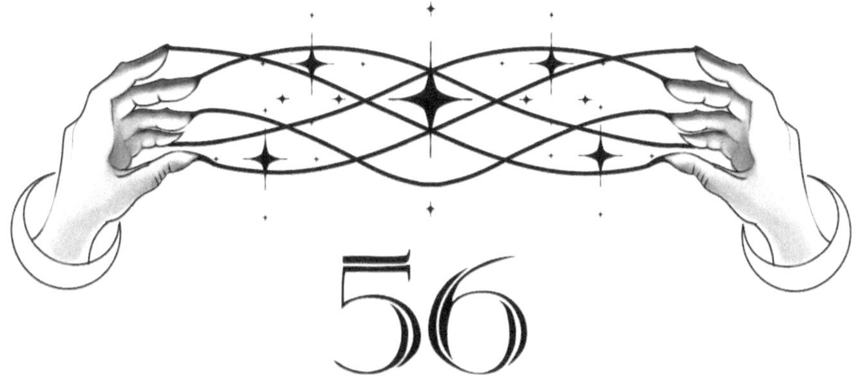

56

STEPPING INTO THE NIGHT-SHROUDED EVESONG—DIRECTLY INTO ITS CAPITAL—was one of the hardest things Lunara had ever done. Like she was leaving Brand behind with every added inch between her and the portal, though the entire purpose of coming here was to do whatever it took to find him again.

A practice in torture.

A tug at her sleeve, and Lunara looked over to see Fern gaping, mesmerized as her steps slowed. She wished she could see Nachthelliae that way again, through fresh eyes. Could behold Starkeep with none of her history and feel the same awe.

It was a truly stunning place.

Galaxies flowed like a river above them, cutting through the black of night and casting their light down over the cityscape. In answer, the buildings and streets hummed with a vibrant glow, everything crafted of glimmering moonstone that sparkled in rainbow prisms like the skin of her people.

Sharp, needle-like spires shot out from the rooftops and reached for the cosmos, stacked in endless, crowded layers. They stretched higher and tighter with each level of the city streets, thinning out to a single peak at the very center.

The Elder Halls. Illamiata's resting place.

From the top of that tower, one could look out and behold the

Evesong, dark and vast, every acre twinkling with luminescent flora and fauna. It was a dizzying view, even for experienced Sorcerit. Up was down, down was up, the sky and the ground mirroring each other so closely that it distorted perception and twisted the mind.

Others, creatures who'd never been and didn't know, might climb up to look out for the first time and be utterly petrified when they realized the truth—that Starkeep hovered in thin air, jutting up like a mountaintop missing its base, the entire city suspended miles and miles above the shadowy forests below.

All to be closer to the celestial light the Evesong and its people fed from.

Lunara fucking hated it here.

"This is your home?"

Lunara threw a glance over her shoulder to check the progress of their companions. Brand's brothers had insisted on coming. On being here for her when he couldn't. It was enough to bring her to her knees, going from no one to the entire Imperial Family calling her their own.

Are you sure you should trust it? Are you sure that it's true?

She wasn't. Not yet. Not… quite.

Magnus and Thaddeus were a few yards back, dodging the crowd that was ever near the Upper Portal, Araxis just behind. Vann came through next, followed by Amal. The *ajma* darted her keen eyes over everything, spear at the ready as Amunkar entered behind her.

All far enough away that they shouldn't be able to witness her seemingly speaking to no one.

"You don't have to whisper, Fern," she said out of the corner of her mouth. "I'm the only one who can see and hear you. Just stay close and try not to run into anyone. And no, this is not my home. Not anymore."

Home was smiling hazel eyes and fiery hair. Home was the way he said her name and stole her breath. Home was missing.

Gone. Gone. Gone.

As far as anyone knew, Lunara had put Fern back into a deep sleep to help her mind heal, and had been left behind on her stone pallet. With any luck, the spell she'd set on the Fae's room might help them identify the one who'd harmed her. Who'd massacred an entire village and lured them to the aftermath. Who'd probably helped to steal Brand.

She wanted to see their likeness so she could ruin them.

Magnus reached her side, eyes dancing over the space around her. "All is well, witchling?"

He was the only one who knew what she'd done with Fern. He'd howled with laughter when she'd told him about her antics at that first dinner, and later with Brand at the Occurrence. A relief, to see him mischievous again, if only briefly.

One of them needed to smile, and she didn't have it in her.

He'd supported her plan wholeheartedly, but they'd both been worried the spell might break through the portal crossing. Hence the anxious look in his eyes.

"Perfect." She nodded her head towards Fern to show him where she was.

His shoulders slumped. "Thank the Sisters."

"I really wish he'd tell me who the fuck he's always talking to," Fern muttered, her brown eyes focused intently on Magnus. "It's irritating to hear only one side of a conversation, especially when it's about me half the pissing time."

Lunara had no idea what she was talking about. "What do you mean?"

Fern blinked at her for a second before sighing. "Please tell me I'm not the only one hearing a disembodied voice whenever his arse is around."

No way.

Before she could respond and find out whether that voice was the same as her own, a crotchety grumble reached her ears.

"I was sure you'd be halfway up the spire by now, Moonweaver."

Lunara's heart stopped and thudded over, galloping when it resumed its beating. Seeing her would make it real. Would make it so there was no going back.

She turned and found Cordelia, of all people, holding fast to Araxis as they approached, her arm looped through his. Her hair, pure and white as starlight, was braided into a thick rope over her shoulder. She was mindlessly running her fingers down the plait as if it were some kind of pet, and Lunara had the sudden, disjointed thought that perhaps Cordelia was where she'd picked up the habit of twisting her own curls.

"I'm told you've come to claim your rightful place." She stopped in front of Lunara, a head shorter, and peered up. "Good. About time."

So few words, and yet there was so fucking much to unpack from them.

"About time?"

Oh, sure. You've not seen her in years, and that's what you lead with?

A year. And yes. Fewer words were better where Cordelia was concerned. It hurt less.

Stormy eyes perused her. That they looked glassy and hopeful must've been a trick of the light. "Don't you remember this wasn't here before?" She grabbed Lunara's hand in hers, twisting her palm up and running a finger along that one strange freckle on the inside of her wrist.

The one Brand had been so drawn to the day they'd formally met, his thumb passing back and forth over the spot and making her shiver. The one he'd kissed so many times since then.

She had to fight not to snatch away from Cordelia's touch. "That's always been there," she argued, hardly able to understand how she'd gotten here. How she was even having this conversation.

"No." Cordelia dropped her hand, her eyes closing. "I remember the shock of seeing it there like it was yesterday, your arm raised to hold the door open when you finally let me in the first time—years after *he* was already dead—glaring like a beacon. The mark of a Keeper."

Her voice was hardly audible, but Lunara still jolted and looked around to see if anyone had heard. She was here to claim the stone and its power, not announce herself.

The second the terror wore off, Cordelia's words sank in. "You knew?"

Lunara examined the oblong spot, mind racing, only just realizing the fleck looked alarmingly similar to a large teardrop.

"I did, and I've never breathed a word. I had my reasons. And before that, I knew you were special. Different, in all the ways that mattered." Cordelia stepped closer and reached up to cup Lunara's cheek. "Araxis has told me everything. I'm here to help."

They shouldn't be having this conversation, not where anyone might hear, but she couldn't bring herself to break away. To detach herself from a moment that felt a whole lot like she was healing from something.

String music started up and floated on the air from somewhere nearby as Vann, Amal, and Amunkar finally joined them. The crowd swelled as more and more people poured in from the portal, making their way to dinner or the theater. Some headed towards it, jumping right through or stopping at one of the many stalls selling tolls.

No matter which direction they were going, nearly all of them took a stumbling moment to gape at her companions.

"We have to move," she said, nodding at Cordelia. "If you're here to help, then you know I can't be found out. Not yet. I have to take it and go."

Cordelia gave her a pat, tucking her hair away. "We'll figure out the rest later, as we always have."

Swallowing, Lunara picked her way through the surging mass, leading the others past countless Nachthellians in their finest robes or glittering dresses. When she reached the central fountain—a grotesque thing depicting the Star Goddesses on their weeping deathbed as it rose up—she climbed the steps to its rounded oasis. There were far less people milling around the marble monstrosity, and it would be easier for them to talk.

Conversations over wine and under the stars filtered up to her from the outdoor restaurants, rife with tittered laughter and vapid murmurings. The sound of it made her skin crawl.

Lunara could probably throw a stone and hit her childhood home from here. Or, the rebuilt tower that'd replaced it.

Thad plopped down onto the fountain's edge with a contented sigh. Unbeknownst to anyone but Lunara, Fern hopped up too and crouched beside him, a thoughtful look on her face as she beheld the young wolflord.

"I fucking love Starkeep," Thad said, splashing the water and wholly unaware that a Fae was only inches away from his own face.

"Makes one of us," Lunara mumbled, crossing her arms.

Thad gasped dramatically. "How could you not?" he demanded, incredulous. "No matter what time it is, there's that evening promise in the air. A dark frivolity, waiting at the edges to snatch you up and carry you away. It's perfect."

"It's wretched," she countered. "And weren't you forbidden from being here?"

He waved her jab away. "I left a note. Besides, Da's so overwhelmed with everything, he'll never even notice I'm gone."

Thad held Fern's attention for about ten seconds before she stood and began pacing, dipping her booted toe into the fountain and glancing up at Magnus every so often.

"We need a plan."

"No need. No one of note is in there tonight."

"What?" Lunara narrowed her eyes on Cordelia. "Why?"

Her look was impish. "Someone may have told the Council that the Keeper has been found. They're all at a party celebrating the young male before he receives the Tear Stone tomorrow morning. And because they're desperate, no one has thought to check that the mark on his arm is real." Her wink was wicked, and Lunara had the insane urge to laugh.

It can't possibly be that easy. Why is she suddenly helping? How do you know it isn't a trick to capture you?

She didn't, but there was something in Cordelia's face that drew her in. A mix of sorrow and love and regret that—paired with the twinge in Lunara's gut—said she could be trusted.

Lunara looked up to gauge Amunkar's reaction just as his stately image manifested in front of the towering building behind him.

Sorcerit were obsessed with power, even if it wasn't their own—especially the Imperial Line. They showed their appreciation by enchanting sparkling particles of light to rise up and form colossal, statuesque versions of the people they were honoring. Every evening, for as long as she could remember.

First, each Elder would be displayed in succession, followed by the Imperials. She used to cheer when her parents' images appeared, longing to see herself there. The last time she'd witnessed the spectacle, the Sons had been as young as she, only included in a family portrait where all of them had gathered together as one.

It had likely been many years since they'd stood for their individual renderings to be captured, but Lunara hadn't been in this part of the Upper Block since her parents had died. She'd clung to the shadowed alleyways instead, only staying as long as was necessary to determine whether her skills were truly needed before escaping just as quickly, without being seen.

In a bizarre twist, Amunkar was currently standing in the exact same position as his massive, rotating likeness—arms crossed, eyebrow raised, feet planted as he gazed upon Starkeep like the emperor he would be.

The portrait disintegrated, bits of light falling to the ground and quickly reforming in Vann's likeness. "Sisters save us, not me too," he groaned. "They never get my eye right."

Instead of wholly black, the particles had concentrated there to make his one eye entirely gold, which was somehow even more unnerving than the reality.

The lights had barely finished shifting again before Thaddeus was gaping. "Ach, Mag," he groaned, pretending to gag. "That's just not right."

Magnus was entirely too proud of himself.

Lunara could hardly believe her eyes. If Amunkar's had been stoic, and Vann's slightly unsettling, his portrait was suggestive. At best.

His arms were crossed in his as well, but the cheeky Wolflord had sunk his teeth into his bottom lip mid-smirk and tilted his head just enough that it had made his eyelids heavy. The sleeves were torn off of his ceremonial battle robe, and his tattooed biceps bulged bigger than her head beneath the tattered hems.

He looked like he was trying to tempt all of the Upper Block into going to bed with him.

"Oh, Magnus, that's..."

Unfortunately, they all realized too late.

The particles fell and rose, and a giant, golden Brand was staring back at her.

"Ah, fuck," Magnus whispered.

Indeed.

Brand's arms were down, hands fisted at his sides, like he had no idea what to do with them. His arched brows were furrowed slightly, eyes a little wild and jaw clenched, like he'd barely forced himself to stand still long enough for the image to be rendered.

He looked savage, like every inch of the brutal warrior he was, but Lunara knew in her soul how intensely uncomfortable he'd been. Knew he'd stood there wishing he was anywhere else—somewhere filled with peaceful quiet.

Shitting stars, it hurt.

Fern appeared like a ghost. "You'll find him, I can feel it."

Before Lunara could sift through the emotions choking her to formulate a response, Araxis was in front of her. "Come," he said, gripping her shoulder and turning her away. "I already know what I look like."

He herded her towards the other side of the fountain and the stations there. She stepped onto one of the levitating platforms waiting to whisk them up to the Elder Halls and forced herself into a mindless state—easier to ignore the thought that it was like being lifted up by her father, his greatest creation thrumming beneath her feet. Still here, though he was long gone.

Gone. Gone. Gone.

Fern slipped through the crystal barrier and pressed in close as Araxis joined them, leaving the others to follow on another platform.

A tear slipped down her cheek as they shot into the sky like a shooting star.

Up into Illamiata's domain.

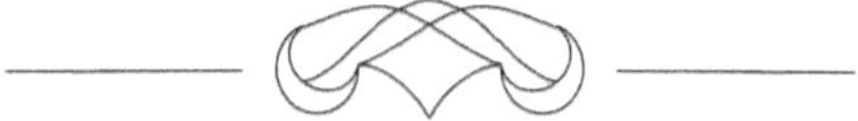

"It's even bigger than I remember," Lunara whispered.

She was hardly breathing as she gazed down at Illamiata, nestled in a maroon velvet pillow on its carved pedestal. The clear, drop-shaped stone sparkled beneath the lights, almost fluid, like the glittering Serpent Sea in Straelon.

And yet, even as it dazzled, there was something dark about it.

Fitting, since the bauble was allegedly the first tear each Sister cried, joining together and solidifying as they hit the ground, holding the deepest of their sorrows within.

It made her nervous. There was too much power in that first drop of regret. That first piece of glimmering evidence that the ones who'd released them had changed their hearts and been willing to admit it through their weeping—before they'd died.

Legend said it had been swept away as the Realm Rivers formed, riding the current all the way to the Evesong. Some claimed it was the reason for the endless night here, their despair radiating out from Illamiata and denying Solyrian's shining rays.

If that was true, then Nachthelliae was nothing more than a shrine of sorrow. A tomb of funereal darkness, ever mourning the loss of its creators.

As if reading her mind, Cordelia sidled up to her and said, "It's a rock,

Moonweaver. An important rock, yes, but don't give it influence it doesn't have. It holds enough already."

"What do I do, Cordelia?" She blew out a slow breath through pursed lips. Another. Calm settled over her like a too-thin blanket, panic thrashing beneath the surface. "Just… grab it?"

It's fine. You're fine. Breathe.

"Come," the Elder said, moving away. "Take a moment to find your focus."

The Tear Stone was held in an enchanted room above the Elder Halls, at the very top of the central, solitary spire that crowned all of Starkeep. It boasted no windows, no walls—nothing more than a mystical barrier that blocked the wind and weather, and kept visitors firmly inside its confines.

A monstrous ring of crystal was suspended in the air overhead, sharp shards of the same resting on its edges—six massive splinters that shot upwards and joined together like a dagger made of glass, the spaces between left open to the sky. From down here, the peak mimicked a brilliant star as it loomed and glimmered against the perpetual night.

When the moons aligned during Nachthelliae's Occurrence, their light would shoot down as if forcibly pulled to that highest point, power refracting from every piece and funneling into whichever Keeper held the stone. Or, at least, so she'd been told.

All that power in your body, at your fingertips. What if it eats you alive? Burns you up? Breaks you apart?

Shaking herself, she followed Cordelia to the low wall serving as an infinite bench around the room. A place to rest and absorb the unimpeded, full-circle view of Starkeep and beyond.

She'd only been up here once as a young girl, and it felt exactly the same as the first time.

Dizzying. Nauseating. Breathtaking. Like one wrong move would send her spinning away into the unending cosmos.

She sat near Cordelia, ignoring the yawning drop behind her. "I came barreling in, so sure. Now, I'm terrified all over again."

The others had stayed behind, distracting the guards with the honor of their presence as she'd slipped by with Cordelia. A good thing, she'd thought. She'd wanted to do it alone, as she'd done almost everything else in her life. To climb the steps and face her *fear* in peace. If Brand couldn't be here, she didn't want anyone else.

Lunara wasn't sure how she'd found herself surrounded by so many she cared for. How she suddenly had the choice of whether to do something on her own or have companions to support her. How she had four brothers waiting below for any word they were needed.

She'd wanted to do it alone, but she'd been wrong.

"For what it's worth," Cordelia said, resting one elbow on the bench-back, "I have never, in all my long life, felt power like yours." She sighed and met Lunara's eyes. "It's bundled up inside you, screaming to break free. Even before you found your Brandir and accepted his gift, the bond, it was a force. Now?" She scoffed, a breathy sound that encompassed her disbelief. "You could probably feed the Evesong on that well of power alone. For *years.* After the trial all Keepers must face, Illamiata will only help you, and I have reason to be confident your fate does not lie in the culling. You are different. Trust me on that."

Something in her eyes…

'Only poor choices shaped the others, and you are not the same… Trust me, I would know.'

Shitting stars.

"You hear her, too. The Oracle."

Cordelia hummed, looking away. "A story for another time, but yes. Since just before you were born. Not that the mad creature made much sense. Not until—" She shook her head. "Another time."

For some reason, Lunara couldn't muster even an ounce of surprise.

Brand first, answers later.

Illamiata first. Or have you forgotten why you're here?

Right. Yes. Face her greatest fear to find her fate. Easy.

Sure. Keep telling yourself that.

A hand landed on her shoulder. As if she'd summoned him, Lunara looked up to find Magnus standing above her.

"Thought you might be needing us about now, witchling," he murmured.

"H-how?"

He smiled and sat beside her, allowing her to see everyone else filtering up from the stairs as he hiked a thumb at Amunkar. "Ask him."

"It was the right time." The First Imperial Son had a strange look as he gazed out over the city. "It *is* time."

Magnus shifted, his arm wrapping around her. "Besides, did you really think we'd let you do this without keeping an eye on you?"

One-by-one, Brand's remaining brothers crowded in close as Amal guarded the stairs, Fern unseen beside her.

Vann knelt and laid a hand on her knee. "Brand would be right here, if he could be. We'll do no less in his place, little sister."

"I'm scared," she admitted.

"Ach, you're the fiercest lass I've ever met." Thad gripped his nape. "You'll be fine, aye?"

He sounded about as sure as she felt.

Araxis threw his shoulders back, clearly uncomfortable with the sentiment thickening the air. "You are the rightful Keeper, and the stone will not harm you. Not once have your predecessors suffered ill effects in the beginning. The rest will come later, and we have time for that if or when it happens. Brand…" His jaw clenched. "Brand does not have time for you to be afraid."

No. He didn't.

"You'll stay? You'll be here when it's done?"

Magnus gave her a little shake. "Aye, witchling. Right here."

Looking at them, tucked in close and supporting her, gave her the strength to rise on trembling legs. They parted, clearing the path that would take her to the pedestal.

One foot in front of the other and she was suddenly there. Somehow, Illamiata didn't seem quite so large anymore. Didn't feel as daunting as she stretched her shaking fingers towards it.

For Brand.

As if from a great distance, she faintly heard Cordelia say, "Keep to the perimeter, Your Highnesses, and brace yourselves."

Just before contact, Lunara heard the faintest laughter.

And then the world exploded.

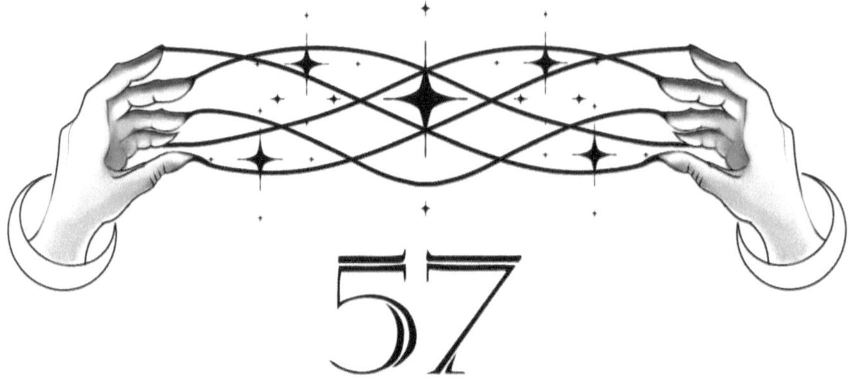

57

So warm. So bright.

So empty.

Lunara couldn't tell whether she was moving. Everything was white on white, as far as the eye could see. No ground. No horizon. No sky.

No way to tell how long she traveled, or gauge the time. It wasn't until she saw a dark spot in the distance that she had a goal.

She ran, sprinting for that far-off thing until the details cleared and she stopped dead in her tracks.

Two rows of doors waited, angled slightly in to face her. Different shapes and sizes, different colors, nothing between or behind them.

Her steps were tentative as she walked between them, eyes darting. More than once, her feet stumbled when she recognized one of the panels, long lost memories jumping up to accompany the sight. They followed her life, aging with her, the recollections becoming more and more recent. She nearly fell over when she reached one that was an exact replica of the carved double-doors in Lyriat's great hall, a vision of Nyri's laughing face as she showed her around flashing in disjointed stills.

That was all fine.

What surprised her most was the gilded door at the very end. Teeming with intricate designs, a massive, curving handle in its center, it was the one from her dreams. The one she was never allowed to pass through.

It stood front and center, like an end to all things.

And there, lying on the floor in front of it, was a female—twiddling her thumbs as she looked up at absolutely nothing. She wore a plain white shift that blended with the landscape so completely it gave the impression she was naught more than a head, arms, and legs. Her feet were bare, crossed over each other and rocking back and forth with seeming impatience.

"Hello?"

The female froze, her only movement a smile stretching across her face before she bounded up in a blur and rushed for Lunara. "You're here!"

Shitting stars. You know that voice.

She didn't bother to mask her shock. Couldn't have even if she'd wanted to. "It's… you. The Voice."

For the first time, those familiar giggles reached her ears, instead of banging around inside her skull. "It's me!" She swept Lunara into a crushing hug. "Though, I wish people would stop calling me that."

The female released her, stepping back with an exuberant look. She was tall and lithe. Ethereal. *Beautiful.* Her violet eyes were wide and excited as they danced over Lunara, as if she'd never seen another person before and had been waiting ages for her first glimpse.

"Where are we?"

"The actual explanation is incredibly complicated, but—very simply and for lack of a better description—this is a pocket of your mind."

Would have thought there was a bit more to it, honestly.

The female laughed, as if she'd heard her thoughts. Then again…

Lunara swallowed. "You don't… live here, do you?"

You might be even crazier than you ever thought.

It was strange to see the sad look that flitted across her face, like it didn't belong. "Sometimes, yes. Sort of. When I wish to feel safe or see the light." She snapped out of her melancholy so fast that Lunara recoiled in surprise. Bouncing on the balls of her feet, she said, "So this is it—the moment we've all been waiting for. What do you think? How are you feeling?"

"Um…"

Lunara didn't know *what* she was feeling. Sort of nothing. The last she remembered, she'd been brushing Illamiata's glassy surface with no idea what to expect.

Certainly not this.

Are you dead?

The female threw her head back and laughed, a wild sound that had Lunara's lips curling in response. "No, little moth. You aren't dead. Well, you might be soon. It depends on you."

Comforting.

"It really isn't," the female said matter-of-factly.

So many pressing matters, but only one thought was able to solidify in her mind. A mystery that had been burning within her for decades. "What's your name? Who are you really?"

Her smile morphed into a thoughtful frown. "One moment, please." Her eyes went to the middle distance and began to glow, swirling with the very fabric of the Unknown before she blinked and it disappeared, muttering, "How interesting." She shook herself and smiled again. "I remember now. I can answer one of those questions without consequence, but not both, and only if you choose the right one. Which is it to be?"

Oh, sure. Zero pressure.

"It's really not. It's actually quite a lot of pressure and now you *have* to decide on one because, if you choose neither, it will… bring…" She grimaced and gripped her head. "Um, never mind that last bit."

"O-kay…" Lunara picked up an errant curl and twisted it in her fingers.

"Lots of choices today, I know, but you're doing wonderfully so far." She leaned in and narrowed her eyes, her brows raising as she pinched her lips between her teeth, as if she could urge Lunara in the right direction with the bizarre look.

She searched her face. This creature had always given her the answers, even if Lunara had been too dense to understand them. She was clever. Cared and helped, for whatever reasons, and Lunara was almost certain she already knew most of the answer to one of them. It made her hesitant to waste the chance on a confirmation, and—

Ah ha! *'I wish people would stop calling me that…'*

Both of their faces split into matching grins at the same time.

"What's your name?"

The air moved as the female rose from the floor on majestic, feathered wings, her hair defying gravity to float around her face and body. How Lunara had missed those attributes was no wonder—both were white as snow, as the rest of this strange place, blending perfectly like her shift had. Golden light poured from her skin when she spoke in a voice that boomed with infinite layers. "I am called Endellion," she proclaimed.

Sweet baby Sisters in a cradle…

Endellion's power was all-encompassing, all-consuming. It sucked the breath right out of Lunara's lungs and forced tears to her eyes. The warmth of it was staggering.

When her feet touched down again, she reverted instantly back to normal—as normal as she was capable of being—and Lunara sucked in a heaving gasp at the loss of it.

"Yay!" Endellion squealed. "Two out of three!"

"It's… lovely to finally meet you." Lunara was having trouble staying upright, her own power thrumming down every nerve ending, alive and buzzing, and growing by the second. "What's the third choice?"

Endellion's brow furrowed, suddenly serious. "The one that matters most." She turned to the golden door. "Two are there, without a doubt." Her voice was layered again, though less overwhelming than before. She pointed to Lunara, a crushing weight settling over her. "Two go in, but one comes out." Her voice dropped as she gripped Lunara's shoulder. "Is the light filled with love, or spiteful and mean? It is peace for the world, or the end of all things?"

Lunara buckled, her knees crashing to the floor. "What's happening to me?"

"*Things* are happening, moth, outside of our control. The dawn dwindles. You feel its crown slipping. You're out of time. You must choose, or die."

"Choose what?" Lunara grunted through clenched teeth. It was like being ripped apart at the seams, her flesh waiting for the moment it could spill free. "I think I'm already dying."

She crumpled fully to the floor, curling in on herself.

"Sweet, little friend. It's not you who's dying. The fourth tower has lost its heart and its hope. Its loss is yours."

The regret in Endellion's tone snagged her attention through the agony, even though she couldn't decipher the words. Not with the weight settling down and trying to snap her bones.

All this way, all this drama, just to die inside of your own damned head. Great.

"It really isn't," Endellion whispered. "Now you have to choose *quickly,* or die."

Lunara forced herself to all fours and drew jagged air into her lungs. Endellion had led her to this door—the door she'd dreamt of—and it had to mean something. Maybe the choice was to go through it.

She crawled, slipping over and over, losing her balance. Face-planting as she reached her arm out to touch it. More and more pressure bore down on her, her neck bent at a sickening angle as she cried out.

Cracking an eye open, Lunara found herself staring at the floor—and at the faint lines she hadn't noticed there before, creeping along and up into the gilded frame of the door. What had seemed so perfect from a distance was actually decaying, gold flakes sloughing away as veins of blue worked to dismantle it.

Blue, like the sea on a clear day.

'Turns out, little moon, that you are my favorite color.'

It suddenly didn't matter that her insides were liquefying, or that her skull was about to explode. Lunara scraped her body up and threw herself at it with a sob. Blood poured from her nose and mouth to splatter against the unending, pristine white as she reached the jamb and dug her fingernails into it, attempting to pull herself up.

Endellion was at her side in an instant, breathless and urgent. "Do you wish to go through?"

Lunara tried to answer, but all she did was cough up more blood.

"You must answer me, or I cannot help you!" Her hands hovered around Lunara, desperate, waiting for permission to move.

With what felt like the final gulp of air she would ever take, she choked out a garbled, "Yes."

Endellion gripped the back of her dress and hauled her from the floor like she weighed nothing, using her free hand to shove one of Lunara's against the knob.

Peace settled into her like a sigh. Certainty. Rightness. This was exactly where she was meant to be.

"You must go through of your own volition, moth." Endellion's voice was pleading. "There's nothing more I can do. Just go. The final choice awaits on the other side."

Lunara thought she nodded, but couldn't be sure. She did as she was told, leaning heavily against the panel as she finally cranked the handle and fell into a midnight sky with a scream—belatedly making sense of Endellion's last words.

Endellion sighed as Lunara slipped into her innermost mind. The darkest parts of herself.

Getting her here had been the most difficult task. The most unsure move in the game she was playing, the pieces she was arranging. She watched through the Sight as possibility after possibility died, narrowing down to two, side-by-side.

To one of the most pivotal moments she'd foreseen.

The Moonweaver had been perilously close to succumbing to the fracturing of her bond with the Demon. Of crumbling beneath the weight of his utter desolation.

A problem for later, but not *too* much later.

First, Lunara had to face the split in herself. The moth-shaped divide.

"Tell me, Sorcerit," she whispered to herself, "will your answer be right? Or will you consign us to doom-colored Night?"

Two were there, without a doubt. Two went in, but only one would come out.

The question was, which would it be?

If she was smart… If she was fast… If she trusted herself…

They'd make it just in time.

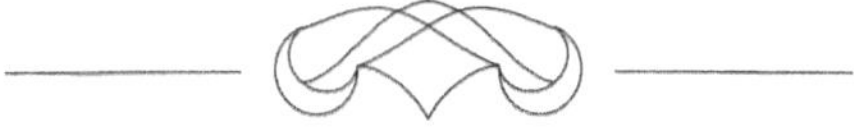

Lunara plummeted for an eternity. Stars and nebulas raced by on the edges of her vision, infinite galaxies bleeding into one another, until a blackened ground appeared below and rushed up beneath her.

Dust and debris flew as she crash-landed, knocking the air from her lungs. Staring up into the endless void, she took stock, fighting to steady herself. The impact hadn't hurt, and the pain from before had been erased the second she'd fallen through the door.

Endellion had assured her this was all in her mind, so Lunara wasn't fooled into a useless panic at finding herself back in the chasm—especially since this one was lacking all of the things that made the real one terrifying.

Little more than a dense, weighted emptiness, every breath thick and heavy.

She far preferred the blinding white from before to this stifling black and grey—aside from the faded orbs of dim light hovering drunkenly in a poor imitation of the spell she herself had cast in the actual chasm.

This bleak place was *inside of her*? Probably best if she didn't think about it too long.

Standing, she brushed the dust away from her hands and body, finding exactly nothing when she looked both ways down the rift.

"*You* are nothing."

She jolted, her insides clenching as the hair on the back of her neck rose. Maybe she'd imagined that rasping voice, scraping like cracked nails against the deepest parts of her.

"You are weak."

O-kay… Not imagined, after all.

"Who's there?" she called into the darkness.

"Such a disappointment. How can you even bear to look at yourself, Moonweaver?"

A hot, prickling wave of shame washed over Lunara from out of nowhere. She pressed shaking hands to her burning cheeks, confused as her chest tightened.

"Pathetic."

She hunched unbidden, her body making itself as small as possible, limbs tingling with fear.

Still, some small part of her rebelled against it, and anger spiked. Enough to clear the dark thoughts away. To remember this was *her* mind, and there was no more room for anyone else inside of it.

The only shame would be to listen to yet another fucking disembodied voice spewing unwanted vitriol.

"Show yourself!"

The air stirred violently, more dust and dirt flying as a dark swath gathered in the distance. Twisted laughter echoed all around her, rife with scorn. "You are worthless and broken, you daft witch. You wish to confront me? I dare you."

Lungs heaving, she tried to make sense of the creature bathed in shadow and gloom as she went forward on unsteady feet.

It turned to mist and rushed her, cackling as it pulled her hair. "Useless fool," it whispered directly into her ear. "How many have been hurt because of you? How many have you let down? Your parents, your mate. Even entire realms. Dead or suffering, because of you."

Lunara spun in place as it whipped like a cyclone around her, an elusive *something* pounding in her skull.

It manifested again mere feet away, looming above her and poised like a snake ready to strike. "Why do you even bother when you do nothing but fail?"

"What do you want from me?" Her demand sounded far more steady than she felt.

More hideous laughter rippled out, every mirthless chuckle slicing through her like a hot knife. "I want you to admit what a waste of space you are. That your life has been utterly pointless. Maybe I'll leave you alone. Maybe not. Only one way to find out."

Lunara fucking hated the tears that sprang forth, despised that she'd had that exact thought on lonely nights, even as she welcomed the seething piece of her that wished to *fight.*

So many stars-forsaken voices, slinking in and thinking to control her. Telling her what to do, who she was, how to be. Even Endellion had been a torture at times. Now this? No more. Her own damned thoughts weren't even—

"We speak to ourselves in the cruelest tone, don't we? It's your voice, but… not. A mantra that you beat against yourself, murmured painfully in the silence of your own mind."

Every jagged, horrible whip.

Shitting, fucking stars.

Lunara stumbled back, nausea swirling as the creature stepped into a pocket of light and showed itself. She'd said those words to Brand what felt like a lifetime ago, and here they were—a monster staring back at her with dull eyes and sallow skin, a sickening grin exposing sharpened teeth waiting to tear her apart.

A monster that was *her.*

"Yes. Now you understand." It crept forward until it was only inches away. "*You* did this. You wish to fight yourself? You're even crazier than we thought."

It was like looking into a cursed mirror. Lunara tried to keep her breaths even, tried not to sob, as she took in the lanky, stringy hair framing its grotesque visage. The tattered scraps of fabric barely covering gnarled and wasted limbs.

Reaching out a clawed hand, it ran a finger down Lunara's cheek. "Now you see how truly helpless you are." She finally heard the familiar notes of her own voice being twisted into something obscene. "Give in. Accept it. We will never be more than this."

Sisters help her, but part of Lunara believed it, even if she didn't fully understand. "What is *this,* exactly?"

The creature swelled, growing until it towered above her. "*This* is every lonely hour and unbearable day. Every horrific memory. Lost innocence and forgotten dreams. Isolation. Belittlement. Ignorance. Failure. Betrayal. Pain." It bent and gripped Lunara by the front of her dress. "This is hatred, and there is nothing more powerful."

With a flick of its wrist, Lunara was thrown across the chasm and into the cliffside, crumpling to the ground in a breathless heap. Its taloned foot was digging into her chest before she could right herself, pinning her to the ground. "Give in to the bitterness. Accept your spite. I will nurture it and wield a power so mighty that the realms will quake before us."

Lunara raised her eyes and met the familiar gaze staring back at her—blue orbs swirling and hypnotizing, pulling her in to their darkest depths.

Loathing filled her, sizzling down every nerve ending. Resentment wrapped itself around her like an old, beloved blanket. Power winked at her fingertips, deeper than before, drawing as much from the misery she held close as it did from the well.

This part of herself had saved her countless times before. Protected her, kept her company.

"Yes, let the darkness flow. Let it refashion you into something greater, so we may crush all in our path and have our vengeance."

She wanted vengeance with every fiber of her being. Wanted to scream it out over the land until her mate was returned to her.

Except, Lunara didn't want realms to quake before her. She hardly wanted to leave bed most mornings. Crushing all in her path would make her no better than Malachyr and the Council. And darkness? Darkness was the fucking problem.

This part of herself had saved her, but it had hurt her, too. Had convinced her so many times that she was *less.*

She wanted her vengeance, but not like this.

Not when she could still hear Brand—louder, stronger, more fierce—telling her she was all that was lovely and blessed in this world. Everything that was good. Not when he'd plucked her from the edge of death, over and over, and held her through the worst of herself.

Not when she had a choice.

Even if it killed her, she would be worthy of him—worthy of the love he offered at every turn, that she might give it back tenfold—and to do that…

'Is the light filled with love, or spiteful and mean?'

It crashed like a wave. Brutal, unforgiving in its heartbreak, stunning clarity in its wake.

To do that, Lunara first had to love herself.

She was the monster. The monster was her. She'd created this broken, horrific thing, and she was the only one who could fix it.

It was time to embrace the truth. It was time to embrace *herself.*

"Join with me." Its milky stare was crazed as it released her and offered a hand. "Give me control. Together, we'll wreak glorious havoc on our enemies. Together, we'll be unstoppable.

Lunara pushed to kneeling, peering up into a ravaged face so like her own. She hadn't noticed before how childlike it seemed. How fragile it really was. Hadn't heard the pleading notes. The absolute suffering in its tone.

A thought from before, so different now…

"There is untold power in that first, glimmering shard of regret." Her voice was soft as she stood. Soothing. "Such mighty strength in that first step towards changing your heart for the better."

It bent and roared into her face, spittle flying. "Stem this weakness, you arse-brained bitch. It will not help him." Shrieking, it backhanded her with enough force that her feet left the ground.

She landed with a thud, immediately pushing herself upright with trembling arms. "You deserved so much more than the poison I fed you." She planted her feet, already braced for the next attack.

Lunara wasn't scared. Not anymore.

It flew towards her, serrated claws slicing across her body. Blood poured from the wounds, but Lunara refused to back down.

"You are not a bane." Its other hand slashed down her face. "You are not a curse." It shoved her to the ground and straddled her, wrapping its long fingers around her throat. "You are not a ninny, or a halfwit, or an eejit. You are not a fool. You are not mad. Not crazed. Not ridiculous." It squeezed, choking her. "You are not a monster," she wheezed, black spots dancing in her vision. "You... are not... alone."

The creature reared back and leapt away, malformed muscles straining as it bellowed to the sky.

Lunara didn't pay her injuries any heed—just blinked back the haze of blood loss and regained her feet.

"What are you doing?" it hissed, panting as Lunara inched closer.

She was moving on instinct. Doing something she should've done a long time ago.

Reaching out, Lunara grasped the creature by the face. "I'm sorry," she whispered, smoothing a greasy lock of hair. It wailed at the contact, trying to jerk away, but Lunara held fast. "I'm so sorry."

Its features were a mask of confusion, chest heaving as Lunara stepped even closer. "Don't do this," it rasped. "Don't—"

Lunara pulled it close and—for maybe the first time in her life—wrapped *herself* in loving arms.

"Please forgive me." Tears flowed unchecked as she tightened her embrace. "I would have us whole again, dear one."

The creature tensed in her hold. "What is this?"

"You are strong." She spoke over its growls and the snapping of its teeth. "You are lovely." Over its gasps and whines as it weakly thrashed, uncertainty in the splintered sound. "You are worthy."

Silence. Such deafening, wondrous *silence* in her mind.

So slowly it might have taken hours, crooked, emaciated arms lifted around her with a whimper.

The smile starting to spread across Lunara's face was wiped away by the searing agony that engulfed her body, her mind ceasing to function.

Gathered over decades and bottled in this nightmarish place, it was her own pain that battered relentlessly against them. Worse than any healing she'd done before, than any physical wound she'd experienced.

They held on with clenched fists as a storm picked up—a tempest that tangled hair and clothes together. That merged breaths and skin, even as it tore ragged sobs from their throats.

It lifted them, pulling their feet from the ground with suffocating intensity, but she forced herself to speak—to scream—the final, most important thing above the howling wind.

"You are loved, Lunara!"

Light exploded from within them, shattering the darkness and landscape in one, fell swoop. Both versions of her rose above the sweeping damage. Boulders plummeted and cliffs crumbled, brittle as it all disintegrated beneath the beams of their power, until nothing was left but blinding warmth.

Only one thing left to do.

Lunara wept as she took the damaged creature into herself. Into the safety of her heart. Her skin stretched and her skull ached, ribs and limbs cracking beneath the pressure…

The slightest shift melded the two battered pieces of her and locked them perfectly together. Two halves of a greater whole, joined as one.

She pressed a hand to her chest—to the glowing stone now resting there—and laughed.

58

It was like air and breathing. Cool water in the heat. A lover's kiss amidst down feathers.

Lunara had never known true ease. Had never known herself.

Until now.

Gleaming below the hollow of her collar bones, it was like Illamiata was always and only meant to be hers. Like it had been waiting since the creation of the world to be nestled there. The hum of it was a song in her bones she hadn't known how to sing before. A chorus that drowned out every twinge and ache and swell. Silenced every weakness. And the power?

It was *consuming*, and it was hers.

"Weeping, fucking shite." Magnus stood stock-still before her, his eyes wide as saucers.

Araxis appeared at her side, gripping her elbow as her feet touched down. "Behold, the blessed Keeper of Illamiata. You did well, Lunara. Very well."

Had she ever even felt the floor before? Had her nerves ever fired thus, sending every sensation as they should?

No. Never. And it's glorious.

Yes. Glorious to feel not just the coolness of the stone beneath her bare soles as she took her first steps, but every worn crack and crevice. Every tiny hole. Every thrum of the energy it had to offer.

"Are you alright, witchling?"

Her laugh tinkled in a manner she'd never heard, delighting her. "In some ways, I feel as though I have never been well until this moment." Stars above, was that her voice, trilling and warbling like a flock of songbirds?

Yes, you have. With him, you were more than well—you were perfect. Else, what was it all for?

She was right, of course, and a blanket of melancholy tempered the heights of her exhilaration.

Brand. He, his love, was the only thing better than this.

She wanted him back.

Then you *need to come back.*

A blink, and she centered. A breath, and she settled into corporeality. Into a freshened mind and body that finally knew who it was and what it wanted.

"Thank fuck." Magnus sagged, cheeks puffing as he loosed a forceful sigh. "There you are. I was worried you were going to be eldritch forever."

Lunara recoiled. "Eldritch?"

"Aye, everything was glowy and shite. Silvered. Even your hair. And that smile? Ominous as fuck." He shuddered, even as he smirked at her. "It wasn't right."

She shoved her hand in his face, pushing it away. "Mangy arsehole."

"Aye, most of the time." He laughed, batting at her arm. "You're fine, though? Truly?"

There was a spark of worry in his golden stare that pulled at her heartstrings. "I'm…" It was her turn to exhale, melting a bit. "Let's agree to never do this again."

She practically fell over when Araxis chuckled.

"As warming as this is," Cordelia piped in, still sitting in her same spot on the rounded bench, "you've only got minutes before half the Evesong comes barreling up here, Moonweaver."

"Aye, it was quite the spectacular light show you put on, witchling."

"She's right," Thaddeus said, head tilted towards the stairs. "I can hear them already."

Shite.

Darting a frantic look around, she spotted Fern, perched on the pedestal where Illamiata had been resting like she owned the place. "Where are Amunkar and Amal? Vann?"

"Our future Emperor said he would know when to find us later, whatever the fuck that means. Likewise, Vann said there was something he needed to do before he met us back in the Montrealm. Again, cryptic and meaningless."

Lunara didn't have time for the small twist of disappointment in her gut. She'd done what she came to do, and the Tear Stone was hers.

It was time to find her mate.

Murmurs started up from the stairwell, growing louder. The way was long and winding, so they had a few minutes yet, but they were trapped.

"Calm." Araxis rounded her, his hand on her shoulder. "You already know what to do."

Leave finding out how in the arsing realms he knew what you were thinking for later.

Right.

"I don't." She squared her shoulders. "Tell me."

"We're going to mist, obviously."

It's fine. You're fine.

For the first time, those four words uplifted and encouraged, instead of being bitten-out with underlying impatience. For the first time, she believed them.

"Show me."

"Reach your power out and latch on to mine. I will carry us this first time. Pay attention. It should come to you fairly naturally if you let yourself feel it." He gripped her hand and gestured for Magnus and Thaddeus to come closer. "We were born for this, Lunara. Use that knowledge to your advantage."

She did as he said, sending out her threads—and had to stifle a grimace when the magic swept out and away from her and actually *slammed* into him, rocking his body backwards.

Araxis grunted, but gave no other sign he was offended by her lack of control. "Think of it like there's ten of you now, and adjust."

She nodded and pulled some of it back, the invisible particles surrounding them greeting one another like long-lost friends.

"More like a thousand," Cordelia murmured, "but who's counting?"

Lunara chewed the inside of her cheek and retracted even more of her power, one ear on the advancing racket. "Are you coming with us?"

It was odd to find herself hoping the answer would be yes. That they might have more time to mend the rift between them.

"I am not." Cordelia looked away, out over the sparkling city. "Someone has to make excuses and smooth ruffled feathers. Might as well be me."

"Then… I will see you soon."

Her eyes glittered. "Yes, Moonweaver. You will."

With a pointed look at Fern, who hopped down and wrapped an arm around Lunara's waist, they were ready.

She was ready.

"Remember"—Araxis's fingers tightened around hers—"let yourself feel it."

The smallest parts of themselves began to vibrate, shimmying into the space *between.* Into the invisible pockets and thoroughfares of the ether's expanse. She sensed Araxis's control over their particles, his steadfast hold. Sensed the moment he chose their destination, and held the vision in her own mind. And, as they leapt away to travel the ancient, teeming pathways…

Stars above. She *felt it.*

In the end, it was too much.

The constant begging and screaming and sobbing in his ears. The agony between bouts of blackened nightmare. The frailty preventing him from snapping his chains. The snippets of memory that wrenched up stinging bile before they were buried again.

The certainty it was all his fault.

She'd promised to make it all disappear if he was good. If he just did this one, little thing.

He'd held on for as long as he could—right up until she'd come to dance over him, chanting ancient songs, the razored darkness sawing something vital from within him and taking its place.

The loss of that intangible thing had hurt worse than any of the physical pain.

By the time he saw her again, he was nothing. No one.

So, he gave in.

The shame would have to haunt him later, for all it hadn't really felt like a choice.

At first, he hadn't been able to hold himself upright or take more than a few stumbling steps before collapsing again. She'd been confused, unhappy about the extra days. Or weeks, maybe? It was so hard to tell, but he was here now.

Feeling Solyrian for the first time since he could remember was almost worth his weakness. He might've laughed if he could remember how. Heard the birds and felt the wind. Thrown his arms out and plopped back into the grass to take it all in.

But he couldn't, and he didn't.

Instead, he stepped up to the void and looked across the chasm, at the Ghostwood looming just beyond the opposite edge, and grabbed onto the land with his power.

Bring it together. Close it up. That was all he had to do for her to cease the incessant torment. She'd keep him safe until then.

The earth rumbled beneath his feet, rock cracking and dirt crumbling. Beads of sweat dotted his brow and trickled down his back, his muscles straining as he brought himself right up to the limit of his considerable abilities.

A roar ripped free of his lungs as he pulled and pulled, the gap slowly shrinking. Shouts sounded in the distance, shapes drawing closer, but he ignored all in favor of his task.

Bring it together. Close it up. Make it go away.

Something elemental thrashed within, fighting from behind invisible bars. He felt its warnings, its rage. Wanted to embrace that inner being, but he couldn't. Not anymore, no matter how hard he tried. Not unless he did this one thing. Not unless he was good.

The world shook with a cataclysmic shudder and the Ghostbor Dread Chasm was no more.

He turned his face to the sky and sunstar, allowed only a single, deep breath before the shadows engulfed him and whisked him away.

Soon. He'd be back with them soon.

The smell of burnt roses preceded her voice raking over him. "You've done so very well, my darling boy," she crooned, running a hand over his hair as he laid down, exhausted from his labors.

He still didn't understand why she kept calling him that. Who she was meant to be to him.

When the shackles closed around him once again, he didn't bother with his usual threats. Didn't fight or scream obscenities. Didn't notice it was too quiet. That he couldn't hear *her* anymore.

"Sleep. You've earned it. We still have a few more things to do, my love."

He had no idea why a knowing smirk would try to twist his lips, but he fought against it and the unbidden closing of his lids. There was something wrong with her words.

"A few… more things?" The sound that left him could hardly be called a voice.

"Oh, sweet." She bent down and kissed his brow. "You didn't think closing the chasm was it, did you?"

But he'd been good.

Hadn't he?

"No. No!" Why was he laughing? "I was good! I was *good!*"

Thrashing, he ignored the horror contorting her face and blinked, trying to stave off the dark spots crowding his vision.

He had to get back. Had… to…

THE GREAT HALL WAS FULL TO BURSTING, COUNTLESS DEMONS ALREADY IN their rage and gathering from every direction.

Lyriat paced on the dais above the din, a harried male she didn't recognize speaking below him. His arms flung out, the gesture frantic, and Lunara spotted the tattoos marking his body as the sleeve of his battle robe slipped back. A Wolflord, then.

"Move!" Magnus pushed through the crowd, cutting through them like a knife and dragging her along. "Andreus?"

The male turned, slumping in relief. "Your Highness, thank the Sisters," he breathed, bending at the waist with a fist to his chest.

Lyriat rushed straight to Lunara, offering his arm. "Come," he said under his breath. "You'll want to sit for this."

"Please." Her nails sunk into his flesh of their own accord. "Tell me they've found him."

He led her up the steps and urged her to sit in Brand's throne. "Yes, but steel yourself." To the Wolflord, he said, "Again, Andreus. From the beginning."

She focused all her attention on listening, instead of the furious pounding in her chest. Against the desire to fly out into the realms right away, tearing them apart to find him.

"Aye, Your Majesty." Swallowing, he gathered himself. "A few hours ago, scouts returned to Fanghold to report that the Ghostbor Dread Chasm was rapidly shrinking. Caius went to the border immediately, a contingent of warriors with him, to stem the droves of Forgotten leaping across. When they got there, they found the missing Son, Brandir, instead. *He* was the one doing it, closing the chasm with his power."

Lunara's pulse throbbed in her ears, a deafening sound that threatened to devour her. She could hardly eke out the words, "Where is he? Where is my mate?"

"We don't know exactly, my lady," Andreus admitted. "Before anyone could reach him, the two lands slammed together, and he disappeared within a cloud of shadow. The only certainty is that he… he did not look well."

She barely held in the scream clawing its way up her throat.

"The rest, Andreus," Lyriat snapped.

"Aye, sire. Caius and two others followed the shadows, all the way to the Thodelemaia Dread Chasm, but were unable to follow when it went over the edge and into the darkness."

The world stilled, then shifted. Perked up. Looking at her. Waiting.

"Where on the Westrealm's southern border did this happen?"

Somehow, she already knew the answer, but she needed to hear it spoken.

"Directly south of the lost village of Glynmor, my lady. Also overrun with Forgotten, but Caius and his warriors paid them no heed, since they were too few against so many and there was no one nearby to need help."

Magnus was vibrating with fury, features twisting as his beast rose up, but it was Thaddeus who spoke. "Where is my father now?"

Andreus cleared his throat. "Back in the Westglen, battling Forgotten and other monstrosities, the likes of which I've never seen."

Magnus and Thaddeus pinned her with mirrored looks of alarm. Lunara tried to tame the churning in her stomach, but it was no use. She might actually be sick.

Dreadbeasts—and Brand had helped to bring them over.

He would never. It isn't what it seems. It can't be.

"Have messengers been sent to the other realms to beg for aid?" Magnus asked.

"Aye, Your Highness. Only the Imperial Heir has promised his support. The Elder Council of Nachthelliae have refused, citing their own complications. No word from the Kohamaian Queens."

Araxis misted to her side and bent to her ear. "I know we just escaped. I know you think you aren't ready to be known, but controlling Illamiata means controlling the Evesong. As Keeper, you command *legions* now, Lunara. Unconditionally. Every adult Sorcerit will gladly do your bidding, if you have the strength to call upon them."

What!

It was a struggle to slog through the hatred. To toss aside the bitterness rising up over the fact that, mere hours ago, she'd been dead to them —and that a majority of the Elders knew themselves to be partially responsible for her and her parents' deaths. This male included.

That's for later.

Right. Still.

"That's disgusting," she hissed. "I can wield their loyalty, hold their lives and futures in my hands, because of *what* I am? No training. No knowledge or guidance."

"That about sums it up."

"That's fucking wrong. Unspeakable."

"Yes, well..." His jaw ticked, eyes falling to the floor. "What is unspeakable power for, if not exactly this?"

"*Change.* As soon as this bleeding shite is over with." Lunara stood, a cold calm suffusing her bones even as her heart sought to hammer its way out of her.

You can do it, just this once. For Brand.

"You will go to the Evesong, Andreus." She was amazed her voice could sound so steady. Reaching through the ether, she plucked up the crimson pillow the Tear Stone had just been resting on and stepped down to place it in his hands. A message. "You will tell them the Keeper sent you and orders the legions to Thodelebor—half to the Ghostbor chasm, half to the Thodelemaia." She looked back at Araxis. The details of rank were muddled, beyond her, but it was his own words forcing her to act, so fuck him. "The Fifth Imperial Son will lead them in the west. I will meet the others near Glynmor, in the fields."

Andreus darted his gaze between Magnus and Lyriat, clearly unsure of what to do, and something in her snapped. "Don't look at them, Andreus. Look at me." Her tone was far more gentle than she felt. When he did, she let some of her new power surge to the surface, to harmlessly batter against all who were present in the hall. "I am Lunara the Moonweaver, Keeper of Illamiata, and blessed mate to Brandir aht Bordoroth. I hold as much sway as any of these other males, and *I* am telling you to go. *Now*."

Impeccably dramatic.

The silence was deafening.

Thaddeus cleared his throat. "I'm with you, Andreus," he said, stepping forward to clap a hand on his shoulder. He looked older, somehow. So serious. "First to the Evesong, and then back home. My father needs us, aye?"

Andreus blinked rapidly, awe written on every line of his young face. "Aye."

"Ach, get on with it then. We've got work to do."

Shaking his head, Andreus drew himself up and nodded, spinning and sprinting for the portal.

"I'll see it done, Lunara." Thaddeus backed away, a fist to his chest. "You bring my cousin back." With that, he and Andreus were gone.

Hedda and Faldir appeared through the throng to take their place, towering over her.

Lunara let her power die and stumbled down the remaining steps as Hedda knelt in front of her and leaned in close. "Bloody well done, Sorcerit."

"Thank you, I think. Except now, what?" She'd exhausted the limits of her wherewithal. Had no bleeding clue how to proceed. "I don't know what to do."

"Good thing I am their Second Commander, then."

Hedda and Lyriat shared a look, the king giving a firm nod. "I will lead half of ours with Araxis," he said, then turned to Lunara. "The other half is yours."

Umm…

"Mine?"

Hedda gifted her with a savage smile. "Another lesson for my pupil—motivation and inspiration are important in warfare. Trust me, my friend. A little bravado goes a long way. Try to play along." She stood, her voice booming over the chaos. "Demons of the Montrealm! The Wolflords of the Westrealm need you. Our *Son* needs you. Who will follow Lunara the Moonweaver in his stead? Who will bleed for Brandir's mate in glorious battle?"

Lyriat's markings appeared, his chest heaving as he grew and grew, stepping down from the dais and into the crowd as he began to chant.

The room erupted alongside their king. Weapons beat against shields. Against the flagstones. Against horn and fist.

"Hoo, hoo, hoo!"

Over and over, building in volume until the windows shook. Until it joined Illamiata's song in her bones and that same feeling from before—when she'd felt the ground for the first time after accepting the stone, felt its latent energy—whispered again to her now. Begged for her to reach out.

There was no need to fake it. No need to *play along,* as Hedda had put it. Not when Lunara followed Illamiata's silent nudging—its request to answer the call and burn free—and instinct, deep and ancient, took hold.

With a cry, prismatic power poured from her—a shockwave of dancing threads. They touched down on each and every Demon gathered, sipping from their essence and giving a piece of herself in return.

Red seeped into her vision, a fire that spread to her veins. Bloodlust and fury boiled in equal measure and, for just a moment, she was changed.

She was Straelon's sparkling sea and its crashing waves. She was the wood these creatures worked and the stone they shaped. She was their whorling power. Their colossal might. The righteous devastation of their rage made manifest.

For just a moment, Lunara was Demon.

Lyriat's grin put Hedda's to shame, his brutal bass rumbling beneath the roaring cacophony. "We will tear them limb from limb."

"Limb from fucking limb," she growled. "For Brand!"

"For Brand!"

59

VANN FINALLY RETURNED AS PREPARATIONS WERE BEING MADE.

His first and only words had been a hurried, *"A word. Bring the Fae,"* in her ear, before he marched his way out of the great hall.

He stood before her now, staring down at Fern's likeness on the slab, more serious than she'd ever seen him. "Is she here?"

"Maybe." Lunara resisted the urge to glance at the actual Fern where she hovered nearby, examining Vann with a furrowed brow. "Are you ready to tell me what you've been hiding?"

"Yes, and no." He straightened, unperturbed. "How much damage would forced remembrance do?"

Interesting.

"Hard to say. Depends on the person, and what they're ready for. Under the circumstances, I would suggest that less is more. I don't have the time to fix anything you muck up." Without looking away from him, she said, "Do you mind being revealed, Fern?"

The Fae arched a sardonic brow. "What do you think? I didn't want go through with all this pissing foolery in the first place."

Right.

Breaking the spell barely required thought. The well within had ceased being such a paltry thing the moment she'd taken Illamiata. She wasn't even sure *sea* was an appropriate description. It was far more vast than that. Than any physical thing she'd ever beheld.

Vann sagged with Fern's appearance at his side, her image disappearing from its faux repose. "Thank the Sisters."

His relief irked Lunara. "We're needed elsewhere, so make it quick."

"Yes, I'm aware." He tossed the pillow on Fern's sickbed aside, plucking up a small, bumpy thing from beneath it.

"What is that?"

Vann held it up between pinched fingers. "A storm seed. I'd hoped it would help her before, to have one close and feel its familiarity. It didn't." He tossed it at Fern. "Swallow that."

Fern caught it, eyes narrowing. "Why do I trust you?"

"We're friends."

More interesting.

"Hmm." She shoved the seed in her mouth without so much as a blink.

Shite.

What is happening?

Excellent question.

Before she could ask it, Vann was pulling something else from a deep, inner pocket of his long jacket.

Lunara recoiled. "Is that a *mace*?"

"Yes." Fern stepped forward like she'd been hypnotized, fixated on the plain, battered weapon in Vann's grasp. "It is."

"Give her some space, Luna." The tone in his voice brooked no argument.

Her back hit the wall as he handed it over, joining her in a blur. The second Fern's fingers wrapped around the handle, the mace transformed. Bronze bubbled up from beneath the steel, morphing it into an ornate monstrosity. The spiked end lengthened as a grey, stormy cloud gathered around it, and yellow sparks shot down to strike the tip and flanges like a lightning rod.

Everything about Fern was magnified. Her curls defied gravity to float around her face and shoulders in a lavender halo. The gold dust in her skin twinkled above and below the edges of her bandeau dress. The green of her wings deepened. And, when she looked up at them with wicked eyes, there were roiling clouds in her dark gaze as well.

"Yes," she hissed through her teeth, grinning as electric arcs danced over her skin. "This feels *right*."

"Behold the Spring Rain." Vann spoke under his breath, barely a sound. "I'll be traveling with you. She needs me nearby to use her powers." He shrugged. "Cost of Fae magic, which I'll happily pay since we're going to need all the help we can get if the rumors in the Tempus-realm are true."

Too much information to sort through.

"What was the seed for?"

"To help her body remember what she is, without having to explain anything."

That… sort of makes sense?

"Wait—"

"That's all I can say, for now." He gripped her shoulder, his mismatched eyes earnest. "I didn't like the secrecy, but it was—*is*—necessary. Just know… You have found yourself with an extraordinarily powerful ally. The rest of her truths are hers to give, when she finds them again. For now, keep her close and trust her intuition. It is unmatched."

ACCORDING TO ARAXIS, MEMORY WAS ITS OWN SORT OF REALM TOLL FOR those who could mist, and there were few places Lunara remembered more emphatically than Glynmor.

Being back sent a shiver down her spine. She'd come alone, hidden in the space between, to see first by herself what awaited them before delivering the Demon host to its cursed soil.

In the month since they'd been there, the fields between the village and chasm had failed to heal themselves. Veins of black spread out from the ruts through the land, and—where the dreadbeast's blood had spilled—festering decay was slowly eating away at the grass and flowers that dared to remain.

Solyrian mocked her from above, casting its warmth on a scene that didn't deserve it.

Invisible within the shimmering ether, Lunara stood atop the rocky incline Brand had made and watched the swarm of Forgotten wandering aimlessly below, seeping shadow and towering like trees. White and bony, cracked and gangling, they trampled the ground with their careless, clawed steps. Their brittle moans crackled through needlepoint teeth and shattered the silence in intervals, like branches as they snapped and fell.

As far as the eye could see. In every direction.

Good thing Hedda had thought for her to come. There'd be no time to gather themselves. No time for finding their feet.

Magic floated in on the soft breeze, running familiar fingers through her hair. The Sorcerit were coming.

This is it.

They just had to get to the steps at the chasm's edge. Sisters willing, they would lead her to Brand.

That thought burned away any lingering fear. Lunara would have only moments once she acted. She had to make them count.

"Sisters, bless me. I am yours, as I am his, as I am mine." She urged her fangs to lengthen and took a shaky breath as she recalled the details of Hedda's instructions. "And I am not afraid."

She sank her fangs into her wrist, ripped the flesh away, and stepped through the ether to the far side of field below, outside the forest's edge.

Her blood hit the dry ground in a waterfall of red as the dreamlike quality of her hiding place dissipated. Heads snapped to the air, sniffing, and she smiled as the droves of Forgotten took the bait and surged towards her

"Come and get it, you fucking filth."

Just before the first claws could rake across her torso, she misted back to the Montrealm.

When Lunara reappeared in Straelon, everyone was already joined in any way they could manage while keeping one fighting hand free. Fern stood right at the front, Magnus and Vann's hands on her shoulders, Faldir behind with a hand on each of theirs.

And so it went, the towering Demons of the Montrealm holding fast to their brethren, their numbers staggering as they filled the courtyard and spilled down onto the road.

Hedda was waiting, asking quietly, "How was it?"

"Exactly as you thought it would be. Your idea worked."

"Then we have no time to waste."

Before leaving for the Westglen with Lyriat, Araxis had hastily guided her through what to do. How to feel the connected bodies and join them with her own. After a couple of practice runs, and with Illamiata guiding her, it was the most natural thing in the world to grasp Fern's outstretched fingers and grab onto every particle of every creature.

It was amazing the things one could learn in a matter of hours when fueled by desperation.

Hedda gripped Lunara's nape as she turned to the gathered horde and raised her battle axe. "Be ready! We follow the mist into mayhem, to the Forgotten awaiting on the other side. Rip them apart!"

Gritting her teeth, Lunara wrenched them into the ether.

Their voices were still blaring, "Limb from fucking limb!" in answer to their commander when they emerged in Glynmor as one.

The violence was instant.

Demons roared as they swung their weapons, descending upon the throng of Forgotten where they were still crawling in a seething mass over her pool of blood.

"Get us to the incline!" Hedda shouted over the chaos.

With a nod, Lunara misted again, bringing their core group with her. Hedda had tasked warriors from her First Legion with leading the battle here. The chasm, finding Brand, was up to them.

Releasing Fern, she brandished her whip… talon… things, ready for the final trick Araxis had shown her. Well, mostly ready.

Magnus pointed at the spot where the grass and dirt at the chasm's edge were drooping. "Brand's steps, and our destination."

"Do we await the Nachthellians?" Hedda asked.

"No need." Magnus stripped his robe away, keeping his eyes trained below. "They're here."

Lunara pushed past him, panicked, as Sorcerit spilled from between the longhouses of Glynmor, magic leaving their hands in bursts as they joined the fray.

She wasn't sure whether to laugh or cry when she spotted Cordelia already in the midst of single-handedly beheading one of the Forgotten and setting it on fire. "I didn't know she still had it in her."

"Ach, I fucking did," Magnus scoffed. "There's a gleam in the eye there, witchling. Cordy will be just fine."

...Cordy?

"Mist down," Vann asked, "or fight our way through?"

Faldir twirled his axe. "I say we butcher as many of these bastards as possible."

"Agreed," Magnus growled.

Lunara's breaths came shorter, nerves ratcheting.

A hand on her shoulder. "No fear, Sorcerit," Hedda murmured. "Stay close, follow your instincts, and let your body remember what it knows now to do."

Fern grinned. "You'll be fine, eh? I can feel it."

Trusting the *feelings* of a Fae with secret powers who couldn't even remember her own name was—

Your only choice. Let it happen. For Brand.

Right.

"At my word, jump and make for the steps." Hedda toed the drop, glancing down. "We'll clear our path, but that has to be good enough."

"Aye. See you on the other side." Magnus spared one lingering glance at Fern before he shifted, howling to the sky as he settled.

Answering howls sounded in the distance. The Wolflords were coming.

Vann's smile was not in the least bit comforting. "Life or death, little sister?"

What the...

"I should think life would be obvious!"

Is he trying *to scare you? Honestly!*

"I rather agree," he answered, though why it sounded sad was beyond her.

Between one blink and the next, Vann's platinum hair flowed with green. The black bled away from his one eye and revealed an emerald iris to match the other. Even his skin brightened, deepening as a healthy pink suffused his cheeks.

Riotous flowers and teeming vines flew across the battlefield below. They filled the rotting places with life and rose up to seize Forgotten by their multi jointed legs, holding them in place for the Demons and Sorcerit to slaughter.

Well, alright then...

Shouts from the bottom of the incline, and Magnus let out a snarl. The

Demons guarding it were being overrun by the Forgotten concentrating there. They slashed out with teeth and talons, and Lunara watched in horror as one of the warriors was impaled and devoured.

"No!"

"Ah. Time to go." Hedda wrenched her back, stopping her from trying to help. "They have their job, we have ours. Sadness has to be for later." Jaw tight, she shouted for the Demons below to clear away. "Ready?"

Not even a little bit.

"Go!"

Fern was a blur as she shot past, hurtling towards the ground. Mace raised, she brought it down in an arc, thunder booming when she connected with her first target. The earth shook with every hit she landed, shockwaves rippling out and sending the Forgotten sprawling. From nowhere, rain poured around her in a tight circle, never touching Fern even as it doused their glowing ember gazes and flowed up into their mouths. Twitching, gurgling, *drowning*—just before she cast out hot streaks of lightning to electrocute and disintegrate them.

Faldir whistled. "Fuck. I think I'm in love," he said, and joined her.

Vann followed with a wink, riding a wave of flora that churned the soil. Pastel petals scattered and sank into the Forgotten, eating through their woody flesh like acid. Thorns shot out and embedded themselves in fiery eye sockets. Vines lashed out like clawed hands, gripping the maimed at each limb and tearing them apart before burying the pieces in their wake.

Magnus leapt from the incline and landed on the back of a Forgotten. His massive jaws closing over its jagged skull and tearing it away in a single pull, shadows spilling from the decapitated torso like blood. Its needlepoint teeth were still snapping when he fed the severed head to Vann's violent maelstrom of plants. She could hardly track him as he moved on to the next, and the next.

Shitting stars.

"Araxis showed you what to do, and we're running out of time." Hedda gave her a nudge, eyes darting between her and whatever was happening behind them. "Let go, my friend. You must."

With a deep breath, Lunara unfurled her whips. Araxis's voice in her mind, she commanded the particles in the air to lift her body, holding her suspended—safe—over the pandemonium.

Yesterday, she'd been nothing. No one. Now, she was the Keeper of Illamiata and she was fucking flying over a bleeding battlefield.

It's fine. You are *fine. You were made for this by the Sisters themselves.*

She hated when she was right.

Let them guide you. Let them feed you, like the Demons did.

Insanity.

She loosed Illamiata the tiniest bit, joining with the others—feeling out their intentions, their movements. Again, their rage was hers. Their strength and fury. Their vengeance.

Lunara didn't have to understand it to *harness* it.

With a scream, she threw a surge of power behind her first attack, her taloned whips cracking as they landed. The first kill echoed, boiling her blood.

That they'd taken him… That they'd fucking dared…

Lunara unleashed. She fell willingly into a pattern of alternating swings, obliterating Forgotten and filling the craters she left behind with piles of bone and shadow.

It wasn't perfect, and she didn't hit every time, but it was enough. It helped.

The others delivered Forgotten into the devastating paths of their comrades in perfect harmony. Vann's vines would hurtle one into the air for the twins to decimate it. Fern struck hard enough to send them flying—right into Magnus's waiting fangs. On and on they went, closer to the chasm's edge with every hammering blow, every twining stem, every savage bite.

Just as they reached the steps and she touched back down, a shadow fell over them and Lunara glanced to the sky.

A colossal dragon flew above, blotting out the sunstar. Its scales glittered in shades of the deepest orange and gold, its clawed wings beating a steady rhythm as the quadricorn serpent threw its head back and roared. One of the riders on its back stood in their saddle and pulled down the swath of linen wrapped around their head and face.

Amunkar, Amal behind him, on their way to the Ghostbor.

"For Brand!" he shouted, spurring his dragon onward. Flames gushed from its maw as they flew, incinerating the enemies on the hillsides.

The Demons answered, *"For Brand!"* as he disappeared over the horizon.

Tears in her eyes, Lunara looked down into the gloom.

Throwing out her shield, she encompassed her friends—battered, a little worse for wear, but still standing tall and ready—and pushed the shadows away.

"For Brand," she whispered, and led them into the abyss.

WHERE BEFORE THE SHADOWS HAD SEEMED CURIOUS, NOW THEY WERE volatile. Deranged. Slamming themselves collectively against her shield with harsh, repetitive strikes before recoiling with what Lunara would swear were screams. Like they'd been burned.

Still, they came back. Battering. Lashing. Biting. All of it focused on *her* —not the barrier or her companions.

It felt personal.

"I thought there'd be more to it," Hedda murmured at her side, the gash above her brow seeping anew when she raised it.

It was hard to ignore the deep lacerations in Magnus's bloodied muzzle or the matching claw marks on Fern's bare shoulder and opposite thigh, her bandeau dress muddied and torn between. Faldir was sporting a particularly spectacular black eye, emphasizing the twisting scar down his face. Vann looked utterly exhausted, his limp more pronounced than she'd ever seen it.

All of them had rejected her offers of healing. She didn't need to waste her time on their scratches, they'd said, but Lunara had heard the words between—she needed to be ready for Brand. For whatever state they found him in.

"Yes, well…" Lunara frowned at a pocket of dribbling ooze and tamped down her shudder. "Fortunately or unfortunately, the only thing we found was the army of cursed creatures at the bottom. It's empty, otherwise."

"Disappointing, honestly." She gaped at Faldir, and he shrugged. "What? I was hoping for a challenge."

"You Demons." Lunara shook her head. "I, for one, am grateful it isn't worse. Leaving the steps here was an egregious oversight."

"I'd say you had more pressing matters to see to at the time." Hedda swiped at the blood dripping from the cut in her swollen lip. "All the more reason to find Brand"—she leveled Faldir with a pointed look—"*without* any unnecessary drama."

They lapsed into a heavy silence, Hedda's quiet words settling over them as they descended ever further into the chasms's bowels.

Over and over, Lunara searched for the bond as they trekked. For anything that would tell her where her mate was in this foul place, and—again and again—felt nothing.

It's fine. He's fine. Everything will be fine.

No, it was too much. Too much. She was so fucking *tired.*

Tears sprang to her eyes, a wretched, consuming hopelessness with them. What if there was no point to this? What if he was already gone and she was doing nothing more than leading the rest of the people she cared about into ruin? What if they all—

Something isn't right.

Of course something wasn't right. *Nothing* was right. This was futile.

Stop it! This isn't right! Don't you feel it?

Lunara blinked, sniffling. Only then did she notice her breaths were coming in shorter and shallower. That there were fingers in her mind. Insidious tendrils digging in and searching through her.

"Wait." She stumbled to a stop. "Just wait."

Sweat dotted her brow and soaked the neckline of her fighting linens. When had that happened?

"What is it?" Vann asked, searching her face as Magnus loosed a low whine.

"I…" A hand was closing over her face to smother her. She was sure of it. "Something is wrong."

No sooner had she said the words than the presence multiplied and a horrific pressure filled her skull, threatening to crack it in two.

"You would bring that trinket here, into my domain?"

Weeping fucking Sisters. Not another one.

It wasn't herself. It wasn't Endellion. It wasn't even the monster who'd stolen Brand.

This was something else. Something old. Something *evil.*

She felt it in the tiny hairs on her body as they stood on end. In every particle as they cowered within her, begging her to run.

"Interesting choice, little one. If only you understood what it was you had. The gift you were giving me."

Piss. Shite. Arse. It *hurt*. She was going to shatter apart. Was going to disintegrate into a million tiny pieces.

Illamiata flared in her chest, vibrating as prismatic light flashed out from her.

The being chuckled. ***"Ah, yes. Very interesting, indeed. Not to worry. My children will thank you when they feed on your marrow. I will thank your barren bones when I am free."***

Lunara fell to her knees as it left her, gasping for air. The relief was so stark, so sudden.

She doubled over, vomiting, as if her body wished to purge any lingering traces of whatever *the fuck* that had been.

Who. Who it had been.

"Lunara!" Hedda was crouched in front of her, panic etched onto her face. "What is it? What happened?"

The shadows lightened, the black going tepid around them. Lazy.

"Something… something was here," she rasped, still retching. "*Someone*. I don't—"

The entire chasm shuddered around them, and went still.

"I don't like this," Fern said, her head cocked to the side. "It doesn't feel right."

Another shudder, dust and pebbles clattering against the stone. Time slowed as she watched the crack form, and yet it happened so fast.

Before Lunara could move, they were hurtling down into the darkness, the step gone from beneath them.

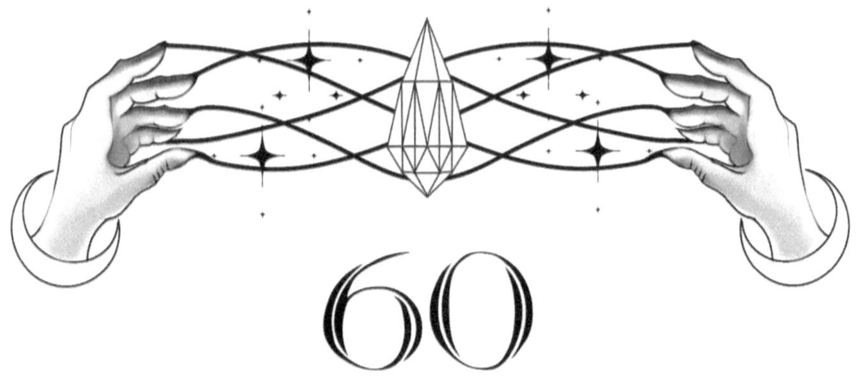

60

Lunara flung her power down as they plummeted, the wind whipping by.

Fern shot like a verdant arrow past her, reaching Hedda first and grabbing her by one horn, then Faldir. Vann's vines shot out in two directions, snatching Magnus to himself before winding around Faldir's outstretched hand and arm.

She grabbed onto the group of them and wrenched their particles to herself, grunting with the effort of being stretched in so many directions—the shield, the air, their bodies.

Fern's wings worked to help her, pulling them to a nauseating stop.

It was ridiculous, the way they hovered, wrapped around one another in a tangle of limbs and fur and flora. Worse still when Magnus—*Pet*—panted in her face and drew his rough tongue across her and Fern's cheeks.

"Fuck off, you hairy bog troll, or I'll drop you."

Hedda let out a choked sound as Fern let go of her to shove a hand in Magnus's muzzle, pushing his massive head away, and a huff of nervous laughter escaped Lunara.

"We should've jumped from the get-go." Faldir pried Fern's hand from his own horn with a slow breath. "Next time, maybe try to catch me somewhere else though, gorgeous."

Magnus growled low at that. Fern seemed… intrigued.

"Honestly, Fal. Not the fucking time." Hedda's eyes were still wide and blinking, like she didn't quite believe they were alright. "Now what?"

Vann cranked back and looked down into the murk. "May as well finish our descent, eh?"

A good idea as any, but not what they'd planned.

"Are you sure? There's more going on than we thought. I can take you all to the surface, come back alone and—"

"None of that." Vann pinned her with his emerald stare. "We stay."

No one refuted the statement, though a part of Lunara wanted to beg them to go. Wanted them to be far, far away from the *thing* that had spoken to her.

"We stay, little sister."

As it turned out, they were much closer to the chasm floor than they'd realized before she and Fern had stopped their fall.

"Bloody Solyrian," Hedda muttered, swiping a hand down her face. "I never want to be high up again."

Lunara felt that sentiment to her damned soul.

"Brace yourselves and be ready. I'm going to give us some light and—while I don't sense anything living—there's no telling what we'll find."

She ignored the twinge in her chest at the thought of the last time she'd done this, Brand at her side, and pulled from the well. Power concentrated between her hands and she threw the gathered sparks free, the shield blasting out.

And revealing nothing. Well, *almost* nothing.

The ooze had multiplied ten-fold, a hundred-fold, since she and Brand had been here. It bubbled up from cracks and crevices. It gathered in puddles and piles. Writhing. Crawling. More alive than she'd ever seen it.

Magnus shifted in a flash, bringing an arm to his face as he gagged. "Ach, that smell. Can't fucking take it."

Lunara plucked his robe from the ether, handing it over as she drew in a deep breath—the scent of burnt roses with it.

It was visceral, the way her senses locked onto the horrible, familiar stench and everything clicked into place at once.

Meliora. Baldrir. Glynmor. Fern. The Horned City. Nyri. Brand.

All connected. All hers, in a way. She'd known, but she hadn't *known*. Not in the manner it was solidifying now. Not looking at all of it through the lens of the Prophecy and her presence within it.

A prismatic aura enveloped her, dancing up to tease her hair. To whisper in her ear.

"A shadow, once living, abides in bleak places." She was in a kind of trance, Illamiata humming as the words left her unbidden. "A vengeance, once loving, on five towers gazes."

The sludge churned, more agitated with every syllable that left her lips.

She had to find Brand, yes, but she also had a responsibility. A place in this mess that was bigger than just the two of them. She hadn't understood before, but she did now. Could hear the song of it in her blood.

"Fuck, witchling. Not again."

Her feet were moving without being told, out into the center of the chasm. To the worst of the pooling black.

"Their hate is consuming, biting and bruising. Eating and rotting and writhing and oozing."

Fern and Hedda flanked her as the ground shook, rock crumbling from the cliffside. All of that *oozing* filth retracted, falling from the walls and racing towards itself—merging, growing—before shooting away into the distance.

The others joined them as Vann said, "That doesn't bode well."

"Naught more than the dark, being called by its darker master." Her voice was back to its warbling tones, both the sound and the knowledge not quite hers.

"Well." Hedda brandished her axe, eyes darting. "That's ominous as fuck."

"Hmm." Fern grinned. "I love it."

From high out of the far-off gloom, an object flew towards them. Closer. Closer.

"Ach, no."

A severed leg landed with a wet slap a few feet away, bursting as it tumbled.

"What. The. Fuck." It felt like a privilege to see Faldir so rattled, shock on his slack-jawed face.

A hand next. A head. A torso. All *inside* of her shield.

Vann made a canopy with his vines. The twins and Fern batted chunks away with their weapons. Magnus placed his body between her and the onslaught.

Except, she didn't need his help.

A warm giggle sounded in Lunara's mind.

Hello, Endellion.

The greeting didn't come from her own conscious mind, it came from—

Illamiata pulled at her center and she shoved her way past Magnus. When he reached out and grabbed her hand, she turned around and locked eyes with him.

"Let go of me."

He recoiled but didn't release his white-knuckled hold. "Lunara, please. You can't—"

"I can, and I will," she whispered. "It was always meant to be me, from the very beginning."

Of time. Of creation. Of her life. She felt the truth of it.

Magnus must have seen it in her face, that there was no stopping her. "Be careful. Brand would never forgive us if something happened to you."

"Don't worry." A roaring thunder started up, shaking the fabric of the world. "I won't be letting anything happen to *us*."

"Weeping fucking Sisters," Magnus breathed.

The others regrouped beneath Vann's rudimentary structure and went still—resigned, almost, as they gaped at the sky behind her—and Lunara closed her eyes.

She had friends and a family now. A mate and a life worth living. Love. So much fucking love, she hardly knew what to do with it.

They needed her. Whatever was there, she would not be afraid. Not anymore. Not ever again.

With her hands clenched into shaking fists, Lunara turned and faced her destiny.

Hundreds of feet high, a tsunami of darkness was hurtling straight for them, churning with bodies and bones and blood.

A cataclysm of rotting death.

"This is the moment we planned for. It's time. Time to accept your bright place in the sky. Burn, sister. Shine. Unleash fire on night. Release all your fear and wield vengeance that blinds."

Release *all* her fear.

One foot in front of the other, Lunara flashed her fangs and tore the top from the well. The barrier was no good to her anymore. Had no place in her life. She loosened the nervous, spectral fingers she'd kept wrapped around Illamiata since claiming it, letting them slip away and finally unlocking the cage she'd built around herself all those decades ago.

"Yes, moth. That's it. Let go and stamp your name upon eternity."

She was free. At last.

As the darkness hit, Lunara *erupted.*

Power exploded from her in a tempest of wind and searing light, and she screamed into the descending void—screamed and screamed, releasing the torment that had followed her every day for decades, until her throat was raw and shredded.

As bits and pieces of cursed creatures rained down, she swam amongst her rage. Let it shine out from every particle and pore. Let herself burn.

Hotter than the sunstar and brighter than the moons. More staggering than the galaxies. More infinite than anything the cosmos had ever held within themselves.

She was a celestial fire of divine retribution. The Unknown made manifest.

A Star Goddess in her own right.

Illamiata pulled from the essence of the world and gave it back to her, and she used every drop to administer its vast destruction.

Her incineration was accompanied by shrieking death throes—quieter and quieter, less and less—until there was nothing left but ash and afternoon sunlight, beaming all the way down to the barren chasm floor.

Just before she collapsed—before her knees could hit the dirt and her body could crumple—Lunara looked up past the charred remains and at the scorched chasm wall.

At the perfect doorway carved there and the reddish glow shining from within.

At the cave he'd made to save her, where her life had finally begun.

Just before she collapsed, Lunara found him.

Brand.

Araxis spat, the misty fog of his midnight power drawing back and away from the *thing* he'd just suffocated with it. Not quite a Forgotten, not quite a creature—some abomination in between that curdled the blood in his veins.

Seeing was different than hearing. Brand and Lunara's storytelling had done little justice to the reality.

Pandemonium reigned around him, the stink of death mixing with Nakarat's wafting smoke to burn like acid in his lungs with every putrid breath. His brother's dragon roared in the sky, pummeling the land in front of the Ghostwood with its fire.

The flaming wall was going a long way towards stemming the flow of monsters, but it was almost too little, too late.

Dead. So many were already dead.

And it did nothing to dispel the writhing pocket of darkness within the otherworldly trees of the 'Wood. It had been there since the beginning. Unmoving, but watching. Waiting.

Doing an excellent job of matching Lunara's description of the one who'd taken Brand.

His lips peeled back as he fought the temptation to go after it and see for himself whether it was as all-powerful as his brother's mate had depicted—or if it bled and screamed like anything else that took air into its lungs.

Fuck. No. They didn't need another one of them missing because he'd misjudged.

Lyriat's wings beat a steady rhythm as he bellowed another command at his legions from the air, regathering them near a grouping of dread-beasts screeching their way past the blaze.

A pack of Wolflords raced by him, one nipping out at his shoulder as the others howled to the sky. Thaddeus. Or Sorcha, technically.

Araxis misted his way alongside her as they moved to join the Demon front, gathering himself for another round of mayhem. He was beginning to flag. He'd never expended this much of his power at once—not without a gift to temper the aftermath.

He needed night, if nothing else.

A blink and he was through the ether and perched atop the crystal peak of the Elder Halls, the cosmos stretching above him.

One breath. Two. The stars and galaxies reached down with a

welcome caress, embedding their magic—their life—into his skin. Not enough, but it would have to do.

Another blink and he was once again within the chaos of battle, Demons towering above him as they swung their steel and battered their horns and fists in every direction.

"Araxis! To me!"

He dodged a hurtling talon and misted into the sky, the matter in the air holding him aloft as he searched the seething mass of bodies for Amunkar.

There, back-to-back with Amal, a ring of Forgotten around them. With a thought, he was in the circle, his power blasting outwards to latch onto some of their enemy.

"Get us to Lunara!" Amun shouted, his fiery spear jabbing out.

His fog popped the head off of a Forgotten as Araxis fought not to roll his eyes. "How do you propose I do that? I don't know where she fucking is."

A blinding flash of light overtook the southern horizon, rising up like a thousand sunstars to blot out the sky and turn the world white.

"What the—"

Araxis was thrown to the ground along with every other creature in the vicinity by a shockwave of searing heat, the grass and soil overturning in its wake.

What he did not expect was the absolute power that welded itself right onto his bones.

"*That's* where she is." Amun stood above him, his brow furrowed as he bent to pull Araxis to his feet. "We need to go now."

Someday, he would convince his brother to admit how *the fuck* he always *knew* shite.

Araxis spared a single glance back to the Ghostwood—to the empty space where the darkness used to be—and cursed.

"WHERE IS SHE?"

Magnus looked up and blinked, still trying to find his way back into his useless body. Even Pet was content to remain quiet within, curled in on himself and too stunned to comment.

He wasn't the least surprised to find Amun and Araxis standing above them, his oldest brother demanding answers he didn't really have. Shite, he'd probably never be surprised by anything ever again for the rest of his damned life.

Lunara had made fucking sure of that.

The witchling had become something else. The stuff of myth and legend.

Somehow, she'd protected them. Leveled their group to the ground and tried to turn them into flattened hotcakes, aye, but she'd kept them from harm.

Saved their fucking lives.

Amun pounced, gripping his robe to shake him. "Where, Magnus?"

Only then did he spot Fern hieing away over his brother's shoulder, her wings a blur behind her, and followed her path to its logical conclusion.

"My guess would be there." He pointed past her to the hole in the chasm side, his voice little more than a burnt husk.

"We have to go." Amun hefted a muttering Vann from the ground, then the dazed twins. "Quickly."

"What's the fucking rush, Amun? Give a lad a moment to breathe, aye?"

"No. Not aye." Golden scales rippled to the surface of his skin, eyes shimmering with amber and jade before his irises lengthened vertically.

The Serpent.

Shite. He was pissed if he was losing control of himself.

"Where's Amal?"

Amun ignored him as he gathered everyone close. A bad sign.

Most didn't realize that her place as his *ajma* wasn't only for his protection—it was to protect others *from* him, if necessary.

Smoke curled from Amun's nostrils, lips peeling back as his teeth sharpened to lethal points. "You get us there now, Araxis, or Lunara dies."

The witchling's scream echoed across the empty chasm.

Weeping fuck.

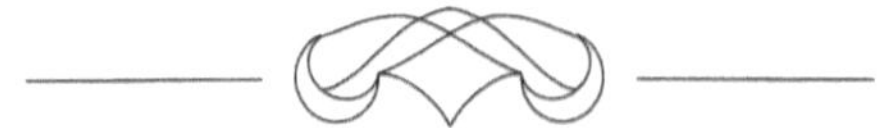

WHEN LUNARA FINALLY DID HIT THE DIRT, IT WAS ON THE FLOOR OF THEIR cave.

She felt hollowed out as she stumbled her way upright, the place foreign to her now. Their haven had been reduced to a torture chamber. A dungeon for her mate.

Black smudges lined the walls, and torches made of bone flickered with a sinister light. It reeked of the dreadbeasts' venom and that same hateful, cloying scent of burnt fucking roses.

None of it mattered. Not when she finally spotted Brand, and the rest of the world dropped away.

She misted to the platform, a cry breaking free when she beheld him up close. It was the nightmare from Argoph, every detail exactly the same.

His eyes were closed and swollen. Barbed chains had been wrapped around his beaten body, holding him down. They'd carved through flesh and bone, and rivers of blood had caked over him in layers, seeping from the uneven wounds. One of his hands was almost completely severed, his wrist broken.

It was the tears, though—the ones that had dried along his temples and still dampened his hair—that splintered something deep within her.

"I'm here. I'm here, Brand."

She was already moving as she sent out a thread of power, her fingers barely brushing over his shoulder when—

"No."

His skin was so cold, his heart barely beating. She tried to tell herself his breaths were just slow, her mind playing tricks, but the sound that tore out of her was pure agony.

"Sisters, no." She scrambled onto the platform. "Please, no!"

She gripped the chains and willed them apart, chucking the shattered pieces to the ground and ignoring the puncture wounds they left behind as she laid her palms to his ravaged chest.

"Please, please, please." Lunara had no other words as his pain became hers.

She dumped power into him and bore every wretched second of his torture. Gladly. Willingly. Flooded him with everything she had left to give.

Anything. Anything to have him back. He could have all of it.

She never let go of the dying beat as choked, anguished utterances finally pushed themselves past the ache in her throat. "Please, Brand. This heart is mine, remember? You gave it to me right here. You gave it to me again and again." Agony of a different sort twisted within her. "I was so scared—so hopelessly scared—but I took it anyway. I took it for myself and I never said it could stop. Please, I'm here. I'm here now. Don't let it stop."

Ever so slowly, Brand's wounds knitted themselves together. Bones cracked and blood flowed backwards. Color rose in his cheeks and his muscles thickened. All the while, she clung to the resonant *thump, thump, thump* in her ears as it grew stronger. Steadier.

Lunara could hardly see him through the sheet of her tears. Hardly trusted the hope she felt building.

When his body was as healed as it could possibly be, she commanded the filth of his captivity to fall in dusty flakes, until his hair shone and his skin glowed. She plucked a tunic and a pair of his trousers from the ether to cover his nakedness and keep him warm.

And then she collapsed, spent. So utterly spent and in more pain than she'd ever been.

It was worth it to be able to press her ear to his chest and feel him moving beneath her. To know he was alive.

She was weeping freely when a strong, familiar hand landed on her back and pressed into her, dragging up her spine and tangling in the wild, matted mass of her curls.

"Shhh."

Sweet Sisters, to hear his voice again, even saying so little…

Lunara fisted his tunic, pressing her face into his chest and gasping out a sobbed, "I thought I'd lost you."

His other arm came up around her, squeezing. "No more crying. Please. Shhh."

Her nerves sparked with the added pressure, breath hissing through her clenched teeth. "Brand?"

"We don't need to cry anymore. I was good."

She didn't have it in her to make sense of his words. He was still squeezing.

"Brand, that h-hurts."

And *squeezing.*

"Please. Please, stop." She started thrashing, as much as she was able in her feeble state. "Brand, stop!"

"No. No screaming," he growled. "Can't listen to any more screaming. *I was good.*"

Even when her ribs snapped beneath the force of his violent embrace, and she couldn't drag air into her own lungs, she didn't believe it was really happening.

It couldn't be happening.

Probably why she didn't notice his hand wrapping around the back of her neck and digging into the base of her skull, or the scream he tore from her lips, even as he begged her to be quiet.

As he crushed the life right out of her.

"Shhh."

Shouts and hands and chaos reigned between one slow blink and the next.

Lunara found herself being wrenched away and thrown into Hedda's waiting arms, Fern's breaths heaving as she turned a seething glare at Brand, still murmuring on the slab.

All of his brothers were there, somehow. Faldir too, but so what?

She was numb to it. Didn't actually care.

Because Lunara found absolutely nothing when she stared across the short distance and into his stunning, hazel eyes.

Brandir aht Bordoroth, her blessed, perfect mate, didn't know her at all.

61

"I know what you're thinking," Endellion murmured into the absolute darkness of her prison, a soft sigh escaping her, "but weren't you paying attention?"

It was so hard when no one listened. Nigh impossible to get anything done.

The split vision shimmered and fused itself into one, the swirling pool of apocalyptic possibilities drying up that much more.

Good thing her moth had come around, or this would be an entirely different story.

"Don't worry. Victory isn't always pretty at first, and this isn't the end. This isn't even the middle." A giggle bubbled up to bounce around the dank cavern. "We're still at the beginning, remember? Just like I said."

AUTHOR NOTES & ACKNOWLEDGEMENTS

I know. I *know*, and I'm sorry. Please don't hate me. Instead, allow me to offer you some reassurances:

Despite that wretched ending, The Towers of Bordoroth *is* a romantasy series. As such, I promise you—from the bottom of my hopelessly romantic heart—that all of my couples will eventually find their happily ever afters. They just have to go through some shit first. Don't we all?

You may have noticed that Luna was allowed her "glow-up"—space to come to terms with herself and her past, and an opportunity to dig up the dormant strength and bravery she'd buried in order to face her greatest fear—but what about Brand? Well, unfortunately, he was using our heroine and their binding as something of a bandaid for his deeper (and some as-yet-undiscovered) issues.

This, my beautiful readers, is never a good idea. Ask me how I know.

And so, Brand and Luna will be continuing their journey together in the next book, *Of Dusk and Daybreak*—coming in 2026.

Now, on to the part where I attempt to express my appreciation for everyone who stayed by my side throughout this harrowing process, despite the fact that a few measly sentences will never be able to do them justice.

This would have been far more difficult to accomplish if I hadn't had the epic fortune of marrying my very own living, breathing book-boyfriend. So, to my husband, who's already given me the perfect HEA: Thank you, my darling. For every morning you let me prattle on, listening and asking helpful questions. For every late night you went to bed alone without making me feel guilty. For every week you set me free, so I could grow into my own. For every day you loved our children enough for the both of us. For every hour you held me while I cried, both good tears and bad. For every minute, every second, of the years you've called me yours… *Thank you*. I love you more than I could ever hope to express in a single, paltry paragraph. Hopefully Brand and Luna's story will go some way towards making up for it.

To my sisters, who inspired an entire fantasy world: "Thank you" doesn't feel like enough. How could two words possibly encompass a lifetime of fierce and feral solidarity? So I did the only thing I could think of: I used *hundreds of thousands* of words to immortalize it. And—from its half-cooked inception in my notes app, to the physical book in your hands—you've read *every. single. one.* Earnestly. Honestly. Brutally. Tenderly. Fairly. You didn't just inspire Bordoroth—you are the solid and stunning foundation upon which I built it. You are every incredible thing I am not. Thank you for seeing me in the same way, and always making damn sure I know it.

To my brothers, who give me hope for all male-kind: Thank you for breaking the mold and proving that heroic, intelligent, complex, romantic, wonderful men do, in fact, exist. If only more of them were exactly like you.

To my best friend: Thank you for being who you are. For knowing me as well as you know yourself, and offering every drop of your infinite understanding while I followed my dreams. For always being the perfect body double. And for a lifetime of memories and the kind of friendship most people can only imagine. I'm not sure I'll ever deserve you.

To my parents: Thank you for passing on your love of reading, and never denying access to the many laden bookshelves in our back room. For your excitement when I told you I was going to write my own stories. And for asking every time I saw you how it was going and *when* (not *if*) it would be released.

To my other parents: Thank you for loving me like your own, and for all of your encouragement, even as I disappeared into the realm of my own imagination.

To my editor, Casey Harris-Parks: Thank you for taking a chance on me. For seeing beyond my social anxiety to the potential beneath. For every call/email/text. For every wine-soaked, sticky-note-riddled retreat. Your willingness to hold my hand through everything has made all the difference. You are more than an excellent editor—you're a stunning human being, and I'm honored to call you my friend.

To Uncle A and Aunt J: Thank you for showing us—even from so far away—what true, lasting love looks like. You've inspired all of us more than you probably know, and it has meant everything in our own lives.

To the Dream Team: Thank you for dragging me up out of my introverted mud and giving me a safe place to be myself. For being the kindest, most supportive void for me to author-scream into. You've loved and understood me as only fellow writers can, and I will be forever grateful.

To Jennifer and Hannah: Thank you for always being honest, and for being willing to say the hard things so that this book could be the best possible version of itself.

To Beck and Taylor: Huzzah, lettuce! ILU.

To Destinee: Thank you for everything. Who knew that a single comment about my left tit would make me a new friend?

To all of my alpha and beta readers: Thank you for being some of the first humans who believed in me—especially those of you who read v1.0 of OMAS and were still willing to come back for more. LOL.

To my early ARC readers: Thank you for being the sweetest, wildest bunch, and for screaming about OMAS far and wide. I don't know what I did to lure you all in, but you're mine now.

To all of the artists I've worked with: Thank you for bringing Brand, Lunara, and Bordoroth to life in all of your unique and wonderful ways. Believe me, I look at them and cry more often than I care to admit.

To LJ, Penn, and Melissa: Thank you for your generosity. You helped my life-long dream come true, and I look forward to the day I can follow your example and do the same for someone else.

And to you, my readers: Thank you for taking a chance on a debut indie author, and making this all worthwhile. I hope, above all, that I didn't let you down.

LINE OF BLESSING
AND SERVICE KEY

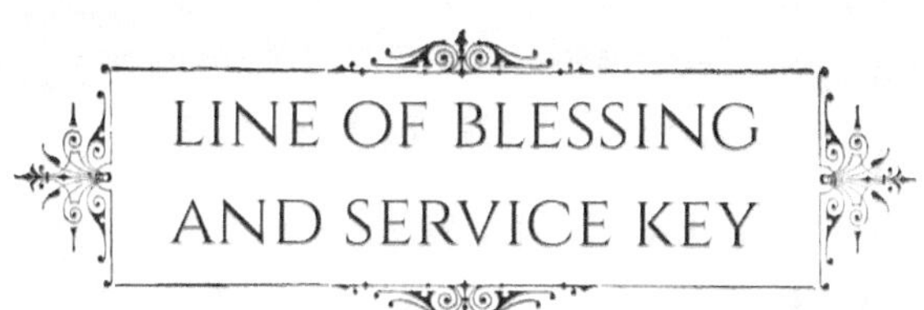

REALM
ALT REALM NAME

IMPERIAL

IMPERIAL MATE

IMPERIAL SOVEREIGNS
OF BORDOROTH AND
THE FIVE REALMS

IMPERIAL CHILD
-BIRTH ORDER-
-BLESSING REALM-
-TITLE/POSITION WITHIN REALM-

IN SERVICE TO:

REALM RULER
OFTEN THE CREATURE WHO
CLAIMED THEM FOR PEACE
AND SERVICE AT BIRTH

ARRAJNEKKAT
THE SOLYREALM

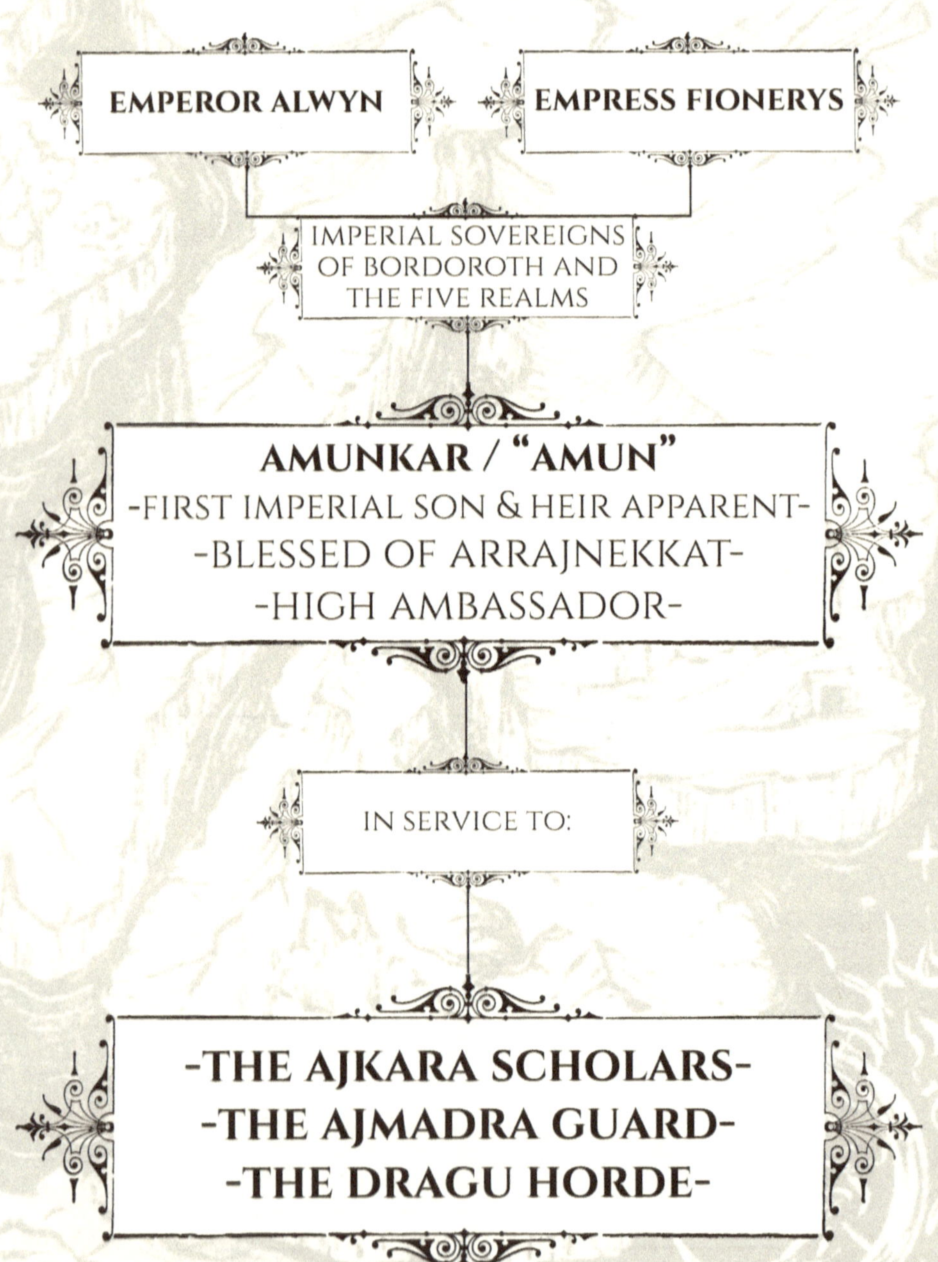

[uh-*razh*-neh-kaht]

A desert realm of sand and sun. home of the arrajnekkatti riders—warriors, scholars, and elemental wielders that long ago befriended the dragons of their land, forming unbreakable bonds with them. Known for its extensive libraries and centers of learning, if one can find them.

CAPITAL:

THE OASIS, WHEREVER IT IS AT THE MOMENT.

CURRENT RULERS:

THE AJKARA SCHOLARS PROTECT THE KNOWLEDGE.
THE AJMADRA GUARD PROTECTS THE PEOPLE.
THE DRAGU HORDE PROTECTS THE LAND.

CURRENT HIGH AMBASSADOR:

AMUNKAR AHT BORDOROTH
BLESSED OF ARRAJNEKKAT
FIRST IMPERIAL SON OF ALWYN AND FIONERYS
IMPERIAL HEIR APPARENT

KOHAMAIA THE TEMPUSREALM

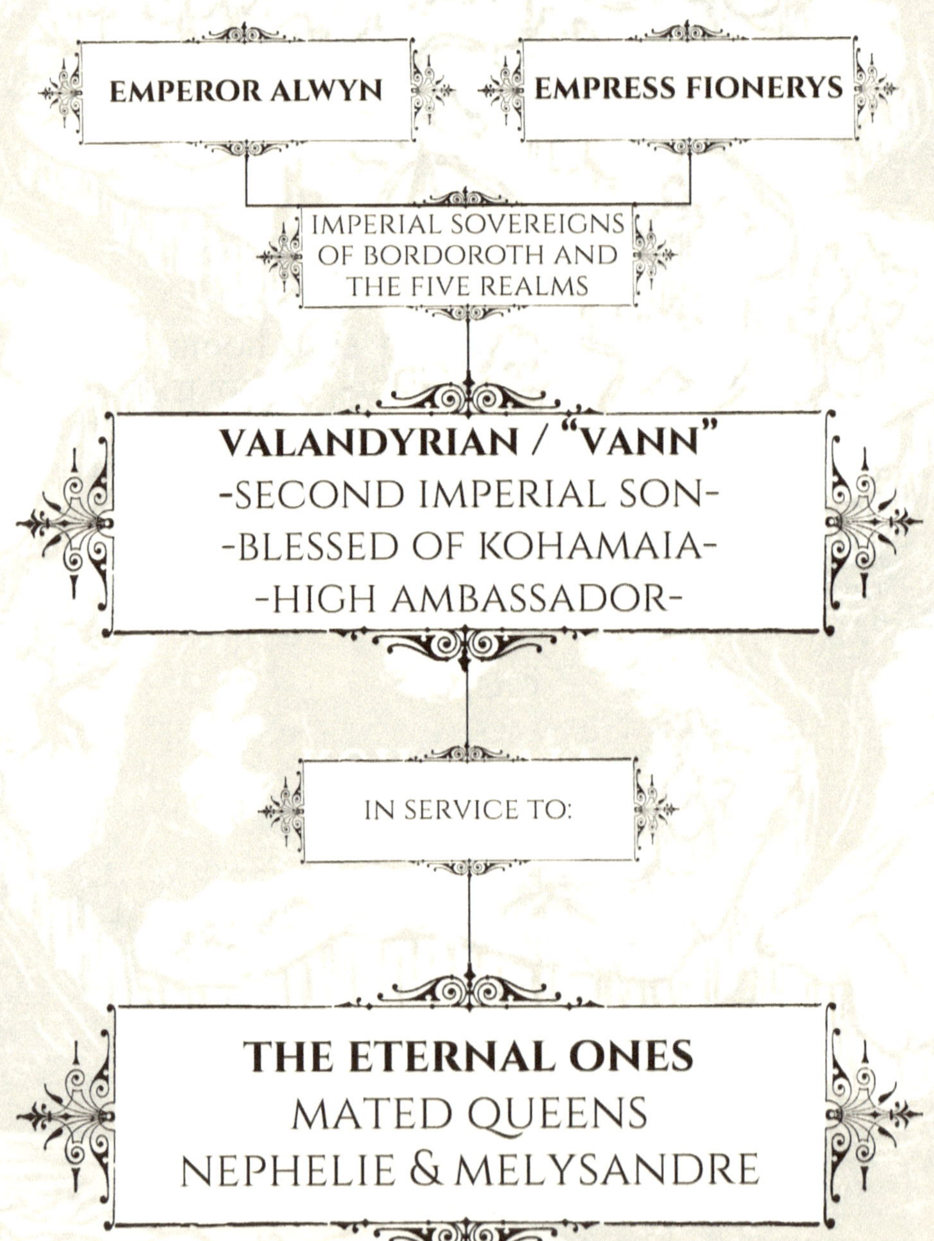

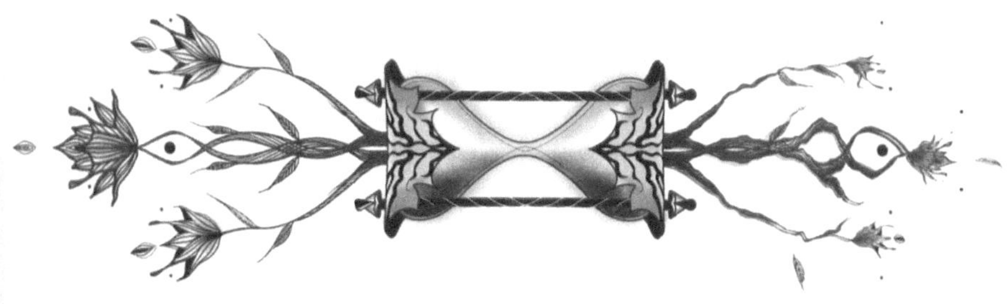

[co-uh-*my*-uh]

A teeming realm of countless Domains, each holding unique creatures and characteristics. Home of the Kohamaian Fae—a diverse, mysterious people that work hard to keep their many secrets. The only officially matriarchal realm of Bordoroth, much to their chagrin.

CAPITAL:

FALWARREN

CURRENT RULERS:

THE ETERNAL ONES
MATED QUEENS
NEPHELIE AND MELYSANDRE O KOHA.

CURRENT HIGH AMBASSADOR:

VALANDYRIAN AHT BORDOROTH
BLESSED OF KOHAMAIA
SECOND IMPERIAL SON OF ALWYN AND FIONERYS

THODELEBOR
THE WESTREALM

[tho-*del*-uh-bore]

A picturesque realm of rolling hills and fertile farmland. Home of the Thodeleborian Wolflords—shapeshifters that use their powers to protect their land and livestock from the creatures of the Ghostwood. Farmers and shepherds mostly, warriors as needed.

CAPITAL:

THE KEEP AT FANGHOLD, IN THE WESTGLEN

CURRENT RULERS:

LYCIDAS AND URSULA À BOR
MATED CHIEFTAINS OF THE WESTREALM

CURRENT HIGH AMBASSADOR:

CAIUS AHT BORDOROTH
BLESSED OF THODELEBOR
SEVENTH IMPERIAL SON OF STENNYX AND GILDAT

AMBASSADOR APPARENT:

MAGNUS AHT BORDOROTH
BLESSED OF THODELEBOR
THIRD IMPERIAL SON OF ALWYN AND FIONERYS

STRAELON
THE MONTREALM

[*stray*-lahn]

A mountainous realm that cradles the Serpent Sea, blanketed in towering evergreens. Home of the Straelani Demons—horned berserkers with the ability to grow into colossal warriors when they rage, possessing powers over the earth and stone of their homeland. Famous for their quarries and stunning woodwork.

CAPITAL:

THE HORNED CITY

CURRENT RULERS:

THE DEMON KING LYRIAT

CURRENT HIGH AMBASSADOR:

BRANDIR AHT BORDOROTH
BLESSED OF STRAELON
FOURTH IMPERIAL SON OF ALWYN AND FIONERYS

NACHTHELLIAE
THE EVESONG REALM

[nock-*thell*-*ee*-ay]

A bioluminescent realm of endless night. Home of the Nachthellian Sorcerit—fanged magic wielders who rely on blood and the celestial light of the cosmos to fuel their power. The only creatures in Bordoroth capable of using their abilities outside their own borders, aside from the Imperials. The other realms often seek their services, as both healers and mercenaries. Sorcerit must prove themselves worthy through various trials, displaying possession of a unique power, before they may be counted among the Elder Tier.

CAPITAL:

STARKEEP

CURRENT RULERS:

THE ELDER COUNCIL

CURRENT KEEPER:

MALACHYR THE MISTWARDEN

CURRENT HIGH AMBASSADOR:

ARAXIS AHT BORDOROTH
BLESSED OF NACHTHELLIAE
FIFTH IMPERIAL SON OF ALWYN AND FIONERYS

THE GREAT PLATEAU

FOUNTAIN OF ALL LIFE

A massive plateau ringed by mountains and forests in the center of Bordoroth. Home of the Palace of Argoph and the Imperial Line—creatures with the unique ability to change once in their lives, taking on the characteristics of the Realm Ruler who "Blesses" them. They possess greater power than the creatures in other realms and are not hindered by the magical boundaries between them, able to use their abilities anywhere.

CAPITAL:

THE WEEPING CITY

HEART OF THE FIVE REALMS AND PERPETUAL SOURCE OF THE REALM RIVERS

CURRENT IMPERIAL SOVEREIGNS OF BORDOROTH AND THE FIVE REALMS:

EMPEROR ALWYN AHT BORDOROTH AND EMPRESS FIONERYS O KOHA

OF NOTE

THE FORGOTTEN LANDS

Mass of land to the west of Bordoroth, completely disconnected from its magic. No Realm River flows there, and no creature has ever successfully used the portals to reach it. Home of the infamous Ghostwood, also known as the 'Wood—a dead forest that runs the length of its eastern-most border, teeming with all manner of vile beasts. Most notable among these is the Forgotten, the towering monsters that spring from the bony trees and leap across the chasm to hunt in Thodelebor's pastures.

CURRENT RULER:

UNKNOWN

OCCURRENCE

A semi-centennial, mystical event that draws power from the cosmos and feeds it into the realms and their people. Each one is unique to its realm, taking place on different days over the course of two years, until the cycle is complete.

NEXT OCCURRENCE:

THE MONTREALM OF STRAELON

K.R. Fryatt is a former opera singer who finally put her foot down in order to realize her childhood dream—becoming a published author. Now, she writes epic, swoon-worthy romantasy novels about complex characters finding their inner strength, experiencing radical self-acceptance, and meeting their true, fated love.

She resides in the mitten state with the real-life book boyfriend she married, their three amazing kids, and an aging Samoyed who's afraid of his own shadow. When she's not writing whatever her characters tell her to, you can find her cursing over crochet, learning how to let go and cry during movies, eating spicy food, and daydreaming about long, tropical vacations.

@author_k.r.fryatt

krfryatt.com

www.ingramcontent.com/pod-product-compliance
Lightning Source LLC
Chambersburg PA
CBHW021930110726
47901CB00003B/776

9798999330109